Missus

Penguin Books

The Harp in the South Novels

Born in New Zealand, Ruth Park came to Australia to take a job as a journalist. Here she married D'Arcy Niland and travelled with him through outback Australia working in a variety of jobs from shearers' cook to fruit packer – all of which provided a rich source of material for her later writing.

Her reputation as a writer was established when her first novel *The Harp in the South* was published in 1948, and its sequel, *Poor Man's Orange* in 1949, neither of which has been out of print since their first publication. More recently *Missus* completed the trilogy.

She has written almost forty books, including ten novels and twenty-seven children's books. Her many prizes include the prestigious Miles Franklin Award for her novel *Swords and Crowns and Rings* (1977) and The 1984 Australian Children's Book of the Year Award and The Boston Globe Award for *Playing Beatie Bow*, available in Puffin.

Other books

Novels

The Witch's Thorn
A Power of Roses
Dear Hearts and Gentle People
The Frost and the Fire
Good Looking Women
Serpent's Delight
Sword and Crowns and Rings

Children's Books

The Muddle-Headed Wombat Series
Callie's Castle
When the Wind Changed
Playing Beatie Bow

Non-Fiction

The Drums Go Bang (with D'Arcy Niland)

Ruth Park's

Harp in the South Novels

- Missus
- The Harp in the South
- Poor Man's Orange

Penguin Books

Penguin Books Australia Ltd
487 Maroondah Highway, PO Box 257
Ringwood, Victoria 3134, Australia
Penguin Books Ltd
Harmondsworth, Middlesex, England
Viking Penguin, A Division of Penguin Books USA Inc.
375 Hudson Street, New York, New York 10114, USA
Penguin Books Canada Limited
10 Alcorn Avenue, Toronto, Ontario, Canada M4V 1E4
Penguin Books (N.Z.) Ltd
182-190 Wairau Road, Auckland 10, New Zealand

The Harp in the South – First published by Angus and Robertson Ltd, 1948
Published by Penguin Books Australia, 1951
Copyright © Ruth Park, 1948
Poor Man's Orange – First published by Angus and Robertson Ltd, 1949
Published by Penguin Books Australia, 1977
Copyright © Ruth Park, 1949
Missus – First published by Nelson, 1985
Published by Penguin Books Australia, 1987
Reprinted 1988
Copyright © Kelmalde Pty Ltd, 1985

First published in this edition by Penguin Books Australia, 1987
10 9 8 7 6 5

Typeset in Garamond by Leader Composition
Made and printed in Australia by Australian Print Group, Maryborough, Victoria

National Library of Australia
Cataloguing-in-Publication data:
Park, Ruth.
Ruth Park's Harp in the south novels.
ISBN 0 14 010456 9.
I. Park, Ruth. Missus. II. Park, Ruth. Harp in the south. III. Park, Ruth.
Poor man's orange. IV. Title.
A823'.3

One

The old Queen was dead, and King Edward well settled on the throne of England. In far away New South Wales, in the town of Trafalgar, Hugh Darcy and Margaret Kilker were born. There were but a few months between their ages, Hugh being the elder.

Trafalgar was first settled by a veteran of that battle. He used his prize money to go out to New South Wales with a cargo of sheep and horses. He applied for a grant on the well-watered tablelands, and was assigned thirty convicts as slave labourers. It was his fancy to give them Jack Tar uniforms to remind him of his glorious days in Nelson's navy. He called his property Trafalgar, and the four creeks that ran through it Victory, Aboukir, Copenhagen and Nile.

The natives were a trouble at first, believing the sheep to belong to everyone, and much more easily speared than kangaroos. But the master of Trafalgar made short work of them, by inviting them to hang around waiting for white man's titbits, and then feeding them flour cakes primed with strychnine. The survivors did not connect the deaths with the white men; they believed the water had gone bad, as it sometimes did after a dry season. One old woman tried to warn the white people not to drink it, but they did not understand. She went away with the two or three others and that was the end of them.

Martin Darcy came to Trafalgar in the mid-1880s. It was then a small town; already a single railway line ran through to freight out the timber milled in the encircling hills. Martin bought a horse and shingle scoop and set up on Aboukir Creek, hauling out gravel for the new roads. He was a sober, virtuous man, working as long as daylight lasted. The horse broke down before he did.

When he was forty years old he began thinking about a wife. For some time he had been corresponding in formal terms with a young governess on a New England station. They had met on a train. He now went courting this girl and in due course brought back to the dilapidated shanty beside the gravel works a frail, dark-haired bride called Frances.

Frances entered upon her hard life with hope and gaiety. She had

3

no knowledge that it was always to be hard because her husband knew no other kind of existence. He loved her, there was no question of that. For a short while his iron face softened, a little red crept into his cheek. He thought he might stroke her hair but feared his calloused hand might catch in it and hurt her. He took off the leaking bark roof and replaced it with corrugated iron. He bought a small bowlegged stove so that she should not have to cook on the open fire. He promised that, should he have a good season, the dirt floor would be replaced by planking. Frances, bemused by love and the conviction that at last she had something of her own, thought it all an adventure, like camping. It was some years before she understood that she had been brought to Aboukir Creek to become a part of her husband's life, not to have one of her own.

Soon she had a boy child, dead at birth. Though she had no family, she wept, homesick, for her native city and the girls with whom she had attended the orphanage school. Martin said nothing; he did not know what to say. He went to a nearby farm and came back with a sleek young fox terrier.

'I've brought you a bitchie,' he said, 'for company.'

At first Frances ignored the dog, seeing in her no substitute for her infant. But soon, noticing the sweetness of the creature's disposition, her delicate humour, she became devoted to her. She named her Witch. The two were together all day. There was great empathy between them, more than there was between the married pair. Frances believed Witch understood everything she said. She often talked to the dog of her dreams for the new child she was to have, and her growing terror that nothing would ever be different for her.

During a flood, Martin having gone to the town to help pile sandbags on the levee, Frances's pains came on. She was able to persuade Witch, a note tied to her collar, to go out into the night to a neighbour's house.

Frances brought into life a strong boy, black-haired and blue-eyed. Martin named him Hugh. Frances was feeble for a long time, restless and tearful. She believed she owed her life to the little dog, and doted on her more and more.

When Hughie was two years old, a neighbour shot Witch, saying the terrier had chased his hens. Perhaps that was so, but nothing could now be done. Martin came home from work to find his wife nursing the baby in the midst of her undone housework, and the

4

bloody body of the dog stiff in a sack.

'Eichhardt shot my Witch,' was all Frances said. Martin could not find a word. As though there were, indeed, words of compassion struggling to get out, he suffered pain in chest and belly. He took away the dog, instead of burying her he sent the body to a taxidermist in the nearest large town.

It was an expensive business, it took most of his savings, but when Witch was returned to Trafalgar Martin was satisfied. The taxidermist had posed the dog sitting on her hind legs, begging, her dainty white paws turned down. Her hide was as pure as snow; her eyes, looking through a black mask, as dovelike as in life.

Martin's excitement at the thought of his wife's joy was so profound it was almost sacred.

When he brought the stuffed dog into the house Frances seemed to take a fit. She was unconscious for a long time. When she came to her senses her gaze wandered fearfully to the corners of the room.

'Is it gone?'

'Didn't I think you'd be pleased,' said Martin.

'Dreadful, dreadful,' muttered Frances.

The doctor said she had a goitre, made worse by Hugh's birth. He prescribed the painting of her throat and chest with iodine, and laudanum for her nerves. The skin peeled off her throat, and she became addicted to the laudanum.

She became very excitable, flushed and flirtatious with casual visitors, flying into frenzies over trifles. She had abominable nightmares and was afraid to go to sleep. The doctor increased the dose of laudanum. Often she was fantastically merry, though falling suddenly from laughter into tears. Hugh's earliest memory was of his mother dancing with him. She wore a cherry blouse with high sleeves and many tucks, relic of her teaching days; it sagged from her emaciated shoulders. To the little boy she was beautiful.

His wife's rejection of the resurrected Witch wounded Martin irrevocably. He had wanted to please and console and she had reacted like one half-crazy. He did not know what to do with a mad-woman. The pungent smell of the iodine and the bandages she often wore around her flayed throat filled him with a desire to leave Trafalgar and never be seen again. Nevertheless he got her with child once more.

With great difficulty it was born, a dark elvish thing with its feet

5

back to front. Martin had decided that the child, if a boy, should be named Oliver for his father, but after he had looked at it he said curtly, 'Name him what you will.'

Frances called the child Jeremiah. In a month or two it was plain he had fine features, dark eyes, and a questing look. From the beginning she impressed on Hughie, now robust and turbulent, that he must look after his brother, love him more than anyone else in the world.

Hughie promised he would do so.

After the birth of this child Martin Darcy fell into morose depression. He was poisoned by suspicion. He accused his wife of fathering a cuckoo on him. He stared at his neighbours until they backed away in embarrassment. But being mostly Irish and German they were fair-skinned and pale-eyed. The suspicion fossilised into certainty; he could think of nothing else. The doctor and the parish priest remonstrated with him, pointing out that Frances herself was brown-eyed and olive complexioned, but this did no good. He had the idea on the brain.

He settled at last on an Indian hawker, a consumptive in a pink turban, smelling of patchouli and curry, who sometimes came through the district with his pack of cheap cottons, baby clothes, pins, ribbons and corset tapes. Frances, in hysterical rage, mimicked herself flirting with the Indian, and the Indian making big eyes in return.

Martin punched her. After that he never spoke to her again. Jeremiah grew, learnt to scuttle, to walk with crutches. Hugh never queried his responsibility for his brother. When Jer was small and weak Hugh pushed him to school in a handcart; later the child became as nimble as a sparrow. The schoolchildren teased Jeremiah unmercifully, partly because he was clever and outshone them all, but mostly because his feet were knotted like tree roots. His difference offended them mortally. They would have killed him if they had dared. At eight years old Hughie was fighting for his brother, shaping up to short and tall, being thrashed, humiliated, bloodied. The parish priest, seeing that Martin would do nothing about it, took Hugh aside and taught him how to dodge or land a blow. By ten years of age Hugh had fought every boy who tormented Jer and was given living space by his schoolfellows. He grew up a feared brawler. But he was not truly a fearless person. Approaching adolescence brought a trembling diffidence. He often found a lump in his throat for no reason. He began to look at things, stars, girls' hair, the way a paddock of cabbages was not green but blue. He practised using his tongue or his quick wits to get out of a scrap if he could.

The boys did not question the situation between their parents. They thought all fathers were like that. They never spoke of their mother, protecting her by a conspiracy of silence.

But Frances often talked with them. Sometimes she was so out of the world with laudanum they could not understand her. Other times she spoke of Sydney, its statues, the buildings so grand, steepled and turreted, the sea so blue, swarms of richly dressed people, busy important people. The brothers liked best to hear of a bridge that opened in the middle to let tall-masted ships go by. They could not decide whether Sydney was like London or Babylon. Still, they yearned to go there.

Hugh recognised that his mother had a voice different from other women. Pretty he called it, when he meant refined. A nervous understanding came to him that she, too, must have begun life as a preparation for something wonderful. But all she got was a shanty for a home, constant illness, and two boys, one a cripple and one always in mischief.

He promised himself that when he was in work he would take his mother back to Sydney where she would be happy.

When Hugh was twelve, and already truant and tearaway, Frances went out one night to the creek. She knew a deep hole above the gravel pits. Filling her pockets with shingle she jumped in. During the day or so she rolled in the swirling mud, her jacket was torn off and lay with its weighted pockets at the bottom. So it was thought her death was accidental, which was a good thing in Trafalgar where suicides were looked upon with dread and condemnation. Long afterwards, after a flood, Martin's scoop dragged up the muddy jacket, but he dried it and burned it. The boys always believed their mother had died by mischance.

After their mother's death the boys had a terrible two years. Later Hugh was to think of that time as a kind of dark country they had perforce to pass through in order to become independent. After the funeral Hugh did not go back to school. The nuns pleaded with him not to leave, and the priest pleaded with Martin Darcy. Hugh was smart, wrote a good hand, and in spite of his wildness was a cheerful likeable boy.

But Martin put the boy to work on the scoop. Jeremiah, now handy with crutches, got to school by himself, though he was adept at sitting beside the road looking pitiful so as to get a lift in any cart going that way. Once he even got a ride in a motor car. There were now at least a dozen in Trafalgar.

The War had started, but Hugh and Jeremiah knew nothing of it. When Jer came home from school he cleaned up the shack as best he could. He took to cooking like a duck to water and, crumpled up like a spider on a chair in front of the stove, he turned out far better meals than Frances had ever done. Mistakes earned him a thump on the ear, which cleared his brain with regard to burning the eggs or over-salting the porridge as nothing else might have done. He was in deadly fear of his father and longed to poison him.

Hugh became strong and stocky. In spite of the long hours of toil he managed frequently to get into trouble. Though thrashed by his father he went on seeking out mischief, occasionally coming home drunk and silly. He had no money himself but his mates were generous. Like them he believed to be a man was to drink, and ardently he wanted to be a man.

At last he took Jer for a joy-ride in the doctor's car. In lieu of a year in Borstal, the sergeant birched him, delivering him sullen and stinging to his father.

'You'd do better, Martin, to let him work in the town,' he advised. 'He's a big lump of a lad and there's plenty of work, with the fellows away at the fighting, and all. There's little harm in him at the present, but he's knocking around with all the roughs. You know what that comes to in the end.'

After the sergeant had gone, Martin took down the piece of harness he used to larrup the boys. 'I'll touch you up a bit more,' he growled.

'You won't, Dadda,' said Hughie. He caught hold of the strap as it came down and jerked it out of Martin's hand. Martin, blanched with rage, rushed him, his hand extended to take hold of the boy's throat. Hugh caught the hand with both his, turned his back and tried to throw Martin across his shoulder. But he was too short and the father too heavy; the two of them crashed through the door. Hugh was up first. Jer, poised on his hands, his crooked feet up around his belly, swung and jigged, screaming hysterically, 'Kill him, kill him! Hit him with the axe!'

Martin was winded. He crawled to the shadow of the tank-stand. Something terrible and irrevocable had happened. He was fifty-seven and his son was fourteen. He was still a man built like a tree but nothing could take the stealthy arthritis from his joints or restore the steel of his muscles.

'Get!' he said.

'You bet I will,' shouted Hugh.

'And take that black bastard with you.'

Jer had never thought that if Hughie should go away to a job he might be left defenceless with his father. His face became yellow, it shrivelled before Hugh's eyes. He wept, he begged. Hugh saw no way of leaving him behind.

'Course you'll come, Jer. You go and shove our things in a sugar sack.'

The sergeant put them up in one of the empty cells at the station, and his wife fed them. He wired a friend at a sheep property that he had on hand a good strong lad who could buck in at anything.

'I didn't have the heart to mention the brother,' he said. 'You got a big burden there, son. Better let him go to a Home.'

'He sticks with me,' said Hugh.

As it happened, after the first row when the squatter laid eyes on Jer, the young boy was sent to the homestead kitchen. He was so handy peeling potatoes, washing dishes and plucking and skinning that the Chinese cook asked for him as steady offsider. Also Jer made him laugh with his chatter.

In Jer's good-looking head was a sharp brain and a burning imagination. There was not a story he heard or read that could not be turned roundabout and inside out and arranged around himself.

Where this could not be credible because of his deformity he applied the yarns to Hughie or to fictitious uncles and aunts. Their poor mother now had her loneliness enriched with sisters, brothers, cousins, many of extreme eccentricity but undeniable interest. As he often found himself yarning to men of Irish descent, Jer commonly made these kinsfolk Irish, picking up names here and there as berries from a bush. In fact, Frances's grandparents had been Americans, refugees from the war between the States. It was as well Jeremiah was ignorant of this, or he would have had himself and his brother descendants of Abraham Lincoln.

Hugh clipped his ears for him. He threatened to send him back to Dad, to put him in an institution. Jeremiah cringed, smiled placatingly, promised, and at the next opportunity was off again. Hugh was profoundly embarrassed by his lying brother. He thought it must have something to do with his handicap, that poor Jer was scrambled at both ends. He had not an idea in his head that work was plentiful for him not only because he was a strong willing lad but because everyone in the country knew that where Hughie Darcy went Jer went as well, and he was such an entertaining beggar.

The often illiterate ruffians of the timber camps and sheep stations recognised what the elder brother did not, that Jeremiah was a come-ye-all, a storyteller, kin to those performers who had enthralled their emigrant parents at fairs and cattle sales.

They believed him and they didn't believe him, and it did not matter either way. All they knew came from their own experience and that of others like themselves. With their own eyes they'd all seen strange things, the tall parentie lizards, upright on splayed legs, curvetting in ceremonial circles in desert moonlight. Upside-down lightning leaping like dazzling twigs from the ironstone plains of North Queensland. Blackfellows dancing a thunderhead into the sky, and drenching rain to follow it.

Some of Jer's stories were told years afterwards by bushmen, having become part of campfire history. There was his grandfather's brother Archie, funeral director in a one-horse settlement out west. He had a dummy son he couldn't stand the sight of. Any old how, here are the pair of them working on a departed, dummy going ooo-gah and bugger-bugger in his usual way, trying to let the Dad know that a black kid he was friends with had finger-talked him that a flash flood had burst a few miles to the north.

Now everyone knows that the wilder sort of black has this funny power, this bush telegraph as they call it. Someone important dies in Darwin, and in ten minutes every old gin around Wilcannia is gassing about it. So the dummy's friend knew that the creek, which had had no water in it for eight years, was due to flood. Archie understood the boy quite well, but he always went on as if the dummy was wrong in the head as well as deaf and dumb. So he paid no attention. Anyway, corpse in coffin, peaceful as hell, rosary beads twined in fingers, boyish flush on cheeks. Suddenly there's this fearful roar and down comes the water, thirty foot high, wipes out the town in an instant, shacks, telegraph office, everything gone.

10

In a flash Archie tips out the deceased, leaps in the coffin, and is off. Poor dummy tries to get in as well, but Archie bashes his fingers, makes him let go. Good riddance, he yells, and away he whirls, riding the flood like a champion. But he was also the settlement's carpenter, and he'd bodged up that coffin out of old grocery boxes. It busts at the seams, it leaks, down it goes. Holy gee, gurgles Archie, I'm for it. And as he sinks below the raging tide what should he see but the dummy, safe as houses, sail past him riding the stiff. Help, help, my son, shouts Archie, but the dummy gives him some finger talk the like of which the innocent Aboriginal never knew.

As Jer grew older he became more accomplished. Even Hugh began to believe his stories. Had he or had he not had an aunt who was married to a hangman? Had his father indeed seen the tracks of a bunyip on the muddy banks of Aboukir Creek?

Hughie never thought of his father at all. Let the old devil rot, was his feeling. Yet when he received a letter, much addressed, from Mr John Kilker of Trafalgar, he was disturbed, and concealed it from Jer. Memories rushed back, the stony odour of the Aboukir, his mother dangling her feet in the yellow yeasty water. White feet, nothing to them but bone. Half blind with old anger he read and re-read the letter.

Hugh scarcely recalled Mr Kilker, who wrote a stately, long-tailed hand. He said that Martin had been ill a long time; the boys had better come home if they wished to see their father alive.

Hugh was working at Brit Brit, out of Helena, at the time. He felt all at once young, unable to sort out his emotions. Fury swamped him. He almost died of it. He was so distraint he got himself bailed up by the station bull. He was gored only in the shoulder, but the squatter was as mad as if it had been a fatal accident. He called Hugh every kind of careless hound, not fit to be in charge of a vealer. He would not hear a word against the bull. Hugh was afraid he and Jer would be kicked out, so he blurted that his father was dying. The squatter turned soft, had Hugh attended by the women, carried him till he was fit to work again. Hugh hated himself for using the old man as an excuse. He didn't want Martin to be good for anything, even in death.

Jer was happy and excited. He took it on himself to write a grave reply to Mr Kilker. He had Hugh at death's door, praising his brother's courage and fortitude to the skies. He told of their filial

11

yearning to have a last glimpse of their father, and their sorrow at its unlikelihood. Should things come to the worst, he begged, would Mr Kilker take their place at the graveside.

John Kilker was impressed and moved by this letter. Martin had two loyal sons in spite of all the disorder of that household. The good Catholic man had not told the brothers the half of it. After they left Trafalgar Martin had given up work, living on his savings and the charity of others. He, who had always been temperate, took to drink, the cheapest rotgut. It was almost as if he wanted to kill himself. But his strong body stood against all the abuse he handed it. It gave in reluctantly, taking three years to do it. Martin's teeth decayed and fell out; his bones filled with arthritis and his muscles with rheumatism. Something was going on in his chest; he felt it was full of boiling water.

The drink did not make him happy. He had always been quiet; now he was a hermit. The doctor went to see him and was driven off with curses. The ladies of St Vincent de Paul knocked, offering food and comfort, but went away with their soup all over their skirts. They said that rats were running races in broad daylight over the roof.

Martin was in and out of jail for drunkenness, bad language, and resisting arrest. The sergeant welcomed these interludes so that he could be sure the man was properly fed. Martin was much the same age as himself, but he looked seventy, toothless, thin as a rake, his eyelids hanging scarlet like an old ewe's.

During these bad years John Kilker, the iceman, and his wife had done what they could for Martin. He had never been a friend. Had he indeed ever been a friend to anyone? Still, in a small town everyone knew everyone else's business, and Mrs Kilker welcomed the challenge of doing Martin good even though it should be by violence.

John Kilker and his wife were fire and gunpowder. They had been wed in 1888 and not a day since had passed without a fight. Yet the wife never saw John come through the back gate without a wickedly warm tickle in her vitals, and the sight of Eny waggling her bottom as she stirred a pot on the fire made John feel quite astray. The result of all this was that they had eleven children, of whom eight had survived infancy. The two deaths amongst these had been terrible to the parents. One child died of chickenpox. May had been only five, a darling child. The mother, pregnant with

12

Delia, was almost demented. It was no wonder Delia was such a devil. The parents, May torn from their arms, had turned their passionate love on Kathleen, aged four. She was their jewel, and indeed she grew up a flashing creature, joyful and giving joy, until God took her away in a fall from a horse, she being not quite sixteen.

John and Rowena were older then. They did not make so much noise, but the wound was deep and never healed. They tried not to curse God, but in their hearts they never liked him again. Eny felt they must have done something sinful for God to punish them so.

'I think I'll turn meself to good works,' she told John.

'God in his mercy help the poor and needy,' thought John, for his wife had no patience at all, and a tongue that would take a splint from a horse's leg.

'Sure, darling,' he said soothingly. 'Don't I already belong to St Vincent de Paul's? But maybe you'd find the time for a helping hand for the poor women who've lost their men in the fighting.'

Eny did better than that; she was a generous woman. For most of the War years, when so many young men died, John frequently found at his table a destitute widow or a clutch of mute, bewildered children. She gave them beds, food, comfort, and occasionally curry in the shape of a good talking-to. She stuck with Catholic families, not because of bigotry, but because she felt at home with them, all the brave strength, and the trusting silliness, too.

Tears came to the parish priest's eyes at the edifying sight of Mrs Kilker kneeling in her parlour, surrounded by her own younger ones, and six or eight children and a widow or two, all in black, but stuffed to the craw with stew, floury potatoes and apple doughboy. No one in her house went to his bunk without a round of the Rosary.

Mrs Kilker, slender and upright still, her fine hair untouched by grey, spoke the Aves in a voice like a purling stream. Still without missing a word, she could lash out and land a thump on the ear of some child absentmindedly picking its nose.

The priest thought with soft pleasure that God would surely bless John and Eny, a credit to Dublin and Derry respectively.

But God had not yet stayed his hand, and almost in the last week of the War Owen Kilker fell before a bullet. He was their third son, twenty-five years old, and taken by the Army only in the last years because he was duckfooted and had a slight squint. The perfect young men, strong as bulls, incandescent with life, had already been killed or wounded.

It was easier for the parents to be resigned to Owen's passing. He had been a slow, gloomy boy. In fact, John had sometimes thought he was not the full quid.

'I wager he walked up to a German and asked for the lend of a match,' he said sadly.

After Sunday Mass it was John's custom to take a little tobacco to Martin Darcy and have a few friendly words. He asked his wife to accompany him, saying it might take her out of herself. But Eny was too wretched. She was ashamed that she could not feel for poor Owen the unbearable woe the deaths of her daughters had brought her. She hated herself for her cantankerous ways with the boy in life. The vehement names she had hurled at him!

Snivelling a little, she went home with her young girls Margaret and Josephine, the tail of the family. Margaret was blooming in all directions, her face full of blushes. She burst out of her bust bodices as if they had been made of paper. Josie was disgusted and never ceased pestering her mother to get Margaret into stays.

Margaret thought of nothing but love; she was feverish with dreams of love. The powerful sentiment was part of her blood and bone. Even when she and Josie quarrelled she still loved her sister. Now she took her mother's hat and coat, wept with her for Owen.

'He was that slow on the uptake,' mourned Eny. 'Didn't he have me on my hind legs most of the time. Ah, what was the poor boy born for?'

'To obey, honour and serve God in this world and be happy with Him for ever in the next,' spoke up young Josephine. She was a neat little girl with big eyes and a small chin. Eny was bored with children by the time she came along and had greeted knowledge of her pregnancy with storms, yells and curses. Somehow this had filtered through to Josie. She was aware she was a cuckoo in the nest and the awareness made her sad, clever, and spiteful.

Her mother gave her a brooding look. 'In the name of God, Josie, don't show off. Get out into the kitchen and make us all a cup of tea.'

Josie sulked out. She thought, and she was right, that if Margaret had given a correct catechism answer she would have been praised as a good Catholic.

Meanwhile John had found Martin Darcy so close to death he

14

wrapped him in a blanket, put him in his own wheelbarrow, and ran him to the hospital. There he died.

John Kilker took it badly, not that he was grieved for Martin, who for years now had been like a tree eaten out by dry rot, still standing but dead as a doornail. He felt somehow that Owen and Martin had been similar, decent men both, but inexplicably deprived by life. John was so low spirited he had to take a week off from the iceworks, the first time ever. Rowena fetched the doctor who thought in dismay that perhaps the Spanish influenza had come to Trafalgar. But it had not. John was up and around in a few days. What had bowled him over was a glimpse, as it were, of the indecipherable shapes of the future.

Later, but feeling that this no longer mattered, he sent a telegram to Hugh that his father had died.

A month or more after Martin Darcy was buried, Hugh awakened with a sudden, fierce resolution. It was as if someone had tapped him on the shoulder as he slept. He told Jer he was going to Trafalgar.

'Get out,' said his brother. 'The old shit's dead.'

'I'm going,' said Hugh.

Jeremiah begged and wept; he did not want to be left alone. At the back of his mind always was the fear that he would be abandoned. Hugh said he would be back in a few days.

'But why, why?' lamented the cripple.

He was afraid he might take the influenza while Hugh was away, that he might die all in a day as people said could happen.

The plague had enveloped the earth like a poisonous fog. The world had lately seen such anguish, such catastrophe, so many millions of people dead in the War. Then, as if Death gripped humanity as a cat a mouse, came the epidemic. How it raged in Australia! The people scarcely had the heart to rejoice that the War was over at last. They went to their work wearing cotton masks soaked in disinfectant, not knowing if they would ever return home. A man could fall down in the street, marked for the grave. A housewife might exchange a few words with her neighbour at noon, and a day later everyone in her house was blackened and stiff. Every old wives' tale in the drawer came out. People wore around their necks little bags containing garlic, asafoetida, saints' relics, or private amulets such as a lucky bean or a blessed medal.

The authorities did what they could, but since they did not

know how or why the pestilence had come, they were helpless. Town councils took matters into their own hands. A brutish, instinctive knowledge told them that in this crisis law had nothing to do with anything; all was between them and Death. In Trafalgar, which had had no case of Flu, the people gathered and decided that no strangers should be permitted to enter the town for the duration of the epidemic. This was easy to do. It required only four shotguns. The town lay low in a circle of hills. There was a road in and a road out. The railway track appeared through a tunnel in the north and speared into another in the south. Men patrolled the road day and night, others with shotguns were on duty at the station. Trains could unload and load freight, but the townsmen did the work with no contact with passengers and crew.

Hugh wired John Kilker of his arrival, but it was not until the guard came through the train that he learnt he would not be allowed to alight at Trafalgar station.

He argued with the man, explaining that his father was dead, it was his duty to see the grave. The man pitied the boy, fresh-faced, wearing a Sunday suit, straw boater on home-cut curly hair.

'God knows I'm with you in your bereavement, son,' he explained, 'but it would be as much as me life was worth. Them Trafalgar men are tigers.'

As the train pulled into the station, all the carriage doors and windows closed, Hugh made a bolt for it. A shotgun's grim snout shoved him back. Hugh had never been held up by a gun; he could not believe it. The rage which had driven him on his journey blazed out.

He had something of the eloquence of Jer. Shouting defiance and expostulation, he ran through the train and slipped out into the goods yard. A jet from a firehose punched him in the chest.

'Get back, get back!' he heard above the snarl of the water. The jet chased him as he dodged; when he fell it whacked him like an iron bar across the seat of the pants. He staggered to the guard's rear van, where he was hauled inside.

'You can't beat the beggars, son,' commiserated the man.

The passengers, moved by sympathy and pleasure in the commotion, began to shout and jeer. The stationmaster feared a riot, and signalled for the train to pull out of the station. A heavy man ran shortwindedly beside the van. Hugh recognised the artless red face of Mr Kilker.

'The funeral was real lovely, son,' gasped out Mr Kilker. 'St

Vincent's, the Hibernian brass band, Masses, all respect.'

The train gathered speed. Hugh, hanging out the van door, saw a young girl, curls down her back, run up and take Mr Kilker's arm. The old fellow looked as if he might throw a fit, he was so red. Hugh vaguely recognised in the girl Margaret Kilker, who had been in a class below his at school.

The guard took Hugh's clothes and dried them off somewhat near the boiler. He gave the boy a cup of tea.

'What you gonna do now, mate?'

'Get off at the next station and wait for the next train back to Helena.'

'You go back to Trafalgar after the Flu's over,' advised the guard.

On the return trip, damp, humiliated, Hugh felt his chest stuffed with tears. He could not remember why he had come on this journey, unless it were to make certain his father was dead and underground. But now there was no freedom or relief in that thought.

He felt unreasonable hatred of Trafalgar as well. The town had done nothing for him while he lived there, and now it had driven him out with abuse and a torrent of water. While he fumed thus, one side of his brain commended the townspeople's attitude. He would have felt the same way in this time of plague. But Trafalgar had cast him out, like garbage. He was to hate the town for the rest of his life.

At Helena he had a five-mile walk out to Brit Brit station, but he welcomed it.

It was night, winter, sky gauzy with stars, waterfalls chirring in the dark. Hughie left the road and went into the bush. For an hour he wept, howled, tore up the grass. He did not know why. His mother, his childhood, the lasting burden of Jer? All those things, and something more profound, more horrifying: if his father could grow old and die, so could he.

Jer tenderly cleaned and pressed his brother's suit. In no time he had turned Hugh's misadventures at Trafalgar into an epic. The station boss, thinking the boy had had a rotten deal, his Dad gone and all, gave them a small bonus cheque when they left Brit Brit. Hugh, holing up in a small pub in the middle of nowhere, was drunk for a week.

'Don't you die, Hughie, don't you never leave me,' Jer pleaded day after day.

After that Hugh went on regular sprees. He was under age, but

17

that was no problem. He became a shearers' cook, with Jer as his offsider. The team was a well-known one, and the men were glad when they saw the Darcy boys turn up at a station instead of some Borgia. These men mostly had stomach trouble and ate bicarbonate of soda by the spoonful. They said their guts were ruined by the stooped positions in which they shore. But the real reasons were too much booze, and the unskilled, dirty cooking.

Jer now had a guitar. He was taught to play by a shearer so cracked about music he had once made a viola from a kerosene tin. Jer learnt countless songs; once through and he had the tune, twice and he had the words. He had a pleasing breathy voice and did best with succulent ballads. Often he was given a few shillings for playing at smoke-ohs or weddings and it did not take him long to become ambitious to earn enough money to have his feet fixed.

'But you'll stick with me until I can manage for myself, won't you, Hughie?'

For as Hugh became interested in girls, often on a Saturday afternoon riding thirty miles, his good duds tied up in an oilskin behind him, to attend a dance, Jeremiah became more and more panicky.

'Them girls,' he said, 'they wouldn't have me in the house, and you know I got to stay with you, Hughie.'

'I ain't getting married ever,' answered his brother. He crouched before a looking glass, rubbing the softened end of a candle into his top lip, where a downy moustache faltered.

'You will, you will,' mourned Jer. 'And what will become of me then?'

'You keep moaning,' said Hugh, 'and you'll cop what you're looking for. We had this out two, three years ago when I got that guitar for you. What I said then I mean now.'

He rubbed his palms, glistening with brilliantine, over his hair, put on his hat, and left.

Jer could have cried. He began to play sadly: 'I dreamt I dwelt in marble halls with diamonds and pearls at my feet.'

A passing shed hand looked in the window.

'I seen marble once,' he said.

'Where?'

'In a bank. It looked like liver.'

'Bloody nong,' shouted Jer. 'When would you be in a bank unless you were holding it up?'

18

He was agitated, banging his crutches on the floor, scratching catlike cries out of the guitar. He got out the holy picture the little girl Bridget had sent him, of a poofter angel hoicking a kid in a nightie back from a cliff edge, and said a Hail Mary. He was in his heart religious and often prayed.

The little girl's father had given Hugh the guitar for Jer, on the only occasion Hughie had gone away and left his brother by himself.

The child Jer had known that his only weapons against the world were his wits and his two funny feet. When Hugh was sixteen or seventeen, and became infatuated with that girl and this, the lame boy began to stage fake suicides. The first time Hugh was almost demented, the small crumpled figure, the empty bottle of Lysol, the burn or two around the mouth. The second time he stood off and watched until Jet cautiously opened his eyes to see what was happening.

The third time Hugh threw him in the creek. The water was shallow but Jer was mortally afraid of drowning. Hugh watched the boy flounder for a while, then hauled him out. He said:

'You and me got strife, Jer. You can't go on all your life hanging onto me like a tick. I'm going to take a job somewhere, and you're going to stay here.'

Jer screamed, wept, begged, but Hugh was firm. He had a word with the boss, a fatherly man who agreed with his decision.

'I've made up my mind to do a spell farmhanding, up Juno way,' Hugh told Jer. 'You'll be offsiding for Charley. You'll be on a good thing. He thinks the world of you.'

Charley was the homestead cook, an old Chinese. It was a step up for Jer, a little room of his own, lashings of good tucker, the missus to keep an eye on him.

Jer gaped at Hughie who said uneasily, 'It's only for two months. I'll send you a postcard every week.'

'I'll do meself in, I really will this time.'

Jer was greenish yellow. Hugh, at seventeen, was hard put to it to stand his ground.

'Right. You want to do that, you do it. But you'd be a real nit. Why, you might have your feet fixed by the time you're twenty-one, dancing and playing football and everything.'

But Jer would not be consoled, until the boss threatened to kick the seat of his pants through his teeth.

Hugh could turn his hand to anything. Pruning trees, digging spuds, disorganising a tomcat, fixing a feed for the men when the cook came down with the staggers. On Butt's property, a few miles out of Juno, they liked him so much the old man said he could have a regular job if he felt so inclined.

'Like hell,' thought Hughie, though he answered pleasantly. Juno put his hair on end. It was like a thousand other small country towns. At five when the shops shut their doors and put their lights out it began to croak. When the pubs closed, it dropped dead. One stray dog trembling in a doorway, a horse trough half-full of scum and Mintie papers, a yellow light shuddering above the crossing. Not in a million years would you think that anyone lived there.

On his day off Hugh couldn't wait to get into town, and he couldn't wait to get out of it either. Its voice was the voice of everything lost and pointless in his life.

He had a postcard to Jer in his pocket. He shoved it through the slot at the post office. It wasn't much of a picture, just the local forge with a draught horse and dray beside it. He had a sudden vision of young Jer in another smithy, patching someone's dungarees with rivets. Or sitting on his bunk, stitching on a button. Handy with a needle Jer was, and always willing to do a job for some hamhanded mate. He made a few bob out of it, too. Working men were not mean.

Hugh missed his brother. He could see that he'd spend the rest of his life being haunted by Jer, resenting him when he had him on his back and miserable as hell when he hadn't. He was glad he was on the last week of his job at Butt's. The Butts had several daughters, all too young for him, mad with the giggles, and the only woman in the kitchen had her front teeth missing and a husband as jealous as if she still had them.

Mooching about in Juno, Hugh was in such a stinking temper that when he heard the sniggers and growls of male voices around the corner he broke into a gallop. If there was to be a brawl he didn't want to miss it.

Six or seven men, mostly young, mostly full to the gills, had an old fellow bailed up behind a parked truck. The half light showed grey hair, but he had his fists up, businesslike.

'Hey, give the poor old cow a chance!'

Hugh hopped in, showing off right and left, chopping and

jabbing, until an uppercut lifted him clean off his feet. As he hovered, for a split second his mind like crystal, it came to him that it was the old cow who had dropped him.

When he returned to the world he found a school kid bathing his eye and a tubby policeman in shirt sleeves sitting beside him drinking a beer. He was in someone's kitchen. His assailant glared at him from beside the stove.

'You can go a bit,' he said grudgingly.

'Not as far as you,' said Hugh.

The man looked like a retired gladiator, thick ears and eyes stitched in deep by old blows.

'Old cow, is it?'

'Well, Chris'sake,' said Hugh, checking that his jaw was still on its bearings, 'you must be forty if you're a day.'

He could scarcely imagine anyone older than that and still alive.

'My Dad is fifty-five,' spoke up the kid, 'and it was because those men said things about me that he was fighting.'

'Well, I was on his side, dammit,' said Hugh.

'You got one peeper bunged up, too,' said the tubby cop, pleased. He turned to the girl. 'You forget all about it now, Bridget. Them blokes just wanted to get a rise out of the Dad here. It'll all die down now they've had their fun. I got four of them for disturbing the peace, and that Dave Crookall, the splinters will be working out of his elbow till next Christmas.'

Hugh found it comfortable in the kitchen, though it had the queer look about it that spoke of no woman being around. Even the kid, who was about twelve, had that look. Her black hair was scraggy, and the school uniform she wore had a blue button sewn on with white thread. An argument was going on about the school dance. The father said she didn't have to go, and she, her eyes flashing, said she would and be damned to the lot of them.

'And if no one will dance with me,' she said, 'I'll spit in their eye.'

She was at that age when her body could make up its mind about nothing, legs too long, hands too small, little breasts like new potatoes and teeth too big for the tender, trembling mouth. She was as hurt and upset as a twelve-year-old could be, and she was not going to let anyone know about it.

'I'll take you,' said Hugh, 'if you don't mind a bloke with one eye and a busted lip.'

21

Hugh never knew what it had all been about, nor did he care. He meant to ask the Butts what people had been saying about the girl but he forgot.

He kicked himself for offering to take a twelve-year-old schoolgirl to a dance, and he a man of seventeen. Jer could scarcely believe it.

'You must have been nuts. What'd you get out of it?'

'Not a cracker, you crude bugger. But you got the guitar, didn't you?'

The father had fetched it out from under a bed, saying a mate of his had left him with it when he went off to the War in 1915. He'd copped his. Maybe the young brother of whom Hughie spoke could have some fun with it.

Jer caressed the instrument lovingly. Now and then he looked at the holy picture Bridget had sent him. Just like a kid to give him something like that, he thought. She probably thought he still went to church. All that stuff.

It was a funny thing to have happened, thought Hughie. He recalled the shy thrill of the skinny half-child body in his arms. Oh, she was triumphant amongst those awkward Juno kids with their puffed sleeves and frills and frizzed hair, that she alone could flaunt a handsome stranger, a grown-up man, a king!

'You did a real decent thing there, taking my girl Bridget to the dance,' said the old man as he gave him the guitar in its dusty case. 'She won't forget it, and neither will I. And you can handle yourself well in a stoush, too.'

Separation from Hugh settled Jer down a little. But as he grew older he developed other habits. Because he was deprived of living fully, he had intense curiosity about other people's lives. There was not a man in any camp whose swag or duffle bag he had not examined. He was a knowing little fellow. He knew the man whose clothes were well made, old, dirty and ragged though they might be, was possibly running away from something, even if it were only a wife. He sought for clues in the man's letters, the photographs in his wallet, his subjects of conversation. Jer was so astute, so intuitive, that he often hit on the right answer to his questions. He knew a great deal about everyone; it pleased him to sit in the circle about the fire at night and think: 'You with your legs! I could dob you in to the cops tomorrow if I wanted.' He called this Jer power. It was his secret strength.

Once or twice he was caught ratting a man's belongings, and slapped over the head. Strangely, these men seemed to understand what he was after. They did not accuse him of thieving. They were indulgent towards him. Jer did not care, but Hugh was humiliated.

When the last shed cut out for the season, Hugh said 'What say we go back to Trafalgar for a couple of weeks, look up some of the old mates?'

He longed to make that town envy him. He wanted to bust up his cheque there, flaunt his money around, let people see his cream flannel waistcoat with the cornelian buttons. He wanted his old companions to see how far a man could go when he left Trafalgar.

Jer did not want to return but he had no choice.

In Trafalgar Margaret Kilker still thought of Hugh Darcy. She had schoolgirl dreams about him, taking him from the train carriage and having him walk down the grassy road with her, his arm around her waist. She could not reconcile the loud, dirty schoolboy she indistinctly remembered with this stunning young man. His face was not with her day and night, her mother kept her too busy for that; but when it was it was as clear as a picture, the straight black brows, the bloom in his cheeks. For Hugh had a skin as fine as a china cup. The ravaging Australian sun had done not a thing to change his Irish heritage. A long triangle of carnation suffused each cheek.

'You'd think he painted,' thought Margaret.

The girl never expected to see Hugh Darcy again. She went to socials and dances with other boys. But at the back of her head Hugh remained, not as real as a movie actor, but a good deal more solid than someone in a story.

Two

None of the Kilker children took after their mother except Margaret, a little, and certainly Delia. She was so wayward her father described her as going through life in a series of crosswise leaps.

The mother was a creature of electric sparks. She had the fatal Irish temperament, knocking your head askew one moment and the next not thinking twice about giving you her last crust of bread. In Margaret these traits had lessened and declined. Eny's dauntlessness was muted into the ability to endure and endlessly forgive. Eny scored forgiveness. She left all that class of thing to God.

When Hughie and Jer returned to Trafalgar Margaret was grown up and had forebodings about many things. When she was twelve Auntie Alf had read the tealeaves for her. She said Margaret would never get married.

'What will happen to me if I don't?'

'You'll have a peaceful life like me, and devote yourself to the Church.'

Margaret got the horrors. Fifteen, sixteen, eighteen, and she was still imagining herself like Aunt Alf, trying to make ends meet in a threadbare rural presbytery, getting excited over the parish bazaar. Josie, present at the tealeaf reading, had worked very hard to keep this dreary picture before her sister.

At fifteen Josie was a valued junior at Capper's Universal Providers. She wore a black skirt and white blouse, and the blue enamel watch on a black cord that Auntie Alf had given her. Three evenings a week she attended accountancy instruction at the local High School. Eny thought she was out of her mind. Noel Capper, of some importance as the son of the firm, had already made application to John Kilker to begin walking out with Josephine when she turned sixteen.

Where the other Kilkers were broad and soft, Josie was narrow and hard. She tormented Margaret, the credulous lump, with thoughtful vindictiveness. Though she longed obsessively for her mother's favour, she rubbed Eny up the wrong way with everything

24

she did. The unhealed wound within Josie bled every day.

Josie knew her worth. Her bones were made of iron, her brain sharper than any other in the family. She had eyes like blue porcelain and elegant feet and hands. Still, her mother did not love her, or, if she did, did not show it. When young, Josie had sometimes thought of drowning herself in the creek, or even the cesspit. She had confessed this to Auntie Alf, her only friend within the family except her father. Aunt Alf loved and supported Josephine. She knew that the girl's mother, so wicked-tongued, so swift to judge, could never understand a child so different from herself. Alf knew, too, the secret damage inflicted by the indifferent parent.

Rowena Kilker had begun as a Mullins. Her father was a slight man with beautiful, treacherous blue eyes. It was not his fault he started with a large head and dwindled down to a pair of wasp legs: his poor mother was carrying him during the Famine. She had nothing but a daily handful of Indian corn with which to build his bones and nerves. All his features jostled together in the middle of his face and he was never seen without a downpour of a cold.

Still, Eny loved him, and as soon as she was old enough she applied for emigration papers for them both. As he was an actressy little fellow, he put on a great show of lamentation for the neighbours, referring to the departure from his starving country as a white martyrdom.

'Won't I make it a red martyrdom if you don't shut your face,' said his daughter. She was a grand girl but altogether too forthcoming with the back of her hand. It was a mystery to all how Willie had begotten her.

'Come on, Dadda,' she persuaded, 'isn't it the strong climate that will lay waste your catarrh? I hear they have sunshine even at Christmas.'

Her father put on a stubborn lip.

'And the very minute you're on the ship,' coaxed his daughter, 'you can set about growing dundrearies!'

Mr Mullins's long ambition had been to grow fine tresses of hair at the sides of his clean-shaven face. He had seen pictures of the English parliament which looked like an acre of seaweed. Even in Ireland the dandies swanked about between feathery sideburns so long they sometimes blew over the curly brims of their hats. Mr Mullins's master had such dundrearies, and he took jealous care

25

that none of his servants sprouted any of the same.

'The dishpot!' brooded Rowena's father.

Escape from this despot and the prospective grandeur of dundrearies was what brought the father to Australia. Unfortunately he was light-fingered and, having been caught ratting his fellow passengers' kit, he was given a rough deck trial and sentenced to a pitch cap. It was only the chaplain's eloquence that saved him from this severity, for the painting of the head with tar meant that the scalp as well as the hair was destroyed. Peevishly, the emigrants compromised by shaving him, face and head, as bald as a skull.

It was a brutal blow to old Willie. He sulked in his boarding house bed until Rowena had to fetch the priest to him. It was this man who found a post for the pair of them on a farm north-west of Sydney, the father to work with the crops and Eny to milk and help cook for the homestead. Still Willie would not venture forth. He said he would lurk in the town till his hair had grown decently. It was arranged that Eny would go on to the situation at Chandadah, near the settlement of Juno, and Willie would follow her as soon as possible.

Eny left her father with misgivings and tears. He was just the kind to use all their savings to take the ship home and never leave her a word. But once she was in the train, her straw hamper on the rack above, her Rosary beads in her pocket, and her hatpin held ready on her lap, she forgot her worries. The hatpin was there on the advice of the Father, who warned her that colonial men were airy beyond belief.

Autumn was on the land. The sky might have been like blue enamel, but the wind had a tweak in it. Eny had been told that in New South Wales the trees were always green, the grass brown, and water was not to be seen. But this was not true. The train drummed many times over the suave coils of great rivers. Amongst the freckled gums shone steely trickles between huge rounded rocks. Skewbald cattle crowded around them, thick as flies about jampots. Rows of poplars, yellow as sovereigns, marked out the boundaries of vast fields, velvet black, some being harvested for potatoes, others with the dry haulms still standing. Eny marvelled.

'A body wouldn't go hungry in a million years,' she thought, and said a Hail Mary on the strength of it.

The railway led between the hills. Eny fell asleep, waking some time later to find herself alone in the carriage except for a party fondling her ankle and about to make free with her garter. Instead of being an airy colonial lad, he was a small Dresden china knick-knack, with a baby face and a tall hat like an unlicked cat.

Rowena sent him tumbling with one blow. She had a moment of guilt at hitting so venerable a man, but that soon passed, and she shied his hat through the window.

Apparently expecting a murder, with himself on the wrong end, the granddad grabbed up his portmanteau and fled the carriage. Still, Eny was shaken. She sucked her knuckles and thought how right the priest had been. She was still ruffled when she got out at Juno, where she was to be met by someone from Chanadah homestead. Juno was a siding where the slow north and south trains stopped once a week. It served half a dozen small settlements, placed like potholes amongst the melon-green hills. Not a thing moved at Juno. The noble landscape was so silent Rowena thought she'd been struck deaf. She washed her face and hands at a tank beside the tin shed with the fine name on it, and shook the dust and smuts from her hair.

She now saw a ball of dust bowling down the thin road from the hills. In a few moments a horse and trap emerged from the cloud, and Steve Tookey was with her.

'You took your time!' she burst out.

Words of music and poetry rose to Steve's lips, for he was a terrible fellow for the girls. When he saw this one, the red mane down her back taking fire from the sun, her face clean under the stiff straw boater, but a watermark around her white neck from the train soot, everyone else in the world vanished and he knew he had to have her.

They drove through the big beaming landscape in a daze, a shared folly of delight. Eny did not even notice as they passed Juno, two horse-troughs, a farrier's shop, a general store and a tin church. The idea of being kissed, ever, ever, by anyone but Steve Tookey made Eny's teeth shudder. The impact of his nearness upon her innocence made her feel a trifle out of her mind. She dared not open her mouth lest some foolish unexpected sound came out, a giggle or whimper. There was not a thing about him, from his tan highlow boots to the strip of court plaster on his nose where he had run into someone's fist that did not wound her heart deliciously. Her body, that all unconsciously for some years now had been alert

27

to every young man who came along, saying in its own way, 'Is this the one? Is this he?' burst into bloom.

She was so discomposed by love that when she finally met the mistress of the farm the woman thought she was a bit thick in the head. She looked with distaste at Rowena's bold tail of hair.

'Haven't you put your hair up yet, my girl? We'll have none of those old country ways at Chandadah!'

She commanded Eny to get it bundled into a cap before supper that evening.

The girl had been well trained at the Big House in her Derry village. She was an excellent dairymaid and could in a pinch wait on table. She was also required to clean, wash, assist the cook, feed the hens, dogs and cats, and do a multitude of other jobs, all this for twelve pounds a year and her keep. She must have given satisfaction, although looking back at those months Rowena perceived she had lived in a dream. She could think of nothing but Steve.

Their meeting was more like a collision than anything else. Her passion, her bliss, was so private, so much a part of her, that all her life she kept it to herself. She never gave as much as a hint to any of her girls when they idly chattered about romance, not even Kathleen, her dearest. She did not dwell on it herself; its primitive holiness must not be defined by words. Only when she was being married, and she heard the words 'with my body I thee worship' did she cry out silently 'Oh, Stevie, wasn't that the truth!' and weep inside her for what could not be.

For, like so many roaring affairs, this one came to nothing. Steve Tookey, foundering in love as he was, believed he would be betraying his manhood if he changed his ways in the slightest. Bravely he fought his inclination to do what Rowena expected, to settle down and take a steady job and in due course wed her.

At this time Steve was twenty-four and had been in the Colony six years. He had arrived as an apprentice wheelwright, and found work immediately. But he was a devil to fight. In fact, his nickname around the country was Leather, because he threw it so often. No sooner did he hear of a likely scrapper at some peppertree town in the inland than he was off. It seemed he could not rest until he had licked every man within riding distance.

He broke his indentures and was brought to court for that, but his master the smith, a Salvation Army man who liked the boy, paid his fine and released him.

'He's like a tomcat or one of them tumultuous dogs, Your Honour,' he explained to the magistrate. 'It's in his nature and only prayer will cauterise it out of him.'

Steve led a wandering life, mostly working as striker in whatever forge he came across. He was of middle height but built like a blockhouse, honest, cheerful, with not a thought in his head beyond the next fight or feed or kiss.

Eny could not turn her head without his disappearing some-where, his gloves on a string over his shoulder. In two or three days he'd be back, sometimes with both eyes bunged up, though mostly unmarked. Rowena tried everything, tears, reproaches, seduction, rages.

She went privily to Steve's great friend, Constable Jim Oyster.

'Has he got you into trouble, my girl?'

'He has not,' she fired back. 'But he's the one for me and I don't want to waste time.'

'You're not going to change Leather Tookey,' warned the constable. 'Take him as he is, Eny. He's a lovely fella.'

But Rowena could see no future for herself or any possible children with her husband disappering all the time, never in regular work. And what would happen when his strength went and he could no longer lift the hammer? There was, too, her old father to consider. Any husband of hers must be prepared to take him into his house when Willie could not or would not work. The quarrels with Steve grew more frequent, more cruel. It was as if they had moved into a country where a row of thunderheads always towered upon the horizon. The fights left Eny with a hopeless ache in her breast. It was not only fear but anger that he did not find her more diverting than knocking the head off some blameless fellow thirty miles up the line.

At last Steve did not come back. He had been taken into custody for brawling with his opponents' supporters. That was bad enough, but he stretched the arresting sergeant as well, and got six months in the local jail. Rowena was so upset she lost her head entirely, told the mistress a few home truths, and was turned out without notice and no reference. She decided to go back to Sydney to her father, but a hundred miles down the line she was too distrait to travel fur-ther. She left the train at a town called Trafalgar, and went to a boarding house, where she got a job as a skivvy within a day or so. She tried to calm herself and think everything out. But Steve's fresh ruddy face was before her night and day. She longed and longed for him. She turned and twisted on her bed, the hot darkness full of her memories of him. For the first time the Irish songs had meaning for her, they filled her heart with anguish. Their words, dear dark head, swan-white breast, true grey eye, applied to no other man but Steve Tookey.

At last she made the usual excuse of the illiterate that her eyes were troubling her, and got the mistress to write a proud postcard to the jail where Steve was serving his sentence. The old woman saw the pathos in it, the droop of Eny's bright lip, and said impulsively, 'In the name of God, girl, why don't you go to him?'

'Indeed I won't,' retorted Eny. 'I wouldn't give him the satisfaction.'

She was prepared to fly to Steve the instant she had word. But the postcard was never answered. Her self-respect grew cold, her pride dim. She remembered what Constable Oyster had said and wept painful tears. But she was not one for self-pity. Instead she fanned her anger against Steve Tookey, too wrapped up in himself to know a good thing when he saw it. Her chest ached as if it had a skewer stuck in it, but she tossed her head more often than she hung it.

As always in the Colonies, there were far more men than women, and at every dance men cavorted with each other, he who was the lady wearing a handkerchief tied on his arm. So in no time every variety of young man from the chemist's educated son to the butcher's delivery boy began to call.

Also Rowena was a beauty then, skin like a petal, waist as small as a whippet's, blue eyes full of fire.

It was fortunate that the boarding-house missus was like a mother to her young servant. She advised her, should she want to settle down, to take John Kilker.

Rowena had already recognised that John Kilker was in all ways the reverse of her own father, solid as the Vatican, an employee of the Trafalgar iceworks, a man whose strong arm would never be in some other place massacring a stranger when a woman needed it to lean on.

'There's that sister of his,' she objected.

John had emigrated with his elder sister. As she was as plain as a box she had ended up as a presbytery servant. The Trafalgar parish had drawn the short straw. John took a job in that town to be near by.

From the time she was born the world behaved to Alf as if she had chosen to be homely out of sheer spite. When she was nine her mother, who was also John's, went to heaven. Her stepmother made no bones about letting the child know she'd crack a mirror. The stepmother had made a mistake marrying the father and took it out on the children. She was a great one for putting them in dark cupboards and not letting them out until they owned up, though they had no idea what they had done wrong. She refused to lay her tongue to the fancy name of Alfreda, and called the child Agnes. But Alf knew who she was. She fought this woman until she was twenty and John fifteen. The father did the best deed of his life when he gave permission for them to enlist in a Church drive for emigration. The stepmother hit the roof. How could they manage without the young ones' wages? she squealed. The father shut her up. He intended to desert the woman as soon as the children were safe on the ship.

Alf was as flat as a stoat, and yellowish, too. John could lift her with one hand. Yet, like many people starved in childhood, she was an indefatigable worker.

Inside Alf there was someone valiant and resolute, a majestically big woman. If it had not been for the stepmother, the big woman might have been all there was of Alf. As it was, the stepmother had left her mark. Alf had a stomach that took the huff at anything. She feared confined spaces. Even sticking her head in the wardrobe to get out her Mass-going coat was a feat of courage for Alf. She had fearful nervous spells: trembling, distraught, so irritable the sound of a bird chirping nearly drove her crazy. Alf had learnt to control these periods of suffering by becoming silent, going about her work step by step, leaning on God. The priests thought she was sulking. Not one of them realised that every time he spoke he narrowly escaped a good rap on the hooter.

The turnover of priests at Trafalgar was extraordinary. The Bishop might have speculated there was a Delilah in the parish had he not known Miss Kilker's worth. Once when he was scolding a frail incumbent who found it impossible to raise money for the church debt the big woman came raging out and scourged him for his unkindness to the meek old man who had more holiness in his big toe than His Lordship in his whole lardy body. The Bishop thought it over and had to agree. Besides, Miss Kilker was a fine cook and economical housekeeper.

31

Alf's diversions, as her brother called them, were catching. They put everyone else on edge as well. In its own way, the house was eerily affected. Handles came off saucepans, the lavatory cistern developed a soprano wheeze, the cat got a fishbone in its gullet. The troubled coming to the presbytery for advice slipped on the steps and gave themselves something worthwhile to fret about. The priest suspected Alf generated some kind of malefic electricity.

Rowena had never met Alf, but she had heard plenty.

'Ah,' sighed her mistress, 'a man who falls over himself to be kind to such a cranky old article of a sister must be one of the saints.'

Rowena thought little of John's saintliness. He'd made a few powerful grabs for her that made her believe otherwise. She put the bargain squarely to John.

'If you offer up Dadda I'll offer up Alf.'

John thought that as fair as any man could wish. He chose a time when Alf was not having a diversion, and took Eny to the presbytery. Alf looked her over. Rowena had thought the John's sister must be a bit of a crawthumper, going to daily Mass and all. But when she summoned up enough boldness to look into those small, deep-seeing eyes she knew that whatever Alf did was an honest thing. Still, she remained in awe of the woman. She was never truly at home with her.

Alf, for her part, had some misgivings. She could see that Rowena was a warm, volatile girl, only touching the earth in an odd place. Still, she liked her. She chided herself for the jealousy she found in her heart, and stuck her head in the scullery meat-safe for five minutes as a penance. She knew she would probably be jealous of any girl who married her brother.

So, shortly after her nineteenth birthday, when she had been little more than a year away from her own country, Rowena married John. She went into the marriage with the strong intention of making a good thing of it. Before the ceremony she prayed that God would help her never to think of Steve Tookey again. Though she was not in love with her husband, she liked him; so it happened that only two or three years passed before she realised she loved him dearly.

She had her father come from Sydney, and John did his best with him. In the city Willie had spent too much time with homesick Irishmen, and now proclaimed a sentimental yearning for the country which had barely fed him. He announced he was going to turn his face to the wall and die, and John told him he could do that in the henhouse.

The older children recalled him as an old-fashioned looking little man, with bunches of grey wool distributed without rhyme or reason over his countenance, and a soft cozening voice. The Kilker children grew up with this voice, a Dublin voice, for Willie as well as John had been reared in the capital. As he grew older he believed himself irresistible to women, and informed everyone of their amorous advances.

'I'm ate alive with them,' he told the priest, who rather enjoyed Willie's confessions.

One day he said, looking frightened and excited, 'Me belly's full of goss.'

They took him to the hospital, where he lowed and bellowed for a week or two, said 'I'm done', and died.

His funeral was a poor, scanty thing. He was buried on the day of the old Queen's Diamond Jubilee. Though Trafalgar declared a public holiday and hung out flags and ribbons, all those citizens of Irish descent were away at the football field, holding a protest meeting.

Rowena felt her father's death keenly. Her grief was not the same as it had been with little May. She bewailed her father's wasted, empty life.

'Ah, God, John,' she sighed, 'what's it all about?'

John lay in his bed listening to this, Eny nestled on his chest. Very content he was that Willie had gone to his long rest. Many a time he could hardly stay his boot from giving the old creature an urge in that direction.

'Didn't he give me you?' he murmured. 'If it hadn't been for your poor Ma marrying Will Mullins you might have been a Brady or Lenihan or any other one of them awful things. And your hair nothing but donkey brown.'

Eny conceded the biological justice of this.

'Still,' she said dolefully, 'I can just see Dadda in heaven this moment, criticising everything and complaining that St Teresa put the hard word on him.

'Ah, may the poor old coot be as happy as we are,' murmured John, putting Eny's hand where it would do the most good.

So the years went on, and Eny had child after child, sometimes as easily as a cat and sometimes in mortal agony. By the time Josie was

33

born the older boys Dan and Emmet were working away from home, and never writing except, as was their duty, at Easter. Delia had not yet flown the coop with that married villain, and beloved Kathleen was still alive. After Josie was born Eny lived with bated breath for a year or so. She was sick to death of letting her skirts out and taking them in.

At last she knew she was safe and she and John had a real Christmas of a time. She used to sit in church listening to the priest raving about the evils of birth control and the sorrow of empty cradles and think he was off his head, and the Pope with him.

Eny was a happy woman. It was true that now and again her tongue shaved John's dignity too closely and he flung off and got bawling drunk. He was none the worse for that and neither was she.

So the year and the day came when the Darcy brothers returned to Trafalgar. They soaked in the pub bath, getting rid of the stinks of greasy wool, sheep dip, cookhouse fireplaces where the flames were fed half with wood and half with the fat that drizzled from roasting mutton. Hugh's face came up so rosy it was a picture. Jer's, being aquiline and brown as a nut, was the more interesting, but girls didn't think that.

The elderly maid awakened them with cups of tea, and excitedly reminded them it was the King's Birthday holiday.

'We got a patriotic march and a merry-go-round and a travelling show about a murder,' she boasted. 'Wasn't we all cursing last night with the rain, but today's fine. Want me to iron your good duds?'

The rain had thrown Trafalgar into distress.

'Didn't I fear the worst,' said John Kilker, 'when I saw them three kookaburras last night on the washhouse roof, hoohooing like devils.'

Every important event in Trafalgar was held at the Domain, a flat low-lying area to the west of Copenhagen Creek. For many thousand years before white settlement it had been the ritual battle ground of the blacks. Now it was the football field, the showground. Political meetings were held there, and once in a while it was a racecourse. It turned green or brown in season and was often churned up like a mud glacier, for the Copenhagen had a temperament like a mad goat.

'She rose a trifle last night,' reported John. He had been away at first light with the other organisers to see how things were going. 'The tug o' war pitch is all skilly mud. We'll have to move the mat nearer the bandstand. God willing, we'll have a fine day.'

It was time for him to get into his Sunday clothes. His wife watched from the bed, her expression enigmatic.

John hoped that Eny had finished surging at him. In his starched white long-tailed shirt, socks and garters he stood at the wash stand shaving, pulling a long lip as he nicked at the hairs in his nose. He could see a bit of Rowena in his shaving glass and his hopes fell.

Every year since his arrival in the town, John had attended most public sports meetings. He had started off sprinting when he was a youth, and then when he began to put on beef he competed in the tug o' war and the hammer throw. The cry 'Johnny Kilker does it again!' gave him such a kick, every time. Once Eny had been proud of him, shouting encouragement and glowering at folk who did the same thing for other men. But now she considered him too old. Before each King's Birthday he had to endure a week of strong recrimination.

'You'll leave wife and children to mourn you, and all for vanity!'

'I'm as good as I was when I was forty,' growled John.

'Good is it?' she scoffed. 'Look at the varicose veins on you. You're within a prayer's distance of a wooden leg.'

'I've had enough from you, you battleaxe.'

'My Dadda had legs like a little white pigeon.'

'No wonder in that. He went the full of a lifetime without doing a stroke of work.'

By this time he had donned his best black trousers with the scarlet braces which showed up so well when he formally removed his coat for the sporting events.

'You're as contrary as a mule, John Kilker. I think that if I wept salt tears to persuade you to throw that great hammer you'd refuse just to spite me.'

'If only you would, you thick-headed woman,' was what John thought in his heart, for there was nothing he could do about his contrariness. That was the way he was. But there was no doubt he had sometimes felt a trifle light-headed of late, and there was a heavy pounding in his ears when he put his hand to the bigger ice blocks. But the sports events were a test of manhood for him, in a way he felt Eny could never understand.

His good humour returned; it was never away for long.

'Ah, Eny, one of these days I'll be an aged old fella, but that isn't yet. Stop looking like Rent Day and we'll enjoy the holiday with the girls, for who knows whether we'll have another?'

'True for you,' said Eny lugubriously, looking so much like a parson at a funeral that John burst out laughing. So, after a moment, did she. He gave her a smacker, saying, 'You knock spots off all the women I've ever seen. I wouldn't die for fifty quid!'

His wife's fears for him were genuine. The thought of life without John was a nightmare. But she was not one for brooding, and jumped out of bed exhilarated by the holiday, the band music, the murder. If there was one thing she liked more than another it was a play, and this one had blood enough in it to curdle your spit.

'Pip pip!' sang out Josie. Away she skimmed, sleek as a bird in a green dress belted at the hips, her bobbed hair hidden in a fashionable tea-cosy.

Eny could hear Margaret muttering and groaning.

'There's one in,' she heard her daughter say. Auntie Alf, always with a few shillings to spare for her nieces, had bought Margaret a pair of stays. Margaret knew very well Josie had put her up to it, but she loved her aunt too much to protest.

'Don't be upset, dear,' Aunt Alf had advised. 'You'll get used to them. We all need support for the burst. Your clothes will hang better and you won't be embarrassed with gentlemen staring.'

Margaret was mortified. Did people, let alone gentlemen, stare? And why was that so bad? Josie had made her feel it was coarse to have a big front, but Aunt Alf seemed to think it sinful.

Made of pink coutil, stiffened with metal busks, the stays had no space whatsoever for the female body as God designed it.

'They're a cruel shape,' complained Margaret.

Eny squashed her into them. There she stood, her top converted into a cushion hard as rock, with an unnatural hollow underneath.

'Was there ever such a Guy Fáwkes?' she mourned.

Margaret had put up her hair the year before and it had been falling down ever since. It was a turmoil of curls and wisps and no hairpin would hold it. It unravelled from under her new hat, a blue jelly mould with fluted ribbon for handles, as if it had life of its own. In the end she wore her flowered summer hat, with her hair spilling down her back, tied with a ribbon.

Her mother gave her a hug. 'I'm off!' she said. 'And it's a fine day after all, blessed be God.'

The sky was the larkspur of summer rather than early winter. The sun sent out a roaring heat, drying up the puddles on the Domain, letting the flags lighten and blow out with a crack from their poles. The sunshine was so blinding on Herbie's brass buttons, straps and tassels when Eny met him at the door that she teased, 'Ah, wouldn't I like to pawn you!'

He was baffled. But there was Margaret, ready to be escorted to the Domain. She greeted him nicely, though if she had had a magic wand she would certainly have hit him with it and turned him into almost anyone else. Margaret was not officially walking out with Herbie Lennon but she always found herself doing so. He could have been worse, being a decent boy with buck teeth. He hated the Masons and was active in the Hibernians. He was as bare of romance as an egg, but what was Margaret to do? She was at the age when life came at her like a bull charging. She knew what was expected of her, to marry someone respectable, have a family, be a good Catholic, and not bother other people. She was a daughter. A daughter became a wife. But how was she to do that when only Herb Lennon showed signs of wanting to wed her?

Herbie had been sweet on Margaret since they left school. He had made up his mind to marry her and that was that. Once or twice he had a desire to fling her to the ground and teach her what it was all about. Shame had followed these lustful thoughts. Soberly he confessed his sin, and listened attentively to the priest's warning that he who looked upon a woman with lust had done the same as committing adultery. Father Driscoll thought this scandalously unfair, but Herb quite saw the point of it. Anyway, would he wish to marry Margaret if she permitted him to fling her to the ground and teach her what it was all about? He believed not. He had no idea that Margaret, warned against possible flinging by her mother, had felt her stomach heave. This was not prompted by virtue, though she was a virtuous girl, but by physical aversion. Herb had woolly hair like kapok. For some reason it turned her right off.

The young man had tried many times to propose to her. The moment he got a certain throb in his voice Margaret broke out in a sweat and made an excuse, however fatuous, to escape. Something desperate inside her, unrecognised, undefined, let out a screech of horror. Nothing, her desire to be married, her mother's sensible advice to take him while he was still warm, Josie's jibes, silenced that screech. Somehow she knew that if Herbie proposed she wouldn't know how to say no, and to marry Herbie would be to become someone who was not herself.

For Herbie, in spite of his red bandsman's uniform, his good manners, his devout Catholicism, was a great boy for domination. Tirelessly he applied pressure. He was critical and parental.

'I prefer you not to wear those vulgar pink stockings,' he said. 'Black is more ladylike.'

However, he cast a furtive glance of approval at Margaret's bosom. He had never actually seen breasts since he was weaned and was upset by the look of them. He much preferred the cushion.

'They're not pink, they're flesh-coloured and all the rage,' retorted Margaret tetchily. Herbie sighed. She was not in the best of moods. Nevertheless, he intended to come to an understanding with Margaret on this auspicious day. He wished to be engaged. His job was steady, his morals superior, his mother willing if not enthusiastic, and he had fifty pounds in the bank.

'Well, dear, away to the bandstand!' he said forgivingly.

Three bands were playing this King's Birthday. The Salvation Army had made a bit to participate, but the Council banished them to a corner of the Domain where they put up a marquee and dispersed rock cakes and cups of cocoa to the indigent.

As Margaret stood amongst the happy crowd wondering what to do next her sister sauntered past on the blazered arm of Noel Capper.

Josie looked at Margaret's front, and mouthed, 'Oh, you do look a scream!'

Margaret tilted her chin, but she went off with a dart in her heart, a desire to pull Josie's hat down over her eyes, or kick her in her champagne-coloured shins. Well she knew she looked a fright.

'I won't be miserable, I won't,' she commanded herself.

Ahead was the twinkle, the red and gilt, of a merry-go-round. Tragically she flung herself upon it and began to go up and down, faster and faster.

Cruel, hurtful Josie! Why did she do it when she was so lucky, able to become engaged to Noel whenever their fathers gave permission? Margaret didn't care for Noel herself. He had little weak eyes made into big weak eyes by glasses, and he thought the world of himself. But still, he was already Josie's. Margaret hated being alone when all the other girls had boys with them; from her eminence she could see them everywhere, strolling, laughing. Even when she was with a boy it was only old Herb Lennon with his funny lip like a frill of steak. She supposed that was because he played in a brass band.

Still, even thinking about Herbie's lip made her feel squeamish. With horror she realised she *was* squeamish. Her unsophisticated ears and stomach were not used to going up and down and round and round. She slipped off the dappled horse; its teeth were like Herbie's. She sent up a prayer that the machine would slow down, and it did, just as she saw Hugh Darcy standing on the grass watching the merry-go-round.

Hugh had no sooner emerged into the main street than depression hit him. He'd been mad to come back to this hole. He didn't even have Jer with him. Jer wanted to see their mother's grave, and had gone off on his own. Hughie recalled that at Frances Darcy's funeral no one had cried but young Jer. He had sobbed and gasped until he had been led away to be cleaned up and comforted.

No one had thought to comfort the elder son but Mrs Kilker. She had the reputation of being a hard lady, but she'd come over and said some kindly things to the big yahoo he'd been then, morose, hands shoved in trouser pockets. He had been so embarrassed he could have punched her face in.

Hugh had never come to terms with the cruel mutilation of his mother's death, as Jeremiah had. His grief was never expressed, never admitted. Coming back to Trafalgar brought it perilously close to the top of his mind. He was tense with anger, both at himself and his mother, for different reasons.

He stood there watching the merry-go-round, wondering if pubs opened on public holidays, when this soft thing fell into his arms. Actually she was a fair-sized girl; they collapsed together on the grass. But he had this feeling of softness, as if a pigeon had hit him in the chest. She was nowhere near as pretty as some of the girls he'd known, but there was something about her that told him he'd better look after her. Now she sat up in a flurry of skirt, pulling it down over her shiny stockinged knees, white as a bone, speechless.

'Did you fall off? Are you hurt anywhere?'

'Don't speak to me,' she gasped. 'I'm going to throw up.'

'Sit still. You'll be right as rain in a minute.'

In a moment this was so. Colour came back in her face; it was almost as brilliant as his own. She had a nose within an ace of being a saddle, blue eyes amid a lot of lashes and tobacco-coloured hair. The very image of a country mug, a real bunny.

'You with anyone?' he asked.

'No,' said Margaret, feverish with excitement. To meet Hughie Darcy this way! He didn't know who she was, let alone the things she'd dreamt about him. She was in torment from the stays, her stomach was still uneasy, in a moment or two she'd be dying to go to the lav. But oh, the bliss!

Hugh could see she was knocked out by him. The way she blushed, lost her breath, fiddled with her hair! Indulgently, a conqueror, he introduced himself.

'I know,' she said. 'We used to go to the same school, ages ago that was. I'm Margaret Kilker. Gee, I like your moustache.'

'Want to see the show?' he asked carelessly. Margaret squealed as if he'd pinched her.

'Oh, Lord,' she cried. 'I'm not allowed, but I'll die if I don't see it!'

Eny herself would not have missed a play for a guinea, but she maintained that the theatre heated girls' blood. John backed her in this; he knew that most travelling showmen were rough as bags. And the plays were a lot of trash, blood and thunder. But, like Eny, that was what Margaret yearned for, thrills, frights, handsome men and loud posh voices. It was wonderful how flexible her conscience had become in the few minutes since she met Hugh Darcy, for she did not hesitate.

The formless, protective feeling had left Hughie's consciousness and was forgotten. The girl was as silly as a turkey.

'Come on then,' he said. 'My word, you've got pretty hair.'

She floated off with him. The band made heavenly music. The sideshow barkers had voices like silver trumpets. The clash of the Salvation lassies' tambourines far, far away was like bells.

'Ah, bugger it all,' thought Hughie, shutting his mouth on the words. He had seen Jeremiah, and Jer had seen him.

'It's my young brother,' he said sulkily to Margaret. Jer swung towards them, full of pleasure and welcome.

'I remember now,' said Margaret. 'The little cripple boy.'

She tried to smile, to be agreeable, but she could hardly keep her eyes off Jer's bare feet, they were so blackish, thin, and shaped like walking-stick handles. Their strangeness made Margaret ill at ease; she longed for him to go off on his own.

But Jer stuck with them like a burr. No sideways glances or scorching words from the corner of his brother's mouth shook him. Margaret could have cried. She wanted with all her might to be along with Hugh. But how could she let the poor boy see that? She smiled and chatted with him, shared with him the fluff of spun sugar Hugh bought her.

At last Hugh took Jer aside and gave him three shillings to keep out of their way.

'Don't you cotton on, you silly bastard? I might be on to a good thing there.'

'Five bob and you tell me all about how she was,' bargained Jer. 'Shove it.'

'Well, then,' said Jer. He won, as he always did, and moved away laboriously, hoping Margaret was watching him and feeling bad. He was excited. Now he could see the travelling show. If he looked pathetic enough the showman might let him in for half fare.

Margaret could have wept happy tears. Hugh's relief made him blithely reckless. He wanted to show off. Soon her arms were full of rubbish, dolls on sticks, a coconut, paper roses and two balloons. The girl was drunk with pleasure. She heard cheering from the cricket pitch, where the tug o' war contestants had taken up their stand, and did not remember that her father was in one of the teams and she was supposed to barrack.

She longed for Josie to see her. She looked around proudly, nodding to those she knew, until her eyes alighted on her erstwhile escort Herbie.

Herbie had come off duty, deafened by Strauss and Sousa, his cheeks cramped and his lungs as dry as flannel. He sharply refused beer, supplied free to the bandsmen, and strode about looking for Margaret. He was irritated not to find her waiting for him beside the bandstand, and more so to espy her arm in arm with a Valentino in a cream waistcoat with showy buttons. Herb was more puzzled than disturbed.

His strongest reaction was to the stranger's waistcoast, common in the extreme. Margaret did not look like herself, her cheeks were crimson, that unruly hair had sprung out of its ribbon. When she introduced the two young men she tittered like a flapper.

'It's almost lunch time,' Herb coldly informed her, extending his crooked arm.

'I don't want to have lunch,' blurted Margaret. 'I've made other plans, I've changed my mind.'

41

She looked as if she might cry, her eyes glistening, her lip tremulous. Herb was so taken aback he broke into expostulations.

'Stop right there, sport,' said Hugh. 'You heard the young lady.'

The girl now became frightened and stammered:

'I just don't feel like it, don't you see? Oh, stop bothering me about it. I can do as I like!'

All she wanted was for Herbie to take his big disapproving face away.

'You don't own me!' she cried, almost in tears.

'Move on, fella,' said Hugh. Herbie now noticed he had big fists and a thickening over one eye that looked as if he were often in scraps.

'Certainly, Margaret, if that's what you want. I daresay you have some reason for behaving like this.'

He put on his braided cap and moved away with dignity. He was more disturbed than angry. How pretty she had looked! He had a rare pang of desire for Margaret. That yob! That larrikin! She didn't know him; Herbie was acquainted with all Margaret's friends. To think that she would jib at doing something they had agreed to do! It was inexplicable.

'If we hurry we'll make the second show,' said Hugh. He gave her a squeeze.

Hugh knew the phenomenal effect of theatrical presentations, however crude, upon rustic people. He was not beyond it himself; sometimes he and Jer talked for days on end about some melodrama they had seen. Men said that girls got so highly strung they scarcely knew what they were doing. The show was as effective as a travelling revival mission, always blamed for a crop of illegitimate children in the district. Certainly Margaret was giddy with excitement.

'I'm shaking like a leaf,' she whispered, 'and it hasn't even started!'

In the twilit dusty tent every seat was filled. Suddenly a lemon ray shone upon the curtain, painted with a castle and a snow peak. Behind Margaret and Hugh arose an animal bray of pleasure from the sweaty mob shoving and trampling one another in the Standing Room Only area.

Meanwhile Hugh had spotted Jer, his insatiable stare upon him and the girl. Outrage boiled in Hugh. He shuddered all over. Margaret thought it was with passion. He kissed her cannibalistically, ignoring catcalls and cheers.

'Bloody Jer!' he thought despairingly as the curtain cranked aside. Margaret fell against him as if her backbone had gone. She felt things she had never felt before.

Having arrived late, Eny stood amongst the rabble in flat hats and flared pants at the rear. When she spied her daughter in the audience she was irate enough, but when she saw the young man with Margaret give her a kiss you wouldn't see out of a bedroom she uttered a yelp.

'What's the matter, Ma?' asked the flat hat beside her. 'Jealous?'

She lamed him with her sharp-heeled shoe, glaring all the time at the miscreant in front of her. Such misgivings she had when she saw it was not Herbie Lennon but a stranger!

'If God spares me I'll scorch her to the ground,' she said, adding to the whinger beside her, 'Ah, shut your trap and watch the play!' She made up her mind she would catch Margaret and the villain she was with outside the tent. She then put them both out of her head.

There was an actor up there in the ruby murk who had once been good. Never did he speak his fatuous lines without being aware of the mental tumult of the audience. They were riveted by melodrama. He could see their eyes, glassy red as those of animals caught in the glare of headlights. As he slew the victim in the barn he was almost wafted upwards by a vast moan, as though he had murdered them all.

Margaret's head swam.

'It's awful, awful!' she moaned in an ecstasy of enjoyment, and hid her face on Hugh's sleeve. He had seen 'Murder in the Red Barn' twice before: it was a standby of the travelling shows; yet he too could not take his eyes from the stage.

He intended to take Margaret down to the casuarina groves beside the creek before the spell of the play wore off. He stole a sideways glance at her. She looked bemused enough for anything. Somehow he must avoid Jer.

The moment the curtain fell and the pianist began to slam out 'God Save the King' Hugh grabbed Margaret's hand and bolted for the side entrance. Emerging into the horrid whiteness of day both of them felt grumpy, up in the air, half-sick.

Jer had thought fastest. Jer was waiting, teetering on his crutches, pathetic lonely little fellow.

'Stop haunting me, you bastard!' Hugh said savagely, seizing his brother by the shirt. Jer fell skilfully off his crutches.

'Come on!' commanded Hugh. Dragging Margaret by the hand, he whisked behind a sideshow. Water gurgled from a tank: there was a querulous mutter from the unseen audience.

'You shouldn't have shaken him,' remonstrated Margaret. 'Him a cripple and everything.'

'I've had my full of him following me around,' said Hugh. 'Bloody gooseberry.' He turned a melting look on her and said humbly. 'Didn't mean to swear. It's just that I want me and you to be alone.'

Margaret swallowed it all. Blushes came and went; she squeezed Hugh's hand.

'Can you spot him anywhere?'

Margaret peeped out. She did not see Jer, but she instantly observed her mother, standing to one side of the emerging crowd, looking like thunder.

'Oh, Lord, Hughie, there's Ma! Someone must have told her I went to the play! She'll slaughter me, she will, honest.'

The girl was so alarmed Hugh saw that indeed Mrs Kilker would murder her, or something very close.

Hughie pondered. As he did so three mermaids waddled past them, their blue feet sticking out between tail flukes, their sequinned costumes held up in dripping ruckled folds. They were bulky girls, aggrieved and cold. Hugh and Margaret fell in at the far side of them.

'Whatever happened to you, beautiful?' he asked sympathetically of the nearest.

'Some rotten swine took the plug out of the tank,' she chattered. Hugh put on a face of dismay and condolence, pushing Margaret along in their shelter. At their dressing tent he left them and, with Margaret, made a dash for the House of Horror.

'Can you see your Mum anywhere?'

'No. But I can see Jer.'

'Never mind him, he won't have any money left.'

Hugh and Margaret ran through the yawning entrance and found themselves in darkness.

Not far behind them Mrs Kilker snatched her ticket from the box, shoved through the turnstile and the creaking door. She was immediately assailed by a skeleton. Blue light shone, the thing's hollow jaws chomped at her, and she let out a whoop like a steam

44

whistle. She floundered around, intending to go out where she had come in, and bumped into something with long arms like a wooden octopus.

The pair of them fell over together, and were borne on a travelling platform through a dark hideous hell.

The ticket seller had made a gallant effort to prevent Jer entering the House of Horror. He had visions of a crutch getting stuck in the mechanism and the whole thing cranking to a halt. But Jer smartly cracked him across the shin, and shot up the ramp with the agility of a mosquito. The ticket seller heard the shrieks and hoped if anyone was dying in there it was the hoppy.

The travelling platform was made of circular plates that glided back and forth across each other. Eny scrambled at last to her feet. Lightning flashed, and she was whirled around to find a dark devilish face looking up at her from the level of her knees.

'I've lost me crutches, I've lost 'em, moaned this face. The pair of them went around together for a moment, yelling, then night fell and a velvet spider as big as a puppy dropped on Eny's hat.

'I found one!' said the phantom voice gladly. Eny shrieked her head off. Some distance away she could hear Margaret doing the same thing, but the girl was big enough to look after herself. Eny's spider jerked away into the roof, the side of the tunnel lit up fierily, and she saw a man hanging by the neck with his tongue out like a bit of red flannel. She fell back against Jer, who had now recovered the other crutch and teetered precariously on a moving plate. Eny saw he was a live boy.

'I thought you was a ghost too!' she confessed.

Jer did not recognise Mrs Kilker, she was just an old squealing lady. But something about his twisted legs was familiar to her.

Before she could ask a question, a phosphorescent shape, somewhat after the style of a human form, swept up the dark tunnel and enveloped them both. Jer struck out with a crutch. Eny clutched the wall, where a vast hanging spiderweb netted her. She might well have stayed there for ever, but the platform carried her, lurching and staggering, through ghastly blue light and worse green, past dim caves where monsters threatened, and finally precipitated both her and Jer into a dull cloudy afternoon.

'I'm that nervous I could jump the height of a tree,' she confessed to the boy. 'My hair is standing on end!' Embarrassed, he scuttled away, touching his cap and murmuring goodbye. She had him now.

45

He was the little boy who cried so much at poor Mrs Darcy's funeral. Eny looked about for Margaret and her escort, but there was no sign of them. Only of Josie, dishevelled and breathless, half in tears.

'I've been looking for you everywhere,' she cried. 'Pa's taken a queer turn. They've fetched the doctor.'

As for Jeremiah, he found his brother and Margaret in no time at all, eating buttered saveloys on the steps of a caravan. They stared at him guiltily. Jer beamed. But the House of Horror had unnerved Hugh; he was beginning to wonder if Margaret was worth the trouble.

'Get away from us, will you? You're like a flaming sticking plaster. Clear out. I mean it. I'll see you back at the pub.'

Jer put on a heartbreaking expression and Margaret was ashamed.

'Well, of course I will, Hughie. I didn't know I was in the way. I'll go and spend some time with the Salvation Army, they're real nice people.'

He moved away, hanging his head. Hugh's blood ran cold. Always Jer managed to get him by the short hairs. All desire for the girl left him. He had to get to the Army's tent before his brother started repenting.

A smart little girl hurried up to Margaret. She gasped out:

'Where have you been? I've looked and looked all over the place, Pa's awfully sick, you've got to come.'

Hugh blessed the good fortune that enabled him to get shot of the girl. 'You go off to your Dad. Go on, I want you to. Tell you what, we'll meet later, by the suspension bridge. About five.'

Josie ran him over with her clever eyes, summed him up as a bush lair and took her sister away to the St John's Ambulance station.

Strange things had happened to John Kilker. He went through the tug o' war as easy as a bird. He knew that the younger men took the strain; all he had to do was to allow his vast weight to connect with the earth. He had sailed through the event without a problem.

'I'm not even breathing hard,' he pointed out to Eny.

There were terrible depths of frivolity in his wife that even now almost brought a joke to her lips, but she said. 'Your face is such a colour, John. Black as the ace of spades. I'm asking you not to throw the hammer, John.'

But he went off defiantly and, when the time came, took the

great weight, felt his muscles crack, whirled, and let go. He sensed the hammer fly away, the world was speckled red, he felt light and floating, and knew he was still alive and Johnny Kilker. He opened his eyes and saw the doctor and his wife with their heads together above him. The pain in his chest was so great he could spare no time for them. It was a fearful cramp. He could hardly breathe. The doctor raised his head a little, and he was sick over the man's good suit. He was a little better then, whispering, 'Ah, God, doctor, I've destroyed you!'

Eny was not crying, but he had never seen such a face of terror. 'How do you feel, John?'

He pondered a little. 'I feel all right.'

This was so. John had a great sense of his body; it had laboured willingly for him, given him joy and pleasure. Now he could feel it trying to steady itself, settle back on an even keel, get the blood flowing soft and smooth and the heart ticking at the right pace.

'I'll just have a bit of a spell,' he said.

'That beer upset me,' he apologised to the doctor. 'Shouldn't have guttled it down right after the tug o' war.'

'That's probably what happened,' agreed the doctor. He thought what a sad thing it was that nothing could be done for heart attacks except leading the life of a turnip.

'It'll kill old John,' he thought, 'just as it would kill me.'

He was a good man, the doctor, deeply rooted in the complex life of that small town. He had known John for ever. He thought of the way people said, 'The kettle's always on the boil at Kilker's,' and wondered what would happen now.

Robustly he reassured the frightened Eny, said he would call at the house in an hour, and left John to the ambulance officers.

Margaret and Josie stood to one side crying. Margaret blubbered heartily, finding relief in her tears. Josie's might have wetted one corner of her handkerchief; all the others ran down inside like drops of acid.

'She's got cement for a heart, that one,' thought her mother.

Josie suffered for her father far more deeply than Margaret. If he had died! If there had been no more Pa in the house!

Noel tried to comfort her but she dismissed him, saying she wished to go home alone. In truth she was distracted by a premonition of eventual loss, and did not know how to cope with it.

At home, Margaret fussed over her mother, bringing her brandy, tea, and simple comfort. Josie sat for long gazing into the face of her sleeping father, the strong, immortal rooftree of the house. If she had been a religious girl she would have prayed. As it was, she tried to transfer her immense vitality to him so that he should be as he was before.

Mrs Kilker felt the worse because she had slipped away before the hammer throw, and all for a murder play. She confessed to Margaret, and Margaret confessed to her, and they both felt the better for it.

Before five o'clock Margaret returned to the Domain. The King's Birthday was over, the tents and caravans gone, the merry-go-round dismantled. The Domain was dirty, the damp ground trampled into muck. The Boy Scouts ran around picking up bottles and papers.

A chill wind blew from the south, bustling the swans on their homeward flight. They were so high the light from the vanished sun picked them out like a trail of sparks. Their sombre voices struck an echo from Margaret's heart, for already she was certain Hugh Darcy would not come.

Though the suspension bridge over the creek was condemned it was still used. Its planking was coated with dense yellow clay from the last flood, the supporting wire ropes rusty and split. It had been a great place for dares in their schooldays. He who crossed the creek on the outside of the bridge, hand over hand along the rail, was a hero, in the school idiom a bottler. Hugh Darcy had done it with his little brother clinging to his back. He was a double bottler. Margaret looked over the rail now, at the inch of plank which had supported the boy's toes. He had been a brave youngster, and was probably braver now.

Standing there, gazing into the darkening water, she found every excuse for his not keeping faith. She was clumsy, too fat, her bust had turned into a pillow, she shouldn't have worn her hair down her back like a school child. She waited till she heard the Angelus faintly ring in the convent on the other side of town. It was six, too late to wait any longer. She went home through the dusk, feeling upset about her father but more upset about Hugh.

'You're well out of it,' said her sister a day later. 'That brother of his, the lame one, got up at the Salvation Army rally and shouted out he was saved.'

'Maybe he is,' said Margaret.

'Yes, but you should have heard what he repented of,' said Josie gleefully. 'It's all over town. He and his brother, they're just wasters. Your fellow drinks like a fish. He gets into fights, too.'

'Don't call him my fellow,' said Margaret angrily.

'And he's got girls everywhere, they say.'

'So what?'

'Then Hugh came and hauled his brother away. He smacked his head for him, too. The Sally major said he oughtn't to, and Hugh said he'd smack his for him as well.'

'What's it got to do with me?' yelled Margaret. She caught her sister a stinger on the ear. She began to sob: 'Anyway, he's a double bottler.'

Eny thought nothing of the blow; young Josie had got down on her knees and begged for it. But she, too, had heard the talk around town. Also now she recalled Hugh Darcy at his mother's funeral, dark, glowering, a wild goose of a boy. God be between him and my Margaret, she thought.

'It's no use your dreaming about that one,' she told her daughter. 'He's got flighty feet. You'll not see hide nor hair of him again.'

'I know,' said Margaret, continuing to weep.

Eny could have slapped her for letting Josie guess her feelings. Josie was still holding her scarlet ear, but smiling all the same.

'Don't stand there gawking,' the mother said sharply. 'Go and take a look at your father.'

'Even now,' thought Josie, 'with Pa so sick, she's thinking of Margaret.'

But Eny was not consciously thinking. She was feeling what she had felt many times before, that her girl needed placidity, kindness, no hullabaloo such as she herself revelled in. She thought Herbie as dull as dead flies; she wouldn't give tuppence for him; but he was fond of Margaret and he was the sort of man who would look after a wife and children. No wild boy ever looked after anything, let alone a wife.

She forgot her daughters, and went to sit beside her husband.

Jer had humbly begged his brother's pardon. He said he couldn't stand a bar of Trafalgar, and asked wretchedly if they could leave. Hugh knew that, for once, he was telling the truth.

He wanted to have a few words with old Mr Kilker, find out how he was. The old joker had been a trump taking care of the father's funeral and all. But he did not want to meet Margaret again. There was something about her that worried him.

'Sure we'll clear out,' he agreed. 'Bloody hole in the hills. Who'd want to live here unless he had a slat loose?'

He could not think why he had wanted to come, unless it was to make things different in some way.

'What say we clear out for Sydney?'

This was the way all their quarrels concluded, with a turning of their thoughts towards the dreamland with its spires and big clocks as wide as two men turned endways, and whisps of work for willing boys.

'That bridge that opens in the middle.'

'I never could work that out. Maybe Mum had it wrong.'

Hugh felt a renewed passion of protectiveness towards Jer. It was love, although he did not recognise it.

Jeremiah saw it at once. Happiness made him sentimental and warm.

He took his guitar and began to sing: 'Meet me tonight in dreamland, Under the silvery moon . . . .'

After a time the elderly maid knocked. She said shyly, 'Boss says he'd take it kindly if you boys came down to the kitchen and gave us a tune. We got a cup of tea on.'

The landlord was a fanatic Irishman who had never seen Ireland. Reared on an isolated selection by emigrant parents, he spoke as pure a tongue as was ever heard in Monaghan. From his point of view Australia was a small piece of Ireland itself, a bit of acreage that had slipped its moorings. During the Troubles of 1917 he had gone to jail for confronting a policeman in Pitt Street, Sydney, and flattening him merely because he wore a helmet.

He had the reputation of such hardness that a nail couldn't be driven into him with a six-pound hammer. But Jer soon had him pulling a long lip and pretending he had cigarette ash in his eye. He did it with Stephen Foster songs.

The landlord said gruffly, 'The wife died on me last year and it's leaned upon me.'

'God rest her blessed soul,' said Jer, 'as for certain He will.'

The maids gushed he'd make a fortune on the vaudeville, he was that soft and lovely with the songs.

'Ah, I'm nothing at all,' said Jer modestly. He let them know that all he wanted in the world was to get his two feet turned around the right way.

'There's operations,' he said. 'Marvellous things them doctors can do. But ah, it takes money.'

The landlord was back to normal the next morning. Still, he waived half the bill, and he gave Jer an envelope with a pound note in it from the girls. 'Privately he said to Hugh, 'That brother of yours is a bit of caffler. But to be sure, he's a nice one.

Hughie knew that a caffler was a cunning little fellow who got around people with his tongue. He thought yeah, that's Jer all right. But he's a nice one.

Three

The year went by, a hard winter with frost so severe the main street had to be covered with sawdust to keep the horses from breaking their legs. The spring was noisy with floods, the Domain a sheet of brown water with the trees standing like islands. But the old naval officer who settled Trafalgar had chosen well. By early summer the feed was thick on the hills, fruit setting in the many orchards, stock looking prosperous. If a sudden wind shook a tree the air was, for a moment, full of butterflies.

John Kilker was depressed for a while. It was the way he was when Martin Darcy died, not speaking, grey and shambling. Eny didn't know what to do to shake him out of it. But gradually he recovered his strength. The sun and warmth helped him; he was able to look at his bed-shrunken arms and legs and think that soon they would be back to what they should be. He leant heavily on his wife, though he did not realise it. When he saw her haggard with anxiety he was sorry, but humbly glad too, to know she loved him so dearly.

He thought he might turn to religion. He was a Catholic, of course; he would have knocked down any villain who said he wasn't. He had always dutifully done what the Church told him to do, but to be honest he didn't know the why or wherefore of much of it. Eny herself was Catholic to her marrow. She was hung all over with medals and scapulars. She got Father Driscoll down to see John. John listened to him with anxious intent. Oh, he was a dextrous man with the words, John thought. He could see the holy Faith was a ladder all right, but could not see where it would take him. He didn't want heaven. He wanted the simple contentment of earth, and his family around him.

'You pray for me, lovie,' he said to his wife. 'I can't seem to get the hang of it.'

He was very pleased to have two postcards from young Hugh Darcy, hoping he was feeling better and thanking him for his goodness in looking after the Dad's funeral.

'He's a decent lad,' he said. 'And I daresay that lolly-legged brother is too.'

One postcard had a photograph of a bore windmill, and the other a picture of the railway station at Moree where the brothers were working. Margaret studied both pictures but there was not a thing she could read into them. Josie teased her:

'What, not a word to you? He probably can't remember what you look like.'

But at Christmas Margaret received a card all to herself. On the reverse was written: 'Jer and me wish you the very best. Now at Wales Flat cutting prickly pear, stinking job. Got a bike now. Jer rides pillion. Like to have a line from you. Love.'

'You needn't think that "love" means anything,' pointed out Josie. 'Anyway, he's got no business putting it on the card where everyone can read it. Especially when you hardly know him. Cheek!' The teasing went over Margaret's head. She was so happy that Hugh had not forgotten her. She put the card in her prayerbook. She longed to write to him immediately but by the time she had thought what to say a month had gone by.

What she wanted to say was too forward, what she could say was dumb and boring, about the prickly pear and what was Wales Flat like, and her father on his feet again and talking about going back to work. She expected never to hear from Hugh again.

Eny raised a din about John's going back to work.

'Don't barge at me,' he said, 'there's the grand girl. I can feel me joints seizing up. Besides the manager's putting me on light jobs. A child could manage it.'

Eny wasn't giving up. She asked the doctor's advice.

'Don't try to stop him,' he said. He took her hand. He knew very well how she felt. 'That old pump may last another ten years. Even more. Don't make a sick man of him; it won't help. You must have the guts to let him live as he pleases.'

'I haven't,' cried Eny, anguished.

'You'll find them. Don't show the whites of your eyes at me, woman. You go home and think over what I've said.'

But Eny was showing the whites of her eyes at fate that had struck down her man and brought the fear of death into their house and bed. It was there all right. John looked fine; the loss of weight made her remember the fine contours of his face when young. His eyes were sharp and his step swift. But the thought of death was always with her, a sorrow, a painful fear. Nevertheless she did, as the doctor had foretold, find the fortitude, bared to the bone, never to fuss or cosset, to support him in all he did. In bed she had become the lover; her skill saved him exertion where she thought it perilous; she turned their impetuous passion into something slow and mellow. Did John notice? She did not know. There was between them, she felt, a web of loving lies, a conspiracy to make the best of whatever was left to them.

'I'll fight you for him, God,' she thought. 'Every inch of the way.'

Hugh was surprised at how tickled he was when he received Margaret's letter. To get away from the others he put it in his pocket and went out into the empty blaze to pot a few rabbits for the cookhouse. Sitting on a stump, the rifle across his knees, he read her girlish lines and thought what a gentle, simple thing she was. The sort of girl that life would unfailingly knock around. His mother had been like that. She had been educated sufficiently to become a governess, and had been treated like a family member on that distant property. What made her leave that pleasant existence and live such an abominable life in the shack beside the Aboukir? She must have loved Martin, but Martin did not seem to love her. If he had there might still have been a home for Jer and himself to return to now and again. Hughie did not often wish for a home, not even when sheds cut out and he saw the men gladly hastening off on horses, or driving traps or old cars. It was Margaret who made him think of one now, for it was impossible to separate her from the warm family life that plainly was hers.

Sad bewilderment filled him at the thought of his mother, dancing in her cherry blouse, skeletal and mad.

As he returned to the camp one of the rouseabouts, scrubbing his dirty clothes in the creek, called out, 'Hear you cracked it with a stunner at Trafalgar.' Hugh nodded. Jer had been at work. Still, he was not displeased.

'Had a letter from her today. Burnt holes in the pages,' he said. He put on a sly grin and refused to respond to the good-natured chiacking over supper. Jer, emboldened by his brother's acquiescence, changed Mrs Kilker into a hot little cow of sixteen, and pruriently described their experiences in the House of Horror.

Hugh wrote to Margaret. He described how he had read her letter on the edge of the grotesque green army of prickly pear that marched down from the north, taller than he, impregnable, all queer arms and heads like monsters. He said he had taken the bunnies home and stewed them in milk, with bacon and onions. The men had thought him a snitcher cook.

Slowly their brief stiff letters became real communication. Hugh looked forward to hearing from her, and if the store truck brought nothing for him he felt cheated and evil-tempered. He had realised that, free and all as he was, there was no one else in the world, except for Jer, who would write him a letter.

Margaret's heart jumped when she saw Hugh's writing on an envelope. Joy made her tremble.

'Oh, Lord, I'm a goner all right,' she thought. She prayed about it: 'Holy Mary, let me have Hughie Darcy, and I'll try to be such a good wife. I don't know why I love him, but I want to be with him all the time. Didn't you feel like that about St Joseph?'

She was a girl of quixotic faith. It gave her an artless grace. She went about the house singing, and Eny, observing, shook her head. She had done a deal of singing herself when she first met Steve Tookey, and then again, a year or so after she wed, when she looked at John and knew he was the treasure of her life.

After a period of the huff, Herbie Lennon began once again to call upon Margaret. She looked on his reliable countenance despairingly. If only he'd been a wag! If only he had a bit of the devil in him! He was so worthy and respectable. How could she hurt his feelings by telling him to push off, as her mother had advised her to do if she honestly could not stand a bar of him. At the same time, her mother had let her know that if she followed this advice she'd be the fool of the world.

All she could bring herself to was a sulky mutter: 'I don't want to get serious.'

But nothing knocked him back; he knew what an excellent catch he was. He put her reluctance down to maidenly modesty and liked her all the better. But Margaret was greatly confused. Perhaps Herb really would make a good husband and she would learn to love him, as Josie said. Josie! Margaret's thoughts flew to her sister. If Josie championed Herb Lennon it would not be for any kind reason.

This emboldened her. When Eny gave her a talking-to about writing to Hugh Darcy – making it plain that Margaret's head was so full of romantic ideas there was little room for anything else, and that she'd better realise that Herb Lennon could traipse off any time he chose – the girl answered testily.

'Don't I write to Hugh only because he has no family of his own except poor Jer?' she retorted. 'And if you want to know, the boys are to be home in Trafalgar for the Icemen's Picnic, and I think it would be the charitable thing to ask them to have their dinner with us that day.'

Eny was not fooled by her daughter's bold demeanour, but she put the anxiety aside. There were other things to think of.

Josie passed her eighteenth birthday and Noel Capper asked her father if they could become engaged. John experienced the sudden indignation of any father asked for his daughter's hand by a watery-eyed stripling.

He thought Josie still a child. He remembered her, scrawny and shivering like an unfledged bird, sitting on the gatepost to welcome him when he came home from work. Look at the size of her, he thought, them straight up and down hips. He did not let his mind stray as far as the improper thought of Josie getting pregnant; he kept it tethered to the idea that up and down hips were not a good thing for a married lady.

But Josie did not want to get married. Josie wanted a long engagement.

'It's so romantic,' she told Margaret, 'and I can plan everything to the last detail. The wedding will be on Noel's twenty-sixth birthday.'

Josie easily passed the first accountancy examinations and Noel made further application to her father. He pointed out that they were both very level-headed. Reluctantly, then, John gave his permission for the engagement.

Margaret was pleased for her sister, though the thought of Noel in an intimate situation gave her the sicks. Yet she was envious too, finding it hard to keep a smiling face when friends commiserated with her about her little sister's wiping her eye. Rowena thought the whole situation unnatural.

'I could no sooner have been engaged to you for years than fly,' she confessed to John. 'Either I would have gone off with someone else or we would have had three christenings before the wedding bells.'

John was more prudish than she, but he agreed that might well have been the case.

'Still, not everyone's a gladiator like you, lovie,' he whispered.

Eny pummelled him, cherishing him body and soul and anything else left over.

About this time Aunt Alf received a letter from Delia. No one had had a word from Delia since the Great War, when she cleared off with that stock agent who had a wife and four children and sang tenor in the choir. John and Rowena did not speak of her except to each other. Their hearts were still sore over that girl.

Delia had been a plump little thing with a round pearly face and downy hair. There was no teaching her anything; what Delia wanted to do she did. She scarcely knew there were people outside of herself. They were all there to support, serve, pleasure Delia. Auntie Alf, who loved her, said she would settle down as she grew. But that did not happen. At ten years old Delia had no eyes for anyone but boys; as far as anything in trousers was concerned she was as single-minded as a tomcat. In her sleepy eyes there was a flicker that fascinated most but gave others the creeps.

By the time she was eleven fathers were coming round to John and barking: 'Keep that damned fool of a girl of yours away from my Colin, Frank or Bert, or you and me'll mix it.'

John and Eny were mortified and greatly anxious. John was for ever out looking for Delia, home late from dances, dress torn, green grass stains, but bold-eyed just the same. She was in and out of work, cheeky to customers, hand in the till, passionate scenes with the boss, often slapped stupid by the boss's wife.

When she ran off she left a note for her parents whom she loved in her own way.

'I want to experience real life,' she wrote, 'and there isn't any in this burg.'

Eny recognised it as a caption from a motion picture she and the children had seen.

They heard no further news. Delia could have been alive or dead. If asked, Eny might have said bitter words about this delinquent daughter, but she never failed to pray for her.

When she saw the signature on the letter Alf experienced joy and gratitude. She had made up her mind that Delia had succumbed to the Spanish influenza. What happiness the news would bring to John and Rowena!

But Delia asked her to keep the letter a secret; she wanted to cause no more grief to her family. She was in a bad way, worn down by suffering and misfortune. The stock agent had abandoned her soon after they reached Sydney; she had lost her health and gone from bad to worse. Delia blamed it all on her own wicked foolishness. She hadn't known when she was well off. She humbly asked Auntie Alf to forgive her, but said she would never forgive herself. She was now in abject poverty, deserted by her husband but hoping to get well again so she could return to work and support herself and the child. She asked for Auntie Alf's prayers at Mass.

Alf longed to fly to Delia at once. But the shock brought on such a diversion Father Driscoll thought it would never end. Pictures descended from walls, taps spurted brown water, pot plants withered, the entrails of his fountain pen came out and stuck quivering in a page of the parish ledger.

When Alf came to herself again she sent £50 to Delia to help with expenses. She explained she could not leave Father Driscoll, old and unwell.

Delia, who had written her letter as a try-on, to find out what the stick-in-the-mud Trafalgar lot thought of her after the silent years, was flabbergasted. She recalled Aunt Alf as a queer old toad in a black apron down to her boots. Where had the old girl got fifty smackers? Well, she hadn't them now. Delia threw on her glad rags and set off for the racecourse, for she was an addicted punter.

Delia had dumped the stock agent a month after she ran off with him. He had marble teeth and indigestion and tended to whine about his children. She emptied his wallet and flitted. Sydney during the War was a noisy, disorderly town; there were soldiers for ever coming or going. Delia never did a tap of work until after the Armistice; there was always some fellow or other to look after her. When she looked back at those years they were a gorgeous blur, full of dance music and laughter, with herself perched in the middle with a cocktail glass in her hand.

'Oh, I've had a divine time!' Delia said, hoisting her skirts and painting butterflies on her knees. Though the translucent delicacy of her complexion had vanished, and her fine hair gone frizzy since she bleached it, she was still a peach. She stuck kiss curls on her cheeks with gum, and wore a gold snake bracelet that wound from elbow to armpit.

Delia laid eyes on a respectable widower belonging to a girl chum and soon had him by the wool. He was a little dusty from being on the shelf so long, but he had no family, a steady job in a china factory, and was as biddable as a dog. After they married Delia found that his salary was only middling, but that scarcely mattered now that she had stumbled upon a goldmine.

'God bless the old dingbat,' she sang of Aunt Alf, and she wrote a letter of such eloquence that tears came to her eyes. She was brave about both the bolting husband and her little retarded boy. He was a mild little fellow and attended Mass with her when she was well enough to go. His name was John after his grandfather. The letter was so full of meek faith that Alf longed to show it to Father Driscoll. But he, under certain circumstances, was rash in his speech, and Alf had promised poor Delia secrecy.

The deprivations of his early life had passed peaceably from John Kilker's mind. He dimly remembered his step-mother as a sourfaced old tot, and his father as a big smell of whisky. Alf recalled her Dublin life very well, but she had long ago put it away from her. She was satisfied to be alive, the full list of her blessings would have made her nightly thanksgiving last the livelong night. Her only prayer for herself was that she would last long enough to see Father Driscoll into his grave.

This poor man had been a problem to the Bishop, for he had no resistance whatsoever to the bottle. A devoted priest, he had spent the prime of his working life in the outback, riding, riding, days between homesteads sometimes. The land looked like dry shoals. Shiny blanched pebbles worked their way to the surface, lying there like frost. Greasy air hung just above the ground, flawed by heat, making jokes of natural shapes to tease travellers. All over that country were the old shores of old seas strewn with little shells, webbed with salt so bright you'd think it thrown there yesterday.

But so it was, thought Father Driscoll, the continent's yesterday is still with us in those places.

He remembered the immaculacy of the inland sky, not a cloud, not a grain of dust between the earth and the planets. Yet at night, as he lay on his groundsheet, staring upwards, he had known he was wrong. The sky was crowded with stardust. Swift streaks of white chalk scratched soundlessly across the heavens, swarms of bees scintillated for a second or two and were gone. These meteorites, celestial mayflies, accompanied him to sleep every night. To him they were a sign of God's continuing creation.

The Far West settlers were what he lived for, the hard, pared-down men and shy uncomplaining women. No matter what he could bring them, the Sacraments, comfort in the frequent deaths, mail, medicine, news, it was never enough for him. These unbeatable self-reliant people filled his heart to such an extent that when at last his age caused the Bishop to place him in an easy parish he found there was nothing left for him to live for. He had always drunk freely, but the ferocious heat had sweated it out of him. Now he became a whisky priest, a potential scandal. At the end of six months in Trafalgar the Bishop came to see him. His Lordship felt it must be a personal duty to tell this man whose labours had been heroic that he was to go into a retirement home.

Father Driscoll was at the tail of a spree, sick as a dog. The Bishop was waylaid in the parlour by the housekeeper. He always thought of her as a small woman, but after that he recalled her as large, a woman of authority. He found himself agreeing that Father Driscoll was still a grand priest who could hold his own with the best of them if someone kept an eye on him. Alf won Father Driscoll a reprieve of six months that time. When he came to himself she frightened him out of his soulcase; she had the poor man sobbing with repentance and shame. In spite of the Bishop's warning letters he had never thought it would come to his being put in the cupboard at fifty-five.

Alf's methods of keeping Father Driscoll a respected and able man were her own. She consulted the doctor and her brother John. Both were often seen at the presbytery in the early days; Alf put it around they played chess with the Father. She built up his physical strength, got him busy on useful projects, such as building a new fence, painting the church, reflooring the vestry. At first he was as slippery as an eel as far as the booze was concerned, but Alf and John gradually got that under control. The doctor dosed him with something a fiend couldn't keep down. Father Driscoll had both a frightful time and a good time. The six months stretched into twenty years.

The only times of real peril during this long period were when Father Driscoll went off for his annual holiday. Aunt Alf dreaded his holidays. He visited his old seminary chums and Inland co-workers, and more often than not came back in a lamentable condition. The last five years Alf had controlled him by threatening retirement if he got on the grog while in the city. Being very dependent on her, he was alarmed. So he went on the spree during his first week of vacation, and was more or less recovered by the time he faced the long train journey home.

During the first decade the priest's young sister, Mrs Butler, often visited Trafalgar. She and the housekeeper built up a quiet, oblique friendship. It was oblique in that not once was the brother's weakness and courageous battle referred to by either woman. Mrs Butler had some ailment; she was as frail as a feather, with melancholy eyes. Fortunately her husband was wealthy and looked after her like a doll.

She died during the Great War, and to Alf's stupefaction left her a large sum of money, in appreciation of faithful friendship. She laid no conditions on Alf, but Alf silently promised Mrs Butler, who had suffered so much herself, that she would look after Father Driscoll as long as she lived. After much thought, Alf decided she would not tell anyone about the legacy. She believed God would let her know how best to handle it.

When Delia came back into her life, sick and poor, Auntie Alf accepted that God had spoken. After the letter about the retarded child, she sent Delia a blessed medal and £10, and much news about the family.

It had not been all good lately. Aunt Alf was anxious about Josie and her prospects. Mr Capper senior had gone to Sydney on business and died in haste under a tram. Within two months his widow took in a partner at the Universal Providers and presently married him. The bridegroom was godless and virulently anti-Papist. Rowena was aghast to hear that he had ripped the Sacred Heart off the wall and used the frame to enclose the photograph of a racehorse. She was more aghast to learn that Mrs Capper had thrown her religion overboard and wed in a Registry Office. She was an agreeable big heap who would have done anything for a quiet life, but Eny raved on as if Mrs Capper had driven the last nail, blunt at that, into Him on the Cross.

She felt this with intense sincerity; her faith was part of her blood and bones. Hers was a family that had faced death by hunger rather than turn colour for a bowl of broth. She often boasted that there were no soupers amongst the Mullinses, and John, who came of a long line of desperate soupers, kept mum.

Tragically she said to Josie, 'That's the end of it with your sheik, my girl.'

'But, Ma, they love each other!' protested Margaret.

Josie was frightened, but no one would have guessed. She said calmly, 'If you want to know, Noel has turned, too.'

She could have added that Hatch, the new stepfather, had

threatened Noel that if he did not he could leave the Universal and take his holy water with him. How could she explain Mr Hatch's implacable hatred of the Pope to her mother? She did not understand it and Mr Hatch did not either.

Eny gave a scream to wake the dead.

'You'll never lay an eye on that Judas again!'

'I will,' said Josie, 'and I'll marry him, too.'

'But, Josie,' said Margaret, awed, 'you couldn't have a church wedding; you'd have to be married in the vestry where they wash up the teacups.'

'I'll marry him in the Registry Office,' stated her sister.

Josie was panicky over the turn of events. She saw Noel being tossed out of his father's firm, and perhaps even herself. Mr Hatch, a small maggot of a man with power for the first time in his life, had already eyed her assessingly, and made a few uncalled-for remarks about idolators. Still, Josie had to turn her mind to the present, for her mother looked as if she were going to leave the ground. The girl took a grip on herself.

'It's no use, Ma,' she said. 'My mind is made up.'

She had a face chilly as snow; pride was written all over her. Margaret forgot all the spiteful things said and done to her and thrilled at Josie's dauntlessness.

Eny went for her daughter hammer and tongs. The battle raged intermittently for weeks. Eny enjoyed every black word of it, and yet made herself sick with weeping. She imagined Josie scythed down in her youth, dying in her apostasy and going to hell for ever.

'God be with us,' expostulated John. 'Isn't the girl only a child? She can't be wed until she's twenty-one if we say no, and long before that she'll hate the very sight of that long streel.'

John was dejected. He could no longer stand up to the uproar. When the fury was at its height he had to go outside and take a blast of his pipe. He took to visiting his sister more often than he had throughout the years. He confessed that the donnybrook was getting him down.

Inside his sister the big woman hammered at the walls, ground her teeth. Nothing shut her up, not the Rosary Alf said every evening, not early Mass. At last she strode into Eny's kitchen, fixed her with a daggerish glare, and gave her the father and mother of a telling off.

Eny had the frying pan in her hand but it did not occur to her to swing it. The tears began to stream.

'God forgive me, I didn't think for a moment of what the upset was doing to John.'

'It's a crying shame you don't do more thinking,' burst out Auntie Alf, burning for her favourite. 'For what are you doing to Josephine, hacking away at her day and night? You're doing to her what you did to poor Delia.'

Rowena looked at her with consternation. What did the old woman have in her mind?

'For the love of God, Alf,' she said, 'have you no idea what John and me suffered with that girl's misbehaviour? Do you think we haven't cried our eyes out wondering if she's alive or dead?'

'Fine words,' cried Auntie Alf in trembling rage, 'when you drove her away with your unkindness. Don't think I don't know all about it.'

The big woman flew away in a puff. The small old woman subsided on a chair, all of a heap.

Rowena had little trouble getting out of her that Delia was alive, ill and repentant, and that she, Alf, had been helping her with money. The mother was white and shocked. She was all for setting out and bringing Delia home. But Alf dug her toes in there.

'She made me promise not to let on to you she was alive. I've done wrong there, with my unruly tongue, and I won't forgive myself. But I won't tell you where she is.'

'I'm her mother!' cried Eny hoarsely.

She hammered away at Alf, she begged, cajoled and wept. She used every persuasive tactic in the world, and she had a headful of them, all well worn.

'You're denying her mother, Alf. The wickedness of it!'

But Alf was adamant. 'Delia knows you're her mother, but she does not want you coming after her.'

Alf was strengthened by all the things Delia had told her about Eny's indifference. 'Fine mother you were, passing her over all the time in favour of Kathleen. A darling girl Kathleen was, and none has mourned her more than myself, but there's no place for favouritism in a family, Rowena. And aren't you doing the same with Josie, poor child, making a pet of Margaret the way you do?'

Eny felt so queer in herself, Alf's voice buzzing in her ears like a mosquito, the pot boiling on the stove making a noise of thunder, she thought she was going to have a heart attack like John. She found herself shoved into a chair, and her head pressed against Alf's flat front.

'Ah, God forgive me, I'm that sorry I spoke,' said Alf. 'You've been a good wife to John, and no one knows it better than me.'

'Don't speak of this to John,' whispered Eny. 'Mightn't it kill him?'

Alf went away, not knowing whether she had done right or wrong. She knew that Rowena would spend days arguing with herself, finding good reasons for wrongdoing or ill-judgement, blowing up her virtues and sacrifices to the skies, justifying herself to God in the most vehement manner. But in her heart would be the cruel, unchangeable truth the Irish could never get away from, wriggle as they might.

Alf was right. Eny wept scalding tears. She castigated herself for being, perhaps, neglectful of Delia. But the truth she found in her heart was that Delia had been turned towards wickedness from the start. She never cared for anyone but herself, just like Will Mullins. The grandfather had laid his weak greedy character upon the granddaughter, and all Eny could do now was to hope time and God could make something of her.

She visited Alf at the presbytery. The pair of them were very stately, sitting up like Jacky drinking tea. Eny had the look of one with a fortnight's crying bottled up inside her. She asked Alf's advice about Josephine. The girl was not happy at home and neither was anyone else.

Alf suggested that Josephine should take a room at a family boarding house they both knew. It had strict hours and a pious mistress. The strength of Mrs Kellerman's character was known up and down the line. Rollicking young sports avoided the Mount Carmel like the plague.

'Josephine has a good position and can well pay her way,' said Aunt Alf. 'And please God Mrs Kellerman will shame her out of the Registry Office. She's got that much of a tongue on her.'

'There's another thing,' said Eny. 'I'll say no more about Delia until you tell me yourself. But you'll send no more money, if you please. All the world knows a priest's housekeeper gets only a pound a week and her keep.'

'A friend left me a fortune,' said Alf, 'but I'd be obliged if you kept that between our two selves.'

Rowena now thought that Alf had gone out of her head entirely. Her heart lightened. Probably she had imagined hearing from Delia; the whole thing came out of her poor spinster's brain.

'Fortune or not,' she said, 'Delia would soon have it away from you. There was a vicious streak in that girl, though it destroys me to say it. I'll say no word of the carryings-on with men. There was something beyond that that made me and John ashamed to see.'

Josie left home. It upset her very much, though no word or look indicated this. She did much secret crying, and often found Noel's grizzling about his problems insupportable. She set her mind to passing her examinations. Every Sunday she and her fiancé had dinner at home. For a while Eny was nice as pie to Noel, so much so that even Margaret eyed her distrustfully. But soon she was unable to stop herself giving the occasional flick of the tongue to the turncoat.

John it was who was wounded. 'Ah, God, girl,' he said to his wife, 'youth passes like the clouds. Let things be. Josie's a great girl at heart. She'll do the right thing.'

Most of this drifted past Margaret, she being in a happy dream of her own. She could not wait for the Icemen's Picnic.

But Jer Darcy dreaded it.

Whenever Jer saw his brother getting into his blue suit, finicking the gold dog's-head pin through his tie, his heart thudded with apprehension. Jer power had failed him; he still did not know how to deal with Hugh and girls.

It was not that the younger brother did not yearn after girls himself; his dream was that some day he would find one to take care of him. He and Hugh had once seen a picture: handsome young fellow wounded in the War, stunning girl gives up own life to marry him and look after him. Eventually the hero decides her sacrifice is too great. Lips firm, eyes steady, he precipitates his wheel chair into the deep lake. But Jer always stopped this movie halfway through, where the bride fervently pushed her husband's chair through a romantic landscape, and the pianist played 'O, Promise Me'.

When Hugh came home from a dance guilty and puffy-faced, Jer was sick all night, his belly stiff as a board, his ears ringing with fright. When Hugh was grumpy, saying the girls were all bikes or great lumps with cowshit on their boots, Jer visibly relaxed, eager to listen to whatever disappointments his brother had to relate.

He watched with dread Hugh's interest in mail days. Jer had read all Margaret's letters; there was not a hiding-place he could not ferret out. He panicked when he divined that this girl was honestly stuck on Hugh; and when Hugh told him they were going back to Trafalgar for a break he lost his head.

Jer screeched, 'You want to be there for the bloody Icemen's Picnic. You're after that bloody Kilker mare!'

Hugh got him on the bunk with his hand round his throat; he cross-hackled Jer until he confessed he had read the letters.

'I'm that scared you'll get tied up with her, Hughie,' he wept. 'And she won't have me in the house and God knows how I'll live.'

The tears did no good. For the first time Hugh backed away, would not listen, went for days in freezing silence. It was killing for Jer. His world had fallen down. He apologised abjectly, said he was a curse to his brother and himself, he wished he were dead. Hugh ignored him.

One Sunday afternoon the cook angrily shook Hugh awake. The brother had cleared out, he said, and what was he to do for an offsider? Hugh could not believe it. Jer setting out under his own steam? He saw then that Jer's few belongings had gone, all except the guitar. He found out eventually that he had canvassed a lift to the main road, where the motor coach passed on its way south. Hugh castigated the shearer who had provided the lift.

'Gawd, what's biting you?' protested this man. 'Jer's entitled to go where he likes. You own him? Any old how, he'll be back. That coach won't have left Steinbeck. Look at them skies.'

The coach was lower-slung than the old Fords. The road south was disastrous, crossed by many creeks, bankless and boiling over when heavy rain hit the hills. Hugh agreed that the driver, who had often been bogged for hours in the fords, would have chosen to stay overnight in the nearest settlement. He pictured Jer labouring back that long way on his crutches.

Hugh set out at once on his bike. He had not travelled a mile before the churning skies fell on him. It was worse than a thunderstorm; it was a cloudburst. He had to shelter. An hour later to took the bicycle lamp and butted through the roaring wall. The road surface was ankle-deep skilly mud. It sucked off one shoe. Hugh left it. It might come up again when the road dried. He took to the paddocks, up to his knees in water. He knew no other vehicle could have passed along the main road in such weather. Jer must still be there.

He reached the road at last. It slobbered clay and yellow water as far as he could see. There was now little visibility. Twilight had come with the storm. The wind was a vast fist punching him towards the south. The trees lashed like seaweed, roared, slapped at the earth.

He found Jer at last in the lee of a streaming bank. The lamp's last light showed the boy huddled under a slicker plastered with clay.

'You silly bugger.'

There was no moving from the bank until daylight. They huddled together, freezing, the bush howling, the water glugging and muttering. Towards dawn the storm rushed off, spattering showers trailing it. All over the hills they could hear new waterfalls crashing into the gullies.

Hugh untangled himself from his brother, went out on the road to see if walking were possible. Jer's big black eyes gaped from a pinched face.

'Where are your crutches, Jer?'

'I got one here. The other got stuck in the mud over there.'

He gestured at a drowned run-off beside the road.

'God, you're a crucifixion to me.'

When he said it, Hugh was sorry. Jer wept, coughed, choked that Hugh should leave him to get home his own way.

'Shut up, you silly bastard. If I gotta carry you, that's it. And don't bother coughing, I'm up to your tricks.'

He carried Jer through the paddocks to the one-mile post where he had left the bike. He heaved the helpless boy onto the seat and wheeled him through the sludge towards the woolsheds. It was a fearful business; the wheels would not turn; he could scarcely hold Jer on the seat.

'What's the matter with you, you useless bastard?'

Jer's eyes were glazed and mad, his face yellow. Hugh was relieved when several men splashed to meet him, the squatter with them. Jer was carried to the homestead. The squatter's wife took one look at him and rang the doctor. There was no getting in or out of Steinbeck until the road dried. The woman, who was used to emergencies, packed Jer in blankets and hot water bottles, and fed him sips of brandy. When the road was passable they put him in the back of the truck and slid and skidded into Steinbeck to the hospital, meeting the doctor on the way.

Hugh was in a desperate funk. He thought Jer was going to die. Jer's face had become so small it looked like an orange; the eyes had gone back in his head. Hugh did not know what to do, pray, or weep, or get drunk. The sister finally understood that he too had spent a night exposed to the cold and wet, gave him a hot whisky toddy and put him in a spare bed.

Neither of the brothers came out of the experience very well.

'He can't do any more country work,' the doctor told Hugh. 'His chest is always going to be weak. If he gets another attack of pneumonia I wouldn't guarantee his chances. Why don't you send him back home to Mum and Dad?'

'Got no home,' said Hugh. 'I'll look after him. Always have, haven't I?'

He had no idea what to do. At last he told Jer they were going back to Trafalgar.

'I'll get a start somewhere. It's boom times. Must be plenty of work even in a mudhole. And you can lay up a bit and get strong.'

Jer nodded submissively. 'We'll do what you think best, Hughie,' he said.

Hugh was uneasy and fretful. Death had passed them closely, and he did not like it. A trembling started up in his inside whenever he recalled the look of Jer in that hospital bed. It was not altogether because he had almost lost his brother. Probably his mother had looked like that, certainly his father. I'll look that way when my turn comes, he realised, and was filled with horror. He felt alone; he could not speak to the other men of his fear of death. Death made everyone embarrassed. Margaret would listen. He sensed in her a great deal of kindness and sympathy. He wished she were there with him, right that moment.

He almost wrote and told her that. But he had enough sense not to. Already he knew her well enough to understand what she would make of it. He wrote a postcard instead, saying he'd see her at the picnic.

Four

The Icemen's Picnic came late in winter, when the plant closed for maintenance. The hills showed blank, bright dribbles of snow. In the high valleys ponds and bogholes smoked amidst the unmelted frost. Yet the sunshine had the sting of heat in it; in sheltered places winter wattle bloomed in heaps of gold.

'It's a moral you won't need your jacket,' said Eny to Margaret, who was slowly turning before her in her new costume. The scalloped hem of the black skirt came to the middle of her calves. The baggy matching jacket was ornamented with whorls of silk braid. Margaret wanted to leave the coat behind so that the stunning cape sleeves of her new blouse could be seen.

Her father thought she looked a picture. Those cheeks! He kissed one of them, thinking, 'Ah, God, I been lucky in the kids I've had.'

Delia crossed his mind, poor little monkey. He hoped that life had been kind to her, and he would see her again before he dropped off the perch.

Sometimes John was devil-may-care when he thought about dying. Other times he was not. But he tried to put on a good face for Eny's sake. He had a tussle with himself when he faced up to the fact that never again would he throw the hammer and hear the crowd yell for Johnny Kilker.

'You're an old pot now, me boy,' he told himself, 'and you have a worn-out ticker. But, God willing, there are plenty more years left in you still.'

The Council held its picnic at the same time as the Icemen, as did several lesser trades. It all made for a jollier day. Thus the Mayor's secretary wrote to John Kilker, respectfully asking him to be in charge of the pudding and wear the blue sash of officialdom. This honour assuaged his regrets. He was as cocky as a dog with two tails.

Eny was delighted. 'You're more famous than jam!'

The four Trafalgar bakers had fretfully collaborated to produce a monster plum duff. The entire town had gone to see the mixing, contrived in the Council's brand new concrete mixer. A barrel of brandy was poured into the sticky black batter, which was, at the end, enriched with many valuable gifts: babies' bangles, silver teething rings, heart lockets, thimbles and coins. The grand prize was a diamond ring, reputedly worth more than a hundred guineas. Margaret longed for that diamond ring, and her friend Herbie Lennon said he would get it for her.

'It's five shillings a serve,' warned Margaret. Herb waved a careless hand. In spite of her craving for the ring, Margaret was peeved. She did not want to be obliged to him.

'I don't want Herbie to take me to the picnic,' she said querulously. 'Can't you say I have to be with you and Pa?'

Eny was irritated by her ingratitude.

'Tell him yourself! But if that Hugh Darcy doesn't turn up you should give thanks to God.'

'He'll turn up,' said Margaret complacently. 'I made a novena.'

Eny was a great one for the power of prayer. But she thought it would take more than a few Hail Marys and aspirations, said nine days running, to turn that cockalorum into a steady fellow. The girl had a lovely faith, a pretty thing to see, but she hadn't the gumption of a young chicken. The mother didn't know whether to be vexed or sad.

'Ah, dotie,' she said gently, 'do all in your power to put that one out of your mind. I know how you feel, but something tells me there's no good in it.'

'I can't help it, Ma,' said Margaret.

Eny could have wept.

'Well, then,' she said resignedly, 'hang on to Herbie for the time being. An extra pint of stout never goes to waste.'

Margaret was ashamed of her mother's cynicism.

'As to the ring, Herbie's your man there. He's as thin as a lamppost, but he has a desperate appetite. I never saw a man wire into a pig's head as that one did last Sunday supper.'

She brightened. 'If Hughie does shows his face, odds on there'll be a scrap.'

The previous noon the giant pudding had been put on to boil in a corrugated iron tank. All night long relays of men had watched and replenished the fire, occasionally adding water to the tank from a cauldron bubbling near by. A publican with Council ambitions donated a couple of barrels of beer, and the evening and freezing night were boisterous. About 2 a.m. one of the watch awakened, smelt something alarming, and scuttled up the ladder beside the tank: It had boiled dry; the pudding was flumped on its burnt bottom.

His cry of anguish brought the rest awake. They worked like madmen filling the tank once more, building up the fire, and swearing one another to secrecy.

John Kilker and Hugh Darcy wandered through the throng, never meeting, both thinking of other days.

Hugh heard the chonk-chonk of the woodchops, the snore of a crosscut saw. Kids ran races, their sunburnt parents roaring. Once he had almost won a three-legged race. His partner fell on her face and he just walked away, mortified to death, leaving her laying on her freckles.

John recalled that on this ground he had first seen Rowena. As a youth he'd had a shot at goldmining, scarcely seeing colour at all. But still he wore the red silk neckerchief, the wideawake hat, and the beard of the goldminer. These things gave a man class. 'Them whiskers!' thought John, grinning. They'd been an inky waterfall. He'd singed himself with his clay pipe more times than he could count. Anyway, there he had been, sitting on a stump, quiet as a lamb, when up limped this young girl.

'Move over, King Herod,' she said. 'Me feet are dropping off.'

The sun shone on her hair as if it were copper wire. On it was a bonnet like an upside down lettuce, tied under her chin with fresh green ribbons to match.

A rush of affection for that bold girl filled old John's heart. By hokey, he'd been the lucky one to get her! He went off to find her.

But Hugh, looking for Margaret, found Eny first. It was some time before he recognised her, sitting on an upturned barrel drinking beer with her little finger sticking out. But she knew who he was. She looked at the young man in the straw boater, his ruddy face and big knocked-about brown hands, his fancy vest and celluloid rosebud buttonhole, and she could have given anyone his history. He was like hundreds of other young rowdies in Trafalgar, or any other country place you could name. Knockabout jobs, never anything skilled, always in fights, drunken brawls, getting thrown off properties, resisting arrest, language, clocking a policeman, respectable family, mother's a saint, all her boys went to the bad. It was a story so common Eny could have made a song out of it.

And this was poor Margaret's fancy.

'Pardon me,' she said winningly, 'but you have something stuck on your lip.'

Hugh's moustache was dear to his heart. It was not a moustached era; he had to put up with a lot of slack from his friends.

He reacted as any other man of Irish blood would have done; he slipped a riposte between her ribs.

'Isn't it fine that your sight is so good at your age, missus?'

Eny's eyes sparkled. She had a liking for him from that moment, though she never allowed it to alter her conviction that this boy would make Margaret unhappy. She felt that in her inerrable bones.

'Sit down and have a beer,' she said.

Hugh shook his head. 'It's Margaret I'm looking for, missus.'

'Over there listening to the band,' said Eny airily, not worrying at all. She could skewer him some other time.

Hughie drifted over to the bandstand. Margaret saw him coming. Her excitement was so intense she felt suffocated. The young man looked at this dumb blushing creature almost with pity. It was her transparency he was sorry for, though in an objective way, as if he had seen a dog run over.

'You came,' she said.

'Yeah. Here I am.' They stared at each other.

'Your letters,' he said. 'I liked them. Honest.'

'I'm not much of hand with a pen, really,' she said, blushing. 'Young Jer with you?'

'He's at the pub. Didn't want to come. He's been crook lately.'

Margaret said she was sorry, but she was delighted to have Hugh to herself. She trembled with anticipation.

'Hey,' Hugh exclaimed, 'your figure's different!'

Margaret had such a shock she turned beetroot red. 'You've got your nerve. I never . . . Cheek!'

Her hand flew up to her bosom as if to defend it. She didn't know whether she should walk away or not.

Hugh gave her a long cozening look. She thought she'd never seen such black eyelashes in her life.

'Aw, come on, love, don't be angry. It's just that I like you better this way. I don't want you all parcelled up the way you were last time.'

He had such a smile. He took her hand and rubbed it against his cheek.

'It was them rotten stays of Auntie Alf's,' confessed Margaret. 'Hurt like crazy they did. So I left them off.'

His smile said he was glad. Oh, Lord, though Margaret, what has he in his mind?

'Come on,' he said, and she went like a lamb down to the creek.

'I've missed you real bad,' he said. 'Wonder why?'

She melted into his arms as though that was her place in life. All the long months were forgotten; all was worth while. The muttering water, the red-berried trees, the willows dropping dry leaves in Hughie's black hair, all were straight from the Garden of Eden. After a while she opened her eyes, and stared across Hughie's shoulder at a gnomish face gazing through the willow fronds.

'Agh!' cried Margaret, ungluing her lips in a hurry. 'He's spying on us, your brother, that blasted Jer!'

Hugh ran raging through the willows. Jer scrambled up the bank like a crab, throwing his crutches before him.

'All right, all right,' gasped Jer. 'I'll go back to the pub!'

'I'll do for you yet,' roared Hugh. 'I'll wring your flaming neck!'

He was so mad he could have done it. But Margaret was laughing, fixing her floppy hat with a long pin, flushed and blissful.

'Ah, let him go, the poor thing. Did you hear me swear? I got such a start!'

He kissed her again. But the magic had gone, Margaret knew in an instant. He pulled her roughly towards him and began to undo her blouse buttons. His face was fierce as though he was angry with her instead of with Jer.

She pushed away his hand. 'You stop that!'

Even in her surprise and confusion she was struck with his dark, glowering good looks. She grabbed his wrist with both hands as he jerked open another button.

'I don't like you doing that!'

'Why not?' A dozen well-worn sneers were on his lips.

'I'm wearing an old singlet,' Margaret blurted out, 'and it's awful.'

Hugh laughed. 'Christ, you're a seed. I've never met a sort like you before.'

He held her arm above her head with one hand and continued unbuttoning with the other. 'Come on, let's see what you've got.'

'You leave me alone!'

'I want to.' He was enraged with her. He forced her wrist back painfully; he looked as if he would bite her rather than kiss her. 'Bloody little stick in the mud.'

Margaret stamped down hard on his toes. She jerked herself away. Blazing-eyed, she yelled, 'I know what you want to do. What I want to do doesn't matter, does it? You go to hell!'

'Straight out of the cowshed, aren't you?' he shouted as she turned away. Margaret faced him. 'I don't care what you think I am. People have feelings, you know. No one is going to make me do things I don't want to do.'

She began to run. Her head buzzed. She was faint with dismay and consternation. I've lost him, I've lost him, he'll never look at me again, I'll kill myself, I will, I will.

'Going my way, miss?' asked Hughie beside her. He raised his hat, in all ways calm and composed. Margaret, trembling, about to break into sobs, laughed instead.

'You bloody, bloody fool!'

'Careful, miss, I was well brought up. I don't want my ears soiled.'

She burst into tears. The water spurted out of her eyes as if she were four years old.

'Why did you treat me like that? Horrible things you said. Just because I've written you a few letters you think I'm cheap. What do you mean, cowshed?'

Hughie did not touch her. He let her cry herself out. Then he said, 'God, I been lonely!'

'I've been lonely too.'

'You've got your family.'

'Not the same.'

She wiped her face and smiled tremulously. They each had something to say, something big, important, but neither knew how to say it. They laughed instead. Margaret took his arm, and they went off towards the circling crowds.

'Hey, you still going around with that droob in the band?'

'He sort of hangs around,' Margaret excused herself.

'You tell him to sling his hook, you hear me?'

Margaret thrilled to this masterly tone. 'He's not my boyfriend; he just thinks he is. But he's going to get the diamond ring for me. The one in the pudding.'

'No,' said Hughie. 'I will. See if I don't.'

At the stroke of noon the Council crane hoisted the pudding out of the tank and dropped it thunderously on a wooden platform. The pudding cloth was four double bed sheets sewn together. John

Kilker, majestic in his official ribbon, solemnly directed the bakers, nervously picking away at the string that bound the Colossus. Eny, a dab hand at boiled puddings, thought it smelt as if it were a sod and was not backward in telling the bakers so.

Still the crowd pressed merrily around, anxious to get at it. There was not a young man present who did not desire that diamond ring.

Herbie Lennon was enraged to see Margaret arrive with Hugh Darcy. She was flushed and excited, paying no attention to his glowering glances at the upstart to whose arm she clung. She introduced them all over again, and once again they grunted and looked the other way.

'Guess what, Herbie,' cried Margaret gaily, 'Hugh is going to try for the ring, too. And he hasn't had any breakfast!'

'If you're thinking of giving it to Margaret,' said Herbie stiffly, 'I'd like you to know she's my young lady.'

Hugh shrugged, grinning in a sophisticated way that made Herb long to job him one. But the odds were against him. The chap looked like a scrapper, and Herb had to be careful of his lip. He looked to Margaret for support. But she was red of face, eyes sparkling with temper.

'I'm not your young lady, I've told you over and over and you won't listen.' She began to laugh. 'Oh, don't take things so seriously, Herbie! I came to the picnic to have fun. You two silly things, to get all worked up as if it's a duel. You'd think you were on the pictures.'

She struck a Norma Shearer pose, flung out her hand and cried, 'I shall fall in love with the boy who gives me a diamond ring!'

Herbie was outraged. He thought he would give the pudding the cold shoulder. To think that Margaret would make such fun of him! But at that moment Mrs Kilker thrust a plate of plum duff into his hands.

'I'm barracking for you, Herbie!' she cried. 'Aren't you the lovely boy! Hoe into it now, for isn't the butcher's young fella a plate ahead of you already!'

Herbie ate mechanically. Fickle, fickle girls! He was so abstracted he had eaten two servings before he realised the pudding was indeed a sod.

The butcher's lad had hollow legs and a gob like a steam shovel. Hugh soon recognised that here was his true rival, inhaling the plum duff as if it were light as air, instead of black and solid as mud. But he was young and hungry. Nevertheless the pudding was a calamity. If he had served it to a shearing team they would have woodheaped him. Still, he was not going to be licked, either by the bandsman or the butcher's boy. He commended his belly to God and got on with the job.

'Fast and steady wins the race, my boy!' He thought it was someone encouraging him, but it was Mrs Kilker, fanning Herbie with her hat and cheering him on. Hugh noted with alarm that the bandsman ate neatly but with inexorable speed. As fast as one plate was finished he reached for another. People now bought servings for the contestants; betting was hot.

'He's onto his seventh and he's found a thimble and a two-bob bit,' crowed Eny into Hugh's ear. 'Ah, you've such a face on you,' she added, 'you're halfway to a fit, there's not a shadow of a doubt.'

'Piss off, you old faggot!' cried Hugh's heart and soul, but his mouth was too full to utter the words.

One by one the competitors dropped away. Suddenly the butcher's boy moaned like a calving cow and fell sideways. He was towed off to fresh air and privacy by his backers.

''Twas a fearful sight,' said Father Driscoll to his housekeeper, who had not attended the picnic. 'Three young men making beasts of themselves that way. Won't I skin them alive on Sunday in my sermon, that's if they're fit to attend Mass, which they won't be. Hugh Darcy I wasn't surprised at, deprived of a mother as he was, dragged up by the scruff by poor unfortunate Martin. But Herbie Lennon!'

Herbie was now a few mouthfuls behind. He felt somewhat swimmy, his hearing was going. The yells of the excited crowd, the whoops of Mrs Kilker close to his ear, all seemed as if in a dream. He finished his eighth plate of pudding and feebly took the ninth. Something in his brain said, 'You're going to die.' He stood there swaying.

'I'm buggered!' It was an inhuman cry. Had he said it or not?

Perhaps he had found the diamond ring, or maybe Hugh Darcy had. The crowed surged away from him; he was left alone.

'It's all over!' The crushing news made Herbie sit down suddenly on the grass.

'What's happened?' he quavered to a passer-by.

'Fellow taken to first-aid tent. Stomach pump, they say.'

The passer-by, who was Father Driscoll, added scathingly, 'As for you Herb, I'm disgusted. Bloated. Stuffed to the gills. The amount you young fellas put away would have choked Cromwell. You're a hog. And, anyway, Mrs Pettifer's young Nora found the diamond ring in her first toothful.'

Herbie floundered home. He was in torment all night, but the disorder of his head and belly was as nothing to the disorder in his heart. The Margaret of the Icemen's Picnic was not the Margaret with whom he had been walking out for so long. He went over and over his behaviour and could not fault it. Certainly she had told him many times she did not want to be serious, but that had been merely girl's talk. He had been let down, betrayed. As well, he had been publicly humiliated, less by Margaret's brazen behaviour than by the indignities of the contest into which she had lured him.

His employer gave him dog's abuse, not only for the hideous exhibition he had made of himself, but for using an improper word in public.

'I'll have you know I run a respectable family business, Lennon,' he said.

Herbie resigned. When Mrs Kilker called on him, he had almost finished packing.

'You wouldn't be going away!' she cried. 'Aren't you going to fight for her?'

'Fight, fight!' said Herbie passionately. 'That's what you're after, is it, Mrs Kilker? Margaret led me on to make a holy show of myself with that rotten pudding, but that's not enough. Now you want me to get my lip split. Well, let me tell you, Mrs Kilker, I saw the way your daughter was all over that Hugh Darcy and so did everyone else. She went for him like a mad hen. Downright common it was. She's making the mistake of her life. He's a drifter, he's a load of rubbish.'

'You never said a truer word,' lamented Eny. 'Put up a battle for her, Herbie. Stand up for yourself and your rights.'

'I wouldn't have her if she was given away with a pound of prawns,' he shouted.

The astonishing thing was that this was true. All in a moment he had finished with Margaret as a cat might have finished with its dinner. His long courtship meant nothing to him. It belonged to the past. He saw Margaret as a plump, unappreciative girl with hair that wouldn't stay tidy. Ordinary, that's what she was.

Herb felt stronger, more alive, than he had ever felt before. Rage had awakened him. The catastrophic sickness had stirred up his slack metabolism. He looked at Mrs Kilker, who had so often teased him so meanly, and his blood grew hot.

'If you want the plain truth, I don't like a bone in your body, Mrs Kilker, and never have. So go before you're pushed.'

'He's nowhere near the molly I thought he was,' mused Eny admiringly.

Herb returned to Jasper, where his family lived. Back there, his mother and sisters so solicitous, he hardly spared a thought for Margaret. He began to court another young lady, far more suitable. Before the year was out they were married.

In fact he lived happily for another forty-eight years, the father of a respected family. But Margaret's chagrin could not accept this, and neither could Eny's. Gradually Herbie died of the Big Flu. There was no one to contradict Rowena's romancing: 'Of course he *could* have, thousands of people did. And weakened as he must have been by a broken heart! Ah, the poor boy, God give him peace.'

The pair of them knew perfectly well it was only a story to make Margaret feel better, but as time went on the tale seemed so real, so tragic. The letter Herbie's mother wrote, saying that his vitality had been drained away, he had no will to live now that the one he adored preferred another; ah, it was a sad, sad letter! In Margaret's middle age, when the whole thing had passed into the unshakeable truth of myth, she even sometimes looked for that letter. She knew she would never have thrown it away.

Hugh spent three days in hospital. While Herb Lennon was bowed down with humiliation in his boarding-house room, Hugh was bowed down likewise on his bed of pain. Jer was so tearful Hugh sent him away in disgust. The doctor was no help.

'You drink?' he demanded. Hugh nodded. The doctor prodded, palpated, mumbling, 'All you itinerant workers are the same. A few more years and you'll have a liver like a bust brick. Get off the sauce, you young bonehead. You've got all your life before you, why not live it?'

Hugh thought he would never drink again, or eat either, come to that. He was as weak as a cat, his throat had been scoured with gravel, his stomach an orchestra of rippling squeals and resonant gurgles.

Mrs Kilker came to see him.

'Margaret's too nervous to come in,' she explained. 'She will have it you're due for the long box.'

She gazed at him with eyes hard as diamonds, and he gazed back.

'Would you fancy a pork chop fried in engine oil?' she inquired.

'Gah,' moaned Hugh. 'Go away, go on, quick!'

She laughed. 'Ah,' she said, 'you tried hard to get that ring for her. You're not such a bad class of poor fella. I've got the brother over home, you know. Mr Kilker, he said he was not to stay all alone in that dirty den of a pub. And you're to come too, when they let you out. Just till you get yourself settled, mind.'

'It's real good of you and Mr Kilker,' said Hughie sincerely.

She jumped up, nimble as a young woman, good looking still with her fresh skin and lively glance.

'I'll send Margaret in.'

Margaret came in with a rush. She looked as if she had been crying her eyes out. Hughie, already reduced, felt a gush of tears to his own.

'It's all right, it's all right,' he said soothingly.

'I thought . . . I thought . . . oh, Hughie!'

He smoothed his hand over her hair. It was such a bright pretty colour.

'I guess you're my girl, aren't you?'

She nodded, not looking at him.

'Reckon we'll end up together?'

He could see that she did. A feeling came over him that he'd said something rash, wrong, kunckleheaded, but he was too frail to care.

Mrs Kilker said it couldn't rightly be called an engagement, more an understanding. But John said it was: a finer young fella never walked the earth, and he was getting a treasure in Margaret. Jer was ceremonially embraced. He could see quite well that Mrs Kilker had her doubts. Every now and then she wheezed out a sigh meant to be noticed by all present. But he was satisfied, himself.

Alone with her daughter, Eny wept. She begged her not to do it.

'Don't rouse on me, Ma,' said Margaret. 'There's such a feeling in my heart for him. Didn't you feel like that about Pa when you were young?'

'I still do,' her mother might have answered. 'More so now that he might be taken away from me.' But aloud she said, 'It's for better or worse, you know, dotie.'

'I know it might be for the worse,' said Margaret. 'I know he's a wild sort of one. Don't cry any more, Ma, because I won't ever again.'

'Oh, girl,' said Rowena. 'God be good to you in your foolishness.'

In due course Hugh joined Jer in the Kilkers' spare room. Their house was the old colonial kind, with a veranda all round it, shaded with wistaria, passionfruit and choko vines. Out there the Kilker boys had slept before the War. Rowena said neighbours had complained of the bedtime rumpus for half a mile.

As hospitality in the country towns stood high amongst the virtues, the back bedroom was the best furnished in the house. In the unaccustomed surroundings Jer and Hugh were all feet, pickily washing at the wash stand, speaking in whispers. They lay side by side in the high-legged iron bed, gazing at the marcella quilt, white as swans, smelling sunshine and dry grass on the sheets, and feeling like two sore thumbs.

'This is giving me the rats,' said Hugh.

'They're lovely people, lovely,' said Jer unctuously.

'I don't care. I'm getting the shits with all this fancy stuff. I'm clearing out in a day or so.'

'Course you are,' said Jer. 'Mr Kilker said it wouldn't do, you and Margaret being gone on each other the way you are. Not proper to be under the same roof.'

Thoughts raced through Hugh's head. They were all ahead of him, all of them.

'She's not like that. She's a good Catholic girl,' he said. 'Go to sleep for God'sake, flaming earbasher.'

Margaret had wound her toes in the hem of her nightdress. She heard her father shoo out the cat with Hun-like threats, give the last clang to the poker as he banked the fire. There were a few squeaks and door clicks and a rhythmic murmur as her mother recited what she called 'a decker' of the Rosary before she went to sleep. Margaret could guess what the current decade was in aid of, an engagement going up in flames.

'Fat chance,' murmured Margaret. She felt languorous and melting, her hair long and silky, her skin like velvet. She rejoiced in her own body. Oh, she had a lovely shape. Josie might look better in fashionable pleated skirts and long cardigans , but once their clothes were off, she, Margaret, was like one of those old statues. Suppose Hughie came to the bedroom window right now, and

80

tapped quietly, asking her to come out across the moonlit lawn, into the shadow of the trees?

'I'd go like a shot,' thought Margaret. She clapped hand to mouth, shocked.

'Jesus, Mary and Joseph, help me to be . . .'

But what did she mean? Strong, good, sensible? Whatever it was, she knew that the three of them would be of no use whatsoever.

Jer lay awake in the comfortable darkness. This was the life – a clean bed, and white curtains tied back with cords, and no steam whistle blowing in the cold dark morning. Things had turned out his way and no mistake. He had already sounded Mr Kilker out on whether Margaret was the sweet-natured Christian girl he'd picked her to be, one who wouldn't mind a cripple around the house. Mr Kilker was offended to think Jer had even doubted it.

'She'll be as pleased as Punch,' he assured Jer. 'Won't I ask her about it today.'

Margaret knew Jer and Hugh went together like finger and thumb, and readily agreed. She felt confident he'd scramble away quick enough as soon as the children began to arrive.

Once Jer accepted that one day Hugh would marry, he saw that Margaret Kilker, easygoing and religious, was the one who would best look out for him.

It was a good thing for Hugh to get married; he understood that now he was a man.

'Oh, yes, I know you all right,' he thought. He placed an affectionate hand on his sleeping brother. He loved him devotedly, but he knew himself superior in intelligence and foresight. Hugh had cheek and courage; you'd never come to the end of his charm. But somewhere in his character he was flimsy. Jer saw him bowling for ever around the State, like one of those uncanny bundles of dry grass and thorns, a rolypoly, rolling this way and that before the wind until it fetched up against barbed wire and fell to pieces. Wherever he and Hugh had worked there were jokers like that, in all stages of disintegration. Drifters, they called themselves, free men, sons of liberty. Jer knew how they felt. Their way of life provided them with one long open door; whenever responsibility threatened they ducked through it. But the barbed-wire fence was always there, always. They came up against it because of age, failing health, too much booze. That's when they looked around for someone to go home to, and found there wasn't a soul in the world.

Besides, marriage wouldn't keep Hugh at home, if he wanted to remain a seasonal labourer. Jer knew the routine of too many of those: hard workers, but free and easy, back home three or four times a year, get the wife in pod, teach the boy how to pass a football correctly, dig over the garden, tell the young daughter she'll get her teeth kicked in if she goes too far with the boys, lay some new lino in the kitchen, kisses all round and off again grape picking, cane cutting, fencing, or whatever the game was.

Besides, thought Jer, it might be the world's best fun living with a newly married couple. What price Jer power then?

Within a few days Hughie moved out to a working-men's boarding house, saying firmly that that had been his agreement with Mrs Kilker.

'Certainly you've been very good to me,' he said, 'and I won't forget it.'

Neither Rowena nor John would hear of young Jer going as well.

'The amount he eats wouldn't choke a sparrow. He's as welcome as the flowers in May, what with his light spirits and all.'

Margaret put a good face on it, but she feared that Hugh might vanish from Trafalgar overnight. She saw plainly that he was made uneasy by order and system. He was like a wild dog coaxed briefly into becoming a pet. The moment backs were turned, over the fence with him. But still, his last words to her were that he would see her on Sunday.

The truth was he did not know which way to jump. One part of him feared that every marriage was like that of his parents. He could see, of course, by looking at John and Eny Kilker, that all marriages were not. But the panic was there.

There was in him a craving not to be lonely any more, to have a place of his own. He didn't like the boarding house, which had curtains so old mason wasps had built their clay skyscrapers in the folds. Margaret might have starched white lace curtains like her mother had. Yet, as he thought this very thing, something feral in him capered with glee at the chance of escape from such pussycat domesticity.

In the end he came to the conclusion that Margaret was as good as anyone else to get engaged to, and that even if they got married some day (and most likely, they wouldn't) he need not change his ways.

The Kilkers gave Margaret and Hughie a family party. Josie was chagrined to see Margaret wearing a ring, a small ruby in a heart of brilliants. She yearned to tell her sister it looked like a rat's eye. But she was too uneasy in her own life to risk unpleasantness with her parents. She had frequent misgivings about her love for Noel Capper. If she loved him truly, why did she want to screech at him every time he opened his mouth? The worst had happened. Noel the urbane boy had grown into Noel the man and a calamitous stodge he was.

Hugh visited the Trafalgar employment agency, and accepted a job offsiding at a woolshed two hundred miles away. He said he had to put together a bankroll before he could think of getting married. It was the proper thing to do.

He kissed Margaret heartily, told Jer he'd get his tenner for the ring back at the end of the month, and that he was the luckiest coot in the world that the Kilkers wanted him to stay with them and build up his health.

'Imagine me going off on my own and you not even letting out a yip!' he said to Jer.

'Things are different now. Our luck's turned.'

'Well, maybe you're right.'

Hugh was embarrassed and pleased by Margaret's tears when he left. He felt much more the parting with Jer, but Jer was as carefree as a bird. Hugh was aggrieved. At his destination, he had to wait for the station truck. He met some of the team in the local pub, got as full as a boot and passed out. When the station boss arrived he said curtly, 'Leave that one. We got a champion cook and I'm not giving him no boozer for an offsider.'

Hugh hung around the town for three days before someone took him on as a rouseabout. Morosely he sat on the truck tray, bumping over a road made with a knife and fork. The wind went through him like a needle. Well, this is the way it is, he thought. He had always made do with rough rides in store lorries, wind biting your nose off, getting in through the holes in your pants. And if it wasn't cold, it was hot, cycling through empty, exhausted villages, the day on fire, blackfellas leaning against the one listless tree, dust puffing up around the shoes of anyone who dawdled down the street.

Hugh knew several of the men at that shed. He was taken aback when they frankly expressed their disappointment that young Jer wasn't along.

'Jeez, he's a wag,' they told the others. 'The yarns he comes up with! Go on, Hughie, tell the one about the ringbarker from Gatha.'

Hugh told them the scabrous story about the loner so fabulously endowed that he was known as the Gatha Entire. He put in all the funny bits the way Jer did it, the wheelbarrow, the way the Palmer Street trotters ran screaming when they saw him coming; but he didn't get a grin.

'Doesn't sound right somehow, coming out of that kewpie mug of yours,' grunted one.

He detested mucking around with raw dirty wool after the years cooking or offsiding. His hands softened while he was in Trafalgar. Instead of having the usual spine-bash on his bunk, he spent too much of his spare time with a needle, picking burr tips out of his puffy fingers.

He missed Jer more than he would admit, the clean mended socks, greasy clothes washed without his asking. Companionship. Jer's gossip and jokes. He had an impulsive desire to tell Margaret what his brother meant to him, pain in the tit as he was. He wanted to tell her about himself in every detail. It was as though the girl could supply definitions and boundaries to his life.

'Be damned to that,' thought Hugh, going off to join the other jokers at the cookhouse fire.

Jeremiah lost no time in making himself useful about the Kilker place. There was no end to the things he could do, weeding the garden, peeling and scraping, getting a meal on that would tempt a nun.

Eny took a great fancy to Jer. Their experiences in the House of Horror were a bond. She thought that if someone put a rope on him and stretched him out a couple of feet he'd be the finest looking boy in the district. Added to that, he was such a clever little nab in the house.

'You'd make someone a jewel of a wife!' she complimented him.

Swiftly Jer put on a wan look, and then a plucky one. He allowed his dark eyes to grow moist. Eny could have kicked herself.

'Ah, boy dear,' she lamented. 'I've a tongue that could skin ferrets. I'm that sorry. I didn't mean that by any manner of means.'

Jer forgave her with a smile and a wistful look.

'It's just that I like to feel useful. As far as I can, that is.'

As he left the kitchen it seemed to Eny that he was less spry than usual on his crutches, and she wondered if he endured pain, never letting on, like the heroic soul he was. She was hard on herself all day.

Jer knew women to a T. If he could arouse their sympathy he had them tight in his fist. He did not admire them for this; he considered that women's urge to protect and aid came from a yearning to make great big benevolent ladies of themselves.

He was, at this time, quietly looking around to see where he could employ Jer power.

He was already thick with old John. He wouldn't hear of Jer's looking for a little job for himself somewhere.

'Aren't you here to build yourself up after the illness?' asked John testily. 'You're that thin you're like death on wires. You let my old girl pet you a bit.'

John was fascinated by Jeremiah. He could not get enough of his music, or his stories either.

He asked his wife: 'Did you know their grandfather was a statue? Poor Martin's Dad, he was a great man in the old country, and there's a stone statue to him some place in Galway.'

Rowena was cynical. 'I'll believe that when I see it. Why, last Sunday Jer sang me a song he said he'd made up himself, and God knows it was one I heard me father's Fenian uncle sing many a time.'

She did not hold Jer's weakness against him, but admired him for his audacity.

'Wouldn't any living soul amongst us do the same thing,' she demanded, 'should we be all scrunched-up as poor Jerry is, God help him?'

Aunt Alf told Father Driscoll the Darcy boys had a statue for a grandfather, and Father Driscoll challenged Jer.

'He's Robert Emmet, no doubt,' he said sarcastically, 'or maybe Dan O'Connell.'

But Jer was too fly for that, saying that he fancied the grandfather was only a poor tenant farmer who died for freedom during one of the Risings.

'God rest every manjack of them, martyrs that they were,' said Father Driscoll. 'And are,' he added darkly, for the latest troubles in Ireland were far from over.

Jer had a flock of Irish songs. He was invited into the presbytery office to sing them. This den was the priest's own. He was supposed to say his Office there as well as make the parish books balance.

'She never sets foot in here,' boasted Father Driscoll, jerking his head towards the kitchen, 'not even to clean.'

It was a dingy lair, stinking with the pipe smoke of fifty years. The varnished walls were covered with photographs – seminary groups; two Popes, the current Archbishop, all with ringed hands upraised in remote blessings; Father Driscoll's mother, a severe Corkwoman with a bald head and a lace fantod on top of it; and Father Driscoll himself, on horses, mules, camels. Jer looked at each intently, and listened to the story about it. He saw he would be able to adapt several of them. Father Driscoll became quite excited, his flat cheeks flushed. He wished like hell he could offer the young fellow something more manly than tea.

Jer cherished his guitar. It was battered and beaten, but his fingers and its strings loved each other. Father Driscoll looked at the lad with pity, poor little gammy. Then Jer turned his educated glance on him.

First of all he knocked the stuffing out of the priest with 'Twenty Men from Cork', and completed the work with the antique tune of 'Slievenamon'. He picked him up and filled his heart with fire with 'Who Fears to Speak of Ninety-Eight?' The old priest rose to his feet and sang in a quavering roar:

'Some on the shores of distant lands their weary hearts have laid,
And by the stranger's heedless hands their lonely graves were made.
But though their clay be far away beyond Pacific foam,
In true men, like you, men, their spirit's still at home.'

'Jesus, Mary and Joseph,' thought Alf, listening beyond the door. 'He'll blow out a blood vessel.'

Father Driscoll felt his heart lurch. He sat down carefully. Jer filled his pipe and lit it for him.

'Did you notice, lad,' said the priest when he had his breath back, 'I changed Atlantic to Pacific because of the many of us laid here in foreign soil in the penal day?'

'You did it well, Father,' said Jer. 'Is the pipe all right?'

'Ah, this pipe would draw in a blowfly. Herself gave it to me, her out there listening at the door.'

Alf smiled tolerantly.

The priest smoked for a while. Jer observed the throb in his thin old neck.

'Ah, my boy,' he said at last, 'that music of yours would start up a paralytic. I ask your pardon if I am too forward, but is there no way your poor feet might be straightened?'

'Oh, there is,' said Jer instantly. 'There's operations, I've been advised. But it would take five hundred pounds. Oh, at the very least, Father. So I have put that out of my mind.'

The priest grunted. Auntie Alf, waiting beyond the door, went back to the kitchen, shaking her head over the boy's wonderful resignation to the holy Will.

Father Driscoll thought young Jer worth a stack of gold. He couldn't have enough of him.

Very soon Jer had the run of the presbytery. He was the pet of Auntie Alf. Jer did not know quite what he was aiming at, but good friends never went amiss. He cleaned the silver for Alf, sang her touching songs like 'Eveleen' and 'Eileen Alannah', and when she went to do the shopping slid into her bedroom and examined her belongings. There he found a bankbook recording an amazing sum of money and a bundle of letters from her loving niece Delia. He saw at once what was happening. He committed Delia's address to memory and scratched his head over what he could do with this new knowledge. Jer power worked in hidden ways which might well be revealed to him later.

To Father Driscoll Jer praised Auntie Alf to the skies. The priest said maybe so, grunted, or looked secretive. He got sneaky enjoyment from putting down a person who had been so good to him.

'Ah, she's not a bad old dealer,' he admitted.

'And then there's her niece, Delia,' said Jer, ready to look concerned, happy or interested as the case might be. Father Driscoll told him the shocking story of Delia, transparently wrapped up here and there because of Jer's youth.

Well, thought Jer, no fish without a trifle on the hook, and, swearing the old man to secrecy, told him about the money going to Delia at such and such an address in Sydney. He went off well satisfied that he had started a pot boiling, although whose pot he was not quite sure.

Father Driscoll was, of course, privy to his sister's will. At the time he had seen through the dear soul's stratagem and known that Miss Kilker would take care of him until he went to his reward. He was well aware that many of the comforts about the house came from Miss Kilker; the parish fund would never have sprung to the hot water being laid on in the bathroom. He took these benefits for granted. After all, that was what the legacy was for. And, too, Miss Kilker being eight or so years younger than himself, there would be a few pounds left to look after her in her dotage.

He now became agitated. He could have gone out into the kitchen and scragged the woman, except that the lad, with his delicacy and trust, had sworn him to secrecy. He stamped up and down the office, smoking like a flue. The witless old chook was going to dribble the money away, and to Delia Kilker, of all people.

'Why,' he groaned, 'if she had to give my poor sister's money away, it could have been to Jer Darcy, to have his feet fixed.'

His heart gave a single sodden thump, then fluttered so erratically he had to sit down and ring his little bell. Alf flapped in, undid his collar, put a cushion under his head and gave him his angina tablet.

'You're a desperate colour, Father,' she said. 'I'll fetch the doctor.'

'You will not,' he gasped, angrily waving her out of the room.

As soon as she heard him snore, she looked in at him. His nose stuck up sharp and pallid as that of a dead man. She called the doctor. He put Father Driscoll into bed at once and said he was on no account to leave for his holiday, which was due in three weeks. Father Driscoll went off like a firecracker.

The doctor gazed at him and remarked, 'No doubt you're a good old box of tricks and ready for heaven any moment, but would you say this moment?'

Father Driscoll could not let go of his disappointment and bit Alf's head off every time he saw her. She thought it was because she had fetched the doctor, but in reality he was festering about Delia and the money. As he had grown old, he had become very self-centred. His vital powers had drawn themselves about some central fount of life, and would so concentrate more and more until death squeezed his heart into silence.

Truth to tell, there had never been much to him except his obsessive, pure love of the people of the Inland and the way he served them. His devotion to his native land was nothing compared with that. He would have sunk Ireland, Cork to Coleraine, if it had benefited his outback parishioners. His life in Trafalgar was a cosy, trivial routine except for his priestly duties. Sometimes he realised this, remembered the vehement idealism of his young life, and was fleetingly sad. Oh, his heart was a furnace then!

'There,' he said to himself. 'I've done my dash and God won't be hard on an old man.'

Five

It was near Christmas, an ardent day, Sydney gasping under a sky violet from the smudge of industry. When the watercart passed there was for a moment a string of puddles blue as iris, and then nothing but whiffs of steam. Under the pleasant odours of ripe fruit and fried fish was the dankness of wet coal, heated metal, the stink of engineering.

From his window the night before Father Driscoll had seen a thousand columns of seething smoke, each sitting on the rosy light of a factory chimney. He thanked God he had ended up in the fresh air of Trafalgar. Oh, he felt a countryman when in Sydney! He who had studied in Rome here felt like a lost dog with low antecedents. His heavy black clothing stuck to him, his collar was iron itself, his feet balls of fire. He cursed the doctor for delaying his holiday so long.

In Jersey Road he asked the way to Delia's from workmen with black singlets and sweaty faces; they were hanging out a pub door with schooners of beer running with dew. He wished he'd had the gall to ask one of them for a swig.

The houses were pushed together in a wall. Dolls' houses they were, with frontages ten feet wide, balconies ornamented with ringletted wrought iron. And here was Delia's.

He banged the knocker, and leant his forehead against the door. 'I'm whacked,' he thought.

'I'm looking for Mrs Delia Barry,' he said to the man who opened the door.

'She's out Christmas shopping. Here, you look done in. Come in out of the sun, Father, and have a cold drink. It's a scorcher today, no mistake.'

The husband was a chatty man, glad to have someone to talk to. The priest pressed the cold glass of lemonade against his wrists and listened. The front room was dim, a paper fan in the small arched fireplace. Moquette upholstery overheated the back of the visitor's legs; a palm fountained in the window between the plush curtains.

'She's got it that nice,' said Mr Barry. Father Driscoll looked perceptively at him. He had uncertainties, this man, so much older than Delia could be. He had a mouth too eager to please.

'Blessed Mother,' thought Father Driscoll, 'I can't put the Jezebel's pot on with this poor man . . . And has God given you the happiness of children, a son perhaps?' he inquired. Mr Barry said no. Delia had a boy by an earlier marriage, but he was a mental case, so afflicted that she had put him in an institution and had not seen him since infancy.

'But maybe it's just as well. I'm a bit long in the tooth for kids, and Delia likes a bit of fun, going out and that. I've a steady job in the crockery. I do glazing. Won't you wait till she comes home? I'll put the kettle on.'

'I won't,' said Father Driscoll. 'It was just that her aunt, Miss Kilker, my housekeeper, asked me to call and see that all was well with her. Her aunt will not be writing to her again.'

'Why, I didn't know they corresponded,' said the husband. 'Is something the matter with Miss Kilker?'

'Arthritis in her hands,' lied the priest fluently. 'Can no more pick up a pen than a ton of bricks. Poor woman's a martyr. But of course Delia can send me a line if she wants news of her aunt's health.'

Returned to his guestroom in a city presbytery, Father Driscoll considered telephoning some of his old friends. But he was sick and shaky. All the anger against Alf – and now against Delia – that churned inside him demanded outlet. How he could have lashed into that deceiving, wicked woman, playing on her good aunt's compassion and natural affection! Lies, lies, lies! She, so well off, a home of her own, a decent husband, cheating money out of an old maid presbytery housekeeper! But wasn't it Delia all over, greedy and grasping, caring for no one but herself, taking that simple soul Barry down as well?

His heart sounded like a pot boiling. He put a capsule under his tongue and lay down, praying for charity. Somehow it had deserted him. All he wanted to do was to choke Delia Kilker.

Father Driscoll went home without having had as much as a beer with his old mates. Those who were alive were very old now; he'd always been the youngest and strongest in that group. Parched thin faces they had, soft scanty white hair, trembling hands. He embraced gently each one of them. God keep you, Patrick, William, Brendan. He felt it was the last time they would meet.

91

All the way home in the hot dusty train he considered the manner in which he must tell Miss Kilker of Delia's perfidy. Every style seemed wrong and cruel.

He prayed, but no enlightenment came. It was necessary at last to go into the kitchen and ask her for a cup of tea and tell her to sit down and have one herself. Alf was pale; she knew he had something on his mind. Perhaps he had seen a Sydney doctor and received frightening news.

He told her baldly what he had seen and heard.

'She's been codding you, Miss Kilker, she doesn't want for a penny. And as for the son, she left him in an institution when he was two months old and has not seen him since.'

It was a mortal blow for Alf. She looked like neither the big woman nor the little woman. Father Driscoll feared she might faint or have a seizure.

'Here, Miss Kilker,' he said nervously. 'Drink your tea. It will put heart in you.'

He thought she would strike it from his hand.

'Why did you have to tell me? Wicked. Heartless. That's what it is.'

'Why . . .' stammered the priest, 'to save the money you were throwing away on her. Wouldn't she have left you with half nothing, she's that rapacious and unprincipled.'

'Money, what does that matter?' asked Aunt Alf. She could feel furious pain in her stomach. But it was not there she had been stabbed.

'You leave my kitchen,' she gasped. 'I don't want to look upon your face.'

Father Driscoll made the sign of the Cross as he left, but whether on her behalf or his own he did not know. He went to his study and groaned out a few prayers. He had meant to do right but somehow he had done wrong.

Alf went through a bad time and so did the presbytery. The drains blocked, and a sheet of roof iron blew off in a breeze that would not tip the coal from a pipe. A possum fell down the chimney and Father Driscoll had to get a man in to pull the fireplace to pieces to let the creature loose. Something drowned in the water tank and gave them both a sickness not to be mentioned.

Aunt Alf did her duty in the presbytery as well as usual. She spoke only once to Father Driscoll.

'How did you know about Delia, that I was sending a little money?'

'I have my ways,' replied the priest loftily, hoping to awe her with Holy Orders.

'Chah!' said Alf.

She wrote him a note. 'I wish a Mass said for her and for her husband.'

She enclosed a ten shilling note. Since five shillings was the usual Church offering, and that by no means a law or rule, Father Driscoll was insulted. He saw what husbands had to put up with from hostile wives. She intended the offering to mean that he was over-interested in money, that was why he went spying on Delia. He was using that word to himself now, ashamed and repentant.

Sometimes he wondered how Jeremiah had come by his information. He had believed that Alf had told the boy. But perhaps it had been Eny or John.

The whole thing had taken a great deal out of Father Driscoll. He felt more and more a little old lame duck of a man, short of breath and pluck. It took days before he could screw his courage to the point where he could remind Rowena and John that the Church forbade their attending Josie's civil marriage.

In spite of her uncertain feelings, Josie had squirrelled her trousseau together, saving, hunting bargains, sewing. Josie had a chest of drawers at the Mount Carmel, packed with bed linen, tea towels, table runners with edges of fluted crochet.

'If Noel has not saved enough for a home by my twenty-first,' she said firmly, 'I'll postpone the wedding. It's the principle of the thing, a man's responsibility. What's Hugh doing about your future home, I'd like to know?'

'He's saving,' protested Margaret. 'You know that's why he can't come back to Trafalgar often.'

Being engaged had made Margaret touchy. The slightest criticism of Hughie made her fly at the throat that had uttered it. She did fatuous things like refusing milk in her tea because he took his black. She choked down rice pudding because it was his favourite. She threw out dresses she thought made her look fat. She was extravagantly happy and as morose as a wet cat, huddling in corners and crying because he hadn't written for a week. She thirsted for spoony phrases in these letters and found every excuse in the world because they were not there. Her eyes got bigger and her waist smaller, she went for hours without a sensible thought.

'You'd think you were addled!' scolded Eny, but Margaret only looked at her with a dazzled gaze. There was a glow around the edges of everything.

'Of course he could come home between jobs!' scoffed Josie. 'Tell him you won't marry him unless he is more considerate.'

'He's just right as he is. You shut your big mouth.'

'Soppy, that's what you are.'

Josie held up against herself a tiny satin camisole embroidered with daisies, and put a secret look on her face. Margaret gazed with wistful envy. She often had disgraceful daydreams about Hughie; she couldn't imagine where she got them. She was ashamed to confess these thoughts to Father Driscoll, burning with mortification when he enlarged on his belief that no unmarried Catholic girl would possibly lower herself to indulge in such immodest fantasies. Margaret accepted these castigations meekly, but on the way home she thought, 'What an old sap!'

Father Driscoll lived in a kind of holy fairyland, she thought, and her mother and father pretended to.

She and Hugh, when he did return to Trafalgar, were not left alone for a moment. They escaped to the outdoors with clumsy scufflings, groans, and ecstatically chewed lips.

'Stop it, Pa'll hear.'

'You've got to. Take your hand away.'

'I won't, I'm scared. You mustn't . . . oh, God!'

Margaret tried to hide her bruises, her guilty eyes, from her mother.

'Have you and that young tomcat been up to mischief?' demanded Eny.

'No, we haven't, retorted her daughter haughtily. This was true. Hughie had departed grumpy, evil-tempered, saying he ached like hell and it would do him no good. All his hostility was focused on her, the cowardly squib.

Margaret accompanied him to the station; he answered her only with grunts and monosyllables. He called from the train window and Margaret hastened to him, sure that he would give her a kiss and a few sweet words to be going on with. But all he wanted was some new socks sent after him.

She chose the socks with passionate care, and wrapped them likewise. She even loved his clothes; she couldn't get enough of him.

Still, Margaret often cried. She had not known that being engaged was so difficult. It had not seemed difficult for Josie.

However, no matter what kind of a face Josie put on for Margaret, she had misgivings. Every now and then she sat bolt upright out of sleep, clammy with sweat, her head stuffed with tears. Suppose her parents had been right, she had been too young to get engaged, there were more pebbles on the beach, people changed as they grew older?

Why had she wanted to marry so young? Josie knew it was to pip Margaret. And she had. She'd shown them all.

Josie blamed herself for her disaffection. Noel was no different from what he had always been, agreeable, dull, and gentlemanly. Deserting the religion of his forefathers had not worried him. He was never piqued with her, even when she was tart or silent. She went to the doctor, saying she was nervy. He gave her an iron mixture, with an assurance that she would feel quite herself when she was married and had commenced her nuptial duties.

Josie resigned herself to frustration, which was what the silly old goat was trying to say, and blamed everything else on that. But she was restless and uncertain. She expressed this to Noel. To her astonishment he banged his fists on the wall, said she was letting him down and he would kill himself if she called off the marriage.

Josie was impressed by this display. Perhaps there were, after all, fire and passion in Noel and the nuptial duties would make up for years of waiting.

On her twenty-first birthday she married Noel in the Registry Office. John Kilker was so upset he would not even attend the wedding reception.

'I'd be bound to say something to that blackfaced bowsie Hatch, for he's at the bottom of it all,' he muttered. So Rowena went alone.

There was no enjoyment for Eny at the reception. Mrs Hatch was flushed and guilty, fearing that her old friend would lash into her as a turncoat. Mr Hatch was in a fume about something, ruby-faced and jabbering. He had a swallowtail of orange ribbon in his buttonhole.

'Not a word about the Pope, Mr Hatch,' advised Eny. 'This is a happy day for us all, and God knows I don't want to send you home with a broken nose.'

She swept a glance around at the teetotal punchbowl, the glum faces, the blanched bride, and went away. Her heart ached for that girl. Something was wrong, cold, hard as nails. But for John's sake she pulled herself together, cooked a fine supper, rallied Margaret that she would be the next one, and twice as beautiful a bride.

Margaret rushed from the table.

'Will you never learn to take your foot from your mouth?' scolded John.

'You're right there,' said his wife dolefully. 'If Margaret ever gets that Hugh up to scratch it'll be the wonder of the world.'

'Ah,' said John, 'he's young yet, and so is she, come to that. Josie was engaged to her sweetheart for years before they wed.'

'Josie was not Margaret's age,' pointed out Eny. 'God knows what the girl sees in Hugh Darcy, shifty article that he is.'

'He'll settle down,' said John placidly. 'Like me.'

Hugh had written Margaret such an inflammatory letter she could hardly sit still. The thought that he could not carry out all he promised or threatened was torment to her. She wrote begging him to name the day. What did it matter that they had little money? They had been engaged more than a year and waiting was so hard.

'No', he said. 'A man has principles. People would look down on me if I didn't provide properly for you.'

Jer, privily reading this before Hughie posted it, rolled up his eyes.

Margaret's eyes filled with tears. It wasn't fair. Nothing seemed fair. She was terrified that her mother or Josie might get hold of the letter. Her father would feel it his paternal duty to knock Hugh's block off for writing dirty things to his daughter, and then he would drop dead. She had no good place to hide it, so she tore the pages up very small and regretfully flushed the bits down the lavatory.

As Jer's health had improved, he sometimes went on jobs with Hugh when the conditions were good and the weather warm. When he was away, Jer wrote letters to everyone, full of fun and jokes, making light of his difficulties. He wrote more personal letters to Auntie Alf, saying his heart was often heavy, he would never save enough money for his operation and would she pray for his intention, since she understood him better than others.

John went off to visit Father Driscoll, who was not well, and Alf took the opportunity to see Eny. Alf told her sister-in-law about Delia, not mentioning the girl's deceit, but that Father Driscoll had visited and spoken to her decent poor fellow of a husband.

'I don't think you need worry about her any more, Eny,' she said.

'She's landed on her feet. And as for the money I sent her, well, no doubt there was some little emergency and I'm glad I could help.'

'Ah, Alf,' said Eny, 'you're a good woman, a saint off the wall, and I hope you get your reward. I'll tell John and set his mind at rest.'

So she did. The pair of them lay in bed, holding hands, wondering why it was that some children turned out waywards, and others were straight from God's hand.

John had never ceased to hope that one day Delia would walk in. At Christmas or on his birthday, perhaps. He said this to Eny, adding, 'It'll be like the boys, I suppose, off leading their own lives and hardly sparing a thought for the old people. It's Nature, my dear, and we're powerless against it.'

Eny snapped 'Why does God give us children, when they all go away from us one way or another? There's no justice in it.'

'Isn't that the truth of it?' said John. 'When I left Dublin, I never sent a line to my old Da. The young have no hearts.'

'Oh, him!' snorted Eny. 'Giving you that Nero for a stepmother. Serve his bones right.'

'Young Jer writes letters,' she thought. 'It might be good and it might be for purposes of his own. He's got some plan or other at the back of that head of his. Sharp as a butcher's knife, he is.'

Not long afterwards, Father Driscoll died. His heart banged like a drumstick, twice, three times, and off he went. He was seventy-eight and had been marking time for a long while. His funeral would have gladdened that Bishop, long gone, who had reprieved him from the retirement home.

It was a great blow to Aunt Alf. She could not eat or sleep. She became so thin you could blow her off your hand. Jer was home again, and if it had not been for him, keeping her company, rousing her spirit with music, telling her jokes and stories, it might have been the end of her. John was grateful to Jer; there was nothing he would not do for that boy. Eny sometimes looked at Jer suspiciously, but she kept her tongue still.

Auntie Alf was now sixty-seven, and so was pensioned off by the diocese. Saint off the wall or not, Eny was frightened that John might now call their bargain of many years before and take it for granted that the old sister should live with them until God called. She felt that if Auntie Alf was to have one of her diversions in the kitchen she'd fly up the wall.

But Alf rented a little stone cottage near the church.

'Won't you be lonely, my dear?' asked her brother, after he had dug her garden for her and put a nail in the sitting-room wall for a picture of Our Lady of Perpetual Succour. Alf's delicate digestion had come against her since the priest's death. She looked like a dry twig in a black dress.

'Haven't I God always with me?' she said. John, who had intended to suggest a nice housewifely cat, was defeated.

Nevertheless Alf hankered for Josie to visit her and not stand on her dignity the way she did. Her niece's final decision to marry out of the Church was a grief to Alf. How could the girl bear the thought of life without grace, without the Sacraments? But she had never, by words or look, indicated this to Josie or the family. Still, Josie, because of the empathy she had with her old aunt, knew how she felt, and stayed away.

When she wed, Josie resigned from the Universal Providers. It was the custom; no one employed married women. Josie had often questioned this tradition. Why should a wedding make any difference? Her diligence turned inwards on itself; she felt deprived and resentful. In no way did she enjoy marriage. She learnt more about Noel in a month than she had in five years, and none of it was to her liking.

Noel too found his life in disarray. There were scenes of passion, sulks and recriminations. Much talk of frogs, freaks, beasts and savages filled the honeymoon house. Aside from the private shocks Josie sustained, she discovered that her husband was a gambler. How was it possible she had not guessed, not heard a rumour? She raged at him.

'Where the blazes do you think I got the money for this house?' he asked defiantly.

Before six months had passed, Mr Hatch proved that his stepson had been embezzling money for years. In a thunderous scene, staged before the shop staff, he dismissed Noel, demanding that the new home be sold to help defray the debt. Noel saw that Trafalgar offered him no future except legal proceedings and prison. He coaxed from his mother all the cash she could raise, and left for Sydney.

He was fond of Josie and thought that his desperate crisis would bring her to her senses, which it did. She saw it as a way out of her miserable marriage and repellent nuptial duties. She let her husband go alone. She told no one of Noel's pleas. She allowed gossiping Trafalgar to believe he had cruelly deserted her.

Eny wanted to rush to Josie. She didn't know her own feelings about it all, but Josie was her daughter. But John said, 'No, let her come to us. She knows she's welcome in this house always.'

Josie needed all the spirit she had. It was true she had chosen the lone way herself, with fair knowledge of what it would mean. People would righteously condemn her. No matter what Noel had done she was expected to stand by him, her hands clasped and her eyes turned up like the Mother of Sorrows. If he was sent to jail, as well he might be, she must be standing outside the prison gates when he was released.

Josie recognised the injustice and hypocrisy of this moral attitude, and scoffed at it. But scoffing did not alter it. She would have to face it just the same.

Nevertheless, bitter chagrin consumed her. To be left penniless by a thief and gambler like any silly woman around the town! She could not understand how it was she had never seen through Noel Capper. Blackness welled up in her. Bile or hatred or despair, it half drowned her night after night. How could she survive, neither married nor unmarried, twenty-two years old? She felt changed, bent over, her hair in snaky locks like Medusa's. Yet when she looked in the glass in the morning there she was, her girlish face clear and unmarked. Dainty as a doll. Josie thought that if her youth survived such anguish it could survive anything. And so it must.

Margaret helped her pack. She could not help weeping into the enviable tablecloths and underwear of her sister's trousseau.

'Oh, Josie, what will you do? Please come home,' she pleaded. 'Ma and Pa want you, they really do. And I do too, Josie.'

'Stop bawling, for goodness' sake,' said her sister. It's not the end of the world. Noel turned out a flop. I'm relieved to be rid of him.'

Margaret did not believe her. She thought Josie was hiding a broken heart.

'She's just like Joan of Arc,' she told her mother.

Auntie Alf heard a familiar knock at her door and was glad. There was Josie standing beside the hollyhocks.

'Please help me, Auntie Alf,' she said. For the first time Alf saw tears in her niece's clear eyes.

'I will,' said Alf.

The new priest was radical-minded. He said nothing to Josie

about getting her just dues for marrying out of the Church. He pulled rank and found young Mrs Capper a position in the accountancy department of the butter factory.

Knowing she had no means of support and was desperate for work, the manager offered her less than the single girls, who were receiving only half of the male rate anyway. The pittance was enough for food but not for lodging. Josie set her teeth and accepted it. The manager had not relished being bullied by the priest, and promised himself he would give the young madam curry.

Aunt Alf offered her niece a home, and Josie accepted. John Kilker was disappointed and bewildered.

'You've a right to come back to your own family,' he protested.

But Josephine defended her independence. She had made a mistake and must find her own way out of it. She told her father than when the required number of years had passed she would divorce Noel for desertion.

'We've never had a divorce in the family,' he muttered, scandalised.

'Don't tell Ma yet,' she asked. 'She must never hear what I had to put up with. Noel was not the kind of man you are, Pa.'

John could not bear to think what she meant. He resolved to defend Josie against her mother's fire and sword. But Eny was not over-wrathful. She had one blazing hour of recrimination, maternal sorrow, and hopes that Josie had learnt her lesson. Josie said not a word. She looked almost as though she were praying. Margaret admired her generously.

'If it was me,' she said rashly, 'if Hughie left me, after we are married, I mean, I'd pine away.'

'Get the meat in the pot before you cry over its loss,' snapped her mother.

Margaret tossed her head huffily. But in reality her mother's sharp tongue had not touched her. She breathed and dreamt happiness. Hughie had written to say he was coming home for a week's spell before going on to the next job. Work was getting scarce; he had had to take on the hard labour of scrub-cutting. Margaret floated on a sea of romantic love.

'Jer's not coming.'

'I thought them two went together like the two legs of a peg,' said Eny tartly.

'He's gone to Newcastle to see a specialist, to find out where he can get his legs straightened.'

'If he's saved as much money as all that he's a better man than his brother,' said Eny. Margaret remained silent. No matter how hard Hughie worked, he seemed unable to keep money in the bank or even in his pocket. Now and then he sent ten or fifteen pounds to put in their wedding savings account, but no sooner had she gloated over the balance than he borrowed it back again.

When Hugh knew that Father Driscoll had left Jer £100 he tried all in his power to borrow it.

'I'll pay it back right after the wedding, my first cheque,' he said.

'Like hell,' said Jer. He thrust out a twisted foot, waved it under Hughie's nose. 'I know your promises. Where's my ten quid for the ring? You guttled that down like the rest.'

'I've been a good mate to you,' shouted Hughie. 'I stuck with you like Mum said when anyone else would have shoved you in a Home.'

Jer said nothing, staring, peaked face and hollow-eyes, rubbing his knotty toes. Hugh flung out. He was ashamed of himself, but relieved, too.

'Tell that Margaret to get a job, if you're so hard up,' yelled Jeremiah after him.

It was just a spat. After grumpy sparrings, offhand favours done, they were as before.

Hugh broached the question of a job to Margaret. She, the daughter at home, had never thought of work outside the home. She had taken for granted her mother's belief that a girl's work in the house was a rehearsal for her inevitable life as wife and mother.

'I'm not trained for anything,' she said doubtfully. 'I can only do housework.'

Rowena hit the roof. 'No daughter of mine is going out scrubbing boarding-house stairs!' she stated. 'No word of this to your father, Margaret. The very idea would kill him. I suppose we'll see you working in a factory after you're wed, expecting or not, and my lord at home with his feet up.'

She was abrupt and unfriendly with Hugh when he spent his next layoff with them. Prevented from tearing his ears off because of John, she made do with slamming the pots around, never serving rice pudding, and sarcastically snorting whenever he made a remark.

'What's up with the old girl?' he asked Margaret.

'It's me being supposed to get work,' she said hesitantly. 'She's that old-fashioned,' she added apologetically.

'Well, I've had a crawful of it,' he said, and went away three days earlier than he had to.

'I will get a job,' she vowed. Shyly she tried for this situation and that, and at last found one, three days a week helping at the kindergarten.

There they treated children like short adults. Briskness, discipline, no sentimentality were the rule. Margaret did too much kissing and cuddling.

'Are you broody or what?' demanded the teacher acidly. Margaret was removed from the children and set to scrubbing the classroom, sweeping the playground, washing the nappies of those marked on the roll as WET. She might as well have worked in a boarding house.

Still, she stuck at the job. She saved her wages, and the bank account began to fatten a little.

'Where'd Hughie's brother get a hundred pounds?' Josie asked. Margaret told her.

'I wish Father Driscoll had left me something,' said Josie.

'Well, there's Aunt Alf's fortune,' said Margaret, laughing.

She told her sister about the old lady's fantasy. Josie smiled deprecatingly. Still, she thought seriously about that fortune. Aunt Alf was a great one for holding to the truth.

After Father Driscoll went off to God, Alf predicted that she would not be long after. He work was done. She thought of herself as looking more and more like a pressed pansy and, like it, fraying away into dust.

But Nature had other plans. Certain glands in her insides shut themselves off; chemicals in her brain dried up for ever or flowed more copiously than before.

'Alf's getting fat around the middle,' commented Eny. 'You'd think she was four months gone.'

Margaret blushed crossly. Since she had become engaged her mother often said vulgar things to her, as though breaking it gently that marriage would be a sight more indelicate than she dreamt.

Alf's physical health was now better than it had ever been. But her mind was turbulent. Memory patterns dormant for years were activated. At night she woke suddenly in her dark room, the hollyhocks kissing the window, and was back in Dublin, that woman's iron fingers twisted in her hair.

'Get in there, you ugly beast of a thing!'

She was thrown into a cupboard, pitchy, stinking of mice and mothballs, John already in there, crying, wetting his pants with fright and misery.

'I'm here, dotie, Alfie's here,' she had whispered, fondling him, his unbrushed hair, his mouth crusted with sores of dirt and neglect.

Alf, in her old age, hissed, growled, ground out: 'I hate her, I hate her, I pray the pigs will chew her bones.'

She fell back on the pillow, her ears buzzing, frantic with rage. Her heart walloped. It was some time before she calmed herself, falling then into a passion of repentance.

How could such thoughts return? She had forgiven her stepmother over and over again. She had rooted out from her memory the clothes she wore, the face she grinned with, the voice with the venom of snakes.

But there she was in Alf's mind, hard, flat, a woman not for little children inside or out, slapping away and screeching: 'Now will you own up that you done it, you bick, you dirty useless slut?'

Old Alf cowered, hands up to protect her head. It had always been her fear that the woman would break her ear drums as she threatened.

Josie, candle in hand, opened the door. Instantly Alf was back in the present.

'Don't you look like a fairy standing there in your nightie!' she said. 'Did I give you a start, Josie! I had such a nightmare!'

Though such nightmares went away, the memory of them did not. Alf was consumed with fear that she had never forgotten the stepmother, never given over hating her and wishing for vengeance. She was obsessed with the idea that she had made bad Confessions and, worse, bad Communions all her life; that wickedness, unconfessed, unrepented, had been with her all along. She asked the priest about it, crying and agitated, but he was too young. He said it was just her age, she must pay no attention. She returned angrily to her cottage. The man was nothing but a clown. They were hard up for decent, devout young fellows to ordain nowadays. Not in a million years could she image Father Driscoll telling any poor troubled soul it was her age.

To whom could she speak? Only John. She made him swear never to reveal their conversation to a living soul. John, alarmed, promised.

'She's dead, isn't she, John?'

'Who?' asked her brother.

'Her. The one who married our father.'

John stared in consternation. If Alf was going astray in her wits he felt he couldn't stand it.

'You haven't been seeing her, Alfie?'

'No, no, no,' she snapped at him. 'Only in dreams. But she's in my mind all the time and the things she did to you and me, John.'

She confessed her worries, the hidden sin of intractable hate, the bad Confessions, the unsympathetic young priest. John soothed her.

'Ah, Alfie, it's just bad old memories swimming up, that's all. That woman is dead the dear knows how many years ago. Wouldn't she be about a hundred and twenty if she was still kicking?'

'But how can I get her out of my mind?' asked Alf piteously. John was stumped.

'Say an aspiration. That's it, my dear. Say Mary help, Jesus save, and try to think of something else. Now tell me about Josephine. Is she happy, do you think?'

But the stepmother stayed in Alf's mind, an obsession. The realisation of her unabated hate caused Alf more misery than the memories. The hate thrived. Murder was not beyond it. It followed her around like the reek of foul water.

Although she loved the girl so much, she was not altogether at ease with young Josie. Josie did not behave as if she were in disgrace. 'Did I expect that?' Auntie Alf castigated herself. 'Badly treated and all as she was by that Noel Capper. The tattle she has to face, the way that plague of a manager at the butter factory treats her!'

Aunt Alf had never in her life lived with a young woman. At first it was quite thrilling, new fragrances in the bathroom, nail polish in the kitchen, a little orange lipstick called Tangee falling out of Josie's braided dolly-bag. Auntie Alf looked at the lipstick, perturbed.

'I didn't know you used that stuff,' she said reprovingly. 'I'm sure it's not right. Our Lady didn't use lipstick.'

Josie explained that Tangee was very ladylike. On the lips it changed to your own natural colour.

'I'd look such a freak if I didn't make up a little. Everyone does,' she explained.

Josie persuaded Auntie Alf to let her cut her hair, saying it would grow thicker and stronger and maybe even have a curl. Alf had always worn her hair pulled back to a little bun, first brown, then grey, and finally yellow-streaked white.

Such alarm she had as the thin locks fell to the floor and a cold draught blew on the back of her neck! Josie shampooed her hair, putting a little laundry blue in the rinsing water, and set it with clips. Alf had to sit in the sun until it dried. 'Whatever will I say to Eny?' she worried. 'She's sure to torment me with the teasing.'

Finally Josie took out all the metal clips, brushed and pushed the hair around, and told Auntie Alf to go and take a look at herself.

The old woman could not believe it. Waves rippled in the shining white hair.

'It's just like white satin,' said Josie, pleased. 'You look beautiful!'

Alf lived on those words for a day. She then plucked up courage to visit Eny, who lavished praise.

'Oh, won't the boys all be after you now!' she cried.

The months went past, and Josie began to make changes in the cottage. It was a cold, dark tunnel, with windows as big as tea trays, and a back door opening in winter into the glacial south wind. The interior walls had been varnished in Queen Victoria's day and, what with smoke and dirt, had become almost black. Josie persuaded Aunt Alf to let her get them papered.

'You'll never know yourself, it'll be so light and bright,' she coaxed. 'Well, just let me do the hall!'

She sold two or three wedding presents, the EPNS cutlery, the Westminster clock from the Hatches. Paperhangers were cheap. Times were getting hard, and men jumped at the chance of extra work. She sent Aunt Alf over to her brother's for the day. When Margaret escorted the old woman home the house was filled with the smell of flour paste and turpentine.

Margaret saw a long hall papered in cream, a frieze of green leaves and yellow buttercups at both ceiling and floor. The ceiling was white, the plaster rose in the middle touched up with green. Alf was overwhelmed, and so was Margaret.

'It's just stunning,' gasped Margaret. 'I feel I'm in a garden. Oh, I wonder if Hughie will have our place papered too?'

But Aunt Alf felt unsettled. She had become used to grainy

varnished walls and smoke-stained ceilings. Every presbytery she had known had had the same.

'It's terrible light,' she said doubtfully. 'Won't it mark?'

'Oh, we'll be careful,' said Josie gaily. 'Say you're pleased, there's a dear!'

One by one the rooms were papered or painted. Auntie Alf gave her permission, but she always felt dubious.

'It doesn't feel right somehow,' she confided to Eny. By the time Josie began to make new curtains Alf was in the depths of her obsession with the stepmother, and when she saw the red material tossed over the sewing machine she was horrified.

'People will think it's one of them bad houses!' she cried.

'They're just for the kitchen, Auntie,' said Josie. 'They'll make it so warm and cosy. And in summer we'll hang a nice muslin.'

But Alf felt herself skim over the precipice. She was going to have a nervous attack and she could not do a thing about it. Josie was white as a sheet; she was saying something, but Alf couldn't hear. The tea caddy fell from the mantelpiece and scattered the tea; down came the picture of St Rita, patron of the kitchen, and smashed on the hearth. A blue flame ran like St Elmo's fire around the edge of a stove plate.

'You're always making me do things I don't want to do. You bully me,' shrieked Aunt Alf. 'You made me cut off my hair!'

'I did not,' she heard Josie say clearly. 'You thought about it for months. I've done nothing without your permission.'

'Delia took my money and you're taking over my house,' said Auntie Alf. She fell into a chair quite exhausted. She knew she had been dreadfully upset about something or someone, but she could not remember. The stepmother had blown away like a bat. Alf could not recall the torment she had suffered for so long on that woman's behalf.

She said feebly to Josie, 'Oh, my darling girl, did I say bad things to you?'

'You just got upset,' said Josie. She made the old woman lie down, covered her with a rug, made her tea. Alf was blanched and shaking for a long while.

'It's time for me to go to the Little Sisters,' she said sadly. 'It's in my mind that for a while I've been not quite right in the head. I've had thoughts that dreadful you wouldn't believe.'

Josie embraced her. 'But you've got me, Auntie Alf! I'll look after you for as long as you need me. You need never go to the Little Sisters as long as I'm here. Fancy us letting you to to a Home in Sydney, away from all of us, away from Pa! And besides, you're not old enough for a Home for the Aged!'

Auntie Alf looked at her tremulously. 'But I said cruel things to you, I know I did. You had tears in your eyes.'

Josie hugged her again. 'You were cross about having your hair cut, that was all. But it will grow again in no time. There, there, lean against me, I'll look after you, Auntie Alf.'

Alf had leant against no woman's breast since her mother died. How strange it was, putting her cheek against something so soft, so vulnerable and yet so protective.

'I think I'll go to sleep now, Josie,' she said. 'Aren't you like a dear daughter to me?'

'Yes,' she thought with wonder, 'I've never been a missus, but I have a dear daughter just the same.

'Still, I've been a kind of a missus,' thought Aunt Alf drowsily. 'Spending my life looking after men, putting up with their sulks and funny little ways, making ends meet, being lonely, darning them thousands of black socks, always being there when they wanted a cup of tea or an ear to complain into, being respectful. Not much different from other women.'

At this time Josie had not questioned Auntie Alf about her fortune, nor had she examined the old woman's private papers. She was not desperate enough. Nevertheless, the thought of the money was always at the back of her mind.

She continued with her studies, and swept triumphantly through her final examinations. She was now an accountant, though working as a disgracefully low-paid clerk in a butter factory.

Six

Hugh Darcy leant on the bar of the Royal Duke at Juno, depressed and not knowing how to handle it. Both gloomy and gritty, he was ready to fly out of his skin at anyone. He swept a snarl along the bar, inviting trouble. But the drinkers were all country boys, crushed hats, broken teeth, skin like roses. Not wanting to get into a scrap, they behaved as if he were not there, genially shouting at each other above the roar of the rain on the iron roof.

Life for Hughie had become a weary dream. He had worked on one near-bankrupt station after another, his life made wretched by fretful bosses, skimped food, the curse of wet sheep. Three times he had been booted off properties for drunkenness and insolence. He had been forced at last to take on stump-grubbing at a mean farm south of Juno. Again he had been dismissed. Same song, different verse.

Unemployed for three weeks, Hugh was now coming to the end of his cheque. He scarcely knew what to do, except return to Trafalgar, his tail between his legs.

The talk in the pub was of slump, the coming bad times. Men were being paid off all over town, the match factory bankrupt, most of the landowners in the district in hock to the banks. The younger men believed a crash couldn't happen in Australia. The older men recalled their Dads talking about the calamitous slump in the nineties, poor devils cutting their throats by the drove.

Someone stood in the half-open doorway, slicker streaming. The figure took off a collapsed hat, and slapped it against a leg. Hughie saw it was a woman, hair chopped short like a man's.

'Hey, any of you jokers want to drive me back to Mt Yatala?'

'That you, Pal? Come into the dry.'

'Women ain't allowed in public saloons.'

'The hell with that. Come in and have a snort, keep out the cold.'

The woman advanced, middle-aged, with a hooped back. She held a bloodstained cloth to her mouth.

'You been fighting, Pal? What's the other bloke look like?'

'I come into town to have me top teeth ripped out; been giving

108

me jip for weeks. I was a mug and had gas. Now I feel real weird. Wouldn't trust meself to drive.'

She bolted for the door to spit blood. When she returned the sunburn blotched her pale face like a map. The publican gave her a brandy. She winced as she drank it.

'Ghost, that stings like nettles.'

'Camp overnight, Pal. The missus'll be glad to find you a shakedown.'

'No, got to get home to the Boss, you know that. Ain't there anyone here who can drive me?'

But it was horse country. Few boys had the opportunity to learn to drive motor vehicles. They looked at her, sympathetic, and muttered excuses.

'Sorry, Mrs Biddle, going to the housie with me girl.'

'Don't know one end of a lorry from another, Mrs Biddle. Real sorry.'

'I can drive,' said Hughie. She looked at him searchingly.

'You been grogging on, boy?'

'Only three middies. Ask him. What's in it for me if I get you to Mt Yatala?'

'Here, fair go,' protested the publican.

'Not your business, mate. What's in it, missus?'

'What d'ya want?'

'A job.'

'You're on.'

'You'll have to show me the road.'

'Only one. It's about twenty miles.'

Motor vehicles were still comparatively rare. Hughie no more thought of ever owning one himself than he thought of flying. Still, he liked being around cars. Aside from illicit jaunts as a boy, he had practised driving station utilities. He had a natural affinity for things with wheels, and soon got the hang of their workings. But when he saw the tall grunting monster, its headlights steaming and hissing in the rain, he backed off. He looked around for the woman to tell her so. She was vomiting blood and brandy into a puddle.

'Christ,' she groaned, 'I feel crook. Get in, boy. If we don't get a move on Second Creek will be flooded and she's a brute.'

Hugh jumped in. Recklessly he shoved in the clutch, stumbled around the gears, and truck groaned off. The thing was full of inexorable power. It stood high off the ground, its tyres were solid

109

rubber. To wrench its steering wheel around took strong arms and shoulders.

'How'd you manage the wheel, missus? Cow weighs a ton.'

'Used to it. We're coming to the first creek. Should be pretty low still. Get into third and charge it.'

They roared through the water, the wheels slipped and clutched at the far bank, and they lurched onto an unmade road, running with water but still firm under the tyres.

'You ain't driven one of these big jobs before, eh?'

Hugh admitted he had not. She was calm.

'Then you're doing real well.'

Now and then she opened the celluloid side flaps to spit out blood. It came whistling back at her, borne on the wings of the weather.

'No worry. It'll all wash off in the rain, if we get stuck at Second Creek.'

The rain swarmed over the landscape like an army. Hugh could not see the road, just a few yards of mud and hurtling water. All around were trees, a sopping amorphous cloud, blacker than the night.

The woman kept up running directions. Change down here, keep away from the left, there's a breakaway bank, keep in first, we're coming to a hill, up we go, dead ahead, lad, you'll be right now. On the flat, so let her out a bit.

In between times she rested her head against the clammy celluloid, muttering with pain or disgust.

'Mouth feel bad, missus?'

'Could be worse.'

The air was full of wild cries, trees squawking, the surfy roar of the low scrub flattened before the blast. They came to Second Creek and stopped. The brown water lurched past. Mrs Biddle climbed down and tried the depth with a fallen bough. She returned, blinded with rain, to the truck.

'Too deep. I'm going to hoof it. You want to stay here?'

Hugh chose to go. The truck cabin offered little comfort. He was already wet to the skin. He backed with difficulty and got the vehicle partly off the road. The woman took a storm lantern from under the wooden seat and lit it. She folded her slicker and tied it on top of her head with its belt.

Hughie wondered if he should offer to pickaback her across. In spite of her large hands and wrists, she was a small woman. But she plunged ahead, holding up the lantern, and floundered through. The water, up to Hughie's armpits, was chill as death. It plucked his feet from under him and rolled him like a log. A powerful hand seized his, he scrambled to his feet and up the bank. The woman had hooked her other arm round a tree.

'Come on, it's only three, four miles.'

Like drowning creatures they struggled along the road. The wind dropped, the rain dwindled. The hills showed themselves against a lightening sky in sable domes, steeples, and shattered dykes. Far away shone a spectral star. Mrs Biddle gave a satisfied grunt.

'That's the homestead. The Boss has had them put a hurricane on the gatepost.'

She waved the lantern she carried. 'They'll be watching for me.'

Hugh fell into bed and slept like the dead until seven, when a gargoyle with a swollen shiny face awakened him.

'Yes, it's me all right,' she uttered with difficulty. 'Got a chill in me gums or something. Tucker's ready. Boss wants to see you when you're finished.'

Hughie ate on the veranda. The tranquil day knew nothing of storms. The homestead tank spouted white water into a series of lesser tanks. In the smallest, a barrel, a black child as big as a radish washed its face.

Hughie now saw he had come to real blackfellow country, all mysterious glens and sudden rich pasture, paddocks turned over in long glistening furrows for the frost to break up, creeks where wild ducks showed upturned feet, quail toddling in long files across the home garden. And over all the grey wall of Mt Yatala, a broken ridgepole, falling abruptly into the bush with the sound of waters, birds, wind in caverns, the rattle of scree.

He went to see the Boss. He expected a big man, his shirt tight in the chest and the shoulders, face like a butcher's block.

Biddle lay in a basket chair. He was only half a man, one leg gone, the other eaten with sores. His lungs were sick, it seemed, for he spoke in a strained wheeze.

'Mustard gas,' said Pal.

She was not his wife, merely his pal. The countryside gave her the title of Mrs Biddle because all respected and admired her. But in fact there was a Mrs Biddle somewhere. Joe Biddle had gone off to war in 1914, the fittest young man the Army doctor had ever passed. He was newly married. A dispatch rider, he was caught in a low-lying pool of mustard gas, clinging to grass and harrowed earth like yellow steam. He was invalided home. His wife would not or could not care for him after he left hospital. Yet she would not divorce him.

Pal was years older than Joe. She had inherited Mt Yatala station because her three brothers were killed in the war. But she had always more or less run the property, anyway.

'Never had no trouble,' she said. 'It's either in you or it ain't. The land, I mean. Brought Joe here to look after him. Good air, good tucker, me on hand when he has a bad turn.'

She turned to the man, a look of such love upon her swollen face that Hughie turned his eyes away. He felt he was spying.

'But don't you make no mistakes, boy. Joe's the Boss and always will be. What he says goes. We breed shire horses, got more blue ribbons than you can shake a stick at. It's Joe's stud. Any credit goes to him.'

On the way down to the feedshed, stumping along in her gumboots, she said abruptly: 'Them two black house girls – don't you lay a hand on them. They're Joe's. I'm too old for kids, have been since me and Joe hooked up. Them little boys you see running around, they're Joe's. Mine too, come to that. You got that clear?'

Hugh nodded.

'You got to live while you can,' she said, trudging away.

'Gawd,' said Hugh. He couldn't think straight. He longed to tell someone, Margaret perhaps, about Pal. He felt there were lights shining about her. She'd never go sour on that poor devil, never. Joe was right for life. And maybe she was, too.

The sick man could walk with crutches. Hughie sometimes heard his stammering footsteps moving slowly along the veranda. He had a fearful, choking cough.

'He ain't got long to go,' Pal informed Hugh. She had a curiously fierce, aristocratic gaze. He wondered what would happen to her when Joe died, and could answer it. She would carry on as before.

At Mt Yatala Hughie thought a great deal about the nature of love, not love like you saw at the pictures, or read about in newspapers, but the real thing. The older Kilkers had it in a way. He wondered self-consciously if he might ever find it himself.

Margaret now, she was full of it. If he was knocked out of life like Joe Biddle, she would look after him, be his meal ticket somehow. He did not doubt she loved him. She had cried when at last he had been permitted to make love to her, she being worn down by pestering. He had been sportive, laughing, tickling, caressing, excited. Her crying had spoiled his style, but he could understand it. She was religious, she didn't want to commit sins. He knew it was good for women to be religious: it saved men worry after marriage, even if it was a damned nuisance beforehand. But Margaret was Margaret, a lovely armful, even if she was hung with medals and scapulars. Somehow she had become part of his life, he didn't really know how. He experienced a soft kind of feeling, homesickness for Margaret. Maybe that feeling was love, too.

'Live while you can,' Mrs Biddle had said.

He saw a photograph of Corporal J. Biddle, AIF, in the parlour. Hugh could scarcely believe it. What a beautiful bloke! Straight nose, clean-cut mouth, the kind of smile that made you want to take him away and shout him a beer. Curly hair showing under the slouch hat.

'Twenty-two,' said Pal, watching him. 'A real dazzler, wasn't he?'

Hughie was shaken. He often played euchre or poker with the sick man but that day he could not bring himself to it. He stared at his own youthful face and saw the marks of life upon it, marks of the past years. He'd been passed over for work, sacked several times, thrown bodily off properties. He was getting a bad name amongst the trumps. Some of them were already thinking twice before taking him on at all, though they did not demur if Jer was with him.

'By God,' he said, 'I'll have to give the grog away.'

He had already lived a month without a drink, but he knew it was because he had not left Mt Yatala. As soon as he got to town the fatal desire for companionship and jollity would get him into a pub, and that would be the end of him.

'Am I that weak?' he asked himself wonderingly. He could not believe it, even though he was looking at the pattern of his life for six or seven years.

Disturbed, he wrote to Jer that he was going on the wagon before the bottle sickness got him. He was surprised to have an answer from Newcastle, where Jeremiah had been sent to have the operation on his feet.

'I wish it had been Sydney,' wrote Jer, 'so I could have a look around. That bridge and the statues. I wish you were here, Hughie. I feel a bit scared, hospital and all that. The doctor say's there's a good chance I'll get to walk. I was thinking the springtime it brings on the shearing, like the song says. It would be good if you and me could go on the circuit again. Like old times. But me walking around this time. Thanks for the tenner back again. I have nearly all the cash I need now. The doctor is so interested in my case he is going to do the surgery for a reduced fee. There'll be other doctors looking on and learning. Margaret said she will pray for me, and Mr and Mrs Kilker too. Mt Yatala sounds a real nice place.'

Hugh had an impetuous desire to be with Jer during this ordeal. He could think of nothing else. He even went as far as packing his swag. Then good sense halted him.

'Jesus, I'm a bunny. The kid isn't twisting my arm. He can manage. He's grown up now.'

But he was anxious for Jer. He needed a drink. He knew Pal had liquor in the house. She wouldn't refuse him a drink, especially when she knew about Jer. He caught himself rehearsing what he would say. He felt his face taking on disarming expressions, wistful, anxious, rueful – and was disgusted. He saw himself turning into a dispenser of charm like Jer, smoodging, flattering, manipulating.

He spoke to Mrs Biddle, asking if Jer could come there after his operation and recuperate.

'I know it's a lot to ask. I could move to the bunkhouse, and have him with me. You needn't even see him.'

Mrs Biddle said that if the other station hands did not mind, she was agreeable. Once Jer was on his feet he might like to help in the kitchen, as the older house girl was returning to a tribal marriage in the spring. Hugh was relieved. He wanted to have Jer under his wing again. He imagined Jer yarning with Joe Biddle, his music sounding through the house.

The kindness of these people moved him. He wrote to Jer telling of their good fortune. But, the operation over, Jer had been moved to a convalescent home. He said they had broken and reset bones, something like that, and he was in plaster. But he'd come later.

Hugh felt as if a great load had been lifted from him. The operation was over and, with luck, Jer would be able to walk and lead a normal life. Maybe he would even get married, have kids. Hugh felt deeply thankful, almost religious.

He was happy in those days. In that freezing air, with no liquor and plenty of good food, he began again to feel strong and optimistic. His body was springy with vitality. His letters to Margaret became more expansive. He wanted to tell her that he had been off the drink for many weeks; but she did not know that he got on the grog. He was always temperate in Trafalgar, mostly because he wanted no hassle with old John Kilker. He had constant thoughts of Margaret. He wanted her in his bed.

One day when Mrs Biddle was about to leave to pick up the weekly stores, he said impulsively, 'Hang on a minute.'

He scribbled out Margaret's address and a few words.

'Send a wire for me, will you, missus?'

'Something wrong, boy?'

'Read it. You'll have to, later, anyway.'

She read: 'Missing you something terrible. What say we get hitched on your birthday. Hugh.'

Hauling herself up into the truck, she called, 'Catching, ain't it?'

The telegram was delivered at Trafalgar at midday. Flushed and sparkling, Margaret flung down the yellow slip in front of Eny.

'There you are!' she said with insolence foreign to her. Then she broke into tears and blundered out of the room.

'She's surprised, too,' observed Josie.

'Oh, shut up!' said Eny. She was angry and defeated.

'That bangs Banagher!' she exclaimed.

John was pleased, but wistful. 'It's desperate the way daughters go away from a man.'

'She'd better not see the priest just yet,' said Josie. 'It's a long while to her birthday.'

Those were the only words she said that could be construed as spiteful. Josie had exciting news of her own.

'I'm opening my own business,' she announced.

They looked at her dumbly, their thoughts with Margaret. She perceived it had been foolish to blurt out her plans so soon after the arrival of Hughie's wire.

'An accountant's office,' Josie went on. 'I've leased that empty shop in Hardy Street, the one where the dressmaker used to be.'

Eny now paid attention. She said impatiently, 'What in the world do you know about business, and you just a slip of a girl?'

Her father said doubtfully, 'It's in my mind that a businessman

115

would not take his books to a young lady.'

Disappointed and chagrined, Josie went away. She was no more chagrined than her mother. Eny was unable to conceal her apprehension. Her heart ached at the look on Margaret's defenceless face when she was sarcastic or cruelly prophetic, but she could not stop her tongue.

'God help you,' she cried. 'You'll have six yowling kids before you're thirty-four.'

'Aren't you the one to talk!' retorted Margaret, between tears and heat.

Eny shook the stirring spoon at her. 'I had a man in a steady job, a roof over my head and porridge in the pot. Never mention your father in the same breath as that one!'

She reduced her daughter to a blubbering mass of conflicting emotions. The girl loved her mother and she loved Hughie. She saw that if she settled for the one she must give up the other, for the fireworks were beyond enduring. She flew into a panic at the thought of it.

'I can't do without Ma,' she wept into John's sheltering chest. 'But I'll have to.'

Eny had almost forgotten the compelling nature of young love. But John remembered. There had been a small, fiery brownheaded thing on the goldfield. Even yet when he thought of her his throat ached, he felt again the insatiable longing of more than fifty years before. She had died, that one. But he remembered how he had felt.

In the privacy of their bedroom he reproved Eny.

'You've gone beyond all decency, the way you're making Margaret unhappy,' he said. 'I won't have it, Eny.'

His wife burst out passionately. It was all for the girl's good, she had to be shown once and for all that Hugh would be useless as a husband. His chancy nature was written all over his face. Margaret had to be saved from a terrible future.

'But it's what she has chosen,' he replied. 'And who's to know it will be terrible? God's good.'

He hushed Eny's dozen arguments, he put his big hand over his vehement mouth.

'I want no more of it,' he said. 'It's our girl's life, and if she wants young Hughie to share it, that's the end of it. I'm desperate ashamed of the way you're going on, and that's the truth of the matter.'

Eny wept as if her heart were broken, and indeed it almost was, for John had never before spoken to her in such a manner. She could not bear that he should be ashamed of her.

During this weeping he did not comfort her. He said not a word. At the end of it he demanded her promise that she would accept the situation and cease barging at Margaret.

'And I want you to tell her you're sorry, for God knows you've made wretched this time in which she has the right to be happy.'

He called Margaret into the bedroom and told her what had occurred. Margaret took one look at her mother's red, fierce, repentant face, and threw her arms around her.

'There's no need for any apologies. I just want us all to be happy like we've always been!'

'Ah,' thought John, 'you'd have done better to have screwed a beg-pardon from her, my girl. She'll be off again if we're not careful.'

But Eny turned her attentions to Josie, uttering tragic predictions of failure and humiliation.

'We'll see,' said Josie equably.

The moment Josie had inspected the dressmaker's shop she saw the possibility of being her own woman. It was as if some calm presence took her by the hand.

Without trouble Josie had got the money she needed from Aunt Alf. Examining the old woman's papers while she was asleep was an act which did not rest easy on Josie's conscience. But what was she to do? She loathed Noel Capper for putting her in a position where she had to do dishonourable things. More and more she realised the perils confronting a young woman on her own. The factory manager made timid but determined overtures. They were timid because his wife was a tartar, and determined because he knew Josie needed her job. Josie used every method of avoidance known to women. The affair had reached the stage when she felt sick in the stomach as he approached.

'I'll have to resign,' she confided to Alf. 'And work is so scarce, especially for women.'

Alf deplored her niece's situation. She complained to the priest and received a lecture on evil gossip.

'I think he's dotty, that young fellow,' she decided. 'Some of them go that way, you know.'

Josie, dreaming aloud, said that if only she had £250 she could set herself up in her own business, with typewriter, adding machine and everything. She was well qualified and not afraid of hard work. Then she laughed.

'But Pa has nothing like that. If he had, he'd lend it, he's so good.'

Auntie Alf had looked upon her bank passbook as a goldmine. When the £250 was given to Josie, she regarded the balance with astonishment.

'I thought I had more than that,' she said. She became a little anxious and told Josie it was the £300 she had given Jer Darcy that had made the great hole. He had promised to pay it back, but of course she would never ask for that.

'I hope there'll be enough to keep me for the few days I have left,' she said to Josie. 'That's all I want. But there, God's good.'

Josie was furious to hear about Jer, not even a member of the family. But she kept her tongue between her teeth. In six weeks she opened her office. It was bright and clean, flower prints on the wall, steel filing cabinets.

'It looks like something you'd see in one of them photoplays about modern girls going to business and making millions,' reported Eny. She didn't know whether to be shocked or admiring. 'That Josie, she's a goer, all right.'

Josie visited several religious organisations, telling them she would do their books for nothing. They eyed her askance, but could not resist. The work gave Josie an appearance of industry while she waited for clients. The weeks passed and clients did not come. Nothing of Josie's panic showed on her face.

It was a stark world, built on social deceptions. As a girl, she had been shielded from the vulgar and wicked. She had to wait until marriage to learn about that. She had thought in her trustful idiocy that during their long engagement Noel had been as faithful to her as she to him. It was only when he attempted to practise on her the gross arts he had learnt in the town's several badhouses that she understood his values were different from hers. The factory manager had persecuted and harassed her, yet she was the one who had to resign.

Now she sat alone with her intelligence and skills in an office, as good an accountant as any in Trafalgar, and nobody came.

She went at last to the woman owner of the drapery shop, a competent brusque personality, and asked if she might handle the shop's books for a reduced fee.

The proprietor said instantly, 'I would never take my business to a professional woman.'

'But why?' asked Josie desperately. 'You're a professional woman yourself.'

The older woman did not know. She echoed tradition. Not having an answer, she said, 'That will be all, Mrs Capper. Good day.'

Josie began to feel reduced in health as well as spirits. What did all this madness, this injustice, mean? She considered her sister. Was it better, after all, to be like Margaret, with no more thought for the morrow than an animal? The idea stuck in her throat like a lump.

At Mt Yatala the hands went off in the truck to Chanadah, the big woolgrowing property a few miles east of Juno railway station. Chandadah always began and ended the spring season with a shearing-shed dance and a campfire spud roast. The Chanadah boss believed a little fun put everyone in a willing mood.

Hugh loved to dance. He looked with anticipation at the long woolboard that had been scrubbed and made slick with candle parings. The walls of the cavernous shed were decorated with pine boughs and blooming branches of acid yellow wattle. The odour of fresh leaves, sweat, and hair tonic filled the air, overridden only by the smell of the sheep pens.

Hugh watched for admiration in the girls' eyes and found it. He knew how good he looked in his best blue suit, his black dancing pumps, his cream waistcoat. He looked into their shiny overheated faces and gave them the full benefit of his blue gaze. He held them close until they wriggled and their eyes grew hot, and whispered, 'Meet you by the bonfire at supper time? Remember now.'

None of these innocents ever saw him again. Between dances, fetching lemonade for his partner, he saw before him a girl in a yellow dress. He saw the dress first; it had a scalloped, gauzy kind of hemline that fell in points. The girl in it had dark eyes, a flare of red in olive cheeks, and a fluff of black hair.

'Thanks for the lemonade, Hugh,' she said, taking it from him and drinking it.

'You've got your nerve,' said Hughie.

She had a kind of high seriousness, a mitigated arrogance that sat charmingly upon the face of one so young.

She set the glass down. Someone had put another record on the phonograph, a waltz.

'Come on, let's dance.'

119

In a moment they were gliding about the floor. The girl had a melting grace.

'Better than last time?' she asked mischievously.

'You've got me beat,' answered Hughie. He reversed and bore her away down the board.

'When you were at Butt's.'

Something flickered in Hughie's mind. 'Cripes, you're the kid!'

She laughed. 'Eight years ago. Bridget Tookey, remember?'

If Hugh fell in love with Bids Tookey he also loved her. It was his belief that this love would stay with him all his life, and in this he was right. But in those early days she was an obsession. They became lovers within a week, for Bids was not one to hold anything back. She matched him in passion. They took each other to another country, hectic as a dream, and yet with more substance than the real world.

Hugh was in such a haze of delight he did not know what to do. Peremptory, plain spoken, puritanical in her concepts of honour and truth, in no way did Bids resemble the servile, cozening girls he had known. Nevertheless, he was in a rage to gobble her up, to make her part of him for good and all, have her looking out of his eyes.

On another level he was a little afraid, humbly marvelling. In the dead of night he shed strange, exalted tears, the overflow of worship. He sensed in the girl a mysterious strength, a centre of gravity different from his own. Common phrases came to him: 'She'll make a new man of me.'

For in truth he now despised the man he was, seeing himself as a nobody, governed by chance and self-indulgence, his wastrel's life already, at twenty-six, showing on his face. Unconsciously he turned to prayer, hammering at God or whoever it what that ordered human lives:

'I've got to have her. I need her. She's all the world to me. Let me have her!'

Bids took Hugh to her father, Steve Tookey.

'I'm going to marry him,' she said.

Steve eyed Hugh, bigger and tougher than he recalled him, marks of dissipation on his face.

'It could be worse,' he said to his daughter.

Because of their family situation, Steve had always been jealously possessive with Bids. By the time Hugh came into her life he was aware of this bitter taste to his character and tried to control it. He knew men, and he distrusted Hugh, yet he liked him as a man. The boy could fight like a broken windmill; he had looked after that hoppy brother of his.

Steve knew that the time would soon come when he would lose Bids and faced it with grim composure. He knew Bids was strong, and consoled himself that she would be the making of Hugh.

When he and Bids were private he asked, 'You been playing up with him?'

'Yes,' answered Bids, with her direct glance.

'You thought about what might happen if you fall? He's the kind that clears out.'

'Hugh wouldn't clear out on me,' said his daughter. 'And if he did, more fool him.'

'It's not a nice situation for any girl to be in.'

'I'd have the baby and be damned to the gossips,' said Bids. 'You'd stand by me, wouldn't you, Dad?'

Steve smiled.

'Then why would I need to be anyone's missus?'

Steve lumbered his painful leg out to the veranda. He sat there thinking of Bids, thinking of youth, marvellous moonlight nights, that time by the lake with all the islands like green butterflies, lone sunny valleys, and hidden ones made for lovers, secret cracks in the earth. He had no right to blow up Bids, or Hugh either, the things he'd done.

But it was different for a woman.

And Bids wasn't just a woman. She was his daughter.

He said to Hugh, 'I hear you've had the best of her.'

Hugh was abashed by these words. He blurted out admission.

'It's Bid's decision,' said Steve. 'But I know blokes and I know you. You duck out on her and I'll find you and do you.'

The whole of Juno knew about the love affair. Pal Biddle came to Hugh, awkward and uneasy, and said, 'It ain't none of my business, boy, and you're welcome to the truck to go into town any time you can, but I can't help thinking of the other girl, that Miss Kilker.'

'She turned me down,' said Hugh.

'That's all right then. You going in to fetch your brother today on the midday? You take this blanket to wrap him in. He mightn't be a hundred per cent yet.' She turned back. 'Sorry I spoke outa line, Hugh. The Boss and me have got real fond of you since you came.'

121

Hugh, as he waited on the station platform, thought he would have to come to grips with that problem sooner or later. It seemed far away. The train appeared in a mist of steam, and Hugh sprang forward joyously, anxious to see his brother. Two passengers carried Jer off the train. He propped himself up on his crutches. Hugh was aghast at the look of him, yellow, wizened, his feet and lower legs in bandages under thick socks.

'What's all this? You're not walking yet?'

Jer was silent, gesturing at his baggage. Hugh threw it in the back of the truck and lifted his brother into the front seat. They were scarcely out of the station yard before Jer began weeping hysterically. The operation had not been a success. He was worse off than he had been before.

'It's early days yet, you got to allow time,' protested Hughie. 'Why, I suppose you even have to learn to walk, like a baby.'

Jeremiah was distraught and ill-tempered. Everything upset him. When Pal teased Hugh with love madness when he did something clumsily, Jer exclaimed, 'What's this? Who's Bids Tookey? What about Margaret that you're going to marry?'

Mrs Biddle got it out of Hugh then. He said sullenly that Margaret would break it off when she heard from him.

'Well, boy, ain't no one's business,' she said.

He was ashamed to have had his perfidy revealed, and so created within himself a dislike for Mrs Biddle.

'Interfering old chook. Bloody cheek. Think I'll move on, Jer. Got to get some bigger money together, if I'm getting hitched. Going into town to see what jobs are offering.'

He secured a job cooking at Prospect Yards, across the Queensland border. Bids saw the sense of his move, and so did Steve. The old man thought that perhaps he had misjudged Hugh, and then again perhaps he hadn't.

'He's not doing a flit on you, girl?'

Bids shook her head. 'No. I trust him.'

Hughie gave in his notice at Mt Yatala. Mrs Biddle was disquieted. She asked him to stay another few weeks, the Boss being on his last legs, the mares to see to. Hugh gazed at her stonily. This woman, whom he had so admired, meant nothing to him in the face of his tumultuous desire to marry Bids as soon as possible.

'They're expecting me at the Yards, missus.'

Mrs Biddle said no more except that Jer was welcome to stay on until he recruited his health. She'd keep an eye on him.

'Well, that's between you and young Jer, missus. But thanks, anyway.'

Jeremiah did not know what to do.

He did not let the Biddles know how he felt. He put a grin on his face and told a few preposterous stories to Joe. A choking bray came from the man's ruined chest.

'The Boss says you're a real dag,' translated Mrs Biddle. 'Go on, Jer, give us a song. Sing "Red River Valley", he likes that, or "In the Evening by the Moonlight".'

Jer sang, giving the Biddles all the benefit of his big sad eyes, his valiant smile.

But inside he was not valiant.

He sat on his bunk, face all eyes, like a spider's. The operation had left him not only with his feet as useless as before, but occupied by pain. Up and down the shinbone it went; his unused child's toes cramped and pricked. Bones broken and reset, though to no avail, cried out, saying they remembered the torture and always would. Things had gone wrong for Jer. Jer power had failed. Hughie would throw over Margaret and marry the bitch Bids, who would not have him within a hundred yards of her and had no hesitation in saying so. Jer feared Bids. She did not giggle or smile, she was not submissive or solicitous, she had a strong face like a boy.

'What will I do, what will I do?' moaned Jer.

He had had a cough and a sore throat ever since the operation. He felt they had done something wrong with the anaesthetic.

'My ankles, my ankles,' he whispered, as the throb rose like a wave of fire.

All the money was spent. Doctors were expensive and hospitals more so. Would Miss Kilker give him more money? He had never told Hughie she had given him £300. He had told that yarn about the doctor reducing his fees. He didn't want Hughie to know all his business.

'That bloody Bids!' Jer moaned with hatred.

She had said plainly, in front of her father, that she would not take Jer into her home when they were married.

'I'm sorry, Hugh,' she said. 'But he turns my stomach.'

'That's a rough thing to say, girl,' remonstrated Steve.

'I know it is, I know it. But it's the way things are, and Hugh should know it now rather than later.'

Hugh began to speak to Jer now and again about going into an institution. Kindly, reasonably he said it, as though a Home for the handicapped were the bathroom or the picture palace. Hide yourself in there, Jer, I've done my bit as I promised Mum when I was four. We've been through a lot together, but Bids can't stand a bar of you, you give her the creeps, and I can't have that.

'I'm over twenty-one,' said Jer. 'I can do as I like.'

'If you can manage without me to shepherd you,' said Hugh with hard eyes. At least, Jer thought they were hard, but in reality Hugh scarcely thought of Jer at all.

'What about Margaret? She's a decent sort; you haven't done the right thing by her.'

'She'll get over it.'

Hugh had not done the right thing by anyone. Bids did not know he was due to be married to someone else; the formidable old man Steve did not know either, and a good thing that was as he would chop Hugh up for firewood. Or try, anyway. Margaret at almost twenty-six was on the shelf, and Hugh had put her there with his backing and filling. He was leaving the Biddles in a hole.

But Hugh, gluttonous, gorged with love, thought of none of these things. He was in another place altogether and cared for nothing but himself and Bids Tookey.

Jer raved at him, begged, spoke eloquently of the scrapes and difficulties they had survived because they had been together. It was like listening to someone else's story.

'Yes,' he said, 'we've had a blazing good time, Jer, but it's all over now. I reckon you ought to come to the Yards with me. You don't want to be under no obligation to these Biddles.'

Jer thought with a pang that he had spent his life being under obligation to someone, and he'd better look out for his future. He said he would remain at Mt Yatala for a while.

'Suit yourself,' said Hugh.

Not for a moment did Hugh think that Jer might tell Bids, or worse, her grim father, that his brother was promised to a girl in Trafalgar. Loyalty had been the climate of their lives, the bond between them since Jeremiah's birth. It was a fact of life. Jer had never, by word or hint, said anything to Hugh's discredit. His escapades with girls, his drunkenness, the many times he had been tossed out of sheds for slackness, the nights he'd spent in pokey, bombed out of his skull – none of these had been mentioned by Jer, even when Mrs Kilker, skilled at the task, interrogated him. He told lies about Hugh by the hundred, grand tales of this and that, all to the brother's glory.

But now things were different. Jer felt as he had never felt before.

'My heart must be broken,' he thought, half in awe that a thing which happened in stories and songs could happen to him. He could not bring himself to say goodbye to his brother.

Pal observed his downcast looks.

'Don't fret, boy,' she said. 'And don't be too hard on old Hughie. He has to live his own life.'

What about my life, cried Jer's heart. I got to live too. But how?

'Me and the girls'll tidy up the kitchen,' suggested Pal. 'You go along and give the Boss a singsong.'

The Boss was familiar with very few tunes, mostly sentimental ballads and marching songs from the Great War. He liked to hear them played over and over – 'Roses of Picardy', 'Hard Times', and 'Tipperary'. There was little left of the Boss these days. He was not much more than a raucous whisper and eyes that had almost relinquished life.

Jer played the Stephen Foster songs he loved. Pal quietly entered, and sat smoking and listening, now and then patting the hand of Joe, who had fallen asleep.

Stephen Foster had been down on his luck, too, deserted by everyone, dying alone in a gutter, in a cold wind. Jer saw himself in that gutter, in that wind, and unexpected tears sprang from his eyes.

Pal put her arms about him. 'It's Hughie clearing out, ain't it?' she said.

'Course it isn't,' gulped Jer. 'My ankles are murder. That's what it is.'

'Long as the Boss and me are around you got friends,' she said. 'And like I said before, don't you be too hard on your brother.'

But the young man was hard. His sense of betrayal made him ferocious.

Some time after Hugh left Mt Yatala, Jer wrote a long letter to Auntie Alf.

Auntie Alf read it with consternation. Her hands shook so, she had to put the paper down. She prayed for courage to go on. Jer wrote soberly that he found it hard to resign himself to being handicapped for ever.

'I had a dream,' he wrote, 'of coming to Trafalgar and walking with you to Mass. But God knows best.' He went on immediately to say he was worried out of his mind by Hugh's goings on. He explained fully what had just happened.

'I don't excuse Hughie,' he wrote. 'I just want to ask you what to do. Do you think Margaret ought to be told about this or not?' He added, 'Please let me have your advice quickly, because I want to do the right thing.'

Josie found Auntie Alf distracted to a degree. The old woman did not know what to write to poor Jer. She gave the letter to her niece.

'Do you think it's just a fly by night thing, Josie? Tell me what you think. Because if it is, it would be best not to tell Margaret. You're young like her, you know about these things. Oh, the poor girl, looking forward to her wedding.'

Josie was distracted by worry. The bitterness of failure permeated her whole body. Perhaps it was this that made her take revenge on Margaret for her own unhappiness. But at the time she believed she acted for the best.

'Of course she must know,' said Josie, going straight to her parents' home and telling Margaret and her mother as they sat at their dinner. Margaret turned as pale as death, her spoon fell and splashed over the table. She looked to her mother for help.

'I'll scrag you, Josie, God be my witness I will.'

The glitter in Eny's eye was frightening. Josie stepped backward. From the corner of her eyes she saw the door, which she could reach in one spring if her mother lost her head altogether. She felt she had been rash. She should have told Margaret privately.

'Margaret ought to know,' she protested. 'You've never trusted Hughie. Well, now you know you were right. And Margaret's well out of it.'

Margaret gave a moan so loud, so ghastly, Josie's hair almost stood on end.

'I might have guessed,' she said. 'His letters have been different for a while now. Skimpy. I'll kill myself,' she said.

Her mother caught her by the apron tapes.

'You'll do nothing of the sort. Sit down. Josie, make fresh tea. Lock the back door. We don't want every nosey parker in the street to know. Stop that noise, Margaret. I won't have your father upset by this.'

126

'He'll have to know,' said Josie, perturbed but still calm. Eny shot her such a look. 'I'll tell him my own way.'

Seven

When Rowena heard the name of the fast little cat who had got off with Margaret's sweetheart she felt a thump in her chest. Then she thought, 'Aren't there Tookeys all over the place?' Her second thought was a spring of hope that this would be the end of it with Hughie and Margaret.

But these things vanished from her mind when Margaret went entirely to pieces. When Eny saw the big cuddlesome lump collapsed on her bed, crying night and day, her face swollen and ill-looking, scarcely able to speak for grief, her impulse might have been to shake the girl till her teeth bounced in her head. But instead the tenderest love flooded her, love like that she once felt for Kathleen, protective love for this vulnerable child now hurt, it seemed, beyond repair.

'I'll see to it, my dotie, I'll get him back for you.'

'He won't come,' blubbered Margaret. 'Jer said she was a peach.'

'Aren't you a nice looking girl, too?'

'I'll be twenty-six before you know it,' said Margaret, and her woeful look added: 'And on the shelf already.'

'And who put you there?' thought her mother bitterly. 'Isn't it just like that tripehound of a Hughie to tie you up for years and then waltz off with a girl in her first bloom?'

'He's all the world to me, Ma.'

Eny knew very well this could be so. Like an arrow through her heart she remembered her love for Steve Tookey. Passion, disillusionment and loss came back to her from the past. She was amazed to find herself weeping. Margaret looked up at her mother's firm, often severe features and saw them all awry. It was wonderful for the girl to see that her mother could cry for her. Though she was mistaken in this belief, Margaret felt supported, stronger. She was able to pull herself together a little.

'She'll take no argument,' Eny reported to her husband. 'It's Hughie or no one. I've fear for her, John.'

The parents could not decide which way to move. John defended Jer, saying he had acted like a gentleman in leaving Aunt Alf to judge whether Margaret should be told of Hugh's betrayal. It was true, he added sadly, that Alf should never have opened her big gob to Josie, knowing the latter's wicked tongue where her sister was concerned.

'I'll bake that one's bread, too,' said Eny vengefully.

Josie moved through all the tumult with her secretive eyelids lowered, her face composed. She had justified herself a dozen times to everyone but none would listen.

'My conscience is clear,' she said. She believed it was. Josie bore with equanimity her father's reproach, her mother's crabbing. Aunt Alf's distress was another matter, but Josephine thought she could assuage that in time. The deep unease that fretted her came from Margaret's appearance. All in a week her sister looked as she might look when old – sallow, fallen away, ugly. Josie scoffed, told her she was better off without a philanderer for a husband, she was lucky she had found out in time. But Margaret only said woefully, 'I love him, just like he is.'

The truth was that something was happening inside Josie. The invincibility of her youth seemed to be crumbling. She had always felt herself superior to the rest of them; she had foresight, self-control, resolution. It came to her now, confusedly, that she lacked something Margaret had. She recognised that she had never loved Noel as he was. Perhaps she had never loved people as they truly were.

She pushed these thoughts away.

'It's in my mind to go to Juno and see this girl's father,' offered John. 'Couldn't I explain how it's all a bad business? For how do we know that Hughie told her he's promised?'

'That's it, of course,' said Eny, light in her eye. 'Very likely this Bids Tookey is a decent girl. Wouldn't it be best then, John, if I went myself and spoke to her?'

She told John then that there had been a Tookey working at Chanadah station when she was there, though perhaps this was not he, seeing that one had been a footloose kind of boy.

John was relieved. He knew that such talk between fathers often led to one or the other being knocked rotten, and he felt he was past that caper. Retired now, he was happy enough, but never quite feeling his old self.

How many years it was since Eny had boarded a train!

Preoccupied with memories, she lent only half an ear to John's cautions about not losing her temper, not being too hard on the girl in case she was as innocent as a daisy. The Railways had not changed the old dogboxes in the interval, the hard seats, the clouded drinking-carafe with the water sloshing around, the dust sifting everywhere like talcum – these things brought back her flight from Juno as nothing else had done in the years between. How desperate the anguish she had suffered on that journey!

She had kept her marriage vow and never willingly thought of Steve again. It had been hard at first but no trouble at all later. Forty years and she had not raked over the memories of him. She was not thinking of him now except as a shadow. What she remembered was herself, as gormless as Margaret for all her pride. She had allowed her love for Steve to balance, life or death, on the edge of a postcard. Why hadn't she stormed away to the lockup and got the truth out of him? Her grief was impersonal, arising from her recognition of the stupidity and fatally stiff necks of the young.

It was hot weather, rainless, the country the hue of a honeycomb, hills streaming away into tarnished bronze. The forest and the potato paddocks were replaced by thousands of fruit trees. At every little station the platform was piled with crates of plums and cherries. Rowena recognised nothing from the two journeys of her girlhood. Even the brimming rivers, green as stone, had shrunk to dark dribbles in a waste of gravel and sand. She began to think that the past had been a dream.

When she reached Juno she could scarcely believe what she saw. The solitary siding, marooned in warm silence, had become a tidy station. All around were houses, streets, shops with pretentious gables and painted signs.

It was as if someone had rubbed a magic lamp. The town as it grew had rushed towards the railway. The sweet valleys where it had begun were now farmland. Now and then a farmer made use of a fallen stone wall to rebuild the pigyard, or felled a hoary fruit tree. On the original site nothing was left of the settlement but a roofless church with treeferns crowding the nave.

The change, the passing of all she had known, unnerved Eny. But she owed it to Margaret to do what she could. She went to a hotel and, after booking in for the night, asked the clerk if he knew a family called Tookey.

There was only old Mr Tookey and his daughter. They lived close to town. Miss Tookey worked along the main street in the Bank of New South Wales.

'Would it be Mr Steve Tookey, do you know?' inquired Rowena. The clerk nodded.

The words 'old Mr Tookey' had shaken Eny, but she was more shaken by the news that Bids was employed in a bank. How could her simple Margaret compete with a smart young business girl?

And old Mr Tookey! 'Why, Steve is no more than six years older than myself,' simmered Eny, who thought of herself as thirty-seven or thereabouts.

The anger did her good. With her mind settled, she went downstairs and ate a robust meal. In her bedroom she examined the wardrobe to see if the last person had left anything behind, washed herself from a jug of hot water, said her prayers, and went to sleep, confident that a Mullins born could knock the stuffing out of anyone behind a bank counter.

In the bank next morning she was taken aback: she could see no young ladies in sight. She asked one of the men if she could speak to Miss Tookey. He frowned, saying Miss Tookey worked in the office and could not come to the front.

Eny put on a tragic face, saying she had travelled a hundred miles. Since there was no customer in the bank, the young man said, 'Just for a minute, then,' and went to an inner door.

The girl who approached the inquiry counter was puzzled. 'I'm sorry, I'm not supposed to . . .'

Eny held onto the counter. She thought she was going to keel over, for the girl, this Bids Tookey, was so like her Kathleen they might have been sisters. If Kathleen had lived she would have been like this, black curly hair, a dimple in the creamy cheek.

The girl put a hand over hers. 'Are you all right?'

Eny nodded. 'It's just that for a moment you looked like someone I knew.'

Rose flowed over the girl's face. She said eagerly, 'You know my mother?'

'I do not,' replied Eny, puzzled. 'It's about Mr Darcy I'm here.'

Bids said, 'But he left for Prospect Yards some weeks ago.'

'It's important to me and to you that we have a few words about that gentleman.'

Bids hesitated uncomfortably.

'I get off for lunch at midday. I'll meet you in the Windsor tearooms down the road.'

Eny spent the intervening time in the church. It was a place of gaudy simpering statues and banks of candles, but that was what she liked. She prayed for a while, and then she had a snooze, and very soon she heard the Town Hall clock strike half past eleven. She went along to the Windsor and drank a cup of tea while she was waiting. She had had a great start when she saw Bid's resemblance to Kathleen but she had worked it out while praying in the church. Kathleen had been a sport in her family. She was one of the black Irish, with large bow-shaped Spanish eyes, and a torrent of silky hair. She was the only Kilker with black eyes as far as anyone knew. But Aunt Alf said she remembered a tradition that their grandmother, hers and John's, was black-eyed too. She came from Galway, where the Armada ships were wrecked, many of the seamen being drowned or murdered, but others taken into Irish homes.

And Steve, too, had begotten this rarity, tall, slender and airy on her feet, coming towards her now and looking so like Kathleen Eny could have let the unsealed sorrow in her heart out in a howl.

The girl had been thinking over the visit of the stranger and did not like it. Eny could see by the set of her red mouth, the way she kept her neck proud and stiff.

The waitress brought more tea, Bids all the time gazing at Eny with a direct shining look.

'I don't know you, do I?'

'I'm Mrs Kilker, from Trafalgar. I'm that sorry I nearly turned up me toes when I saw you first . . .'

'Never mind that. What have you to say about Hugh Darcy?'

The girl plainly thought her as old as the hills, and maybe astray in her mind into the bargain, but she was not giving or taking anything on that account.

Eny thought it best to come out with it. 'That young hero is engaged to my daughter and has been for some time. They're to be married in two or three months.'

The girl made a hardy try at composure, even boldness. 'I don't believe you. You're making it up. How dare you annoy me this way?'

Eny thought her grand. She flew the red flag in her cheeks, she came back fighting.

'Ah, girl,' she said, 'there's no need for me to lie. I can see how Hughie would tumble for you; I've not a thing against you. But Margaret, she's taking it badly; her heart is broken, the flesh is shrinking from her bones. Didn't I come here only to appeal to you, not to make trouble?'

As she spoke, she put in front of Bids the engagement pictures of Hugh and Margaret. Bibs did not want to look at them; she looked away and around the tearooms, she cast a piteous cornered look at Eny herself. Then her mouth set firmly, and she turned over the photographs.

'Why haven't they married then? All this time!'

'Didn't our man keep dodging. He's that class of fella.'

'These pictures don't prove anything. He might have been engaged to your daughter for a fortnight, all those years ago. He would have told me.'

'I'm asking you to give him up and tell him so.'

'On your word?' retorted the girl. 'Not in a hundred years. I don't know you. You could be crazy for all I know. A mischief-maker.'

'You ask your father if I ever laid me tongue to mischief in my life.'

'You know my father?'

'I do, and if you won't listen to me maybe he will.'

Eny slapped down some money and swished out. She thought Bids would follow her and so she did, putting a hand on Eny's arm, showing a glisten in her eyes.

'Please, they were all listening in here. But we have to talk, get things straight. There's a memorial park along here; we'll sit there. I'm sorry if I was impertinent. You gave me a shock.'

She did not cry, sitting there near the War Memorial, so smart in her short skirt, her shiny silk stockings and pointed shoes. She gazed at Rowena with eyes that demanded she should deny the whole thing, go away, drop dead.

'I rather care for him, you know,' she muttered.

'I'd sooner you had him than Margaret, if the truth is told,' said Eny sadly. 'It will take a sturdy woman to manage that scamp. And she's soft. Soft as butter.'

The trouble was that Mrs Kilker had not said a word that Bids's father had not used about Hugh time and time again.

The girl told herself she did not believe any of it, but she did. She rubbed the base of her throat, which was hurting, and said, 'I have to get back to the bank.'

'I'm that sorry to be bringing you such news,' said Eny sincerely. 'I'm at the Royal Hotel for the next day or so if you want to see me. Now, do as I ask girl, and write to Hughie and get the strength of it all, for your own good and Margaret's.'

Bids was so distrait she could scarcely do her work. She longed to fly round to the Royal and examine those damnable pictures again. Hugh with a glass in one hand, his other arm round the shoulders of a pretty, bashful girl with untidy hair. She was holding up her ring towards the camera.

'No,' she thought. 'I'll go home and see Dad.'

When she went into the kitchen, her father was peeling potatoes. Bids, who was a quarter boy, came straight out with it.

'Do you think it true, Daddy?'

'I do.'

She spoke to him about it over supper and as she washed the dishes. Steve said little. What could he say that would make things better for her? She kissed him and went to bed.

Steve sat on the veranda in the cool darkness, smoking. He had not told Bids that Eny Mullins had visited him that afternoon.

Eny was so surprised when she recognised Steve Tookey in the short old codger who opened the door that she blurted: 'God help us, Steve, you've got as old as Moses!'

'And a man would be looking at a chicken a long time before he thought of you!' he retorted.

The interchange was so like those of many years before that both burst out laughing.

Her visit had set him back, though why, after so long, he could not tell. He had lost his place in time; the years had come down in an earthquake.

He was not a well man; his body was full of small distresses, his heartbeat had a stammer. Seeing Rowena again had shaken him up. That was it.

When Steve Tookey had returned to Chanadah so long ago his job was gone and so was his sweetheart. The lack of communication had not disturbed him; she was as ignorant of letters as a blackbird. But not for a moment had he imagined that she would not be waiting for him at the railway station, ready to tear his ears off with fiery words. The mistress told him the girl had taken the south train only a few days after they had news of his jail sentence.

'She said she was off back to Sydney. Good riddance to her. She had a big opinion of herself, that one.'

Eny's defection hit Steve on all sides. He was the one who always left the girl lamenting. She'd run out on him, the redhaired squib. His mates knew it was a comedown for Leather, but they held off chiacking him about it. He took it as if it didn't matter in the least. Easy come, easy go, he said. Still, he felt bereft, as though something was missing.

He went back to his job as blacksmith's striker. Although he intended to move on in three or four months, he dallied. Soon it was a year since he had seen Eny. In that time life had changed for him, it had lost colour and reality. On slack days he would sit outside the forge yarning with passing horsemen, thinking, Why am I here? Who are these jokers? He couldn't get up off his stern long enough to have a fight or go to a dance. People said that a few months in pokey had taken the sting out of Leather Tookey something woeful.

His friend Jim Oyster took him in hand. 'Is it Eny Mullins you're fretting over? Because if so we'll find her somehow.'

But Steve could not truthfully say that was so. He had been incensed that Rowena had left him no word, no sign, but his anger had subsided into the indifference that now seemed to fill his life.

'Snap out of it before you take to the sauce,' advised Jim Oyster.

He straightened himself and said in his official voice, 'I call upon you in the Queen's name to assist me in a matter of the Law.'

Steve laughed. But Constable Oyster meant it. In country districts this was legal procedure.

'You bastard, Jim,' exclaimed Steve. 'A man has a right to his own troubles.'

Constable Oyster took him to the courthouse to be sworn in. He signed for a rifle.

'What's this for?'

'You know Quilley's, up past The Narrows? Raving bloody looney taken off to the asylum a few years back? Well, them silly snots down at Sydney let him out last month.'

It was raining as they rode out, and they moved into a rainstorm thick as dense fog. It was fantastic stony country, gorge walls straight, flat like the walls of a house, spouting waterfalls. They got the wretched horses through The Narrows, the single pass leading to the grassy uplands, and a watery sun opened the landscape to them, the faded green, antique highland rifted by pine windbreaks casting long-legged shadows. There they met Lyall, the neighbour who had given the alarm.

He said they had not seem Mrs Quilley or the child for a week. Just before that the wife had heard shots, though it might mean only that Quilley had potted a rabbit or duck. He, Lyall, had gone over casually the day after, and been driven off by Quilley with a shotgun.

'He looked pretty queer, didn't say much, just "Get!" So I got, and went down to report to you. Mightn't be anything, of course.'

Lyall was not young but he was strong and willing, with big hands and a body that the shirt went over like a cloth skin, tight and breathing. Jim Oyster did not have to ask his aid; he rode ahead of them. He too had a rifle in a saddle holster, and a big ironbark waddy slung beside it.

They approached the farm. They saw no smoke from the chimney. The place bore the signs of a property long looked after by a lone woman – rust, cobbled fences, things mended with string and fence wire. The cows had been milked but there was a dead dog on the end of a chain.

The constable gave the customary hail: 'Anyone home at Quilley's?'

Silence. He directed Steve to the back of the house. He and Lyall approached from opposite sides of the front veranda. A child's toys were scattered there, and a dish of blackened potatoes with a peeling knife amongst them.

Steve kept to cover, moving cautiously past the chicken pen. Amongst the bodies of a dozen hens lay Mrs Quilley in a bloody apron. A pair of crows flew up as Steve drew near; they glared from a dead branch.

There was the blast of a shotgun and chips scattered at Steve's feet. A man had come through the darkness of the back doorway into the sun. He carried a gun, not aimed, resting across his arms. But his eyes were aimed, fixed in a furious stare.

'Good day,' said Steve.

The sun ran up and down the barrel like quicksilver. The man stopped. The two men looked at each other. Steve had no idea what to do. He could only hope Oyster and Lyall were coming through the house from the front. He knew this man was an implacable enemy, not only of himself but the world. Whatever had happened in his head had fixed it so that he was never to be won over by any human means.

'I'm Steve Tookey. Been out after rabbits.'

'Drop the rifle.'

Steve did so.

'Now clear out, or I'll blow a hole in you.'

'Mrs Quilley all right?' Steve ventured. 'My old lady told me to ask.'

He thought he could see movement behind Quilley but kept his eyes from it.

Quilley was not forty years old, tall, with the tough wiry body of a farmer. But something had gone wrong with his face, soft and ruckled, anxious eyes small as pills. It was the face of a sorrowful man.

Steve himself was in a strange place he had not been in before. He looked at Quilley, scarcely breathing, not moving, not afraid but suspended in time. He thought afterwards he had been waiting for death as though he, and it too, were unreal.

The man began to speak of the monstrous grief of life, how he could not allow his wife and daughter to continue in it. He said the girl was only four, but she had suffered enough already.

'She's under the house,' he said fretfully. 'I've put everything there to get her out, food, her toys, but she won't come. She ain't had a bite for three days. I thought of firing under – I know she's in the corner by the chimney – but I might only wound her.'

He turned his attention to Steve, shouting that people had taken him away three years ago, preventing him from looking after his wife and child as was a man's job.

'They think I'm mad,' he said, amazed. He gestured to the young man to come closer. There was only the gun's length between them. Steve thought his last hour had come.

'Do you think I'm mad?'

He was from some English county. He pronounced the word 'mahd'. Unexpectedly a manic humour seized Steve.

'Well, Mr Quilley, there's one sure test. They say that if a man's mad his tongue turns black.'

A harrowing look of hope, fear and consternation passed over the man's stubbled face. Steve knocked up the gun; it exploded, blowing the top out of a nearby tree. At the same moment Lyall and

Oyster seized Quilley from behind. He broke free, ran shrieking into the bush. They had to subdue him with Lyall's waddy. All three men were aghast and sickened, Steve most of all, for he had read the madman's last look. Quilley had not wanted to be mad, but he knew that if he was sane he had murdered his wife and possibly his little child.

'Poor cow.'

Though he could not hope to reach Juno before dark, Oyster decided to take Quilley down to the town. He was afraid the afflicted man might escape. Since Lyall was familiar with the track, he accompanied him. Steve was left with the task of burying the dead birds and the dog, and covering Mrs Quilley. He did this, often calling the child meantime. Mrs Lyall had come to help, but he asked her to stand at a distance until he had finished his gruesome task.

'Her name's Evie,' Mrs Lyall said.

There was not enough crawl space for a man under the house. Both Mrs Lyall and Steve thought the child might well be dead from exposure. It was early morning before they heard some faint sounds, and midday before they coaxed her out. The feeble filthy child could scarcely crawl. Her eyes had the glazed blind look of a treed kitten.

Mrs Lyall was allowed to adopt the orphan. She was a wild little creature, frightened of other children, passionately devoted to her foster parents, terrified by the sound of guns. When the Lyalls sold their farm and moved down into the growing town of Juno Evie went to school. She became loving and high-spirited and the joy of her parents' hearts.

'Why don't you join the Force?' asked Jim Oyster of Steve. 'You handled that Quilley business pretty well.'

Steve thought he'd like it, plenty of action and change of scene. But he failed to make the height. If there had been a lack of volunteers for the Force at that time he might have scraped in with Oyster's recommendation, but it was the terrible depression of the nineties, ruin and worklessness all around, and there was no scarcity of fine big six-footers hungering to get into police work. Still, Sergeant Oyster, as he presently was, often called on Steve as a special. He remained in Juno, beginning to look upon it as home, until the Boer War.

He came through that lot without a scratch. When he returned

Juno had put out arms in all directions but mostly towards the railway line. The whole country looked astonishingly prosperous.

'Well, it's the twentieth century,' everyone said, as though that had brought some variety of magic with it.

Steve called on the Lyalls. Evie was fifteen, a scraggy delicious thing as shy as a bird.

'What a shame I'm so old,' he said jokingly. 'I'd marry you tomorrow.'

'You're not too old,' she said.

Steve had had plenty of love in his life; women naturally liked him. He did not try to charm them. He just had to look around and there one would be at his elbow. He had never seriously thought of marrying. Even Jim's domestic felicity, his clutch of healthy children, had not made him conscious of anything missing in his life. Yet seven years later, when Steve was forty-three and Evie twenty-two, they were married. Steve was lame, having been whacked on the kneecap with a pick handle by a drunk and disorderly.

He worked in the local woolstores. To go home to Evie became the comfortable aim and design of each day. He loved her, and yet it could be said that he did not fall in love until his daughter Bridget was born. The dark-haired infant cast a spell on him the moment she opened her filmy blue eyes. Those eyes swiftly became large and black, shining as water. She stared at him all the time; it seemed she too was besotted with love. Evie used to laugh at the pair of them.

Evie was reasonably happy for some years. At first she was busy. The house and garden, and then the baby, took up her whole time. Bids was two before Evie realised that for a long time she had not really thought about anything beyond her daily responsibilities. The kind Lyalls had educated her as far as they were able. Mrs Lyall had an idea that every woman needed to be able to do something to keep herself. She taught Evie needlework and simple dressmaking.

'No woman ever knows whether she will be left a penniless widow,' she explained. At great sacrifice, she and the father gave Evie a sewing machine for her fourteenth birthday. Evie was disappointed: she had wanted a bicycle. But she was a tactful and obliging child; dutifully she learnt dressmaking.

Steve could not understand Evie's fits of restless abstraction. Everyone had said a woman settled down when she had a child.

Evie was the same as she had been when he first courted her. She had fanciful ideas. She suggested that they should move to Sydney, where he might find a more interesting job. There would be better schools for Bids, more places to see, more fun.

'What's the matter with Juno?' he asked, baffled.

She was not able to say. It was not till Bids went to school that Evie realised she was in bondage. She looked at other women, how they had become identified with their housewifely functions. The occasional woman who had assumed a dominant position in the family was called a battleaxe, and often was just that. Evie wondered what the battleaxe had been like when a bride. She knew that married partnership was a possibility; her own intelligence told her so. Also, she had evidence from her foster parents, the happiest, most mutually considerate people she had known.

She asked Steve if he would mind if she got a job. He was fearfully affronted.

'Do you know what other men would say about me?' he growled.

When she pleaded that whatever they said could not, in reason, be true, he retreated into a dark silence. She saw that the good opinion of his peers meant more to him than any desire of hers.

However, she tried to persuade him. For the first time he shouted at her. He thought she was behaving badly in not believing what he believed a woman should be.

Nevertheless, Evie might have settled down and made the best of things if she had not been so sexually frustrated. She was in physical and nervous distress almost all the time. Her foster mother was now dead; she had no other kin. She was not one to make close women friends; she felt she could not consult any of her acquaintances. The few times she had tried to speak about her feelings with Steve he had looked at her strickenly, as if she had shouted obscenities. He would not answer her pleas; he slammed out of the house or pretended to be asleep. She understood that their sex life was a subject she could not bring up with her husband. There were other subjects, too, that Steve refused to discuss – death, the British in Ireland, whether there would be a war with Germany.

Timidly, after much thought, she asked the priest in confession if there was any book she could read to make her marriage better. He barked at her and gave her a Rosary as penance, to purify her thoughts.

The doctor also was very offhand, the implication being that there was something physically amiss with her. He made veiled statements about inflamed organs and the possibility of a hysterectomy.

She saw plainly that she, and possibly many other wives, were looked upon as she herself looked upon the old tomcat. Like his, her unruly instincts were in some indefinable way wrong, disgusting, and a nuisance.

Steve was not only much older than herself, for which she could not blame him, but he knew little about women. His early reputation as a ladykiller, which had so bothered her foster father, took on new meaning. She imagined his leaving a long line of frustrated, maddened girls behind him. Poor things – who could have talked or complained about such things in the nineties? She was not permitted to do so even now. Even while cursing his ineptitude, she loved him all the more; he was so honest, so manly, such a doting father to their child. Was it his fault that he was as innocent and unskilled as a ram? Possibly most men were.

'Yes, but he isn't a ram,' she thought. 'He ought to wake up to the fact that he isn't.'

She got out her sewing machine and began to sew children's dresses and other small items for money. The neighbourhood women eagerly connived at secrecy. Their husbands were similarly pigheaded about their earning any money except by selling eggs and chickens. The husbands and Steve thought Evie sewed out of neighbourly kindness and to fill in her time. Slowly she scratched together a few pounds. She did not truly know why. She told herself she had to have a little money of her own in case some day she became a widow. It was a long time before she faced her secret: that she needed money, however little, if she ever hoped to be free.

During her married life there was the feeling that she was in a lightless, confined space. Frantically she longed to escape, but if she did a person whom she loved would hurt her. She recognised the symbolism. The Lyalls had never kept from her the circumstances in which she had come to them. Once again, it seemed, a man whom she loved had driven her into confinement. Yet if she came out she would have to face an unknown, frightening future.

When Steve found out that she had been charging for her dressmaking he was outraged. Glaring at the machine, he said, 'I'll put an axe through it.'

141

'You do,' she retorted, 'and I'll poison you.'

Her face was crimson, she felt the whole word was crimson; a fine internal shaking made her wonder if she were going to die or start screaming. Steve regarded her with consternation.

'You sick or something?'

'No, I'm not sick, I'm unhappy. I've been unhappy for years. I want a separation.'

Steve was thunderstruck. He was so knocked over he said something that was not truly in his mind.

'You're as mad as your old man!' he jeered.

Children had sometimes said this to Evie when she had frolicked more capriciously than usual, and it had gone over her head. When Steve said it, it did not. She was wounded fearfully. Yet the pain of the wound hardened her resolution.

Before that she had been half playing with the idea of leaving her home. It had been a game to comfort herself. Even now she was full of apprehension. Could she really look after Bids and herself, alone in a city? She had a womanish hope that Steve would give in, that he too would fear being alone.

He did not argue with her, but turned away, half laughing. She felt the impact of his derision.

'Bids and I will leave at the end of the week,' she said furiously.

'Bids will stay here. As for you, bloody well go if you wish. I'm finished with you.'

Bids was very perceptive. She had long ago given over crying when she heard her parents arguing. But it still made her feel sick and weak. She went out to the kitchen now and asked, 'What's this?'

Her mother told her they were going to Sydney.

'Without Dad?'

'Yes.'

'Then I won't go. I'll stay here with him.'

It was the crisis of Evie's life. She looked at it carefully, though all in a flash, and she saw that this was a matter of life or death for her. She argued with neither the girl nor her husband.

Bids went with her to the station. She felt as if an earthquake had happened to her. Evie felt the same way.

'I'll send for the sewing machine when I have a place to live.'

'I'll look after it, Mum.'

'Queer this, isn't it? Me going away, I mean. I'll write to you, I'll send you a postcard.'

It seemed to the mother that all Bid's soul was in her dark bright eyes. The girl's face was white. All at once she looked spindly and gawky,

'Oh, Lord, I must be mad, like he said,' Evie suddenly sobbed.

Bids said nothing. Not waiting for the train to pull out, she walked away. The girl was equally devoted to mother and father. As an infant she had sometimes sat sobbing between them, unable to make up her mind which one to run to.

Steve was fifty-five. Jim Oyster, looking at his friend, saw a historic thing happen. Leather Tookey, the unbeatable, the good-humoured, the leg-puller and joker, became an old Irishman. He was so like Sergeant Oyster's own father it was unsettling. The flesh dried and tightened over the bony frame, built for hard work. The thick brown hair turned into a grey scruff like a terrier's. But the face was heraldic. It had not only belonged to Oyster's father but to other men middle-aged when he, Jim, was a child. They were men born of famine mothers. Their lives had been little beyond bitterness, hunger and rage.

Here was Steve Tookey, escaped from Ireland as a youth, leading an entirely different life from that forced on the old Irishmen, and yet he had the same face. A winter face with bleak, keen eyes, protruding cheekbones, lines cut with a knife from nose to mouth.

Jim Oyster wondered if that face were his destiny likewise. He took to staring into his shaving glass. But sedentary life had inflated him. It had turned him into a mudguts, and he had a mudguts' face.

Steve Tookey was now foreman at the woolstores. He became despotic to the point where the men looked forward to his retirement. It was probable he would have been tyrannical with Bids too, if the girl had been of another disposition. But she stood up to him like a Trojan. Gradually they became not father and daughter but mates, constant companions. Each knew what the other was thinking or about to say, and often answered it. Bids grew up knowing more about men from a man's point of view than other girls. She had a boyish way, too, very blunt and uncomplicated, devoid of the obliquities of women. She rarely caused Steve anxiety, and when she did it was not her fault.

There was one occasion when she was twelve. The school had a bush picnic, and Bids and one of the boys became lost. They were lost for two days and a night. That was a bad time for Steve, unbearable torment. But almost as bad was what came after the lost pair were found; the boy boasted about Bids and his own prowess.

Steve heard the gossip, which ran like a scrub fire about that little town, and was angry to the edge of frenzy. He was in a dilemma. The boy was too young to be thrashed. He had no father whose face Steve might have rearranged. He went to the parish priest. There was a tough one in Juno then, a chaplain in the late War. He had a face spattered blue with shot, and a temper like a tiger.

He advised Steve man to man. The next Sunday Bids and Steve went to Mass. The girl was pitifully humiliated by the looks she'd had, the things people had said to her. She heard the whispers as she and her father walked down the aisle, but no one would have guessed it from her expression. The congregation then saw that Steve had his boxing gloves slung over his shoulder. As the pair seated themselves, the priest swung round on the altar. There was no sound in that church save the starlings tick-tocking about on the iron roof.

The priest said, 'There has been wicked gossip in this parish. Much damage has been done to an innocent girl and a respectable family. Let each one of you know that every man or boy over seventeen who repeats a word of this gossip will be the business of Steve Tookey. As for the women and children, they are my business, and their names will be read aloud at each Mass until Christmas.'

He then preached a roaring sermon on calumny, slander, backbiting and such things, glaring all the time at the boy who had been the cause of it all and his poor weeping mother.

About this time Hughie Darcy, a station hand out at Butt's place, took her to the school dance. He had given Bids courage to face all the trouble she had at that time. When she grew older she knew his action had just been a whim, a bit of fun. But she remembered gratefully.

Yet, well as she understood her father, Bids made a mistake when her mother returned to Juno. Evie had kept in touch with Bids. Steve never asked the girl how her mother was. He had not troubled to get a judicial separation, and neither had Evie.

Though these things were never spoken of, Bids knew that her father did not hate her mother. He simply could not see where he had gone wrong. As Bids grew older, and began to feel in her own body clues to what the young Evie might have felt, she thought she understood why her mother might have left home.

144

When Evie first went to Sydney she had a desperate time. She found a job as finisher in a dressmaking shop. It was little better than a sweatshop, but it paid her rent. She could scarcely afford to eat, but one day it occurred to her that her thinness made her appear more elegant and well-bred than before. She was a pretty woman, not young, for she was then thirty-six, but she had a peerless country complexion and a twist of dark hair. Resolutely she tried for positions in the big shops, and eventually was taken on at a toiletries counter. Maquillage was still considered fast and theatrical, but lipsalve, rouge and face cream sold well. On her own skin Evie used only rosewater and glycerine, but she lied charmingly.

The toilet goods and perfume buyer found her pleasing. One thing led to another, and three years after her departure from Juno she owned half shares in a tiny dressmaking shop in King Street. She could see that before long she would be making a comfortable living, and set her sights on buying her partner out. Her personal business with him had already lapsed. Evie pined for her daughter. She felt she could afford to send the girl to college. Or she might care to train in the beauty business. Evie knew what a future there was in that.

In Juno Evie went unobtrusively to a hotel. That was a year for wearing velvet-spotted veils, conquettish and concealing. But she had no need to worry. There was no one in the hotel she knew. The town had grown enormously; there was even a picture theatre. Evie rested in the hotel until it was time for Bids to leave the convent school she attended. She waited in the shadow of trees until she saw Bids emerge. Even in the lumpy serge tunic, the black woollen stockings and heavy shoes, the grace and beauty of her child were identifiable.

The mother realised then how much she had needed her daughter. She called the girl, but was unable to speak. It was Bids who held the fragrant familiar stranger in her arms and comforted her. They talked for a long time. Evie asked Bids to come back to Sydney with her.

'Not now, not this minute, not till you're sixteen if you wish.'

Bids knew no other way of answering except to speak her mind. She seemed cruelly outspoken to Evie.

'No, I have to be with Dad. He means so much to me.'

'Don't I mean something to you too?'

'Yes, of course you do. I think about you a lot. You mean something to me, but I don't know what it is. Dad is the person I live with: that's what he means to me. And now he's getting old he needs me.'

Evie returned to Sydney. Bids told her father of the visit. She thought Steve would be delighted and proud that she had chosen to remain with him. But instead he broke down for the first time in her life. She was aghast. Later she asked him why he had cried.

'I think your mother wants to come back to us. She was only sounding you out.'

'Would you have had her back?' Bids could not believe it, even when she saw her father's expression. The mystery of these grown-up people! Not for a moment did she believe that her mother wanted to return to Juno. How could he possibly think that? It occurred to her that her father was getting a trifle unworldly. She looked at him critically. At a pinch he could have been her grandfather. Still, he was the best man in the world. She became more protective towards him, a little domineering. In those years after she turned sixteen she and her father were closer than ever.

Bids finished her education with a commercial course, and began to work in the bank. She was much admired and constantly courted by Juno's young men; one by one they fell in love with her and one by one they slid away. Bids was too blunt for them. She knew what they were thinking, and did not hesitate to tell them they were wasting their time.

Steve watched these courtships warily. In his heart jealousy was waiting to come to the boil. Bids saw her friends of twenty and twenty-one marrying, and it did not disturb her at all. She had confidence that somewhere there waited for her the perfect husband, a friend like her father, the lover for whom she was born. If he did not come along she'd manage to make a life on her own.

'I'm not crazy keen to get married,' she told her father. 'I'll not take second best for anyone.'

'How did they come to met, her and Hugh?' asked old Rowena of old Steve.

'At the Chanadah shearing-shed dance, last spring,' he answered shortly.

'Chanadah!' marvelled Eny.

The despotic-looking old man suddenly burst out: 'Why did you run out on me like that? It wasn't the decent thing to do, Eny. A man cops a batch of trouble and you run like a cur.'

Eny looked at him sheepishly. 'I did, that's a fact. I was nearly off my head with worry about you, and the missus threw me out. But what about my postcard? I sent you a postcard from Trafalgar, saying I'd come like the wind if you wanted me.'

The grief of that old happening came over her suddenly. Her eyes filled with tears. 'Never a word did I hear ever again.'

'I got no postcard,' he said. 'Never.'

She looked at him dumbly.

'Did it go astray or what? Who wrote it for you?'

Eny told him. She felt an old woman, and a feeble old woman at that. She sat down. He made her a cup of tea but the cup rattled against her teeth.

'It would have turned out different, Steve. And Bids would have been my daughter. But something went wrong.'

Not that I don't think the sun shines out of John, and my kids are the world's best, she thought. But something went wrong. And here's Steve, the core of my heart for so long, handsome as a hero, an old cranky limping man.

'Who would have guessed it, Steve, that we'd get old like everyone else?'

'We made a desperate fine couple while it lasted,' he said ruminatively.

Rowena drank her tea, spoke awhile of her children, those who had lived, those who had died.

'My missus run out on me, years ago.'

'I'm real sorry, Steve.'

She gathered up her handbag and rose.

'Will you see to it that your girl gets it straight with Hugh Darcy?'

For a moment the old fire came back into her eyes. Steve had a moment's vision of how she had looked, how he had looked; he felt a cruel pang in his breast.

'The vagabond!' Eny said. 'Two fine girls and both crying their eyes out over him.'

'Bids won't cry,' said Steve.

'That's all you know, you old fool,' thought Eny as she walked back through the heat. The hotel was airless. She undid her corset and lay down.

Her head was stuffed with memories, anxieties, fears that she had failed. Thoughts flew in and out like flies before she could give them attention. The bitterness of Steve's voice! How had it happened, the calamitous change in his body and face? Age came, God knew, and none could stop it; but there was more to it than age with Steve Tookey. He was as glum as a bear. A hard, disappointed man.

She remembered young Jer singing 'The Kerry Dance'. Didn't that hit the nail on the head! Time goes by and the happy years are dead, and one by one the merry hearts are fled. Eny put her hands over her ears to shut it out. O the days of the Kerry dancing, O the ring of the piper's tune. O for one of those hours of gladness, gone alas, like our youth, too soon.

The maid knocked on the door.

'Young lady left this message for you, Mrs Kilker.'

Eny opened it. As the years had gone by she had learnt to read well, though she was still shaky with the writing.

Bids had left a brief note. 'I've wired him at Prospect Yards to come back here at once to straighten things out. Bridget Tookey.'

Eny shook her head with admiration. Wasn't that just like the girl to command the double-dealer to come galloping back to Juno to face the music? Margaret would have gone to Prospect Yards to plead for the truth, or written him a letter full of tears and prayers. But Bids, she was the one. 'Come back here, ye blaggard,' said Eny with spirit. 'Come back and give me the truth of it.'

She hastened downstairs to the desk clerk. He got her a seat on the midnight mixed, and some time in the lovely summer dawn she arrived on the deserted platform at Trafalgar. She told the yawning stationmaster she'd leg it home, and someone would come down for her suitcase later.

It had rained within the last two days. On the golden hills already showed a ghostly green. Hughie had showed her how the infant grass hid itself in the dry roots of dead clumps until it was strong enough to face the sun. Hughie knew a few things. Perhaps, with the nonsense knocked out of him, he mightn't make such a bad husband for Margaret. She strolled down the empty main street. A huge black sow raised her snout from the Chinese greengrocer's rubbish tin and pointed her ears at Eny.

'Get on with it,' said Eny. 'Your business is your own and so is mine.'

John was asleep. He awakened to find Eny beside him and had a fit of joy.

'Didn't I miss you, my dear! The days were all a week long.'

She told him what had occurred.

'And this Tookey, the father, was he the same man you knew long ago?'

'Ah, a different class of fella altogether,' she said.

Eight

Shortly after Hugh's departure from Mt Yatala, Joe Biddle had died. Pal shrivelled. Her rough wiry hair lay flat and cottony. Only her man's hands remained powerful and impressive.

'You'll stand by me, boy?' she entreated Jer. Joe's funeral was on a blowy day, the air full of yellow dust and tattered dragonflies. Not being able to stand, Jer sat on the gravedigger's barrow and sang 'Nearer My God to Thee'.

'Now sing Joe's song, Jer,' said Pal. 'That one you played one night, and he said that was him all over.'

Jer shot a look at the parson's pursed, inquiring lips, but he sang it just the same.

'Tis the song, the sigh of the weary,
Hard times, hard times, come again no more!
Many days you have lingered around my cabin door,
Oh, hard times, come again no more.

But those in the crowd knew that hard times had come again. They said Joe was well out it, him being sick. He had done his duty for his country, but it looked as if the country soon would not be doing its duty by anyone, let alone those such as Joe had been. A monstrous shadow hung over the nation. The people looked at it fiercely. They recognised its menace but not its identity. It had come mysteriously from overseas, and the servile Government had allowed the invasion. How could hard times seize a sumptuously rich country like Australia?

Jer sat with Pal all night. He besought her to cry.

'No good holding it in, Mrs Biddle. I know about things like that. Just you listen to that housegirl. She knows what's natural for a woman who's lost her man.'

The housegirl Kitty sat out in the dew, letting loose long howls with the precise quality of music. Her sisters in the desert would in the same circumstances rip their breasts and arms with stones.

'Don't you leave me, Jer. I'm in a bad way.'

She drank herself into a stupor. Jer sat with her, huddled by a dead fire, until it was dawn. He experienced true grief for Mrs Biddle. It was of the same quality as his own. Hugh had deserted him and Joe Biddle had gone off and left her. He wept for Pal and himself.

But there was the other thing, too. Jer had misgivings about his letter to Aunt Alf. He had wanted to stir up trouble, not to let Hughie get away with it. But what trouble, where? Hugh might come raging back and tear his head off. Worse than that, he might never see or speak to him again. Jer examined all the possibilities. Aunt Alf was a holy old lady. She wouldn't tell Margaret. But she might tell her brother, Mr Kilker. Or would she write to Hugh? But she didn't know where Hugh was now. Jer was in torment. He had to know what had happened; he would have no peace until he did. Face to face with facts, he could produce some ingenious story exonerating himself.

'Oh, dear God,' prayed Jer, 'why did you let me do it? I didn't really want to. Make it all right for me now, amen. I've had enough to put up with,' he moaned. 'I don't want any more.'

He didn't know how to tell Mrs Biddle he must return to Trafalgar, especially now when she needed him. After a week or so he blurted it out. She said not a word, but he knew she was bereft. He gabbled out the truth, blaming his impetuosity.

'You did a wrong thing there, Jer,' agreed Mrs Biddle. 'You better see what you can do to fix things. And, later on, you come back here. There'll always be a bite and a bed for you here.'

In Trafalgar he got himself into an obscure boarding house. He thought he'd lie low and think things out. He heard no gossip in the town. He was not functioning in top gear. His money was running low. He would have to write to Hugh at the Yards and tell him he had reached his hard times sooner than other people.

He continued to write to Mrs Biddle as he had written to Aunt Alf, pouring out his thoughts, his ambitions, his dire disappointment that now he would never walk. Pal returned terse letters about the horses, the weather, Joe's grave looking a treat, come back soon. One day her letter contained a telegram. Jer read the telegram first: 'So you put me in. You're wiped. Hugh.'

Nervously Jer took up Pal's letter. She apologised for opening the wire. 'I thought it might be bad news and perhaps I should try to get you on the phone. I'm real sorry.'

Jer was in a panic. He had lost everyone. He swung himself round to Auntie Alf's house. He had to know what had happened after she received his letter.

When Hugh found the telegram from Bids on his bunk at Prospect Yards, he had a feeling of disintegration. The other men moved around him like shadows. His thoughts centred on Jer. Who else could have told Bids about Margaret?

He went to the boss. 'I'm shooting through.'

'What for?'

'Personal.'

The man blasted him, told him he'd never get another job in Prospect Yards, leaving them in the soup this way.

'Too bad.'

He sent Jer a wire from the railway station telegraph counter. He did not intend to see his brother.

In a state of intense agitation, Hugh travelled southwards over the Queensland border. The belt of the wheels rattled his very brain. The first day was breathlessly hot, the sun boring down from aluminium skies. Hugh's thoughts were like veering winds. How, when, what did Bids know, what did she feel about it? He could not lose her; his life would be over.

He arrived at a time when Bids was at work. Hugh dropped his swag amongst the trees, kept an eye on the house. The old man, her father, sat in the shade on the veranda, podding peas. A stubborn, selfish, possibly jealous old man, not wanting his daughter to marry, he had hidden his feelings for civility's sake.

Hugh slept a little, exhausted by travel and anxiety. The cooling shadows alerted him. He saw Bids turn in at the gate.

'Here I am,' he said.

With love he saw the moistness of sweat on her brow and neck, under the tied-back hair.

'So I see,' she said. 'Come inside.'

Three days later he boarded another train, going south to Sydney. In the extremity of loss he thought again of the talismanic city, where even his mother might have been happy. He wanted to submerge himself in noise, bustle, ceaseless traffic. He needed to be with strangers.

'I can stand it,' he told himself. 'I've stood worse.'

But the pain was so fresh and cruel he could not bear the

152

journey, the people around him, the joggling familiar landscape. Suddenly he leapt up and swung down his swag. He left the train at a wayside station called Gaines. There was a short main street, a garage, a timber mill rasping and thumping peremptorily in the background, several hotels. He crossed the road and entered the first he saw.

The next day, awakening on a thin mattress, a flyspecked window glaring daylight into his eyes, he lay for a few moments in drowsy contentment, nothing in his mind at all. He was in pain. In truth, he felt as if a horse had rolled on him. There was not a muscle or ligament or bone that had not been jerked, stretched or bruised. Nevertheless, for half a minute he had not a worry in the world.

He heard the timber mill's knock-off whistle, became aware that the light was blackly barred, and thought without interest: 'I'm in the cooler.'

Hugh had little memory of the events that had put him there. He could remember a big looking glass, gold printing on it, crashing down, bits flying everywhere like stilettos. Himself slugging away toe to toe with a beefy fellow wearing a flat woolly cap like an omelette. He had a cloudy idea that cap had something to do with the brawl. Getting doused in a horse-trough, pulled out, punching a policeman. His face felt as if it were scalded, his neck was surely broken.

He managed to crab over to the bucket. He heard locks clang, footsteps. His eyes would not focus on the sergeant.

'Get this down yer, son.'

'What am I in for?'

'Bitta fun. Go back to sleep.'

The sergeant was a mild man; he looked down the list of charges and whistled. The stranger had no money for bail. The sergeant thought he might well have had plenty before the donnybrook. He'd lost his coat and his money had gone with it.

Hugh was not sorry to be in the station lockup. It was a place to crawl into and pull sleep over his eyes. As the day passed he felt better, even was able to eat. The sergeant got his name and address.

'Want me to notify anyone, son?'

'Yeah. My young brother. He's at – ' Hugh thought confusedly – 'Mt Yatala. How much will the beak hit me for, you reckon?'

The sergeant named a sum, and added, 'That's on top of costs.

And you may have to sport the publican a new mirror. It couldn't be less than seventy quid, or the option.'

'Hell! My brother could never find that. Unless he can borrow it. There's a real good boss at Mt Yatala.'

The sergeant agreed to put full details in the telegram, and send it urgent, collect. Hugh rolled over, groaning at the new pains that fired up, and tried not to think of Bids.

But she was there, vital as sunshine, hardy, unquenchable. Bids, one moment looking at him limpidly with love, the next staring at him so strictly, so severely.

'Bids,' he had pleaded, 'Bids! Listen to me.'

'You fooled me, Hugh,' she accused. 'When we danced at Chanadah, last spring, I asked you if you had a sweetheart and you said no.'

Hugh admitted it. 'But, Bids love, I can make it all right. I'll talk to Margaret. She'll break it off.'

'Yes, and when you're tired of me,' she answered, 'you'll do the same thing.'

How could he explain that she was the core of his heart? He muttered, 'It's different with you; you're for ever.'

'That girl,' said Bids. 'I saw the engagement snaps, and she was happy. And her mother said she is fretting herself to death.'

'The old chook would say that, wouldn't she? Stands to reason.'

'I believed her.' She suddenly cried, 'I can't stand doublefaced people, Hugh. I can't trust you any more. Oh, you've got the words, yes, that's the Irish in you I suppose, but I'd never know when to believe them. You're more like Jer than I thought.'

Hugh lost his head then. Adrift and confused, he grabbed at any words or phrases that came his way. They said terrible things to each other. He jeered at her that he was not the first man in her life. Bids leapt to her feet, seized the old man's stick that stood near by and caught him a stinger over the head.

'You bastard, you low bastard, you know better than that. And if it was true, what business would it be of yours?'

He seized the stick as it stabbed at his brisket, and wrenched it from her. He dragged her close.

'Bids, you know I'm mad about you, I want us to be married.'

But she would not listen. Crying, struggling, spluttering, she pushed him from her. He had stung her beyond healing, he had said fearful things to her.

154

'Go, go,' she cried. 'I'm not taking a risk on a man who is two-faced whenever it suits him.'

He went back again the next day and the next but she would not see him. Steve Tookey met him on the veranda.

'She's made up her mind, Hugh. And she's not one to change it.'

'And I bet you helped her make it up,' said Hugh bitterly. 'I know you jealous old buggers. It's a crying shame I can't thump an old man.'

'I can thump a young one,' was all Steve said. 'Better clear out, son. It's finished.'

Hugh misjudged the father when he believed Steve Tookey had influenced his daughter's decision. Steve had said, 'You're rattled, girl. Leave it for a month. Hugh will hang around and wait.'

But Bids, with the hard streak of resolution he had unremittingly fostered in her, said, 'No. I can't face instability in a man's character. I don't know how to handle it.'

Steve pointed out that people misunderstood each other, judged too harshly. She listened with an unsparing, tearless face. He wanted to tell her about Rowena's postcard, all those years ago. Eny should have sought him out, he should have gone looking for her. Neither did the sensible thing, even though they had lived for each other. But he could not say anything about this to his daughter. He could not break the reserve of years.

He muttered, 'Maybe love isn't as important as you think, Bids.'

She looked at him as if he were mad.

Her nights were full of questions. 'What have I done? What do I want?'

On his hard bed in Gaines, Hugh thought the same thing and moaned aloud.

Mrs Biddle received the telegram for Jer and paid the collect fee. Doubtfully, she opened it.

She realised that Jer had to hear at once about his brother's trouble. She had no telephone, so she drove into Juno. There she found that the boarding house, where she had hoped to ring Jeremiah, had no telephone either.

'I'm stumped,' she said. She went outside and sat on the post-office step and smoked a cigarette. Then she recalled that Jer was a Catholic. She thought she would ring the parish priest at Trafalgar.

Through crackles and a din of thready voices, she got the message to the priest. Thus by one means or another Jer soon learnt that his brother was in the lockup and might well end up in jail.

Jer was at his wits' end. He did not hear a word of Mrs Kilker's castigation of his making himself a stranger to them.

'All this time back here in the town and no one knowing but Alf!' she scolded. 'You get yourself over here and into our spare room or I'll never look meself in the face again.'

'How can I get seventy pounds?' he cried, distraught. 'I'll have to let him down. What'd he have to go on a drunken spree for just now when I haven't got a bean?'

He confessed that this was not the first time he had been called upon to bail Hughie out, or pay his fine. John got the whole story from him.

'Ah, my dear,' he said privily to his wife, 'is our girl going to marry a drunk?'

Eny was deeply troubled. She had given her word that no longer would she oppose her daughter in her love for Hugh Darcy. But in her heart and head she longed to see the young people turn their faces away from each other.

Nevertheless she said to Margaret, 'I did what I could for you when I travelled to Juno, and I'll do what I can again.'

'You don't have to do anything, Ma,' said Margaret. 'I'm going to Gaines myself.'

Eny argued with her, forbade her, saying she had never been on a journey in her life. It was up to Jer to go.

Margaret showed a mulish face. 'It's not Jer's business, it's mine. No matter what has happened, Hugh hasn't broken the engagement and I haven't either.'

Jer, though anxious for his brother, was profoundly relieved. He had no wish to confront Hugh's accusations of perfidy. He said he thought Margaret would be a comfort to Hughie, a wonderful comfort.

The parents marvelled at Margaret's resolution. Was this the girl who had refused food, sat inert for hours, wept like a cloud for so long? Margaret could not explain that all those things had happened because that had been her trouble. This was Hugh's.

'God knows what's the right thing to do,' lamented John. After Margaret's departure for Gaines he had another slight heart attack, nothing like the first hammer-blow. Still, pains sharply twinged chest and arm, a deathly feeling blanched him with dread. Rowena put him to bed, and sat by him holding his hand.

Margaret had listened intently to the account of her mother's visit to Juno. She had asked only one question: 'What's she like, this Bids?'

'Kathleen all over again,' said Eny. 'I had to turn me face away for the tears when I looked at her.'

The journey for Margaret, shy and nervous as she was, was an ordeal. All through the racketing, swaying night she silently recited the Rosary, asking that her resolution be firm, that she would not say or do any stupid things. It was cold, coming into autumn; the water in the metal footwarmer had soon lost its heat. Margaret sat shivering, remembering Kathleen who had died when she was young. To Margaret's backward glance that slender girl was saturated with light, her glistening hair, the glassy skin. Always she had seemed poised on tiptoe, as if to take flight. And she had. Perhaps she had known she was but a guest in the Kilker family. And Hughie's Bids was like that, like Kathleen.

The train arrived at Gaines in the sleepy morning. In the waiting room Margaret washed her face and tidied herself. She thought she looked gaunt and old, not a girl any more but a woman with many burdens.

The station-master banged on the door. 'Make you a cuppa tea, missy?'

She was glad to have it, sitting with the ruddy man in the waiting room. The mill whistle blew.

'You come to visit someone?' he asked.

'Sort of,' said Margaret, not liking to ask him the way to the police station, but knowing he would watch where she went.

The police sergeant was watering his garden. Margaret explained who she was and why she had come.

'I've got money,' she said, 'to pay his fine. You'll have to tell me what to do, Sergeant.'

'He comes up tomorrow. The beak arrives this afternoon. You better come into the station and see what your bloke has got himself into.'

With a stupefied expression, Margaret read the charge sheet. The sergeant thought with pity: 'Poor girl, silly as a tin of fish where that young scamp's concerned.'

'Did he do all that?' she asked. 'He must have been dreadfully upset. They won't send him to prison, will they?'

'Not if he can pay the fine.'

'Can I see him now?'

Hugh looked up as the sergeant unlocked the door of his small open-barred cell. When he saw Margaret he felt like banging his head against the wall.

'What are you doing here?' he shouted. 'Where's that bloody Jer?'

'That's no way to talk to a young lady come all the way from Trafalgar,' remonstrated the sergeant. 'You can sit on the other bunk, miss. Call if you need me.'

He locked them in.

Margaret looked at Hughie, face swollen, his clothes in dirty disarray, his lip split, and began to laugh. She had no idea why she did. For the moment she lost her nervous distress. She sat down almost gaily.

'Aren't you the dog's breakfast?' she said.

Hughie again asked angrily where Jer was, and she replied, 'He's back in Trafalgar, with my people. He's not too well. And anyway, this is my business.'

If Hugh had been free he would have walked away. But all he could do was to crouch on his bunk and look at her dumbly. He saw she was thinner, the sweet pink that had always pleased him had gone from her face. He could not tell whether she was vengeful, hostile or what. She seemed her usual self.

'You brought any cash?'

'Yes, I brought all our wedding money.'

'Gawd!' Hughie buried his head in his hands. But there was no shelter there.

'I suppose your mother told you everything? Funny, I thought it was Jer who spilt the beans.'

'Well, in a kind of way it was. I suppose he meant well,' she said. She added: 'What happened after that? Have you seen Miss Tookey since Ma spoke to her?'

As she spoke that name she observed the change in Hughie's face – rage, loss, a deprivation that cut her to the heart. But she went on steadily: 'I have the right to know, Hugh.'

He told her, turning his head away, mumbling.

'That's it, all of it.' He burst out: 'What have you come here for? To give me the ring back, tear strips off me, tell me what a no-hoper I am, eh?'

158

He took refuge in aggressiveness, glaring at her, slamming his fist against the wall.

'I just want to know what you'll do after. You know, after you get out of here.'

'I don't know.'

She was silent. He rushed back and forth in his mind, unable to think. He asked her to go away, he was seedy and half-poisoned still, he had a headful of wool.

'But I'm glad you came,' he mumbled. 'Thanks. You're a trump.'

Trump, thought Margaret desolately, walking up and down the grubby room in the hotel to which the sergeant had sent her. He still loves that Bids. But he might come back to Trafalgar just the same. He's that upset he needs someone, even me or Jer. It's up to me, I suppose, to take second best or nothing.

She had her pride, yes. Now that she looked at it, damaged and bleeding, she saw what a complex thing it was. Hughie had wounded it almost mortally, and yet she needed it to save him from a wasted life.

'Why do I think I can save him?' she wondered. 'I'm just ordinary, not clever at all. But I love him. I don't know why I love him, but love is there and always will be.'

She was apprehensive of the court case, the magistrate, the witnesses. She might herself be called as a character witness, the sergeant told her. When she reached the police station the next morning she shook like a leaf; she had to go to the lavatory every five minutes. She rushed into the Women's, clean but suffocating with the smell of that disinfectant people used to commit suicide. She could not remember the brand name and it worried her.

The courthouse was no more than a formally arranged room under the same roof as the police station. Dismayed, Margaret stole glances at the bald man peering like a cormorant over the high desk, the portraits of King George and Queen Mary, the subdued demeanour of witnesses and plaintiff. Three of the witnesses were in as much bodily disarray as Hughie. One, his eyes lost in green and yellow puffs, his nose taking a south-west direction, said cheerily the whole thing had been fair and square, a first-rate stoush enjoyed by all. In truth, no one seemed to have any grievance against Hugh except the publican.

Margaret was called. Her composure had deserted her. Trembling, she held to the rail before her. She was croaked at to speak up, speak up, speak up, madam. Asked about Hugh's general reputation as she knew it, she said he was a decent boy, much liked in his own town, Trafalgar. She had been engaged to him for nearly four years and would marry him soon.

'What made your fiancé go berserk?' she was asked.

'I was not there, sir,' she replied.

'Well, there goes all our dough,' said Hugh glumly after he was freed. 'The fine, and that bloody mirror in the pub – it couldn't have cost all that. Bastard's having a piece of me.'

'Of us,' said Margaret tartly. She was extremely fatigued. She had not eaten properly for days or even weeks.

Hugh took her into the town's one tearoom.

'You'll have to pay,' he said. Margaret counted what money she had.

'If you're coming back to Trafalgar with me, I've only enough for your ticket. I've got my return.'

'Oh, great,' said Hugh. 'We can't even afford a cup of tea.'

He was so humiliated, enraged with himself, bitter towards her, he longed to tell her to stick the flaming ticket up her jumper.

'Might as well wait at the station then,' he said grumpily.

'Suit yourself,' said Margaret. 'I'm going to sit in that little park and look at the flowers. Here, take this and buy your ticket.'

She walked away. Hughie was open mouthed. Never before had Margaret stated her own preference. He had taken it for granted that she was all too happy to do whatever he wished. He entered the station. He still felt unwell, stiff and sore. What could he do without a penny in his pocket? What did Margaret intend he should do? He could not think straight. Best go to Trafalgar, hole up a bit and puzzle it all out. He bought the ticket and idled over to Margaret.

'Bit windy on the platform.'

They circled conversationally around the blue and yellow flowers, when Jer had left Mt Yatala, the twang and screech of the saws. Margaret seemed withdrawn, almost enigmatic, to Hugh; she was so unlike herself, no tears, no stumbled reproaches, no real interest, it seemed.

'You make it damned hard for a man,' he said at last.

'To do what?' she asked, looking directly at him. He was struck by the gentle blue of her eyes, after the dark candour of Bids's. He shrugged: 'Well, if you're going to take that attitude.'

'Don't try that on me, Hugh,' she said without rancour. 'You face up to things. You treated me rottenly, and that other girl rottenly, too. You got no call and no right to get up on your hind legs.'

'Why did you come here then?' he asked in a fury.

'Because I love you, of course,' she said, reasonably, as if she had to set him straight.

Hugh saw at once that she had put herself into his hands. It was the thing he dreaded most, a responsibility he was powerless to reject.

'I'm grateful, Margaret, for everything,' he said.

She did not acknowledge this. He had the impression she would have done the same thing for a dog.

Irritably he burst out: 'Well, don't sit there like a mummy. We got to talk some time.' When she remained silent he said loudly, 'We got to talk.'

'I can't, Hughie,' she said. 'I'm tired. I'm tired of worrying and wondering where I stand.'

But in the train he put his arm around her and she did not draw away. She slept against his shoulder. Hughie looked at the lakes sliding past, the trees black brooms against the light sky, and wondered what it was all about. He did not want to think about anything.

Back in Trafalgar Hughie dumped his swag on the Kilkers' veranda, where Jer sat cutting up onions and cauliflower for winter pickles. Jer looked at him beseechingly.

'It's all right,' said his brother, aiming a cuff at him. 'You're not wiped.'

Jer stuttered out explanations. Hughie cut him short.

'That's it. Forget it, eh?'

Jer appeared shockingly delicate. The bones of his face seemed about to jump through the skin.

Hugh said, 'I'm real sorry about the operation being a flop. Maybe some other time, another doctor. When I get some money together again.'

'Yeah, sure,' said Jer. Hugh saw his brother did not believe him. No one seemed to have faith in his word any more.

'I got to get a job,' he said.

'They're scarce,' said Jer. 'Everyone says there's a real daddy of a slump coming.' He heaved himself up and took the basin of vegetables into the kitchen.

Hugh faced up to John Kilker, sitting like an old grandpa in a chair before the fire.

'I'm real sorry it happened,' said Hugh. 'It was just one of them things that hit a man.'

John had been prepared to give the young fellow a good talking-to, but he did not feel like it. He was struck by Hughie's dejection and said kindly, 'You were caught between a rock and a hard place, lad. But what man isn't, some time in his life? There was a little girl I was spoony about before I met Rowena. She died of the typhoid fever. I was all broken up and hanging down for the best part of a year. But I got over it. The thing is, are you still fond of Margaret?'

'I am,' admitted Hughie.

'And what does she think about it?'

'I don't know,' Hughie had to confess.

John looked clever. 'Ah, she wants to be courted all over again. That's the way of them, you know.'

With John's help, Hughie got a job in the iceworks. He lived elsewhere in the town. He wrote to Bids a dozen times, pouring out his despondency, huge incoherent letters full of excuses and justification. But he had no answer. He told himself she was unforgiving, hard as nails, he was well shot of her. He was like one bereaved, living in a matter-of-fact way for much of the time, at other times suffering such anguish, such a tumult of emotions, he thought he must die to find peace.

During this time, ironically, his only source of comfort was the Kilker household. He sat by the fire with John, like an old man himself, listening to Jer and Mr Kilker swapping yarns, Jer singing bits of songs. Sometimes Margaret came to sit there as well. She was a peaceful presence, never speaking of Juno or Bids. Whatever clamour there was in her heart, no one ever heard about it. Eny was driven mad by curiosity and impatience. She was all for Margaret's having a grand conflagration with Hughie and getting the whole thing off her chest.

'You let us alone, Ma. He's getting over it. Let him do it at his own rate.'

But Rowena could not see that Hugh was getting over it. She was nettled that her daughter so disregarded her sage advice.

'She's praying for you,' she said vengefully to the young man. 'We're all praying for you.'

'A man hasn't a chance in this place,' thought Hughie ruefully.

He asked Margaret to come to the pictures: Greta Garbo, whom she loved. In the darkness, he squeezed her hand and whispered, 'You're damned good, Margaret. I'm glad you're around.'

It was a contrary thing that in this time of his dejection Margaret should be a comfort. He did not wonder what was going on in her head.

Margaret had made the great offering. She had placed her future life in God's hands. Not my will but Thine be done, she had said, and frequently experienced a terrible panic in case this should be so. All kind of things seemed to her to be bad omens. There was a story Jer told her father that put her spirits under a cloud for days; it seemed mysteriously directed at her, though not by Jer.

A twice great-grandfather of the Darcys it was who, wandering along the Galway strand, found a rich coffin. Lying within was a beautiful young girl, alive but speechless. The only jewellery she wore was a silver ear stud. The twice great-grandfather, his heart overborne by this strange waif, deeply desired that she should speak, so that she could make the marriage vows. He went for advice to a saintly hermit and was told the girl had been stolen by the sea people long before. She could not speak until the silver ear stud was removed.

Gladly the great-great-grandfather did this. But alas, what the lost girl said was that she belonged to someone else; and so the rescuer was left to marry someone else and to fret his life away.

'For the love of God, child,' exploded Eny when Margaret confided the uncanny feeling she had. 'There's not a shadow of likeness.'

'But I did rescue him,' said Margaret.

From afar Josie Capper watched the gradual rapprochement of her sister and Hughie. Josie had time on her hands; she had been forced to close her office for lack of work. Continued adversity had disheartened her. She was grieved, shaken. Somehow she could not come to terms with the disappointment.

Aunt Alf, who within a few months had grown frail and shaky, tried to console her.

'It's just that people don't consider young ladies can do that kind of work.'

'Why?' cried Josie. 'What has being a girl to do with anything if a person is properly qualified?'

'People are like that,' said Aunt Alf helplessly. 'They get ideas.'

She thought of mentioning to her niece how she, a new immigrant, had been turned down for many situations in decent households because she was Irish and a Catholic. 'But I'm a good cook,' she had protested. 'I work like a Trojan. I've a good character from the Emigration Office.' No use. No use at all.

'It's what you call prejudice,' she said.

Josie's struggles with the mindless injustice of her world were beginning to show on her face. Only halfway through her twenties and already there was a cynical droop to her mouth. Aunt Alf's heart was sore for her.

'Perhaps you could make up with your husband,' she suggested timidly.

'I'd sooner go and ask that swine Hatch for a job,' said Josie. Her face softened. 'Ah, dear Auntie Alf, I'll never forgive myself for losing your money. I tried hard not to, I really did.'

'What's money, my treasure?' said Aunt Alf, kissing her. 'Did Our Lady worry about money?'

All very well, thought the girl, but Our Lady had a good husband. If she hadn't, I don't think she would have made it, and everything in our world would have been different.

Josie applied for positions wherever they offered, but without success. Those with responsibility and opportunity for promotion were given to male applicants; the lesser jobs went to young girls who could be paid the minimum wage and dismissed when they turned eighteen. There seemed no place for a woman of Josie's age.

Josie caught a bad cold in the winter wind. It settled on her chest and she went to bed. The doctor suspected pleurisy, but in reality she had some kind of breakdown. The world pressed in on her. On every side it attacked her with its traditions, its false concepts and self-righteousness. At night she wept inconsolably, knowing that some part of her must be defeated. She could not think what else she might do. The bright flame of independence seemed to have no heat in it now. Again and again she went over the errors of her life. The common lot of womankind had been there in front of her nose but for some reason, bumptiousness, innocence, romanticism, she had not believed it. Why had she thought that life was fair? Had her mother, long ago, been like her, a wild foal, kicking up her heels at the deliciousness of being alive? Was disillusionment the secret of Delia's disregard for all others?

There was her sister Margaret, who would never learn, no

matter how many foul blows fate dealt her. Margaret thought that because she loved the world, the world loved her. She had faith in the goodness of God.

Here she was, blushes coming and going, telling her sister that she and Hugh Darcy had made up. In two months they would marry.

'Aren't you scared Bids Tookey will come back into his life?' Josie, though so unhappy herself, could not resist trying to prick her sister's bubble.

'She's been,' answered Margaret, 'and she's gone.'

Steve Tookey had scolded his daughter when he saw her putting Hugh's letters in the stove.

'Fair go, girl.' He knew she was eating her heart out.

'No,' she said, her lips a firm line. 'It's finished. He's not going to get around me twice.'

Steve said, 'You're feeding your anger, Bids.'

'Maybe I am,' she flashed back. 'Just like you fed your anger all these years against my mother.'

It was the first time she had ever deliberately wounded him. In his pain he turned away.

'That's true, girl. And that's how I know anger is sour pickings.'

In vain she wept her contrition, hugged his spare body to her breast. A little uneasiness grew between them, not coolness, not embarrassment, but rather a shared knowledge of guilty pride.

One evening Bids said to her father, 'I've applied for a transfer, Daddy. Sydney.'

Steve heard the sound of farewell, and nodded.

'It's come through.'

'You'll see your mother. Living with her maybe.'

'No, I thought I'd get a flat. Whatever I can afford. Because I want you to come too, Dad.'

'Leave Juno?'

He was amazed. He, who had been born with such itchy toes, had not thought of leaving Juno since he returned from South Africa. Bids, kneeling beside him, her arms about his bent back, pleaded ardently. She was eloquent about the pleasures of the city, the easier climate, the comfort they would have.

But Steve did not hear that beloved voice. He saw himself as a young man, a real cock o' the walk, labouring in the smithy.

165

Crowds of Steve Tookeys, dissolving, appearing in a magical progression, middle-aged, getting lamed by that drunk, married, Evie, Bid's coming. The town did the same thing, houses flowing up the hills, the dark fur of the long gentle slopes shrinking, vanishing. He was alarmed. If he left Juno he would not have anything. All that he was and had been was here.

'Ah, no, Bids, I couldn't do that. I'm too old.'

His face was like reddened wood. There was the unresilient look of wood about it, as though he had grown into a tree, a tree with roots in Juno.

'Then I won't go. I won't leave you here alone.'

They argued back and forth for a week.

'You fetch old Jim Oyster for me. I feel like a yarn and a beer,' said Steve.

Jim Oyster had been retired for three years. He lived with his daughter, and the noise of the kids drove him dotty. Steve put it to him to come and share the cottage after Bid's departure. Jim gladly accepted.

'The daughter will help out with cooking, and keeping the draughts out of our socks and things like that. She'll be real glad to have the extra room now the boys are growing.'

Steve called Bids and gave her the news.

'Us old pots'll look after each other. Yes, I want you to go, girl. It's right for young ones.'

He promised Bids he'd come for a long holiday after she was settled, but they both knew he would not.

Bids felt it was the end of the world. But she was driven forth by something inexorable, a passionate instinct.

She suffered more than she believed possible. Losing her mother had been a fearful amputation; for six months she had wandered in a half-world, no anchor, no holdfast except her resolute will. Losing Hugh was another blow, one with which she could not come to terms. And now she was leaving this old man, the centre of her life.

On an impulse she sent a letter to Hugh Darcy.

'I'm going to work in Sydney. The express stops for a few minutes at Trafalgar. I'd like to say goodbye and good luck.'

She gave the date and the time of the train. Bids told her father what she had done. She expected him to be disconcerted, but a grin slowly spread over his features.

'You're trying yourself out, Bridget.'

'That's right. I want to finish clean.'

Hugh received her letter. His longing to see her again was so intense he had to plead sick and take a day away from work. All day he wandered the hills. That evening he called to see Jer. His brother squatted in a chair, rubbing his ankles. He listened querulously to what Hugh had to say, then with terror. Hugh was going to make up to Bids Tookey again, and he, Jer, would never have a home with his brother. But Hugh continued: 'I want you to meet that train, Jer. I got no one else to ask. I want you to say good wishes from me and I hope she'll always be happy.'

'I will, I will,' gabbled Jer, almost in tears.

'You won't say anything else, Jer?' entreated Hugh. 'You won't make up any big stories, or tell lies about what I did or said? You promise just to say what I told you?'

'May I hope to die if I don't keep that promise,' said Jer.

Hugh went away without seeing any other member of the household, and Jer rolled around in his chair with relief and ecstasy. That would be the end of the bitch. Margaret had won out and so had he.

He did as Hughie had asked. Hughie did not question him about that fleeting encounter, but Jer knew he was awaiting a message.

'She said good luck and she'll never forget you.'

'Right. Thanks.'

Hughie took Margaret to the pictures. Coming home across the suspension bridge, they stopped to peer into the dark water, alive with wagging, jostling star reflections.

'This old bridge is going to fall to pieces one of these days.'

'It's stood up to just so many floods,' said Margaret. 'It'll be here when we get grey hair.'

'I want to tell you something,' said Hugh. He told her about Bids Tookey passing through on her way to Sydney, and Jer carrying his farewell. Margaret was silent for a while.

'Did you feel bad?'

'Yes. But I'll get over it.'

Pain seized him suddenly, in the way it had. Silently he shouted: 'I won't, I won't. Never.'

'I suppose I will, too,' said Margaret. They walked across the Domain to her home.

They sat for a while on the veranda, arms around each other.

'What do you reckon it is about us?'

'I don't know. I suppose it was meant somehow.'

Jer, spying through the crack in the curtains, went back to bed. Deep religious feeling flooded him. He was sorry he had thrown Bids Tookey's holy picture away. God had been watching out for him all along, just like that guardian angel. He was safe at last.

Nine

Hugh and Margaret rented a small weatherboard cottage for seven shillings and sixpence a week. Empty houses showed their bereft faces all over Trafalgar. People overshadowed by the coming Depression were scuttling together, sharing roofs and household expenses.

'It's nothing to write home about,' grumbled Hugh, kicking the wall and watching fine borer dust trickle out of a rash of holes.

'It's ours, though,' murmured Margaret. She had become gentle-voiced and slow-moving these last weeks. She lived as if absorbed in a dream. Hughie found this languor strangely erotic. It seemed he had at last overcome in the girl some resistance he had scarcely known existed. She was powerless before his desire; everything wavered, upbringing, conscience, Church. The defeat of the Church brought him a mean, small triumph. He had swept away that powerful and ambiguous presence in Margaret's heart. He was therefore more of a king with this girl than he had been with Bids Tookey, who recognised the final jurisdiction of none of those things. He seized Margaret roughly.

'Bloody emperor, aren't I?' He preened himself. For a moment something lenient and sage looked out of her eyes. So you think I'm just for ransacking, it conveyed. You'll learn. Still, there was a strong feeling for life in Margaret. She sensed sweetness and drama in the empty house, the slant of sunlight in which they lay, the smell of must and dead ashes overlaid by that of sappy grass. She did not answer and he forgot the question.

In the unkempt garden bloomed freesias and grape hyacinths. The eucalypt twigs flushed red, the four creeks overflowed, lambs appeared on the hills, white as mushrooms and as sudden.

'Them two had better wed quick,' said Eny ominously, 'or I won't answer for Margaret.'

'Ah, my dear,' thought her husband, 'if we could have our time over again!'

John sold the old cow paddock next his house, and gave the money to the young people as a wedding present. Hugh was both pleased and obscurely angry.

'It ought to be my Dad giving us that, not yours,' he said to Margaret. But the gift removed a weight from his shoulders, for he was aware that his iceworks job was insecure. The firm were not taking on any young fellows; older men were pressed to retire early.

'I break into a cold sweat to think of being out of work,' he admitted. Margaret was optimistic.

'If things get too bad we'll go to Sydney,' she said. 'There's always work in a big city; everyone says so. Isn't that right, Jer?'

She saw the city swim like a mirage out of the sweltering smoke of industry. Always hungry for workers, cities were, otherwise how did the wheels keep turning?

'God's good. You just have to trust Him,' she told Hughie.

Half of the young man's brain marvelled at confidence that was both artless and relentless. The other half drew support and comfort from this very thing. Perhaps she was right. She had got what she wanted, hadn't she, and who was to say God had not given it to her?

With a satirical eye, Jer watched the expressions chasing each other over his brother's face. He knew Hughie's present mood of resolution. He had put Bids Tookey and what he felt for her into some closed place, and he thought she would stay there. There was no guarantee that his resolution would last. Well, what does? thought Jer without rancour. All things in life, or so he had found, were transient. He began once more to write to Mrs Biddle. If things went wrong between him and the lovebirds, he required a bolthole to slip into without delay or fuss.

The thought of a marriage in the family gave John renewed vitality. He knew he was not the man he had been. A shelly rim showed around the iris of his eye and every time he washed his face he felt the skull pushing against his fingers.

'Be damned to that,' said John to himself. 'I'll see my treasure married and I might last long enough to see young Josephine settled as well.'

The night before the wedding the house was thronged as six in a bed, Dan, the eldest, having brought his seven children, great cackling louts all under eighteen years old. Eleven o' clock in the evening it was, and they were still talking at the tops of their voices, the jabber interspersed with squabbles and sudden blasts of temper.

Eny and John lay like nested boomerangs, her back cosily fitted against his stomach, her head under his chin. It had been their

170

favourite sleeping position for forty or more years.

'I can't warm to them children and that's a fact,' confided Eny. 'They must take after Myra.'

Silently they meditated on the lucky accident of Myra's having put her back out. They had met Dan's wife only three times and liked her on none of them. She was a plaintive woman with an eccentric stomach.

'The age of that Dan!' continued Eny with wonderment. She failed to identify the burly, lavender-chinned farmer with the rose-petal infant she had loved with such passion.

'It's the wonder of the world how they grow away from you,' agreed John. 'It's a shame Emmet couldn't make it after ten years. Likely we wouldn't even know him except for the freckles.'

They said their prayers together, John giving out and Eny answering.

'Who did you offer for?' whispered Eny when the last amen was said.

'The other one, our Delia, that she's happy wherever she is,' said John. 'She had hair that nice, like a little duck.'

'God bless you, my darling,' thought Eny of John. 'God reward you for what you've been to me and the children.' But all she said was, 'Them rowdies of Dan's are all roosting, be the sound of them, so let's go to sleep.'

Hugh and Margaret stood up together in the crowded church and were married. Hughie had been away from his religion so long that the ceremony tricked him altogether, the standings up and sittings down, the priest turning his back or his front at unpredictable intervals. The altar was ornamented with white flowers, there was a snuffy odour of candles. The morning light through the coloured windows had the bloom of fruit.

Hugh recalled that his father, when he first came to the town, had helped build this Church. Every plank was pitsawn by Irish immigrants, every shingle hand-chopped from silky oak. The poor devil Martin had been only a year or two older than he, Hughie, black stiff hair, eyes blue as glass marbles. And then, ten years later, he and his bride had stood here in this very place, hoping for and expecting happiness.

'Hughie!' Margaret jogged his arm.

'I do,' he said, hurriedly.

It seemed to Margaret that all roads had led to this place, this moment, since she fell off the merry-go-round on the King's Birthday. But it wasn't her planning any more than it was his. It was just the way life turned out.

Jer began to sing 'Oh, Promise Me!' and one of the female guests uttered a neigh. She was not the only one. Halfway through the ceremony Rowena began to cry. This was because of a number of things: the arduous preparations for the wedding breakfast; the desperate night she'd spent because of Dan's bog-trotters; John's going away from her. Yes, she felt that any year now the great blow would come, she would be left alone.

Josie sat beside her mother. Margaret had wanted Josie to be her attendant, but the priest had raised Cain. In the Church's eye Josie had an anomalous position. What could she be, bridesmaid or matron of honour? He felt the question should be submitted to the Bishop. Josie stepped down from the honour, and Margaret had for bridesmaid Dan's Mary, fourteen years old and crimson with fright.

Josie now put her arm around her mother, expecting it to be shrugged away. But it was not.

'Aren't you all I have now, Josie?' choked Eny. Josie left her arm where it was. She thought the remark arose from her mother's sense of the dramatic occasion, but received it tolerantly. Her mother was now over sixty, she had white hair with sulphur streaks; lately her fine straight back tended to bend at the shoulders. Josie felt pity for this woman who had impaired her sense of worth, left despoiled her childish pride of self, but had no comprehension of the damage she had done. It occurred then to Josie that she had always expected her mother to be more than human. She had confounded the woman with her motherly function. She had given no scope to the wrongheaded, wilful spirit that inhabited this familiar body.

'Will you come back home to live?' whispered Eny.

'There's Aunt Alf,' pointed out Josie. 'She needs me more.'

'Much you know,' said Eny, sorrowfully.

When Josie told Margaret of Bids Tookey, and seen the almost fatal wound she had given her sister, she became aware of a shift in her concept of life. It was as if some power had decided she was getting nowhere the way she was. In the moment of forgiveness for her mother, there was a second veering onto a new road.

'I know you're thinking of Pa,' she said. 'But I'm sure he'll be with us many years yet.'

172

At the house, she sat quietly at the table amidst the jolly uproar. She realised clearly that she no longer possessed the combative spirit of her youth. Perhaps malice had been the sparkling stream that energised her. She had put her heart into becoming someone freer, more independent than her mother or Margaret; she had done everything possible towards that end and she had failed.

'If you're a woman,' she thought, 'in the end someone always arranges your life for you.'

She wondered what the end would be for her.

Her eldest brother Dan had an eye on her. Stunned to hear of her calamitous marriage, he had been outraged when his Pa told him that Josie planned to divorce the scoundrel. Dan let his father know what he felt, what Myra would feel, about this disgrace to the family.

'Ah,' said John charitably, 'can you blame the young ones, wars and depressions and picture shows and all? But she's a good girl for all that.'

Dan gazed at Josie, surreptitiously looking for signs of sin. He thought she looked moody, far from well, thin as a fishbone picked by a gull. Well, she'd made her bed and she knew what to expect, a life spent hanging around with the old people, neither married nor unmarried, one of those disconsolate leftover women.

'Ah, but God's good,' thought Dan, cheering up. 'She'll always be on hand to take care of Aunt Alf and Ma and Pa. The way things are, she'll be in no position to say no.'

In fact, Josie's future life was remarkably different. Shortly after her divorce a gusty wind struck her, bowling her head over heels. This vital, self-engrossed man, hair in a bush, a boot-shaped nose, forty-five if he was a day, was nothing more than a house painter but could, if he chose, have been a rich or powerful man. Nature had endowed him with that mysterious voluptuousness which irresistibly calls forth the folly of women. He was affable to the creatures, leaving them melting with nostalgia, their hatboxes and other hidey-holes rich with mementoes, dried flowers, chocolate wrappers, tram tickets. Not being wealthy, he could give them no more, though he would have if circumstances had allowed. He was a generous man. Now that he was middle-aged, and by nature indolent, he looked about for a wife.

Josie realised she had never known what love was. Vehemently she wrote to her married sister Margaret in Sydney. Every time she set eyes on Harnett Gore she could faint. She could not sleep, she would rather starve by his side than live in luxury without him. For the first time, she confessed, she understood how Margaret had felt about Hugh Darcy.

With the clarity of experience Margaret realised that Josie was sunk. Josie married Harney and in no time at all had four children, cystitis, and never a spare moment to brood on her past ambitions for success and a tidy life. Had she really become a qualified accountant, had she tried with anguish to establish a business of her own? The whole thing was a dream, something she had read in a women's magazine.

Josie subsided beneath the flood. It was warm and safe down there; she loved her children ardently; everyone said Harney was a lucky man, she was a wife in a thousand. It was hard to go against the approbation of everyone she knew. Josie realised this was called settling down. She no longer had the time to think about it, or try to work it out, but it was, she supposed, Life.

As with Josie's unpredictable future, so with Auntie Alf's. At the wedding breakfast guests looked sidelong at the dry wisp of a woman, and if they had any saucy jokes up their sleeves they kept them there. They thought she looked like a nun out of place.

As the beer circulated and noise began to lift the roof, Auntie Alf felt in her head the frightening dislocation that preceded one of her nervous attacks. Eny had put away stout at a great rate. She and Jer were well away on the forty-three verses of her favourite song:

Brian O'Lynn was a gentleman born
His hair it was long and his whiskers unshorn,
His teeth were far out and his eyes were far in,
'I'm a wonder for beauty,' says Brian O'Lynn.

Sweat broke out on Alf's parchment brow; she staggered to her feet. Immediately the teapot tipped over and flooded the Father. The crimson bridesmaid got a pig's toe caught in her throat. Josie flew around the table and half carried the old woman to the kitchen.

Brian O'Lynn was in want of a brooch
He took a brass pin and a fine cockroach . . .

174

'Ma!' said Josie sharply. 'You're needed in the kitchen!'

The sight of Alf lolling in a chair, her eyes adrift, her chin fallen, drove the fumes from Rowena's brain.

'God in heaven, has she been called home on us?' she cried.

The breast of his shirt he fixed it straight in,
'They'll think it a diamond,' says Brian O'Lynn.

Margaret rustled in, a big doll in her white tulle and orange blossom, to find her mother beside the chair, holding Auntie Alf's head to her breast in the tenderest manner, and firing off a command to Josie to haul in the doctor. But the doctor was astride Dan's daughter, trying to hook out the pig's toe.

'Wasn't she enjoying the trotter, poor Mary; she was always a terror for a pigsfoot.'

'Hail, Queen of Heaven, the ocean star, guide of us wanderers here below.'

'Can you get a purchase on it, doctor?'

'Fetch the holy water, one of yous, and be quick about it.'

'Serve her right, tearing into that pigsfoot like a starving sheepdog.'

'Will you stand back!' roared the doctor. 'Throw that holy water on me once more and I'll job you. Someone get a holt on her teeth – she's like a shark. Ah, got it!'

Mary, weeping and retching, was led into the air. They could hear her ow-owing all the way across the lawn. Jer took up his guitar.

Faith of our fathers, living still
In spite of dungeon, fire and sword . . .

Auntie Alf opened her eyes.

'Them words,' marvelled Eny, 'they've the power of magic.'

But Alf had been coming round at her own speed the past five minutes. Very comfortable she was against Eny's breast, though the smell of stout was fierce. Eny looked down at her anxiously. 'Ah,' she thought, 'the old thing is the weight of a feather. And pale! You could drop snow on her face and you wouldn't see it.'

Eny had never missed her mother, or could not recall doing so, but now she did. Give or take a few years, Alf Kilker could be her mother, needing loving care in the extremity of her life, a religious hand to close her eyes at the last.

'Alf,' she said, choking with impetuous tears, 'you're coming to live with me and John, I'll not hear a word against it. Long ago I promised to look after you in your frailty, and here I stand fast to keep that vow!'

That was how it happened, and a great comfort Alf was to Rowena for several years after John went to his eternal rest. The pair of them would sit on opposite sides of the fire, knitting socks for the grandchildren, talking about old times, Eny sometimes taking a blast of the little clay pipe she had become attached to after John's departure, Alf often knocking off the chat to say a silent aspiration or turn her thoughts to God in sweet gratitude. For she was not far from being a saint off the wall, as Rowena believed.

But now it was time for the bride and groom to leave. Margaret kissed her aunt and her mother, and went to her old bedroom to change her clothes. The married pair were not going away.

'I'd rather spend my honeymoon in our own little house,' said Margaret.

She and Hugh said their goodbyes. The company wanted to escort the bridal couple, banging tin cans and roaring all the way, but John forbade them.

'It's a moonlight night,' he said. 'They'll never forget it.'

Such was his majesty, the respect in which all held him, that no one followed Hugh and Margaret. John sat down and took off his shoes.

'Well, my dears,' he said, stretching out his clenched toes, 'if ever I wear them grand boots again it'll be to my wake, and that's a promise. And now if young Jer will strike up we'll have a sing-song to round off the evening.'

Hugh and Margaret heard the yips and hooches nearly all the way to their home.

'They might as well have come with us, the row they're making,' said Hugh.

His wife was both shy and excited. She longed to have a good cry, or a talk with Josie.

'I'll make a cup of tea,' she said.

'It won't be too bad,' thought Hugh, surveying the double bed with the marcella counterpane patterned with ribbons and bou-

176

quets. 'The Kilkers are real good people, respected. They's stand by us if things get tough. But I'm not having that old faggot of a Ma sticking her nose in our affairs.'

'Maybe we will go to Sydney,' he said when Margaret came into the room. She was wearing a long nightdress.

'Not yet, though,' she answered, banking the fire in the small curved bedroom grate. 'I wouldn't like to leave my people yet.'

'Take that bloody shroud off!' he commanded. She did not like to. He repeated his order, threatening to chase her out on the lawn and rip if off there. At last he had the nightdress on the floor and Margaret in bed.

'God, you're an armful and a half!' he said.

Before midnight, though lulled by warmth and delicious ease, Hugh was still wakeful. He had rarely spent an entire night with a girl. It occurred to him now that this was one of life's near perfect experiences, a drowsy, relaxed involvement with a sleeping girl's body. He bit her shoulder gently, tickled her breast, but she did not wake. He ran an exploratory hand over her. How delectable all those plains and hills! She was a landscape all on her own. He ran the sole of his foot up and down her calf. It was slick as glass, with a defenceless feel to it. He tried his own calf. Quite different, hairy as an old sock and hard as a brick.

Well, she wasn't such a bad buy. He hugged her more closely, remembering Mrs Kilker's pointing out a rosebush beside her kitchen door. The more blooms you picked, she had said, the more the bush produced. It was a good giver. That was Margaret, a good giver.

How had that fightable old girl produced a gentle soul like Margaret? He had a sudden desire to protect his wife from her mother's nipping and niggling, to show the old woman she was wrong in her estimation of him as a husband.

Bids now. He would have tried, have broken his neck in the effort to be a hero of a husband to her! But it wasn't to be. She'd find someone better, someone more her own kind. He caught his breath, his eyes filled with tears. Something inside him that had strained, panted, struggled to open its wings, folded those wings and seemed to sleep.

He turned his thoughts away from Bids. But still sleep did not come.

Drowsing, he lay and watched the fire, a red wink, a crack of sparks. Well, he mused, he had Margaret for better or worse, and she had him. I won't get on the grog again, he thought. A few beers with the boys. But not on the grog.

The curtain wafted gently from the window, and the full blaze of moonlight filled the room, not white, not blue, unearthly. A dark knob, roundish in shape, seemed to sit on the window sill. Hugh looked at it indifferently for a while, then realised with a start that it was a human head.

'Oh, boy!' he thought. 'That little tick!'

He coughed, and the head sank out of sight. Hugh slipped from bed, dragged on his trousers and boots, and raced outside. Jer was crouched in the deep shadow of the chimney; the moonlight glinted on the metal tip of a crutch.

'Come on out, Jer. I can see your crutch, Jer,' he said gently.

Jer came out, beaming, full of explanations. He had just been passing. The party was still going on at Kilker's, so he'd gone out for fresh air. Hughie swooped on him, seized him by the scruff, and dragged him down the yard.

'I'll go home, Hughie, I will, I swear,' babbled Jer.

'You peeping Tom, I couldn't trust you. I'm going to lock you in the dub until morning.'

Now Jer let out a strangled shriek. 'It's cold. I'll die of cold. You know I'm delicate. I'll go home, honest I will.'

No use. Hughie hurled his brother into the dark depths of the outside lavatory and shut the door. There was a bar to keep chickens and other creatures from sheltering in there, and Hugh slammed it home. He stood there grinning. It was freezing. Winter still hung around, thin and splintery, in the night air.

The lavatory stood under a fruit tree in early flower. The blossoms drifted downwards, inconceivably fragile in the moonlight.

'Hughie?' Jer's most charming, conciliatory voice.

'Yeah, what?'

'Let me out, mate, it's bloody awful in here.'

'Let you out in the morning.'

Hugh stalked away, frozen. His sockless feet rattled about in the unlaced boots like blocks of ice.

He thought: 'I'll let the little bugger out in ten minutes. Don't want him coming down again with pneumonia.'

He had hardly reached the bedroom before he heard the distant crash of wood. He watched through the window.

'Did you hear something?' murmured Margaret.

'Branch fell off the pear tree,' answered Hughie. 'Go to sleep, love.'

Grinning, he watched Jer emerge through the broken door and crab away over the paddock. The moonlight was so sharp Hughie thought there might be a frost.

He went back to bed and warmed himself against his wife. If he had some faint feelings of longing, perhaps regret, he put them out of his mind. A man made his own choice. He went to sleep.

Margaret, who had been waiting for him to return, relaxed and drifted contentedly between dreams and reality. Mrs Darcy. Missus.

The Harp in the South

One

The hills are full of Irish people. When their grandfathers and great-grandfathers arrived in Sydney they went naturally to Shanty Town, not because they were dirty or lazy, though many of them were that, but because they were poor. And wherever there are poor you will find landlords who build tenements: cramming two on a piece of land no bigger than a pocket handkerchief, and letting them for the rent of four. In the squalid, mazy streets of sandstone double-decker houses, each with its little balcony edged with rusty iron lace, and its door opening on to the street, or four square feet of 'front', every second name is an Irish one. There are Brodies, and Caseys and Murphys and O'Briens, and down by the corner are Casement and Grogan and Kell, and, although here and there you find a Simich, or a Siciliano, or a Jewish shopkeeper, or a Chinese laundryman, most are Irish.

Even the names of the streets tell the story of those old emigrants who came looking for roads cobbled with gold, and found them made of stone harder than an overseer's heart. There is Fahy Street running off Riley Street, and both of them branching from Coronation Street, which had the name of Kelleher before they changed it to honour Queen Victoria. And there is Ryan Street running down into Redfern, and Brophy Street, mean and horrible, flowing into Elizabeth Street, which leads to the city.

This was the place where the Darcys lived – Plymouth Street, Surry Hills, Sydney, in an unlucky house which the landlord had renumbered from Thirteen to Twelve-and-a-Half.

It was the oldest in Plymouth Street, a cranky brown house, with a blistered green door, and a step worn into dimples and hollows that collected the rain in little pools in which Roie and Dolour, when little, had always expected to find frogs.

There were many houses like Number Twelve-and-a-Half, smelling of leaking gas, and rats, and mouldering wallpaper which has soaked up the odours of a thousand meals. The stairs were very dark and steep, and built on a slant as though the architect were drunk, so that from the top landing you couldn't see the bottom.

On the top landing hung a little globe, very high up, so that the tenants could not steal it. It was as small as a star and as yellow as a lemon.

Downstairs there was a dark bedroom without windows or skylight, a kitchen with a broken floor, and a scullery with one window overlooking the flagged yard, where a drunken garbage can stood with its lid over one ear. Upstairs were three cramped attic bedrooms. Hughie and Mumma had slept in one of these for a long time, but it had a sloping roof, so that anybody bouncing hastily out of the left-hand side of the bed hit himself a terrific blow on top of the head, and fell prostrate again. Hughie had done this a thousand times, both drunk and sober, and it was the main cause of his frequent absence from work; as he pointed out to Mumma, by the time he'd shaken his brains back into their proper place it was past the hour and no use going to work at all, seeing that a man was fined for every minute he was late. He had promised himself time and time again that he'd move the bed, but somehow it never got done, for it meant rearranging all the furniture, and that would take a full afternoon of time. He could not afford that, for Saturday afternoon he always spent at the pub, and Sunday afternoon he spent sleeping off Saturday afternoon.

So the simplest thing was to move the children into the attic, while he and Mumma took the dark bedroom downstairs.

Once Roie and Dolour had had a little brother, Thady. When he was six, and Roie nine, and Dolour two, he had been sent out on to the footpath to play, for the backyard was too small and dirty and sunless. And he had just disappeared. Nothing was ever heard of him again. No one had seen a man or woman leading him off, or a car carry him away. There was just a little box cart left lying on the roadway, and that was all. Hughie had rampaged round the streets and through the alleyways like a madman; he had accompanied the police as they patrolled the sewers. Grim-lipped and devil-faced, he had sworn that God and he would never be friends while the agony and mystery of Thady's disappearance hung over them.

But Mumma had never given up hope. She often stood at the gates of boys' schools, looking and looking, adding the slow years to Thady's stature, and maturity to his little round face. It was ten years since he had disappeared. Dolour did not remember him at all, and Roie only a little, but he was a living presence in that house. He was like a ghost who is not dead.

In the other attic rooms, which Mumma let, furnished, for seven and sixpence a week each, lived Mr Patrick Diamond and Miss Sheily. Mr Diamond was a real Irishman, born in Ireland, an Orangeman who was friendly with Hughie and liked all the Darcys except on St Patrick's Day, when his Orange blood boiled up, and he called them all pope-worshippers and mummers, and stamped upstairs and slammed the door, and banged on the wall if Roie or Dolour gave as much as a squeak. He had been christened Patrick in error by a gin-bemused neighbour, and all his life it had been a cross to him and a confusion to his friends. But his pride and his stubbornness forbade his changing it to William or James, much as he would have liked to.

Miss Sheily was a tiny thin woman, as bitter as a draught of alum water, with a parchment face and subtle black eyes. She had been well educated, and consequently Mumma always felt a little shy of her. Hughie tended to become rumbustious, just to prove that he was as good as she was, and a damn sight better. But he liked her more than the others did. Roie and Dolour were a little bit frightened of her. It seemed to them that Miss Sheily, with her piercing eyes, and birdlike sophisticated voice, knew a world wider than theirs. It would not have surprised them if she had one day thrown open her attic window and darted out on a broom, over the narrow canyon of Plymouth Street, and into the maze of alleyways which makes up the Hills.

The funny thing about Miss Sheily was that nobody knew her Christian name, or had even seen her initial. When she left a note pinned to the door for the iceman or the butcher's boy, she always signed it 'Miss Sheily'. Roie and Dolour and Mumma often had guessing competitions about Miss Sheily's name, but nobody had ever proved her guess correct. Dolour thought that Agnes or Amy was most likely, and Roie said scornfully that Belle or Grace was right up Miss Sheily's alley, seeing that neither fitted. But Mumma, with the stubborn and unpredictable romanticism that she sometimes displayed, voted for Stella.

'Oh, Mumma! Fancy Stella!' cried Roie. 'Why the dickens should she have a name like that?'

'Because she's a lady,' said Mumma obstinately. And, although both Roie and Dolour, as well as the rest of Plymouth Street, knew that this could not possibly be so, they did not dare say anything, for Mumma hated the mere mention of illegitimacy. So they could not quote Johnny as an argument against Miss Sheily's ladyhood.

For Johnny Sheily, the poor unfortunate with his crooked back and great square box of a head, was Miss Sheily's son, and she did not make the slightest attempt to hide it.

'Johnny!' she would scream down the stairs. 'Johnny, where are you?' and to Mr Diamond, who might emerge across the landing just then, 'Have you seen that great lump of a son of mine, Mr Diamond?'

Johnny, sitting beneath the mangy-leaved phoenix palm in the backyard and gently moving some incomprehensible cipher of pebbles back and forth in the dirt, would raise his buttermilk blue eyes and call back: 'Ike ummin, Umma', for his tongue, like the rest of him, was twisted.

Roie was one of those who cannot bear to see the deformed. The dark little currant eyes of an idiot, his chinless face, and thick neck and bowed legs, was enough to fill her day with horror, though she saw him but passingly from a tram. And every day she walked a quarter of a mile out of her path so that she would not have to pass a certain doorway where an old legless man with blind milky eyes sat in the sun.

She tried to conquer this, for it was against the principles which had been instilled in her soul from the time she began to speak. Mumma had always said: 'God has struck them as the wild lightning strikes a tree, and no one knows why.' And she had said: 'It might be you with the hare-lip, or the nose like a strawberry, and if ever I catch you calling names or hurting the feelings of the misfortunate, I'll beat the bottom off you.'

So when Roie shrank from Johnny Sheily, or turned away her face when he mumbled some mysterious greeting, she committed a double sin, that of uncharity and that of pride. For almost unconsciously her hand would go up to her own small slender face, and trace the contours of slanting eyes and soft chin, and the little delicate mouth that had its outline slightly raised as though it were in relief. It was almost as though, with that very gesture, her hand said: 'Thank God that I am not as you. Realizing this, she was always trying to atone, offering Masses for poor Johnny Sheily, and forcing herself to look in his bleary eye and smile as she passed.

But Mumma loved him in her own acidulous, contrary way, and never once did she hear Miss Sheily beating him that she did not shed a tear of mingled grief and rage.

186

Johnny was often naughty, for all that he was twenty or more, for his poor bewildered brain, that saw a sparrow as big as a goose, and peopled the air around him with butterflies and other things that needed to be snatched at, and caught, did not take in every word he heard, and consequently he was always doing the wrong thing, and being walloped for it.

'The woman hates him, it's my solemn belief,' said Mumma one day, staring at the ceiling, her cup of tea growing cold and curdly on the table.

Hughie laughed, 'Hate her own child? What are you talking about?'

Mumma shook her head. 'It's possible, Hughie. He's the cause of her shame, and she blames him for it.'

'Better blame herself for getting all hot and bothered when she didn't ought to,' chuckled Hughie coarsely. Mumma flushed.

'Shut yer big trap,' she snapped, and Hughie laughed uproariously and put his arms round her wide waist and mumbled in her ear. She brought the side of her hand in a sharp chop across the back of his neck.

'You're a dirty old man, Hughie, and that's a fact.'

'I'm not, now. I'm neither dirty nor old. I'm just a man,' protested Hughie. Mumma opened her mouth to retort, but almost instantly the whimpering wails of Johnny upstairs broke into shrill shrieks.

'She's murdering him, the old hag, that's what she's doing,' cried Hughie. His eyes blazed, and he burst through the doorway and pounded up the stairs. There in the darkness he stood, hammering on Miss Sheily's door and yelling to her to open up. Mumma pounded after him, protesting, for in the live and let live law of the slums there is a clause that nobody shall interfere in anybody else's fight.

'Open the door or I'll kick it in,' yelled Hughie, the brilliant white light of the crusader filling his heart. There was a split second's wait, and then Mumma quietly tried the door. It was not locked. Hughie burst in, and Mumma caught a glimpse of Miss Sheily's room, its streaky blue kalsomined walls, the sloping ceiling stuck with pictures, and the gas ring flaring yellow and smoky in one dim corner. The air was thick with the fumes of burnt fat, stale food, and old unwashed clothing. On the floor was a litter of scraps of paper and crumbs of food that had been trodden flat into the grease and dirt.

187

And there against a wall was Johnny, his hands tied around a disused gas jet. As soon as Mumma saw his grotesque figure she gave a shriek and her anger surpassed Hughie's.

'Why, you old Borgia,' she cried. 'Tying the poor kid up to slam the daylights out of him.'

Beside Johnny Miss Sheily stood trembling, thin as a piece of wire, her drooping black skirt hardly hiding the bones which stood fragilely beneath it. In her hand was a piece of knotted electric flex. Her white face was a smudge under the dim light which filtered from the skylight, but Mumma could easily see the hatred and passion which glared from it. It was almost as though Miss Sheily were as transparent as a light globe, and the very force of her bitter spirit illuminated her.

'Get out of here,' she spat. 'What do you mean by it? By God, if it's the last thing I do I'll see you in gaol for this. It's forced entry, that's what it is.'

'What have you done to the poor little devil?' groaned Mumma, her fingers running over Johnny's bare back, wet with oozing serum from a dozen wounds. He sluggishly turned his head, and his bristly hair brushed her face. His pale blue eyes had an opaque opal sheen in the dimness.

'The Red Cross'll hear about this,' promised Hughie. 'Yeah, and the R.S.P.C.A., too. You can talk about putting other people in boob, you old vulture.'

And, indeed, Miss Sheily did look like a vulture standing there quaking with temper, her long white nose curved downwards and her blue lips as thin and bitter as a snake's. Out of those lips came no words, only shrill birdlike sounds that spoke as no words could of the maelstrom of loathing in her soul. Mumma gave a yank with her strong hands and broke the bootlaces which linked Johnny's hands over the gas jet. He stood there giggling under his breath, his great oblong head cocked over one shoulder and his long arms dangling like an ape's.

'You should be black ashamed, Miss Sheily,' said Mumma.

Miss Sheily's fury lapped over as a river in flood brims its banks. She began to speak in a high, hoarse voice upon which her refined accent sat grotesquely. 'I'm sick of him! I'm sick of the look of him!'

Mumma put her arm around Johnny. His shoulders were so broad that her fingers barely grasped his other arm.

'It's not his fault he's a cripple. And you shouldn't be reminding him of it,' she reproached.

188

Hughie had a mindful of scintillating sentences which he could not wait to utter, but every time he opened his mouth one of the women took advantage of the moment and spoke in his place.

Miss Sheily's eyes blazed so much they were like the eyes of a mad woman. 'I hate the way he looks. Every time I realize he's my child I could cut my throat.'

'Easy to do,' cried Hughie hurriedly, before anyone could snatch the moment from him. 'Easier to do than lashing the hide off him.'

'Hating your own child,' said Mumma, shocked to her heart and yet exultant, because she had suspected it all along. 'You shouldn't ever have had a child.'

'I didn't want him,' screamed Miss Sheily. 'I tried every way I knew to get rid of him before he was born. And then when he came he was like this, a monster. I hate him. I hate him!'

'Why don't you put him in an orphanage, then?' said Hughie. Miss Sheily answered sulkily, 'I don't want to.'

'No,' said Hughie astutely; 'and you can get a pretty big pension for him, can't you, so that you needn't go to work. Oh, no, you're quite the lady. You may as well say that Johnny's hump is working for you, Miss Sheily.'

He laughed uproariously. Already he was tasting the applause of the boys at the pub as they listened open-mouthed to his recountal of the story. To Miss Sheily his wide mouth and little screwed-up eyes looked like the mask of a devil. She lashed out with the flex, but before the blow fell Hughie grabbed her thin arm, as dry and mummified as that of a skeleton, and warded it off.

'Oan urt umma,' croaked Johnny, throwing himself upon Hughie. His great weight thrust the man off his balance, and Hughie rolled in the dirt with Johnny on top of him. But the boy had no strength, and squatted there with tears bubbling out of his eyes in a stream, his blubbery mouth pursed in a ludicrous parody of a child's.

'Ah, God in heaven,' said Hughie in disgust, scrambling up and thrusting his face close to Miss Sheily's paper-white one, 'if I hear one more yell from this room I'll report to the cops as sure as God's up there.'

He pointed a dramatic finger at the ceiling and stumped out of the room. Mumma hovered a moment, then followed him.

That night, in the silence Roie and Dolour, lying cold and uncomfortable in their bed next door, heard Miss Sheily crying – faraway, hiccuping sobs which told them she had her head buried in a pillow. And then there was a muffled bellow from Johnny, and sharp sentences from his mother in a voice which was nasal with tears. Dolour whispered:

'Crumbs, she's a funny old tart. I say, Ro, do you reckon Miss Sheily is really his mother?'

Roie was on the verge of sleep, caught between consciousness and unconsciousness; she replied in a voice which seemed to come from down a long corridor: 'I guess that's why she hates him so much.'

Dolour scoffed: 'But she couldn't have hated him when he was a little weeny baby, even if he was all bumpy and queer.'

'Imagine if Miss Sheily loved someone,' said Roie, her voice laden with sleep, but her mind clear and remote. 'Imagine if he threw her up when he found she was going to have a baby . . . and then she tried to get rid of it . . .'

'How can you get rid of a baby?' asked Dolour. The little clear voice coming out of the darkness made Roie feel ashamed. She remembered the shock and horror she had felt when she first learned about abortion. She said quickly: 'Oh, ways.'

'Oh,' said Dolour. They were quiet for a while. Beyond the violet-blue oblong of the window, rimmed with the blowing shadows of the ragged curtains, a flight of white stars slanted across the sky. Dolour said dreamily: 'Have you ever been in love, Roie?'

Immediately she was sorry, and the blood beat in her ears, for she knew she should not have asked, and she was frightened in case Roie rebuffed her stingingly, and hurt her feelings. But all Roie said was: 'No, never at all.'

'I wonder if girls feel about boys like they do about film stars?' asked Dolour shyly.

'I won't,' said Roie. 'It'll be all different.'

'How do you know?' asked Dolour curiously. She felt Roie's slim body move beside her, and felt the faint scent of her talcum powder. All of a sudden Roie wasn't her sister any more; she was in some queer way mysterious, like a strange woman. Dolour realized sinkingly that Roie was grown up and she was still a child. She wanted to ask some more questions, but it was no use, for Roie was asleep. Dolour sighed and turned over.

Next door Miss Sheily, her head feeling as through it were swollen and yet filled with a most malignant emptiness, buried her face in the lumpy, ill-smelling mattress and tried to shut out the

190

sounds of the night; Johnny snuffling in his blankets near the window, Mrs Darcy rattling about washing supper dishes downstairs, Mr Diamond clumping on large bare feet down the stairs to the yard. She could also hear a tied-up dog howling, the vagrant song of a drunken man, and the distant rattle and clang of a homegoing tram.

As the darkness grew deeper the bugs came out of their cracks in the walls, from under the paper, and out of the cavities in the old iron bedsteads, where they hung by day in grape-like clusters. They were thin and flat and starved, but before the dawn they would return to their foul hiding-places round and glistening and bloated with blood, so fat they could hardly waddle.

Captain Phillip brought them in the rotten timbers of his First Fleet, and ever since they have remained in the old tenement houses of Sydney, ferocious, ineradicable, the haunters of the tormented sleep of the poor.

Two

Next door to Number Twelve-and-a-Half was an empty shop. It had been empty for so long that Mumma often groaned and grunted her way through a hole in the paling fence and hung her washing in the back yard. When Roie and Dolour were little they had often peered through the black glass, clotted with spider web, that lighted the little kitchen, cavernous and forlorn; and they had scampered, naked and joyous, under the rain that spouted from the gutterless roof.

When the rent man told Mumma that the shop at last was to be occupied, it was a great blow to the Darcys. What sort of people would come to live there? Someone with lots of children, forever yelling, and lobbing stones on the roof? Someone with a curious profession like fishmongering, which meant that they would get all the smells?

But it wasn't. It was a Chinese, a small, neat, compact, elderly lemon-yellow creature with polished shoes and eyes as glossy as jet. He appeared one day in the yard, bowed to Mumma across the fence, and proceeded to clean the tumble-down dwelling with energy and intensity equalled only by a cyclone's.

'There!' wailed Mumma, peering out of the upper window at the clouds of dust which billowed from his. 'Chow gramophones miawing all night. Prawns lying around the yard. Heaven knows what goings on.'

The next day the Chinese, having spent a mysterious night of bumpings and thumpings, and sharp staccato hammerings, cleaned out his window. To Dolour and the other children, standing spellbound before his door, he was at first only a ghost amidst the yellow dust. Then, before his polishing cloth, crystal lanes and highways appeared on the coated glass, and they saw him, calm and ivory and smiling, chasing the last cobwebs and dirt clots from the window.

'Wonder what his name is?' whispered Dolour, and one of the Drummy kids, cheekier than the others, yelled out: 'Hey, you! Your name John or Charlie?'

The Chinese did not reply. He picked up a small brush and pot of black paint, and trotted outside with a step-ladder. In precise and level letters he inscribed across his window the words, 'Lick Jimmy, Fruiterer.'

Dolour and the others were delighted. They had never before seen so exotic a name. An old woman, doddering past with a billy in her hand, stopped and blinked her little dead eyes.

'What's he givin' us? An invite?'

Ever afterwards, Lick Jimmy was the delight of every wit in Plymouth Street. Even the tiniest child, going to his shop for a penny soup-bunch and thrippence-worth of mandarins, inquired: 'Where do you want to be licked to-day, Jimmy?' And never once did Jimmy fail to smile, for he was not destined to learn the intricacies of Surry Hills English.

How Dolour loved little old Jimmy! A lonely hermit of a man, he did not appear to have either wife or friend. His heavily curtained windows might have concealed almost anything, and occasionally Mumma, who was legitimately curious about her neighbour, reported that she had seen lights bobbing about in more than one room at a time.

Also, occasionally, there were wild bursts of fire-crackers from the upper room, for which nobody could account, but when Hughie irascibly asked Jimmy the next day what all the bang-o had been about, all he got was a silken smile, the offer of a splendid brown pear, and the beguiling words, 'My blirtday, misser.'

Jimmy had a great idea of colour, but none at all of form. He liked to pile everything higgledy-piggledy into his window, the carrot-tops feathering out of the apples, and the celery, like pale-green ivory, mathematically grooved, lying side by side with a heap of crimson cherries. Jimmy counted the change on a worn black abacus, sliding the beads very swiftly with his smooth creamy fingers. Dolour could not work it out. Did the big beads represent the shillings and the little ones the pence? Then she realized that Jimmy thought in Chinese, and heaven alone knew what queer hieroglyphics the beads stood for.

The St Patrick's Day when she was thirteen, her mother gave her a shilling and said: 'There now, God bless you, and for his dear sake get out from under me feet until I get the stew going.'

It was a fine March day, with amber in the sun, and the leaves on the plane trees blotched with clear bright yellow. Reluctantly the summer was departing and after it whirled the leaves on the rising wind. Joyfully, her shilling so hard and substantial in her hand, Dolour ran down the hall to the door. She heard someone shouting upstairs, in a thick, coarse, wine-soaked voice, and as the top door swung open she caught a glimpse of Patrick Diamond standing in front of the mirror and toasting himself with a tumbler of something. He saw her white triangle of face, and lurching to the stair-rail, he yelled: 'Gert, yer little pope-worshipper!'

Promptly Dolour yelled back: 'Garn, yer old proddy-hopper!' She ran blithely down the street, not bothering to wonder why it was that Mr Patrick Diamond hated them all so bitterly on St Patrick's Day. He had been that way as long as she could remember. Dolour bought thrippence-worth of acid drops, lime-green and sour, currant-red and sweet; a twisted liquorice strap, four large leathery-brown buns with coarse sugar grains glued to the top. Then she returned to Lick Jimmy's to spend her remaining threepence. There was much to choose from there, for it had been a good fruit season, and oranges as red as a setting sun were two for a penny. And there were rich autumnal pears, too, and Queensland sugar bananas like little fat fingers. Dolour pondered for a long time, for there was always the problem of getting for your money something that would last in spite of many suckings or nibblings. At last she decided on the bananas, for Hughie loved bananas, and that would mean he mightn't eat his bun, and then she could have that as well as the rest of her share.

Lick Jimmy, patient and tranquil, sat and watched her, stuffing long silky shreds of pale golden tobacco into his little pipe at intervals, and caressing the back of his maternal cat, which lay at ease in a box half full of rhubarb. He had no curiosity whatsoever about Dolour Darcy; he knew all about her, for Lick Jimmy, too, liked to stand behind a dark curtain and watch the life of his neighbours.

'It's me birthday, Jimmy,' said Dolour apologetically, to atone for the delay in her purchase.

'Oh, yeah?' chirped Jimmy. He rose and flip-flopped into the inner room. When he came back he bore a kite, a lovely rose-red thing of finest paper pasted on bones of white wood. It was all there, the thick bank of string, and the fairylike tail like a procession of butterflies, for Jimmy had used the torn-up pages of an old Chinese calendar. Dolour was so overcome that she didn't know what to do. She stammered:

'Not for me? Oh, gee whiz!'

The lovely thing vibrated in her hand. It was like a pair of wings, disembodied, with lift and eagerness in them, ready for the tumult of the wind, and the placid lakes of the upper air.

'You like?' inquired Lick Jimmy, his face a web of smiling lines.

'Oh, Jimmy,' stammered Dolour. 'I *do* like!'

She dropped a kiss on the hand that rested on the counter, and ran from the shop. Lick Jimmy, a strange inscrutable expression on his face, slowly rubbed the kiss away, then went back and sat in his corner behind the window, puffing quietly at his pipe, and rubbing the back of the happy cat. And nobody knew what he thought.

Dolour tore pellmell into the kitchen 'Mumma! Oh, look!'

She pulled up short, for there was Patrick Diamond, and in a perfect devil of a St Patrick's temper. His attitude was that of an early politician immortalized in stone, one hand thrust inside his waistcoat, and the other pointing waveringly to the smoke-stained ceiling.

'Bowing and scraping to heathen idols, that's all you're doing, Mrs Darcy, and taking wilful pleasure in scarlet mummery not fit to be performed, that's what.'

It was a strange thing that every time St Pat's Day came around, and the Orange blood rose rich and rare to Mr Diamond's head, he wanted to convert Mumma. Dolour had long ago got used to it, but Mumma never did. She gave Mr Diamond a look that would brand a pig.

There she stood in front of Puffing Billy, the coal range, who, unheeded, hiccuped and belched against the back of her skirt. Her face bore two brick-red banners of anger, but unfortunately Mr Diamond spoke so fast she did not have the chance to get a word in sideways.

Dolour, however, did. 'Look what Lick Jimmy gave me, Mumma!' she yelled, waving the kite like a monstrous poppy-red moth before Mr Diamond's loathing eyes.

'It's no better than a heathen show you've got here, with your holy pictures on the wall, and your holy water in the bottle. Does it cure Hughie of the D.T.'s when he's got them, or does it take the rheumaticks from your own bones, Mrs Darcy, tell me now?'

Puffing Billy suddenly gave a croaking sound deep down in his throat, and panted rhythmically. Great puffs of soot-laden smoke curled out of every crack in his God-forsaken front and filled the kitchen with stinging fog. Mr Diamond reeled away, and Mumma burst into tears of anger, for she had all the preparations for dinner laid out on the table, and now everything was freckled thickly with smuts. She seized the potato-masher and beat Mr Diamond over the head with it.

'Go on, get out of here, you old bastard, or I'll smarther yer! Coming into me own kitchen abusing me about me holy pictures! Get out of here or I'll brand you!'

She crashed the potato masher down on Mr Diamond's bald head once more, and he with a growling oath caught her wrist and twisted it.

'Smarther me, it is, and you not far from the brink of hell yerself with yer curses and whatnot to call a decent working man.'

Puffing Billy suddenly gave a great sobbing inhalation, and all the smoke vanished as though by magic from the room, disappearing in thin wreaths and rings through the rifts in the iron. Dolour saw her mother and Mr Diamond with sudden clarity. She gave a shriek and flung herself upon the drunken man, yelling at the top of her voice and beating his stomach with her clenched fists.

At this moment Hughie came in, considerably the worse for St Patrick's Day, for he had been shouted by more than one of his friends. He seized Mr Diamond by the back of the collar, and it seemed as though all the fury of the Battle of the Boyne were in his grip. Mr Diamond glugged and gripped his throat, the words coming in spurts from his lips:

'She called me a bastard, she did, Hughie.'

Hughie gave a snort of admiration: 'Do you tell me so! Yer dirty swaddler, and what are yer but an illegitimate, to put it in a gentlemanly way. Coming in here to make up to me missus, no doubt, yer Calvinist.'

He hurled Mr Diamond into a corner, where he lay in a huddle of arms and legs. Dolour flew into her father's arms, breathing in the fumes of liquor with an almost reverent air: 'Oh, Dadda! Dadda! You fixed him.'

'It just goes to show what an Orangeman will do when he's left alone with two defenceless women,' said Hughie, very loudly, so that Mr Diamond would hear no matter how battered he might be. Mumma wiped some of the soot off her face with the corner of her apron. She was trying to hide the tears of anger and fright that were in her eyes.

'Mumma called him a "bastard",' whispered Dolour with a

shocked giggle, for she had never before heard such a word from her Mumma's lips. Hughie frowned.

'Don't you let me hear you repeating such things!' he roared, and Dolour wriggled down from his arms in terror. Mumma whimpered:

'I'm sorry, Hughie love. I am, so. But I was so angry with the soot and everything, all over me apple charlotte. And now you've killed him!' She burst into hysterical sobs.

Hughie turned to the prostrate body of his friend and snorted. 'You can't kill an Orangeman with an axe!' he said derisively. Then Dolour saw his eyes widen.

'By God, me girl, maybe yer right!' He turned Mr Diamond over on to his back, and peered down into his face. It was plum-red; more than that, it was claret, and a great purple swollen vein ran down the side of his temple from scalp to eyebrow. Mr Diamond was snoring so hard that his upper lip fluttered with every breath; his mouth hung open and showed his tobacco-stained teeth. It was a sight not only hideous, it was in some way terrible. Dolour, breathless, held on to her mother's skirt.

'God be between us and harm, the man's had a stroke!' whispered Mumma, blessing herself. 'He'll die on us, Hughie. Get a doctor, quick!'

Hughie turned a face from which all the flush and the bravado had died. 'And have to say that I hit him, and maybe killed him dead?'

Dolour was still clutching her kite. The rustle of it broke through the frozen layer of terror which filmed her consciousness. Suddenly she broke from her mother and plunged out the door.

'Dolour! Come back here!' she heard her Mumma cry after her, but she did not stop. She flew into Lick Jimmy's shop.

'Jimmy! Come quick! Mr Diamond . . . he's dying!'

Without a word Lick Jimmy rose and followed her. He padded as quietly as a tiger down the passage and into the room where Mumma and Hughie still stood in a tableau of indecision.

'Ha!' said Jimmy. He brushed past Hughie and knelt by Mr Diamond. 'Ha! Him plenty sick.'

He looked up at Hughie, and in a moment his whole face was different. The tranquil pale yellow mask was gone; there was vitality and energy in that face, and the black glossy eyes were full of intelligence. Hughie felt a passing wave of chagrin that he had been so cheated into believing that Lick Jimmy was just the same as any other Chink. He stammered: 'What do you think we better do, Lick?'

Lick Jimmy rolled up his sleeves. He said curtly to Mumma: 'Fetch basin. Plenty hot water. Stleng.'

Without a word Mumma vanished into the kitchen, and Hughie asked fearfully: 'What you gonna do, Lick?'

'Take blood,' said Lick Jimmy. 'Him have stloke soon. You watch. Him have stloke and go sssst!' He snapped his fingers.

'Oh, God, it was me that hit him,' babbled Hughie. 'And he had plenty of wine in. Oh, God, I've murdered me mate. Patrick, man, I've killed yer.'

Mumma ran back with an enamel basin and a kettle of hot water. She said no word. Somehow the demeanour of the Chinese had filled her with trust.

Jimmy and she rolled back the sleeve of the unconscious man. There was a soft click, and Dolour, with dilated eyes, saw an open penknife in Jimmy's hand.

'My God, what you up to?' croaked Hughie. Jimmy did not answer. He thrust the tip of the knife firmly into the big vein which throbbed in the crook of Mr Diamond's elbow. Dolour, frozen to the spot, saw the blood come trickling, then throbbing, then spurting, hitting the side of the basin as the milk from a cow's udder hits the side of a bucket. She couldn't turn her eyes away. All she could do was to stare at that rising ruby flood. Mumma turned her face away, and her shoulders heaved. Jimmy did not look at anybody. He saw the colour of Mr Diamond's face turn from burgundy to claret, and then to pink. As it became a sickly mushroom colour, Jimmy put his thumb upon the vein, and the blood, diverted, splashed in a great dark star upon the floor. As he applied pressure, it became a driblet, and then merely a series of reluctant beads.

Hughie ran outside and was sick in the drain. 'Oh, glory-lory-ory!' he kept moaning, wiping the sickly sweat from his brow, and trying to be ill again. When he returned Lick Jimmy had already applied a tourniquet to Mr Diamond's arm, and a square of sticking plaster was on the puncture in the skin.

'Fline, fline!' chirped Lick Jimmy cheerily. 'Come, puttee Misser Dlimon on sofa.'

They lifted the man and put him gently on the old horse-hair

198

couch. He looked very ill; his head sagging heavily, and his eyelids shivering rapidly from side to side. He looked old and pathetic, and Hughie suddenly remembered that Mr Diamond did not have a soul in the world to care whether he lived, died, or berated Catholics about pope-worshipping.

'You give cuppee tea,' suggested Jimmy. He gave the suggestion of a bow, and the Darcys had the definite impression that the whole incident was at an end and Lick Jimmy was required in his shop. They did not say a word as he padded quietly away. Hughie, pale-faced, and no longer even slightly drunk, burst out:

'He mighta killed poor Patrick!'

Mumma's face flushed. 'Don't go covering up yer embarrassment that way, Hugh Darcy. It's gratitude you ought to be feeling to Jimmy. Ah, it's a sad thing to think that poor little yeller heathen won't ever see the face of God in heaven,' she ruminated.

Mr Diamond opened his eyes and said feebly: 'What am I doing lying down in yer house, Hugh Darcy?'

Hugh replied soothingly: 'Yer fainted, Pat, and cut yer arm on the chair. But I fixed it up for you. Be quiet now, and the missus'll have a cup of tea for yer in a minute.'

Mumma threw a tea-towel over the basin of blood and whisked it out of the room. Dolour followed.

'Gee whiz, can I look? All that blood!' She peered under the tea-towel. The blood was as dark as wine, already starting to become jellified where the air touched it. The rich colour, the smoothness of it, fascinated Dolour. It seemed to her to be the most wonderful stuff she had ever seen. It was hard to believe that only half an hour before it was pulsing through Mr Diamond's heart. It was almost like looking at life itself.

'Ain't it beautiful, Mumma?' She dipped a finger in it, and the next moment received a stinging slap across the ear.

'Don't be filthy, yer dirty strap!' said Mumma hysterically, as she poured the blood down the drain, holding her face away in nausea. 'Now, get a cloth and help me flick the smuts off me charlotte.'

Dolour, with trembling lips and smarting eyes, groped around for the cloth. Then her mother's warm breast was against her shoulder, and arms went around her and held her close.

'Ah, Dolour, me darling, I'm sorry. I shouldn't have slapped you and you only a little inquisitive child. But I'm upset.'

Dolour's hot heart flamed with love for her mother. 'I should think you would be, with that old coot knocking you around.'

Her mother dumbly shook her head. 'No, it's not that. It's because I allowed a bad word to cross my tongue.'

Dolour's wide eyes were astonished, 'You mean "bastard"?' Mumma blushed.

'Will yer please forget, Dolour! I won't be content till I get it off me soul in confession. It's no word for a woman, and no word for a mother. Now, forget it, or I'll clip yer ears good and wholesome.'

So Dolour obediently did, but she never after saw Mr Patrick Diamond without muttering under her breath: 'Dirty old proddy-hopper. Old bastard.'

Three

One Friday it happened that Roie had a half day, for the machinery at the box factory had broken down, and the two hundred girls who were its slaves were liberated into the mellow afternoon. Roie had almost forgotten what a weekday afternoon was like, so much more magical than Saturday afternoon, which was noisy and drunken, or Sunday afternoon, which was dull. She walked along, saying to herself: 'I'm married, and I've been doing the shopping, and I'm going home to cook the tea for my husband, and then we're going to the pictures, and he'll buy me an ice-cream, and put his arm around me.' For Roie's heart was full of sweet timid yearnings for the security and contentment of love. Then she laughed, and forgot all about it for it was an exultant, promising afternoon. The road curved upwards and down in a long, graceful bow. The sky was purest blue, not convolvulus, or harebell, or cobalt, nor the happy vapour-laden blue of the sky over the sea; it was as though the air had at last become colour, burnished by the dauntless dying sun, and scoured to brilliance by the vast sandy winds from the desert inland. Roie felt as though anything might happen, and to ensure that it would be good, she ran up the hollowed sandstone steps of the church and into its chilly duskiness. Even there the excitement of the unexpected afternoon off did not leave her. She took no notice of the lame old woman limping around the Stations of the Cross, or of the queer man with his hat still on, who sat counting something that clinked. It was as though Roie spoke to a young and understanding person, not at all as if she were praying to God who had been hoary when the world was still a thought.

'Dear Lord, don't let Mumma get sick. Don't let Dad be drunk this weekend. Let Dolour get her arithmetic right in the exam. And Lord, don't let me get too old before anyone wants to marry me.'

Mumma was pleased to see her come in. She said:

'Dolour will be out of school in a moment. Why don't you and her go down to the Paddy's Market and get me enough vegetables to last for the week?'

Roie groaned: 'Oh, gosh, lugging pumpkin and things all that way?'

Mumma winked, and reached into her little flat black purse that was always being lost under cushions and mattresses, and at the back of the knife-box.

'Here's five bob I've been scrimping from the house money. If you see anything pretty down there, you buy it for yerself, seeing that it's yer birthday next week, Roie love.'

Roie took the two florins and the shilling. She felt their slipperiness and their clean milled edges, and a gush of love filled her heart. She hugged her mother and said roughly: 'You're an old rat stealing from the house like that, but thanks, Mumma. I guess I'll buy a lace dress from the old clothes stall and go out and get myself a millionaire.'

Dolour was so excited at the thought of a visit to the Paddy's Market that she ran round and round the kitchen like a wet puppy. She had lived in Surry Hills all her life, but she had never been to the zoo, the museum, the circus or the market.

Roie and she took a sugar-bag, rolled up in newspaper, and walked down into the city, past the smelly stable where the brewery horses, big white whiskery old fellows, spent their ammonia-scented nights, and through the narrow, drab lanes where the old ochre-coloured tenements shouldered and frowned. Washing hung out over the upper iron railings of the balconies, and dirty-nosed children darted like rabbits in and out of the warren-like alleys.

Soon they had crossed George Street, and were headed toward Darling Harbour. Everywhere there were barrowmen, with lean bowed horses plodding along in front of barbarically painted little waggons laden two and three feet high with fruit or vegetables. Here went a man with a cargo of radiant hothouse tomatoes, blushing beneath a gauzy counterpane of fern which shielded them from the sun. There a gipsy-like fat woman with a black moustache backed a frightened white pony and a barrow of lettuces between two gigantic drays laden to the gunwales with leaden, staring-eyed fish. The noise of people calling their wares became louder and louder, as an increasing tide becomes louder. The girls passed little shops of which the floors were golden with spilt wheat, or silver with spilt barley; there were others where young russet-faced Chinese peasants who could not speak English, but never made an error in the change, sold dried octopus and seaweed for the delectation of budgerigars.

'Cripes!' gasped Dolour. She had never heard so much noise, or seen so much simultaneous movement.

And there was the market, with wide gaping dark doors through which a surf of sound was flowing. Roie tried to look blasé and unconcerned, but even she felt excited, for she hadn't been to the Paddy's Market since she was a little girl. Thady had been with her and dadda that time, and they had stroked the little yellow chicks at the livestock stall, and laughed at their thin cheepings.

'What do they sell?' gasped Dolour.

'Everything,' answered Roie. They hurried forward, and were submerged in the endlessly flowing crowd. The stalls were arranged on long counters which stretched, seemingly interminably, from one end of the vast building to the other. Above each pitch, on a wooden notice-board which swung like an inn-sign in the gust of cold air from the street, was the dealer's name. 'Miss Emily Heplinstall, Licensed Old Clothes Dealer,' and 'Jose Halmera, Old Silver and Chinaware,' or just plain 'Jack Hoop, Fruit Man.'

The passages between were crammed with a seething mass of people, hot, loud-voiced, but always good-tempered. Some of them bore perforated cardboard boxes of yellow fluff . . . baby Orpingtons going home to a suburban foster-mother. Others clutched immense sheaves of dark russet chrysanthemums or held above the heads of everyone else little green enamel pots of velvety-leaved begonia. But the majority of the customers had fruit or fish.

Roie felt as though she were only twelve instead of nineteen, and she let the giggling, sparkling-eyed Dolour lead her, darting from one stall to another. Their greedy, grubby hands pawed over the collection of red and yellow and purple and green macaroni necklaces, all enamelled and strung for an hour's flaunting. They looked idly at the vast array of old books, limp and battered and inconceivably dirty, which had reached the last stop on their *via crucis* to the incinerator. Astute book dealers were here in dozens, pawing over the wrecks, calculating how presentable they would be when cleaned and mended and fumigated – and buying them six for a shilling. Dolour picked up one book with a faded brown inscription on the flyleaf: 'From Ernestine to dear Papa, 1873.' In her dirty, bitten-nailed little hands the old book seemed to protest its lost gentility and gave forth a tiny odour of violets and mothballs. Roie sniffed.

'Funny. Wonder what happened to Ernestine?'

203

'Got óld and conked out, I guess,' said Dolour. She threw the book down and picked up an odd volume of Shakespeare; she fluttered the torn pages and said: 'I like that bit about the billows curling their monstrous heads and hanging them with deafening clamour in the slippery shrouds.'

'What's it mean?' asked Roie. Dolour felt suddenly embarrassed, as though she had been showing off, and said: 'I just learned it off by heart, silly tripe. Look, ain't he got a dome!' The book thumped down on to the pile, and the portrait of Shakespeare went on staring out into the crowd which was so much like his own loud-voiced, unruly Elizabethan one.

Best of all, Dolour and Roie liked the old-clothes stalls. There were dozens of these; some of them sold shoes, all neatly arranged like lines of cargo vessels drawn up at a wharf, and every one plainly bearing the imprint of the corns and bunions of someone's feet. Here was a broad-bowed merchantman that had plainly gone hundreds of miles on shopping tours; here was a dainty triangular-toed pair of wrinkled black patents with a heel worn down the way a fat woman wears it, into a fray of broken wood. And there were tiny shoes, too; little white ones with scuffed toes and needle marks on the straps where the button had been moved back and back until at last there was no more room for expansion. And there was one pair of Russian boots with a haughty furry top and a long aristocratic toe. Dolour stared in hypnotic fascination; it seemed to her that at any moment the boots would leap forward and begin kicking in some wild Cossack dance.

'Gee, look,' breathed Roie suddenly. She pushed aside an Indian lascar in a red velveteen fez. He looked at her with glazy burning eyes and remarked: 'Chi-chi.'

There on the counter was a lovely red silk shawl with a trailing fringe knotted in a strange and exotic pattern. Seagreen flowers bloomed on the silk, and the softness of their padded needlework was like a jewel amongst all the dross of black Italian cloth bloomers and darned lisle stockings and faded print working dresses.

'How much?' asked Dolour timidly of the woman behind the counter, a delicate, genteel little woman with a peculiar cloche hat made of rusty black rooster feathers. She gave Dolour a sharp look, and said in a high, noisy voice: 'Whatcher want it for? To cut up and dress up with?'

Roie stammered: 'Oh, no, I just thought that . . .'

204

The woman's eyes were sharper than needles. 'Whatcher think?'
Roie said boldly: 'I just wanted it to look at.'

The woman patted the shawl. The sharpness went from her face.
'It's pretty, ain't it? Me sister made it. Ten years on her back, she was.
'Ip disease. I didn't want to get it destroyed, that's why I asked.' She
added with sudden briskness, 'Ten shillings.'

The light died out of Roie's eyes. 'I only got five,' she said.

Dolour nudged her elbow. 'There's the other five Mumma gave
us for the vegetables,' she reminded. The woman's acute ears caught
her hoarse whisper, so she said obstinately, 'Ten bob. Take it or
leave it.'

Roie felt a pang in her heart. She knew she could not leave the
lovely shawl. Wordlessly she handed over the two five shillingses,
and with them went all Mumma's potatoes, the soup tomatoes, the
good piece of ironbark pumpkin, the sixpenn'orth of yellow belly,
and the strip of barracouta, nice and thick, which she had down on
the list.

With the money safe in her possession, the woman pushed her
hat up on her forehead so that the tips of the coq feathers mingled
with her eyebrows, and said in a friendly, relieved tone: 'I'm real
pleased you're taking it dearie. It's been knocking around on the
counter ever since me poor sister died, and getting dirtier every
week. Two pounds I was asking for it to start with, and I wouldn't
let it go to any old trollop who'd wipe the floor with it quicker than
kiss yer foot. Here, dearie, try it on, and see how it looks on yer.'

She pushed a brass-rimmed mirror over towards Roie. Dolour
giggled:

'How would you wear a shawl, Ro? Like an old granny?'

Roie did not say a word. A thousand Irish girls who had
bequeathed to her their blood and manner of thinking guided her
fingers. She draped it gently about her head, and looped the fringe
over her shoulders. Oblivious of the crowd that looked at her, and
then looked somewhere else, at odd boots, or patched buckets, or
other things that better merited attention, she gazed into the mirror
at the pale creamy face, with the strangely clear glossy skin of the
underfed, the dark blue eyes, and the little scarlet rosette of a
mouth, so much darker than the silk.

'I'm awfully glad you bought it, Roie!' cried Dolour, her eyes
shining. Roie looked shyly across the counter for the woman's
approval, but she was gone, and was showing some underpants to

an old man further along. In her place was a young man. He was not much more than a boy, with black tousled hair and a thin, sallow Jewish face. One felt that some exotic accent should touch his voice, but it was broad Surry Hills, with every vowel lengthened into two.

'Oh, rose of all the world,' he said. Roie stared, taken aback. He might have said: 'Cripes, you look grouse in that,' or 'Trust a sheila to try a thing on as soon as she buys it,' or even 'Get a move on, willya. Yer blockin' the customers' way.'

Any of these things Roie would have accepted as natural, but the other made her blush painfully. She snatched the shawl from her head, rolled it up haphazardly, and said furiously: 'Shut yer big mouth will you?'

The young man did not seem to mind. He said: 'I've seen you before.'

'Oh, yeah?' flashed Roie. 'I've never been here before.'

'I didn't say it was here, did I? I seen you in Coronation Street.'

Roie was confused. She muttered something and began to move away. The young man called: 'What's yer hurry? Scared I'll bite?'

Dolour meantime had been staring very hard at him. Then she glanced at the board above his head. 'Joseph Mendel,' it read, 'Licensed Vendor of Old Wares.'

'Mendel!' squeaked Dolour. 'You ain't old Joseph Mendel?'

The young man seemed to find the question distasteful. 'Hell, what do you think? I'm his nephew, Tommy.'

It was almost as though they had been introduced by some close friend and relative. Both Roie and Dolour had been in and out of the Mendel establishment in Coronation Street a score of times, for the Darcy family was always popping something, and then popping something else to redeem the first pledge.

'Gee,' stammered Roie. 'I'm sorry if I was rude. You just got my goat laughing at me.'

'I wasn't laughing at you,' he protested. 'You just looked like a picture my Uncle Joseph has in his shop.'

'Oh.' Roie did not know what to say. She looked away foolishly, and pretended to be watching a lascar pawing over the garments at the next pitch. Dolour chirped: 'She's Rowena Darcy and I'm Dolour Darcy.'

The two girls stared at him, and he stared back. Dolour noticed that his hair was loose and curly, and he had a little yellow scar under one eye, and the marks of three boils on his neck. He had a gay green-printed tie, and a tweed suit which seemed too cumbrous and important for his slender boyish body. Roie noticed only that his eyes were dark and melancholy. She had the strangest feeling that her blood was running backwards; down arteries and veins it cascaded where it should have climbed, and through the valves of her heart it pulsed in reverse. She felt quite giddy and lightheaded, but it was a wonderful, intoxicating feeling. All the beauty and promise of the day seemed to come to fruition in this moment.

Tommy said: 'Can I come round and take you to the flicks some time?'

Roie said ungraciously: 'Oh, I suppose so. I live at Twelve-and-a-Half Plymouth Street.'

'Can I come tonight?'

'I'm not doing anything,' said Roie.

She wanted, and he wanted, to say words that were not crude and banal, but their imagination fell flat, unsupported by education or intuition. The boy, shy and sidelong with adolescence's indecisive shames and inferiorities, wanted to say something that would show this girl that he was a man. She, simpler, wanted nothing more than that he liked her. But inarticulate as most of their class, they could do no more than utter bald phrases forgotten as soon as they were spoken. He said harshly: 'First I gotta show you something. Take a squiz over here.'

Puzzled, Dolour and Roie craned over the counter, and they saw that he wore a heavy boot on one foot. For a moment Roie unconsciously felt the same sickness of repugnance and fear that she felt when she looked at poor Johnny Sheily. But it was only for a moment. It was different with Tommy Mendel. She felt a vast surge of pity which so filled her throat she could not speak. She stammered, and the boy's eyes closed to a pinpoint of bitter blackness.

'Now's yer cue to say you ain't going to be seen with no hop-and-go-fetch-it,' he said. Roie blushed. She did not know what to say. She looked away and laughed, saying: 'Gosh, you do say silly things, don't you?'

Dolour cried eagerly: 'There's a whacko cowboy pitcher on at the Palace to-night. Why don't you go to that, Ro?'

'I'd like that,' said Roie shyly. The boy laughed out loud with relief.

207

'Me, too,' he said.

Roie said awkwardly, 'Well, I better be going.' She backed out into the flowing crowd and walked rapidly. Dolour trotted beside her, skipping to catch up.

'You forgot to say what time he was to pick you up,' she cried anxiously.

'He knows the pitcher starts at eight. He isn't a boob,' answered Roie with tranquil assurance. 'He'll be around about a quarter past seven. You see.'

Dolour was so excited one would have thought that Tommy was going to be her boy. 'He's handsome, ain't he?'

'You reckon?' asked Roie proudly.

'What give him the boils on his neck?' wondered Dolour. Roie gave her a look of angry scorn.

'What are you talking about? He ain't got no boils. You're crazy.'

'But he has, Ro,' persisted Dolour. 'I saw them. Little marks . . .'

'Ah, shut up!' snapped Roie. She, too, had seen the scars, but she steadfastly shut her mind to them. Boils did not fit in with her dreamlike and exhilarated mood. She thought: 'I'll wear my pink dress, and do my hair up in front. I'll clean my white shoes . . .'

In silence they walked through the long lanes of little primitive bazaar-shops, each with its flapping sign above. All the way home Roie spoke little save cross and grumpy monosyllables. She had the feeling that worshippers have had at the portals of great temples, that to make a sound is to commit a sacrilege. Inarticulate, dumb at her heart, Roie could only feel that the chapter of her girlhood was nearly closed.

'You're going to get it,' promised Dolour, half-fearful, expectant, as they entered the long dark hall of Number Twelve-and-a-Half. 'Wait till Mumma sees what sort of vegetables you've bought!'

'Well, it's your fault too,' answered Roie unfairly. 'You give me the idea.'

'Well, by gosh!' exploded Dolour. 'You're a squib, if ever there was one, Roie.'

'For the love of heaven will yer stop squabbling like magpies under me very nose?' bawled Mr Patrick Diamond from the landing. He was at that time on very good terms with Mumma and Hughie, as St Patrick's Day was safely behind, so Dolour and Roie, glancing at each other, and muttering 'Old stinker!' and 'Dirty old proddy-hopper!' under their breaths, went silently into their own apartment and slammed the door.

Mumma had been waiting their return impatiently, for Hughie was due home, and she feared that he would be drunk, and anxious to start a fight.

'You've been a time, you have!' she cried. 'Give me the fish so I can get it started before he comes in. And Dolour you start skinning the pumpkin.'

Dolour giggled. 'Go on, show Mumma the pumpkin, Roie!'

Roie silently unrolled the newspaper in which she had wrapped the shawl. The silk, lustrous, poppy-red spilled upon the table, and under its glossy fringe the old heat-marked timber looked as cheap as deal. Mumma, amazed, picked up a corner of it.

'It's pretty,' she said. 'It'd knock the two eyes out of yer head.'

'I didn't get any pumpkin,' confessed Roie.

'Or fish, either,' added Dolour, greedy for sensation.

Mumma wanted to be angry, but she couldn't, for she remembered the time when her Ma had given her a shilling for some sausages, and instead she had bought a little cup of glossy blue china she had coveted for a long time. She gently stroked the silk with her raspy fingers.

'Ah, well,' she said, trying to sound as though they were some justification for Roie's action, 'I suppose this will last.'

She dug in the little black purse and gave two shillings to Dolour.

'Here, now, go to the fried fish shop and get a couple of thick battered pieces for your Dadda's tea. Potatoes will do us.'

Dolour could hardly wait until she had finished speaking, for she wanted to break the news before Roie did.

'Roie made a hit with a boy, too,' she boasted, her eyes dancing. 'Didn't you, Ro?'

'Aw, shut up,' answered her sister angrily as she turned away and began folding the shawl. Mumma shut her lips tight and nodded with a pleased, knowing look, as though this were the beginning and it was no surprise to her. Dolour pranced to the door. 'He's got brown eyes and a funny foot.'

'Quit that, or I'll clout you!' shouted Roie, her temper flaming with the swiftness common to those who know little about the simulation of feelings they do not possess.

With a jeering giggle Dolour vanished up the hall. On the way she passed Johnny Sheily, who was squatting in the shadow of the stairs. She peered down at him and he smiled shyly, ducking his head away. Lately he had taken to making strange grimaces, pulling down the corner of his lip until it was two inches long, and showing the whites of his big aimless eyes until he looked like a bloodhound. He did this now, and Dolour protested: 'Oh, crumbs, Johnny, you give me the creeps.' She patted him on the top of his huge bristly head and skipped onwards, hearing from the top of the stairs the suspicious voice of Miss Sheily:

'What're you doing down there, Johnny?'

'Nothing, umma,' crooned Johnny from the darkness.

A few minutes later Dolour ran out of the fish shop, a grease-stained, pleasantly warm parcel in her hand. She had ideas of tearing a hole in one corner and extracting some of the salt-encrusted bluish potato chips that nestled about the little knobbly yellow lumps of fish.

It was five o'clock and the street was full of traffic. The tramp of a thousand factory workers sounded like a hundred drums – beat, beat, beat – the tributaries of the lanes and alleyways resounding sharper and hollower, all running into the central channel of Plymouth Street. Great red trucks laden with empty milk cans, oil drums, jolting planks, or scattered with the dropped cabbage leaves and the odd carrots of a load sold at the markets, rattled and boomed down the streets, and amongst them darted the fleet-footed starveling urchins, bearing billies of milk and unwrapped loaves of bread.

Dolour was fifty yards from her gate when all of a sudden out came Johnny Sheily. It was the very first time she had seen him outside the house or the backyard. At first she thought that Miss Sheily was going to take him for a walk, and then she saw that he was alone. He stood there, confused at the tumult of traffic, his big oblong head cocked sideways and his lip pulled long and straight.

Dolour yelled, half anxious: 'You'd better go back before your mother catches you.'

He turned slowly on his big flat feet and stared up the road at her, waving his fat sausage fingers. Several little boys barging past stopped and jeered: 'Lookut the loony! Lookut the loony!'

Johnny did not like their voices. His lips trembled. Perhaps they seemed as big as elephants to him, or small as rats, with dirty leering faces and little red mouths open to bite. He backed off the street into the gutter, and a car moving out from the kerb caught him with its fender and threw him into the path of a heavy brewery truck that was jolting homewards. He fell sprawling before the wheels.

Dolour heard the skip and crash of the barrels in the truck as its

210

wheel rose and fell. She stood as still as though she had been frozen, her mouth open, her hand raised, even a smile still upon her face. She stood still and stared at the red squashed melon on the road, with the little teeth scattered about like grains of bloodstained corn. It was truly like a dream, seeing his poor tattered body lying there, and no head at all. She was not aware of the screams of passers-by, or of police whistles, or of the truck-driver tumbling out of his cab and being violently ill quite near her, moaning all the time, 'Oh, God forgive me, I didn't mean it. Oh, God forgive me, I didn't mean it.'

Dolour turned and walked stiffly inside. Miss Sheily brushed past her in the hall, saying shrilly, 'Have you seen Johnny? Have you seen Johnny?'

Dolour still with a smile fixed immovably on her face, did not answer. She walked sedately into the kitchen and stood in the doorway. She saw Hughie's red face and Mumma's worried one, and then she began to scream and scream, on a thin high-pitched note, like a rabbit in a trap.

'What's the matter with yer?' bawled Hughie in alarm.

Mumma ran up to her and shook her. 'For God's sake, darling, what's got into yer?'

Dolour's mouth was wide open, her eyes staring blindly. She went on screaming. Hughie brought the flat of his hand in a sharp slap across her cheek, and she stopped screaming instantly. Slowly she rubbed her cheek, and then toppled forward in a dead faint.

It was not really a faint; it was a nightmare, an ebony thing blotched with scarlet, that flapped about her with roaring and fading sounds that nearly deafened her, and then shrank away to a tiny niggling noise like a mouse at the end of a long passage. Dolour fought to remain unconscious, but it was no use. She became aware of something cold and prickling on her forehead, and the bitter stifling smell of ammonia in her nostrils. Then her mother said, very loud and close: 'She's over it now. She's coming out of it now.'

Then Dolour heard the sound of someone sobbing loudly; and with astonishment she realized it was Roie.

'What's the matter with Roie?' she asked with a sort of feeble irritability. The sound of her voice was at first shrill, then hoarse, and then, as though shaking itself into focus, was normal. The room seemed to be full of people. Mr Diamond, pale and aimless, was wandering about falling over chairs and begging people's pardon, and then rushing out to the kitchen to get a cup of smoky hot water from the kettle, for the shock of the accident had brought his indigestion on.

Mumma's face was streaked with tear-marks, and Dadda's nose was red, and not only with wine. And Roie was crying in the corner, all huddled up like a wet sparrow in winter.

'What's the matter with Roie?' asked Dolour. 'She didn't see the accident. I did.'

'She ran out and saw it afterwards,' said Mumma stroking her head. 'But you mustn't worry about Johnny any more, darling. It's all over for him now, God rest his poor soul, and maybe it's a good thing he's out of it, him being as he was.'

Dolour said to herself: 'I saw Johnny killed. I was right there.' She tried it over two or three times, but already the shock and horror of it was fading from her resilient mind. She found that she could even feel a certain pride that she had been there. Of all the people who had been walking up and down Plymouth Street she had been the last one to speak to Johnny.

Roie went on crying. She did not know what for. She only knew that the ache in her throat and the constriction in her chest needed tears. The picture of Johnny was before the eyes of her mind. She closed her lids, and it was there; she opened them, and it was bright as paint upon the wall.

'Ah, darling, it's all for the best,' soothed Hughie, putting a distraught clumsy hand upon her hair. 'Who'd want to go on living like Johnny, him all minced up at birth and never got over it?'

'He was happy,' sobbed Roie. 'He didn't know there was anything the matter with him.'

'I'll bet Miss Sheily's glad. I'll bet she's up at the hospital laughing like anything,' cried Dolour, sitting bolt upright and saying the words with a sour intensity that mated oddly with her childish voice.

'Shut up that talk,' said Hughie fiercely.

Dolour yelled: 'She always hated him! She did! She did!' She burst into savage tears. 'She was always beating him.'

'She was a good mother,' said Mumma contrarily. 'She always fed him well, and he was never allowed out when there was danger. Nobody can go slinging dirt at Miss Sheily and saying she neglected him.'

'Now, Mrs Darcy, missus' protested Patrick Diamond. 'And you only a few weeks ago going up there and finding him tied up and lashed like a dog.'

But Mumma in the strength of her sorrow for Miss Sheily refused to remember it, and they argued inconsequentially, punctuated by Roie's weeping.

Roie wanted to go out and find a quiet, dark place amongst the trees somewhere, and lie down and think it all out and ease the hurt in her chest. But there was nowhere to go. Like all the poor, she had nowhere to be private except in the lavatory, and even that had no lock on the door, so she could not be sure of being uninterrupted. The sorrow of this, so intimate a need for solitariness, that had never in all her life been satisfied, became all mixed up with her grief for Johnny and she cried: 'I can't stand it! I can't stand it!' Just as she had done when she was a little girl with the toothache.

There was a knock on the door. Mr Diamond answered it, with an air of subdued importance mingled with trepidation, for he feared that it might be Miss Sheily back from the hospital. But instead, it was a strange young man with dark sombre eyes and hair sleeked down with oil.

'Excuse me,' he said, 'but does Miss Darcy live here?'

'Two Miss Darcys live here,' answered Mr Diamond. 'Which one do you want to see?'

'I want to see the big one,' said the young man, losing his careful composure and looking for an instant as though he were inwardly trembling with nervousness.

Dolour's eyes glistened through her tears. 'Gee,' she croaked, 'I forgot. It's him, Ro.'

'Send him away,' sobbed Roie. 'I can't see him tonight. I don't want to see him.'

'Of course you do,' said Mumma practically, for she had made up her mind to see this young man who wanted to be her daughter's escort to the pictures. She marched to the door, opened it wide, and said: 'Come in, son. You'll have to excuse the mess, because there's just been a terrible accident and we're all upset.'

'Not in the family,' said Hughie, gruffly, seeing the reluctance upon the boy's face. 'Just in the house.'

'I saw it happen,' said Dolour proudly. Roie hid her swollen and tear-blotched face in her hands. She felt a hand on her shoulder, less assured than her father's, yet warmer, and more comforting. The tears welled unbidden out of her eyes.

'I'm sorry I can't go out,' she choked. 'Please, please go away now.'

She rose and ran into the bedroom, throwing herself on her face on the bed. The young man looked at Mumma.

'Please can I go in and see if I can do anything for her?' he asked. Mumma was pleased and proud at his delicacy in asking first. She said: 'I wish to heaven you would.' She explained about Johnny. The young man's face grew sickly. He shook his head silently.

'Crook business. Kids are always getting run over in these streets.' An idea sprang into his mind. He shyly extended his foot with the big boot. 'A motor bike did that to me when I was a nipper. One leg grew shorter than the other.'

Ready tears welled into Mumma's eyes. 'You poor boy. Go on in to Roie, and I'll get a cup of tea for yez both.'

The boy felt warm and exultant. It was not everyone who would have thought so well on the spur of the moment. He felt proud of himself, and for the first time since his foot had been paralysed a few years before, he almost looked upon his disfiguring boot as an asset. It had gained him attention and sympathy. He went through the glass doors into the bedroom.

It was dim and cold in there, for there was no window, and the sun had not touched its walls for nearly seventy years. There was a smell of old clothes, and mustiness, and down one wall was the great map-like stain of last winter's rain. The dressing-table was a litter of rubbish, old powder-puffs and broken boxes; a grubby, balding hair-brush, and some cheap photographs. From one wall the melancholy face of the Madonna looked down into the half dusk.

Tommy sat down upon the bed. He was trembling with excitement. The way the edge of it swayed and dipped under his weight, the dim intimacy of the room, and the long slim body of the girl, lying there face downwards beside him, made him feel as though he were taking part in something curiously dramatic. He was twenty, and had never had a girl. Shy, sullen, and tormented with the frustrations and brooding ambitions of adolescence, he had longed futilely for a girl of his own, about whom he could boast to his pals, and thus prove himself, in spite of his foot, a man amongst men.

He put a hand on her back. It was damp with sweat, though the room was chill. He tried to think of something to say. He formed two or three sentences in his mind but none seemed memorable enough. Finally, he said: 'Forget it, kid.'

214

Roie wiped the back of her hand across her wet face. 'I'll never forget it as long as I live' she choked.

Tommy said: 'I did.' She stared at him, sitting up beside him, knowing that in the gloom he could not see her disfigured face. He told her the same lie he had told her Mumma, elaborating on it until it seemed to him so real and vivid that a momentary shock of horror filled his soul. It was almost as though it had really happened . . . the little dark Jewish boy running across the street, and the motor bike crashing into him . . . the crush of bone, and the screams and the blood trickling. Tommy's voice shuddered into hoarseness. Ah, God, it might have well happened that way!

In an instant Roie forgot all her own pain, and flung her arms around him. Clumsily he returned the embrace. They put their soft cheeks together.

'Ah, Tommy, Tommy . . . you must have got a terrible fright.' Her voice broke again.

'Yeah. I still dream about it.'

She held him tighter. In a moment their position had changed. She was comforting and protecting him, who had so wanted to comfort.

Four

The day Miss Sheily came home from her sister's place, where she had gone for a little rest after Johnny's death, was a great one for Number Twelve-and-a-Half. She did not look much different. Her black suit was as neatly pressed, the big round gold brooch at her collar just as precisely fastened. Only her face, as white as dough, gave the impression that Miss Sheily had died some time before. She came in the front door without a word and stumped upstairs on her sharp-heeled shoes. Mumma ran to the door and stood there panting for a word. But there was none. Mumma was very disappointed. She had secretly expected something dramatic and surprising to happen, such as Miss Sheily drinking phenyl and dying in convulsions, or perhaps hanging herself from the very same gas-jet where she had tied Johnny.

But Miss Sheily did none of those things. She made toast, for they could hear her scraping the burnt pieces with a knife; she went out and did her shopping down the mean street, as she had always done; and on Saturdays she disappeared for the whole afternoon and came home late, as had been her custom for years. And if she met anyone she spoke ordinarily and that was all. Yes, Mumma was disappointed.

'She's got no heart, that one,' she said to Hughie. 'No doubt she's pleased the poor misfortunate is gone. The puzzle to me is why she don't go and live at her sister's.'

'Because probably her sister won't have a drunk on her hands,' said Hughie bluntly. Mumma scoffed. Miss Sheily was a lady, even though she had had an illegal child. Miss Sheily didn't drink.

'You ain't heard her at night-time, clinking bottles,' said Roie.

'And you ain't met her in the hallway, either, and smelt her breath,' added Hughie.

'You're the one who'd recognize it, then,' flared Mumma. 'Drinking her breath in like perfume, there's no doubt, you old tosspot.'

'Tosspot or not,' bellowed Hughie, aggrieved, 'Miss Sheily knows how to throw up her little finger, you take it from me. And I'll thank you to keep me own weaknesses out of the conversation.'

216

But Mumma did not give up hope, and the next day when Miss Sheily came down to do her bit of washing in the copper, Mumma went out and fussed about there with the broom, looking yearningly meanwhile at Miss Sheily. Ah, she had a queer face, that one, with a beaky high-class nose, and eyes deep back in like jet pieces. Mumma's mind, which was innocent and fiercely chaste, in spite of the life she had led, tiptoed down avenues of inquiring thought about Miss Sheily. Somehow she could not imagine her being kissed or beloved by any man, no matter how remote. And yet she had had Johnny, and on the wrong side of the counterpane, too. Mumma blushed, and dragged her errant mind back from its wanderings, scolding it ferociously. Suddenly Miss Sheily turned around and said:

'You're not going to get any change out of me, Mrs Darcy, so you needn't be snooping around for any information about my feelings.'

'Well, indeed . . .' stammered Mumma, so taken aback her mouth fell open. Miss Sheily's eyes sparked cold glitters.

'I'm not sorry he's gone, if that's any use to you,' she said, watching Mumma's consternation with an icy interest. Mumma's mother-heart burned for poor Johnny.

'Ah, the dirty drop's in yer, there's no mistake!' she exploded, and waddled out of the laundry. All the morning she repeated to herself the things she might have said to Miss Sheily, brilliant, cutting things, but in the afternoon when she saw her again, the rancour had all gone, and they spoke civilly to each other, with a sort of wary politeness.

But if Mumma were curious, the rest of the establishment cared little about Miss Sheily's strange and secretive character.

Dolour was happy, for the end of the year was approaching, and though examinations were yet to be faced the brightly-gilded picture of Christmas filled her mind like a lovely ghost.

In the schoolroom they were already making preparations. All the year's drawings and mottoes and scrolls had been rubbed off the blackboard into a cloud of mingled red and yellow and green dust which vanished for ever as Dolour shook the duster out the window. It was just as though she could see the year vanishing, first brilliant, and then vague and dispersed, whirling and scattering, day after day, and hour after hour.

'Dolour, what are you dreaming about?' inquired Sister Theophilus from her desk. Dolour withdrew her head and blushed.

Sister, a tall slender figure in a classically designed brown habit, her wide sleeves rolled up a little so that her slim sallow arms showed, went to the board, six beautiful untouched, velvety-pointed sticks of coloured chalk before her.

'It is two months to Christmas,' observed Sister Theophilus. 'But I think we will decorate the blackboard so that we may have Christmas in our thoughts.'

Spellbound, the children watched her draw in one top corner a large five-pointed shape. Upon this she stuck a star she had already cut out from silver foil. It fitted perfectly, and to her pupils this seemed to be a good omen. Some of them shivered with joy, for already they could scent in the air the peculiar smell of orange peel and boiled pudding and incense which was Christmas's.

Sister Theophilus took the blue powdery chalk delicately in two fingers, and a thumb, and shaded in a long strip of sky. As she did so, chalk dust fell in a soft rain to the floor.

'What you going to draw in the other corner, Sister?' called Harry Drummy, who was busy pricking his name on the top of his desk, and knew that silence would draw suspicion upon him.

'You'll see.'

Dolour sat up and stared intently. She saw a strange snake-like thing grow under the mole-coloured chalk in Sister's hand.

'It's . . . it's a dragon.'

'No.'

'It's a lizard.'

'No.'

'What is it, then, Sister?'

'You'll see.'

The serpentine head grew; it had big heavy-lidded eyes and a sardonic shaped mouth. It had a long neck which swooped upwards into a hump and downwards into a tasselled tail.

'It's a camel! It's a camel!' shrilled Harry Drummy, who had seen one in a circus.

'It's the Three Wise Men,' said Dolour softly. The picture grew rapidly under Sister's fingers. It was beautiful to see how the blunt chalk made delicate little lines, and how blue smudged into green to make a twilight sky, and how the Wise Kings had each a different turban. And soon there they all were, travelling over the lonely brown desert to find the little Child whose house wore a star above its chimney.

218

There was a sharp rap at the door. Sister put down her chalk and dusted her fingers.

'Now,' she said. 'You all know the story of the Three Kings. Write down all you know about them. Harry Drummy, what are you doing with that compass?'

'Nothing, Sister,' answered Harry promptly.

'Then you can write an essay on that, too,' said Sister, sweeping to the door. She closed it firmly behind her, but Dolour caught one glimpse of the visitor.

'Crumbs!' she breathed. 'It's old Delie Stock!'

'What's she seeing Sister for?'

'Someone's been bunging goolies through her window.'

'She's going to tell on someone.'

'She might get tough with Sister. She might call her somepin.'

They were all dumb at the thought, for although terms that in better districts would have caused disgust and shock were used in nearly all their homes, and certainly on every street corner, the idea of them applied to Sister Theophilus was alien, and somehow frightening.

But Delie Stock hadn't come because of stones bunged through her windows, though there were plenty of them. She had come with a purse full of money.

Sister knew her, of course. Hurrying home through a winter afternoon, long ago, she had seen a young Delie Stock squatting on the church steps and being sick between her shoes; and another time she had seen her violently hammering a policeman on the head as he half-carried, half-dragged her to a small dark green van that was waiting. And, even in the seclusion of the Convent, Sister had heard the rumours, the legends and the fabulous scandal that had sprung up about this woman.

Her heart beat a little faster, for though she was secure in the poise and tranquillity of her profession, yet she felt a little frightened. She looked at the other woman, and in the second before she spoke a welcome she had taken in the expensive coat and hat, food-stained and dribbled all over with cigarette ash: the grey hair frousled and yellow at the ends; the old humpy black shoes; and the face. Above all she saw the face of Delie Stock.

Delie Stock's was an interesting face, not yet fifty years old, but with a sort of ancient, timeless air about it. It was not really dirty, and yet one felt that Delie Stock had not washed it for a long, long time. It had a grey-ivory look, and wrinkles like tiny vertical lines sketched with a fine pen, covered it in a net. Out of this, rimmed with short spiky eyelashes, looked Delie Stock's eyes, furtive, small with middle-age, brazen with amorality, and yet with a queer habit of scuttling away from the stare of the beholder. They might have been the eyes of a number of people ... of a woman with no sense of morality at all, whose conscience never kept her awake at night ... of a devil who chose their opaque brown to hide his greedy ferocity ... or just of a dirty old prostitute with no mind, no soul, and not much body.

Sister's own eyes, fascinated, kept returning to them, as to a window through which could be seen some mysterious and appalling scene. It was only by the utmost effort of politeness that she looked away.

'How do you do? Do you wish to see me?'

'I'm Delie Stock, Mrs Stock,' said the woman, her voice deepened and rasped by gallons of rough native wine. Sister bowed slightly and extended her hand. Delie Stock looked surprised, and giggled awkwardly, looking away to cover her momentary embarrassment.

'I'm Sister Theophilus.'

'Well, it's this way, Sister. I was thinking of the kids the other day ... all the kids here, the Drummys and the Stevenses, and the Brodies and all the rest, poor dirty-nosed little arabs. And I said to meself, Delie, it's time you did something about them little bastards. Give 'em a bit of fun. You see what I mean, Sister?' The hot eyes looked into the nun's for a moment, and then hurried away.

Sister said, yes, she did, but what ...?

Delie Stock gave another chuckle, a pleased, proud guffaw. It was plain that some mystic psychological change was taking place in her mind. She was growing in stature as her charity unfolded itself. 'So I'm going to give 'em a picnic, see? The whole shebang. Hire a bus. Two buses. Ice-cream, plenty of tucker. Beach and everythink. And maybe we can get a magician bloke to give 'em the works. How many kids in this school, Sister Theoctopus?'

'Why ... there's ... there's ... two hundred odd,' stammered Sister Theophilus.

'Here, then,' said Delie Stock. She opened her stuffed shabby purse, and it was crammed to the lip with notes.

'Holy Mary, Mother of God,' said Sister Theophilus, but it was a prayer and not an exclamation. She had never seen so much money before. Delie Stock shook it all out on the bench amongst the children's hats and caps and lunch-packets. There were dirty, crumpled green notes, and smooth blue linen ones, and lavender ones which had faded to tobacco-stained lilac. They fell in a rustling heap which the wind riffled and teased. Delie Stock wished that she had taken another nip before she left. The tall, brown-faced nun, old and yet young-eyed, with her clean face that had never known powder or even scented soap, somehow made her feel all feet, and too loud-voiced. She gave a hitch to her coat collar and reminded herself that she owned six houses and more than forty girls, and she had the right to hold her head up with anyone. So she gave the notes a slap and cried loudly:

'There they are, take 'em or leave 'em.'

Sister Theophilus had a temptation to say: 'Oh crumbs!' like Harry Drummy or Dolour Darcy, for her whole mind was a circus of delight. In the space of twenty seconds she saw the whole picnic, Deewhy perhaps, or Collaroy, and the great double-decker buses, pied red and yellow, drawing up, and all her two hundred children pouring, shrill and hysterical with excitement, towards the biscuit-brown beach and the great majestic foam-topped breakers. She smelt the sea, and she saw the sunshine of gum-leaves, glossy and curved like a rooster's tail-feathers; she shook sand out of sandwiches, and smeared liniment on stone bruises; she taught the little ones how to make forts, and she gathered tiny yellow grooved shells like grains of wheat. Then she said: 'Oh, Mrs Stock! Oh, Mrs Stock! But how much is there?'

'A hundred and thirty,' said Delie Stock. Then she boasted a little, for she was feeling proud and happy. 'I would have made it more, but . . . well, perhaps I can put another tenner to it.'

'Oh, no,' cried Sister Theophilus, aghast. 'It's more than enough. Oh, Mrs Stock . . . the children will . . . I just can't say thank you sufficiently.'

There was a firm step on the porch, the brush of boots on the mat, for Father Cooley had never lost the Irish habit of scraping the bog off his feet. Then in he walked. He was a stout, compact man with pleasant red face and silky white hair. His feet were large, and his strong practical boots showed strangely prosaic under the skirt of his soutane.

'Oh, pardon me, Sister, I didn't know you had a visitor.' His eyes flickered with quiet civility over Delie Stock, for though he knew all about her, he had no dealings with her, and she was no business of his. Then he saw the notes on the table.

'The Lord look down on us!'

Sister Theophilus clasped her hands. 'Isn't it wonderful, Father? Mrs Stock has donated all this money for the children . . . for a picnic for Christmas!'

'Ice-cream for the poor little . . . beggars,' said Delie Stock.

The priest put his hand on the faintly crackling notes; they were like dried leaves, impregnated with the powder and dirt and tobacco crumbs of a thousand pockets. He did not have the rapid imagination of Sister Theophilus; his, tranquil, silent, slow, saw only the entry in his ledger: 'One hundred and thirty pounds donated to school by Delie Stock.'

'Hope there's enough,' blared Delie Stock, with something of defiance and preparatory argumentativeness creeping into her voice, for she did not like the priest's silence.

Sister Theophilus, with clasped hands, rushed in: 'I thought perhaps Collaroy . . . I went there once for a holiday . . . it's a lovely beach . . . and a nice ride in a bus . . .' her voice trailed away. For the priest shook his head. He chased his imagination back into its cubbyhole in his brain and shut the door sharply.

'I'm sorry, Mrs Stock. Sister and I do appreciate your offer, but we cannot accept it.'

'Oh, Father,' said Sister Theophilus. Then a faint red crept into her smooth sallow cheeks and she dropped her glance. Delie Stock's dark eyes became snapping pinpoints. She knew what was coming. Hadn't she had it a dozen times, whenever she'd tried to give some money away to one of these boneheads in an upside-down collar?

'Why not?' she demanded roughly. Unconsciously her arms, in a habitual way of the slum women, tired-backed from too many babies and too much carrying of heavy loads, folded themselves over her bosom and in this belligerent attitude she waited.

'Mrs Stock, your generosity will long be remembered by us, but I'm afraid that what you suggest would be quite impossible.'

Delie Stock did not blush; she could no longer feel shame, but she could feel anger and bitter resentment against those who thought that she should. Her tight wrinkled mouth fell open and showed the narrow, yellow-stained bottoms of her lower teeth.

'So, you ain't taking me money, is that it? You don't want old Delie's tainted dough. There's a hundred and thirty good quids there, and no mangy old bible-banger is going to keep those kids in there from getting it. See?'

Father Cooley gathered the notes into a bundle, tidied it up, and offered it politely and calmly.

'Mrs Stock, you are frank, so I will be as well. I am afraid it would be against my principles to take this money. It is tantamount to stolen property.'

'Stolen from who?' flamed the woman.

'Stolen from the wives and children of the men who spend it in your foul places of pleasure,' thundered the priest. Then abruptly he turned to Sister Theophilus and said: 'Please leave us, Sister.'

Sister Theophilus, with trembling lips, flew back into the schoolroom. There was a subdued sort of bedlam there, but not so much that the children did not notice her expression. She said sharply: 'Harry, have you finished your essay?'

Harry muttered: 'Can't think of nothing.'

'Sit down and do it, or I'll give you the cane,' commanded Sister Theophilus. Abashed, he sat down. Ashamed of herself, she seated herself and forced her hands to move slowly over the desk in their little accustomed tasks. Calm, calculated movements, like rhythmic words, soothed her mind, and it was soon tranquil again. Her mind was like a deep pool, which the wildest wind might ruffle only for a minute.

Father Cooley's, however, was not so easily subdued. All his life he had deplored, and battled, and scourged his temper, but it was still like an electric wire, forever ready to be charged with extra voltage. Now he felt it rising in him, and ignored it, keeping his voice low and his manners gentle. But it was no good. His face grew crimson and his white hair bristled almost perceptibly. He felt sick with passion and remorse at the same time.

Delie Stock, on the other hand, loved and petted her temper. It was like a horse that she caressed and fed and teased when necessary. When it suddenly rose and took control of her, it gave her an exhilaration comparable with that of drink. Now it was well away, in a tossing gallop, upsetting one more restraint each split second. She longed to see shock and disgust come over the red face of this respectable man, and to hate and despise him because it was there.

223

'Ha!' she yelled. 'So you're going to diddle those poor little bastards in there out of a bit of fun, are yer? Just because you're too damned pure and holy to touch my money, that was earned honest. Yeah, yer call yourself a Christian. Do you think God would have done that? Yeah, when Mary Magdalene came along to him, did he tell her to take her precious hair-oil somewhere else? Go on, answer that, you old buffalo.'

Father Cooley choked. He stared at the woman with her sly beetle eyes, and her face that knew everything and respected none of it. How could he preach about hell when this woman had been there? All the knowledge and disillusion of the devil was hers; her bawdy houses were filled with poor Surry Hills and Redfern kids that grew up starved and ignorant, knowing nothing, trained for nothing, and cast out to earn their livings by their own instincts. She peddled dope; she sold liquor that was manufactured in her own backyard, laced with foul fuel spirits and given a tang with tobacco . . . liquor that filled the brain with madness and murder, and had been the cause of dozens of terrible bloody brawls in those dark back alleys. Did she really know what she was doing? On her deathbed, would she feel horror and fear, or would she feel she had been a successful business woman? Father Cooley, wondering, did not answer. Delie Stock leaped into the silence.

'You call me a bad woman. Yeah, I'm the worst woman in the district, the coppers say, and I'm not ashamed to repeat it. But who comes across with fifty quid when there's a funeral? When Johnny Sheily got hit with a truck, who gives his ma enough dough to go away for a good holiday to get over it? You? No, old Delie Stock, that's who.'

Father Cooley said swiftly: 'Just to square your conscience? Is that it?' And as soon as he said it his soul shuddered and he inwardly prayed: 'Oh, Lord, when would you have said a thing like that?' And simultaneously his Irish blood remarked gleefully: 'Now, there's one in the eye for the old pig.'

Delie Stock half-closed her eyes. A dozen rich and luscious phrases, thick with imagery and laden with obscenity, rushed into her mind, but she discarded them all. She felt like playing with this man, like bringing him down so hard that he would kiss her feet. She caressed the head of her temper softly, and it stamped its feet and shook its mane, but did not bolt.

She said in a hoarse, sad voice: 'It's a nice thing when a minister says things like that. I thought you was different, Father, from all the others.'

'What others?' asked the priest, doubtfully.

'The reverend over at the Methodist Church, and all the others, I've been around to them all at some time, and they all think they are too good to be in the same room with me.'

'Mrs Stock, if you think I can help you to make a new start in life you know I am at your service. But still that has nothing to do with the moral question of whether I should accept your donation.'

Delie Stock suddenly felt grieved and utterly alone. The alcohol in her bloodstream affected some part of her brain where melancholy lurked like a raven. Here she was, the worst woman in the district, trying to give away some money for a cause that ought to get into the papers. And this evil-minded old codfish wouldn't look at it. She was a character; she had a whole book of police court clippings about herself; drunks got out of her way, and kids thought they were gutsy to chuck a few stones through her windows. She sniffled, and a lone sticky tear rolled down her withered cheek. It wasn't fair. It wasn't fair.

'I was just a little bit of a sheila when I started,' she said, her voice breaking into a croak. She leaned against the table and played with the shabby purse, clicking the broken clasp in and out. 'Just a boy here and there . . . never got a bean for it. And then I got into a good house. Up on the corner of Murphy Street it was. You wouldn't believe it, but no customers were allowed after twelve at night. Well, when the old girl died, she left the house to me, and that's how I got me start. It's been hard work and good business brains that done it. You've got no call to be looking down at me, Father Cooley.'

'Start!' exploded Father Cooley. 'Start on the road to hell!'

'You wouldn't say that if you were a girl,' said Delie Stock, still quietly and sombrely. 'You don't know what it's like being a woman. Everyone's got it in for you, even God. Even God,' she repeated sadly. 'What chance does any woman get around here? Starved and dirty and walked on to the end of your days, that's all, unless you kick over the traces and make the most of what yer got. I'm as good a woman as anyone else, and what's more,' bawled Delie Stock, sticking the spurs into her temper and giving it a slap on the rump for good measure, 'that money wasn't earned the way you think. I won it in a lottery, and if you want to know which one, just stick yer beak in the newspaper and read me name amongst the prize-winners.'

Father Cooley realized once more that he was a lamb amongst goats, and hardly knew more than his prayers. He resolved that he would go without a smoke all the next month in order to atone for his sin of uncharity against one who should be pitied. Perhaps even admired. Had he been so great a sinner, would he have bothered to throw such drops of water into the flames of hell as fifty pounds to a widow at a funeral, or a hundred and thirty for a children's picnic?

He thought humbly: 'No, I wouldn't. I'd go the whole hog and be damned to me, there's not a doubt.'

Aloud he said: 'Please pardon me, Mrs Stock. Indeed, and the children will be most grateful to you.'

'Well, now,' said Delie Stock, 'that's better talk.' She shook her shoulder like a ruffled parrot, and marched out.

Father Cooley took up the money and stuck it in his wallet. There was more than would go in comfortably. For the very first time he could not get his wallet shut. Usually the flap wrapped over three times. He rapped on the door, stuck his head in, and beckoned Sister Theophilus. She said a word to the children and came out with her gliding step.

'Do you think they heard, Sister?' whispered Father Cooley with an anxious face. Sister understood instantly what he meant.

'I got them reciting, Father. But she did shout a bit now and then,' she answered. Eager expectancy was in her face.

'Well, I found out that the money was earned honestly enough, even though in a lottery. For if the Government condones it . . .' Father Cooley drifted for a moment into puzzlement about the ethics of lotteries, and then he shrugged his thick shoulders and continued: 'We'll be having the picnic.'

Sister Theophilus clasped her hands like an excited child. 'Oh, Father, thank you, thank you. I've been saying ejaculations under my breath all the time.'

The priest said rather sadly: 'You never can tell with people, can you Sister?' She said, flushing: 'We can pray for her. Nobody is beyond help.'

'No,' said Father Cooley. Then, more heartily: 'Well, I hope you good Sisters will get together tonight at recreation and jot down a selection of ideas for the picnic.'

'Oh, we'll do that gladly, Father,' she cried, and a dimple split her

226

cheek for a moment, so that she did not look at all like the headmistress of a poor and difficult school.

'Um,' said Father Cooley. He gruffly added; 'It's strange, the queer sort of people who win the lotteries, isn't it, Sister?'

There was an almost wistful tone in his voice.

Five

And so it was arranged. The children of St Brandan's were to go for a picnic. The whole of Surry Hills knew about it in no time. In every narrow back alley littered with rusty garbage tins and sleeping bony cats, somebody leaned over a bent corrugated iron fence and called: 'Didja hear about it, dearie? Ole Delie Stock's put down a hundred quid flat and give the kids a treat for Christmas. Young Kathie's going, and Mrs Wilson's Bernie is wetting his pants with temper cause he's a Protestant and can't go.'

The feeling was one of pleasant excitement, and geniality towards Delie Stock, so now when her big black car drew up in front of the grog shop in Little Ryan Street, people gave her a jovial jerk of the head instead of an intimidated one. They had always been proud of Delie Stock; she was tough and hard, and she had got on in the world, though there were those who remembered her as a little snivelling fancy-girl being hauled off to the station by the Vice Squad. The people thought, you didn't catch any of them flash night club-hoppers from Rose Bay and Potts Point donating hard cash to give a lot of poor kids a picnic.

Dolour had never been to a picnic in her life. She was not even sure of what it was, except that it involved swimming, and races on the sand, and sunburn, and a great deal to eat. Roie was superior, for she dimly remembered outings with her mother and father and Thady in the country long ago. She remembered a hedge, dark green and speckled with some sweet-smelling bewhiskered white flower, and some mushrooms which she found in a furrow, pale brown and peaked, with delicate stalks. And although she was happy for Dolour's sake, Roie was a little jealous that nobody had sent St Brandan's kids for picnics while she was there. She tried to make up for this jealousy by lending Dolour her new pink slip, which was much too large for the child and had to be held up by four safety pins. But Dolour loved wearing it.

At last the wonderful day came. It was the first of December, an enchanted date, for then the year turned on its axis and a shower of heat and light, and burning, burning blue fell upon Australia.

Already the smell of the scorching hinterlands was stealing upon the city; the odour of river-beds appearing through brackish dwindling water, and of soil dried into dust and whipped into whirlwinds that vanished like smoke. Dolour climbed out of bed at five in the morning, for she had slept lightly and excitedly, and through the skylight the sun was already pouring in a flood of yellow. She rose on tiptoe and looked out through the window, and through the ragged fronds of the phoenix palm in the backyard she saw the stainless sky and the haze on the distant buildings. Like onion-shaped domes and slender spires they rose, an eastern city dreaming in the early morning.

All the children attended early Mass, for as Sister Theophilus told them, God loves to receive the offering of our pleasure as well as our pain. Never before had the old church seemed so lovely to them. They loved Sister Theophilus, kneeling so straight and silent, only the faintly hollowed black wooden beads slipping through her fingers. They loved Father Cooley, strange in his vestments, moving ceremoniously about the altar. They loved each other; Harry Drummy and the seven Stevenses, Dolour Darcy with her petticoat hanging down, all the Rileys and the Archibald boys with their ears rimmed with dirt, the Mulligans, the Brogans, the host of gipsy-eyed Sicilianos, the Brophys and the O'Donohues. They glanced about with the bright unselfconscious eyes of birds, their tousled, home-cut hair bobbing, their clothes washed, and pressed with flatirons that left tell-tale freckles of soot behind, and their bare calloused feet restless with delight and anticipation under the seats. They prayed for everyone they could think of, mainly Sister Theophilus, and one even remembered to pray for Sister Beatrix, who was old and cross and rheumaticky, and laid it in with a cane very frequently. After they had had their breakfasts, they all met on the corner of Plymouth Street. It was now half-past eight, and lots of mothers came down to see the children off, feeling vicarious excitement, and many wishing that they, too, were going off to Collaroy in one of the two big double-decker red and yellow buses which waited like docile monsters at the corner.

'Now, don't you be going too far out,' explained Mumma anxiously to Dolour. 'Them sharks,' she added. Sister Theophilus, who was standing nearby with her big black umbrella shading her face from the sun, said: 'They'll only be allowed in the baths, where it's perfectly safe, Mrs Darcy, so don't you worry.'

229

Sister Theophilus was as excited as the children. She had every intention of finding a secluded spot and making sand castles, and even paddling in the shallow clear lips of the breakers as they spent their force after the long roll in from the Pacific.

Mumma watched the buses roll away. There was quite a crowd gathered on the footpath, even a reporter with a square leather case in which he carried a camera. He took a lot of shots, of Harry Drummy biting into a big apple, of Rosie Siciliano climbing upon the back platform of the bus, and then of all the children waving farewell out of the upper windows. The crowd knew quite well what would be over or under those pictures when they appeared in the paper . . . 'Underprivileged Children at Christmas Treat,' or 'Santa Claus comes to Surry Hills,' which would be self-explanatory. Some of the women felt a little resentful, and glared at the newspaperman, for they were fiercely aware of the fact that they were just as good as anyone else in Sydney, and if the rest of Sydney persisted in looking down on them, then the rest of Sydney could just lump it. But others thought it lovely that their children should be in the papers, for it meant that you could clip the picture out, and that was as good as having a real photograph.

Mumma walked slowly home, for the corn on the ball of her foot was bothering her, in spite of its being a fine day, and she felt hot and uncomfortable. Her winter dress was mended and tight under the arms, for she had not yet saved up enough money to go poking around the second-hand shops after a cotton one for summer. She called in and bought some bread and six-penn'orth of garlic sausage, for Hughie was still in bed, not feeling very well after last night's bottle of muscat, which had not been all it had promised. Mumma though sadly of the lost money, which they could so ill afford, but she was used to going without her full complement of housekeeping money.

She had barely reached the gate before the postman came along. There was a letter for Miss Sheily, and one for herself. Mumma shrieked up the stairs for Miss Sheily, meanwhile shaking the envelope busily to see if it contained anything more solid than paper. She left the envelope on the stair-post and hurried into her own flat. A letter was so rare that she was half-frightened to open it, for it was plain to see that it was from sister Josie, who lived at Albany, and had five children, and looked after Grandma.

Mumma muttered: 'Now, Lord, don't be too hard on me,' as she tore open the envelope. She sat down and read it, and as soon as she had finished she commented: 'Lord, sometimes I can't understand you.'

Then a little excitement filled her mind, and she hurried heavily into the bedroom, crying: 'Wake up, Hughie, I've had a letter from Josie, and she's got important news.'

Hughie was lying sulkily awake, rhythmically rubbing his bristly chin in an effort to smooth down the pain which tickled him in every portion of his face. He did not like Josie, she was fat and putty-featured, with a coarse habit of saying exactly as she thought. The very remembrance of her made his head feel much worse.

'Yeah, what does she say, the old ratbag?'

'She says she can't possibly go on looking after Grandma. She's got fallen arches.'

'Who, Grandma?'

'No, Josie. She says she can hardly crawl from her bed.'

'Well, what about it? Does she expect us to brace 'em up for her?' inquired Hughie, with almost a grin. Then suddenly the significance of Josie's arches struck him, and the top of his head palpitated almost visibly. He sank back with a groan. 'I think I'm getting brain fever.'

'Is that what's the matter with yer?' asked Mumma satirically. She sat on the edge of the bed, feeling bolder.

Hughie whispered: 'Grandma wants to come and live with us again. I can see it writ all over yer ugly face.'

'Well, where else can the poor dear live?' cried Mumma, her temper rising. 'Josie's had her for eighteen months, and if she's sick then she's done her duty and no one can ask more. Grandma'll just have to come back here, that's all.'

'That means to say I've got to go out on the couch again,' protested Hughie, 'while Grandma sleeps in here with you. It's not right. Not by no manner of means. A man shouldn't be separated from his wife.' He added, rather wistfully, 'not that it's so bad now, with me growing older every minute.' He brooded for a while on this, then exploded: 'I won't be having that old dragon breathing fire at me every time I come home with more than one drink in me!'

'She's my own mother, and while I live she won't be turned into the street,' proclaimed Mumma ferociously. Hughie closed his eyes.

'Now, who's talking about turning the old battleaxe into the street?' he protested. 'All right, I'll shift out on to the couch, and

231

when I want to kiss you, I'll have to take you out into the scullery.'

Mumma sniffed. 'And when do you ever want to kiss me, Hugh Darcy? No more'n Lick Jimmy does.'

A brief twinkle was born in Hughie's eyes. 'Ah, so you've been encouraging that pagan cabbage-seller, have yer? Wiggling yer bottom at him, no doubt.'

Mumma refused to be a party to the pleasantry. She glared. 'And what's more, Ma's coming next Tuesday. So we'd better be getting the place cleaned up, and it's a blessing you're home today to give me a hand.'

Hughie groaned. 'I might 'ave known this was me unlucky day. Metho in me booze last night, and Grandma in me bed this morning.'

'Ah, yer poor old mug,' sympathized Mumma. 'Well, I'll bring you in some tea and a nice slicer toast.' She smiled down at Hughie, for now that she had won her battle, such as it was, she felt strongly the affection which always lay in her heart for him.

'Now, would you do that?' asked Hughie, gratified. She was delighted. 'Don't you come smoodging around me. Look at the grey in yer whiskers.'

She bustled off and happily made a pot of tea.

At half-past seven that night Dolour, almost purple with sunburn, and with sand in everything except her mouth, came bursting into the room. Behind her was the brilliant memory of a day at the beach, of bus rides, of yelling 'Waltzing Matilda' and 'Little Nellie Kelly' and 'Hail Queen of Heaven'; of swooping white roads and sudden revelations of cobalt seas iced with foam; of Harry Drummy being sick all over three Sicilianos, and Father Cooley being forced to take Bertie Stevens aside and explain to him about the gigantic hole in the seat of his trunks; of Sister Theophilus sitting calmly hour by hour making high turreted sand-castles which were wiped into spinning dust and pigmy willy-willies by the afternoon wind. There were so many things to talk about. Dolour had experienced them all in one day, but it took her weeks to tell about them.

Roie came in late, having spent the evening with Tommy. She listened with a sort of dreamy content. Having at last found someone who seemed to fit into her ideal of love, she found that there had mysteriously developed in her a sort of divine aloofness. She was isolated in her own happiness, watching from a distance the squabbles and scraps and little excitements of others. A new tolerance grew in her heart. Consequently, when Mumma timorously broached the subject of Grandma's coming home, she was surprised when Roie readily agreed.

'Poor old thing. After all, Auntie Josie's got all them kids to look after. It must be pretty solid for her with Grandma as well.'

'I like Grandma,' said Dolour decisively. 'She's got a nice nose.'

'Hooked like a vulture's,' chuckled Hughie. Mumma's eyes flashed, particularly as Hughie was correct.

'I can remember the time when my mother's nose was as straight as a die. And the skin she had. Like milk. And she never washed it with anything but common old yellow soap.'

'Now she doesn't wash it at all,' observed Hughie.

'You mark my words, Hugh Darcy, when you're eighty-three you won't be bothered with washing your face, neither. You'll be a dirty old man, or I miss my guess.'

'You bet I will,' affirmed Hughie, his voice growing loud and hearty. 'I'll never wash me hoofs once I pass me sixtieth birthday.'

'Where are you going to put Grandma?' asked Roie. Mumma shook her head vexedly.

'She'll just have to come in with me, and Dadda'll have to come out here on the couch again,' she said.

Hughie looked at the shiny, lumpy couch, too short for anyone over the age of twelve, and too narrow for anyone over eight stone weight. He well remembered his sojourn there during Grandma's last visit, with his feet stacked up on a chair at the end of the couch, and the blankets slipping off him all night long, first one side and then the other. At last he sat up against the curved end of the ancient bit of furniture, and reclined there with his chin boring into his second shirt button, so that by the time morning came he had a savage crick in the neck.

'Gawd,' he said dolefully. Roie laughed, and Mumma thought lovingly how beguiling her little teeth looked with those tiny spaces between them, and how the wide white space between her eyebrows emphasized her slanting eyes.

'Couldn't we put the couch up in our room, Dolour, and then you could sleep on it, and Grandma could sleep with me? I don't think it's right for husbands and wives to be separated.'

She lapsed into silence as Dolour burst into loud lamentations and protest, and Mumma saw with astonishment that she was thinking of how she would feel if she were married to Tommy

233

Mendel and was forced to sleep away from him. As mysteriously as though she were right inside Roie's head, Mumma felt forlornness and loneliness because she did not have a tousled dark head to press into the hollow of her shoulder, or a slender, warm, young man's body to relax in drowsiness beside her own.

She thought, protesting: 'It's not like that, Roie love. It all goes after a while, and he's just a man who snores, and smells of tobacco, and hauls all the bedclothes off you every time he turns over.'

'Not that I wouldn't rather sleep on the couch than with Grandma,' Dolour's voice became audible to her. 'I slept with Grandma once, and she stuck her great big bony knees into my back all night. All crooked up like a safety-pin she was, and cold as a frog. And in the morning when I woke up she was smoking a pipe and setting the blankets on fire.'

'Hush,' said Mumma hurriedly, for she liked to preserve the legend that nobody but herself knew about Grandma's fondness for her little clay cutty.

'No,' said Hughie obstinately. 'I'll tell you what we'll do. We'll hang a sheet up in the bedroom and divide the room, and Grandma can sleep in there, all nice and private.'

'On the couch?' asked Mumma, scandalized.

Hughie shook his head. He had a surprise. 'On the stretcher Johnny Sheily had. We'll borrow it from Miss Sheily, and glad she'll be to be rid of it, with the bugs in it and all.'

'Oh, no, you don't,' stated Mumma with determination. 'My mother's not going to sleep in any bed where Johnny Sheily died, poor creature.'

'He didn't die in it. He died right out there in the road,' said Dolour, and her face went sickly under the sunburn. Mumma hurriedly back-tracked, and agreed that it would be a fine thing, and so it was arranged.

On Tuesday Grandma arrived, as fresh as paint after her long journey. Once she had been a tall and slender woman, with lovely white skin and a bun of dark red hair, and blue eyes with the devil in them, and innocence, too. But now her bones had descended one upon the other, and she was a little old creature, not very bent, but giving you the impression that at any moment she would shrink still further. She walked along with a brisk pigeon-toed step, chewing rapidly at nothing at all, and occasionally having a short, sharp conversation with herself, which nobody else could get the

234

gist of. Grandma had lived on and off with the Darcys for years. In Hughie's turbulent youth she had often thrown things at him, and he had thrown them right back, for they were much of a kind, and secretly admired each other. Immediately they heard her step, Roie and Dolour flew out into the hall to greet her, for they loved her very much.

'Ah, you've grown up something splendid, Dolour,' observed Grandma, reaching up to pat her tall granddaughter on the head. Then she ostentatiously rubbed the cheek where Roie had kissed her, and said: 'You'll never get past St Peter with all that paint on your face, Rowena, me jewel.'

'Oh, you're an old hussy yourself,' answered Roie pertly. 'Don't try to kid me you didn't put on a bit of colour to attract the boys when you were young.'

'Oh, maybe a bit of chewed-up geranium leaf,' said Grandma calmly, 'and I'd have them all twirling their moustaches like to drop off.'

The moment Grandma put her nose inside the door Mumma began clucking like a hen. She flew at her and helped her out of the mouldy old rabbit-skin coat which had been referred to from time immemorial as 'me tippet', and unclutched her hand from the canvas kit that held all her belongings.

'Ah, Ma, it's thin you are. What's that Josie been doing to yer?' she asked, smoothing back her mother's coarse shiny white hair.

'Starving me, the baggage, on three good meals a day,' chuckled Grandma. 'Ah, poor Josie, her with fallen arches that bad, and going to have an addition to the family, too. It's a pity she don't go out of business.'

Dolour blushed crossly, for she was getting to the stage where much that had hitherto passed over the head of even her slum precocity was penetrating her mind. It seemed to her that Grandma's tongue was getting what Sister Theophilus referred to as 'piggy', and she resolved on the spot to offer her next Mass for her Grandma, for she had no wish to stop on the road to heaven and see that long nose poking through the bars of the gates of hell.

Mumma suddenly stopped and twitched up Grandma's skirts.

'Oh, Ma!' she remonstrated, 'where's yer warm bloomers?'

'Up there, somewhere,' returned Grandma absently.

Roie giggled. She said: 'It's nice to have you home for Christmas, Grandma, so that you can make the puddin'.'

'Oh, no, she don't,' said Hughie, who wandered in at this moment, vexed and sharp-tongued with dirt and weariness. 'This year yours truly is going to make the pud. How are yer, yer old hellcat?'

'Fit to break your brain-box in,' shrilled Grandma, a devilish glint appearing in her eye. 'And nobody's going to make any pudding in this house barring me.'

Now Hughie had, long ago, been a shearers' cook, and could make a curry hot, sweet and luscious, with surprising bits of chopped-up date, green peaches, and sliced banana floating mysteriously in it. And he could make soup, and brownie, and the curiously named sea pie, which is nothing more than a stew with an oversize dumpling roofing it. But, best of all, he could make a boiled pudding, dark as midnight and rich as Persia, and containing so many dates, prunes, cherries, sultanas, and currants, that, as Hughie himself modestly said: 'You couldn't spit between them.'

This year he had been determined to make the Christmas pudding well in advance, and tie it to the scullery rafters to 'season' before the great day arrived. By that time, Hughie calculated, it would not only be rich – it would be intoxicating. But, as Grandma pointed out, she, too, had a hand with puddings, and had made one every year since she was eleven and living with her dad in Faroe Street, Cookstown, Ireland. And be damned to anyone, said Grandma, if she was going to stop now.

The pudding argument went on for days after Grandma had settled in at Number Twelve-and-a-Half.

It was a strange thing how her advent changed the personalities and outlook of those already in the house. Old as she was, Grandma had some exciting element in her; the courage and restlessness which had driven her forth at eighteen to emigrate to the new colony had not left her; soon Mumma found herself unconsciously giving her speech an Irish twist, and even the girls, brought up as they had been to the quick Irish idiom and wit, discovered that their voices had a new softness and purl. It was as though the real Celticism, not only of blood, but of memory and association, were catching, and the Australian blood, if there was such a thing, were vanishing before the red blood of the Irish.

Grandma unpacked her canvas bag, and Dolour watching, thought nothing of the fact that Grandma possessed in all the world only two winceyette nightdresses, yellowed and ragged around the armholes; an extra pair of moth-eaten black bloomers; a curious maroon garment of the fashions of twenty years before, and known as 'me house dress'; seven or eight strings of rosary beads, all broken, and an ancient prayer-book which had been used so many times that the bottom corners of the pages were yellow and illegible from the grip of Grandma's thumb.

Dolour had never thought about age, but she had an instinctive feeling that as you grew older you needed fewer possessions, and she seemed to see behind Grandma a long road which extended into her childhood, dotted with the discarded treasures and necessities of Grandma's discarded years.

But Roie, with the curious, subjective sensitivity which love had brought her, found her heart filling with sadness. It stung her eyes and tightened her throat. It seemed so strange that Grandma, who had borne so many children, who had worked and laughed and despaired and grieved, should reach the evening of her life with nothing whatsoever in her hands. She was like a little bird in the sunset hour, safe beneath the eave, chirping and cheeping, possessed of complete poverty.

'Maybe I'll finish up like that, too,' she thought. 'Maybe Tommy will.' She remembered the countless dirty old lonely men around the city, living in some cheap and squalid room, or even half a room; with no one to talk to save park-bench acquaintances; spending their meagre pensions on buttered rolls and scanty cups of tea and mean grey Devon sausage, because eighteen bob a week went nowhere at all once you took your rent out of it.

Roie did not understand her thoughts; she hated them, and because she did and was confused she took it out on Grandma.

'Why don't you get some more clothes?' she said. 'Anyone would think you were as poor as a mouse. Look at that filthy old nightdress – I wouldn't be found dead in it. You just don't care any more – no respect for yourself. You just ought to make your pension go further.'

'What am I, a magic-an? I'm dubersome if you'd make me pension go half as far, Roie me girl,' cried Grandma. 'You've taken leave of yer seven small senses, and what manners yer have, too.'

'Ah, God!' cried Roie, and she ran out of the room. Grandma jerked a black-nailed thumb after her.

'Now what's come up her back?'

Dolour jigged her shoulders in a shrug. She was dying to explain

237

all about the Haymarket and Tommy Mendel. Grandma loved to hear about anyone falling in love. Her interest was a combination of vindictiveness and nostalgia. She sat on the sagging bed and nodded her head like a Chinese mandarin. At the conclusion she shook it.

'It's a good thing, it is, for Roie to have a boy. It makes the mind broader to know how the men think, and if you live too long without finding out you grow into a peculiar one-eyed sort of body. But I'm not so keen on the Jewish,' she added thoughtfully.

At that moment a curious odour, half flavour and half perfume, stole through the door, and Grandma's nose quivered like an anteater's.

'Vanilla, God help us – and that fladdy-faced Hughie of a father of yours is stealing a march on me and making the Christmas pudding.'

She trotted rapidly out to the kitchen, holding an agitated conversation with herself as she went. And Grandma's nose had not lied. There was Hughie, his black brows bent downwards into a solid line, concentrating on a series of sticky brown-paper bags before him, the contents of which he was measuring out into the washing-up basin.

'Ah, yer tom todger,' commenced Grandma mildly, in a tone which brought to mind the precise and gentle pacings of a bull before he starts tearing up the earth.

'Go on, skedaddle out of here,' threatened Hughie jovially. He was in a good mood. Ostentatiously and luxuriously he sniffed at a cupful of raisins soaking in brandy. Grandma dipped her nose downwards too.

'Where'd yer get the brandy, Hughie?' she asked.

Hughie smiled mysteriously. 'Guv to me by a friend,' he explained. Grandma looked longingly at it, and her slaty eyes flicked a glance along the mantelshelf and into the dark cubbyhole beyond the sink. But there was no bottle to be seen. Hughie was mean enough to buy it in a cup, she reflected bitterly, for brandy was one of the few pleasures left in her life. It put the marrow back into her bones and the red into her blood, and for a narrow space she was young and tall and the world had a prickle in it again.

'Can I have the cup after you've finished with it, Hughie?' asked Grandma humbly.

'Will yer keep outa me kitchen if I give yer maybe a sip or two?' inquired Hughie cunningly. Grandma dipped her flag without compunction.

'You won't tell herself, Hughie?'

'Never a word outa me mouth, Grandma!'

'Ah, dotie, it's a fine boyo you are, sometimes, and perhaps I've been hard,' she confessed, thinking of the many times that he'd come in rolling drunk and made Mumma cry, when she'd gone for him with anything handy.

Hughie pondered the times Grandma had been hard on him.

'You have that,' he agreed, savouring Grandma's comedown, and pouring a cupful of yellow, wrinkled sultanas into the bowl. He added chopped dates, clumpy with flour.

'But I always liked you, Hughie,' cajoled Grandma, sniffing lingeringly at the brandy cup. 'I remember when you used to come around when you were courting and Pa used to say. "Here comes the lad with the ellafump ears." '

'Ellafump!' jeered Hughie. 'Poor old Pa. Remember the arms of him like blocks of carved wood.'

'That's right,' marvelled Grandma, of the husband she had not thought of for years.

'And the head of him,' said Hughie ferociously. 'Like a block of carved wood, too.'

'He was the finest man that ever brought a block of ice into a house,' declared Grandma loyally. 'And at the icemen's picnic he won the hammer throw and got an elegant brass clock I'd have yet if you hadn't pawned it, bad cess to you, Hugh Darcy.'

'Stop yer nagging, or you'll ruin me nerve and I'll be putting the wrong amount of suet into me pudding,' protested Hughie. He wiped his floury hand down the side of his pants and groped about under the sink. From out of the ill-smelling recesses around the loops and coils of plumbing he produced a medicine bottle half full of brandy. Grandma's eyes glistened. With pursed lips, Hughie poured a tablespoonful into the bottom of the cup she held out to him. Then he decisively corked the bottle and put it on the mantelpiece, high up out of her reach.

'There now, that'll keep your old bones together,' he remarked with repulsive magnanimity. Grandma peered forlornly into the white bowl of the cup to the minute pool of pungent amber at the bottom.

'Ah, Hughie, you're a mullet-headed sheeny if ever there was one,' she cried. There was a short sharp conversation between herself and some person unknown, conducted in a voice inaudible to anyone but Grandma, and she had decided that she would sacrifice the brandy to the cause of war. She put down the cup, well out of Hughie's reach, and then attacked him with tooth and tongue.

'Look at it, look at it, Hugh Darcy. No more than a spoonful, and you call yourself an Irishman. There's not enough there to warm a kitten. Ah, it'll be a glorious day for me when you're old and aching and knobbly in every joint, and some tight-fisted jeremiah of a son-in-law deprives you of yer wee sup of brandy.'

'Leave it then,' said Hughie unconcernedly, 'and I'll season me pudding with it.'

'Your pudding!' shrilled Grandma, 'and me going to sell me soul and me rights for the sake of that wee driblet of brandy. Get away from that bowl, Hugh Darcy, for I'm going to make the pudding meself, and you can make up yer mind to it.'

The lines in Hughie's face went sour and perpendicular; his eyebrows formed themselves into a line as forbidding as any seen on the battlefield. He plunged his arms nearly to the elbow into the pudding basin, and jammed both hands full of suet, sultanas, and flour.

'Now get out of it, Grandma, before I lose me temper.'

'Temper!' jeered Grandma. 'As though the Darcys ever had any temper worth speaking of, barring the dirty bit of liverishness that passes for it in some families.'

She rolled up her sleeves and put her long knobby fingers into the flour. Hughie's face was dark crimson. He shouted: 'I'm warning you, Mrs Kilker. I'm warning yer that I'll bust the basin over yer scone rather than let you make the pudding this year. I've got me mind set on it.'

Grandma went on kneading the flour, pressing the whole lumps of fat in as though her fingers had done it for centuries.

'Mrs Kilker is it now? You've become mighty polite, Hugh Darcy. More so than yer dadda was, I must admit.'

Hughie cracked her fingers hard with the wooden spoon. 'Leave me suet alone, or you'll get worse, you meddlesome old murphy. And leave me father alone, he was a fine man.'

'He was,' agreed Grandma sweetly, 'save for the teeth of him.'

'What was the matter with me father's teeth?'

'Like clothes pegs,' said Grandma sadly, rubbing her fingers under cover of the flour, for they still hurt. 'And the scandalous manners of a pig under a bed. But the Darcys were always like that.

240

Will you ever forget yer Aunt Kathy, her that had eight children and a pillar of the Church for a husband, and then went mad and danced Salome's dance in her skin and an umbrella.'

'I'm not interested in me Aunt Kathy,' said Hughie loftily, stirring rapidly with the wooden spoon, and involving Grandma's fingers with every stir.

'Ah, it's all in the blood,' ruminated Grandma. 'What about Molly Brody, her what was cousin to yer mother, and married a Lanigan from Limerick way?'

'What's the matter with that, to be properly married to a Lanigan?'

'But he was a hangman,' explained Grandma, 'and kept his rope and noose under the bed. That's a fine bed to be laying on. And it was Molly Brody, own cousin to yer mother who lay on it. You can't say there was any good in a woman like that.'

'Listen to who's talking,' retorted Hughie. 'Who was it got bailed up by the skipper coming out from Ireland and was found with six shirts on, and all other people's?'

Grandma's eyes sparkled, for if there was anything she really loved, it was a fight, and one was steaming up in the best possible way. 'Keep your brazen tongue off me father, Hugh, or as sure as I'm standing on me own two feet it'll be worse for you.'

'Brazen, is it?'

'It is. Me father suffered from the cold, that's all, and if any of them passengers said otherwise he was a liar, and I'd tell him so to his ugly face.'

'Fat chance,' jeered Hughie. 'And them all dead sixty year ago, like your dadda.'

'God rest his soul.'

'God rest it,' assented Hughie piously. Grandma had no intention of letting the quarrel get away from her. She grabbed it by its disappearing tail and brought it back.

'It was sad for me when me poor dear husband consented to your marriage with our girl.'

'Oh, is that so? And she was well on the way to being an old maid when I took pity on her.'

He added sorrowfully, for Grandma's breath appeared to be short. 'No, it was me was the mug, and look what I've come down to.' He gestured flourily at the dirt, the drabness, the overpowering poverty of the dark and greasy scullery, scarred with seventy years.

Grandma felt tears of futile fury rising in her throat. In spite of herself her voice quavered: 'Hughie, you're not saying me girl dragged you down to this? Her that's worked so hard, and reared your children and always gone to her duty?'

Hughie was abashed. He had not meant any such thing. It had just sounded good. 'Who said such a thing?' he jeered. 'But it might be true, for all that. It's disencouragement that drives a man to the drink, and if she was a different sort, and not always whining and complaining and crying about me, I wouldn't do it.'

Hughie had a brief vision of a heroic woman, a mixture of Norse goddess and film star and plain everyday mother, who would have listened to his maudlin self-pityings without bothering him with suggestions for a cure. Wistfully he marvelled at the number of women exactly like that there must be in this world, and how bad had been his luck that he hadn't chosen one.

'No,' he repeated, 'taking it right back to the beginning, it's her that drove me to the drink.'

Grandma promptly snatched the spoon out of his hand and hit him so smartly across what she described as 'his long snout,' that tears came into his eyes. She stood there, tiny, blazing, and indomitable.

'Go on now, hit an old woman, Hughie Darcy. Show what sort of a man you are, blaming your evil doings on your poor wife that's worked her fingers to the bone for you and your children, and then hitting her poor old mother.'

'I haven't hit you yet,' protested Hughie, but Grandma behaved as though he had, crying out and weeping, and calling to Miss Sheily and Patrick Diamond for assistance against the big lout of a son-in-law who'd hit her and take her pension off her, and drink it to the last penny.

Grandma was not conscious of maligning Hughie; by the time she had finished her tirade she was righteously angry and as lamentary as if Hughie had actually beaten her up.

Hughie could hardly speak. His rage choked him. He wiped his floury hands down the sides of his trousers, and crammed his hat on his head, hissing:

'I'd like to see your throat cut by a buck nigger, you old morepork,' and strode out of the room. Grandma, satisfied, plunged with eager enthusiasm into the pudding, and by the time

Mumma returned from her shopping it was tied up, a jetty cannon-ball, in its tea-towel, and bubbling and knocking in the black enamel saucepan.

'Where's Hughie?' asked Mumma. Grandma tucked in her lips and tried to look grieved and wise at one and the same time.

'I suppose he's drowning his woes,' she shrugged. 'Flung outa here like a tomcat with a tin on his tail.'

Mumma looked distressed. 'Now, Ma, I hope you haven't been annoying him, when he was so good and all, making the pudding and not a peep out of him.'

Grandma was indignant. 'Him make that pudding! It was meself and no other, though he might have helped a bit with the mixing. And you'll be able to tell from the taste, too.' Grandma was feeling good, not only because she had vanquished Hughie, and at eighty-three, too, but because she had licked out the luscious fragrant brandy cup and got more than a drop. Mumma looked at her doubtfully, and went on with the tea-making. Already a cold and melancholy foreboding was settling over her soul, as though a fog of the spirit were coming down. She felt sure that Hughie was going to go on a Christmas spree.

And so he was. He was already getting drunk. It is easy to get drunk in Australia. Things have been so arranged that a man can buy a bottle of muscat for four and six and get madder on it than a cow on a patch of poison-weed. For it did not come from any vineyard. No deep and autumnal southern sun ripened its grapes; no pungent vat housed it before it was bottled. It was born of an oil-well in Texas, seasoned with wine dregs, coloured with raspberry syrup or beetroot juice, and even, occasionally, pepped up with tan boot polish. It was easy to become a god on it, or a maniac.

There are intelligent drinkers and stupid drinkers. Hughie was one of the first. His intelligence told him that he was weak and without any importance in the world he both feared and loved, and so he drank to drown it. Inarticulate, a man who had many thoughts that were no more than a nebulous, cloudy mingling of impressions, half-memories, and emotions, Hughie was continually haunted by the knowledge that he could not express. When he was half-drunk he was possessed with incalculable sorrow for all the piteous strivings and battlings of humanity. For what? Something better than what it had. But what it was Hughie did not know. He only knew that there was implanted in his soul a fierce hunger for it, as there might be hunger for some beloved who had died a long time ago and left an emptiness nothing else could fill.

But when he was really drunk, Hughie grew six inches and put on four stone; he wore a uniform of red and gold and at the sound of his voice the crowds bowed down. Trumpets blew before him, and there were kettledrums rattling. If he met a respectable woman he hated the look of embarrassment or disdain on her face, and he said something filthy or disgusting to her just to see it replaced by another, no matter what it was; he gave dirty little goitrous kids pennies, because in his eyes he was distributing gilded largesse to beggars; he winked at prostitutes to let them know he was one of the boys; he even thought of rudeness to policemen as he passed their frowning presence on street corners. And when he got home he started in on Mumma.

He hated her then, because in her fatness and untidiness and drabness she reminded him of what he himself was when he was sober.

When Mumma heard his erratic feet stumping down the hall, her heart rushed sickeningly into her mouth and her face went yellow, not with fear, but with hatred and dread of the same old scene, the same old bellowings and crazy talk, the placatory words from herself, the brief spasms of anger, and Hughie's louder and more triumphant bellowings, and then the maudlin last stage when he cried into his food and threw it at the wall with melodramatic expressions of distaste.

And now there would be Grandma putting her spoke in, and getting abused, too, in words which made her achingly remember the same performance from her husband, long ago, and cry the hoarse painful sobs of the aged, not only from self-pity, but from nostalgia.

'I wish Thady hadn't gone,' wept Mumma suddenly. 'He would be fifteen. He'd be big and strong and look after me.'

At the thought of Thady she cried out loud, for the knot of pain in her breast which was his memory never left her, and only waited for such a moment as this to burst into agony.

'Thady, Thady,' she wept, with blinding tears, groping through the fog towards her mother, who held out her arms and cried, too, in sympathy.

Six

Mumma had always loved Christmas with a child-like love. It was like another world suddenly impinging upon her ordinary dull painful one; it was as bright-coloured and wonderful as a country road in the spring-time, where even the shadows were full of light. It was mysterious, too – a unique mystery, for although when regarded in the abstract it was perfect, it was never quite that way in reality. Somewhere, thought Mumma, there was the perfect Christmas Day. They would be all together. Thady sitting opposite her with his little freckled face shining with soap and water, and his silvery hair fluffed up in a triangle off his brow; the dinner would be cooked just right, the pudding hot and rich, and yet not overheating, as it always was in Australia; she would feel well, and Hughie would be sober, and Grandma wouldn't choke on the solitary threepence in the duff. But it never happened that way. Dolour was invariably bilious, and Roie bad-tempered with the heat and the fatigue, and she herself so hot and worn out with cooking a winter's dinner at mid-summer that she was ready to cry with vexation. And invariably Hughie got drunk and spoiled things one way or another.

This Christmas was worse than ever. Hughie spent all of Christmas morning snoring, with intervals of staggering out to the lavatory and being ear-wrenchingly sick. When he recovered he was sullen and quiet, with black hollows under his eyes and a pallid look under his three-day bristle. He looked an old man, and he felt it.

'Gawd, how I hate Christmas!' he said, lying on the hot and lumpy bed and looking up at the ceiling, which was pitted and pockmarked with the plaster falling away. Once it had been a lovely ceiling, delicately ornamented with intaglio designs of grapes and leaves; but now it was clotted with dirt and wounded with age. The old house had perhaps been a good one in its time, way back in the 'seventies. Perhaps some rich or famous person had lived there, Mumma often thought, for she occasionally had the strangest feeling, as though someone delicate and fastidious and beautiful passed by her, said softly: 'This was my house. Have pity on it because it was,' and vanished away again.

'Gawd, I hate it!' snarled Hughie, the taste in his mouth as bitter as gall, and in his soul all the disillusionment of an opium-eater who runs out of his drug. He was all alone, for Grandma was asleep in her cubbyhole and Dolour and Mumma were at church, and Roie was getting ready to go out with Tommy Mendel. He could hear her at the sink, washing sketchily, banging a mirror down, clinking bottles of cosmetics.

'Roie!' he bawled. 'Make us a cuppa tea before you go!'

'Oh, damn! I'm in a hurry!' answered Roie angrily, but he heard the hiss and pop of the gas, and settled back on the pillow tranquil in the knowledge that she would make it. After a while she entered, a sullen look on her little face, her hair tousled and untidy, but her mouth as crimson as a poinsettia with lipstick.

'Ta, Ro.' She gave the cup to him silently, and turned to the mirror to comb her hair.

'Whatcher get for Christmas?' he asked, placatingly, to break the silence. Roie gave a little snort. 'Anyone'd think you weren't here,' she jeered. Hughie groaned.

'Ah, cripes, leave that to your mother, will you, Ro? I feel crook as hell. Come on, what did Tommy give you?'

Roie licked a finger and smoothed her thin dark wing-like eyebrows.

'He's a Jew. He didn't give me anything.'

'What, nothing at all? The little sheeny, eh?'

Roie's face flushed a faint red, and in the mirror her mouth looked sulky and cross. 'He don't believe in Christmas, Jews don't. You don't know nothing.'

'Betcha you gave him something,' grinned Hughie. 'Bet you put out some sort of sprat to catch a mackerel. So yer fell in, eh?'

'God, I hate you!' spat Roie, turning around and piercing him with a look of such fury that Hughie felt it enter his head and come sizzling out the other side. She ran out of the room and slammed the door. Grandma instantly awoke, and at the sound of her complaining voice Hughie pulled the sheet over his head and pretended to be asleep. But there was no fooling Grandma. He heard her clip-clop to the side of the bed, and then a hard old hand hit him in the stomach.

'Ah, hell' groaned Hughie, dragging the sheet off his face. 'Whyn't you leave me alone?'

Grandma, rubbing sleep out of her eyes, gave a wink. 'Do you know what Miss Sheily gave me for a present, Hughie lad?'

'No, I don't know and I don't care,' growled Hughie. 'What?'

Grandma fished in the musty folds of her skirt and withdrew a bottle.

'Cripes!' gasped Hughie. Life flowed back into his eyes, and he sat up. 'Cripes, Grandma! Come on, give us a nip.'

'First-grade Port,' read Grandma with pride, though she didn't have her glasses on, for she had read it before, and remembered. 'Now, they're all out, so we'll have a little drink, just you and me, eh?'

'God bless you, Grandma!' said Hughie fervently. 'You're a good woman, sometimes.'

He lay back and listened to the pop of the cork, and the rich trickle into two cups, and the expression on his face might well have been on the face of one of the Faithful who, having been slain but recently, heard the jingle of a houri's ankle bells, and smelt the attar of paradisal roses.

Roie clicked down the street on her high heels. She was angry and upset because Hughie's reference to a Christmas present from Tommy had come right on the heels of lively curiosity on the part of Grandma and Dolour and Mumma. To each of them she had replied the same, but it had been hard to keep her lips from trembling and giving away the hurt in her heart. She too had forgotten that Tommy was a Jew, and she was very disappointed that he hadn't thought enough of her to give her some little present. She had given him a pullover, bottle-green and shoddy, but costing far more than she could afford. She had three pounds saved up to buy her entire summer wardrobe, and the pullover had cost half of it. But he had been pleased. She remembered the look on his face like a kid suddenly presented with an ice-cream.

'Gosh, he's only young,' she thought forgivingly, with a hot gush of love in her heart. She loved him so much that she justified to herself his every fault; so much could be forgiven Tommy because he was so pitifully young, because he had never had any parents; because he was lame and ashamed of it; because he lived by himself in a dirty little attic room in the Haymarket district, and had to make his own bed and cook his food over a gas ring. Roie took him to her heart as she might have taken a sick bird or a lost cat; she fitted him into the vacant space, forgave him everything, as a mother might.

'Where'll we go?' she asked when they met. Tommy groaned.

'It's so hot, Roie. Can't we just go and sit in the park; find a cool spot and yarn?'

They walked down the burning, deserted Sunday-ish streets, and turned into Moore Park. The great English trees stood bushy and green still, their sap not yet curdled by the alien sun. They cast great umbrellas of shade that was dark and sharp-cut against the bright yellow of the sunshine. About their knotted arched roots there were bare, worn spaces of earth. Tommy spread out his coat, and Roie sat down. She was reluctant. She had wanted to go somewhere, on a ferry-boat, or to any place which was new and different, where they could really be alone. But she put the thought out of her mind quickly, and smiled shyly at Tommy. He was dull and discontented; he slouched beside her, picking out pine needles and building them into a little tepee. Then he lay back with his head on her knees and looked up into the chinks of blue sky that showed through the clotted green.

'I hate holidays,' he said. Roie laughed.

'I do,' he cried. 'I hate them because there's nothing to do and nowhere to go when you've got no money.' He thought of his friends, the horde of larrikins with whom he associated, always inferior to them and good-naturedly chaffed. Their life of pubs and billiard-rooms and two-up schools and endless filthy magpie chatter about women seemed to him to be unbearably far away from his.

'There's the beach,' said Roie timidly.

'Kid stuff. Give me the good old town. Lots of people. Noise. Rowdy trams rattling past. Tarts showing off their dresses. I'd like to go to the races with you, Roie, in a slinky black dress and a great big hat with lace round the brim, and a string of green beads.' Roie laughed again, because she did not know if he were serious enough. Tommy's eyes shone. 'With plenty of money to bet with. God, I'm sick of having no money. I'm sick of having a gammy foot. Where'll I ever get in life?'

'There's your Uncle Joseph,' suggested Roie shyly. 'Couldn't he help you to get a better job?'

'Uncle Joseph! That hook-nosed old scrub,' said Tommy fiercely. He turned over and buried his nose in her stomach. His voice came muffled. 'He don't care the flick of a nag's tail about me. He just has some old Jew idea about an obligation to a dead brother's child. I'm useful down there in the market, that's all. You smell nice, Roie.'

248

'Dolour gave me some lavender talcum powder for Christmas,' said Roie, delighted that he had smelt it. Then she flushed because she thought that perhaps the mention of Christmas gifts might hurt Tommy's feelings. He turned so that one sullen black eye was looking at her.

'I got something for you too. Bet you thought I wasn't going to give you anything,' he said. Roie flushed scarlet.

'Oh, Tommy, I never thought about it . . . I . . . I . . .' He fished in his pockets, first one and then the other, and Roie, her eyes sparkling, her heart beating like that of a child who stands outside the room where the Christmas Tree is kept, waited, overcome with joy and expectation. That old Dadda! Mumma and her mean suspicions! Dolour! She needed her face slapped! And Grandma and her nasty tongue about sheenies and long noses! At last Tommy hauled out of his pocket a little parcel wrapped in blue paper.

'I hope you like it. I bought it up Oxford Street last night, after I left you. I thought it was nice.'

Roie was undoing the parcel with trembling fingers. It felt hard and oblong, and there was something soft wrapped around it. Perhaps it was a little piece of jewellery in a box, or a bottle of perfume. Perhaps it was . . . oh, it might be almost anything. Roie fumbled the last piece of paper off, and there on her lap lay a cake of soap wrapped in a pink wash-cloth.

She was so shocked and abashed that tears rushed into her eyes, and she had to look away carefully so that Tommy wouldn't see them. At first she thought it was a joke, and he had a real present concealed in another pocket, but when she stole a swift look at him she saw that he had an expression of pleased expectancy on his face.

'Gee, Tommy,' said Roie gallantly, 'it's awfully useful. I mean . . . soap . . . everyone needs a lot of soap. And the wash-cloth is awful pretty . . . pink, I mean . . . I like pink things. Thank you so much, Tommy.'

It was terrible. Her heart hurt as though he had stabbed it with a knife. Soap and a wash-cloth; it was one of those nasty little gift packages which the chain store made up at Christmas and Easter and Mother's Day and sold for ninepence or a shilling. But oh, Tommy hadn't meant to be cheap or mean about it. The love within Roie rushed out to protect and defend him. He just hadn't thought. It wasn't the gift that mattered, Mumma always said, but the thought behind it. Roie fiercely winked away the tears. Tommy

249

nuzzled his face into her lap and said happily. 'I couldn't think what to get you. I just didn't think of it until you gave me the sweater last evening. I wanted to get you something you liked.'

'I do like it, Tommy,' sobbed Robie suddenly, dropping tears and kisses indiscriminately on his face. 'And I love you with all my heart.'

As soon as she had said it she was panic-stricken, for although Tommy had often cuddled and kissed her, and they had gone steady for months, he had never said he loved her. Now she had done the unforgivable thing and said it first, which all the girls at the factory said was the worst thing anybody could do. The blood hummed in her ears. She wanted to get up and run away and never see Tommy again.

But he turned over and put his arms around her neck, and pulled her down clumsily and a little painfully. His soft boy's kisses fell warmly and ineffectually on her lips, and he whispered thickly: 'Do you mean that?' Roie nodded dumbly, ashamed. 'Gosh . . . Ro . . . nobody's ever said that to me before.' He whispered in her ear, with an excited voice: 'I love you, too.'

Now that it was out they were silent and embarrassed, each too timid to glance at the other, letting their warm arms lie slackly where they were. Finally they both glanced at each other and laughed ridiculously. Tommy rolled Roie over into the hot brittle grass and tickled her.

'Oh, Tommy, my dress . . . my hair . . . Oh, Tommy, don't! Don't!' she shrieked in a delighted whisper. They rolled about like two pups, relieved at the breaking of emotional tension. When they were tired and breathless they lay side by side, and Tommy breathed into her ear: 'Let me touch you.'

'What do you mean?' asked Roie, startled, shying away from his hand that edged itself softly down the neck of her dress.

'Go on, don't play hard to get,' he said, a little sparkle springing into his eyes. He had no real desire to fondle Roie, but he had heard his mates discuss it at length, and he wanted to experiment. When she refused he found himself growing angry, with an urgent wish to have his own way.

Roie flushed. Her quick temper rose. 'I never let anyone maul me around. I don't like it.'

'But I'm different,' pleaded Tommy. Roie sat up, sulkily, all the joy dying out of her. 'What good does that do anybody? It's . . . I don't like it,' she ended lamely.

'You'd want me to touch you if you loved me, like you said,' said Tommy roughly. He flung himself over on his stomach and began chewing a grass stem. Roie was left in the lurch. She began to feel that perhaps she had been too brusque, that perhaps she had hurt or offended him. Her heart went out in a great flood of tenderness towards Tommy's back, its slimness, his narrow neck riding out of the ill-fitting collar, his badly-cut clothes. He was only twenty. She felt much older and maturer.

'Ah, Tommy, don't be mad with me,' she pleaded. Tommy shrugged a shoulder. Roie put a hand on it, and when he did not move away she felt encouraged. 'Tommy,' she said softly. 'Tommy, darling.' The boy looked up, and he saw the pointed pale face, so youthful, with worried eyes, and the mouth trembling a little, looking at him anxiously. He rolled over forgivingly and pulled her down to him.

'I don't want to maul you if you don't like it, kid.'

'Perhaps I wouldn't mind if it was you that did it,' said Roie, trembling, throwing all her moral teachings and inhibitions overboard in her anxiety to please her lover.

'I can't stop thinking about you,' he said sullenly. 'When I go to bed I dream of you, and I wake up and you aren't there, and I lie by myself in that old lonely bed and stare at the bedpost.'

'How can you if it's dark?' asked Roie.

He cried angrily: 'Because sometimes it's just getting light.'

Roie said, 'Oh.' Then she added: 'I guess it's just because I feel funny about doing that sort of thing, Tommy.'

'You're not like all the other sheilas,' he said, and she did not know whether the contempt in his voice was for her or them.

'There's lots of girls like me in Surry Hills,' said Roie stoutly. 'You don't have to be a rat just because you live in a hole. And besides,' she added resentfully, 'what do you know about other girls?'

'I don't know anything, except what other fellas have told me. Who'd ever look at me with my great clump of a foot?' he asked bitterly.

Roie hugged him tight. 'I would! I would!' she cried, her ardent heart burning with pity and love, and a maternally comforting feeling. The two slender bodies clung together, and so they were when a passing policeman leaned over the fence, tapped Tommy on the foot with his baton, and said: 'Hey, none of that in public places. You go and neck on your old woman's parlour sofa, young feller.'

'Garn!' snarled Tommy, jolted out of a half-doze. 'I was only cuddling her.'

'And very nice, too,' approved the policeman. 'But you go on out of here or I'll arrest you for loitering.'

They got up and fled, brushing the dried grass off themselves as they went, and the policeman looked after them and chuckled: 'Poor kids.' He sighed. 'Poor little rats.'

Roie and Tommy went up the street happily chanting under their breaths to the tune of 'A-tisket, a-tasket.'

'A flatfoot, a flatfoot, I lost me little flatfoot,' sang Tommy. He felt curiously triumphant. He knew that Roie would be more amenable next time he wanted to caress her. He squeezed her arm, and they looked into each other's eyes and laughed and trembled with delight. Roie felt words bursting their way out of her throat; she wanted to say something beautiful and memorable, for she knew that she had stumbled into some new and enchanting land. Life would never be the same again. But she could not shape her thoughts. Like mysterious flowers they bloomed and died without a soul to witness, falling into ashes in the mind that bore them.

'See you tomorrow, Tommy!' she asked. He nodded, started to say something, and changed his mind, for his voice was hoarse with excitement. Roie laughed and darted away with a coquetry that surprised herself. She danced into the hot dark hall of her home, and from its shelter watched him limp away down the street. Tommy! At the very name she shivered and hugged herself with delight. Then she remembered. She tiptoed upstairs, pricking an ear curiously to the cracked duet of Grandma and Hughie from the kitchen, as they socialized over another cup of wine.

'Ow! God blesser and keeper, Mother Machree!' cried Hughie, and Grandma sang in a monotonous treble:

Oh Brian O'Lynn had no britches to wear
So he got him a sheepskin and made him a pair.
With the skinny side out and the woolly side in
Oww! It's warm in the winter said Brian O'Lynn!

Roie let herself into her room. She went straight to the old powder-box where she kept her savings. There was thirty shillings left, which meant that she could get a new cotton frock . . . a yellow one . . . and a pair of white shoes. But Roie had other plans for her money. Wistfully she bundled up all her longings for a new dress, and hurled them out of the window. She scraped the shillings and the florins out of the box, which she kept shoved behind a rotten beam by the skylight. Then she tiptoed out of the room. Patrick Diamond's door was half-open. She peeped in to see him lying on his bed, his glasses jammed on his nose, and a puzzled frown on his brow. She stood in the doorway.

'Whatcher thinking of, Mr Diamond?' He glanced up at the girl poised like a butterfly in the doorway.

'Have a nice Christmas, Mr Diamond?'

'All by meself.'

'You should have come down and had Christmas dinner with us. We had a chook but it was as hard as a football.' Mr Diamond smiled, and there was something in his smile that made Roie want to rush over and kiss him, red nose and all.

'Families ought to be by themselves on Christmas Day.'

'But we've known you and Miss Sheily for so long you're almost part of our family,' argued Roie.

'I'll never be part of any pope-worshipping family, saving your presence,' said Mr Diamond, with what he considered extreme civility. Roie flared up like a heap of dry grass in mid-summer. She stamped her foot on the ragged linoleum and cried: 'All right, you can stick in your old room! And never think that I'll ask you to dinner again, because I won't!'

She rattled down the stairs as annoyed as if she had really asked him to Christmas dinner, and he had impolitely refused. She ran down the street to Jacky Siciliano's fruit shop. It was a heavily odorous place, with a luscious smell of over-ripe pineapples and rotting bananas. Half a dozen black-eyed little Sicilianos played in and out of the packing-cases which littered the backyard.

'Hello, Rosina. Merry Christmas, Gio. Hello, Tonetta,' said Roie. 'Your mumma in?'

'Yeah,' said Gio, jetty-curled, and with most of his brown frame projecting through his torn shirt and ragged pants. 'She's lying down with Pop.'

'Come on in, dearie,' called Mrs Siciliano from inside. Roie caught a glimpse of her through the fly-screen as she came through the door, pulling on a blouse over her petticoat. A second later her magnificent cow-eyes looked around the door.

'Good day, Roie love. Did you have a nice-a Christmas? Come on

253

in, and don't-a mind my old feller. He is sleeping off the big-a dinner he had.'

Roie looked at the bed, and the mound of Mr Siciliano's stomach protruding pinkly from his unbuttoned trousers. His mouth was open, and his moustache gently rose and fell as he snored. He was the picture of a happy Italian man on Christmas Day.

'I'm sorry to bother, Mrs Siciliano,' explained Roie, 'but I thought I'd pop around and ask if you still want to sell that brooch you showed me last week.'

'Oh, my big-a silver brooch!' exclaimed Mrs Siciliano, clasping her hands together, and shaking them outwards in a pleased, expansive gesture. 'You want to buy him now?'

'Yes,' said Roie unblushingly. 'I just thought of someone I didn't send a present to.'

'Buona, buona,' exclaimed Mrs Siciliano. 'It will make a nice-a present for some lady. Antonetta!' she shrieked out the door. Tonetta, small and brown and beautiful as an angel, came running.

'Watcher want, Mum?'

'You run upstairs and get my mother's brooch, the silver one. It's in the cardboard box with my corsets,' explained Mrs Siciliano in rapid Italian. A few moments later Tonetta appeared with the brooch. It was two inches square, with a dark red and beautiful stone in each corner. Both Roie and Mrs Siciliano thought they were rubies, but there were really balas. The centre of the brooch was a thick metal web of silver filigree, and a row of tiny tarnished tassels hung from the lower edge.

'Is it not bella?' demanded Mrs Siciliano proudly. Roie took it reverently. There was no jewellery in her family at all, except Mumma's wedding ring and a horrible, gold-bound shark-tooth that Hughie had once bought from a New Zealand sailor under the drunken impression that it was valuable.

'I've brought the thirty shillings,' said Roie, and as easily as that it was done. The brooch was hers. She ran out jubilantly, rubbing it on the front of her dress to brighten it. The red stones shone like a white rabbit's eyes in the sunshine, and the minutest fairy twinkle came from the swinging tassel.

Roie ran into Number Twelve-and-a-Half just as Dolour and Mumma returned from church. Grandma scuttled into the bedroom with the empty bottle, and Hughie composed himself on the couch, trying to appear fragile, and endeavouring not to breathe when Mumma was close, so that she might not smell the rich perfume of the port. Mumma was suspicious, but when Roie showed her the brooch, everything else flitted from her mind.

'Wherever did you get it? It's real!' marvelled Mumma, scratching with a reverent fingernail at the silver. Dolour squeaked with most satisfactory awe, and Roie said proudly 'Tommy gave it to me this afternoon.'

'Oh, he did not!' cried Dolour sceptically. 'Jews never give anybody anything.'

'All right, if you don't believe me,' flashed Roie, grabbing the brooch and glaring at Dolour. 'He was saving up for it for months and months, just so he would surprise me. You don't know how good and kind he is!'

Hughie, gawking shamefacedly from the couch, said: 'Well, I take back everything I said about him. It's a better present than I ever gave anyone.'

'You're telling me,' said Mumma with a scornful sniff.

'Oh, is that so?' cried Hughie furiously. 'You're a nice one to be talking that way, and you're not out of church ten minutes.'

'You mustn't mention anything about it to Tommy when he comes round,' said Roie anxiously. She blushed. 'He wanted it to be just a secret between us.'

Dolour whistled. 'You mean, like an engagement ring?'

'Maybe,' stammered Roie. Mumma nodded in a pleased way. She liked romantic secrets. Roie continued desperately: 'He thought perhaps people might think he was showing off giving me such an expensive present.'

'There's something in that, too,' approved Hughie.

Roie sat beside him and shook the brooch so that the little tassels rang. 'They're real rubies,' she marvelled, peering into the dark garnet depths of the balas. Rapture filled her soul. Her imagination was so strong that she could easily see Tommy giving her the brooch wrapped up in tissue paper and saying: 'This is a secret for us, like an engagement ring.'

Dolour cried: 'Crumbs, he must think a lot of you, Ro. Maybe he pinched it.' But Roie knew that she had won her point, that her family was admiring and respecting Tommy's generosity and taking it as a tribute to her own attractiveness. She felt warm and excited. It was almost as good as if it had really happened that way. Without regrets, she allowed the image of the yellow cotton dress, with a drawstring neck, to fade from her mind.

'What's that other parcel?' inquired Mumma. Roie said carelessly

'Oh, that's a nice cake of soap and a face-cloth that Mrs Siciliano gave me. I went in to wish her Merry Christmas, and she gave me that, funny old thing.'

So Christmas ended very happily.

The day after Boxing Day, Mumma did her shopping at Mr Jacky Siciliano's, a thing she never did, for Lick Jimmy was both closer and cheaper. But she wanted to thank Mrs Siciliano for being so kind as to give Roie a present. She had hardly ordered her weekend fruit before Mrs Siciliano burst out: 'You see the bella brooch I sell to Roie, eh, Mrs Darcia?'

Mumma's heart jumped in her shabby bosom. She waited a moment, then she answered quickly: 'It is a beautiful brooch.'

'I brought it with me all the way from Milan,' explained Mrs Siciliano. A tear sprang liquidly and brilliantly into her beautful eyes, and she thumped herself on her enormous breast. 'Ah, they are all-a gone now . . . the lace shawl, the turtle-shell-a combs, the white linen pantaletta, and the gold ear-rings with the little bells hanging. But I have to have the money. I am having another bambino, you see.'

Mumma expressed polite surprise, though Mrs Siciliano's habitual condition was such.

The Italian woman continued, 'Only thirty-bob-a. It was bargain! But Roie she look after it for me. No, she say she going to give-a it to someone who had not a present. Well, that somebody look-a after it for me.' Mrs Siciliano rapidly polished the air in front of her as though to wipe out the whole conversation and asked briskly: 'You want-a broccoli to-day?'

Mumma walked slowly home, laden down like a horse with two great kits of foodstuffs.

'Oh, Roie . . . Roie, my little girl.'

The innocence and naivete of Roie made her feel both proud and sorry, for she had been the same herself until she learned that nobody could be naive in such a world as this and not end up with a broken heart.

'I wish she hadn't fallen in love so early,' said Mumma sadly, for to her love meant sacrifice, and Roie's sacrifice both of her truthfulness and her thirty shillings was solid proof indeed that she loved Tommy Mendel.

Seven

The New Year was important in Surry Hills. It was really the great feast of the year, uninhibited by religious thoughts, and with a pagan finality about it. Those people, simple and primitive, but with a great capacity for feeling the abstract strong and vital about them, really heard the Old Year's faltering footsteps, and the clang of the door which sounded in the midnight chimes on December 31st. So they made it a feast, with lots of noise and ribaldry, as ancient peoples did when they were a little fearful, and wanted to frighten away their fear.

Where Coronation Street met Plymouth Street there was a rough rectangle striped silver with tramlines. Every year it was the custom to build a bonfire there, just out of reach of the trams, which rushed past in a fleeting crimson glow from the flames. The authorities always forbade it, and nobody ever took any notice of what they said, but went on lighting New Year bonfires just the same.

It was Thady's birthday on the last day of the year, and Mumma always approached it with a sadness she could not control. They all felt this sadness, in a ready emotionalism which made tears spring to the eyes at the sound of a familiar song.

Grandma always felt a cold wind blow over her, for who was to tell whether this was not her last New Year?

To Roie the whole sweet scroll of the year was there, unblemished and white as snow. Christmas had been enchanted, and the enchantment had driven her on to this day, which she felt, fatalistically, would be important in her life. She dressed herself with special care, washing her body all over in the tub in the laundry. It was only a little tub, and when she breathed most of the water flew out. But when she finished, warm and clean, and dried herself on the hard old scrap of a towel, she felt light and airy and indescribably precious, as though her body had all at once become significant. Roie was a modest girl; she stacked lumps of firewood against the laundry door so that Hughie or Patrick Diamond should not come bursting in. In the dim light she looked down at her slender form and wondered. How strange it was! She breathed 'Tommy!' and stretched out her arms longing to hold him and be close to him.

Dolour and Hughie were the most excited of all. Their childish souls looked forward with wriggling impatience and rapture to the bonfire, and the spuds they would roast in the red embers afterwards and all the yarning, and the camaraderie and the high jinks.

'You like flire!' asked Lick Jimmy of Dolour as she bought the potatoes. 'They bling flire bligade and put him out,' he prophesied gleefully, his satin ivory face breaking into ten thousand hair-fine wrinkles. Dolour scoffed: 'Just as though anybody would be such spoilsports. You're silly, sometimes, Jimmy.'

All the afternoon the kids were dragging refuse to the fire. Most of the mothers thought that it was a good opportunity to get rid of all the old clothes and newspapers around the house, and the kids took their trolleys and trundled all the afternoon, with shouts and jeers at each other, as they spied familiar articles. Harry Drummy, reckless as all the Drummys brought a whole barrow load of paper which would have been sold to Lick Jimmy or Mr Siciliano for the price of at least two Saturday afternoons at the pictures. Dolour Darcy brought two old chairs, which Miss Sheily, in the height of rage, had suddenly hurled down the stairs to her.

'Take the foul things and burn them,' cried Miss Sheily. 'They've got bugs in them, and I'm sick of having my bottom nipped every time I sit on them. Caesar's ghost, a woman can't even sit down in this place without being injured.'

So Dolour bore them rapturously off. Mumma reckoned that they had little to burn at all, for they wore all their old clothes, and used their old newspapers as packing for their beds in winter, as newspaper is warmer than blankets and doesn't require washing.

By the time the clear blue of evening was in the air, the bonfire was twelve feet high, with a base like a redwood tree. It was going to be the biggest bonfire Surry Hills had ever had. Dolour was so excited she couldn't eat any tea, though it was her favourite mince pie with potato crust marked into little channels with a fork. A dozen times she ran down to the bonfire to see how it was getting on, and to exchange pleasantries with the small boys posted there to guard it against the inevitable drunken lout who would want to set it off before its time.

By the time the street lamps lighted into high, far, wire-guarded topaz globes, there was quite a crowd, sitting on doorsteps, squatting on kerbs, and leaning idly against walls. An air of satisfied expectancy was abroad. Father Cooley came out of the presbytery and pottered around amongst his parishioners for a little while, then tactfully went off. Sister Beatrix, on her way to chapel, stood on tiptoe and peered out between the grilles to see if she could spy the yellow spark of the fire.

Grandma had dressed herself as well as she was able, and put on an old cardigan with a huge hole in the elbow. She had brushed her white hair back very neatly, and was hanging over the gate, looking with bright-eyed curiosity at the passers-by, trying to pick out which ones were the prostitutes, the bash-gang men, and the cockatoos from the S.P. joint. Grandma's interest in sin was indefatigable.

Roie and Tommy wandered off early, into the shadow of the alleys, emerging to look astonished at the stars, so bright and enchanted tonight that they threw shadows. Once they came across, in a deserted street, a blind cat with opal-white eyes, walking around and around in a ceaseless circle, mewing pitifully. They stood and watched it moving in its endless darkness. Roie shuddered close to Tommy. A great gulp came out of her throat. Then a man came briskly out of a gate, seized the cat by the hind legs and thumped it six or seven times against a lamp-post. He threw the limp body into the gutter, and rubbed his hands down his trousers.

'Can't put up with that yowling all night,' he said cheerily to them as he walked inside again.

'Ah, God!' Roie and Tommy started to run. They panted down into Plymouth Street again. Tears streamed down Roie's face, and her throat ached with pain. Tommy held her face close to his jacket; he wanted to comfort her, but he did not know what to say.

'It couldn't see! It couldn't see!' was all Roie could murmur.

Suddenly there was a glad roar in the distance, and, startled, they looked up. Tommy, with glistening eyes, cried: 'It's on!' They forgot everything and pelted down towards the bonfire. They overtook Hughie, hurrying along with Grandma, very pigeon-toed, and discussing the whole thing energetically with her invisible familiar; Mumma waddled along behind, and behind her again came Miss Sheily, a look of supreme disinterest on her face, because she thought it beneath her to go to watch a bonfire. As they got there a

259

long red streak of flame licked up the side of the pile, and sparkled across the surface of the scattered papers. A second later there was a yellow glare, as some old books which Mrs Siciliano had saturated with grease and kerosene caught the flame. Whoosh! A ragged blue tongue of fire spurted high into the air, and everyone sprang back and surveyed it with awed excitement.

'Bravo! Bravo!' yelled Jacky Siciliano, and he kissed his wife with pride because she had thought of the kerosene. And all the black-haired little Siciliano brats danced gipsy-like around the bonfire, yelling shrilly.

Roie looked awed at the rose-red tower of flame, and the little hyacinth-blue sparks that showed and vanished. A ruby glow was cast over every face, the good and the wicked, the old and the young – old women with their hair rosy with reflected light; little goblin children, dirty and hungry, with bony brows and big, shining eyes; even babies with grubby wrinkled faces, blinking painfully in the glare. Dolour jumped up and down with hysterical excitement. The old year hovered around them; he was like a shadow vanishing bit by bit under an onslaught of light; all his fears and terrors, his failures and monotonies seemed now something soon to be tossed away upon the stream of time, to be forgotten for ever. Dolour did not feel this; she was only glad that she was one year older than this time last year; that she was almost fourteen, and not a child any longer, and soon would be freed from school and allowed to go to work.

Hughie stood with a grin frozen on his red-lit face. He thought: 'New Year resolutions . . . kid stuff. I'll keep off the plonk, except on Saturdays, because it does a man no harm to have a bit of a gee-up now and again.'

Dolour dreamed: 'Perhaps this year I'll find a diamond ring which nobody claims, or a five-pound note, or get on a quiz-session on the radio and win three hundred pounds and a fur coat for Mumma.' She wanted it so hard that tears gushed into her eyes, and her face turned crimson.

Mumma meditated: 'Thady would have been sixteen today. He would have been a big feller, like my family, because boys take after their mothers. He had blue eyes, and his hair was fair and sheeny-looking. But it might have gone dark. He might have looked like that boy over there . . . or that one.' And her heart cried out achingly: 'Oh, God, where is my little boy? Wherever he is, don't let anyone hurt him.'

Miss Sheily, staring into the yellow tongues of fire, thought: 'Last year Johnny was here. He laughed, and then he was frightened, and crouched down behind me.' Nobody could have told from Miss Sheily's acidly cold face what she was thinking, but the people standing near her moved uneasily away, for they could sense the chill waves of desolation that emanated from her.

And old Patrick Diamond, his stiff white hair roughly brushed over his low brow, his ruddy skin paler than it had been the year before, thought: 'What is the difference? One more lonely year. A long and empty life on the outskirts of other people's families. And no joy in it for a lonely man.'

He felt the premonitory prickling in his vitals, and then his stomach filled with nauseous pain. His indigestion was growing worse. He moved away quickly and stood amongst the crowd, so that Hughie wouldn't see the look on his face.

Suddenly there was a roar of laughter as Lick Jimmy, bent almost double under the weight of a huge humped mattress, trotted bent-kneed down the road.

'Mlind! Make wlay!' he giggled, flashing smiles to right and left as he peered under the drooping mattress. From a rent in its side kapok fell in a snowstorm, littering the street. With a gigantic heave Jimmy tossed it on the fire. There was a white puff of stinking smoke that billowed out and almost obscured a passing tram.

'Hooray! You beaut!' cheered everyone, and Lick Jimmy, taking it as a compliment, shook his clasped hands at them and vanished into the darkness again.

Suddenly, as though the sound fell from amongst the frequent and glossy stars, came the goblin wail of far-away sirens, blowing, blowing, in loops and streamers of sound.

'It's the New Year!' shouted Mr Siciliano, and he blessed himself with great, vigorous thumps. Then he seized his wife around her huge waist, and they danced like two elephants. Hughie gave Mumma a timid, shamefaced kiss on the cheek. She was delighted. 'Oh, Hughie!' she said, and then he kissed her properly. The sound of bells commenced. With harsh, jangling sweetness they swung and clashed in some far-off church tower; they shook out their simple music from narrow slotted windows, and it ran into waves and concussions of sound all over the huge and noisy city.

'Happy New Year!' shrieked everyone, and down in the dirtiest part of Surry Hills two hundred people linked hands and danced like red-lit gnomes about the fire; they forgot everything except the pagan pleasure of dancing in a warm and lighted circle of company and safety, with the dark outside it.

Roie and Tommy broke away. They ran up a dark street and stopped panting by a doorway. Tommy's lips felt their way over her cheek to her mouth. He felt excited and strong but he still did not know how to kiss her. He just pressed his lips on hers so hard that she nearly suffocated. They trembled; their eyes shone and their blood beat fast.

'Let's go for a walk. I'm sick of yammering boneheads.'

'Mumma'll miss me.'

'She knows I'll look after you.'

Two shadows passed swiftly through the starlit patch that slanted diagonally past the huge black bulk of the church, and the street was empty.

Back at the bonfire Mumma was breathlessly trying to disentangle her hands from Grandma's dry horny one and Dolour's hot erratic paw, when all at once there was a loudening shriek, swooping down the distant slope of Coronation Street. It was the fire engine. Almost simultaneously a large policeman detached himself from the fence. 'Move along,' he commanded, authoritatively. 'Move along there. Break it up. Move along.'

'Here,' protested Hughie. 'Don't tell me them cows in brass helmets is going to douse our fire?'

'All fires forbidden,' retorted the policeman. 'You read it in the newspapers, and it's posted up on the post-office wall.'

Beefy-faced, solemn, he inspired instant hatred in the crowd. There were yells of: 'Ole wet blanket. Why the hell don't you go home and go to bed?'

'Trust the bloody coppers to break up a bit of innocent fun.'

'Feet like wash-tubs.'

This caught Mr Diamond's fancy. He was by now slightly drunk having withdrawn to the shadows to have a nip or three from the bottle in his pocket, just to ease his indigestion. He began to revolve on his own axis, quietly chanting: 'Feet like wash-tubs. Feet like wash-tubs.'

The policeman quelled a smile. He prodded Mr Diamond gently. 'Come on, get along home. You've had enough for the night.'

Immediately Mr Siciliano, round as a barrel and dark as thunder, rolled up to him: 'Here, you flatfoot. You leave my friend alone. He has-a done nuttin.'

262

Mr Diamond looked down his hooky nose at him. 'No friend of mine, you black smoke. Go on, outa me way.' He waved an arm, and it struck the policeman across his cap and forced it down over his nose. Immediately an urchin, sneaking between the legs of the crowd, bit the blinded representative of the law savagely on the calf. The policeman gave an involuntary yell, thinking he had been stabbed, and promptly blew his whistle.

The fire brigade stopped further up Coronation Street to put out a smaller fire. Now it came ripping down the road, and stopped in all its splendour of crimson and brass helmets. Its arrival coincided with that of Delie Stock, who had just sidled out of her alley and was standing on the outskirts of the crowd, her eyes sparkling with indignation. 'Can't let the kids have a bit of fun,' shrilled Delie Stock.

'Aw, stow it, will ya, ma?' called back one of the firemen. With a high squawk of rage, Delie Stock picked up a potato from the heap which had been put aside for roasting in the embers. She hurled it with unerring aim, and the next moment a perfect hail of potatoes fell and clanged about the fireman's helmet. The policeman, struggling in the centre of the crowd, was a man besieged. Half a dozen old women battered him around the waist, and the taller members of the crowd clunked him with anything handy. Nobody hit very hard, and the policeman's dignity was hurt more than his head. Grandma, with eyes glittering with excitement, and a red spot in each cheek, was making a great to-do about getting a suitable potato. She picked up two or three before she found a nice round solid one that fitted into her hand. She had her arm raised to throw it, murmuring: 'Great splaw-footed spalpeen,' and 'I'll send it clean through his brisket,' when the horrified Mumma seized it from her hand. Grandma was bereaved, for she came from a long line of wild boys and girls who had specialized in potting King's Men from behind hedges, in the insurrections. While they argued about the justice of the matter, the firemen, with potatoes bouncing resoundingly off their helmets, played their hoses on the fire.

Dolour burst into tears: 'And it was such a lovely fire, the old bastards!'

Hughie was appalled. 'You cut that out, or I'll skelp yer hind shoulders good and proper.'

'You can talk, you and yer swearing,' fired up Mumma in defence of her child. The water cut a glittering white arc, falling in a hissing

torrent across the street. The children wailed: 'Awwwwwwwww!'
and the struggle around the policeman began with renewed fervour, many trying to rescue him before some lout hit him with a
broken bottle, and others trying to commit assault on his person.
There was a shrieked colloquy among the firemen, and all at once
the nozzles of the hoses were pointed right at the crowd. It was
packed too tightly for any one of them to move away quickly.
Grandma was torn from Mumma's restraining hand, and washed
away, a rain-bowed spray of water beating against the back of her
neck and blowing her white hair up in an enraged crest. Delie Stock
was right before a nozzle, and the force of the roaring crystal stream
threw her violently across the street. It was the first time she had
had a bath for thirty years, and she loathed it. She lay in the gutter
bubbling and spitting out curses in a half-drowned tone. As she
pulled herself up to a sitting position another avalanche of water
washed her further down the street, where she lay spread-eagled
over a grating until somebody picked her up.

Grandma was shuddering like a tree in a wind, and talking
rapidly to herself and everyone else in a voice which grew more
Irish every moment. She had never had such a time in her life. Her
enjoyment was so evident that Mumma was not only anxious, she
was furious. She seized Grandma by her stick-like arm and marched
her up Plymouth Street, Grandma pulling back and complaining,
and dripping wet at every step, and finally bursting into tears of rage
and over-excitement.

Hughie and Patrick Diamond, soaked to the skin, and muddy to
the elbow from rolling in the drenched dust, heard the fire engine
start and whirr away to some other fire. In the semi-darkness they
looked sadly at the drenched black mess which had been their
lovely bonfire. A dripping and shivering figure flew up to them. It
was Dolour, her cotton frock clinging to every bone in her thin
body, her hair plastered in dark rat-tails.

'You little chump, why didn't you get out of the way of the
water?' demanded Hughie with angry anxiety. Patrick snarled:
'Why didn't you?' and then all three laughed. The crowd laughed
with them.

'Well, we had our dance and our old langa-syne,' said Jacky
Siciliano philosophically. He gathered up all his chicks. 'Come,
Antonetta! Rosina, Amelia, Grazia, Maria, Violetta and Giacomo!'

Mrs Siciliano, who had been looking as though she were

listening to some elusive sound, very distant, suddenly gave a shrill scream and bent over, clasping her hands to her abdomen. The whole crowd of Sicilianos, chattering and screeching amid groans and ejaculations of 'Dio Mio!' hurried down the road, Mamma Siciliano in the middle like a clumsy hen. Hughie, looking after them, shrugged: 'Ah, well, another one in the basket before morning.'

'They're going to call it Michelangelo,' remarked Dolour with bright, interested eyes.

The evening had ended in the sort of excitement Plymouth Street loved. The kiddies played in the pools of dust-streaked water, and the toddlers chewed bits of charred potato, and had to be dragged shrieking home to dry clothes and bed. The elders said they had never had so much fun in all their lives, and shouting gaily across the streets they straggled home. The New Year was here, and bright and shining it stretched before them, unblemished by any failure, unsmudged by sorrow or ignominy. They found it impossible to think of it in any way except optimistically.

Eight

Down in the park, in the dark spokes of shade which radiated from a phoenix palm, Roie and Tommy lay. It was one o'clock, and very quiet. Only a cricket chirped in the moonlight. It was hard to believe that they were almost in the centre of a great industrial city.

Tommy looked up at the sheaves of rich golden 'dates' which hung above him. He was so troubled he did not know what to do. Although he had received a normal education he had so few instincts of right and wrong that he was morally a savage. He was almost incapable of comprehending another person's viewpoint, or imagining the consequences of his deeds in another's life. So when he desired Roie, he thought nothing of Roie. He loved her only because she induced in him a sense of importance, and a sequence of pleasurable sensations. Most of all, he wanted to have an experience, which he could recount in lingering detail to his mates. They all boasted so much, and though he boasted, too, he always felt that they listened to his lies only through pity for his physical deformity. He knew that they knew he had never had a girl; there had been nothing worth boasting about in his life according to his standards. But he did not know how to go about making love to Roie. His desires choked him, and he did not know how to start the cycle that would release them.

He felt ashamed of himself, knowing that he did not have the forwardness or the coarse male pride that would permit him to take her by force, no matter how much she struggled. Yet, unknowing, his quietness and unease won her as force would never have done.

As he lay with his head on her little breast, a strange and delicate feeling stole over Roie. His soft hair was under her chin, so soft it was like a child's hair. She knew he was not the tender and masterful lover her dreams had built; he did not fit into the mould created by books and films; his words were ordinary, his body was slight and ill-formed, and his clothes were musty-smelling, rough to feel, and ugly to look at. There was nothing admirable, romantic, or even desirable about him. Deep in her heart Roie knew all this, yet she fiercely drove the knowledge back before the force of her love

266

and pity for, and understanding of him. She deliberately shut her eyes to all that was weak or foolish, because in her mind recognition of it would be disloyalty to her love for him. She rubbed her cheek gently against his hair, springy and faintly warm. She said shyly: 'Darling.' He answered nothing, pressing his face closer, and trembling. It was queer; it was like the time when, in the country she had come across a rabbit in a trap, and, running her finger along its silken side, she had felt the minute, continuous vibration of its terror.

She held him as a mother might an agitated child. 'Tommy, this isn't any good for you or me either. Let's get up and go home. It's time.'

He held her tightly and mumbled hoarsely.

'No,' she said, frightened suddenly. 'No, I can't.'

He snarled in a sudden fury: 'It's the same with all you sheilas. Giving a bloke the come-on for all you're worth, and then all at once, biff, it's turned off at the main.'

He put his head down on her breast again and she felt a tear fall on her skin. It was as though she were made of ice, and the warm tear melted it.

'Tommy . . . Tommy, darling, don't . . .'

'God, I wish you felt as I feel. I wish you were a man, just for a minute. Then you wouldn't say no to me again, ever.'

For a brief moment she had a wordless, almost uncomprehended glimpse into his mind; she saw as he did, his drab room somewhere, the chafings of his daily life, the disillusionments that had always been his; the surgings of manhood which distorted his outlook, broke into his sleep, and interrupted the flow of his whole existence. She felt such tenderness her heart nearly broke.

'Tommy, you do love me, don't you?'

He wanted to say 'Ah, hell!' but already he had learned that it was better to say yes.

'Roie, would I feel like this if I didn't? Ah, Ro, only once. I swear I'll never ask you again.'

It was too late to retreat. His breath on her face, his clumsy, uncontrolled kisses on her throat, Roie struggled for an instant. She wanted to yell for her mother. But the black panic which engulfed her became grey, and then faded into nothing at all. Did it matter? Did anything matter but to serve the blinding love and desire to please that possessed her?

'No, Tommy . . . please, Tommy, no.'

But she knew, all the same, as she had subconsciously known when she dressed that evening, that it was the end. The stars swung down, and were blotted out by his shoulder.

Afterwards, walking up the street, they were selfconscious and afraid to look at each other. Roie tried very hard to feel uplifted and thrilled, as she knew people in books and in pictures felt, but there was nothing in her heart but an ache and a terror of realization. She wanted to cry on Tommy's shoulder, but she knew bleakly that he wouldn't understand what it was all about. When they saw an empty tram swing around the corner, an illuminated red and yellow beetle, they were both so glad that they began to run.

'Feel all right, kid?' asked Tommy as she swung aboard.

She smiled. 'Sure, I feel fine.' Her lips trembled.

'I'll be around Wednesday.' He half-pushed her into the tram, and crying 'Good-bye, here's yer fare,' he shoved threepence into her hand.

Roie didn't say anything. She was afraid that the ache in her throat would grow and engulf her self-control. Oh, God! Was it like this with everyone? Disappointment and apathy and a let-down feeling worse than anything on earth? She sat heedlessly staring into the darkness, blotched with faint light, that flowed past the open door. Why had she done it? She began to shake, cold and prickling alarm enveloping her. Forgotten was that moment of pity and understanding for Tommy, and the tenderness which, like something out of heaven, with the dew still on it, had flooded her heart.

But the threepence hurt worst of all.

Crawling into bed later, Roie pushed the whimpering Dolour over on her own side with more than usual ferocity.

'Quit crawling all over me, will you?'

She glared down at the pinched mouse face of the child whey-white in the moonlight, her upper lip raised over two dry and shiny rabbit teeth, her eyelids heavy circles of sleep.

'Stop yer kicking,' wailed Dolour in a thick, sleep-sodden voice, which drifted away into a complaining mumble.

'Yeah,' whispered Roie with unreasonable savagery, raising her swollen face from the pillow. 'You just wait until it happens to you. You just wait until you find out what it's all about.'

Then she put her arm over Dolour and hugged her thin and

bony little body close, vowing that she would never suffer as she, Roie, was suffering.

The next morning it did not seem so bad. It was so strange and unfamiliar a happening that it was almost unreal. Roie lived as though in a dream until Wednesday, when Tommy came around for her. They went to the pictures, treating each other with courteous attention, just like strangers. Roie made desperate efforts to recapture the thrill that had once been hers when she sat next to him, the brush of his fingers on her arm, the sound of his breath. But it was all gone. Strangely and mysteriously it had gone. Tommy looked at her, her lower lip thrust out sulkily, her eyes sombre, and thought with what fast turned to indignation, 'I suppose she wants me to crawl to her – tell her how wonderful she was to give in to me. Yeah, some chance of that. Just like any other sheila. It's true what the boys say . . . they're all alike when you've got to know them.'

He did not feel desire for her any longer. She might have been almost anyone. Any rate, she hadn't been so marvellous; discussing the incident in minutest detail with his mates, he had found out that other girls could provide much more excitement.

Outside the picture show he said, 'Saw my Uncle Joseph last night.'

'Yeah?' trembled Roie, trying to be interested.

'Yeah. He's getting me a job all right. Funny you should mention it the other day. He's getting me a job in a boot factory at Leichhardt; so I won't be seeing you so often.'

Roie instantly recognized the tone in his voice for what it was. She tried to be angry, hurt, almost anything rather than the apathy which possessed her.

'You needn't think I care,' she said, piteously defiant.

'Don't be bats. I'll come over as often as I can,' he said. He felt a little regretful. She was a nice kid; she'd looked pretty in that old red shawl. Even now he was half willing that they should continue their relationship.

'Sure,' said Roie.

She stood there for a moment, her lip trembling, not looking at him. There seemed to be nothing to say at all. All at once, almost violently, life returned to her limbs and mumbling something she did not hear herself, she ran away up the street. She did not want to see Tommy limping away, no longer the centre of her existence, but just an ordinary young man with untidy hair and the mark of a boil

269

on his neck. She ran into the church, for her breath was beginning to come in sobs and she knew that at any moment she might cry. It was shabby and drab in there, but its silence thrust away the street noises until it was as though she knelt in an oasis of quiet and peace.

'Oh, gee,' she prayed, 'what did I do wrong? I tried to give him everything he wanted. But I'm not sorry he doesn't love me any more . . . that's the dreadful thing. I'm not sorry. I don't love him either. We lost it somewhere. Oh, God, why does it happen like that?'

Then her fear caught up with her, and she cried in a mental voice so full of anguish that she felt it would reach to the ear of God Himself.

'Oh, Lord, let me get away with it this time! I won't ever do it again. Don't let anything happen to me, for Mumma's sake. Oh, Lord, please don't!'

She looked at the altar, wishing a candle might miraculously light, or even a flower fall out of a vase . . . anything that would tell her that heaven, with an invisible stream of light, had opened towards her. But there was nothing but silence and the muffled orchestra of the trams in the far distance.

She said over and over again, 'I'm wicked, I'm wicked,' but no comprehension of the words came into her mind. She felt no weight of sin, and she was bitterly ashamed, for it was as though all the teaching she had ever had was gone for nought.

Roie entered upon a period of cruel and agonized waiting for reassurance. Every minute as it crawled by was filled with unutterable confusion. She found it impossible to hide it all, and everyone noticed that there was something wrong with her. Mumma put it down to the bust-up Roie had told her she had had with Tommy, but consoled herself with the thought that it was all for the best, for a Jew and a Catholic are not the best of religious partners. She slept restlessly, so that at last Dolour complained.

'She's still thinking about Tommy,' chuckled Grandma maliciously. Mumma flared: 'You shut up, with yer unkind remarks, Ma. It's more likely them bugs up there in that room.'

'It is, too,' said Roie fiercely, glaring at Grandma, 'chewing the feet off me every night.'

Hughie shrugged resignedly. 'They're in the cracks of the old dump. You'd have to burn it down before you got rid of them.'

'Then why can't we go somewhere where there ain't no bugs?' asked Dolour. 'Are there bugs in all the houses in Sydney?'

'How should I know? Have I been everywhere?' asked Mumma. Roie flung herself down at the table and looked at a newspaper.

'Look at this: "Beautiful Socialite Weds Visiting Actor". Bet she never got up in the morning dead-tired through being bitten to death all night. Bet bugs don't crawl out of her nightdress on her honeymoon. Dirty stinking things. I'm sick of them!'

'Well, what are you yelling about them now for? We've had them all our lives, haven't we?' asked Dolour reasonably. Hughie suddenly thumped the table.

'Let's declare war on the foul creatures!' he cried with enthusiasm. 'Come on, Dolour, go and get the kerosene, and Grandma, you can bring up yer pipe. It'd smoke anything out of its hole.'

'Hugh!' remonstrated Mumma, blushing. She put their dinner in the oven, and they all trooped upstairs, Grandma well behind, because she had had a bad cold since New Year's Eve, and felt a strange heaviness in her bones.

Hughie turned over the bed, and they pulled it to pieces.

'Ah, look at the cows!' he ejaculated. He held his nose, and his blue eyes looked over the knot of his fingers with a disgusted horror. For there were more bugs than could be believed. In every pit and screwhole, every joint and crack they clustered, so thickly that sometimes there were whole marshalled lines of them, hidden cunningly in a twist of the wire or a crevice in the iron. A faint filthy smell arose from them alive. Dead, they would smell overpoweringly, of mingled musk and ammonia.

'Every night's blood transfusion night for them,' said Dolour. 'Whee, lookut them run!'

'Why can't we get a fumigator in?' asked Roie querulously. 'We've done this a thousand times. Washed down the beds with kerosene. Burnt them out of all the cracks, and what happens? A month later we've got them worse than ever.'

'Well, it stands to reason you won't never have no bugs,' pointed out Mumma reasonably. 'Everyone's got bugs around here.'

'Why don't the Government do something about it? That's what I'd like to know,' said Hughie, lighting a twist of newspaper and running it deftly along the thick currant-like clusters. They shrivelled up under his eyes, and fell to the floor, a scattering of dirty

271

little brown corpses. 'A gink from New Zealand was telling me it's a crime to have bugs over there. You get fined if they's found in yer house.'

'A fine thing that is!' said Grandma indignantly. 'As though it's a body's own fault.'

'The point is,' explained Dolour, 'if everyone had no bugs then nobody would have any bugs.'

'Say, you think that up yourself?' asked Hughie admiringly.

'Ah, shut up!' snapped Roie. She dabbed a brush in the kerosene and began painting the wooden parts of the bed. Everywhere before her brush rudely awakened bugs scurried away. Without distaste or disgust she crushed under her shoe the ones that fell on the floor. She was inured to their filthy smell; she had been squashing bugs all her life, for only in the coldest months of winter were the slum houses free of them, as it was then that they hibernated in half-dead transparent clusters in the walls and furniture. Roie could have told you all about them, the tiny white baby bug whose bite is the most vicious; the mature bug, brown like a woodlouse and marked in tiny ridges across the back, which feeds until it is so bloated it is shiny, and disgorges droplets of blood at every step. She could have told you that bugs rear up on their hindlegs in order to bite; that they are terrified of light and move with extraordinary swiftness; she could have described the way they tormented her whilst she was at work, for it is so difficult to find a bug that is adept at hiding under the narrowest seam. Bugs had dwelt with her since she was a baby, as they had dwelt with her parents and grandparents, and the people who had occupied Number Twelve-and-a-Half before them.

Cynically she watched Hughie's enthusiastic efforts, for she knew that nothing short of cyanide ever cleared them out of a house. Even then they were back again in a year or two, migrating from the house next door as soon as the poison died out of the timbers. And who would pay for a cyanide fumigation? Not the landlord; he got his rent even if his property were vermin-infested.

Hughie screwed up the bed again, and Grandma swept up all the corpses and bits of burned paper. Mumma felt happy and satisfied. 'There now, Roie love; you'll sleep better tonight.'

'Nobody cares how I sleep,' complained Dolour.

Hughie gave her a slap on the tail as they went downstairs. 'You sleep like a dead horse. I can hear you snoring every night, right through the floor.'

Late that night Roie lay awake, for the night was hot and stifling,

272

and Dolour restless, kicking her savagely, and lying diagonally across her body and clutching her with feverish nightmare-ridden hands.

'Oh, God,' moaned Roie. 'If only I could have a bed to meself!'

She got up and leaned out the window. The backyard, shrouded in shadows, was beautiful, the white moonlight clothing ugly prosaic things with a milky vapour. A cat slunk, a padding shadow, across the white space, and she saw its eyes like glazy green circles in the darkness. Far away a tug hooted on Darling Harbour. But there was nothing of the sea in the air, only the rising breezes laden with the smells of the cooling earth; dry grass, and night flowers opening and the half-exotic odour of a great sleeping city.

She wanted to pray, but she could not. Her secret terror shook itself and awoke, filling all her body with a cold, prickling panic. What was the use of praying? God had hidden his face; the saints loathed her. There was nothing but confusion and darkness all around. Suddenly Roie heard a strange sound, a swishing, regular sound. And now and then there was a whimper, cut off short, as though it were jerked involuntarily out of someone. Roie's skin prickled; it seemed to be in the room, and then all at once a long way away. Could it be a ghost? For Roie believed most matter-of-factly in ghosts, and would not have been at all surprised to meet one.

Then she realized that it was coming from Miss Sheily's room, through the wall. She pressed her ear against the plaster, and it was much louder, a swish, a thud, a swish, a thud. What on earth was Miss Sheily doing? At first Roie thought of wakening Dolour, and asking her what she thought of it, and then she remembered the peephole.

The peephole was a tiny hole pecked in the wall at the end of the room. Long ago, when Roie and Dolour were children, they had discovered it, and had had a wonderful and illuminating time watching the squabbles and reconciliations of a young couple who lived there; Roie had learned more about the facts of life from the couple than she ever had from her mother's timorous teachings. Then one day Dolour and she had been discovered, and Mumma had blocked up the hole with putty and taken them both downstairs and lectured them for a solid half hour on miserable tom todgers who hadn't the honour to keep their sticky beaks out of other folks' privacy.

'It's worse than looking under the door of the lavatory,' Dolour had miserably confided to Roie later, after they had yelled their way upstairs, holding their wounded bottoms. But now Roie, without a thought of intruding on Miss Sheily's privacy, did something she hadn't thought of doing for years. She took a bobby pin and pecked out the putty and applied her eye to the hole. She could see a jagged piece of the next room, half lit by a bare electric light globe that had an old blue scarf draped over it. There was a dressing-table, and a corner of a shelf with a packet of cheese on it, and something that looked like half a loaf tied up in a tea-towel. And there was also Miss Sheily, kneeling down, her back bare, and her blouse hanging down around her waist.

At first Roie thought Miss Sheily was having a wash, and she was about to replace the putty when the swishing sound began again, and with a shiver of horror, her blood tingling with the shock, she saw that Miss Sheily was whipping herself.

'Oh, God!' thought Roie. 'She's gone mad!'

In her hand Miss Sheily had a bundle of knotted strings. They were tipped with something like sharp little screws of wire, and she was lashing her back with them. The whip flicked over her shoulders with regularity, falling with little thuds on her sharp shoulder-blades and the flat ugly back. And each time there was a thud, Miss Sheily's breath escaped in a little involuntary moan.

Roie was frozen with horror. She could never have imagined so bizarre a scene. She made wild gestures to the sleeping Dolour to wake and look, then she became aware that every time Miss Sheily moaned she moaned a word. It was 'Johnny'. The blood sprang up on her back in dark ruby beads, and a spiderweb of red marks slowly grew under the lash.

'Johnny! Johnny!' moaned Miss Sheily. Roie sat back from the peephole with a shudder of disgust and shock. She jammed back the little plug of crumbling putty and tottered over to the window, feeling sick.

'Oh, gosh,' said Roie. She was sorry she had spied, but only because she had been precipitated into such grief, and Miss Sheily's sour, bitter, determination to atone for the wrongs she had done her son.

Staring out into the desolate backyard, and the ebony channel of the alleyway, Roie wondered about life, and the strange way it revealed itself. Who would have guessed that Miss Sheily, so poker-faced, so consumed by bitter furies and hatred of everyone, was in secret whipping herself in an effort to ... to what? Roie's conjectures fell short, though she was no stranger to the doctrine of atonement. She had been brought up on tales of saints who inflicted pain on themselves in an attempt to atone for the sins of themselves and the world.

'Poor Johnny,' sobbed Roie. 'Poor Miss Sheily.' The tears stung their way to her eyes, and she hung her head, so that the moonlight failed to find her in the slanting bay of the window. When she moved back to her bed, the moon had gone, and all was in darkness.

Nine

Saturday afternoon was the great afternoon of the week in Plymouth Street. The factory girls washed their hair and did it up in perforated aluminium curlers, put on old print dresses with sagging necklines and torn pockets, and sat on the peeling, cocoa-coloured balconies of the tenements, beating off the flies and saying: 'Gawd, ain't it hot!' Downstairs, on the pockmarked steps of the old houses and the drab boarded-up shops, old men sat, legs wide, their stomachs bulging open the top buttons of their pants, hats pulled down over their grey frowsy faces, and talked politics, racing, or lang syne.

Down into the mean canyon of the street the sunshine poured, like yellow wine, and under its magic there was a gleam and a glimmer over everything, so that shadows seemed furry and mysterious, and the iron lace around the balconies Moorish and exotic. Lick Jimmy came out, cleaned his window, scrubbed his step, his little black-clad bottom jiggling energetically as he did so. Then he went in and locked and bolted the door, and sat in his corner by the window, peering over the humped, comfortable back of his cat, which drowsed between two pineapples. Lick Jimmy, too, liked to watch Saturday afternoon in Plymouth Street.

Joseph Mendel came from between the concertinaed gratings which protected his front door from the blow-torch and the exploring hand. His round black velour hat clamped firmly on his white, intellectual head, he walked briskly off down the street. The skirt of his coat had a foreign look to it, different from the hip-hugging coats that the men of Plymouth Street liked to wear if they were young, or the baggy hand-me-downs that they had to wear if they were old.

Joseph Mendel was respectfully greeted as he passed, but there was no friendliness in the eyes which looked at him, for he held so many of the people there in bondage. There was something queer about him, as there was about his nephew Tommy, always a sly one in spite of his deformity, which should have taken some of the reticence out of him. They were both foreigners, Australian born, perhaps, but still with the black and antique seal of their ancestry upon them.

Hughie was asleep with the exhaustion of his heavy work and the heat, which had not ebbed for twelve or fourteen days of bush-fire and drought. Dolour was sprawled on the floor of her room reading movie magazines and chewing potato crisps. Roie was out for a walk. But after they had finished the lunch dishes Grandma and Mumma tidied their hair and went out and sat on the balcony, Grandma with her hair pulled back very tight and smooth from her bony freckled forehead and Mumma fatigued and yellow, her stockings wrinkling down into old dirty slippers, the heels of which had been trodden into pancakes. It was so hot on the balcony, yet there was air there, fresh with the breeze which played fugitive from Darling Harbour and came running over the city. The two of them sat there, rocking in the old, uncomfortable wooden chairs, the rush bottoms of which had poked through and were in the habit of pinching any unwary behind that sat upon them.

Grandma was not feeling very well; there was a drag in her feet as though an invisible anchor had attached itself to her heels. She asked: 'Where's that Tommy these days, love?'

'Oh, they had a fight. He'll come around again.'

'He's an unchancy one, that,' commented Grandma. Mumma took it as a personal slur upon Roie's good taste.

'A gammy foot's nothing in these days of trams,' she said crossly.

Grandma chewed rapidly for a few moments, for she was wondering how to broach a subject that was in her mind. Finally she said: 'You want to wise her up about men, lovie.'

Mumma flushed. She had a curiously pure and naive mind and although every form of sin and obscenity had affronted her eyes while she lived in Plymouth Street she still cringed away from it as though it had been a beast, sly, lithe, and poisonous.

'Roie can look after herself, Ma. Anyway, Tommy ain't her first boy.'

'No,' said Grandma sagaciously, 'but he's the first one she's really liked, and that makes a difference.'

Mumma knew exactly what Grandma meant and because she did and had feared the same thing she became angry and tried to take it out on Grandma.

'Go on, you unnatural old sling-off, throwing mud at your own granddaughter,' she said heatedly. Grandma shrugged one shoulder and they went on rocking with determined rhythm, each intending that the other should see how utterly undisturbed she was. Then down the street came Chocolate Molly.

She was an Indian half-caste; she was a beautiful girl lost in a gigantically fat body. Magnificent eyes as lucent and black as glass flashed and flirted out of a face that was drawn in a succession of little curves, curved eyebrows and mouth, curved cheeks and chins. A green dress was drawn as tightly as upholstery over her bulges and her monstrous legs vanished abruptly into the tiny slippered feet of a fat woman.

'Lord look down on yer!' exclaimed Mumma. 'I wonder she's got the nerve to show her face!'

'What's she done now?' asked Grandma eagerly. 'Run off with someone's husband again?'

'Not her, the dirty little scrub,' returned Mumma, looking with unconsciously jealous eyes at the way all the men's eyes followed Chocolate Molly as she waddled up the street. 'Put the coppers on to Delie Stock's dope peddling, that's all. Fifty pound they say she got out of it. Delie managed to get out of it, but she'll be after Molly with an axe.'

Chocolate Molly was feeling nervous. She knew that pimping in Surry Hills rarely went unpunished. She was stupid and impulsive and had squealed on Delie Stock mainly because she had refused to sell her some wine at a decent price the day before. Still, she felt that little harm could come to her in an open street on Saturday afternoon.

She glanced liquidly at men on street corners draped against doorways and clotted in groups like flies before the pub doors.

'Hello, Teddy,' she called to a lank pimply youth who squatted in a doorway combing his long, oily hair. 'When you coming up again?' He winked and guffawed, jerking his head at the men around to draw attention to the conversation.

'What'll I get if I do?' he called.

'Why don't you come and see?' she shrieked across the street. Mumma blushed and looked away from Grandma, but Grandma chuckled like an old magpie and croaked admiringly: 'The dirty neygar.' Chocolate Molly, her confidence restored, waddled onwards. The lank young man, belatedly, shouted after her: 'You better watch your step, blossom. Phyllis and Flo are after yer.'

'What?' she shrieked. He made gestures, but they were lost on her. She drifted onwards. The young man shrugged, and went back to his rolling of a straw-thin cigarette. If Chocolate Molly chose to stick her fat neck out, why should he stop her?

All at once, just by the little dank alley which ran alongside the ham-and-beef shop, Molly noticed Phyllis and Flo. They were a strange pair. Phyllis was very young, about sixteen with an oblong, solid face lined and grimed with guilt. She had been a prostitute since she was ten. Her eyes were currant-brown, furtive and rabbity, darting away from the onlooker's stare. Her body was thick and lumpish, as graceless as a bath-tub. On the other hand, Flo was a tall, slender, elderly woman, with a face painted into the semblance of gentility. She wore a tight black costume, and her hair was set with steely rigidity into the most elegant of afternoon-tea coiffures. She even wore gloves.

The sight of the two was more sinister to Chocolate Molly than that of a man with a knife in his hand, for they were both employees of Delie Stock. She noted the gloating greed upon the moronic face of the younger girl, and the cruel, vulture-like expression in the yellow eyes of Flo.

'Why, hello, Molly love,' said Flo in her tight, genteel voice. Mumma felt quite sick. Her hand closed over the withered arm of Grandma, in order to take her inside. But Grandma let out a yelp of indignation and shook it off.

'What are yer, yer wet blanket, spoiling the only bit of fun I get?' she complained.

Chocolate Molly, cornered, attempted to brazen it out.

'What you want, eh? You get outa my way, you bag of bones,' she said, for she did not lack courage. Phyllis swore explosively. She was like an animal trained to maul and kill, and she was chafing at the bonds of Flo's restraint. Her pig-like eyes roamed all over Molly's luscious and defenceless frame, as though choosing a vulnerable spot.

'Yer stinking stoolie,' remarked Flo softly in her strange cracked voice. And beside her Phyllis jerked and reared like a tethered hound hungry to get in for the kill. Molly stood her ground.

'You touch me, and I'll tell the coppers,' she said loudly, glancing back at the men who stood watching.

'Yeah, if we leave yer lousy tongue in yer lousy head,' jeered Phyllis. Molly gave up all pretence of boldness. She gave a loud anguished squawk and tried to run, but Flo's long polished shoe shot out and she tripped headlong over it. She hit the ground with the squashy sound of a ripe fruit falling, and the men in the distance laughed. It did not occur to them to interfere, because in that district it is neither polite nor politic to get into other people's quarrels.

Not only did Phyllis remember the reward held out to Flo and herself by Delie Stock if they beat Chocolate Molly up. She was aching to slam into her for her own sake. In her ferocious and deadly unmoral little soul there was a love of violence. She threw herself upon Molly's quaking body and hammered her head upon the pavement. She rubbed it this way and that, grinding the brown girl's nose into the burning asphalt and making her squeal with agony.

'Go easy, love, you'll hurt her,' remonstrated Flo. Phyllis gave a strong heave and hurled Molly face upwards on the pavement. Her lips were purple, and her thick mouth open in a dark O of dust and blood. Phyllis punched her in the teeth a dozen times, then stuck one finger in her eye and wrenched it sideways. Molly shrieked 'Help! Help!' at the top of her voice, but nobody took any notice. Phyllis's face was a horrid, doglike mask of ferocity, her stained false teeth showing and her porcine eyes red with lust. She jumped to her feet and began kicking Molly in the stomach.

Mumma cried: 'Oh, oh, oh!' but Grandma merely murmured: 'Sure and she's got a boot on her, that one. She's wasting her time in this street. She ought to be on a football field.'

'They'll kill her! They'll kill her!' gasped Mumma, but she was too fascinated to turn her face away.

Then all at once Flo, who had been negligently leaning against the wall, took off her gloves and arranged them fastidiously upon the window sill. Then she sprang upon Molly's broad body, and holding on to the sill for balance, she began to trample her with her high heels, digging them deeply into her soft breasts and abdomen. Stamp! Stamp! She was like a savage tramping out the brains of his fallen enemy, and yet all the time there was a sort of polite smile upon her face. It seemed to Mumma that there was more cruelty in her action than in all Phyllis's wild beast attack.

When Molly was unconscious, Flo stepped daintily off, gave a few touches to her still perfect hair, and put on her gloves. She touched the reluctant Phyllis, and they moved off, to look for customers in Coronation Street. A drunk weaved up and hauled Molly into a laneway, where she lay for a long time. Hardly anyone else took any notice, for the pub was open, and so was the S.P. shop, Bert Drummy's. Grandma awoke to instant action. She dug eagerly in her skinny black purse.

'Run down with this and put threepence each way on Black Marlin for the third, will you, love?' she asked. 'Or maybe Dolour will do it.'

'I'll do it meself,' answered Mumma wearily; she would not have thought of allowing Dolour to go to Bert Drummy's, for he was the sort that liked to pinch the bottoms of his customers.

She shook a shovelful of coal into Puffing Billy's maw, pulled in a damper and moved up a slide, shook her finger at him when he started to cough, and went out, her old brown hat sitting on top of her screwed up hair. The burning wind smote her like a blow, and on her way back she was glad to go into St Brandan's for a visit. She trotted up the hollowed sandstone steps into the quiet dimness. There was a scattering of people before the confessional, and now and then the door squeaked open, and someone tiptoed creakily in. Mumma drew a deep breath of the clean, faintly incense-scented air, which she loved. She cast an affectionate glance towards the altar, still a mass of thick flowers, with brass shining amongst them. Dolour had helped to polish that brass, she thought proudly; it was almost as though she had done something herself. She knelt down before the poor little Crib, lovingly fixed up by the sisters, but still a miserable plaster cave with thin-necked plaster cows and horses standing amongst the sprinkled straw. A brown-robed Joseph stood stiffly by the little cradle, and a goggle-eyed Mary knelt by the goggle-eyed, too large Child. But Mumma saw it with other eyes. It was all real to her; the little plaster Baby soon became her own lost boy, Thady. Lovingly she looked once more at his rounded limbs, the gentle paleness of his hair, and the way his eyes crinkled as he laughed, showing his little square white teeth with the spaces between them. Little Thady! It was hard to think that he had often come into this church with her, and once she had smacked him because he had cried during Mass. She knelt in a muse. What could have happened to him? How was it possible for any child to vanish into thin air, the way he had done? He was a big boy, she thought piteously. Six years old, and big for his age. Her mind ran over the well-worn track of ten years; murdered, kidnapped for some inconceivable bad house, stolen by a woman with no child, taken by gipsies for sale ... how could he vanish?

She pulled herself back to consciousness with a start, aware that her heart was beginning to fill with the old mad tumult of grief, and that her face was showing it. She hurried out of the church, quickly, quickly, looking at the ground, so that people would not see her wild, anguished eyes. When she got back to the house, she went into the bedroom to take her hat off. Hughie was awake, staring at the ceiling with sunken dark-shadowed eyes. They turned and fastened on her.

'Where you been?' There was a forlorn sound in his voice, as in the whine of a dog which dumbly asks its master not to reproach it for continued failings. Mumma rushed over to the bed and flung herself down beside him.

'Oh, Hughie, I been thinking about Thady, and it's at me again.'

'Ah, Thady. Me poor little feller,' said Hughie. He held her tight against his thin, lank, middle-aged body, and felt her breast shuddering with unvoiced sobs.

'He was so little to be by himself somewhere,' breathed Mumma. 'Oh, Hughie, what will we do? What will we do about it?'

They clung together, and all the memory of his past transgressions was wiped out in his mind and hers, and they loved and comforted each other, while upstairs Grandma, chewing rapidly, and discoursing irately with no one at all, leaned over the balcony rail and wondered the fate of her threepence each way.

As Roie walked, she thought, her thoughts chasing each other round and round like white mice in a cage. It seemed impossible that a baby could come from the clumsy and ludicrous embrace under the phoenix palm in the park. Roie did not know what to think of it. Sometimes she shuddered away in guilt and shame from the memory of Tommy's slender warm body pressed on hers, and his hungry untutored hands that hurt and fondled in one action. And at other times she thought that it hadn't happened at all; that she'd dreamed it in a sinful dream.

Almost with astonishment she viewed the fact that almost certainly she was to have a baby. Sometimes she thought that it was only because she was so afraid that she felt so sick, but in her heart she knew that nothing in her experience could cause these strange feelings; the swimmy nausea if she turned quickly, the tiny achings in her body, and the swelling of her breasts. But still it seemed impossible. Lots of other girls had babies; lots of them in Plymouth Street had had illegal babies. But not she. Not Roie Darcy, who hadn't mucked around with boys since the time when she was little;

who had always gone to Mass and her duty, who worked hard and paid her board and tried to be good. Roie recounted her virtues with urgent force to God, who seemed to have forgotten them.

'I'm mistaken, aren't I, dear Lord? You will please let me off it this time, won't you? You know I'll never do it again.'

But soon there was no mistake. Roie found herself in a blank terror. She prayed with frenzy that she might wake up and find she had died in the night. Yet she could not show any of this terror on her face. She went to work and came home and went to bed. She even went to the pictures with Mumma and Dolour and laughed. She lay every night beside her little sister and did not sob aloud. But deep down in her chest her grief racked her till her whole body ached.

What was she afraid of? Roie couldn't work it out. It wasn't the pain she was frightened of, nor of having a baby like Miss Sheily, to be a burden and a drawback all her life. She was afraid mostly of Mumma's finding out. It would have been different if Mumma had been like other women in Plymouth Street, bawdy and coarse and rough, even though they were kindhearted. She could have taken all the accusatory screams of a mother of that sort, and screamed back similar abuse. But she felt she couldn't face the shock on her Mumma's face when she told her. And Dadda. He'd go straight out to Leichhardt and get Tommy Mendel by the neck and beat him up, that's what he'd do. Roie felt that she couldn't bear that, either, the whimpering boy, and the sodden, infuriated father, and the ring of faces, and the dirty jokes of the crowd: 'He wants to take it out on the sheeny because he did his daughter in,' and the endless chatter from fence to fence until everyone who knew Roie Darcy even by sight would point her out, not always unkindly, but just with interest.

'It wasn't Tommy's fault,' sobbed Roie suddenly, and she buried her face in the pillow so that Dolour would not wake. 'It wasn't his fault. He was just being like all the other fellers. And I don't want him to know. I don't want to be married to Tommy.'

The horror of that idea became greater than the other. She imagined herself married to Tommy, who didn't like her any more. Perhaps they would have to live in the dark little rooms over old Mendel's shop, and Tommy would get drunk because he hated her, and knock her around, and her life would be the long misery of the unwanted wife's. And Tommy was a Jew; not a practising Jew perhaps, but still a foreigner. Roie nearly went crazy at the thought of marriage with Tommy. It was like looking through a prison gate and knowing that next year you would be looking through from the other side.

She remembered her talk with Dolour, long ago, and her saying, 'It's a wonder she didn't get rid of it,' and Dolour's naive little voice saying, 'How?'

Roie pushed the thought from her, but again and again it returned. The baby wasn't alive yet; it hadn't breathed. She wouldn't really be killing it. Other women did it, most women. Didn't old Mrs Campion next door openly boast of her fifteen misses? She took something . . . Roie remembered giggles amongst the girls at work and whispers from machine to machine: 'She's in trouble. Bet she'll be getting into the Epsom salts.' And there were other things, too, that you could buy at dirty little chemist shops. They slipped them over the counter – packets of pills, and little bottles of bitter black medicine. Roie knew. But they didn't always work. Even Mrs Campion, who found it so easy, said that. And if she did do it, and it worked, she could be sorry and never do it again. It was really the sort of sin you could be sorry about, once it was all over.

There were places you could go to, as well. There was Rosie Glavich at the factory, she was in trouble, everyone knew it, for she had to leave her machine every so often to go to the cloakroom and be sick. Then one day Rosie turned up, as white as a sheet, and spent the day sitting down too scared to move, and she'd told some of the girls that she'd been fixed up. She was sick a long time, but she didn't have a baby. It was worth it, everyone agreed.

Roie was like a girl running down a long dark lane from some pursuing horror. There seemed nothing else to do. Then out of the recesses of her mind came the name of the doctor who fixed Rosie up. He operated at a queer old yellow house in Murphy Street; a house with a genteel row of hanging palms and ferns, so that you dodged under a curtain of depressed and livid green before you reached the blistered brown door. The doctor used to come in the back entrance, and left the same way, and he charged ten pounds. Once Roie had decided, things were a little better for her, and she gradually developed a cold, calm tranquillity. She felt nothing for the baby. It was only an uncomfortable little lump in the pit of her stomach that made her sick if she walked fast. It wasn't really a baby yet; she didn't feel sorrow, or shame, or anything for the baby, only for herself.

She became very crafty at hiding her sickness, and every morning she got up early so that nobody would see her face without make-up. She did a lot of overtime too, and in a couple of months she had put aside the ten pounds. It was not difficult to get some overtime, for the work was so hard at the factory that the girls were exhausted after the day's labour, and did not seek it. Roie did not tell her family she was working overtime, pretending she was going skating or dancing with her girl friends. The lies slid awkwardly off her simple tongue, but Mumma believed them all the more because of that, thinking that Roie was trying to forget Tommy in this unaccustomed gaiety and did not want them to comment on it.

On her way home from work she called in at No. 17 Murphy Street. As she raised the iron knocker her heart thudded sickeningly, and she was afraid that she might be sick there and then. There was an old chair placed at one side of the door, with a sort of sardonic implication that visitors to that house might require it. Roie sat down upon it and tried to control her sickness. When she looked up she found that the door had opened silently, and a face was looking at her out of the crack. It was a face of an elderly woman, cracked into a thousand fine lines, like an old piece of china. Sharp grey eyes looked at her, and then, as she was about to speak, a voice said with a poisonous sympathy; 'Feeling bad, dearie?'

And then Roie knew that she had come to the right place. The door opened wider, in furtive invitation, and she stepped into the tiny hall with a grubby carpet on the floor, and a pot plant sitting spiky and hostile in the corner.

'Is this where . . . I mean . . . does the . . .'

The woman nodded familiarly. 'Yes, dearie, it's here. And he does. I make all the arrangements.'

There was a cold dankness about the house, as though the sunshine had never crept within its secret walls. A depression settled over Roie's spirit, so that she felt dreary and fatigued. The woman gave her a chair, and pulling a thumb-marked note-book towards her, said with a professional air: 'Now love, how far are yer?'

'Four months,' faltered Roie. The woman clicked her tongue. 'Youghta come earlier. Three months is bad enough. But four!'

Roie gasped: 'I couldn't save the money before this. I . . .'

285

The woman said: 'Men!' Then she added: 'What's yer name, love?'

'Beryl Graham,' said Roie instantly. The woman nodded approvingly.

'Better'n Smith or Jones.' She wrote it down. She leaned over and said confidentially, 'The Doctor's a good 'un. Good as a Macquarie Street man. He likes to help poor girls outa their trouble, that's why he comes down here.'

'Does it hurt?' gasped Roie. The familiar woman shook her head.

'Nah, no more'n a toothache. That's if you keep still. Ah, it's a good thing there's men like the doctor ready to help us girls outa our trouble. It'll cost you twelve pounds,' she added suddenly. Roie's heart fell.

'They told me ten!' she hurried out. 'I could only save ten.'

The woman looked at her grudgingly, 'I'll speak to the doctor.'

Roie nearly fell on her knees with gratitude. 'Oh, you must make him. Please make him help me.'

'Ho,' said the woman, sniffing. 'Mighty snooty you are with "make him". The doctor won't be made by no dirty little tart who wants to get outa the trouble she got herself into.'

'I didn't mean that,' gasped Roie humbly. 'I didn't mean to . . .'

'All right,' said the woman, softening, 'you can come on Wednesday evening about ten.'

Roie went blinking out into the blinding sunshine. The door shut behind her with a stealthy click, as it had shut behind dozens and hundreds of other girls. The street looked the same as it always had, smelling of unclean gutters and the sharp pungency of orange peel and rotting cabbage stalks. Roie hurried away, hoping that none of the peering eyes behind the curtains of nearby houses had noticed her, for she was sure that No. 17 and its purpose was known to everyone in Murphy Street.

When she got home, so great was her relief that she felt much better than she had for months. It was almost as though she had already been fixed up, and she was as she had been before she met Tommy Mendel. But during tea Mumma said, 'You're looking peaky, Roie. I bought you a tonic. It looks fine and strong.'

She gestured to the mantelpiece, and Roie saw the bottle, raspberry red, with a surly dark sediment in the bottom, and a chemists' sticker proclaiming it was the tonic of the times.

'Gee,' said Roie abashed. 'You shouldn't have done it, Mumma. Medicine's too dear.'

286

'Cost me five and six,' said Mumma proudly. 'I had to save up for a fortnight out of the house-money.'

Suddenly all the mischief in Roie's chest came to the top in one great bursting sob. The thought of her Mumma buying tonics for her when she was guilty and deceptive and plotting dark shame in her soul was too much for her to bear. She gave a croak of anguish, and burst into tears.

'Whist-awhist!' cried Grandma, staring at her over her fork.

Mumma dropped her knife and reached over and patted her daughter on the back, as though she had choked on something.

'What's the matter with you, child?' Roie jumped up and fled from the room. Face down on the bed, she sobbed with such hoarse rhythm that old Patrick Diamond knocked irritably on the wall and inquired what all the waterworks were about.

'You shut yer big gob, Mr Diamond!' cried Mumma stoutly, as she panted up the crooked stairs. 'Can't a girl even have a bit of a weep without you putting yer big snout into it?'

She looked at Roie with real anxiety. 'Now tell Mumma, can't you, darling, and whatever you've done, I'm on yer side.'

For one wild moment Roie thought of telling her everything, and then she realized that it was impossible. She choked: 'It's just that I'm so tired, and I got into a muddle at the factory to-day and the foreman told me off.'

'Oh,' she felt her mother's breast subside, and the relief come out of her like a wave. 'Then you take yer tonic, lovie, and yer'll feel better. I know what that sort of feeling is, none better.'

Down the road that night, someone stuck a knife into a Dutch sailor, and everyone forgot about Roie's outburst. Murders were not uncommon in Plymouth Street; in fact, on the corner where the sailor was found lying, two bodies had previously been picked up. The sailor lay face downwards, curled up in a gutter, and all evening long passers-by had not given him a glance, for the gutter was a favourite resting-place of drunks. Then someone noticed that he had no hat or shoes, and they investigated, and found the broken-off blade of a knife like a little silver slit in the centre of his adam's apple. He was a young dark man with good teeth, and he had a good deal of money on him before he was murdered.

Hughie stopped and had a look at the spot on his way home from work. There were still a few sticky, fly-clotted black stains in the gutter, and the urchins were gleefully pointing them out to people who went past. Hughie felt sorry for the young sailor, particularly as he had been a mug and flashed a roll of deferred pay in a pub, Hughie considered. His knowledge that he himself would have had more brains than that made him feel doubly sympathetic.

'Come down here after a girl, I suppose,' he said at the dinner table 'and someone sees his dough and invites him in for a glass of plonk and then lets him have it in the gizzard.'

'Stop it afore yer turn me liver up,' protested Grandma.

'I'll bet it had something to do with Delie Stock,' said Dolour, holding up a sausage on a fork and consuming it piecemeal. Mumma scolded: 'Youghtn't to talk that way about Mrs Stock that give you the lovely picnic,' she said. Roie rose from the table.

'I'm going to the pitchers tonight. Is my pink dress ironed, Mumma?'

'It's going under the arms, love. But it's hanging in the cupboard. Who're yer going with?' inquired Mumma.

'Rosie Glavich,' answered Roie. 'I'm meeting her in front of the Palace.'

'Why doesn't Tommy call now?' teased Hughie coarsely. 'Scared I might take a shot-gun to him?' Grandma tittered from the bedroom and Mumma went pink.

'Don't you dare talk like that to yer own daughter, yer piggy old fellow,' she remonstrated. 'Never you mind him, Roie love. He's got a tongue so long someone could tie a knot in it.'

'Someone oughter tie one in yours, and then we'd notice,' roared Hughie. 'Ah, the peace, the tranquillity!'

Roie got dressed, slowly. Because it was the gravest and most important night of her life, she put on her best underwear, her only pair of stockings without cobbles, and polished her shoes, which was a thing she rarely did. She cut her fingernails and brushed her hair carefully. Then she made up her face. Looking in the mirror was like looking at a stranger. She felt so much terror that it had all merged into a cold dreamlike numbness. She was like a woman committed to the guillotine and resigned to it, though in no way was her fear alleviated.

When she said good-bye to her mother, her voice was light and normal so that she marvelled at it. But as she went up the hall complete anguish seized her, and she shrank into the dark recess under the stairs where poor Johnny Sheily had played, so that he would not get in anybody's way. Girls sometimes died when they were fixed up. Roie couldn't imagine death for herself, but she

288

could imagine her mother's face when someone, the slatternly familiar woman at No. 17, for instance, came and told her that her daughter had died in a dirty back room in Murphy Street.

But it was too late now. She walked out into the street. The bright autumn evening, lucently blue in the east, with stars sparkling and in the west the calmest, purest saffron, burst upon her with the shock of some lovely picture. The old plane trees, their boughs mutilated so that they had grown into crippled knobs of intertwined twigs; their bark splashed with white, their wide leaves yellowing, seemed to her to be old friends she was leaving for ever. She remembered those leaves tenderly, piteously green in spring, ready fodder for the ferocious burning winds of summer; she remembered the boughs wet and black and shining in winter. She put out her hand and touched a trunk as she went past; the wood was still warm from the daylong sunshine. It was almost like touching flesh.

She got in a tram and went down to the city, for she had three hours to kill before she went to No. 17. The city was full of life. In the day it had smelt of dust and petrol and heat; but now it smelt of coolness, face powder and wine. Crowds were standing outside the theatres, in gabbling queues which snaked untidily over the footpath. Men were waiting on corners for buses or girls. Roie did not know where to go. She had thought perhaps that she could go to the Cathedral, but there might be benediction on there, or some other service in which she had no part when there was sin on her soul.

'But it's not sin for me,' thought Roie desperately. 'It's the only thing I can do.'

She went down to the Quay and pretended she was catching a ferry. Outside the Manly berth she leaned over the railing, and watched the Bridge outlined with golden lights, with the little twinkling beetles that were trams moving rapidly across it. She saw the dark glossy water, and the fiery chestnut of reflected light dancing upon the ripples. She thought how simple it would be for a brave person to slip into that water, and steadfastly die. She knew she couldn't. She'd kick and yell with panic, and before long some courageous halfwit would be over the rail to rescue her, and her name would be in the papers, and doctors would examine her, and then everyone would know.

With almost a feeling of relief Roie saw the hands of a clock pointing to half-past nine. She went up into the rattling bedlam of the tram station and caught one home.

'I'm not the only girl who has to face it tonight,' thought Roie, but the thought gave her no comfort. The tram journey seemed very short. She got off a stop or two before the usual one, and walked quickly into Murphy Street. She thought that if she hurried perhaps she would feel sick, and then she would be glad for it all to happen, as one panted for the dentist's coming when one had a really bad toothache.

The house was very dark. There were heavy blinds on the windows and the only glass panel in the door glowed dimly yellow like an old kerosene lamp. Roie tapped at the door, and silently it opened. She stepped in to the musty-smelling little hall. There was a faint odour of disinfectant somewhere. The familiar woman was waiting for her.

'Thought you weren't coming. Thought you got cold feet.'

'No,' quavered Roie. Her stomach was sickening already, and perspiration damped her skin.

'That's the kid. Wait in there for me, there's a duck.' She pushed Roie into a little room which opened off the hall. It had lavender-striped wallpaper, and a bobble-edged parchment shade on the light. There was an unused feeling about the room, and Roie knew it didn't like her. She was surprised to see another girl there, a dark, oily-skinned girl with bold Italian eyes and an old food-stained coat pulled around her already prominent stomach. Roie and she looked at each other furtively for a while, then the other girl grinned, showing bad teeth.

'God, I'm scared, ain't you?'

Roie nodded feebly. She was so terrified that she could hardly sit straight in the chair.

'But it's not so bad when it comes to the point. You've always got more guts than you thought,' said the other girl. It was a relief to hear another voice in that secret, hostile room. Roie faltered: 'I'm four months gone. How long are you?'

'God, I'm four and a half,' she boasted. 'I got stuck into the dope, but it didn't work. So here I am again.'

'You mean, you've been here before?' asked Roie.

'Cripes, this is me fourth miss, if it comes off. Somehow I'm always falling in. Course, I'm married. But don't you be afraid, love. It only hurts for a little while. Just put yer hanky in yer mouth and bite on it to stop yelling. It's getting home that's hard.'

290

'Why?' trembled Roie. The other girl looked at her amazed.

'Hell, don't you know anything? Well, if you ain't got no one to take you home in a car, like the flash tarts have, you gotta walk, and things often happen on the way.'

'Things?' Roie just had to ask, although her terror of the answer was almost too much for her to bear. The other girl leaped at the opportunity to tell her, and in a low, greedy voice she gave Roie all the loathsome details of abortion. She had hardly finished before the familiar woman stuck her head in the door and said: 'You next, Stell.'

Stell swaggered to the door, turned, and patted her stomach with a jolly wiggle of her hips. 'Don't take it bad, love. Look at me. In another fortnight I'll be wearing me red dress with the bead flower again.'

'Yeah,' put in the woman with a wink at Roie, 'and six weeks after that you'll be right back here again.'

The door closed. Roie sat on the edge of the chair, trembling like a rabbit in a trap. It was worse than a nightmare. Her mind, shocked almost to the point of insensibility with the information she had just received, was incapable of forming a conclusion about anything. She stared at the wallpaper, until its pattern, a long chain of faded purple diamonds, was imprinted on the air when she looked away. She did not know how long she sat there. She was only aware of her knees joggling under her hands, and the sweat staining the sides of her stockings where they touched each other. Then all at once there was a rapid shuffle of feet upstairs, and she awoke as though from a dream. Opening the door, she listened. There was a low mutter of a man's deep voice; the sound of metal clinking on china; and a horrible gagged scream which diminished into gurgling moans. Feet sounded on the stairs, and Roie nearly collapsed against the door, for she thought that it was the woman coming to get her. But the feet ran on into the kitchen at the back, and Roie heard the hiss and pop of gas, and the sound of something trickling into a glass. There was another hoarse shriek, cut off short as if someone had suddenly jabbed a gag into Stell's mouth. Feet ran up the stairs again. The whole atmosphere of that dirty old slum house was instinct with mystery and evil. It seemed to gloat, and hold to itself all the murders that had been committed within its walls. The smell of blood was there, and the miasma of cowardice and stealth and cruelty.

Roie gave a stifled little groan. She ran at the front door and struggled with it until she wrested the bolt from the socket and pulled it open. Crazy with terror, she slid it back and ran out and down the path. She did not look back, nor did she hear any sound. The street was dark now, save for the pools of topaz lights under the lamps. And there was a cold wind blowing, sweeping up the fallen leaves and whirling them forlornly away. Roie raced down the street, little muffled sobs bursting from her chest. It was then a nightmare; there was no longer any control of her thoughts. She pictured the familiar woman, grown to delirious proportions, with bulging forehead and strange receding chin, coming after her; and the doctor, a faceless, bodyless creature that was nothing more than a low mutter, and the sound of metal on crockery, and a hoarse strangled scream, seizing her and vanishing her out of her familiar world the way someone had vanished her little brother Thady.

Then she was out of Murphy Street and turning into the long dark channel of Coronation Street. Roie slowed down, stumbling with fatigue. Almost immediately she was aware of several men lounging in the shadows of a shop verandah. As she drew abreast, one of them snatched her arm. He was a short sturdy man in a blue overcoat; his fair bristly hair stood straight up from his forehead. There was a smell of gin, and his fingers made no attempt to be gentle.

Roie was too breathless to speak. She wrenched her arm away from the man and started to run again, sobbing under her breath. But another stepped in her path, and a thick and rhythmic voice chanted: 'Good efening, good efening, good efening.'

There was a mutter of drunken foreign babble around her, and Roie, astonished, looked through her tear-blurred eyes at the dark ribboned hats most of the men wore. Some were dark-featured, like Indians; others blonde, with pink cheeks, like dressed-up children.

It was the violent conclusion of the nightmare. Screaming, she fought, beating at their strong arms, their chests, their faces. She was dragged into the deep dark doorway, and a strong and violating hand groped over her.

'No, no,' choked Roie, 'I want to go home. I feel sick. I'm going to have a baby. Let me go home to my Mumma! Mumma! Mumma!'

She was dragged from one to the other; bristly chins rubbed against her soft chin, her dress was ripped from her shoulders. A rough torrent of Dutch poured back and forth over her head, drunken, violent, and savage. As she was slammed against the shop door, a window was flung up overhead, and an alarmed voice yelled: 'Hi, what's going on down there?'

There was a sentence of strange words, and one of the sailors ran into the road, plucked a knife from his sleeve and hurled it at the window above. There was a shocked silence, and glass fell with a loud soprano tinkle on to the iron roof. The shopkeeper began to yell at the top of his voice: 'Help! Help! Police! Where are the bloody coppers? He nearly got me with a knife! Help!'

There were no patrol men within hearing, but the black car of the Vice Squad, cruising slowly along Plymouth Street, silently accelerated. It drew in beside the kerb even as one of the sailors threw Roie to the ground.

One boot grazed stingingly past her ear; the other did not miss. She felt a flood of pain unlike anything she had ever experienced. It was so great it made her eyes blur, go bloodshot and lose their focus. She rolled like a kicked football before the feet that stumbled over her as the sailors raced away up the street. There was a deafening babel of noise, shouts, a shot which echoed up the empty roadway like a whiplash, screams, upflung windows, and vanishing footbeats. She dragged herself up to a sitting position. She could see nobody. The squad car was gone; the men were gone. There was no one to help.

'Mumma! Mumma!' she moaned. She scratched feebly on the peeling door of the shop. There was no sound.

'What'll I do? What'll I do?' she moaned. 'Oh, Jesus, help me. Oh, Jesus, come and help me!'

She lay there for half an hour in utter agony. Finally a drunk came along, picking his way with infinite care from one side of the pavement to the other. He sang in a low, happy voice: 'Flowers all dripping with dew! And they join in the chorus of . . . Gawd, what you doin' in there? You been at the meth, sister?'

Roie gasped, the effort bringing sweat to her deathly face: 'A man kicked me. I've got to go home.'

The drunk came closer, looked at her with owlish eyes. 'I'll go and get a doc.'

'No, get me home. Please, get me home,' she begged in a whisper. He gave a foolish shrug. 'Okay!' It was a gay little chirp. He was a tall, strong man, middle-aged, with a labourer's bullocky shoulders. He lifted Roie easily, and held her against his beer-smelling shirt.

He weaved off down Coronation Street, still chanting under his breath: 'Flowers all dripping with dew, and they join in the chorus . . . loverly song . . . loverly sheila on the meth. Where you say you live, miss?'

'Fourth house around the corner in Plymouth Street,' breathed Roie out of the black mist of unconsciousness. 'Fourth house.'

'Okay!' She felt nothing but the jolting of his slow walk, every movement of which was a delicate and subtle torture.

'Here y'are,' said his voice suddenly. It seemed remote, miles away.

'Carry me down the hall,' breathed Roie. He was a little indignant.

'Charge you taxi rates, miss. No, I won't. It's a pleasure.'

He thrust open the green door with one shoulder, and trod heavily down the hall. He had not gone half-way before Mumma came running to the kitchen door and cried: 'Who's that? That you, Roie?'

At the sound of her voice Roie lost her head. She beat on the shoulder of her rescuer and shrieked: 'Let me down, let me down! I want my mother! Oh, I want my mother!' Then she fell deep into the darkness that was full of strange noises and monstrous, bulging faces, and voices that said: 'Good efening, good efening, good efening.'

Ten

It was three hours later, and Hughie, with scarlet face and eyes that watered, so intense was their glare, was saying to Mumma: 'I'm going to get the quack.'

Mumma's mouth closed into a thin line. 'Keep yer voice down, can't yer? Don't yer know old Diamond's got his ear plastered to the crack in the floor? Keep yer voice down.'

'I'm going to get the doctor,' Hughie shouted in a whisper, like the croak of a magpie.

'You will not.' Mumma's face was as white as paper, with a yellow look around her mouth. 'It's not only a kick in the stomach she got.'

'What d'ya mean?' Because he was frightened, Hughie's voice was rougher than usual, his demeanour fiercer.

'She's losing a baby.' Once Mumma said it, her face crumpled up like newspaper in a fire, and she sat down on the bed and pushed her knuckles into her eyes, with a childish piteous gesture. Hughie was stunned.

'You're mad.' Mumma said nothing, and he repeated, more fiercely, but with a pitiful question in his voice. 'You're mad.' Her silence answered him. 'Cripes,' he whispered. 'Ro! Who'd a guessed it?'

'Nobody ain't going to guess,' replied Mumma, with white-hot determination. 'Whatever Ro's done she's had a reason for it. And nobody's going to know about it but us, see?'

'It's Tommy Mendel, the dirty little swine,' cried Hughie, flaming-eyed. Mumma put her hand on his arm.

'Whoever it was can wait. Roie's very sick. You've got to help me.' Hughie looked at her obediently.

'What'll I do? You tell me.'

Mumma's emotion had subsided. 'Put some hot water on. Get those old sheets out from the port under the bed. Get the bucket and scald it out. Yes, and the couch . . . put the blankets on it off our bed, because I'm going to bring Dolour down before she gets wise to what's happening. And for God's sake, if Grandma wakes up, tell her it's nothing, and give her a pipe and send her off to sleep again.'

Hughie, mumbling over the orders, rushed off to the gas stove, and Mumma returned up the dark stairs to Roie.

The light in the room was burning bare and glaring. Dolour, her face like parchment, perched shivering with terror and cold on the broken-legged chair at the end of the room. Her eyes were glazed with fright.

'Is Ro going to die?' she whimpered as her mother entered the room.

'Don't be silly. Them Dutchmen knocked her down and hurt her, that's all. Now I want you to go downstairs and sleep on the couch for the rest of the night. And take yer rosary with you and say a Pater-n-Ave for my intention.'

Dolour scampered off, tears streaming down her cheeks, her bare shoulders sticking out of the rents in her grubby nightgown.

Roie's fine dark hair was matted into long rat-tails. The side of her face was plum-purple, and her lips were swollen. She groaned: 'I am going to die, aren't I?'

'No, darling love. Don't think about that. Mumma won't let you die. Mumma's looking after you,' soothed her mother. Roie forced her drowsy eyes open.

'Mumma, you know about me?'

'Yes, darling.'

'What's going to happen?'

'You're going to be all right. Everything will be all right.'

In a frenzy Roie beat on her mother's shoulders with feeble hands.

'What's going to happen to my baby? What's happening to my little baby?'

'There isn't any baby now, Roie.' Mumma was pulling Roie's torn garments off, and wrapping a sheet about her slender body that was bruised to the colour of a grape. Roie turned her head away and the bitterest tears she had ever known crept from under her eyelids and slid slowly down her stinging cheeks. Until now she had felt no real moral wrong in what she had done or what she had contemplated, but now, as though she had walked into a great shadow, the world was different. It wasn't that she had been going to have a baby that made her sink down to the lowest depths of grief and shame but the knowledge that she would have murdered it, if it had not been for her own cowardice.

'I killed it, Mumma.'

'No, darling. The Dutchmen killed it. And it wasn't alive. It didn't miss anything of life.'

'I killed it,' repeated Roie monotonously. 'I killed it because I didn't want it. That's why God punished me this way. I want to die. Mumma, let me die.'

'Lie still now,' cried Mumma in anxiety. 'Mr Diamond will hear you. Miss Sheily will hear you. Don't talk like that. Oh, Roie, don't talk about anything until you get better.'

'I got to talk about it. You don't know how bad I am. Tonight . . . I didn't go to the pictures with Rosie Glavich. I went to that place in Murphy Street where the doctor comes.'

Mumma's face went yellow-white again. She stared at Roie with her mouth hanging open, and nothing on her face but blank shock.

'You mean . . . is this the result of . . . you mean . . .' she quavered.

'No, I ran away. I wouldn't let them touch me. But it was only because I was frightened when that girl screamed. I didn't have the guts to face it for myself, but I was going to let them kill my little baby.'

Mumma went to the window. She looked out into the chalcedony-blue sky of the early morning, and the great, glossy stars. The wind blew pure and salt-laden from Darling Harbour, with no hint of the dirty alleyways, and fetid lavatories and the rotting garbage it blew across. She felt as though she were a different woman from the one who had climbed the steps only a few minutes before. Incapable of comprehending the dark recesses in others' natures, to her Roie's confession had come as a deep and abiding shock which was never altogether to leave her. She turned her face into the wind and said: 'Dear God, help me to be strong as mothers ought to be.'

Then she came back and said: 'Such thoughts do nothing but harm, Roie, love. You're my little girl, and whatever you've done, it's over now and nothing to you but the past.'

She leaned over Roie and pressed her head close to her breast, and the poignant pain which had been hers when first she had felt Roie's little downy head at her birth went through her again, and she knew that her feeling was no different.

Eleven

Dolour huddled on the couch downstairs. It was very uncomfortable. Her dirty little heels slid up and down the shiny leather until a clean pink patch was worn on each. She looked at the dim speckled globe burning up near the ceiling, and said a Hail Mary in a drowsy way as though to convince herself that she wanted to go to sleep. But she didn't. She was wide awake. She could hear with sharp distinctiveness the dripping of a tap in the scullery, the creaking of a clothes-line in the yard, and, upstairs, mysterious rustlings and mumblings and footsteps passing back and forth.

'Ah, gosh, I wish Dad would come down,' wailed Dolour. Tears, hot and sticky with lack of sleep, squeezed themselves out of her eyes. Suddenly Grandma, who had been creaking uneasily for the last five minutes, called out in a tired, wheezy voice: 'What's bothering yer out there? Have yer the tooth-ache?'

'Oh, Grandma!' bellowed Dolour, leaping off the couch and running in. She jumped on to the bed beside her Grandma's little humpy form, and the stretcher dipped and quivered. Grandma's vexed sunken face yapped at her:

'Be careful, you big ellafump. Just about shook the kidneys outa me, you did. Time you were in bed, anyway.' She closed her eyes and sank back, chewing rapidly. Dolour bawled: 'But I'm supposed to be sleeping in the kitchen, and Dadda and Mumma are upstairs with Roie.'

Grandma opened her eyes instantly. From a filmy grey they changed to a sharp and discerning blue. 'What are you gabbering about?'

'Roie's awful sick. I think she's going to die,' sobbed Dolour. 'Oh, Grandma, I think she's going to die.'

'What happened?' squawked Grandma, levering herself painfully upwards, and wincing as the rheumatics stabbed her in her slow joints.

Dolour wiped her nose on the sleeve of her nightdress. 'It was them Dutchmen . . . them that came down to Surry Hills looking for the fellers that murdered their mate.'

Grandma had already heard all about the Dutchmen, for they had kicked in half a dozen shop windows and kicked old Bert Drummy's head half in, as well.

'Glory-lory-ory!' she whispered. Dolour nodded.

'They were all drunk, everyone thinks, and they attacked lots of girls, too. They caught Roie when she was coming home from the pitchers.' She dissolved into hiccuping sobs. Grandma asked:

'Has your Mumma got the doctor to Roie?' Dolour dumbly shook her head. Grandma gave a sigh of relief and lay back.

'Then Roie's not going to die, acushla. Lie down with yer old gran and go to sleep.'

Dolour felt as though a huge weight had been lifted from her shoulders. She complained: 'There ain't enough room.'

Grandma snorted. 'Don't then. Go and freeze, you ungrateful young tom todger.'

Dolour snivelled. 'I'm sorry, Grandma. I would like to come in with you.'

Grandma's eyes opened, with a wicked glint in them. She shuffled further over in the bed and left about four inches space. Humbly and gratefully Dolour climbed in beside her and wiggled down under the blankets. Grandma smelt of tobacco, old clothes, and plain old age, but Dolour soon got used to it, and she put her head on the old woman's thin flat chest and asked: 'Tell me about when you were a little girl in Ireland, Grandma.'

Grandma answered drowsily: 'When I was a little girl in Ireland I lived in a house with a fine shaggy roof on it. Our house was right in the middle of the shaky, quaky bog, and there was pools of brown water, for all the world like coffee, right at the back door. When you stamped very hard on our front door sill the whole bog shivered all over. It did so. And one day when I was digging with a stick in the mud I found a golden coin shaped like a shell, with a strange lady's face on it.'

'Was it a sovereign, Grandma?' whispered Dolour, as she knew she was meant to ask, for she had heard the story a hundred times before. Grandma snorted triumphantly. 'It was not. It was a coin of the fairy times, long before any people at all came to Ireland. They was great goldsmiths, them fairy people. And my Dadda took the coin into the town, and he came back with a brown pony and a little wagon with red spokes to the wheel. And it was called "Eny's car", for my name is Eny, though the dear Lord knows what use it is to me, who's always been Ma and Grandma for sixty wearisome years.'

Here Grandma got annoyed, and refused to talk any more, and they both went to sleep. A little while later Hughie came down from the upper bedroom. He lifted a candle and peered around the sheet which curtained Grandma's cubbyhole from the rest of the room. He exclaimed silently when he saw the two faces, both sharpened and yellowish with fatigue and sleep, on the grey pillow. Dolour's two arms were linked about Grandma's neck, and her mouth was open, so that her two front teeth showed over her lip.

'God forgive me, Grandma, that I've often been so hard on yer, yer old skunk,' breathed Hughie penitently. He set down the candle and slipped off his trousers; in his patched underpants he knelt down by the side of the bed.

'Hail, Mary, full of grace, don't let me little girl die. And don't be too hard on her. Hail Mary. It's only the one mistake she's made, and she won't never do it again. And God put fire into the belly of the foreign swine what did it.'

The next day everyone knew that the Netherlands sailors who had beaten up Bert Drummy, and assaulted Kitty Gall and Connie Lock and goodness knows how many other girls that they had met in their vengeful progress along the dark and unpoliced slum streets, had kicked Roie Darcy and hurt her bad. Mumma had decided that it was useless trying to keep it quiet, for it was certain sure that Miss Sheily and Patrick Diamond had heard all the commotion, and would be sure to drop a word or two amongst the neighbours.

'Besides, don't you see, Hughie,' she argued wearily, her eyes swollen with sleeplessness, 'it's a good excuse for Roie being so ill, and nobody need know about the other.'

'How is she now?' asked Hughie. Mumma shook her head.

'It's over now, but she's still bad, and sort of delirious. Moaning, she is. I can't keep her quiet.'

A cold wind swept up the street, lifting the tatters of paper and the crackling leaves. Lick Jimmy was in his window, busily mixing up mandarins and tomatoes, with a few parsnips added for effect. He waggled a finger at Hughie as he slouched past: 'Plenty blad blisnis last night, misser! Dlirty folleners!'

Hughie grunted surlily, but his expression lightened. For once he was in the news. He wasn't just Hugh Darcy, home from work; he was Hugh Darcy, home from work because his daughter had been beaten up by sailors. He hastened his step, and when old Delie Stock hailed him from her doorway in Little Ryan Street, he went across with alacrity.

'Didja hear about poor, stinking old Bert?' she inquired. Hughie nodded. He rolled a starveling cigarette.

'Stinking foreigners,' she said. There was real indignation in her voice. Her parchment face, broken into so many minute hair-like lines that it looked like some strange mosaic, filled with sympathy at the thought of Bert Drummy.

'And them poor girls,' she added. Both Hughie and she forgot entirely all the things she had done to girls in her time, and the old buffers like Bert Drummy whom she had had ruined, bashed-up and occasionally murdered. Hughie's blue eyes sparkled. His news would set her back a step, the old lizard. He put his cigarette in his mouth and drew on it carefully.

'Me girl Roie nearly got murdered, too. They grabbed her as she was coming home from the pitchers.'

'Yer don't say!'

'Yeah. Kicked her in the stomach. Face all out like a balloon. Clothes torn off her.'

'You mean they . . .?'

'No,' added Hughie hastily. 'Vice Squad came along, and they left her. By God, if I could get my hands on them square-heads I'd strew them all over the street.'

'Yeah,' agreed Delie Stock. 'What I say is, they ain't got no business allowing foreigners in this country. Chows, yes. Nobody can wash a collar like a Chow. But not blasted Dutch. Anyone with corners on their head is next best thing to a German, I always say. Cripes, Roie, eh? Here,' said Delie Stock. She fished down the baggy front of her dress, and pulled put a greasy little cotton bag. Hugh tried to look somewhere else, but he couldn't, because the bag was so full of money. Delie Stock pulled out a couple of notes haphazardly, and stuffed them into Hughie's resistless paw.

'Here, you see that kid gets all she needs, Hugh Darcy, and if you're hard up, come around here and get some more. There's plenty where that came from,' said Delie Stock, giving herself a spank on the chest.

'Yere!' protested Hughie feebly. 'What's this? Cripes, I can't do it.'

'Go on, go on,' croaked Delie Stock. She was so overcome by her own generosity that she almost cried. She was a character, if ever there was one, she reflected, her the worst woman in the Hills, and giving this old goon a handout when he needed it most.

Hughie tottered off, looking at a fiver in one hand and a tenner in the other. Beautiful, priceless money! Food and beer and a bottle of good wine, and a baked chook, and new shoes for Dolour and a bit off the arrears of rent! He ran across the road, stuffing the money into his inside pocket as he did so. Mumma'd jump out of her skin. But she mightn't take it if she knew it had come from Delie Stock, for, in spite of her steady squashing of Dolour's criticism of the old girl, he knew that Mumma still feared and hated Delie Stock's profession. All right, then, he'd say he found it. But then she might think he'd pinched it. To make up his mind in a little peace and quiet, Hughie turned in at the open door of the Foundry pub. It was quiet in there, with a bit of water sluiced over the floor, and some clotted sawdust, and the handyman sweeping the two together out the door. The sunlight fell amber and warm on the polished counter and the many bottles. Flies buzzed about the threadbare backs of the two steady drinkers who leaned on the end of the bar.

'Gawd,' remarked the barmaid, winding tow hair around her thick glittering finger before the mirror, 'how's yer poor girl? Pat Diamond was in here telling me about it not ten minutes ago.'

'Pat Diamond had better keep his great gob shut or I'll stick me hoof fair in it,' snarled Hughie. Never before had he felt so big or important. He slapped the fiver on the bar. The steady drinkers at the other end shuffled closer, prepared to listen for as long as Hughie cared to talk.

An hour later he came out into the bright sunlight, blinking like an owl. There were many people about now, frowsy women with their hair in pipe-cleaners, and shopping kits in their red hands; little children with transparent skin and large bright birdlike eyes looking through the grime. Hughie barged through them all. He was wearing his idealistic red uniform again, and was six foot high and was accompanied by the grave and pompous rattle of a drum. Hardly anybody looked at him, though drunken men in the morning were not common. They just shoved him good-naturedly away as he lurched into them, with a laugh and 'Push off, mate, yer off yer course,' or 'Garn, get outa me way, you old crackpot.'

Hughie passed Jacky Siciliano's fruit shop, and Bert Drummy's ham and beef, and the second-hand dump and the fish shop. And there was Joseph Mendel's hock joint, with three brass balls swinging like monstrous grapes from the verandah beam. The window was crammed with old jewellery, coarse garnets and peridots and turquoise matrix set in brassy rolled gold; pewter shaving mugs, tarnished silver buckles, cigarette cases with cameos of coursing dogs and girls' profiles; crystal powder bowls with every facet grimy with dust, diamante inlaid hair slides, gold-rimmed spectacles, naked sets of chipped false teeth, brooches with MOTHER in gold wire, bracelets of square topazes, and little phials full of opal nobbies, like drab pebbles with rainbow veins.

Hughie snorted, and lumbered in through the grille gate. Old Joseph Mendel, his white hair brushed straight back from his sloping forehead, his beak of a nose magnificently jutting, his lips classically curved in the eastern way, looked up from his ledger.

'Good day, sir, what can I show you,' he said automatically, though he instantly noted that Hughie was drunk, that he was truculent, that he had something serious on his mind. Hughie leaned over the counter and blew a gust of wine-sodden breath into Joseph Mendel's face. The old man's expression did not change. He did not even bother to slip his hand along under the counter to reassure himself that the metal-bound cudgel he kept for self-protection was still there.

Hughie exploded into a torrent of filthy abuse. It was filthy mainly because he did not have much vocabulary. He did not have a particularly obscene mind, but the words he used seemed to have the necessity of adjectival qualification, and so he fitted the expressions he knew into the vacant spaces. With hardly an expression save that of polite interest, Joseph Mendel listened until Hughie, sputtering and scarlet and flaming-eyed, had paused for breath. Then he said: 'Be that as it may, what can I do for you?'

Hughie was doubly enraged. The coolness of the man he abused seemed to be a reproach, and to prevent that reproach from being any brake upon his self confidence, he broke into further abuse.

'That little sneaking swine of a nephew of yours has ruined my girl,' he said thickly. Joseph Mendel inclined his head.

'I would not be at all surprised,' he replied courteously.

Hughie bellowed: 'You mean he's done it to other sheilas!'

'Not that I know about,' answered the old man amiably. 'But he is twenty, I believe, and most young men of twenty are seducing young women, either in fact, fancy, or desire.'

Hughie did not comprehend, so he bellowed even louder: 'What are you going to do about it?'

Joseph Mendel registered polite surprise. 'What can I do about it? What is done is done. It is nothing to do with me. Tommy is not even one of my employees any longer. If you wish anything done you had better see him.'

'I'll break his stinking little yid neck,' roared Hughie.

'Perhaps that would be the best plan,' remarked the old man placidly. Hughie, baffled, tried another tack.

'I'll take it to court.'

Joseph Mendel smiled. 'Paternity cases cost money, and you will need considerable proof that Tommy is really the culprit. You forget that you come from a street with a very bad name, where the general standard of morality is low.'

Hughie's eyes flashed. 'You insinerating that my girl is on the town?'

'I am insinuating nothing, my dear sir, I am merely stating public opinion. You are perhaps aware that a Surry Hills girl finds it difficult to obtain a position in the city. She may be educated; she may be more highly moral than similar young ladies in more prosperous suburbs, but her address is against her. Most Sydney people persist, somewhat biasedly, perhaps, in thinking of Surry Hills in terms of brothels, razor-gangs, tenements, and fried fish shops.'

Hughie, abashed, said: 'Swallered the dictionary, ain't yer?'

Joseph Mendel straightened his shoulders. His black eyes gleamed as opaque and stony as jet.

'I am well aware that you came to me this morning hoping that I would, on behalf of Tommy, attempt to buy you off, so that your daughter's questionable honour might be salved. But you might as well know that I do not care the price of one of those leaden trinkets whether my nephew Tommy fathers a dozen come-by-chances.'

'I don't want any of your stinking Jew money,' yelled Hughie, defeated and enraged. He flung the remainder of the fifteen pounds on the counter, and gathered it up again quickly in case Joseph Mendel should pounce on it. 'I can make that any week in the year, if I work a bit overtime,' he boasted. 'Honestly, too, not by squeezing it out of poor old tarts with nothing between them and starvation but a ring or a brooch to pawn.'

'Indeed,' Joseph Mendel bowed slightly and stood at courteous attention waiting to hear the rest. But for some reason Hughie had nothing more to say. He had pictured the old Jew cringing before him . . . he who was six foot high, and wearing a red uniform, and was accompanied by the noise of drums. He had pictured him offering him the shop if only he'd keep his trap shut about his nephew's misdemeanours. But somehow it had all come out wrong, and Hughie couldn't imagine why.

Tears stung his eyes, and angrily and savagely he turned and blundered out. He couldn't go home, for Mumma would be furious with him for getting drunk on a day like that when he was needed; he couldn't stay in the street, for a cop might pull him up. So he went back to the Foundry and 'shouted' everyone, and in their applause and warm good fellowship he forgot his misery and hatred of those who always put it over on him. When closing time came they threw him out into the gutter, and he lay there a long time before one of his mates came along and helped him home. And when he went through his pockets, of course, there was nothing there, for someone else had been through them first.

It was just after this that Grandma got sick, too. She had been a wonderfully healthy woman, with a wiry, whalebone body, and a constitution which had repelled all the bacteria which had assailed it from the moment she was born. Although she had spent her childhood in a damp mud hut on a bog island which was sur-rounded by poisonous vapours for half the day and all the night – although she had decided at the age of eighteen to leave Ireland for a better land and had embarked on an emigrant ship which carried its free passengers between decks in evil-smelling, airless little cupboards lit by oil lamps, she had survived. She had survived measles, scarlet fever, and finally the cholera which had broken out on board. When she arrived in Australia, still eighteen, and not much wiser than when she had left, she married an ex-gold-miner with a splendid square-cut beard and a watch-chain of little nuggets. He gave her eleven children in as many years, and she brought them all up with the money she earned scrubbing out other people's boarding houses. But somehow all but two died before she became an old woman, because they did not have the constitution to face the rigours of existence, as she did.

But now, after eighty-five years, Grandma's body suddenly went tired. She wasn't ill, and she wasn't fatigued. She was just negative where she had always been vigorously positive. It started when she said: 'I think I'll have me dinner in bed today.'

Mumma burst out. 'Don't be loony! And me with Roie to look after! When am I going to get the time to come running in and out to you like a sick hen, with the salt one moment and another cup of tea the next?'

To her astonishment, Grandma, who never cried, burst into tears.

'Holy Mother,' cried Mumma, aghast at her own cruelty in refusing a cup of tea in bed for her own mother who had done everything in the world for her until she was old enough to do it for herself. 'It was only a joke, now, Ma, and you can have yer dinner in bed any time you want it. Sure, it was only a joke, and you're the old blockhead to be taking it serious.'

Whereupon Grandma said: 'I'm not crying because you wouldn't give me a bite in bed, dotie; I'm crying because I want it.'

Mumma instantly understood what she meant, and a stab went involuntarily through her heart. Because she was upset she became cross:

'Don't be talking such tripe, Ma. You're a silly old goat if ever there was one.'

Grandma grabbed her hand with her knobbly old ones and asked: 'You do think so, lovie?'

'Of course I do, Ma,' Mumma soothed.

Grandma relinquished her hand. 'Ah, it's a frightful liar you are, dotie. When I've got time, ask me to tell you how to tell a lie. You just haven't got the knack.'

Mumma went out into the scullery and cried, stirring the stew vigorously all the time. She cried because she was worn out with lack of sleep and worry for Roie, and the deep abiding shock which the revelation of her daughter's escapade had brought her. She also cried because the stew had burned a bit at the bottom and she hadn't enough custard powder to make a pudding without going out and getting extra. And she cried because at last old age had caught up with her sprightly and wicked little Ma, and would never be defeated any more.

'Dear Lord,' said Mumma, looking up at the greasy, dirt-stained ceiling and seeing nothing but vast azure expanses with bright slits through which she could glimpse the cool avenues of paradise. 'Dear Lord, don't let go of me hand now, there's a good Lord.'

Grandma did not often get up again. The slow winter weeks

went by and the roof leaked, and the great map-like stain on the bedroom wall grew into a continent. Near the roof above the wardrobe, fungus sprouted blue-green and exotic. Then came the spring, and sudden heat. Number Twelve-and-a-Half baked and simmered, for it had an iron roof, and concentrated the sun's rays like a magnifying glass. But Grandma did not seem to mind. She lay in her little dark cubbyhole, so smelly, and uncomfortable and devoid of all the peace and tranquillity that should surround one's last days. The sweat lay in heavy drops upon her ridgy forehead, and the old corded arms that projected from her torn nightdress. Now and then she was chirpy, and had short spats with Hughie when he came in unnecessarily drunk, or with Dolour when she persisted in yapping out in the kitchen without sticking her head in at intervals to explain what the conversation was about. But most times she just lay, her eyes staring at nothing at all, talking to herself. Mumma rarely had time to sit with Grandma, for all her energy was taken up with Roie, just crawling into health again. But Dolour loved to sit beside her and listen to the things she said.

To Dolour Ireland was inconceivably far away. It seemed strange and enchanting that her own Grandma had come from that land; it was almost as though Grandma were an old fairy woman from another and more fantastic world. Dolour's own half-digested reading about it had been reinforced by the loyal Irisholatry of the nuns at St Brandan's, who were Australian-born to a woman, and yet kept the memory of their surnames vivid in their hearts. Phelans and Flanagans and Dunnes and MacBrides there were at the convent, and old Sister Beatrix had been a Mullins born. And then there was Father Cooley, with a honey of an accent, and yet Australian too, as though he wore a buckled shoe on one foot and an Australian 'laughin'-side' on the other. They had all helped to make Ireland very real to Dolour, even though it was so fantastic a place.

Grandma had fights with people Dolour couldn't see: 'Keep yer tongue in yer jaw and yer toe in yer pump or it'll be the worse for yer,' she would say, or 'I never did like a bone in yer skin, yer crooked ould disciple.'

And another time she drowsed: 'He was a little queer man in a red, square-cut coat, and he came up to me jiggeting on the toes of his shoes and crying as though the heart of him would be broke in three halves.'

'Who was he?' asked Dolour eagerly, and after repeating the

question three times, her grandma opened her eyes and glared: 'You'd talk the leg off an iron pot, Dolour Mary Darcy. Go off and don't be bothering me head.'

Other times Grandma really talked to Dolour, and into the child's soft-moulded mind went unique phrases, strange bits of grammar, and a smattering of old songs which Grandma had learned at her grandmother's knee, and which went back into the dream-days beyant Napoleon.

One day at school Sister Theophilus called Dolour aside and said: 'How's Roie getting on, dear?'

Dolour did not know what to say, because Mumma had told her never to answer any questions about her home life, if she was asked. Then she replied: 'She's getting on all right now, thank you.' She turned her eyes away from Sister's beautiful brown ones; clear, they were, like a bush pool with sunlight on it, or a setter's eyes, freckled with gold.

'We've just finished a novena for her. Do you think your mother would mind if Sister Beatrix and I came around after school this afternoon for a little visit?'

'No, no, I don't think so,' stammered Dolour, overcome with delight and fear because she didn't know what Mumma would think about it.

'Then run away home, Dolour, and we'll be around about four.'

Dolour rushed up the street very fast. She did not even stop outside the fish shop, as she usually did, to look fascinated at the beautiful blue eyes of the giant pink prawns. She burst into the kitchen, where Mumma, with furrowed brow and soot-freckled face was jamming coal into Puffing Billy's scarlet-lit throat.

'Mumma, Sister's coming round. She wants to see Roie.'

Mumma gave a shriek of alarm. 'Not today? Not today when the house is in a frightful mess and me hair hasn't even been done yet.'

'They'll be coming at four,' gasped Dolour. 'Crumbs, I didn't know what to say.'

'You should have said that Grandma had smallpox,' cried Mumma. 'Anything to keep them away.'

'Don't you dare be saying I've got smallpox, the filthy disease,' yapped Grandma from the bedroom.

Mumma sighed: 'There now. You've got her awake with yer loud tongue!'

'I didn't say it; you said it!' expostulated Dolour.

Mumma gave her a light skelp on the ear. 'There now, get the broom and start sweeping the upstairs room. I'll get a basin of water and clean Roie up.'

Dolour rushed upstairs, falling over the treads in her haste. Roie was half asleep; she was hardly recognizable, with her face waxy pale and sunken, and her eyes smudged dark and purplish and extraordinarily empty. Her hair was ragged and tousled; even her teeth appeared brittle.

'Wake up Ro!' cried Dolour excitedly, beginning to whisk all the litter of papers and hairpins and dust under the dressing-table. 'You're going to have visitors!'

Roie gave a sick gasp: 'Not Tommy!'

'Don't be mad,' said Dolour scornfully. 'That flip. Fine sort of mug he turned out to be, not even coming to see you once.'

'We had a fight. We aren't friends any longer,' said Roie. Then she pleaded. 'I don't want to see anyone, Dolour. Who is it?'

'It's Sister Theophilus, that's who. And Sister Beatrix.'

'But me nightie's awful, and . . . and . . . my hair . . .' Roie's eyes, which had shed so many tears those past weeks, filled again.

'We'll fix that,' said Mumma briskly, marching in with a bowl of hot water and a bundle under her arm. 'Here, I got an idea.'

'My nightie,' wailed Roie. Mumma whisked open her bundle. In it was a pale pink cotton blouse with a draw-string neck. 'Here's yer new cotton blouse. What say you put it on and keep the blankets well up, and they'll never know the difference.'

'Yes, all right,' wailed Roie, 'but . . .' Weakly she levered herself up, and Mumma quickly divested her of the old locknit nightdress. Dolour gasped open-mouthed at the emaciation of her sister, the scrawny yellowish arms and the chest which no longer had the sweet soft eminences of breasts, but only the curving ridges of ribs. Mumma caught her staring, and said sharply: 'What are you gawping at, yer big gawk? Go on, get downstairs and give me a hail when they're coming.'

She slipped the blouse on Roie. The girl fingered it softly: 'Gee, it's pretty, ain't it. I wonder if I'll ever wear it?'

'Don't talk like a goat, lovie. You'll be wearing it before this summer's through. Only you'd better not let Sister see you wearing it in the street.'

She looked for a laugh from Roie, but only the ghost of a smile flitted over her lips. She lay down again, exhausted.

'Now, let me do yer hair.' She carefully brushed the long straggling dark locks into some appearance of tidiness and knotted them back with a bit of brown wool. Then with brisk efficiency she rubbed a hot face-cloth over the girl's face. 'Anyone would think you were a baby, getting your face washed.'

Roie winced, and mentally Mumma kicked herself for putting her big foot in it. Oh, wouldn't Roie ever forget that little baby that had never come to anything but a heartache?

'Now, I thought we'd put this over the blankets.' Mumma unfolded the rest of the bundle, which turned out to be a clean patched towel, and the red silk shawl that Roie had bought at the markets. It glowed like a deep ruby in that drab and squalid mouse-hole of a room; its embroidered jade and turquoise were as beautiful as sea-colours. Roie wouldn't look at it for a moment. She shrank into herself in case she should hear in her mind a voice saying: 'Oh, rose of all the world.' But nothing happened. The memory was dead. She felt grief that it was, the only beautiful thing that anyone had ever said to her. But it was dead; it was dead like the baby it had begotten.

There was a sudden shriek from Dolour up the stairs: 'They're coming! I seen them turn the corner!'

Mr Diamond popped out of his door on to the landing. 'Who's coming, my girl?'

Mumma popped out of hers: 'The good sisters are coming to see poor Roie, and one yip outa you about Popish mummery, and so help me God I'll ram yer false teeth down yer orange throat,' she hissed with such extreme malevolence that Mr Diamond backed into his room and closed the door with extreme gentility.

A few moments later there was the sound of Dolour awkwardly greeting someone at the front door. There was also the stealthy sound of Miss Sheily's door opening, and being left ajar. Dolour fell over the bottom step, giggled hysterically, and said: 'I'm afraid it's dark.'

'Just as though they can't see,' hissed Mumma irately to Roie. 'Go on, pull the blanket up and don't be showing yer stomach.'

There was a gentle jingle of rosary beads, the sound which the world over heralds the approach of a nun. A light step on the landing followed, and into the shabby room came tall Sister Theophilus. Behind her came red-faced little old Sister Beatrix, whose spectacled black glances skipped with facile observation

310

before they came to rest on Roie, who sat, stiff with embarrassment and fright, against her pillow.

'My dear Mrs Darcy!' said Sister Theophilus, warmly. 'And my poor little Roie!' She moved gracefully towards the bed and kissed Roie on her damp forehead. Sister Beatrix unsmilingly shook hands with Mumma, who, hot and flustered, and not knowing whether to smile or imitate the dignity of the nun, waved her to a chair. It was lame on one corner, and squawked reproachfully when Sister Beatrix gingerly put her weight on it. Sister Theophilus patted the bed.

'May I sit here, Roie?'

Roie nodded voicelessly. Sister raised one corner of the lovely shawl.

'What truly beautiful needlework. Yours, Mrs Darcy?'

'Good life, no,' cried Mumma, blushing. 'I can't even put a patch on Mr Darcy's pants without getting it skew-wiff.'

Roie did not say a word. Somehow, with Dolour and Mumma around, all her illness and disillusionment of her knowledge had seemed bearable. Sometimes she even forgot that her room was a poor attic, bug-ridden, damp and malodorous. But now it looked what it was, the poor bedroom of a poor girl, each as soiled and hopeless and unexquisite as the other. All at once tears rolled effortlessly down her face, and she turned her head into the pillow and sobbed. Sister Theophilus looked in alarm at Mumma.

'She's not herself yet. She's very weak. It's a hard time she's been through,' said Mumma apologetically, longing to run to Roie, and yet not knowing whether that would be a polite thing to do. Sister Beatrix got up and stumped over towards the bed. She was mushroom-stout, little and dumpy, her white chin-band probably hiding a multitude of chins, the leather belt girding her waist so tight that the top of her wooden crucifix prodded her in the chest. She had a reputation for hardness, and many was the time her gimlet eye had pierced Dolour to the very marrow. Dolour would not have been in the least surprised if Sister Beatrix had given Roie's shoulder a good shake and said sharply: 'Rowena Darcy! Stop that ridiculous snivelling at once! Get up and dress yourself and go and help your mother to get the dinner ready.'

But instead Sister Beatrix said: 'God has his own ways of giving us experience, Rowena. Don't regret all the pain you have suffered. You will learn in the long run that it gave you wisdom of strength.

Lift up your heart, as Father says in the Mass, and be glad that God thought you worthy to go through this trial for his sake and your own.'

Mumma and Dolour listened with the rapt expression of those who see visions and hear things they do not understand. When Sister Beatrix turned to Mumma and said: 'You mustn't worry any more, Mrs Darcy. Roie will be all right.' Mumma nodded as though hypnotized.

As they left the room, Sister Theophilus gave Dolour's arm a little squeeze, and a kind look out of her lovely eyes. Sister was always kind, even when Dolour's arithmetic was a disgrace to her, but never before had she seemed so utterly gracious. Dolour resolved on the instant that she too would be a nun, and learn how to be adored by her pupils, and would die and become a saint and in time be canonized and known as St Anne of the Seven Dolours. She had concluded this dream by the time Mumma had taken the Sisters to the bottom of the dark steep stair, and she was instantly awakened from it by hearing a familiar voice say: 'Blessed be God, Sister dear. Now come into the kitchen where I can get a good look at you.'

'Grandma! Oh, gosh! Oh, jeepers!' wailed Dolour, pelting down the stairs, for she was fully convinced that Grandma in her hearty hospitality, had climbed straight out of bed and gone to welcome the Sisters in her old flannelette nightdress and faded pink cardigan with no elbows in it. But Grandma had made a determined effort to get dressed. Her legs were bare, and she wore old flapping slippers spotted with candle-grease, but she had put on her best dress, and over it 'me tippet'. The fur collar stuck up with ridiculous pomp around Grandma's uncombed head, but the expression on her face was warm and delighted, and there was no doubt that Grandma was really glad to see the Sisters. In face of Mumma's anguished gestures, she drew them into the disordered kitchen, from which the volcanic upheaval of the bedroom could be seen.

They sat down, smiling, on the rickety kitchen chairs.

'You must pardon my mother,' babbled Mumma. 'She's not very well. She . . .'

'Ah, hold yer tongue, darling,' broke in Grandma determinedly. Sister Theophilus patted her veined old hand.

'It's lovely to hear a real Irish voice again,' she smiled. 'I haven't heard the real brogue since my father died.'

Grandma was delighted. She flashed a look of aggravating mischief at poor Mumma. 'And what was his name, if I may be so bold as to ask a Sister?' she inquired, with every confidence of being answered. Sister Theophilus blushed and confessed: 'Matthew Nolan. He came from Kerry in, . . . I think 1880.'

'God be praised,' exclaimed Grandma, lifting her hands to heaven. 'If that wasn't the year I came out meself. Matthew Nolan! He didn't come out on the *Fair Isle*, did he?'

'No, the *Stratford*, I believe.'

'Ah, I came on the *Fair Isle*. Matthew Nolan. I once knew some Nolans on a farm. Outside Tralee, it was.'

'But I had an uncle near Tralee,' exclaimed Sister Theophilus, delightedly. 'The farm was called Knock-na-gree.'

'Glory be!' marvelled Grandma. 'So it was. There was one by the name of Michael, I think.'

'My Uncle Michael!' Sister Theophilus looked at Grandma with shining eyes. 'I often heard my Dad speak of him. What was he like, Mrs – ?'

'Mrs Kilker. Oh, he was a fine man, with black hair that stood up like a wall. A real, elegant Irish face, and blue eyes like glass marbles.'

'My father had eyes like that,' said Sister Theophilus dreamily.

'And the cut of him! A real gentleman,' added Grandma. 'Now that I'm looking at you I can see you've got the Nolan chin. So I can. It's as plain as the nose on your face that you're a Nolan, begging your pardon.'

Sister Theophilus rose reluctantly, glancing at the clock which stood on the shelf. 'I'm so sorry, but we'll have to go, Mrs Kilker. That's a really Irish name, too, isn't it?'

'Me old man, God rest him,' said Grandma proudly, 'was Johnny Kilker the iceman. But me maiden name was Mullins.'

'Was it?' asked Sister Beatrix with interest. She blushed a little, for Dolour was listening, and she did not believe in the pupils knowing their teachers' pre-profession names. 'My name was Mullins, too.'

Grandma gave a crow of excitement. 'Mullins, is it? Would it be the Cookstown Mullinses, or the Kerry Mullinses, or the Mullinses from Dublin?'

'From Dublin,' said Sister Beatrix. She gave a sigh. 'My father was from Coleraine Street, Dublin. He owned a livery stable there.'

Grandma tck-tcked sympathetically, for she could tell that old man Mullins was no more. Then Sister Theophilus interposed: 'Well, you and Mrs Darcy must come to afternoon tea at the convent one afternoon, Mrs Kilker. I am sure all the other Sisters would love to hear some of your reminiscences of Home.'

She extended a hand, and Grandma bobbed in what Dolour thought must be a curtsy. Then the nuns went. As soon as they had gone, Mumma fell into a chair and fanned herself with her apron. 'Ah, bless them, they're nice, but me heart's racing fit to burst. Run up and see how Roie is, there's a good girl.'

As Dolour disappeared, she turned to Grandma: 'A fine one you are, Ma, coming out in that terrible rig and talking so forward to the Sisters.'

Grandma pulled up the collar of her tippet like a proud old parrot.

'Yer only jealous, dearie, 'cause I made meself felt.'

Mumma gazed at her in admiration. 'You certainly did that. There's no beating the Irish, no mistake. But wasn't it the strangest thing you knowing her uncle?'

'Uncle me foot!' scoffed Grandma, wetting her finger and rubbing at a spot on her black dress. 'Uncle me foot! I only used the brain God kindly gave me.'

'You mean to say . . . you mean to say you didn't know him?' gasped Mumma in horror. 'You unnatural old liar.'

'It was a lucky guess and me own reasoning,' confessed Grandma, her filmy blue eyes dancing. 'But sure it gave the poor locked-up soul pleasure, so there was justification in it.'

'You're a wicked old article,' stormed Mumma, 'but I don't believe it. You described him as though you'd seen him with yer own eyes, and it was right, too.'

'Oh, that,' jeered Grandma. 'All Irishmen look alike. I just described your dadda, that's all, God rest his ashes. And now, help me back to me bed, will yer, darlin', because me legs are aching, something cruel, and I need a pipeful.'

'Shame on you, Ma!' said Mumma crossly. Then she started to laugh. Grandma's high cackle joined in, and Dolour, coming down the stairs, frowned at such unseemly mirth. She had her hands folded in her sleeves, and she was busy being St Anne of the Seven Dolours.

Twelve

Grandma got worse after that, almost never leaving her bed, sinking into a drowse of old age and weariness. It was hard for Mumma, running for ever between Roie and Grandma, sitting with one in the hot and prickling darkness and hearing the feeble cry of the other. Dolour was still sleeping on the old lumpy couch and often when Mumma was getting Hughie away to work in the morning they would stay for a moment in their frantic hurry and look at her mousy exhausted face, yellow in the pure light of early morning, drooping upon the curved shiny back of the sofa.

'Ah, it's tough on a kid, this life,' was all Hughie said, and Mumma turned away to Puffing Billy and stabbed a sausage with her long fork, trying to prevent the scalding words from coming up her throat. For it seemed to her that if Hughie had been a different man, a man who hadn't sat down and allowed life to defeat him, then things would have been better for them all.

Grandma had no teeth, having had them all out when she was twenty. In those days you just sat down on the blacksmith's stool and he pulled them out with his blackened pincers, giving you a swallow of brandy when you were near fainting with the blood and the pain and the horror. So Grandma's purply-pink lips were tucked in under her nose and her chin looked very long and pointed. She lay now with her head turning restlessly from side to side and her long, coarse, shiny white hair, like unstranded rope, lying over the pillow.

Mumma sat by her, smoothing her knotted hand as Hughie came in.

He looked down at the old lady, bending his fearsome black eyebrows at her.

'What's the matter with yer, you old devil?'

Mumma said: 'Hush yer gab, Hugh. She's asleep.'

But a thin thread of a voice came from Grandma: 'It's mortal sick I am, Hughie. Mortal sick.'

'Gah!' scoffed Hughie. 'Here, I'll fill yer pipe for yer and see if that puts some ginger in yer.'

315

He stuffed some tobacco in the little brown-stained clay cutty that lay on the counterpane, but Grandma, with the whisper of a gesture, motioned him away.

'Don't be sending me to a home, Hughie boy, whatever yer do. Say yer won't.'

Mumma blotted up a tear. 'Ah, don't be talking such rubbidge, Ma. As if Hughie would. Now try and sleep and you'll feel better when yer wake up.'

She pulled the blankets up to the ruffle on Grandma's nightgown and they left the room, walking heavily and wearily, for they were both worn out with the work and the heat.

Then one night Grandma ran away. It happened when Hughie came home a little happy, content to have his boots taken off and his bemused and wary body shoved haphazardly into bed. Roie had delirious nightmares that night, sitting up in bed and screaming in a thin squeal that made Miss Sheily thump against the wall and demand what the matter was. Mumma sat beside her, holding her poor tousled head against her breast and hushing her to and fro like a baby.

'There, there, it's all over, darling. Never again. Never again,' she murmured. When the girl was quiet again she went downstairs and found instead of Grandma an empty bed.

Mumma gave a great cry and ran out into the passage where a light blue oblong showed the dawn stealing through the open door. She pounded out to the verandah, looking up and down the street in anguish. But although the wind blew bits of paper along the gutter and a dog slunk from an upturned garbage can on the corner there was no more movement.

Mumma screamed and screamed, beating her hands on the bosom of her nightdress and not caring about the people who came grumbling and alarmed from their bedrooms, Miss Sheily in an old tweed overcoat of Johnny's, Mr Diamond with his gingery bare legs sticking out of an old ragged pair of pants which he obviously used as pyjamas, and Hughie frankly in his shirt, rolling from the bedroom in a fury of fright and bellowing what the matter was.

They found Grandma a long way down the street, sitting on the kerb in her nightgown, with blood all down her face and staining her hair, for she had fallen over several times. Beside her squatted a large, caped policeman, trying to get some sense out of her for his notebook. But Grandma was so frightened to wake up and find herself out on the street that she couldn't say a word.

316

'You ought to be ashamed of yourself, a hulking big fellow like you, tormenting the life and soul out of an old granny!' exploded Hughie, so relieved he found it less embarrassing to burst into passion than into tears. 'Go on, be off with you! The poor old soul's wandering in her head.'

'Then she shouldn't be wandering in the street in her shimmy,' expostulated the policeman.

Hughie gave the policeman a wink. 'You needn't worry, constable. It's into a home she's going as soon as I get me wife's consent. Sure, she's had a good spin, the poor old girl, and I've done me duty by her, mother-in-law and all as she is.'

Mumma cried bitterly as she put her signature to a paper which took Grandma away into a home for the aged and helpless.

'I'd never do it as long as I'd breath in me body,' she sobbed. 'But I can't tie her up, and if she's going to go wandering away, I'll never get a wink of sleep, and I'm that worn out already with looking after Roie as well.'

So Grandma went away, and all the street turned out to see, for it was a great event when the ambulance drew up before Number Twelve-and-a-Half, and Grandma, very shaky, but all dressed up in her tippet, and her tucked black hat with the jet hatpins, was lifted in. She was tremulous with joy, for she thought she was going for a ride in a bus, and she had always loved buses. By the time they reached the hospital, Grandma had forgotten all about her home, and Roie and Dolour and Mumma and Auntie Josie had drifted back into the past, as insubstantial as figures out of a book she had read long ago. Even Hughie looked strange to her. She asked him doubtfully: 'Do you belong to me?' and he had nodded and smiled, and kissed her cheek like soft chamois leather before he left.

'Stop yer whining,' he bellowed exasperatedly to Mumma when he reached home. 'It's a place like a mansion, and she's fine. She's got a little bed, with an elegant white counterpane on it, and there's a cabinet beside it with a bunch of flowers on top. And nurses everywhere. She's lucky, I'm telling you.'

'I know she is,' said Mumma forlornly, and she bent over Puffing Billy again, and prodded him in the stomach with the poker and rattled some coal down his gullet, so that he hiccuped smoke into the kitchen and spat a little shower of soot from the crack in the flue. And Dolour knew that Mumma somehow felt that she had betrayed Grandma's trust and helplessness, for there was no doubt, even if the Home was like a mansion, if Grandma had been in her right sense she would have bashed the nurses over the heads with her handbag and walked all the way home again.

Almost straight away Roie began to get better. She looked like a girl painted in blue and white crayon, her bones like shadows showing through the skin. At first she wouldn't look at anyone, turning away her face and looking somewhere else as she answered questions, but after a while as the blood became redder and her heartbeat stronger, she seemed to forget what had happened. It was almost as though she had gone to the brink of madness, and come back again, without the burden that had sent her to the brink.

In some ways Hughie understood her better than Mumma did, for always in Mumma's heart there lay the memory of that awful night when she realized that Roie was almost a stranger, with distinct and individual experiences and troubles. That realization, in some strange way, was almost worse than the knowledge of her daughter's sin and tragedy.

But Roie hadn't forgotten anything. It was just that now, in the apathy and languor of convalescence, she could drift away from all her memories. She could not even remember the faces of girls at the box factory. Even after she got up, sitting out in the backyard soaking up sunlight, and crawling around the house, she kept up this pretence, until at last it was a habit, and nothing shook her apathetic calm but some fleeting thought which she pursued and threw violently from her.

All the pitifully hard shell which the slums had taught her to build about her gentle, timid nature had disappeared and was never to grow again. She had no defences now.

Her first outing was to see Grandma. It was like stepping out of a dream to see the narrow sweep of Plymouth Street again, the plane trees with their white-pocked trunks, and the familiar houses crammed against their sooty iron-railed fences. Roie saw with astonishment that the trees were heavily leaved, and the starlings squabbling in the gutters were young, with faint rainbows on their dusty feathers.

'Why, it's summer!' she cried.

'Of course it is,' said Mumma. As usual, it had crept up on her, and she was still in her hot winter dress, rough and chafing around the neck and under the armpits, so that she was in a continuous state of discomfort and uneasiness. Mumma had already been to see Grandma several times, timidly attempting the trams, of which she was nervous, and returning home in the flushed and nerve-wracked state of one who has narrowly escaped death. She had said little about Grandma, save that she was well cared for, and seemed to be happy.

'Of course she is,' answered Hughie heartily, 'who wouldn't be, with a nice clean hospital to lie in, instead of a bed full of bugs, like she had at home.'

'It was the best I could give her,' glared Mumma, 'and you couldn't expect poor Josie to take her back again.'

'Who said it wasn't?' demanded Hughie. 'But it's poor fare when you're old and cracking up.'

'It might have been better if you hadn't guzzled every shilling we had to spare, and a lot more beside, these last few months,' said Mumma, her lips cold and stiff and straight.

A crunchy red gravel path ran up to the hospital, and slim-legged flowers swayed beside it. Dolour was in great delight. The smell of disinfectant did not bother her; the hospital was like some great and romantic house out of a novel or a film. It did not enter her mind that within that great white colonnaded building there was suffering and loneliness and death, and the lingering misery of sick old age.

They creaked self-consciously down the ward, looking from left to right at the sunken old woman faces on the glittering white pillows. And, after a while, there was Grandma, so small, so thin, she hardly made a hummock on the bed. Her hair had been clipped off short, and it was neatly brushed. Her corded, sagging neck emerged from the ruffle of her nightgown. She was frightened when they all stood around her bed and stole a look at Dolour who stood stupidly, open-mouthed, staring at her minute and sunken face, the soft skin of which was now mottled with red, and the long, long hands which, like a skeleton's, lay aimlessly upon the frosty counterpane.

But the worst thing was that she didn't know any of them. It was so strange, to look into her familiar eyes and see no recognition there. It was almost as though they had become invisible.

'It's no good,' said Mumma. 'She'll never be any different. The doctor said her memory's quite gone.'

Hughie felt his temper rising in a sparkling, reviving tide. Borne on the surges of it, he said in a loud voice, for he was appalled and shocked at Grandma's condition. 'Do you mean to tell me you knew she was like this?'

Mumma nodded dumbly. Tears were in her eyes. 'I didn't want to tell you. I didn't want you to know.' Hughie understood quite well that Mumma's grief for this, Grandma's final stage in life, had tied her tongue. 'I just couldn't tell anyone, Hughie. It seems so strange. But it's for the best, Hughie. If she knew she was in a place like this she'd die.'

Hughie said foolishly: 'I wouldn't have allowed you to put her in here, if I'd known they'd do this to her.'

Roie whispered: 'Oh, Dad! It's only because she's so old.' She sat down by Grandma and held her hand. 'It's me, Grandma darling. It's Roie. Don't you remember me?'

But Grandma only looked at her with sad, wistful eyes, not knowing what to say to a stranger.

Hughie said slowly, the fire in him dying out: 'It's a fearful thing.' It was just as though he could see Grandma's memory, like a stretched piece of cloth, and it fraying into holes, little useless tatters. He felt a lump in his throat and turned away, frightened that he might break down and disgrace himself before all the other old people, who were so close to the brink of death themselves.

Grandma crooked a knobby finger at Dolour, and trembling, the child went closer.

'Tell me what I'm doing in bed, Kathleen dear? Am I lazy, or is it the sickness has got me?'

Dolour stared. 'She called me Kathleen, Mumma.'

Mumma thought for a moment. 'Kathleen was my sister. She died a long time ago, when I was a little girl. Say something, Dolour.'

Dolour held Grandma's hand, piteously fragile, and feverishly hot. She opened her mouth to say something, but before she could frame the words Grandma was asleep, her mouth fallen open, and her sunken eyelids heavy.

So they went away, the two girls avoiding each other's eyes, and Mumma unnecessarily severe with everyone, because she was frightened she would burst into the tearing sobs which were knocking at her breast.

In bed, in the night, Hughie said shyly: 'Are you awake, dearie?'

Mumma answered thickly, for she had been soundlessly crying: 'What is it, Hugh?' He slid over and put his head down on her shoulder almost as if he were a boy, and soft with love again.

'Would you like us to bring Grandma back here again?'

'It was you who wanted to put her away, Hughie, in spite of what you said today in the Home,' she answered.

'I was wrong then, darling. Sure, it's her home here too. It's empty without her being in the old stretcher and yelling for a new pipeful every now and again.'

She turned to him and held his head closer, his dear, wicked, wasteful head that she loved so much, and it seemed in that enchanted instant that her breast was slim and eager again, and his hair soft and curly, and there was nothing more in all the world that she wanted.

So it was decided and the next day Hughie went back to the Home.

The doctor was a strangely cubic being, with his white jacket falling in still perpendicular folds, and his nose and cheeks all following the same straight up-and-down pattern. His glasses flashed disapprovingly as he said: 'I don't deny that I'm against it. It's on your own responsibility that you do this.'

Hughie, a bright spark shining in his blue eyes, brought his eyebrows together with an almost audible clang and replied: 'We're doing the right thing, thank you kindly,' and added the rest under his breath.

So Grandma came home. It was almost a triumphant procession. Plymouth Street lay drowsy and golden under a heavenly flood of Christmas-month sunshine. You could not notice the smell of garbage and old, old timber, for the sunshine itself had an odour, of the hot acres of the hinterland, and flowering gum, sweet and sticky. Everyone, gossiping over fences, waddling home from the marketing, waiting for the tram, turned and looked when the taxi bearing Grandma pulled up in front of the house. There was a brief painful scuffle as Hughie hauled and lifted her out of the taxi, for Grandma wanted to continue her ride.

Dolour was pleased, excited. She had told her friends of Grandma's departure and her own visit to the Home. Most of them had grandmas of their own, but very few had relations in homes for the aged. It gave Dolour an aloof and important air. So at Grandma's return, as a special favour, Dolour brought Phyllis Gall and Gracie Drummy along to watch. They stood giggling explosively at intervals, in the shadow of the stairs. Mumma was so happy to have Grandma back that she did not even notice, and after a while Dolour became sorry that she so pandered to public curiosity, and coming out of the kitchen, spoke sharply to her friends, telling them that they ought to know better than to hang around where there was someone so sick she was nearly dead.

'Crumbs, Dolour!' they gasped, their eyes big, and Dolour felt an overwhelming sense of importance, so that she went back to the kitchen on tiptoe, as though walking in a solemn procession.

Hughie was on top of the world. His was the feeling of pride and joy which one feels when one has performed, against violent opposition, a purely charitable action. He basked in the adoring glance of his wife, who had in a single instant forgotten all his transgressions of the past, and loved him for what he was, a husband who had brought his old mother-in-law home so that she could die in familiar surroundings.

Nobody thought to ask Grandma what she thought of the change. She lay in the narrow sagging bed, looking at the light with her filmy blue eyes, her puckered mouth tight-shut against food, drink or medicine. Grandma was not in that room; she was walking in some long ago year as another might walk in a meadow. Days and nights filled with swift passions and griefs of youth lay around her feet like the pages of a discarded letter; hours and minutes of memory and sensation brushed her brain like the wings of moths.

Roie came and looked at her there, so tiny that she hardly interrupted the even flow of the quilt. It was hard to believe that from the little worn-out body had come eleven children; it was as though Grandma were a tiny gate in the great wall of life, and through her had flowed being itself.

Roie thought: 'If it hadn't been for Grandma, I wouldn't be here, or Dolour, or any of our cousins. My baby wouldn't have lived or died.'

Grandma began to mutter, and frightened, Roie called her mother. They all came in, Dolour and Hughie and Mumma, and sat about the bed in the intolerably hot room, Hughie breathing aromatic fumes.

'Stevie,' said Grandma; her voice was as tiny and hoarse as the voice of an old gramophone record. 'Stevie agrah, wait till I undo my stays.'

'Who's Stevie?' asked Hughie in a shocked whisper.

'I dunno,' said Mumma, holding Grandma's hand tight between her own. 'Me father's name was John.'

Grandma's face seemed to fade under their very eyes; it was the colour of yesterday's milk, and smaller than they had ever seen it. She looked straight at Dolour and said: 'Stevie, it's wicked you are, and there's hellfire under me feet, but I love you, Stevie. Ah,

322

Stevie!' There came the ghost of a giggle from Grandma, and Hughie rose to his feet and gestured Roie and Dolour from the room.

'It isn't fitting for girls to be here, when there's talk of this nature.'

'Ah, Dadda!' whispered Roie.

Dolour gave a wail, but Hughie was not to be baulked. He gave her a push, an angry, frustrated push, and Dolour, furious, ran out of the room, flung herself down on the mat and listened at the crack, for she knew that Roie was not likely to tell her all that the delightful and scandalous old Grandma said. But all she heard was the mumble of forgotten love-words, and phrases with no more sense to them than the babble of a magpie. Then, all at once, Grandma opened her eyes wide, and said in a clear voice to Hughie: 'Don't be breathing on the candle, yer tom todger, or you'll have us all blown up.' Then she smiled at Mumma and closed her eyes and went to sleep.

Dolour couldn't believe it when the silence came over the room and the house, just as it does over the land between the still and the turning of the tide. Then, as she heard her mother cry out, hoarse and anguished, she ran out of the door and screamed up the stairs: 'Miss Sheily! Miss Sheily! Go and get the priest, for Grandma's dying.'

She waited long enough to hear Miss Sheily's alarmed feet thudding down the stairs, then she ran inside again. Roie, pale-faced, met her. Dolour tried to say: 'I've sent for the Father,' but she could not, for she could see the words already forming on Roie's lips.

She gave a little squeal and ran out in the yard, hiding herself in the great jagged shadow of the phoenix palm and looking up at the cool sky and its wind-washed purity of light and colour.

'Grandma!' whispered Dolour. 'Oh, Grandma, where are you?'

Chained to earth, shackled and bound by her own body, she strained to get some point of contact with that flying timeless spirit which had just been released. The soft air touched her cheek, melting as it touched; the pure light flooded down into her eyes, but Grandma was nowhere, nowhere at all.

Thirteen

There was a man who used to go around Surry Hills with a barrel-organ in a pram. The organ was no more than an oblong box, with a fluted and gilded facade, and sides that were painted with gaudy pictures. When Dolour was very little she loved to stand and look at them . . . there was one of a Florentine blue lake with a snowy mountain behind it, as triangular as a moth's wing, but much whiter; there was another of a gipsy man in a yellow shirt sitting by a stile while his dappled horse grazed, and another, her favourite, of a little boat with a red sail, gliding for ever to a distant blue shore where a dusky castle stood. And, all the time, there would be in her ears the haunting wheeze of 'Come Back to Erin' or 'Land of Our Fathers' or 'Swanee River'.

The man who owned the barrel-organ, and presumably lived on the pennies its music brought him, was an elderly clean fellow with a lot of tidy white hair around his ears and a square, sturdy body. He spoke with an accent that puzzled everybody: Irish they knew, and Italian and Greek, but not his.

'What makes you talk like that?' Roie had asked him when she was ten, and he became cross and sparkled his bright light blue eyes at her, and moved off, playing 'Beautiful Dreamer' very fast.

The morning Grandma was buried, he happened to be coming up Plymouth Street. He wheeled his pram to a stop before Bert Drummy's ham-and-beef, and with tranquil slowness moved the lever and began winding out 'Come Back to Erin'. The music jingled like a harp with a broken string, but sweet and clear it drifted down the road to the church, where a curious sprinkling of people had gathered to watch the tail-end of a poor funeral. There was a strange deep satisfaction in watching a funeral; it made them feel almost smug that they were still alive; that someone else had fallen before the Reaper, while they still stood, not only alive and kicking, but with a good chance of winning the double on Saturday.

There was a chitter of hushed talk: 'Old Mrs Kilker. Her that stayed with the Darcys.'

'They say she was eighty-six, poor old thing. Well, she's better off than the rest of us, that's what I say.'

'Yeah, that's her grand-daughter, that was knocked around by them Dutch bastards. Don't she look pale and sick, poor thing.'

'I'll bet Hughie's got a few under his belt. Ain't like him to carry a pall without getting in a few stiffeners first,' chuckled someone coarsely.

Mumma, awkwardly dressed in someone else's new brown coat and with a stiff, unbecoming black hat wedged on her head, her poor, swollen face averted from the inquisitive glance of her neighbours, climbed into the taxi. As she settled uncomfortably into the corner, the sweet tinny strains of the barrel-organ floated through the open door. Hughie slammed it with a muttered blasphemy.

'Nice time to be playing that now.'

'It's true, though,' choked Mumma. 'She was always wanting to go back to Ireland, and now she knows all about it. Oh, Ma, I miss you so much!'

She collapsed into tears, leaning her wet cheek against the smudgy window of the taxi. Hughie sat gazing mournfully at the pockmarked red neck of the driver and the way his hairy, capable hands gently caressed the wheel.

'Sure, I might have let her make the Christmas pudding without all the fuss,' he said suddenly. Mumma gave a snort of assent. 'And there's many times when she called out in the night that I could have got her a little nip of brandy, and no harm done.' In the depths of his grief, which was nonetheless sincere because it was ephemeral, Hughie searched for more damning statements. 'I had many hard thoughts of her, and said hard things, and now she's gone for ever, and I can't say beg pardon.'

'I wish we could have got a priest in time,' sighed Mumma. Before her eyes marched a succession of little pictures of Grandma . . . Grandma young and vigorous, and skelping kids left and right; Grandma clouting a travelling salesman with a frying pan; Grandma getting tipsy at Christmas time, and having knock-down, drag-out fights with Pa; Grandma telling lies, being proud and hard with sinners, maliciously witty with the unfortunate. It seemed to her that she couldn't remember Grandma when she wasn't committing some sin or another. Then she said, with piteous defiance: 'If I could love her, the good Lord could, and he won't be too hard on an old lady who didn't have an easy life.'

'That's true enough,' admitted Hughie. He put his hand shyly on the sleeve of the ugly brown coat. 'That's an elegant coat you're wearing.'

'It's Miss Sheily's sister's,' said Mumma, comforted. 'It's good cloth.'

The little funeral passed slowly through the crowded streets. More men raised their hats to Grandma dead than ever had while she was alive. Hughie and Mumma felt a little happy because of this. It was almost as if for once she had commanded other people's consideration and respect.

When the funeral left the church, Miss Sheily, spare and white and emaciated in her tight black costume of another generation, trotted hastily down the street with determination in her heels. As she approached the barrel-organ man she said hastily: 'Fine time to be playing, with a funeral only a few doors away! You ought to be ashamed of yourself. Caesar's ghost! Isn't there any decency left?'

The barrel-organ man stopped playing right in the middle of an arpeggio and a tide of red flowed up from under his collar and swamped him even to his bald patch. He stammered: 'I didn't know. I am short-sight. Please pardon. I go.'

'You'd better,' shrilled Miss Sheily, in her high, cultured, birdlike voice. He looked at her out of round crystal blue eyes, sea-blue they were, with simplicity and naivete in them. He gave a duck and a tug at his suddenly assumed round felt hat, and hastily trundled the pram away.

The next day he arrived at Number Twelve-and-a-Half, having inquired in the meantime where Miss Sheily lived. Dolour was surprised and delighted to see the barrel-organ in the pram come jolting over the flag-stone path.

'Hello, you come to play us a tune?' she invited thoughtlessly. The barrel-organ man shook his head.

'I come to see lady; the lady whose funeral it was yesterday.'

Dolour understood at once. 'Oh, you mean my Mumma. All right, I'll call her.'

Mumma, swollen-eyed, and melancholy-faced, came to the door. When he saw her the barrel-organ man said timidly: 'I come to say I sorry I played so loud yesterday while the funeral was on.'

Mumma said; 'Oh, that's all right, and it was very civil of you to call.'

'Mr Gunnarson my name,' said the barrel-organ man.

'Mr Gunson,' muttered Mumma embarrassedly, for she could smell something burning in the kitchen, and beside, any mention of Grandma and she knew tears would gush into her hot and stinging eyes.

'No,' said the barrel-organ man. 'Gunson not right. I am Gunnarson. It is Swedish name. Please, I would like to speak to lady with black dress, white face, who say "Caesar's ghost!" '

Dolour gave a spurt of laughter, and Mumma, frowning, said: 'Oh, you mean Miss Sheily. She doesn't belong to our family. She just has a room.'

'She's upstairs, on the landing. First room on the right,' added Dolour.

Mr Gunnarson replaced his hat neatly. 'Thank you. I go.'

He slipped past Mumma and Dolour, who looked at each other in dismay. His outward pointed boots clip-clopped down the hall. He looked up the dark crooked staircase and without any hesitation ascended it.

'Gosh!' remarked Dolour. 'Bet she pushes him down the stairs.'

'Ssssssh!' said Mumma. For the first time in a week a little smile tweaked at her mouth. Upstairs there was a brisk rat-tat on Miss Sheily's door.

Dolour and Mumma heard an irate squawk from inside. 'Very well, I'm coming. Don't knock the door down,' and Miss Sheily's sharp skinny shoes squeaking across the floor.

'Well?' they heard her say. Mumma rapidly waddled down towards the stairs, and crouched tittering, in the shadows. Dolour's face went scarlet with the effort of keeping her giggles under control. They heard Mr Gunnarson's tranquil voice explaining his sorrow at putting his big hoof in it on the day of the funeral. Then Miss Sheily said: 'Well, what about it? It's all over, and it's Mrs Darcy you want to rub your nose in the dirt to, not me.'

'I'm a lonely man,' explained Mr Gunnarson, 'and I like you. You are a lady, you are not married, and I like to come and see you then and now.'

'Pooh, you dirty old man!' exploded Miss Sheily. 'Using a funeral as an excuse to pick up a woman. It's ghoulish, that's what it is, you dirty old disgrace. Now be off before I push you down the stairs.'

'There you are, I told you,' triumphed Dolour, and Mumma pinched her tail threateningly.

'I do not try to pick you up,' protested Mr Gunnarson. 'I am a man with a good business. Here, I have my bank book. You read. And I am not dirty. I wash my hands many times a day. You look.'

There was the sound of a door jarring on an intercepting shoe.

'Go on, take your foot out of there,' cried Miss Sheily angrily, and they could just imagine her white face distorted with fury and her black eyes snapping and sparkling above her beaky nose.

'I go,' agreed Mr Gunnarson. 'but I come back. I like you. You have kick in you.'

'Caesar's ghost!' yelled Miss Sheily, and there was the crisp sound of someone kicking someone else on the shin. 'I've got kick in me all right.' The door slammed. Mr Gunnarson quietly descended the stairs. When he saw Mumma and Dolour he said: 'I like her. She is Miss Sheily, yes? One day she will be Mrs Gunnarson, no? You see.'

He raised his hat, and his innocent blue eyes, as round as a child's, smiled naively: 'You think I am angry because she kick me in the shin? No, I like woman with fire.'

He slid past down the narrow passage, and Mumma and Dolour turned their heads like one woman. As he trundled the old pram down the road he started to play and the tingling, jingling strains of 'Pop Goes the Weasel' filled Plymouth Street with music.

Down in Hughie's work the men often ran a syndicate in a lottery ticket, a bob in per man, and Hughie always refused to join in. The Government, he said, had enough dough without him sticking in a bob for nothing. And as it had also happened that nobody amongst these faithful gamblers had ever won a fiver, he firmly continued in his belief that the whole thing was a rook.

When at last Roie was well, Hughie was so pleased that he paid a visit to church on his way to work. Hughie was a stranger to his religion. He would have knocked down anybody who announced that it was not the true one, but he never found time to attend to it, personally. He had not been to confession since the day, six years before, when he had been nearly run over by a tram, and in a burst of thankfulness had shed his sins.

Hughie left for work very early, the narrow streets were full of shabby girls hurrying off to the factories that hummed in every alleyway of the district. And there were men in navy work shirts and good tough tweed trousers; men with hard, cracked hands that they were proud of, for they were the symbol of their contribution to labour, and the commerce that made Sydney what it was. Inside the church Mass was proceeding; there was a sprinkling of people in the dusky brown pews, mainly very old or very young, for the middle-aged were engaged either in getting breakfast or in eating it preparatory to leaving for the day's work. Hughie stood awkwardly in the side doorway before he creakingly knelt and prayed:

'Lord,' he said, in a mental voice which seemed to him to be rough and manly, but straightforward and easy to listen to, 'Thanks for making Roie better, and don't ever let her do it again. Lord, I forget how to talk to you; you'll have to excuse me. When I get drunk keep me tongue outa the dirt, will yer please. And for God's sake give me some encouragement so that I'll have something to live for, me and me wife.'

Instantly and mysteriously, there shot into his mind the idea: 'Why not buy a lottery ticket?' It was like seeing the roof of the church split apart, and heaven itself peep through. Nothing could have convinced Hughie that it was not a thought straight from God himself.

'Christ!' he muttered, awed, and hastily changed his tone to a prayerful reverent one, repeating: 'Christ!'

He got up and clumped out on feet that refused to adopt a tiptoe stance, and from the door he looked at the altar and gave that familiar sideways jerk of the head which the man in the street always uses to greet or farewell a friendly acquaintance.

He did not think of the first prize; his imagination went no farther than the hundred pound prize. It seemed to him to be the limit of all wealth. He spent the day in a fever of impatience till he received his pay, for who was to tell whether or not some other clunk, perhaps even a wealthy clunk, was not buying the ticket which had the signature of heaven itself upon it?

When finally his money passed over the counter, and he received the jade green slip into his horny hand, Hughie had a conflict of sensations in his heart. He believed so sincerely that it was the lucky one, and yet at the same time he mentally prepared a speech of denunciation and contempt for God, if it should prove to be otherwise. The days passed slowly by, bringing more excited anticipation with them. It was like being a kid again and looking forward to Christmas, or a birthday.

Yet, finally, when he stood on the verandah, with the newly-arrived paper in his hand, he was too scared to open it.

'I don't ask for fifty, Lord. Maybe that was high-flown of me. Just ten, or even a fiver would ease things up a bit.'

Dolour came prancing out. 'That the paper, Dad? Let's have the pitcher ads. Roie and me are going to the Palace tonight. I earned our fares doing some messages for the Sisters last week.'

'Garn, hop it,' growled Hughie. He opened the paper with tremulous hands. The print blurred. He couldn't read it. Dolour said impatiently: 'Watcher looking for? I'll find it for you.'

'Leave me alone, willya?' yelled Hughie, and to Patrick Diamond, who clumped past just then, he complained: 'Blasted kids. Always around like flies around flypaper. Can't let a man have a peaceful read of 'is paper!' he finished, bellowing the words at the surprised Dolour.

'Oh, okay,' she said, skipping inside again. As Mr Diamond vanished through the gate, Hughie opened the paper again. He forced his eyes to the column headed 'Lottery Results'. The blood drummed in his ears, then faded away to a quiet humming sound. Hughie sat down suddenly on the gas box. For there was no doubt. The print plainly stated, 'First Prize (£5,000) to H. Darcy, Surry Hills.'

'Heaven look down on me,' whispered Hughie, brushing away the little black stars and moons that swung before his dazzled eyes. He looked at the print, and it still said the same thing. He could even read who won the second prize – 'Can't be Me,' Rozelle. Hughie poked his head out between the mealy vines that cloaked the verandah, and looked up into the infinitely high, infinitely clear blue-green sky.

'You're a good man, Lord, you are that. Never would I have believed, disbelieving old bastard that I am. You don't hold any grudges for all that I've been to you. Ah, it's a good man you are, and I'll never forget you for it.'

He withdrew his head, and there was Dolour looking at him. 'Whatever are you gabbling to yourself for, Dadda?' she inquired. 'You look like an old looney.'

'Looney, it it?' cried Hughie hysterically. He burst into a roar of laughter. 'I read a joke,' he explained. 'Here, take yer pitcher ads.' He flung the butterfly of newspaper at her, and she pored over it in the yellow light of the street lamps. He thought he'd tell her then and there; then he changed his mind. It might be better to tell them all together. He rushed down the hall, then paused. How much better to get the money first, and shower it all around the room! Five thousand lovely quids, representing a motor car, a new house, and endless bottles of wine! Or should he go out and buy a fur coat for Mumma, and come in and say he'd found it. Hughie found himself so besieged with delightful ideas that he had to go out and sit quietly in the laundry amongst the smell of soap and wet wood, while he marshalled his thoughts. Sometimes he felt as though he were dreaming it all; people in Erskineville and Mona Vale and King's Cross won the lottery, but never anybody in Surry Hills. Particularly never anybody named H. Darcy.

In the mornings Mumma usually had a job to wake him, for he was much too old for the work he did, and sank into exhaustion every time his head touched a pillow. She hated the sight of him in the mornings, his false teeth sitting on the dusty table beside his bed, and his gums tucked in like an old man's, his exhausted eyelids too sodden with sleep to lift. He looked like an old grandfather, and in some inexplicable way it hurt her, so that often she said, 'For God's sake, Hugh, won't you be getting yer big frame outa the blankets!' and turned away with a tear of love and pity in her eye for him.

But to her astonishment and alarm the next morning she awoke to find the bed empty. She got up hurriedly and clumsily, putting her old coat over her nightdress, and waddled out into the kitchen, twisting up her hair at the same time.

'Hughie!' she called sharply. 'Where are you? What are you doing?'

'Getting some of the scrub off,' called Hughie from the scullery, and there she beheld the unprecedented sight of him, at six in the morning, scraping the stubble off his face.

'Are yer mad, Hughie,' she cried.

'No, I'm shaving,' replied Hughie, unaware of any witticism. Mumma was so angry, she put her hands on her hips and stared at him belligerently.

'What are you shaving for on a workday?' she demanded.

'To get me face clean,' answered Hughie patiently, pulling a long lip and snicking out the hairs in his nostrils with harsh rasping sounds.

'What for?' cried Mumma exasperated. Hughie wiped his razor and turned to her, a white ruff of suds around his mouth and under his chin.

'Because I ain't going to work this morning, that's why, sticky-beak.' He pecked over suddenly and kissed her on the cheek.

'Because I got some business to do. Now, don't be asking me,' he winked mysteriously. Mumma, shutting her mouth tight, stamped off. The next moment he heard the pop of the gas ring, and murmured dreamily: 'All electric.'

All through breakfast Mumma was deeply troubled. What did he mean, business? Was he perhaps buying a present? It was Christmas soon. But Hughie never bought anybody any presents. The only thing he had ever bought in his life had been her wedding ring, and he wouldn't have bought that except that everybody seemed to expect him to do so. She was so baffled and frustrated that she hacked into the loaf as though it was Hughie's neck, so that by the time Dolour wandered down it was the shape of a scallop, with strange fluted edges.

'What's the matter, Mumma?' asked Dolour, sleepily.

It's *'im!'* cried Mumma, pointing the knife into the bedroom where Hughie, in his grey undershirt, stood deliberating. He had two shirts, the khaki one with the holes under the arms, and the blue one with the frayed collar. In her clumsy way Mumma had patched them, and then patched the patches, and now they were beyond all human aid. 'Six white silk shirts with dandy stand-up collars,' murmured Hughie.

Mumma continued to fulminate to Dolour against Hughie.

'Don't ask him,' cried Mumma. 'It's business. He ain't going to work this morning! Just as though we can afford to lose the money. Oh, no, he's the gentleman this morning. Shaving, if you please, and now putting on his good blue suit and his red tie as though he had nowhere to go but to the King's palace itself. And he can go, for all I care!' With that she made a slam with the bread knife, and rushed out into the laundry.

'Gee, Mum,' wailed Dolour. 'You know I'm practising to be a quiz kid. I need nourishment. Where's my breakfast?'

There was a snort of repentance in the laundry, and Mumma came in, flushed and tousled, but ready to prepare breakfast. She did not spare another glance for Hughie as he marched with unbearable casualness to the door. 'I'll be seeing yer,' he offered.

'If you're lucky,' said Mumma rudely. Hughie's temper rose.

'I'm telling you you'll be glad to see me, when I come back!' he cried. Mumma went over and put her arms around his neck.

'I'm always glad to see you, you old tripehound, and you know it,' she said. 'But I wish you wouldn't tease me.' Hughie closed his lips

332

tight and smiled at her mysteriously, so that she nearly swatted him. Then he closed the door and went off.

He took a tram to the city. How lovely Sydney was, all newly washed by the night rain, with her narrow streets brimming with people, and the sun cutting great yellow swathes out of the shadows that still shrouded the tall buildings. Hughie walked in a sort of dream, past the great pillars of the Post Office, and the little stalls with their striped awnings, and the flowers that the vendors were unloading from barrows. Nameless flowers they were to Hughie. Flamboyant bucket-shaped pink things and dark ruby rosebuds, tightly furled, and exquisite sprays of white flowers, with golden middles, and dew carefully applied from a syringe. Hughie thought: 'I'll take her home a quid's worth. Only I'll go in a taxi, in case I meet someone I know.'

He was outside the lottery office as it opened. The clerk smiled the smile he had tried out on a hundred other prize-winners, and hazarded: 'Five thousand?'

Now that he actually heard someone else say those magnificent words, Hughie's spirit began to tremble, and he went red and stammered: 'I'm H. Darcy, Surry Hills, like it said in the paper.'

The clerk was all politeness and congratulations. 'Excellent, sir. Fine. Fine. Now, may I have your ticket?'

Hughie fished in his pocket and got it, faded sea-green now, but more precious than Aladdin's lamp. The clerk took a glance at it, wrote a little in his ledger, and then compared the numbers. A strange look flashed over his face; his spectacles glittered ominously as he raised his eyes.

'Have you another ticket, Mr Darcy?'

Hughie gasped: 'No, have I gotta have two?'

'I was just wondering if you'd bought another ticket and put the same name on it,' explained the clerk. 'You see, the numbers are entirely different.'

Hughie, his face pallid, and his tongue swelling so that he could not even grunt, took the ledger that the clerk reversed for him. There was no doubt. There were only nine usable figures for a lottery ticket, but the ones on the ledger and those on his ticket were so different they looked like words out of different languages.

Hughie cried: 'It's down wrong, that's what.'

The clerk shook his head sadly. 'No, sir. No possibility of a mistake. Didn't you check up with the number in the paper?'

'I was too busy keeping it from me wife,' stuttered Hughie. He felt so sick he wanted to go out in the fresh air and sit down on the steps. But the clerk was inexorable in his sympathy. He took Hughie upstairs so that they might compare the signature on the winning ticket. Hughie was a man in a dream. He did not think to pray any more; he was a miracle man whom God had deserted in the middle of a miracle.

The clerk looked over another file of ticket butts. 'Here you are, sir.' He showed Hughie the line of writing. It was inscribed shakily in black ink. 'H. Darcy, Clarion Street, Surry Hills'.

Hughie barged home like a blind man. He did not even think to take a tram. Numb and light-headed with anguish, he headed towards the maze of alleys and laneways of Plymouth Street. Then he realized that he couldn't go home and face Mumma, so he turned towards the works. It was very late, but the foreman, seeing his good clothes and surmising that he had attended another funeral, was non-committal instead of abusive. And Hughie's mates, who had been straining at the leash for a conversation with him, said nothing more than: 'In the family, Hughie?' He nodded. One of them whispered to another: 'There you are. I told you it wasn't him. The old coot doesn't believe in gambling. Never had a ticket in his life.'

'H. Darcy, Clarion Street, Surry Hills.' It was written on the bench before him; it was written on his soiled hands and his polished boots that were already dulling before the dirt and slime.

'Oh, God!' cried Hugh in his heart, and no more anguished voice had ever risen to heaven's implacable gates. His life seemed almost too much to bear. As soon as the whistle went he took his coat and ran away. His mates watched him go, astonished: 'Musta hit the old boy hard, eh?'

He clumped into the church, looked sourly at the altar. 'All I got to say is,' he remarked, 'you're a poor sport,' and the voice of Judas could have been no bitterer.

He couldn't face his home. He hated Mumma, he hated Dolour, he hated Roie with her fragile face and little bones that cried out for a holiday and a rest in some luxurious place where he could never, never take her. He thought of going to the pub, but he had no money; he hung around the door for a while, longing to ask someone for the price of a drink, then he spat in the gutter with contempt for himself and hurried along to Clarion Street.

It was not much better than Plymouth Street, strongly ammoniacal with the smell of the nearby brewery stables, but Hughie was not cheered with the knowledge that someone badly off was receiving the pot of gold. It made him feel worse that anyone in such poor circumstances should be so ruddy lucky. He hailed a fat woman leaning over a gate.

'Excuse, missus, but where's this Darcy feller live?' It seemed strange to be saying his own name and knowing that it belonged to a person he had never seen. The woman winked.

'You got it wrong, pal,' she said. 'It's Miss Darcy. Miss Helen Darcy. You 'eard the news, I suppose. Ain't one of these reporter fellers, are yer?'

Hughie recovered enough to gesture vulgarly. The woman snorted with laughter. 'They been around all day, like flies after a dirt-box. But she ain't seeing no one. She's that stuck-up, the old cow. Wouldn't chuck a few sixpences out into the gutter for the kids to fight over. Not 'er.'

'Well, I wanter see her,' explained Hughie, bringing his eyebrows down grimly. The woman shrugged. 'Betcher got to crawl through the keyhole, then. She lives in the house with the washing out.'

Hughie went to the little down-at-heel cocoa-coloured house that was squashed between two towering tenements. A string of depressed greyish washing hung from the upper verandah. He knocked at the door, and a curtain was agitated at the window. He knocked louder.

'Come on, open up,' he cried jovially. 'I ain't going to hurt you.'

A little voice breathed behind the door: 'Who . . . who is it?'

'Name of Darcy,' answered Hughie. The little voice hardened perceptibly.

'I ain't got no relations name of Darcy,' it replied. Hughie's mouth formed words, horrible, soul-searing words, but he said nothing. Then he cried: 'I ain't trying to borrow nothing. I want to show you something. Look, I'll shove it under the door.'

He pushed the lottery ticket through the crack. It twitched out of his hand, and he waited patiently, hearing the click of a spectacle-case, and then a silence. The door opened a fraction, and a long nose strangely reminiscent of Grandma's poked through. A timid, faded eye surveyed him. 'I hope you ain't drunk or nothing.'

'Sober as a judge, Miss Darcy,' answered Hughie with bitter truth.

'Well, you can come in, but I'm all of a fumble with people knocking on me door, and the reporters from the papers, and everything.' Hughie slid through the narrow space. The hall was dark and dirty, and smelt of cats.

Miss Helen Darcy was a tiny bent old woman, at least seventy-five. She matched the house in its neglect and grime. One felt that her old fingers found it too long and difficult a task to do her hair properly, or to wash the once-white collar that shrank miserably on her old dark dress.

Hughie explained the position, hope springing in his soul as he did so. He felt sure that he was good for a fiver at least, although his only motive in coming down to Clarion Street was to pour more acid into his wound. What would this old haybag do with five thousand quid? She probably required no more than her pension; she was too old and shaky to enjoy even fifty pounds.

'It was a bad disappointment,' explained Hughie meaningly. She looked at him vaguely. 'You aren't related to the Lismore Darcys?'

'No, I said I ain't.'

'Then I can't think who you might be.'

'I ain't no relation. It was just the funny coincidence,' explained Hughie patiently. 'I thought it was me . . .' Once more he launched into the tale of the lottery ticket, and Miss Darcy listened, her eyes roving into space, and her thoughts obviously somewhere else.

'I'm a poor man, and it came a hard blow,' said Hugh once more, giving her a plain cue.

'I don't know whatever I'm going to do with it: I never thought I'd win. Five thousand pounds; it's an awful amount of money. People'll come bothering me about tax. They've been trying to borrow all day, too. That Mrs Bainter . . . and besides, all them religious people'll be around asking for donations for bazaars and things. I'll never have any peace.'

'You could give a bit of it away,' suggested Hughie roguishly, but she did not hear. She looked at him timidly: 'Not related to the Lismore Darcys, I think you said?'

'No!' bellowed Hugh. She doddered to her feet, pottered out of the room, and recollecting, came back and ushered him to the door.

'We must take a ticket in the lottery together, some time, Mr Darcy,' she said. She put out her hand, and then pulled it back.

'You needn't think I'd pinch it,' said Hughie bitterly, brushing out into the street. Every gate was decorated with a bystander; they all wanted to know if he'd succeeded in borrowing anything.

'How was yer luck, mate?' called the fat woman. Hughie scowled and bitterly humiliated, went home. He was very late for tea, and Mumma was cross and childishly vindictive, giving him the too-hot plate, and the leathery egg, and the dribbling old cracked cup. She had not yet forgiven him for his mysterious goings-on that morning, and though longing to ask him about it, would not give him the satisfaction. Also, he had grease on his good trousers, and hers was the job of cleaning it off.

Dolour and Roie went to the pictures again. Roie was excited, and a pink light shone in her cheeks. It was so long since she had been out anywhere. After they had gone, and Mumma sat sulkily reading the paper and slamming the creases savagely out of it, Hughie said: 'It's a fool I am, dearie.'

'You are, and that's a fact,' answered Mumma composedly, though her heart sank. Suddenly, to her amazement, Hughie put his head down on the table and began to cry. It was the first time she had known him to do so, apart from a few drunken tears. All the nervous strain and disappointment of the day opened like an abyss before his mind, and he sank into it.

'Darling, darling, my boy! My lovie! Were you hurt today, Hughie? Were you sacked? Never you mind. We'll find another job. A better one.'

She pressed his head against her bosom, and comforted him. A wave of tenderness filled her with such panting desire to shield him from the hard corners of the world that she felt quite faint.

He told her the story. It seemed funnier and less tragic when he told it all, his efforts at secrecy, and Miss Darcy's refusal to see the important point. But Mumma's eyes shone: 'Oh, Hughie, a fur coat, and an electric stove!' She was just as delighted as if she had really received them. Hughie felt proud of his generosity, and expanded visibly.

She fussed about him, got him a cup of coffee and a piece of the cake she was saving for Dolour's lunch. Then they went to bed, and he fell asleep in her arms completely comforted. He did not feel the heave of her breast, or the heartbroken sobs that struggled to free themselves from her hungry and disappointed heart.

'It's not for the likes of us,' she breathed. 'Not ever.'

Fourteen

A long time before Dolour had applied for a chance on the 'Junior Information, Please' quiz session from 2MB. Her family had laughed at the time, and Sister Theophilus had looked at the child with misgivings. But Dolour felt that she knew quite a lot. Bits of information of little use to her or anyone else stayed obstinately in her brain, and often she could have answered questions at school very well, if only Sister had given her enough time to find words to wrap up her knowledge.

When finally the letter accepting her application arrived at Number Twelve-and-a-Half, Hughie became so frightened on her behalf that he jeered abusively, trying to shake her out of the idea. Nothing in all the world would have persuaded him to step before a microphone, and for Dolour's sake he suffered more nervousness than he would have believed possible.

'You'll be making fools of us all, showing your ignorance, and the whole world listening-in,' he said angrily. Mumma poked her heated red face out of the kitchen.

'And if the whole world's got nothing better to do than to laugh at a little child's ignorance, then it's time it was boiled down for glue,' she cried. 'And what's more, I'm going down to the radio theatre to see her go on, and if nobody else claps, then there'll be a good one from me.'

'And I'm going, too,' added Roie. 'I'm going to say aspirations all the time that she answers the question.'

'Is that going to help her remember how far it is from here to Perth?' bellowed Hughie.

'Is it scoffing at God now you are?' cried Mumma vengefully, and Hughie remained silent, smarting, for he had not forgotten the lottery, and he felt that much talk about God would lead him to say things both libellous and scandalous.

But when he went to work the following morning he boasted to his mates about his girl who would be on the air from 2MB that night, and showing the big pork-barrel of an announcer that there were brainy kids in Surry Hills, just as there were in Manly and Potts Point.

338

Mumma was worried, for Dolour had nothing to wear except her school uniform, which was old and faded. Dolour herself thought nothing of this, for she had not quite reached the age where the clothes become more important than the person they cover. The tunic was good enough for school, and she could not see why it was not good enough for a radio session.

'You can wear my new blouse,' offered Roie. Mumma was pleased. The incongruity of a pink draw-string cotton blouse with an old serge tunic did not occur to her. It was a good garment, and Dolour would look nice in it, and that was sufficient.

All during tea Dolour was as chirpy as a sparrow. She felt excitement comparable to that of a girl who has tasted champagne for the first time.

'I'll knock 'em all down,' she boasted, and Mumma surveyed her geranium red cheeks and glistening eyes and privately thought she would end up in a storm of tears just before she was due to go on the stage.

Hughie was sulky, because Dolour had taken no notice of his warning, and proud, too, because she hadn't. He sat on the couch and pretended to read the paper, glaring over it now and then at Mumma, who was dressing. First she tried on her old coat that had tomato sauce down the front in a huge ragged stain; then she put on her navy dress. But it didn't seem 'dressy' enough, so she added her red cardigan with a hole in the elbow. Roie hastily cobbled the hole, and by adroit wrinkling of the sleeve they managed to hide the darn satisfactorily. Then came the question of shoes. Mumma was in the pernicious habit of unpicking the side seams of her shoes, just a little, to allow her bunions breathing room, and all her shoes had this peculiarity.

'You can wear my school ones,' suggested Dolour desperately. She was already dressed, the rims of her ears shining scarlet from soap, and her hair combed back with a wet comb into a slick, raggle-tailed mop.

'Think I'm going to be seen in them great canal boats,' said Mumma angrily.

'My feet are no bigger than yours,' defended Dolour. Mumma scolded, and began picking over the heap of dead and gone shoes once more. Roie seized a comb and cried: 'For goodness sake, Dolour, come here and let me do something about your hair. It looks downright frightful.'

'It'll do me,' answered Dolour, shying away. 'I don't want any old sissy curls and things.' But all the same she went, and stood docilely while Roie, her hand trembling a little with the weakness she had never shaken off since her illness, combed her hair into little tendrils which dried into featheriness.

'I can't find none!' cried Mumma in a panic, and stood, a forlorn figure in her mended stockings, her face red, her hair unkempt, acutely aware of the clock inexorably ticking away the too short moments.

'We're going to be late,' moaned Dolour, feverishly rocking from heel to toe. Hughie jeered: 'Best stay here with me, rather then see her bring disgrace upon everyone.'

Mumma instantly straightened her lips, and jammed her feet into Dolour's school shoes, scuffed and slanting of heel. They were a little too small, just enough to remind her in an exquisitely subtle fashion that her bunions were still there, and full of vigour. She crammed on her hat, rubbed a powder puff over her hot damp face and pronounced herself ready.

'Ho!' commented Hughie, with a derisive shake of his paper, as he subsided behind it and all they saw of him as they went out was a cloud of smoke and a pair of stiff defiant legs protruding underneath the white butterfly of the paper.

Dolour hesitated at the door. 'Ain't yer going to wish me luck, Dadda?' she asked expectantly. Hughie flung the paper down.

'You'll never win any quiz session when you say ain't,' he bellowed, and beckoned her over and gave her a smacking kiss on the cheek. 'Good luck to yer, darling, and be sure to show them smart aleck announcers that yer not afraid of them.'

As soon as they had all disappeared from sight, Hughie leaped into action. He rushed into the laundry and rubbed the wet end of the towel around his neck and face, then hurried into his good clothes, swearing at the big toe that popped through the end of his sock as soon as he donned it. He rubbed the toe of each shoe on the back of his trouser-cuffs, and in less than ten minutes was pounding down the hall.

'Where yer going, Hughie, in such a ramtam?' inquired Mr Patrick Diamond, who was leaning over the banister.

'Me girl Dolour's been picked for the junior information session,' cried Hughie proudly, 'and it wouldn't be me to let her go to such a place without the support of her dad.'

Hughie arrived at the radio theatre not twenty minutes after his

340

womenfolk. He sought high and low for them in the crowd, and at last caught sight of Mumma's red cardigan, and Roie's neat black head and white collar, near the front row. He was extremely annoyed, for it seemed to him that if he had been encouraged more he would have gone with them and thus not be forced to sit in the back seat.

He pushed past a dozen knees to a seat in the centre and settled himself against the soft overflowing bulk of a fat woman. Craning his neck, he saw Dolour on the stage, her knees very close together, and her ankles apart. Hughie groaned in spirit when he saw her. Only fourteen, and undergoing this torture. He suffered acutely, and the fat woman, annoyed by his agonized writhings, turned and said: 'Can't you keep quiet?'

'I could if you'd keep yer fleas to yerself,' retorted Hugh vengefully. The fat woman's temperature went up three or four points; he could distinctly feel it. He jammed the soft flesh of her arm against the side of the chair.

'Lout,' murmured the fat woman.

'Tub of lard,' hissed Hughie.

The compere appeared and gave the audience their instructions. They were to clap when he held up a large board with the word 'APPLAUSE' printed on it. Otherwise they were to be silent. He was a glittering individual in a white dinner jacket; his spectacles flashed semaphore messages of hope and cheer to the farthest corners of the theatre. Hughie hated him on the spot; he was just the sort of man to tangle up a kid with some frightful questions on general knowledge, sport or music.

Down in the front row Mumma's lips moved steadily as she murmured Paters and Aves to herself. Roie jammed her hands between her knees to keep them from shaking, and tried to draw Dolour's attention, which was hypnotized by the microphone.

For Dolour had lost all her *savoir faire*, her nonchalance, and her champagne feeling. The marrow had drained out of her bones, and her toes were so cold she could not have sworn that she had any. The other contestants looked much the same, some red-faced and prone to giggle, nudging each other and pushing handkerchiefs into their mouths; others waxy with the paralysis of stage-fright. Every one was wishing he had not been such an idiot as to enter this ridiculous contest.

The announcer, in milky tones, rolled out the commercial; it was all about some sort of washing powder that made laundry days a mere frolic in the backyard. Mumma's raspy red hands twisted in her lap. She muttered the more rapidly. There was a brassy blare from the orchestra, and the session commenced on a high note of jollity and suspense. One by one the contestants went before the microphone, and the compere mowed them down with the simplest questions. It was not that they did not know the answers; they were too frightened to think. But here went a ten shilling prize, and there fifteen shillings, and one terrified boy, potato-pale, walked off with five pounds. Before they knew where they were, Dolour was standing in front of the microphone, a thin, badly-clothed child with bony legs and a sliver of white petticoat showing above them. The pink blouse looked ludicrous. Roie blushed for shame. And Dolour's mousy whey-white face looked even worse.

'Closer, please,' said the announcer. Dolour stayed still.

'Closer, please,' he said, and on faltering footsteps she moved towards the little soap-dish which stood there, looking at her with its single evil eye and sharpening its every wit to catch the least and slightest syllable.

'Now,' said the compere pleasantly. 'Will you have sport, music, history, or general knowledge?'

'Eh?' squeaked Dolour faintly.

'Don't say eh, say wot,' cried some jokester from the audience, and Hugh, fighting his way out of the folds of soft flesh that billowed upon him, shouted: 'Shut yer big gob and give the kid a chance.'

In an instant an usher with a torch was at the end of the row, flashing it up and down, but Hugh, sinking down behind his fat companion, was invisible. Meanwhile the announcer, with a humorously despairing shrug at the audience, had repeated his question. Dolour whispered: 'General knowledge.'

The announcer looked up and down his list of questions. The jackpot was three pounds, and he did not want to lose it to this trembling child, but rather to one of the pert, red-faced adolescents who would be good for a bit of repartee and slick gaggery. He found a nice, simple-appearing question, and put it to her bluntly: 'What is a Dead Sea apple?'

His voice was as far away to Dolour as a cricket in the grass. She stared at him uncomprehending, conscious of the microphone with its greedy mouth wide open to catch her trembling reply.

'Come now, have a guess,' suggested the announcer pleasantly.

342

There was another dead silence which seemed to stretch into interminable minutes. Hughie was overcome with torture for his poor child; he tried to send her telepathic messages . . . 'Come on kid, kick 'im in the belly and come back here to Dadda.'

The announcer repeated: 'Just a guess, that's all we ask for,' and winked at the crowd. All at once Dolour woke up. What was the matter with her? She knew that question. She'd read it in a book once. Things flicked back into focus. She said firmly: 'It's anything that looks nice on the outside and is nasty inside. A real Dead Sea apple is fruit with a lovely red skin and a whole lot of slimy stuff inside it.'

'Wow!' cried the announcer, giving the audience the wave to clap. The crowd cheered, and Dolour, clutching the money like a bouquet, walked off the platform. There was another commercial from the announcer, who infused the most innocent sincerity into his voice; a lot of rowdy music, and the audience rose and clumped out, reassured by the green slot of light over the door that the sound of their feet would not deafen half listening Australia.

Hughie turned and clapped the fat lady on the shoulder. He loved her. But she jerked away from him and glared.

'Sorry if I annoyed you, missus,' said Hughie placatingly, 'but that was me little girl. I was scared stiff she'd burst into tears or sumpin.'

The fat lady tried to glare again, but her curving cheeks and tiny fluffy brows were not made for frowns. She melted into a smile which involved a dozen dimples and four chins.

Hughie was a different man. It was not quite as ego-inflating as being drunk, but well on the way. He grew three inches, and all the mediocrity of his being vanished. He knew that people were looking at him, with tolerant grins, so he spoke extra loudly in a ringing voice, so that everyone might know that Dolour was only fourteen, and the smartest kid in Plymouth Street.

Mumma's pride was silent. She gave Dolour a squeeze, and cast around shy eyes to see if other people were noticing. Roie as though to redeem the disloyalty of her first thought about that frightful pink blouse, lied gallantly: 'You looked as cool as a cucumber. Nice, too.'

Dolour was too breathless to speak. She held up her hand and showed them money crisp and starchy; it was the first she had ever possessed. Together they turned into the retreating crowd, all struggling to reach the door first. Somehow Roie dropped behind. She could not see Mumma's hat anywhere, or Dolour's bobbing head. To make it worse, she was feeling dizzy, with cold pricklings at the base of her spine and perspiration damping her hair.

'Ah . . , ah, gosh,' murmured Roie, desperately trying to get past the mass of people into the fresh air. But it was no good. Her knees melted, and she would have fallen, if it had not been for the fact that she was wedged upright in the crowd. Perspiration streamed down her back. Terror of falling, and fear of drawing attention to herself filled her. Noises were already fast fading into a babble of sound. Then a voice said: 'What's the matter? Are you feeling sick?'

It was a hollow, echoing voice like thunder on a heath. Roie tried to answer it and couldn't. It sounded again, frightening her a little, then she felt someone lower her into a seat. She sat there with her eyes closed. After a while the feeling passed, leaving her limp, but singularly clear-minded. She glanced at her companion.

'How do you feel now?' he asked. He was young and dark, his white shirt collar over the grey one of his coat. Roie said with surprise: 'Your voice sounded so queer. But it doesn't now.' He laughed. Roie hurried on. 'I'm awfully sorry. It was just the heat . . . and the crowd . . . I've been sick . . . I'm so sorry.'

'It's not your fault,' he said. 'Are you by yourself?'

'Oh, no,' said Roie. 'My mother is somewhere in the crowd. And my sister. She was the last contestant, the one who won the three pounds.'

'Well, we'll go and look for them when you feel better.'

'I'm fine now,' Roie assured him. She rose to her feet, still shaky and together they moved up the aisle. Unselfconsciously he took her arm, and unselfconsciously she leaned upon his firm hand.

'Did you enjoy the show?' Now she realized that there was something different about his voice, a soft breathiness that was not in other men's.

'Oh, I did. I thought it was fun.'

They found Mumma and Dolour outside, together with Hughie, who had waited for them. Mumma was offended with Hughie for misleading them so, and delighted too that he had been there to witness Dolour's triumph. Dolour was rushing around amongst the people like a wet hen, searching for her sister.

'Oh, there you are, Roie!' said Mumma. They all stared in embarrassed amazement at the young man, his height and darkness, and the yellow clearness of his eyes. Who was this stranger? Roie stammered: 'I felt a bit sick in there . . . and he brought me outside.'

344

Mumma was blushing: 'It was very kind of you, son.'

The young man said unsmilingly: 'It was nothing. I hope your daughter will be all right now. Good evening.'

'Indeed, and you can't be going like that,' said Hughie beaming. He rolled up to the stranger and clasped him by the hand as though he were an old friend. 'Come on home with us and have a cup of tea.' He winked. 'Or I might find a drop of muscat in a bottle I've got stowed under the bed.'

Roie pulled at her father's arm, anxious to shut him up before he shamed them all. 'He doesn't want to . . . he's got somewhere else to go . . . please, Dadda!'

'Where's yer hospitality!' demanded Hughie irately, shaking off her clutch. Mumma added quietly: 'If you've nothing better to do perhaps you'd like to call in some evening and we could have a little supper and a listen to the radio.'

'I'd like to do that,' answered the young man. He and Mumma looked at each other as though they were old friends.

Dolour chirped. 'We live at Number Twelve-and-a-Half, Plymouth Street, Surry Hills.'

He smiled at them all, and vanished down the street. Mumma eased her heel out of her shoe, which had been giving her jip all evening. Her face screwed into awful lines of agony as she tried to slip it back again. Hughie said irately: 'What you looking like a gargoyle for?'

Dolour waved the money. 'I'll buy you a new pair tomorrow, Mumma. Sixes. So your feet won't ever hurt again.'

Hughie felt this to be a reproach to himself, so he digressed by staring off down the road and proclaiming: 'We won't never see that young sprout again. And he looked a good sort, even though he did have a bit of tar in him.'

'What do you mean by that?' asked Mumma sharply. Hughie glanced at her in surprise.

'A bit of Aboriginal, that's what. Couldn't you see it looking out of them eyes? And them long strangler hands?'

'No, I couldn't,' said Mumma shortly. She fell into silence, and not even the hysterical chatter of Dolour, recounting all the other questions she might have answered just as well, brought her out of it.

Into Roie's timid and cautious mind, so frightened now of anything new or out of the domestic rut of her life, came gentle thoughts of the young man. She had liked his warm hand, and his dark, tranquil glance. She did not want to see him again, but something strange and unusual in him made her wish, almost ashamedly, that their meeting had been more prolonged.

For a week there was no sign of him, and Roie had almost put him out of her mind, when one evening he came, strolling up the flagged path as though he had often done it before.

'Hello,' he said to Roie, who sat drying her hair on the verandah.

'Hello,' she answered breathlessly, looking shyly at him from under its dark fall.

'Sorry I couldn't come before. I've been put on night work. Mind if I sit down?'

'Oh, no,' gasped Roie, moving along the step a little. He sat beside her.

'You've got pretty hair.'

Roie blushed. 'Oh, it's all tangled and untidy now. I'll go and fix it in a minute. Where . . . where did you say you worked?'

'Down in Coogee Street. At the Clarkson printery. I'm a machinist.'

'Oh,' Roie was silent. She had never learned anything about making conversation. She was at first awkward and uncomfortable, but imperceptibly her unease vanished, and she had no desire to talk, or to do anything but sit there. He was a strange restful person. He made her feel remote from the usual muddlement of her thoughts, born of shame and sickness and a terror of the long unknown future.

'What's your name?' he asked after a while.

'Rowena Darcy . . . Roie. What's yours?'

'Charlie Rothe.'

'That's an unusual name.'

'It's Irish, just like Murphy.'

'Darcy's Irish, too.'

'I can see that.' He smiled at her, and it was as if he acknowledged in that smile the extreme Celticism of her dark blue eyes and milky skin, clouded around the eyes. He touched her hair lightly. 'You have got pretty hair.'

'Have I?' Roie melted into smiles. She was happy that he liked it. He saw the ghost of a dimple in her thin cheek, and a delectable crease at the side of her mouth. Almost then and there they fell in love.

Fifteen

Falling in love with Charlie Rothe was different from falling in love with Tommy Mendel. Had she really been in love with the Jewish boy, so shallow, so emotionally brittle, his mind clouded with the selfishness engendered by his deformity? Yes, yes, cried Roie passionately, as she remembered the subtle sweetness she had experienced at the touch of his hand, and the longing, yearning way she had tried to cover up his defects. But there was nothing left of it. It had all been killed that night in the park. Until then she had successfully fitted him into the mould her dreams had created, but her love had been too fugitive, too insubstantial, to survive that experience. She knew that she would never think of him again, other than as a stranger. But surely, surely, thought Roie piteously, all love isn't that, fading in a season, like a rose?

So she said farewell to first love, that had bloomed so swiftly, and died so pitifully soon. There had been pity in her heart for Tommy, his loneliness and despair and youth; but there was none for Charlie. Tommy had brought out maternal instincts; she had wanted to shelter him, to do things for him. Charlie brought out the lover in her; she wanted to be sheltered by him. He was one of those rare people who meet life with a non-derivative mind. He watched it go by with a patient and humorously impersonal eye; observing, he created his own opinions, and acted on them. Charlie would never be a great or famous man; he was not the sort that goes into politics and finally dies and is epitomized in the words, 'Slum Boy Makes Good.' But he had the sort of heart that great men have, straightforward, undeviating and tranquil.

Roie often looked at him speculatively, and wondered what he was thinking about. He had an interesting face, very brown of skin, with uneven eyebrows, one peaked. His eyes, so hazel they were translucent, rarely clouded or altered from their calm expression. His hands were broad and long, large capable hands with rough stained patches from his work.

Mumma had clucked sympathetically when he told them that he had no parents.

347

'They died when I was about seven, I think.'

'Don't you know?' asked Dolour curiously. He shook his head. 'I was adopted about that age. That's all I really know.'

'By kind people?' asked Mumma.

'By a bagman. He just picked me up. I was sitting by a fence yowling my head off, and he asked me to come along with him, and I went. He was good to me, old devil that he was.' Charlie's eyes looked back into the past and saw the endless dusky, dusty roads of New South Wales, linking station to station, and hamlet to hamlet; always the brazen sky above, and the sense of great unfathomable spaces all around, when not even the wind found a barrier for hundreds of miles. He said quietly: 'When I was fifteen we came to the city. We had a lodging together. He apprenticed me to the printery, and said that he would give up the road, and I could support him for a change. I would have been glad to do that, but after a week he disappeared. I've never heard of him since. That was nine years ago.'

'Twenty-four,' added up Mumma mentally, and a dread filled her soul. 'He's just right for Roie. I hope they don't get interested in each other.'

She was desperately frightened that a second love would be as disastrous as the first, and yet she was anxious for Roie to marry, so that the girl would forget the quicker. The stress between her two desires was so great that she became quite cross and upset with everyone, and, leaving the dishes to Hughie and Dolour, she went to Benediction to think it over.

But she received no help there, either. She felt that Our Lord was smiling at her enigmatically, as though to say: 'Now, Mrs Darcy, use your common sense, and no more of this running to me like a foolish child, big fat woman that you are.'

And it was no better when she got home, or during the following month, for Roie went round the house quiet and absorbed, and regaining her health at so rapid a rate that it was almost as though the strong heart that beat in Charlie Rothe's breast pulsed life and vitality through Roie's own body. Once again they heard her little voice, as fugitive and uncertain as the voice of a sparrow on a chimney-ledge, singing in the upper room. This made Mumma angrier than ever, in a muddled, anxious way. She hurled a mouthful of coal down Puffing Billy's maw and went up to tackle Roie herself.

348

She came to the point at once. 'Roie love, I'm worried about Charlie. You aren't getting serious about him, now?'

Roie instantly flew at her, her eyes as wide as a cat's with alarm. 'Mumma, you wouldn't tell him about me and Tommy?'

Mumma's heart sank. She sat on the bed and began rubbing her thumb over the smooth iron rail. 'Ah, Roie, I wouldn't tell a soul. You know I wouldn't tell him. But . . . are you in love with him, Ro?'

Roie's face suffused with relief, and a shy delight filled her eyes. 'Oh, Mumma, I am. And he loves me too,' she added with a delicate pride that tore her mother's heart.

'Did he say so?'

'No, he hasn't yet. But he will.'

'He's not like that Tommy,' warned Mumma, 'Charlie's a man. He's a grown man.'

Roie sat down beside her mother. 'Oh, Mumma, I know. I know that Charlie's quite different. Aren't people queer, Mumma?'

'Why, darlin'?'

Roie couldn't find words. 'People going along, each one like an island, quite separate from all the others. Then you meet someone going the same way, and you find that you don't want to be an island any more.'

Mumma said desperately, blurting out what was in her mind. 'Roie, you aren't ready for marriage yet. That illness, you don't know what it might have done to you. Maybe you'd get worse after you were married.'

Roie laughed. 'Oh, Mumma, I won't. And I do want to get married to Charlie. I do, so much. Isn't it funny . . . a little while ago I was so frightened to think about getting married that I wanted to die. But now it's different. Everything's different.'

'Maybe Charlie won't ask you,' said Mumma brutally, but Roie only looked at her wide-eyed and laughed: 'Oh, Mumma, of course he will!'

'How do you feel about him?' asked Mumma. Roie thought for a long time before replying: 'I want to be with him all the time. I want to do things for him.'

Mumma gave a silent groan, for she knew so well that the sort of love which wanted to serve the beloved was the sort you never escaped. It was around your neck, a silken cord of inconceivable strength, till the moment you died, and probably afterwards.

She went away, and brutally punished Puffing Billy all the afternoon, till Hughie came home, when she started on him. He was in a particularly good humour, having bested someone in a political argument down at the pub, and this irritated Mumma all the more. She had a teasing masochistic desire to precipitate a quarrel between herself and Hughie. She said sharpened things, and when he answered only with amiable chaff, made them sharper. When he finally turned on her and told her that if there was one more crack out of her he'd flatten her out, she subsided, satisfied. It was a good lead up to a timid, apologetic remark that she was worried, and it was a pity she couldn't get any help from him in this matter, which was beyond her powers to solve.

Hughie instantly melted into sympathy and self-importance.

'It's this Charlie,' said Mumma, helplessly. 'She's in love with him and talking about marrying.'

'And why not?' demanded Hughie warmly. 'She's a very pretty girl, our Roie. She wouldn't be my daughter if she had the bent nose and scraggy hair of some I could mention. And Charlie's got a good job, and a fine pair of broad shoulders too.' He saw the look on Mumma's face, and went on, even more warmly: 'And if you're thinking of her little slip-up with Tommy Mendel, then you can forget it, for there's many a girl who has made the same mistake and no worse for it. You would have made it yourself, if I hadn't been the gentleman.'

'Fine sort of gentleman, you with the hands that needed to be slapped every blessed minit,' declared Mumma. Then she blew her nose on her apron and looked at him red-eyed and told the truth. 'It's because there's nigger in him, Hughie. I'm scared of it, and no mistake.'

Hughie said defiantly: 'It's better than Chink. It's real Australian and no matter how bad that is, there's none better.' Then he lapsed into silence, seeing the same picture that haunted Mumma, of himself out on the verandah nursing a sooty grandchild.

He said grimly: 'I'll speak to him about it when he comes this evening,' and immediately fell into a state of nervousness in case his impulsive tongue offended Charlie and ruined Roie's chances.

That night Charlie instantly sensed the awkwardness and worry that was behind Hughie's greeting. His mind ran over one possible reason after another. He looked at Mumma, rushing off to the pictures with Dolour, and at Hughie's red creased face that was making every effort to be as garrulous and hospitable as usual, and yet plainly showed in every line the turmoil its owner was feeling.

Charlie quietly manoeuvred Hughie into a conversational position where he had no option but to ask the question that was bothering him.

'You won't get rumbustious now, Charlie boy, because there's no offence meant, and heaven knows I'm not the one to skite meself, having a hangman in the family, but could you be telling me where the dark blood in you comes out?'

He sat panting, fiercely swiping at mosquitoes, for they were sitting out on the verandah in the shadow of the hanging vine.

Charlie said: 'It comes out all over me, I guess,' and sat courteously waiting.

Hugh blurted: 'I mean, where it comes from?'

'Well, my grandfather was white, and my grandmother was white, so it must have been long before that. It's funny how it shows long after.'

'It is that,' agreed Hughie, baffled, pulling at his pipe and sliding the worn stem up and down a little nick in his teeth. After a while he tried again: 'Perhaps I'm rushing things a bit, Charlie, and no offence meant if I am, but what about the children?'

'You mean my children?' asked Charlie. A soft red crept into his brown cheek. 'Then you think Roie would marry me?'

Hughie said embarrassedly: 'There, now, I can't be telling on me own girl, can I? But it's my belief she likes you well enough, and that's saying it fairly.' He looked carefully at a vine leaf that had fallen near his hand and asked again: 'And now, what about the kids?'

'What do you think?' asked Charlie. Hugh didn't like staring at him, but he did, his own face going red meanwhile. And it seemed to him that Charlie spoke and behaved like a white man, and looked like one, too, except to the wise eye of a man such as himself, who had been in the outback more times than he could remember.

'I reckon they'd be white,' he declared.

'Who would?' called Roie, clattering down the stairs in her high heels.

'Our children,' answered Charlie. Roie gave her father a startled glance and fled past him into the blue dimness. Charlie followed

351

her and, in the shadows away from Hughie's eyes, pulled her close and kissed her, stopping her whispered protests with words of his own.

'What did Dadda say? He's an old devil. He didn't mean it . . . whatever it was.'

'When can we be married?'

'You're making fun of me, and I'm not going to stand for it.'

'Will it be next month, or next week?'

'I'll kill Dadda. What did he say about children?'

'Only that ours will be white.'

Roie stopped, open-mouthed, and tried to walk away from him. He caught up with her, and they went swiftly up the street. Roie stole a sideways glance at Charlie's face.

'You don't mind, do you, Roie? I mean, me having a bit of dark blood in me?'

Roie said scornfully: 'Of course I don't. It's such a long time ago, and it wouldn't matter to me if it was only a generation ago. There are lots of lovely dark people. Even Dadda says that, and he often worked with them.'

Charlie realized that there was no black-white problem with Roie. Either people were nice, or they were not. Her wisdom had deeper roots than that of the people who put colour before character. Laughing aloud for exultation, he stopped her under a street lamp and stood tall and shadowed amidst the yellow circle of light.

'You haven't answered me, Roie. When can we be married?'

She blushed and hid her face on his coat. 'Could it be tomorrow?'

'As soon as that?' he teased. She held him tight around the waist and hugged him.

'I just want us to be together all the time, that's all,' she answered softly.

Something made them laugh, staring into each other's faces with joy and triumph pouring into their minds. The night was inconceivably bright and glamorous, and the saffron flood in the western sky like a reflection from the doorway of paradise. Hand in hand they ran down the street and vanished into the dark maze of alleys that led to the city.

Hughie, who had been watching their light-limned figures from his distant gate, shook his head and wandered slowly indoors, muttering: 'He ain't a buck nigger, and he's got a good job; but it's funny to think of little Ro married.'

A slow hurtful feeling was taking possession of him; he felt old. A man who had spent his whole life in pursuit of the satisfactions of the body, as far as was compatible with the wages of a poor labourer, he viewed with fear and mutinous feelings the approach of age. He was a strong healthy man, and all the gallons of rough wine he had poured into his stomach had not done more than sharpen his temper and slow down his digestive process. When he looked at Mumma, so fat and clumsy, he felt slight and young and superior, and he did not hesitate to tell her so.

But with the prospect of Roie's getting married, he felt worse, as though the shadow of old age and eventual death had become fleshly and well-established beside his daily path. He remembered Roie so well as a dirty, startled-faced little brat who scuttled under the kitchen table at his drunken approach; he remembered her howling on her first day at school, and his bribing her with a penny, the way she had doubled one fist upon the other, and looked at him with grey tear-streaks down her cheeks. And that other time when he gave her a belting for stealing biscuits out of an open tin at the grocer's; he had only done so because the grocer complained, and not because he thought it was right, for who but a bonehead would leave an open tin within the kid's reach? Many, many pictures of Roie, nostalgic and painful in some incomprehensible way, filled his mind, and merged into the picture of the girl she was now, thinking about getting married.

He went upstairs to see Patrick Diamond, wondering whether his friend had a half-bottle that would drown his unease. Patrick was lying on his bed, groaning.

'Now, what's the matter with you, mate?' asked Hughie irritably, sorry that he had come up. Patrick looked up at him with the eyes of a sick bloodhound, drawn down into great sallow pouches.

'It's me bloody indigestion. God, it gets me day and night like a chaff-cutter in me guts.'

'Why don't you go to a quack?' Hughie cast a furtive look under the bed. Yes, there was a bottle, amidst all the clotted dust and kapok from the corn tick. A warmer feeling for Patrick's suffering filling his soul; poor old coot with no one to look after him. Patrick Diamond cursed savagely, clutching his stomach, and rolled over into the pillow.

'It was them that guv it to me when I got me ulcer fixed. Bloody students mucking about with me organs as though they was a bunch of offal from the butcher's'.

Hughie tck-tcked sympathetically. 'What can yer expect in a free hospital? You've got to have a specialist or you come out worse than yer went in. Dirty quacks making a potful outa the sufferings of the working-class.'

'Get me some hot water, Hughie, willya?' groaned Mr Diamond. Hughie rose with alacrity and put the kettle on the grease-clogged gas-ring. The gas shot out in a fanning ring of blue crocuses, hissing and roaring.

'Why don't yer get married, Patrick, boy, and have a bit of comfort in yer old age?' he suggested. Mr Diamond's face showed even more agony.

'And have some old slut up here messing around with me things and making more work than enough? I hate women,' said Mr Diamond bitterly, for well he knew that he was far past the age when any woman, however hard up, would look at him twice.

Hughie shook his head. 'They're a comfort sometimes, Patrick. But not so much of a comfort as a good bottle of spirits,' he added meaningly. Mr Diamond shot him a look and sighed. He knew Hughie had spotted the bottle, and he said hopelessly: 'Go on then, yer old booze-artist. But for God's sake leave me some for when me stomach's better.'

'Indeed I will, Patrick,' came the amiable voice of Hughie from under the bed. 'Pooh, it stinks under here. Why don't you sweep it out?'

'Because I don't want to,' snapped Mr Diamond, wild-eyed. 'Now get me the hot water, Hughie, for God's own sake.'

Hughie lingeringly poured himself a cup of wine, and Mr Diamond a cup of rank hot water from the kettle. Mr Diamond sipped it, haltingly, while Hughie let the stinging aromatic turpentiny flavour of the wine roll around his tongue.

'Ah, there's comfort in the sup, as Grandma used to say,' he remarked dreamily.

There was a slow, steady, clip-clop on the stairs, as though an ascending horse were approaching.

'Hello, now, who's that?' wondered Hughie. Mr Diamond snorted into his cup, and came out wiping his whiskers.

'It's 'im. Miss Sheily's boyfriend.'

Hughie began to roar. 'Don't tell me. That old hag? Who's the mug?'

Mr Diamond gestured towards the door. 'Go and have a look if you don't believe me. No, put the light out first, you fool.'

Hughie did as he was told, opening the door a crack and peering through. And there was Mr Gunnarson, his round grey felt set firmly on his head, and his bright eyes shining milky-pale in the dim light from the infinitesimally small globe the landlady provided to light the stairs. He was dressed most precisely, with a salmon pink bow tie butterflying from his stiff collar, and under his arm was a long, odd-shaped parcel. Hughie sniffed. He smelt fish.

Mr Gunnarson, unaware of scrutiny, knocked on Miss Sheily's door. After a little while there was a furtive scurry inside the room, and Miss Sheily's cracked voice called: 'Well, who is it?'

'It is I, Mr Gunnarson,' replied her visitor, smiling tenderly at the door. There was an irritated mumble from beyond it, and the sharp stamping about of Miss Sheily's wooden heels. Then it creaked open.

'Oh, it's you. Well, what do you want, you old pest-house?'

Mr Gunnarson removed his hat. 'I come to see you, Miss Sheily.' He stood humbly, waiting. Hughie could well see that Miss Sheily was dressed up more than usual, with a bit of yellow lace sticking out from her collar. But her manner was even more acrid.

'I'm busy,' she said. 'You can't come calling on me at all hours. I'm just going to bed.'

'I bring you a little present,' said Mr Gunnarson, tendering the odd-shaped parcel, devotion oozing from his every word. Miss Sheily snatched it from his hand. 'It stinks,' she stated briefly. 'What is it?'

'Lobster,' breathed Mr Gunnarson; Miss Sheily gave a shriek, and dropped the parcel. Hughie, drooling with desire, watched it slide into the shadows, but alas, Mr Gunnarson went after it and picked it up.

'Don't you come around here bringing your off-colour fish with you,' shrilled Miss Sheily, and as the expression on Mr Gunnarson's face grew more and more lugubrious, she suddenly spat: 'Caesar's ghost! Come inside, you poor old half-bake!'

Mr Gunnarson shuffled inside, and the door shut. Hughie, overcome, went back to Patrick, who, his pain ebbing, was now sitting up in bed.

'Who'd believe it?' marvelled Hughie, looking suspiciously into his cup, for the level of the liquor was much lower than when he had left.

'I tell you, he comes nearly every night,' said Patrick Diamond. 'And the poor coot thinks the world of her. He'd give her the eyes out of his head to play marbles with.'

'And she'd do it too,' agreed Hughie, 'for she's just like them old dames who used to sit around the guillotine waiting for the heads to fall so that they could cart them off to make soup of them.'

'Now, you're wrong there, Hughie man,' protested Patrick, to whom the breath of life was returning. 'Sure there's no one in this world, not even the French, who would make soup of a human being's nob.'

'Miss Sheily's that sort,' said Hugh decisively. Patrick gave a sigh and reached for the wine bottle, then he settled back comfortably, warmth stealing over him, and the awful loneliness which severe pain brings fading into the dimmest of memories.

Sixteen

Mumma cried like anything when the shining-eyed Roie told her that she and Charlie Rothe were to be married, but she did not allow Roie to see her tears. She kept them for the night, robbing Hughie of sleep, so that he spent hour after hour explosively swearing and thanking God audibly that he had only two children to get married off with such fuss and clatter.

'I wish Grandma was here to advise me,' wept Mumma.

'She'd tell you to stop roaring like a runover baboon,' cried Hughie furiously, sticking his cockatoo crest out of the blankets. 'She had six daughters, all married, and I'll bet she didn't howl over one of them.'

'I'll be losing her,' wept Mumma. 'She'll go away and I'll never see her any more. And marrying a nigger, too.'

Hughie sat up and glared at her, and Mumma tentatively moved away, for he looked as though he were going to thump her. 'Now, none of that talk,' he said decisively. 'If Roie's picked her man, then she's picked him, black, white or brindle, and we can't talk with a hangman in the family.'

'The hangman's in your family,' bristled Mumma. 'Never was a Kilker to make a living by other people's necks.'

'Be that as it may,' said Hughie firmly. 'There's no talk about niggers. The boy's good and solid, and I'll have nothing said against him.'

He lay down, mumbling to himself, and Mumma jerked the blankets up and tried angrily to go to sleep, saying prayers very rapidly until in the end they were nothing but words that not even her own ears heard.

Hughie said: 'Hey.'

'What yer want?' snarled Mumma. He turned over, and she could feel his stomach, warm and placatory, against the small of her back.

'We'll have to get you a nice dress for the wedding. A nice red dress.'

'Sure, I'd look like a house in red,' protested Mumma, secretly pleased that he had suggested such a bold and flashing colour. 'Black's right for stout people.'

'Not black,' cried Hughie. 'I won't have my wife looking like a morepork's widow.' This pleased him, and he lay there chuckling for some minutes, repeating 'morepork's widow'. Mumma's rage had subsided entirely, and a calm filled her mind.

'Perhaps a nice, elegant maroon, then, Hughie love,' she suggested, and had an instant vision of herself in elegant maroon silk, with tucks here and a few bits of ruching and fancywork there; with navy shoes that didn't hurt, and a nice hat with a flower. Her heart filled with gratitude towards her kind husband who had promised her a new dress for the wedding and she turned and flung her arms around him.

'Four pounds would do it all, Hughie,' she said. 'And I'd be proud to come right out at Roie's wedding and look decent for once in my life.'

'Of course, the question is where the four pounds is going to come from,' reminded Hughie gloomily. Mumma tossed that off lightly.

'We won't pay the grocer,' she said.

'Oh, well,' acquiesced Hughie. 'He's got more money than we have,' and snuggling against Mumma he went to sleep. But before he did he said: 'Betcher we'll have Miss Sheily off our hands, too, before long.'

But Mumma was already asleep.

Dolour was so excited when Roie told them she was engaged that she didn't know who to inform first. Usually girls in that district didn't get engaged; they just went steady with someone and then got married. But Roie even had a ring, a queer little turquoise, rather lumpy on one side, that Charlie had paid six times too much for at a refugee jeweller's in town.

'It's a real precious stone,' said Mumma, awed, looking into the opaque milky blue face of the turquoise.

'I like diamonds better,' said Dolour dreamily, and was amazed when Roie said sharply: 'Well, I don't. Flashy things, they look vulgar. I like little green and blue and red stones. I like them best.'

'So do I,' said Mumma, though when she was young she would have given ten years of her life for an engagement ring with a diamond in it. She thought regretfully of the pink cameo brooch Hughie had given her, and pawned a few years later, to pay for

Roie's birth. That was what Roie had cost, a pink cameo brooch. And Thady had cost his father's gold tie-pin, and his silver watch-chain, and Dolour had been free, as all the assistance Mumma had had was that of the woman next door.

Dolour told Sister Theophilus: 'Roie's getting married soon.' Sister's eyes sparkled. She loved weddings, real white ones. She loved all the flutter and excitement of a marriage, and there was in it no vicarious happiness at all, just joyous faith that here at last was a couple who were really going to be happy ever after. She began at once to say prayers for Roie and Charlie, without the faintest doubt that they would be answered. She had the strange blithe childlike soul that is found so often in convents. Once when caught in a rainstorm she prayed that she might not get wet, and when she found no more than a sprinkle of raindrops upon her habit she was not at all surprised. She lived not in the shadow of God, but in his light. It was as warm and familiar and comprehensible as firelight. So when Sister Theophilus prayed for Roie, grace as impalpable as light itself stole ahead into the girl's life and made the rough smooth, and the smooth pleasant beyond doubt. She was like a magician weaving spells for Roie and Charlie, with complete faith that they would come true.

She also started to work on a gift, a white silk petticoat with handmade lace on it. She copied the design from a picture in the newspaper, blushingly, for Sister Theophilus's own petticoats were made of black material, and had sleeves in them. But she made up the lace out of her own head, with lovers' knots and grape leaves, crocheting with darting swiftness as she walked about the playground. When she had finished she wrapped the slip up in tissue paper, slipped in a holy picture of St Anne with the child Mary at her knee, tied it with pink ribbon, and gave it to Dolour.

Dolour ran all the way home. She had two pleasures in store for her. Roie's excitement, and the praise her dear Sister Theophilus would be sure to get.

'It's my first wedding present,' breathed Roie, scarlet fluttering in her cheeks. She held up the slip. It was much too long, for Sister had measured it against herself, forgetting how small Roie was.

'I'll have to cut the lace off,' she cried in distress. Mumma was indignant.

'A fine way to treat Sister's lovely present,' she cried. Roie looked at the slip helplessly. 'I'll have to turn it up, then, and I can't sew.'

'Anything rather than cutting the good stuff,' said Mumma, who couldn't sew either beyond putting patches on. So Roie wore the petticoat to her wedding, the hem roughly cobbled up with pink cotton, so that it showed bulky under her skirt. But it made her feel happy, and that was all Sister Theophilus had wanted.

A little while after Roie had received her first present Charlie came in. His broad figure made the room look smaller and more congested, but he was not conscious of his surroundings, for he had lived in such nearly all his life. Dolour had never taken much notice of Charlie, beyond thinking how extraordinarily old he was, but now she was conscious of a feeling of resentment against him. It was almost as though he were an interloper at the wedding, that it should have been a family affair, and he was a stranger with no place at it. She thought that he touched Roie so frequently just to make them feel his new possession of her sister; the arm around her shoulder, the hand on her arm, the kiss as they stood wiping the dishes in the scullery, all annoyed her, incomprehensibly, so that after a while she found her self snappy and close to tears.

After they had gone out, Mumma found her sobbing in the laundry, a miserable bowed figure huddled in the soapy-smelling shadows of the tubs.

'What's the matter now?' she asked irascibly, for she was tired and overwrought herself.

'Roie doesn't belong to us any longer,' hiccupped Dolour. Mumma swallowed hard, for she had felt the same thing herself. She gave Dolour a chiding pat on the bottom, and said: 'Don't be sillier than you look now, Dolour love. You need your tea. Come and help me set the table.'

'I wish we was rich, so Roie wouldn't have to get married,' wailed Dolour. Mumma tck-tcked with exasperation, for Dolour's reasoning always had a most naive streak in it which made Mumma feel that she had neglected her daughter's worldly instruction.

They had hardly sat down to tea before Mumma gave them some news.

'Miss Sheily's getting married,' she said. Dolour choked unbelievingly. Hughie was peeved that he had been cheated of the glory of announcing the news himself, and hastened to cover it up.

'I told you as much the other night,' he expostulated.

'You didn't,' argued Mumma. 'It was only ten minutes ago that she told me herself.'

'You're batty,' said Hughie angrily. 'I told you just before we went to sleep. It was just an idea I had, coming from observation.'

'You never said a word about it,' protested Mumma. 'We was talking about me new maroon dress, and that was all.'

'Look,' he said. 'I was lying on me left side, and . . .' he went into a long description of detail. Mumma cast a despairing look at Dolour.

Dolour interrupted: 'Anyway, it doesn't matter, Dadda. She's getting married quietly next Friday, and she's wearing a grey dress and a grey hat with a veil, and she's going to leave the house.'

'So, don't you see? Charlie and Roie can have her room,' cried Mumma. Hughie's face darkened. He pictured himself coming home drunk as usual on Friday nights, and Charlie's presence damping all his performance.

'Young people ought to be by themselves,' he muttered.

'But they'll have their own cooking things up there and everything,' cried Dolour. 'And maybe Roie will ask me to tea.'

This seemed to her to be almost as exciting as being invited to the Governor-General's residence.

Mumma and Roie were equally excited about Miss Sheily's marriage, for that had seemed to be as unlikely as the remarriage of Queen Mary. They fossicked about, and dropped hints, and on the eve of the great event were invited to view Miss Sheily's going-away clothes.

Mumma wiped her hands on her apron and climbed the steps with difficulty, because her legs were troubling her; but Roie and Dolour sprang like young deer from one dark step to another, because they had done the same fifty times a day for most of their lives.

'Oh,' commented Mumma, as she looked at Miss Sheily's going-away dress laid out on the bed. It was dark brown, dark as mahogany, and with much the same effect on Miss Sheily's complexion as a polished table on a white tablecloth. A neat, sharp-toed pair of shoes with bronze buckles and a business-like air, also stood on the bed, and a brown handbag, severely plain. 'It's very tasteful,' said Mumma, disappointed; for she had imagined that Miss Sheily would have piles of lovely underclothing and perhaps a pretty nightdress or two, as brides always had in books. Roie nudged her, for her disappointment was plain to be seen.

'It's really fashionable, Miss Sheily, and you should look very nice,' she said gently, looking at the strange desiccated little woman

361

with pity and interest. Did Miss Sheily love Mr Gunnarson, or did she marry him just to escape into another environment and another sort of life? Miss Sheily shrugged. She was making toast at the gas-ring, and took no interest in their visit. The prospect of marriage made little difference to her; she was as acid and unpredictable as ever.

Suddenly there was a firm tread on the stairs, and Miss Sheily ejaculated: 'Caesar's ghost! Can't the man stay away for five minutes?'

'Oh, it's Mr Gunnarson,' whispered Mumma, like a scared hen, trying to shepherd her daughters towards the door. But Miss Sheily waved the toaster.

'No, no, don't go. He won't stay long, I promise you.'

Roie and Dolour looked at each other with suppressed giggles. A moment later Mr Gunnarson came clumping into the room, disappointment on his face plain to be seen.

'Oh, you've got visitors, Miss Sheily,' he said, flashing his bright light eyes at them.

'I can have my friends up, can't I?' snapped Miss Sheily, turning over the toast.

'Indeed you can, my darling,' agreed Mr Gunnarson, going over and kissing her tenderly on the cheek. Miss Sheily, her eyes glittering like black coals, immediately swiped him over the hat with the red-hot toaster. It left a black criss-cross pattern on the felt, and there was a smell of burnt wool.

'My living heart and soul!' whispered Mumma, swallowing hard, for never in all her life would she have thought anybody capable of swiping their prospective husband with the hot toaster.

'You stop that licking around me, or I'll brand you, you old octopus,' shrieked Miss Sheily. Roie and Dolour fled down the stairs. Mumma went more slowly, but before she left she caught a glimpse of Mr Gunnarson's face. It was almost proud, as though any moment he might say: 'Ain't she the one, now?'

'The wedding's off,' yelled Dolour, bursting into the kitchen and recounting the story with gusto to Hughie who sat washing his feet in a basin.

'Not that one,' said Hughie. 'He's one of them that loves his face trod on. You see.'

And they did. The next day a taxi called for Miss Sheily, and off she went without a word; she even had a shopping basket over her arm, and intended to pick up a few things after the ceremony. Mumma and Dolour, just bursting with curiosity, waited inside the kitchen door for her return.

'I wonder if he'll call her Mrs Gunnarson now, instead of Miss Sheily,' giggled Dolour. Mumma replied: 'I still think her name's Stella.'

'We don't even know his Christian name, either,' murmured Dolour. Her eyes sparkled. 'Sssssh, here they come.'

They heard the two pairs of feet ascend the stairs, and a few minutes later the door slammed and the feet descended. Mumma waddled across the kitchen and sat in a chair, pretending to be darning. Dolour drooped herself over the table and became engrossed in the pattern on the tablecloth.

Miss Sheily's sharp voice said: 'Don't pretend you weren't listening, because I saw your shadows on the wall. May I come in?'

'Oh, yes, Miss Sheily ... Mrs Gunnarson, do,' said Mumma feebly, too taken aback even to become angry at the insult.

Miss Sheily came in. They saw Mr Gunnarson, laden with a suitcase, a hatbox so crammed with goods that its lid wouldn't shut, and with a palm-stand under the other arm, trot down the hall. Miss Sheily was all dressed up in her brown outfit, and they had never seen her look so plain.

'I came to wish you good-bye, Mrs Darcy,' said Miss Sheily. Her eyes flickered from one to the other. 'You were kind to poor Johnny.'

'I loved him, I did,' said Mumma simply, and the ready tears welled to her eyes. A brief flicker went over Miss Sheily's face.

'I don't suppose we'll ever see each other again, Mrs Darcy, so I want to wish you luck. Here's a month's rent ... no, don't be foolish, woman, take it and be thankful. And here's a little present for Rowena.'

She put a white cardboard box on the table. Mumma blushed and stammered: 'It's good of you, Miss Sheily.'

She shook hands with them both, a cold, white, dead fish hand. Then she was gone. Dolour cast a desperate look at her mother. She felt she couldn't bear it if Miss Sheily went without ... She raced after her.

'Miss Sheily! Miss Sheily!'

She faced her in the dark hall, and her courage failed.

'Well, what is it now?' asked the woman sharply.

Dolour stuttered: 'Please, before you go . . . would you tell me . . . we've often wondered . . . would you tell me what your Christian name is?'

Once she had it out it sounded preposterous. She cowered away from Miss Sheily, almost expecting to have her face slapped. But Miss Sheily, after a pause, said softly: 'Isabel.'

'Oh,' said Dolour. The relief was tremendous. She said: 'I just wanted to know.'

'I know,' said Miss Sheily, and it seemed to Dolour that never before had her voice been so kind. She watched the taxi till it disappeared down the street, and coming inside, stood for a while in the dark stair recess where Johnny had played, feeling as though she wanted to cry again.

Seventeen

'She was a mystery woman and no mistake,' marvelled Mumma, looking yearningly at the parcel which Miss Sheily had left. It was a great temptation to open it, but she conquered it, and it was there when Roie came in with Charlie that night. They had been out shopping, and Roie was both rapturous with and doubtful of the quality of everything she had bought. She had a breakfast-cloth in gaudy checks, and a set of blue-rimmed plates, and two knives and forks and spoons in cheap leaden ware from Woolworths. But Roie looked at them as though they were hallmarked silver.

'Gee, Charlie, our very own,' she had murmured over and over again. There was a curious change in him, as his marriage drew near. Many years ago, when he realized that the only way to face a bitterly cold and cruel world was to build refuge within himself, he had fought and laboured to become a content and tranquil person. This he had achieved, and the desolate, frightened little boy he had been vanished as though for ever. But now it was as though the little boy were back again, warm-hearted, excitable, needing to be comforted and reassured of love. Charlie was restless every moment he was away from his girl. Roie felt this, and loved him the more for it.

The present from Miss Sheily was a beautiful, white ruffled nightdress. None of them had ever seen anything like it before. It was like something Lana Turner, or some other delicious porcelain Hollywood princess might wear, not Roie Darcy from Plymouth Street. It smelt delectably, too, of freesias. Nobody knew the name of the perfume, save that it was the smell of the plain little creamy flowers that grew by the Sicilianos' fence.

When Charlie saw it he immediately imagined Roie in it, and because that was disturbing, he put the thought out of his mind and turned to Miss Sheily. Queer little tragic harridan, what had she meant by such a gift? That she, too, might have worn such a nightgown on a bridal night if it had not been for some misadventure? What was her secret? Something had happened to her a long time ago, and a catalysis of the soul had taken place. She was a well of bitter water, and not even the adoring and masochistic Mr Gunnarson would change her, ever. Charlie looked at his own girl, her cheeks like poppies with happiness; her soft sooty hair in disarray, and her little sallow neck vanishing into her cheap cotton blouse, and loved her so much that he felt he would have to shout it aloud to them all. Funny, timid little Roie, whose words faltered so often, yet whose expression told him everything.

They went upstairs to Miss Sheily's room. Dolour whispered to her mother, 'I wonder if she's left anything behind,' for it was the delight of the Surry Hills children to rat empty houses after their tenants had shifted, and come laden home with all sorts of treasurable rubbish.

But there wasn't anything. The room was as clean as a scrubbing brush could make worn and hideous linoleum, and a manila broom the crude blue kalsomined walls. The bed sagged forlornly in the middle, and the blankets were stained with tea and coffee and a dozen other unanalysable things. But it was no worse than a thousand other lodgings in Surry Hills; it was a lot better than Charlie's present room. It had a door which locked, and it had a window which looked out on the alleyway which ran down beside the house, and, across that, into three crammed and hideous backyards full of garbage cans, tomcats, and lavatories with swinging broken doors and rusty buckled tin roofs.

But these were all things they were used to. They didn't mean anything to Roie and Charlie. A stranger in this attic room would have withered and died with the sheer ugliness and sordidness and despair of it; but to Roie and Charlie it was a room of their own.

Mumma pinched Dolour, and taking her by the edge of her sleeve, drew her towards the door. 'I've got to be getting the tea on.'

'I'll come down later,' protested Dolour. Mumma pinched her harder, and with a yelp they both disappeared down the stairs.

Dolour was furious. 'What's the big idea?' she demanded.

'Can't you leave them alone for five mintues?' hissed Mumma, red-faced at her daughter's obtuseness. Dolour asked: 'Whatever for?'

'What do you think for?' asked Mumma, busying herself at the sink. Dolour's face reddened with humiliation, and, more than that, with the strangest feeling she had ever had. She had always come first in Roie's heart; now she knew she had been taken from that niche and put elsewhere. Charlie was in her place, and she would never win it back.

From that moment Dolour hated Charlie. She pictured him upstairs, holding Roie, kissing her, touching her in a way that no one had ever touched her sister, except perhaps Tommy Mendel, for Dolour in her shrewd precocious way had her own ideas about Tommy Mendel. It made her feel sick with disgust and hatred.

The wedding was coming very close, and Mrs Drummy, who sewed, at last finished Mumma's maroon dress. It was in a shoddier material than the frock she had dreamed, and it did not fit very well over Mumma's upholstery, but there were stylish tucks, and a thing Mrs Drummy called a 'slimming panel' floating like a limp scarf from the right shoulder. Mumma did not fancy this much, but everyone told her it was elegant, so she didn't pull it off.

One day Charlie said to Roie: 'Is there anything your mother would like for the wedding . . . I mean, a little present from me?'

Roie said instantly: 'She's always wanted to have her hair permed.'

That was thirty-five shillings, and Charlie had to work many hours to earn as much as that, but he put his hand in his pocket and pulled out the money.

'Now, tell her it's from you,' he cautioned, 'not me, or she'll think things.'

'What things?' scoffed Roie, and ignoring his advice she went off to Mumma and jubilantly announced that Charlie had made her the present of a permanent wave. She was aghast when Mumma took it very badly, fulminating against upstarts who criticized their mother-in-law's hair, and telling Roie to tell him to go and get his own waved and not to be insulting her.

'But you've always wanted a permanent. It was me that suggested it,' wailed Roie. Mumma had known this from the start, but couldn't help seizing the chance to express a little of the jealousy and resentment a mother-in-law feels against even a man she likes. She said, grudgingly: 'Oh, well, then, I suppose I could get it done.'

'You needn't get it done at all if you don't want to,' flamed Roie. 'And you ought to be ashamed of yourself. It was a kind thought of Charlie's, that's all, and I give him credit for it.'

Mumma eyed Roie's hand with distrust, for it looked as if it were going to dart forth and take the thirty-five shillings back, but it didn't, and she said repentantly: 'Don't be listening to me, Roie love. I'm upset because the iceman didn't come, and the meat's gone funny. I'll get me hair done on Friday.'

Mumma's hair had never been done before. When she was young

367

it was rich and wavy and chestnut, for ever tumbling down from the knot in which her clumsy and inept hands twisted it. It was always a surprise to her to look into the glass and find that it was no longer that way, but grey and brindly and tousle-ended. She went to the hairdresser as one might go to the guillotine, frightened into stupidity; but she was happy and excited about it too. Mumma had visions of herself with glossy symmetrical waves like the ladies in the hair-oil advertisements.

But somehow her hair didn't turn out like that. The hairdresser did her best with it, but Mumma came out of the shop with a sort of electrified bolster on top of her head.

'It'll lie down in a couple of days,' said the hairdresser anxiously. She was a neat, harried little body with four children crammed into the dingy living-room behind her salon. Mumma surveyed it doubtfully. She couldn't quite believe that it was the same hair which had covered her head only a couple of hours ago. This had a virile frizziness like the hair on a strong man's chest; it almost crackled when she nodded, so dry and brittle it had become.

When she got home she was frightened to face the critical gaze of Hughie. Roie's sympathy and Dolour's mirth she felt she could withstand, but not Hughie's. As she walked down the passage and heard his loud Friday-night voice, her cheeks flushed in anticipation, but she forced herself to march in without any diminution of spirit in her footsteps.

'Goddlemighty,' gasped Hugh when he noticed her. 'Sweet jumping moses, whatjer done to yerself, woman?'

'I been permed,' began Mumma, with a piteous attempt at dignity. Hughie laughed until he nearly fell on the floor. Roie came out of the scullery and cried: 'Don't you mind him, Mum. All perms are funny for a while. Yours'll be good. You see.'

Mumma looked in the sideboard mirror and prodded the strange cushion of hair which still had an odd elusive perfume of ammonia about it. She felt hopelessly that it would never be any different. She would have to go to the wedding like this and have everyone laughing at her. Probably . . . Struck by a sudden awful thought, Mumma rushed into the bedroom, Roie following. There she was, trying to force her old navy hat down over the mass. It jammed tightly, and then, as though on invisible springs, slowly rose. Mumma looked aghast at Roie.

'I can't get it on,' she moaned. 'Now I won't be able to come to the church.'

Roie took the hat and pulled it down to Mumma's tortured eyebrows, but once again it slowly ascended. In the doorway Hughie rolled about in uproarious mirth. Mumma cried: 'You can well laugh, but what about me, not even able to go to me own daughter's marriage?'

'You'll come to my wedding, if we have to get Father Cooley to perform it in the backyard,' vowed Roie, and then the picture of the robed priest standing amidst the garbage tins and reciting the marriage ceremony overcame them all, and Mumma's first permanent wave ended in roars of laughter.

But that night, as she lay beside the snoring form of Hughie, she touched the tight kinky curls and spirited high-voltage frizz of her new pompadour, and murmured: 'It's that Charlie who's done this to me.'

Then came another thought, apologetic: 'Not that I'm blaming him. And it might turn out very well, for all that. I'll wash it tomorrow.'

So she washed it twice a day until the wedding day came, and by that time it had only a flyaway fluffy effect, which Mumma privately thought youthful, and indeed beguiling. It made her very happy.

Dolour dearly wanted a real wedding, with herself as bridesmaid. She said several rosaries for this end, but with a forlorn feeling in her soul all the time that her prayers were not to be answered. The idea of all the pomp and etiquette of a real wedding, with a best man, and confetti, and presents and breakfasts, and all the rest, terrified Mumma and Hughie and Roie and Charles into numbness. None of them had the slightest idea about the conduct of such a ceremony – who gave whom a present, or who walked on the right side of whom.

'I just want to be married,' confessed Roie to Charlie. 'And I'd like it best with nobody there at all.'

That morning Roie had gone to Communion and afterwards she knelt for a long time thinking of Tommy Mendel. Had it been a sin, or hadn't it? Roie knew that the Church thought so, and so she had confessed it, but she still could not work out the rights of it. She had committed a sin because she loved Tommy very much; there had been no thought of self in it. She felt that if it had truly been a sin then she was not worthy of Charlie. That brought a new idea; had she really paid enough for that sin, or would she, and Charlie perhaps, go on suffering for it ever after?

'I don't want him to be hurt ever,' she gasped, shuddering at the impact of that thought. 'Oh, I wish it hadn't ever happened. Please, please let me forget it.'

But she couldn't, and then she thought that perhaps Charlie was like Tommy Mendel, with the same instability and selfishness and inconstancy, and she felt that marriage with him would be intolerable bondage, and that she must run away from it now before it was too late.

The dread and fear were with her all day, but it was impossible to run away now. Mumma had her new frock, and Dolour a new hat, and Hughie had so steadfastly remained sober. Besides, Father Cooley was expecting them at eleven. These things seemed to Roie to be insurmountable obstacles.

It was a lovely day, very soft, with an autumn pulse in the air. Roie got dressed with Dolour's hysterical help. Through the phoenix palm's radiating vanes she saw the blue sky like a flag, but it didn't comfort her.

'Ah, gosh,' groaned Roie. Dolour viewed her with dismay, for her cheeks were milk-pale and her eyes dark with fright.

'You're not going to be crook, are you?' she squeaked. 'You don't feel sick in the stomach?'

'No, I don't,' snapped Roie. She snatched up her blue halo hat, glared at her sister, and clattered noisily down the stairs. Mr Diamond, who had tactfully accepted an invitation to the 'breakfast' only, opened his door a trifle and peered at her. She looked slender as a wand in her blue dress, and pitifully young.

'Poor little devil,' muttered Mr Patrick Diamond, envisioning all the disillusionment and drab monotonies that lay ahead of Roie. He felt his indigestion coming on, and grabbed his stomach premonitorily as he clicked the door shut.

Mumma had been dressed for an hour, sitting stiffly on a chair so that she would not disarrange the pleats in her skirt. She had refolded the slimming panel a dozen times, for it worried her very much. Hughie's face was red with scraping, and his hair was slicked back unfamiliarly with brilliantine. Roie scarcely knew him. Also there was Charlie, dressed in his best suit, the one with the blue stripe. His tousled hair was already springing out of the sleek order into which he had combed it. He paced up and down the kitchen, smoking one cigarette after another.

'Charlie!' wailed Roie, jumping into his arms. They closed around her, big and warm, and such a good fit that all her fears

370

immediately left her, and she thought: 'Gee! I'm lucky. I'm lucky!' as she listened to the steady beat of his heart through the too-stiff lapels of his five-guinea suit.

'Plenty of time for that afterwards,' said Hughie gruffly, for he was embarrassed and nervous. 'Come on, or we'll have his reverence suing us for overtime. Dolour!' he screamed up the stairs.

So they all went to the church, and Roie and Charlie were married in a very plain and ordinary way, kneeling there at the altar rails in the empty amber-lit church, with the stout red-faced priest standing before them in his black soutane with one button missing at the hem, and over it a surplice starched too much, so that the lace stuck out stiffly like a verandah roof and gave Dolour hysterical giggles.

In twenty minutes it was all over. One might have thought that anything so fast would be unimpressive, but Roie and her husband never forgot that golden morning when their paths met completely and continued as one.

Hughie was more nervous than any of them. It brought him out in a sort of rash of garrulity and exuberance; he couldn't get home quickly enough to toast the bride and drown his qualms in the comforting warmth of alcohol.

As soon as they reached home, Mumma set about laying the spread, and Hughie bellowed up the staircase: 'Come on down, Patrick man! The knot's tied. Come and have a swigg,' and the door at the top of the stairs sprang open as though by clockwork, and Mr Diamond descended.

Roie saw with surprise and a queer feeling of tenderness that he had put on his best suit, and had shaved the back of his neck as far as he could reach, in a sort of makeshift haircut.

While all the preparations were going on, Charlie and Roie sat together on the old couch.

'Happy, Ro?' he asked, softly, so that Mumma wouldn't hear. Roie nodded, and the fugitive smile that flitted over her face filled him with joy and fierce determination that he would shield her from every grief the hard world might bring. For him, marriage was even more of a milestone than it was for Roie. She had known poverty of an inconceivably drab and sordid sort, but she had always had love and companionship, and the warm family circle that was broken only by her father's bouts of drunkenness. Charlie had had poverty, and the desperate panic-stricken loneliness of a small child. He had had homelessness, and the heat and cold and hunger of a bagman's gipsy life, the long silences of his strange eccentric companion, and the vast desolation of the outback. Marriage was for him the ending of all that chapter; it was the commencement of an entirely new life. There would not be much in it; children perhaps, and work and laughter, and sorrow, and eventually pain and separation. But it was a pain bestrewn with jewels for him, for Roie was to make it hers.

'Now you can tell us where you're going for your honeymoon,' cried Mumma, slapping down a dish of subsiding butter on the table. She had steadfastly refused to listen before, on the grounds that it brought bad luck.

'Narrabeen,' said Roie, 'You go in a bus. You can swim there . . . there's breakers.'

'I went there,' boasted Dolour. 'That's where we had Delie Stock's picnic.'

'You didn't, you went to Collaroy,' corrected Hughie. Dolour looked sulky.

'Well, it's near enough,' she said. Her nervous tension was high, not only because of Roie's wedding, but because of Roie's departure with Charlie, into a life in which she, Dolour, would never more have part.

They all sat around the patched and greyish tablecloth, that was set out in a prosaic assortment of hastily-assembled edibles; plates heaped with thick corned beef sandwiches, soup plates full of tomatoes and lettuce, and here and there a dish piled with sticky baker's cakes. Three sherry bottles and a port bottle shouldered each other with clinking familiarity in the middle of the table, and Mr Diamond eyed them thirstily.

There was not much conversation, but many smiles. Mumma was full of yearning for her daughter, so young, and, in spite of Tommy Mendel, so innocent, about to set forth on her new life like a small and inexperienced Christopher Columbus braving an unknown ocean.

'It's so hard, darling,' cried her heart. 'Not now, when there's love between you, but later on when you've got children, and them with the croup and you up all night with your back broken, and your mind crazy with no sleep, and your husband snoring on the bed with his boots on, as drunk as a lord. 'Oh, God, dear,' cried her heart. 'Make it easy for my little Roie.'

And Hughie, warming up with the drink, thought: 'I'm not an

old man yet. There's many men grandfathers at forty, and who's to say I'm fifty-five? Not so long ago I was married . . . and Dad there with his face like a big red moon. God, he had a tongue on him, sweet as honey with the brogue . . . and Ma, too.' He tried in vain to remember his mother, but all he could recollect was a black dress with a sort of plaited gold brooch close up under her chin. 'She must have had hair,' argued Hughie to himself muzzily. 'And eyes . . . she must have had eyes. Funny how I can't remember them.' It seemed to him so ineffably sad that he couldn't remember the colour of his mother's eyes that he put his head down on his hands and wept a tear or two. Patrick Diamond, who was equally muzzy, clapped him on the shoulder.

'Ah, you should have remained a bachelor, mate; there's nothing like it for peace and contentment.'

'I wish I was dead,' sobbed Hughie.

'Then go off, for goodness sake, and cut yer throat and stop spoiling the party,' suggested Mumma hotly, for she had had a couple of glasses of spirit and was feeling full of courage. Charlie laughed. He knew it was all a surfeit of emotionalism, and took no notice of it. He sat quietly with Roie, holding her hand under the table, and looking now and then at Dolour, so as not to leave her out of the fun. But Dolour, stuffing cake into her mouth, thought: 'I hate him! Buck nigger! Buck nigger!'

Roie thought; 'I want to cry, or laugh, or something. Don't let me spoil it. I want to be what he wants me to be. I love him. I love him. I love the back of his neck and that little hollow in his cheek, and his eyebrows. I love you, Charlie, don't you hear me?'

She felt that the intensity of her thoughts was so great that he could not help but hear them. With shyness she looked away, from his lips that silently said 'Darling' above the merry uproar.

Hughie recovered suddenly from his sorrow about his mother, and said confidentially to Mr Diamond: 'I've gotta dance. I've gotta dance, mate.'

Mr Diamond cheered hoarsely, and winking at the company in general, pushed Hughie out into the middle of the floor. He looked all around with a beaming smile, promising all the entertainment of their lives. But because the alcohol had effected a strange sense of distance between his feet and his brain, he did not move, but stood on one leg and waved the other in and out and back and forth in a kind of stationary Highland fling.

Mr Diamond held his nose and let out a wild squeal, meanwhile

373

pumping his left arm up and down against his side, in imitation of the bagpipes.

'Whoopsy-doopsy, oopsy-doopsy, up the leg of me drawers!' bellowed Hughie. Mumma banged the table with a fork.

'You stop that sort of stuff, Hugh Darcy,' she threatened, 'or I'll stick you in the gizzard with this.' Her mild eyes sparkled and her face was fearsome.

'Mumma gets funny when she's a bit woozy,' chuckled Roie.

'Yole spoilsport,' complained Hughie, collapsing, mainly because he was out of breath. 'Lookut ole spoilsport, Patrick. Lookut 'er,' he said, nudging Mr Diamond, who reluctantly gave up his pumping and looked.

'Don't you glare at me, you old tearer down of images,' cried Mumma, turning her wrath on Mr Diamond, who said placatingly: 'Now, now, missus, keep yer hair on. I didn't look at you.'

Dolour pushed the sandwiches over. 'Here, have one,' she invited, and Mumma took one and subsided, a little tearful, sniffing away her tears because she wanted very much to be happy at her daughter's wedding, and couldn't quite manage it.

There was a little precise knock on the door, and Dolour hissed: 'Bet that's the Drummy kids to see if there are any left-overs!'

But it wasn't. It was Lick Jimmy. Small and bowed, and yellow as soap with increasing age, he stood there, a narrow figure in his tight black trousers and coat. He bore a parcel, strangely wrapped in the exotic back-to-front newspapers he read.

'Come on in, Jimmy,' roared Hughie, waving his arm in an expansive gesture. 'Come on in, me old heathen, and join the bun-fight.'

Mumma's hospitable heart smote her that she had not invited Lick Jimmy to the party. 'Come and 'ave a cup of tea, or some sherry, Jim,' she invited.

Jimmy smiled. 'I bling plesent, then I go,' he announced. He gave the parcel to Roie. Roie was covered in confusion and delight. Lick Jimmy bowed.

'Many long years, missie Roie,' he said. 'Many sons. Many lands and houses, misser Charlie,' he said. There was a flicker in the doorway, and the quiet tiger padding of slippers up the passage.

'Gee,' gasped Dolour.

'He's a queer old coot,' said Patrick Diamond.

'Useful sometimes. You oughter know,' said Hughie meaningly, and laughed to kill himself when Patrick looked perplexed.

'Go on, open it, Ro,' urged Mumma eagerly. Roie undid the parcel. Inside was an entire flat bolt of finest silk, thinner than gossamer, a filmy glossy stuff that had unfortunately been dyed a violent salmon pink.

'What a pity. You couldn't wear that. You'd look like a nigger,' cried Mumma, and could have bitten her tongue out. But Charlie didn't seem to notice.

'You could make lots of pants out of it,' suggested Dolour. 'Shut up,' hissed Mumma fiercely. But Hughie unheeding, chipped in:

'Keep Charlie interested.'

'Yer don't need nice clothes after yer married,' said Patrick Diamond superiorly. 'You need good heavy working clothes that will stand up to a lot.'

'Fine life you think the girl's going to have,' flashed Mumma. They could all see that at any moment there was going to be a good old stand-up fight. Hughie said hastily: 'What's that fell out there?'

Roie picked it up; a little yellow card inscribed with a brush in sweeping black letters: 'Good luck from Lick James.'

'Lick James, eh?' Nobody saw the joke but Charlie. Mumma was a little offended.

'Well, you couldn't expect him to sign it with anything but his full name,' she expostulated. 'It wouldn't have been manners.'

And they all agreed.

Eighteen

As the time of going-away grew near, Roie became frightened. She felt the old trembling, prickling feeling rising at the base of her spine, and her head beginning to spin. Charlie noticed it even before Mumma did. He said quietly: 'It's going to be all over soon.'

And so it was. Soon she was jumping down the crooked stairs for the last time, still in her wedding dress. It was blue linen, with an exotic sort of beaded lily on the bodice, under which Roie's little breast bloomed with a pitiful slenderness. Hughie clasped her gingerly at first, and then gave her a good hug, muttering into her hair: 'Good-bye, kiddie. Hope you have a nice holiday.'

Mumma didn't cry. The wine had lent her a self-composure, and she looked long and gravely at Roie and said: 'Remember this is the beginning of your new new life. Start it well, and it'll end well.'

Roie nodded silently, for she was frightened she was going to cry. She looked around for Dolour, and there she was standing with her head ridiculously hidden in the curtain, like an ostrich. Roie went up and peeped around the curtain and there was Dolour's face, twisted up into dumb grief.

'Good-bye, Dolour, darling.'

'Ta-ta, Ro,' choked Dolour. Then she gave a long anguished snort, and everyone laughed, and Roie ran out quickly in case her tears should overbrim.

Soon they were in the tram, and Roie began to feel better. She looked at Charlie, and he looked at her, and they looked away again, each with a little shy smile. They liked the tram, but they liked the ferry better. It made them feel almost as if they were going on a sea-trip for their honeymoon, as lots of young people did. They looked about with awe at the hugeness of the ferry, and when the man with the mandolin came along Charlie gave him three-pence with proud hauteur that was born of pleasure and embarrassment. He played 'Little Nelly Kelly' and 'Concerto For Two' with extreme hurry and eagerness, as though he were anxious to earn another threepence.

They managed to get a seat together in the crowded Narrabeen bus, and it was then that Roie really began to feel excited. The road unwound, white and curving, bordered with green paddocks, and little houses sitting comfortably under the lee of hills. Now and then there was a sapphire flash of sea, and after a while, as they rounded the bluff above Long Reef, a wondrous stretch of beach opened before them. Pale and oatmeal-coloured, curved in a half-circle, and rimmed with the uneven stripes of the great white breakers, it swung around into the far distant haze. Roie gasped. 'This is what Dolour told me about,' she said. Charlie squeezed her hand.

'Pleased I chose this place?' he asked.

'Is it here? Oh, it's like Paradise,' she cried.

The bus spun downwards into Collaroy, past a theatre like an exotic lime ice-cream. And soon it was impatiently chugging, waiting for them to get off at Narrabeen village. Charlie lifted out Roie in one hand and their suitcase in the other. He was excited with an exultant growing excitement. He wanted to laugh aloud.

'It's up this way.' He gestured with the suitcase to the little houses scattered amongst the dunes.

'I'm glad you didn't want to stay at a boarding-house or something,' panted Roie, skipping ahead of him, and looking around her like a delighted child.

'I'm glad *you* didn't,' he replied.

'I wanted our own little place for the fortnight,' she cried.

'I wanted to have you all to myself. Ah, gosh, Roie!' he cried in a sudden tumult of excitement and anticipation. Roie suddenly stopped. Her heart beat fast. She was all at once frightened. She was even more frightened than she had been when Tommy Mendel had wanted her. She wanted to run down to the bus stop again and go back to Mumma, and poor Dolour, who had so hated her going. Charlie put his arm around her, and felt her trembling. He said gently: 'Darling, don't be scared.'

'I'm not scared!' cried Roie angrily. She pulled away. 'Which is our cottage?'

Charlie pointed to a little house a hundred yards away.

'That's ours.'

Roie was delighted. She jumped up and down like a child and cried: 'It's pink! It's pink!'

And so it was, a tiny square pink cottage, with a sandy path, and geraniums and petunias struggling gallantly with the overgrown grass. Charlie fished the key out of his pocket. 'Here you are. You open it.'

Roie took it and ran forward. The key grated in the lock, and the door opened, a little protestingly. The tiny place smelt of the sea, and the white sand had sifted under the door, so that their feet crunched on the floor. There was a minute lounge gaily furnished with blue cane. Yellow and blue-striped curtains flew in the breeze as Roie threw open the casement windows. She cried aloud with joy: 'Oh, the sea! The sea!'

There it was, the whole Pacific, cobalt, glittering richly, tossing itself in foam-laced breakers against the castled Narrabeen bluff. It was magnificent and lonely, and the very essence of all blueness and sunshine, and it was the backyard that Roie and Charlie possessed.

They ran through into the tiny kitchenette, and laughed at the pygmy gas stove, with the row of bright saucepans hanging above it. Everything was clean, and smelt of the sea and the coarse blowing grass.

'Where's the bedroom?'

'Through here.'

There was a white-painted bed, with a blue spread on it, and pink ruffled curtains at the window. The floor was bare but for rag mats, and a big mirror hung on the wall. Roie bounced on the bed.

'Oh, it's hard! No dips!' she sang. Charlie bounced beside her.

'No bugs! and real white sheets.' Charlie pulled her back on the bed, buried his face in the hollow of her neck, and said softly: 'Darling Roie! I can't believe we're really married at last.'

'At last!' Roie wriggled away, because she was timid of the tone of his voice. 'It's only been a few months since we first met.'

'I wanted you right from the start,' he whispered. Roie lay in his arms looking up at his face, dark and beautiful in its odd way. She kissed him on the peak of an eyebrow, fleetingly, so that he laughed and dropped her: 'Let's go and have a swim.'

'I can't swim,' she protested.

'Neither can I. But we can fool around in the breakers.'

He flung open the suitcase, tossed her bathing suit to her, and picked up his own trunks. Unselfconsciously he pulled his shirt over his head. Roie watched, blushing a little because, although her instincts told her to turn her eyes away, she knew that she did not have to do so. It was like watching a stranger undress. Charlie noticed her discomfort, and said: 'I'll undress in the lounge. Hurry up, because the tide's on the turn.'

Roie didn't know whether to be pleased or sorry. She hurried into her own suit and joined him on the step.

They ran into the water. The sea spoke in vast sonorous vowel-sounds . . . 'aaaaaaaaaaaaahhhhhhhh . . . ooooooooo-hhhhhhhhh hhh.' Roie screamed and pranced on the sand. She was frightened to go in, and yet longing to breast the cool and tingling water. When she was wet all over, she felt proud, as a child might, when it had conquered a fear. She became almost hysterical with excitement; it was such fun waiting for the great glossy bottle-green breakers, runnelled and channelled with a thousand gullies and hillocks, to lift her off her feet and carry her irresistibly to the shore. For the first time that year she felt the blood running strongly through her body, and her skin opening like a flower to the hot caress of the sun and the cold caress of the sea. She caught Charlie around the waist, and he stood like a rock before the approaching wall of the breaker. Then they were hurled together, breathless and laughing, upon the sand.

'Oh, oh,' gasped Roie, sitting up, with sand thick upon her swim-suit. 'I've never had so much fun in all my life.' Charlie pulled her to her feet. The water ran in little droplets off his smooth skin. He had a wide chest diminishing into his trunks, and long, well-muscled legs. Roie had never really seen a young man's body before. He grinned as he saw her surveying him.

'Well, do I come up to standard?'

'I think you look better with your clothes off,' she said seriously. She shuddered with a passing chill.

'Come on,' he said. 'You're cold. Let's go up to the house.'

'Oh, no,' she begged. 'Just one more dip.'

'We'll be here fourteen days,' he reminded her. They looked at each other and laughed aloud with delight. Fourteen paradisal days stretched between them and the drabness of their daily life. They ran up the dunes, playing like children.

Ten minutes later Roie saw the sun go down behind the bushclad cliff beyond the village. Her skin smooth and cold, her wet hair brushed into fluffiness, she stood at the tiny stove, grilling the steak and tomatoes which Mumma had packed in the suitcase. She had forgotten nothing. Bread was rolled up in Roie's nightdress, salt and talcum powder sat side by side; the pepper and sunburn lotion rubbed shoulders and the butter sat securely in a spare soap-holder.

'I can cook,' boasted Roie.

'You can do everything,' said Charlie. He ate as vigorously as he did everything else. Roie felt a stirring of vainglory as she watched him. It was good to think she could feed him. She felt scorn for all the brides who couldn't cook at all.

The evening came down, and the village sprang into a sprinkling of yellow lights. Roie was so tired after her surfing she wanted to go to bed at once, but she was frightened. On the threshold of a great experience, she stood tiptoe, timid and hesitant, and wondering, and longing to run away home. For a long time she put off going to bed. After a while, as she went past the couch where Charlie lay at ease, he put out an arm and pulled her close to him. He nuzzled his face into her hair and asked: 'Don't you want to go to bed with me?'

She put her head on his chest, and felt the deep slow pulsations of his heart.

'I love you, Charlie.'

'I know you do, sweetheart.'

'I'm just a little bit scared, Charlie.'

'Scared of me?'

'Oh, no . . . just, scared.'

Charlie was silent. Only his heart sounded in the stillness.

'Let's go to bed, Roie, and let me lie with my arms around you, and you won't be scared any more.'

'Yes, Charlie.'

She went into the bedroom. The light was soft and dim; through the wide windows came the mournful sound of the tide incoming.

She undressed slowly. 'I wish I was fatter. I wish I didn't have so many bones. I wish my hair was longer. I wish I was prettier. I wish I knew what to *do*;' and deep down was the wish: 'If only that hadn't happened, I mightn't be afraid.'

She got into bed and lay there, her little body making hardly a hummock in the blue field of the spread. Her heart was beating fast. She held her hands together to keep them from trembling. Charlie came in, his hair tousled from the shower, mopping the drops off his brown chest with a towel. He looked down at her.

'Are you scared of seeing me with my clothes off?'

'A little bit.'

He dropped the rest of his garments on the floor. He was slender and shapely and tawny-skinned. His neck rose out of his shoulders like a short pillar of bronze; his dark head was beautifully set on it. He looked at her without any selfconsciousness, without any shyness or embarrassment in his golden eyes.

'I'm just like other men.'

She nodded, without a word. He flicked off the light; and got into bed beside her. She did not move for a moment, and then, as his arms went around her, she turned to him, put her head on his shoulder and lay close to him. The warmth of his body lay all along her side; his velvety skin brushed her arm, her ankles, her cheek. Again she felt his heart. It was like some machine that had started twenty-four years ago and never faltered one hairbreadth in its steady throbbing. It was in some way like Charlie himself, deep, wise, undeviating.

'Oh, Charlie,' she trembled. 'I love you so much.'

'I love you and want you so much,' he returned. His hand stole down to her breast. 'You're so little, Roie,' he said inconsequentially. They lay there for a while. Roie's heart steadied. He said: 'I've never held a girl like this before, although I often thought about it. It's much nicer even than I thought it would be.'

Roie whispered: 'Haven't you ever had a girl?'

'No,' he answered.

'I thought all men did,' whispered Roie, shamefaced. She felt him shake his head.

'Lots of men don't. I've never touched a girl yet. No more than you've ever touched a man. I picked you right, didn't I?'

Roie was silent. In that moment the episode with Tommy Mendel, her illness, the baby she had lost, all went spinning away like dust down a corridor. They were a nightmare unreality, as though they had never been. How could it have been true, that silly, clumsy, ludicrous little experience? It wasn't anything like this. It was no more like this than a street lamp is like the sun. This was beautiful, exultant, the most overwhelming thing she had ever known.

She felt for Charlie's lips with her own. 'You're the first man I ever had,' she breathed. 'You're the last man.'

His lips met hers, young and warm and ardent. His arms held her more tightly, and she felt the glowing warmth of his flesh, his very bones. He was hers, and more than the whole world she wanted to be his.

Nineteen

It was strange when Roie woke up the next morning, and yet familiar, too. She woke quietly, opening her eyes suddenly on the bright, light room with the sea-dapple sliding over the ceiling. She turned her head, and right under her lips was Charlie's warm soft hair. His head was on her shoulder, his arm flung across her, one knee over hers. She marvelled that she did not feel his weight; it was not at all like sleeping with Dolour, who had been all awkward angles, and as heavy as lead.

She lay there for a long time, looking at his sleeping eyelids, and his face, relaxed and tranquil. His dark blood was plain now, but it gave to his face an exotic difference, a delicate difference in the line of his lips and the triangularity of his eyebrows.

He was hers and she his; the mystery had been consummated. She was different now, and it was not a physical difference; it was spiritual. Nothing she had ever dreamed had been even remotely like the reality, his passion and strength, his complete adoration of her and surrender to her. Roie had often read books that talked about a bride's surrender, but now she knew that the bridegroom's surrender was just as complete.

Suddenly he opened his eyes, looked at her and smiled. He slid his cheek along her bare shoulder and murmured: 'Roie.'

'What, darling?'

'Nothing. Just Roie.'

They lay in warm quietness for a long time, while the sea light glimmered all about them. Then, with mischief in his eyes, Charlie asked: 'Still frightened of me, Roie?'

She shook her head dumbly, frightened lest he should look into her eyes and discover that she loved him as the saints loved God, unquestioningly and exultantly. The knowledge was in her heart, but there were no words for it yet. Gently, tenderly, they would come to clothe it, until at last she would be able to tell him.

They stayed at Narrabeen for a fortnight. Every moment of it was a revelation to Roie, learning more about Charlie, and falling deeper and deeper in love with him all the time. She grew in mental stature; there were implanted in her the seeds of tolerance and sympathy that were to flower in her adulthood.

The two of them, barefooted, ran along the sand-dunes, sliding and slipping, the little flat bright town on one side, and the steely glimmer of the lakes, and on the other side the wild and lonely shore. A fierce vigour seized Roie; she felt as though she had never been alive until now. She ran and played on the hard oatmeal sands, and taunted the great breakers to come and get her. She was fey, and Charlie felt almost an awe as he watched her. She, so delicately strung, so passionate in everything she did and felt, must surely have great pain and sorrow ahead of her. Where others found valleys, she would find abysses; where they climbed hills, she would climb mountains, and see from their peaks enchanted vistas beyond their comprehension.

Sometimes he felt frightened before this unknown quality in her future; he put his head on her breast and felt the palpitation of her heart.

'Happy, Roie?' She was silent a little, and then her breast shuddered and a sob rose out of her throat.

'What's the matter, my sweetheart?'

'If I died now, this minute, Charlie, it would have been worth it.'

The tears trickled under her closed eyelids, and he kissed them away. He did not say anything, for she knew what he meant. Her feeling was not his, for as much as he loved Roie, he, as a man, had a grip of years as she, as a woman, had a grip of moments; he knew that there was much more to come. But he understood in some wordless way how a passionate soul can achieve happiness so great that there seems no more to be experienced.

The blue sky was low about them on the dunes; they were islanded in air, in aloofness from the rest of the world. 'It mightn't always be like this, Roie. We'll never have much money. We'll have to live in cheap places, down in the dirt and drabness like everyone else. We'll grow old. Perhaps you'll be ill. Perhaps I will. Nobody can tell what life will bring to us.'

Urged by compassion he tried to shake her out of the rapture that might entrap her into so much pain. She shook her head. 'It won't matter. As long as we're together.'

'We mightn't always be together, either,' he said slowly; a premonitory shadow of the agony of their separation drew over him like a chill from the sea, so that he drew her closer and sought warmth from her body. He expected her to shudder, too, but she looked at him with eyes as innocent and unalarmed as a child's.

'You mean one of us will die?' She sat up; the wind flung out her hair. 'Of course one of us will . . . maybe it isn't so far off, either. But nothing can separate us. Souls don't die. Did you forget?'

Looking at her, he marvelled that she could accept so unquestioningly the fact that death would one day tear one from the other. A pang of pain went through his heart at the thought, and he forced it away from him and held her so fiercely that she cried out and protested, her body melting into his even as her words sought to thrust him away.

'Oh, Roie, if I lost you, I'd kill myself.'

She shook her head, smiling to herself, and thinking of her mother and Thady.

The fortnight might have been a thousand years. Every day Roie changed from what she had been to what she would thereafter be. Her pursuing, inward longing to make things what they were not had gone, because she had found that Charlie had changed the world to her desire. His presence made it all she had ever wanted. Her timidity now became a warm and self-contained silence into which she entered when she was with strangers. She was not self-conscious; it was just that she had a world of her own into which none but she and her husband might enter.

She said to Charlie: 'Would you give me a baby?' He was surprised, for he and Roie had never discussed children. He had thought it was because she would, like most girls, like a year or two free before she entered upon motherhood.

'Why do you want a baby? Aren't I enough for you?' he asked, half-humorously, for a tiny jealousy had risen in his heart. She put her head on his shoulder confidingly.

'It's just that I want you to own me altogether,' she said. Words did not come easily to her when she was thinking her deepest thoughts. 'I want you to be part of me for ever and ever.'

He smiled. 'Perhaps it's already happened, Roie.'

Roie shook her head. She felt quite sure.

'Up till now you've only wanted me for myself, because we love each other. Can't you want me because you can give me a baby, and I can give you one?'

Fear rose in him, fear for her health and her life. He experienced in a fleeting instant that sense of loss which had been his when they spoke of death, upon the sands. It was almost as though the dark blood in him, nurtured on superstition for a thousand generations, trembled and was afraid before the doorway of life. Roie felt this. 'You're not afraid for me, are you?'

'You're not very strong, Roie, and it'll hurt you.'

'Oh, Charlie, you don't understand. Having a baby is different from all the ordinary ways of being hurt. It's worth it all. Other pain isn't worth anything, but that is.'

Roie was driven on by something she had to obey. She held herself guilty for the death of one baby; she felt that she had to conceive and bear another, and if God still deemed her guilty he would take that from her. She felt this as surely as if it had been written on a tablet of stone, feeling shadowlike the agony of a childless mother. Yet, at the same time, she wanted to laugh out aloud for delight that she could have a child, the seal of her union with her husband. She took him in her arms as though she were the lover and not he.

'My sweetheart, my own love,' she murmured.

The sea crashed again and again at the foot of the dunes, and the little house moved as though before the breath of the vast ocean. The pale water-glimmer on the walls quivered and wavered and fled before the sinking of the moon. In the bed Roie slept, untroubled even by dreams, her hair like filaments of jet over Charlie's shoulder, whilst within her the soul of her child trembled into existence.

Twenty

Dolour was so excited on the day Roie was coming home that she could hardly sit still in school. All her little memories of her sister merged into one enchanting whole; she felt that never had there been anyone as beautiful or romantic as Roie. Even her name seemed as distant and unusual as that of a film star. 'Rowena Darcy,' muttered Dolour into her geography book. 'Rowena Rothe.' That sounded even queerer. How could Roie have discarded her own name for that of her husband, so easily and unresentfully? Dolour felt suddenly very upset and angry. She was on the threshold of womanhood, borne this way and that by conflicting tides of feeling, often her muddled yearnings and dreamings dissolved into storms of furious tears. She felt angry with and disdainful of Roie, because she had been so weak. She, Dolour, would never fall in love; she felt fierce and pure and fortified against the soft call of the flesh.

'Ha!' snorted Dolour. Sister Theophilus looked up in amazement, and Dolour bent blushing over her book, while Harry Drummy kicked the back of her desk and sniggered inquiringly.

When she came out of school she paused for a while beside the brown stone house on the corner of Plymouth Street, and watched the rubbish men emptying all the tins which stood, like rusty sentinels, in a ragged line along the footpath. The men were great beefy-armed fellows in sacking aprons. They spread out a sheet of hessian in the middle of the footpath and emptied one tin after another upon it, until at last there was a huge stinking heap of week-old refuse. The dogs and toddlers darted in to pick up fascinating scraps, and the blowflies crawled, shimmering cobalt, upon the sticky masses of decomposing foodstuffs. There were cabbage stalks, a barrowload of rotten fruit from Lick Jimmy's, peaches that oozed yellow pulp from the rents in their brown-patched skiṇs; there were old clothes, sad boots with calloused heels, and hats that were just misshapen basins of felt; old books and magazines, stained with tea leaves and the sodden heterogeneous mass of household garbage. Dolour poked away a bit of squashed pumpkin with her foot and picked up an old satin shoe with a diamante buckle. She jerked it off and walked away quickly, her heart beating fast for she had a magpie adoration of shiny things. It was so pretty, flashing diamond showers into the air, and reflecting little rainbows into her cupped palm. It made her feel happy all the way home.

She heard Roie laughing in the kitchen, and with her heart jumping with pleasure she galloped noisily down the passage and threw her arms around her sister.

'Gosh, you're brown, Ro! Isn't she brown, Mumma!'

She did not think for a while to see if Roie were different in any other way, but when her excitement had died down she looked covertly at her sister to see if her honeymoon had changed her. But Roie looked just the same; no consciousness of her new knowledge showed in her eyes, or in the way she moved. It was only now and then, when Roie turned her head and fell silent, that Dolour saw in the pure slender line of her cheek and mouth some elusive difference, some rich and peaceful expression that had never been there before.

She loved Roie more than she ever had, and out of her mind she thrust Charlie, who had taken her place and would for ever more come before her. In her pocket the diamante buckle lay cool and hard and square. Dolour danced up the stairs to her own room, so that she could gloat over it. It was funny with Roie not sleeping in her room any more. Dolour, though she was growing up, and her body enlarging felt little and thin and forsaken in the bed which had always been too narrow for both of them. She missed Roie's grumblings and kickings, and the warmth of somebody to turn to when there was nightmare in the room. Sometimes she cried a little, for self-pity that her sister had left her, and other times she was ashamed to find herself listening to hear what Charlie and Roie talked about when they were alone. For Dolour's mind, less precocious than those of most Plymouth Street children, was awakening to curiosity, and all the formless hypotheses and muddlements of adolescence. It was not that she wanted to pry into Roie's private life; she just wanted to know. The physical manifestations of sex had always been before her, crude and blunt, but she longed to know if there was in her sister's love affair the sense of high glamour that there was in love affairs in books and on the screen.

It was only a few weeks before Roie knew that she was to have another baby. The little sick feelings, the faintness, and the fugitive pains brought back poignantly and nostalgically her longing for that other little baby that had never been anything at all. What had it been, a boy or a girl? A little creature with a face as soft as a petal, and tiny teeth like shells, with fumbling hands and uncertain fat feet . . . like the ghost of a child its memory was always with her. She clutched her stomach, pain gripping her throat like a hand, and tears burning their way out of her eyes.

'Oh, dear Mary, say that I'm forgiven, and that God won't take this one. Let me be brave and not think about anything that might hurt my little one. Let me make up for the wrong I did to my other baby.'

She told Dolour before she told anyone else. Dolour, her heart sinking, and her stomach feeling slightly unstable, stood looking after her. Slowly but surely a wall seemed to be building between Roie and herself. Then all at once she felt glad. It would be nice to have a baby to look after and play with; it might even look like its auntie. Dolour rushed to the glass and examined her face minutely. Melancholy-featured and sallow with adolescence it looked back at her, but Dolour thought her mouth rather pretty, and her eyebrows not too bad at all. They would look well on a baby. She peered at a spot on her chin and rubbed it painstakingly with her finger, as though to erase it. Then she picked up the tube of tooth paste, said solemnly: 'This is a magic cream from the East,' and rubbed a little into the spot. She went downstairs, feeling spellbound, and entirely sure that when next she looked the pimple would be gone.

Mumma was very angry when she was told; she blamed Charlie, most unreasonably, and argued interminably about it with Roie as though the matter could be settled as easily as that. Finally she realized that Roie was very happy about it, and she began to think that perhaps it would be nice to be a grandmother.

'What are you going to call it?' she asked. Roie said eagerly:

'Moira if it's a girl, and Michael if it's a boy.' Mumma nodded approvingly: 'They're real good Irish names. Moira was the name of one of my sisters that died, and I had two Uncle Michaels, one on the Kilker side and one on the Mullins side.'

Charlie had never loved his wife so much. Now and then he came home and found Roie weeping on the bed. He was undisturbed, looking at her quietly, for he knew that she was easily upset, and would be laughing again within a few minutes. Tenderness filled his heart. He did not wish, as a woman might that he could suffer her coming ordeal for her, but he hoped with all his heart that it would not be too agonizing for her little body and slight nervous strength.

'What's the matter, darling? Feeling bad?'

'No, I feel fine,' sobbed Roie. She fumbled for a handkerchief, and Charlie put his inky one into her hand. She rubbed streaks all over her face. Charlie shook his head: 'Lord, you're a goon. You look like a darkie going to a corroboree.'

Roie glared, throwing herself on the bed and sobbing heart-brokenly, kicking her heels in rage because she knew she was crying for nothing she could explain. Charlie laughed and tickled her, knowing that she would soon recover.

'It's just that I feel it's impossible for me to have a baby,' she choked ridiculously. 'I can't imagine me with a baby.'

'Well, I can't imagine myself as a father. It sounds as outlandish as riding a rhinoceros.'

'You sound like an old grandfather,' cried Roie petulantly. She jumped up, gave her face a cat-lick with a washcloth, and put on some lipstick. Feeling much better, she went beguilingly over and kissed Charlie under his chin. 'Gee, I love you Granddad.' She kissed him again, warmth and fragrance rising from her body, and he held her close and hid his eyes in her hair, so caught up in his happiness that he might have stumbled upon paradise unawares.

Everything in the lives of Roie and Charlie was bound up in sex. It was as though they moved in an atmosphere of their own, gentle, spellbound, warm as an island air, far from the rest of the world. It was so subtle that the physical expression of it, beautiful and ecstatic though it might be, was crude and vulgar compared with this spiritual knowledge that had come to both of them. The touch of a cheek, Charlie's arm across Roie's breast at night, her soft sleeping breath, his little murmur of drowsiness; all these things were expressive of wordless delight. During the day they did not always think of each other; it was just that each was in the other's thoughts like a shadow, or perhaps a light illuminating the swift-flowing river of mentation. And this was for all time; it was an actual transformation in their souls. Some love affairs come like extraneous things, and are worn by a personality as a woman wears a garment, to be flung away when worn out. But others are a sea-change, springing out of sex and bearing fruit in the spirit itself. Charlie's and Roie's marriage was like this.

Dolour still loved her diamante buckle. It was so treasured that she had not shown it to anybody. She flashed it back and forth, her eyes chasing the prickles of green amidst the blue and white glitters. It was the loveliest thing she had ever possessed. It took her a long time of anguished indecision, but eventually she bolted downstairs and gave it to Roie.

'It's a little present,' she stammered, her eyes beseeching Roie to take it and treasure it for its beauty as she had done. Roie answered warmly:

'It's lovely, Dolour. I've never seen such a pretty one. Thanks ever so.'

Dolour had for a few hours the exultant joy of the martyr, and when that died away she wished bitterly that she had not been such a fool. When Charlie came home she pressed her ear to the wall and out of the mumble of their talk she heard Roie say:

'Look what Dolour gave me. Funny kid.'

'What for? The baby?'

'I don't know. She just gave it to me,' said Roie with a tender, amused laugh. Dolour knew that it was, but all the same a sword went through her heart. She heard the tinkle of the buckle in a drawer, and leaning her head against the wall she cried silently, not only because she had humiliated herself with a needless sacrifice, but because she knew that nobody would ever fondle and adore the diamante bauble as she had done.

When the months went past without any trouble, Mumma grew easy in her mind, and boasted shyly to the shopkeepers that she was going to be a grandmother. Hughie looked at himself anxiously every time he shaved, to see if the white was coming out in his whiskers, and when they grew black and coarse and virile as ever, he, too, boasted to his friends that his daughter was to have a child. Only Mr Patrick Diamond resented the coming baby. He felt it a slur upon his barren life, and concentrated all his wounded vanity into one premature complaint about babies yowling all night.

'It won't yell at all, you see,' said Roie confidently. Already the baby was becoming a person. Roie's body was still slim, but her breasts were full and aching. She hugged the soreness to herself as though it were a blessing and a privilege. The rich autumn went

390

past; Lick Jimmy changed the yellow chrysanthemums in his window for purple everlastings and the cold winds came from the interior of the continent as bitterly as from a fireless hearth. Roie was always warm; an inward fire made her body glow. She felt a rich and drowsy contentment, like a wheatfield, heavy and burdened with its own harvest. Often she placed a hand on her abdomen and felt her baby quivering. It was so alive; it jumped when a loud noise occurred, as though it heard. Charlie and she loved to lie in bed, feeling the baby between them, moving a tiny foot or hand, perhaps turning its head a little in its cramped and sheltered haven. There was a precious secret feeling about their love of the baby's little movements, so helpless, so pathetic.

'I'll work overtime till I drop,' vowed Charlie. He held her until she went to sleep, the deep protective instinct in him subduing his desire.

Just a few days before the baby was due, Mumma went shopping. Two winceyette nightdresses for Roie, a woollen singlet, for the weather was cold, and a pair of ugly mustard-coloured bedsocks. They had all the baby's little clothes ready, folded and immaculate. Roie fingered them again and again, amazed that a baby could wear anything so small.

As she walked back from the shopping centre of Oxford Street, Mumma's feet were bothering her. She wearily meditated upon bunions, and the way they shot out radiating streaks of pain as a tree might send out roots. As long as Mumma could remember she had had bunions, mainly because from her childhood she had worn other people's shoes.

All at once her heart gave a painful thump, and she stood still, the string kit dragging from her hand, and all her faculties concentrated on the face of a young boy who stood talking to another at a tram stop.

He was fair, silvery-fair, with a wide freckled face, and teeth with little spaces between them. His blue eyes were crystal-pale, with dark blue rings around the iris. He was Thady . . . Thady grown up, and . . . and . . . Mumma began feverishly to count, as she had counted a million times. Ah, what was the use, when she knew it off by heart? Sixteen and six months and three days. Ten years all but eight days since he had vanished, at four in the afternoon. Mumma moved forward like a woman in a dream. She stared at him greedily;

every silver hair on his cheek, the whorl of his ear, his slender neck, his big, hard, clumsy hands. She had no doubt. It was Thady. Her heart fell down in adoration. It was like a miracle.

'After all these years, these long, long years,' sobbed Mumma's heart.

The boy nodded to his friend, and they walked off in different directions. Mumma's bunions gave an awful stab of pain, and for a moment she thought that she might not be able to catch up with him. She hurried her unwieldy body forward, and, losing all sense of judgement, called out: 'Thady! Wait for me! Thady!'

The boy, unhearing, did not stop, and Mumma gave a great gulp of breathlessness and anguish, and he turned and looked at her curiously. 'You calling me?' he spoke roughly and abruptly, like many in that locality.

Mumma panted: 'You're my Thady.'

The boy screwed up his face, looked at her like a suspicious cockatoo.

'What's this? A gag?'

Mumma, seeing him closer, was overcome with love for him. Oh, he was a fine lad, with skin like milk save for the freckles; a real Irish buttermilk skin. She saw fleeting resemblances to Roie, and when he scowled, there was the young Hughie before her. She burst into tears. The boy stared. He wanted to swear, and walk away. But a feeling of curiosity intervened. What was the old hen cackling about, and her looking at him like a ghost just risen from the grave? He said: 'Here, can the waterworks, willya? What are you gabbing about?'

Mumma sobbed thickly: 'I'm your mother, Thady. Oh, me little boy, me little Thady!'

The boy became more and more convinced that the woman was mad. He looked with repugnance at her red, tear-blotched face, the hat pushed lopsidedly over her forehead, and the string kit, distended with odd-shaped parcels, dangling from her fat fingers. He ejaculated an obscene word, and walked off, very fast. Mumma, shocked into self-control, ran after him, crying: 'Don't go away. Don't. I want to talk to yer.'

'Go and cut yer throat,' answered the boy rudely, a little alarmed and annoyed at Mumma's persistence.

'You were taken off the street, ten years ago,' cried Mumma

waddling along so fast that people in doorways laughed to see her. 'You were only six. Oh, Thady! Listen to me, Thady!'

'Go to hell, willya,' yelled the boy, his fair face so flushed with rage that his freckles stood out like a peppering of dark brown spots. 'Get back to yer bombo, yer old hag.'

He dived down a side-street. Mumma, her heart beating like a hammer, had to stop, holding to a fence and panting for breath. She had the sense to step back into the shadow, and she saw him jump a low gate and enter a house at the end of the street.

'God help me. God help me not to lose him now,' she prayed, aloud, so that people passing smiled pityingly, or amusedly.

She came to the house. It was neatly kept, and immediately a hatred for its keeper entered her heart. Here lived the woman who had stolen him, who had plunged his mother's heart into the intolerable anguish of the woman who loses her child. Ten long years of purgatory, of ceaseless worry and yearning had gone past Mumma, and she had never felt any hate for those who had stolen Thady, only wonder for their reason for so doing. But now she felt hate and fury as she never had before. Her eyes were blinded by a red-streaked mist; she had to bend low and fumble for the catch on the gate. Inside the house she heard words: 'God, there she is now. She follered me. Wouldn't it?'

A dark-browed man stamped out on to the verandah. 'Now, look here, missus, what are you chasing my boy for? State yer business and get hopping, will yer?'

'He's my boy,' cried Mumma, her lips trembling uncontrollably. 'He's my Thady, that you stole.'

'I told you she was bats,' put in the boy excitedly from the door-way. The man said with rough kindliness: 'Garn, get home, will yer? And sleep it off.'

Mumma said wildly: 'Thady, darling, don't you remember anything? You were six, Thady, remember? And yer had yer little navy pants on, with the patch, and yer red braces, new ones. You were so proud of them. And you had three marbles in a flour bag, a yeller connie, and a sort of stripy white one, and a big clay one you'd made yerself and baked in me oven.'

The man on the verandah eyed her with a fascinated stare. Her anguish, her earnestness, were beyond doubt.

'I ain't forgotten yer, Thady ... not one inch of yer body, and

393

you're still mine. I bore you down there in Plymouth Street, and I got every little bit of a garment you ever wore. Yer little shoes . . . Thady, darling, say yer remember.'

'I ain't remembering you nohow, yer old haybag,' said the boy sullenly.

A ruddy-faced middle-aged woman, who had been lurking down the hall, appeared with alacrity, her hands rolled up in her damp-spotted apron.

'Elsie,' said the man. 'This lady's in some sort of a mix-up about Brett, here. Get her a cuppa tea, willya?'

He pushed Mumma into a poky sitting-room, heavily over-furnished with sooty net curtains, an over-large chesterfield suite, and many oil pictures. She sat down gingerly on one of the rigidly upholstered chairs. The man rubbed a hand over the seat of his trousers, looked at the hand, and sat down himself.

'Now, missus, what *is* all this?'

Mumma, in a voice from which all the life had gone, explained. A heavy weight, so heavy that it seemed to compress her lungs, pressed on her heart. She was hardly able to breathe. She couldn't find a handkerchief and sniffed with increasing rapidity. The boy, standing awkwardly in the doorway, looked at his father.

'I don't know what she's gabbing about.' His eyes appealed to his father. He had a frightened, uneasy feeling that perhaps the old girl was right, and he would have to go away with her, a stranger, and live with her, and never see his own home any more.

The lady of the house entered, flushed and bursting with excitement. She put down a tray and said with gushing sympathy: 'Do have a cup, you poor thing.'

Mumma flared up, gave a last tremendous sniff and said:

'Don't you dare poor thing me. You'll be poor thinging on the other side of yer face when I get the police on to you for pinching my baby.'

'Now, look here,' began the woman, a brick red creeping into her cheeks.

The man said gruffly: 'Hold yer gab for a while, Else. She's talking the truth, as far as she knows it.'

'Of course I am,' said Mumma indignantly. 'You ask Father Cooley. You ask the nuns at the convent. Anyone. They'll tell you that what I've said is true.'

'You hold your tongue, too,' ordered the man authoritatively.

394

Mumma subsided. 'Now, maybe you're telling the truth, as far as you're concerned, but all the same young Brett here is our son.'

'I had him in Paddington hospital,' interpolated the woman. 'Thirty-eight hours' labour, I oughta remember.'

Mumma scoffed. 'Easy to say that now. But can you prove it?'

'You can call in the neighbours,' cried the boy. 'Mrs Stead next door can tell you that we've been here for years ... since I was seven,' he added lamely. Mumma's eyes flashed. 'There now,' she cried.

'There's his birth certificate,' said Else uncertainly. Mumma jeered: 'Do you take me for a fool? Do you think I'd be mistaken in me own son? Of course he's my Thady.'

She stared at the boy, who looked uneasily away. More and more she could see resemblances to Hughie and Roie, and even, now and then, to Grandma. The man laughed: 'You're batty, missus. It's just a resemblance, that's all.' Relief and triumph suddenly flashed into his eyes. 'Go on, Else, get out all them photos.'

'Oh, yes, I didn't think before.' Else rummaged in the sideboard, and brought out an untidy album bulging with photographs. She sat down by Mumma.

'Now, here you are, Mrs ... er ... here's Brett when he was six weeks.'

Mumma screwed up her eyes and looked at the bald-headed bundle of long clothes. It might have been almost any baby.

'And here he is with me and Dad, on his third birthday.'

Mumma looked eagerly at the fair-haired mite laughing between a smoother edition of the man opposite her, and a younger but unmistakable Else.

'It's me Thady. Glory be. It's me Thady.'

'Don't be a fool,' said the man brusquely. 'He's only three. How could he be?'

Mumma looked again. There was no doubt. The child in the picture was not six. Then how ... her poor muddled brain snatched after the flyaway springs of her assurance, and failed.

'It's the resemblance, you see,' said Else with smug complacency.

She showed Mumma a studio photograph of a five-year-old child dressed in a black velvet suit which made him look like a gooseberry. It was undeniably Brett, but it was not altogether Thady. Mumma felt a slow hard pain at her heart, growing and growing.

She said faintly: 'I think ...'

The man said firmly: 'You don't want to think. You want to *know*.' His wife showed her half a dozen other photos, all like Thady, but all with subtle differences. Was Brett's face wider, his hair fairer than Thady's . . . Mumma dropped the last photograph and her face collapsed into a thousand lines of misery, and she put her head down on the table and wept tempestuously.

Else dropped her mask of complacency, and became the warm-hearted decent woman she was. 'Here, you poor dear, have a cup, and try to forget it.'

After a while Mumma recovered enough to sit up and drink the tea, the cup rattling against her teeth. 'It's the disappointment,' she managed.

'I know. It must have been a dreadful experience. Losing a kiddy like that. Many's the time . . .' said Else, looking at her with grave, screwed-up face, as though to convey that she understood everything. Mumma picked up her hat, that had fallen off, and put it on with trembling hands.

'I gotta go. You been nice to me. I'm sorry I said some things I did,' she said. Else patted her shoulder.

'Don't you think of that, Mrs . . .'

'Darcy,' said Mumma drearily.

'You just try to forget all about it, Mrs Darcy, and I'm sure I hope that next time you find the right Thady.'

It was such a long way home and already the dark evening had come over the streets. The lamps winked out round and golden, and the cold wind blew the dust out of the gutters in miniature willy-willies. Mumma walked very slowly, her feet painful, and heavy as lead. She hardly noticed that the parcel of Roie's night-gowns had burst open, and the dust was streaking itself across the cheap furry winceyette.

'It makes you wonder what a body's born for,' said Mumma to the lucent cold blue sky, so far, so remote, so unhearing of pitiful human prayers.

At seven she reached home. Dolour was on the verandah. As soon as she saw her mother she called out the news. Roie had been taken bad, and had gone to the hospital.

Twenty-One

When Roie felt her pains that afternoon she was all alone in the house, and a little frightened. They were familiar pains, a shivering thrill of sensation through her abdomen. She felt the child lie quiet, as though resting for its ordeal which perhaps was just as great as hers. She knew that first babies are usually slow, and she sat down on the bed and packed her bag and brushed her hair quietly, as Charlie's ways had taught her. All the time she was saying: 'Please don't let me get frightened and lose control of myself. Make me brave. Make me brave.'

At half-past three Dolour came running in, up the stairs like a whirlwind, and banged at Roie's door.

'Where's Mumma? The fried fish man is open and maybe we can get some . . . what's up?' she asked, seeing Roie's white face. Roie smiled.

'I think you're going to be an auntie.' Dolour's face turned as white as milk, so that Roie forgot her own fear and said: 'Don't be silly, now. There's nothing to worry about. Can you walk up to the hospital with me?'

Dolour cried: 'Oh, you'd better not walk. I'll get a taxi. I'll get one right away.'

'No,' said Roie, 'it will do me good. The Sister at the hospital said it would.' She turned away, for the pain was sharper this time, and she did not want Dolour to see her face.

Dolour, sick at her stomach, faltered: 'Do you want to go now?'

Roie answered: 'If you'll just carry my bag, I'll be all right.' Now that the pain had gone, she felt wonderful. She rose and put on lipstick, saying: 'I'm glad I washed my hair yesterday.'

'Yes, it looks pretty,' stammered Dolour. She went ahead with the suitcase, and Roie climbed downstairs one by one, very carefully.

It was not far to the hospital, perhaps half a mile. They walked slowly down the broad street and into Murphy Street. Roie looked across the road at Number Seventeen; the tall brownstone house with all the jungle of pot pants looked as dark and furtive and secretive as ever. Roie had never seen it since that dreadful night when she ran away from the horror it contained. Now she looked at it only passingly. Charlie's love had almost destroyed her memory of that night. It was funny, she thought drowsily, how he could do that; he was something solid interposed between her and the nightmare. All at once her pain returned. It seized her in iron, merciless hands, and she had to turn and hold on to a fence, sweat coming cold on her forehead. Dolour chittered like a frightened bird.

'Are you all right? Oh, I wish Mumma was here! I wish Mumma was here!' there was hysteria in her voice. Roie took a deep breath. As mysteriously as it had come the pain was ebbing away. She relaxed and tried to smile.

'You don't want to take any notice of me, Dolour. Don't let this make you feel scared about having a baby. I'm pleased it's come at last . . . I was getting awfully tired of being big and clumsy and tired all the time. And the pain isn't really bad at all.' She had the age-old instinct of women to lie to younger women about labour pains, so that dread might not make things worse for them when their own time came. Dolour nodded dumbly, and they went slowly on.

The hospital was cold and white and incredibly busy. Roie felt forlorn and anonymous and unimportant when she entered the swing doors. She gave her name and they waited in a barren waiting-room until the nurse came along.

Roie cautioned: 'When Mumma comes home, tell her I'm fine. There's the potatoes on the back of the stove, and the pudding's in the oven. Turn the gas out when you get back. Tell Mumma not to come up to the hospital, for it might be a long time, and I don't want her waiting around with her rheumatics.'

'What about Charlie?' whispered Dolour. She had just heard, from somewhere on the top floor, a frightful rending shriek, and her lips were pale and frozen.

Roie smiled faintly. 'He'll know what to do,' she said. 'Now, you'd better go now, Dol, and get the tea started for Mumma. She'll be tired.' Her cold lips touched her sister's cheek in a hurried caress, for she felt another pain starting. Dolour said nothing, not even good-bye. She tiptoed creakingly out, and ran all the way home, sobbing to herself, and hoping that Mumma would be there to take this awful burden of anxiety from her shoulders.

Now at last Roie was on her own, as she had not been since she lost her first baby. They came and led her away, unresisting, as though she were a puppet, for she was fast sinking into the abyss where one can concentrate on nothing except agony.

The night passed like an hallucination, splashed with violent yellow electric lights, the firm, often rough hands of nurses and interns, and the continual shrieking and moaning of other women all around her. Her baby was born early in the morning. It was the conclusion to nightmare. There was the coarse stinging smell of ether, much too late, and then she came to consciousness again, still muttering, as she had muttered all through her agony: 'Let me be brave. Let me be brave. I want to make up for the other time.'

Daylight was in the ward, blue and wan, and the lurid globes dimmed it into darkness. She saw the white forms of nurses at the bottom of the table, working over the little red body of her daughter.

One of them looked up. 'She's all right. Go to sleep,' she ordered brusquely, and Roie closed her eyes and drifted into the sleep of exhaustion.

Charlie came to see her that afternoon. They sat for a long time, rather shy of each other, looking at the baby at intervals, but most of the time staring at each other with delight and relief and happiness. They had little need to speak; her hand lay in his, and now and then he turned it over and looked at it. It was young and smooth, the nails short with housework, and already the stains of cooking and scrubbing upon it. How little and young she looked in the high white bed. It seemed impossible that she was a mother, that he had possessed her, and implanted his soul and personality upon her. He looked back at his hard and lonely childhood, and beyond that to other ancestors, black and strange, who had felt as he was feeling now, the piteous realization that time is fleeting and flesh is as grass.

Briefly and without words Charlie left his youth behind. He meant something now . . . not only companionship and sustenance to a woman, but everything in the world to a child. He embraced the knowledge joyfully, for it seemed to him that although youth with its blitheness and beauty was to be loved, all of life was to be cherished.

Roie said suddenly: 'I didn't think she would be born all right.'

'Why, darling?'

'I don't know. I just didn't.' She smiled, and knew that instant

that the old doubts and fears, born in her conscience, had gone for
ever. The second child had wiped out the grief of the first. She
passed her finger over its downy cheek, and it screwed up its pink
face and whimpered.

'She's a little grub.'

'She's a little honey.'

They looked at her for a long time.

Until now their marriage had been ten months of careless
happiness, now it became something else. Roie learned what
broken rest was, hanging over her baby's cot until she was crazy
with desire for sleep. She learned what it is to be bound hand and
foot and heart to another human being, and to resent it a little, until
at last mother love welled in her heart and made her slavery a
happiness. Charlie, quiet and contemplative, watched her face;
watched for the first fine tracery of the lines of irritation and
disillusionment and monotony which mark like a seal the faces of
slum women. But they did not appear. Roie had something which
those other women had not, contentment and continued love.
Charlie was the centre of her world. She ran to meet him at night,
always with the same delight. In bed she lay behind the wall of his
back, feeling little and protected and secure, as a woman of the
caves might have felt long ago, as she lay with her man shielding her
from the cave opening, and the great darkness and mystery beyond
it. Charlie was a shield and a refuge to Roie, and she an endless
delight to him.

'You're beautiful, Roie.'

'I'm not. I look like an old woman when I'm tired.'

'You won't always be tired. We'll get out of this, have a lovely
house, and a garden . . . some day.'

They both knew that day would never come. Responsibilities
anchored them, for Charlie's earning capacity was very limited, and
day by day their bonds to the cheap and dirty portion of the city
were made stronger. Perhaps they would struggle against it in their
dreams, but no more than that. There were so many other things to
consider too; their shyness and awkwardness with the people of the
outside world, just as though they were inhabitants of an island
lapped by the roaring traffic seas of the great city; their consciousness of poor, halting speech and inability to cope with any social
standards; their tendency to shrink into and shelter within the
warm, coarse, familiar things and places. They would grow old and

die in Surry Hills, as people have been doing for five generations.

It was Mumma's birthday, and little Moira was four months old. Hughie had found in his nature strange depths of love for the little mite, for although he was Irish, and sentimental, he was also Australian, and thought the exhibition of it effeminate. He often talked to Moira, seeing in her birdlike blue eyes his father's Kerry eyes, and his mother's eyes, for they too had been blue.

'Wait till you're a big girl, little moke,' he said to Moira. 'You don't want a dirty old granddad staggering along in the gutter, being sick all over the footpath. You want a nice grandfather to take you for a walk and buy you an ice-cream. That's what you want.' And he pictured himself, with just a little drink inside to keep him warm, walking very upright, with a fine bushy head of white hair, and perhaps a decent little whisker down the side of his face, and beside him a prancing curly moppet of a Moira. And he pictured, too, all his old mates, purple in the face and bleary-eyed, sitting in doorways and being mighty envious of Hughie Darcy who had stopped when he oughter.

'I'll come right off it. I'm just weaning myself,' he explained to Mumma, as he had explained so many thousand times before. Mumma, since the time when she found Thady and lost him again, had been silent and often pale. For the first time in her life she began to think that perhaps it was not much use wishing and praying that Hughie would come off the drink.

'For what else in life is there for him?' argued Mumma with herself. 'He was a good husband when he was young.' And she convinced herself of this, in spite of all the appalling evidences to the contrary with which her memory presented her. 'I've put up with it for twenty-five years,' said Mumma defiantly, 'and there's no reason why I shouldn't put up with it till the end of me life.'

And because of this she did not argue any more with Hughie when he came home shouting drunk, nor did she demur when at her birthday he produced both Patrick Diamond and a bottle of ripe and turpentiny port. Mr Diamond looked thoughtful, as he usually did when he had a few in, and was considering casting down a few images. So Mumma said warningly: 'Now, not a word out of you, Patrick Diamond, about Pope-worshippers, for it's me birthday, and I'll worship who I like.'

'Not a word, Mrs Darcy,' promised Mr Diamond, and with a twinkling air of suppressed excitement he said: 'I've something important to tell yer later, Mrs Darcy. It'll make yer poor old heart warm, so it will.'

'Not so much of the old,' snapped Mumma, flushing as red as a turkey-cock, for she was only fifty-two. And Hughie burst in with: 'Yes, you keep yer long tongue between yer teeth, you old Orange beggar, or I'll tie a knot in it. Look at the fine figger of a woman all in and out like a pianner leg.'

Mumma said haughtily: 'That's enough of that filthy talk, then.' And so the evening began well.

Dolour came bursting in with pink cheeks and dazzled eyes from the darkness.

'What's the matter?' asked Roie. 'Where have you been?'

'Just to a choir practice in the school hall,' answered Dolour. 'It was good fun.' She looked at Charlie and grinned as though she could not help herself. This was so rare that he laughed aloud.

'What's on your mind, Dolour?'

Dolour blushed and ran outside. She stood outside the phoenix palm in the windy, gusty darkness, and looked up at the bright and piercing stars. Stray cats, empty-bellied and desolate, mewed feebly from behind the alley fence, but Dolour did not notice. Once again there was a spellbound, exciting world before her. She was not fierce and pure and fortified against the world after all, and she did not want to be.

'I know how Roie feels about Charlie,' she chanted under her breath, and giggled, and hugged herself.

'He's nice,' she whispered. 'He's got lovely brown eyes, and he wears a blue suit when he's all dressed up.'

It was a miraculous thing. She had gone to school with Harry Drummy, had yelled at him, kicked him in the shins, and been kicked in return. And now she had fallen in love. It was as sweet as a peppermint stick, and as pink and white. It made everything different. There was no sex in Dolour's feeling for him. It was as pure and fairylike and useless as the love of knights and ladies in antique ballads. But it was something to be gloated over at night time, hugged to her bosom, and cherished until, like a bubble, it floated unheeded away. For the first time Dolour was pleased that Roie wasn't sleeping with her any more. Now she was free to indulge as she wished in dream conversations.

St Anne of the Seven Dolours vanished with a swish of the skirts, and Dolour said softly: 'Mrs Dolour Drummy, Mrs Harry Drummy.'

'Ah, crumbs,' she said. The sweetness and wonder of it nearly overcame her, and she leaned her face against the spiky trunk of the unheeding tree and shivered for joy. Her Mumma cried crossly from the doorway: 'What are you trying to do? Imitate the ivy?' And Dolour, a little cross, and red-faced, marched in. Mumma! How should she know what her daughter was capable of feeling? Her life had only been housework, and babies, and trouble. Nothing like the glamorous, golden, and misty life which stretched out before Dolour Darcy. She drifted in and began handing around cups of tea, gobbling a tomato sandwich meantime, for love had not affected her appetite.

Mumma sat quietly, looking on, for she liked to see other people enjoying themselves. Her feet hurt, and she eased off her slippers under the table. It was nice to have a cup of tea and sit and watch Hughie drinking port, and not care about it at all. She wondered why she had ever worried, forgetting that fierce hatreds and desires belong to youth and not to middle-age, which can at last learn to accept things as they are. Hughie noticed the absence of her cautioning voice, and this worried him so strangely that he stopped drinking, and even chided Patrick Diamond, who seemed to be putting away more than usual.

'It'll burn the guts outa you, Patrick man,' he cautioned. 'You with yer ulcers.'

'To hell with me ulcers,' retorted Mr Diamond blithely. 'I'm celebrating. Here, let me light yer little bit of a bumper, Hughie man.'

With an erratic hand he extended a lighted match to the cigarette butt which was protruding under Hughie's nose. There was an anguished yell, and a squirt of laughter from Roie and Charlie.

'Me nose, God damn it, you nearly burnt me nose off,' yelled Hughie, holding his hand over it. Mr Diamond shrugged foggily.

'It's yer own fault for having such a God-forgotten honker,' he answered reasonably. Hughie swelled visibly, for the nose was the Darcy nose, and had been handed down from one proud generation to another. Mumma interposed hastily:

'Now tell us, Patrick, what are yer celebrating?'

Mr Diamond's air of secrecy grew greater. Dolour said sarcastically: 'He's put a bomb in Father Cooley's bed, that's what.'

'Don't be speaking disrespectful of yer priest,' cried Mumma angrily, making a backhanded gesture at Dolour. Mr Patrick Diamond looked grieved.

'It's you who'll be taking them words back when yer hear me news, me fine young pullet,' he said to Dolour, who sniffed and stuffed half a tomato in her mouth. Then he announced:

'I'm entering.'

'What? A home for old men?' asked Hughie malevolently.

'I'm entering the Church,' said Mr Diamond pompously. There was a deathly silence, broken only by the juicy chewing of Dolour. Mumma gasped:

'You mean the Catholic Church?'

Mr Diamond nodded. Hughie began slowly to turn petunia purple.

'He's only being sarcastic,' ventured Roie.

Hughie suddenly exploded. 'You dirty stinking scoundrel of a scab, Patrick Diamond! To think that I've been nursing this viper in me bosom all these years, and now he does this to me.'

Mr Diamond was bewildered. 'I thought you'd be pleased. I've always had a strange discomfortable feeling in the back of me collar that you've been praying for me to turn.'

'But Orangemen never turn Catholic,' gasped Mumma. Mr Diamond said proudly: 'I do.'

Hughie exploded again. 'Drinking me wine and eating me tomato sammidges and then saying a thing like that. You're not fit for decent society, Patrick Diamond. You can't be trusted to stick to yer own principles.'

Mr Diamond, with the port mounting to his head, and his stomach beginnng to burn ominously, shouted: 'I'll do what I like when I like without the interference of any bone-headed tike.'

'There now,' cried Hughie triumphantly. 'He's blaspheming against the sacred name of the Church. And him talking about entering it. Why, the Church wouldn't have yer.'

'And why not, may I ask? Is it too high and mighty for such as me?'

Mumma flashed: 'It's not too high and mighty for any grey-bearded old sinner who wants to seek grace when he's on his last pins.'

Mr Diamond began to roar incoherently. He made a swing at Mumma, and Hughie clipped him under the ear. Charlie seized one by the shirt-front and the other by the coat-collar.

'Now look here, don't break up the party. Go outside and cool off.'

404

He shoved them both outside and shut the door. There was the anguished voice of a stood-on cat and the stamping of feet and mouthing of muffled oaths. Mumma cried to Charlie: 'Now they'll kill each other, and you'll be a murderer.'

There was silence outside; then they heard Mr Diamond slowly ascending the stairs. Hughie adjusted a triumphant expression on his face and entered the room.

'I gave him a swipe in the brisket,' he boasted. 'He's gone, and I never want to see his blaggard countenance again. The idea of him, wanting to turn at his age. The dirty old turncoat. Nobody would suspect an Irishman of doing such a thing, would they now?'

Mumma was repentant. 'Perhaps he meant well, Hughie love. There was no call to hit him in the stomach, anyway, and it so bad.'

'To hell with him and his belly,' cried Hughie. 'From now on he's wiped. I never want to see him again.'

'He's a poor old man,' said Roie softly. 'Perhaps he just wanted to bury all the differences, Dadda, and never fall out with you on St Pat's Day any more.'

Hughie reconsidered. He took a mouthful of port and let the strong stuff roll around his tongue before he permitted it to scorch his throat. 'Well, maybe I'll go up tomorrow and say I'm sorry,' he conceded magnanimously. 'Not that I am.'

Upstairs Mr Diamond lay on his bed and held his stomach and groaned. His pain was on him, and the agony was almost too much for him to bear. The little ugly room pressed on him as though it had a descending ceiling and contracting walls. He had a nightmare urge to shriek and scream and bellow and roar until someone came and knocked him on the head and put him out of this awful travail. He forgot all the scene he had just experienced; all he remembered was his complete loneliness. Somewhere he had missed his path, and now his only possessions were futile abstracts. Even they had deserted him. He did not care for either the green or the orange – nothing but the blackness and quiet of oblivion.

'One of these days,' said Mr Diamond between spasms, 'I'm going to turn on the gas.'

Downstairs Charlie said: 'Well, it's ten o'clock and I'm on an early shift. I'd better turn in.'

Roie rose, too. 'It's time the baby was fed.' She kissed her mother and father, and gave Dolour a slap on the tail as she passed. 'Happy birthday, Mumma, and I hope we're all here for the next one.'

They climbed the stairs. Near the top they stopped, and Roie leaned against her husband's shoulder and he kissed her soft, eager lips.

'Gee, I love you, Charlie.'

He whispered in her ear, and in the warm tingling darkness they clung together, exchanging kisses and whispered fugitive phrases, desire enveloping them both. Roie laughed, and ran into the dark room and flicked on the light. She picked up her baby and collapsed on the bed with it, holding it above her and laughing into its crumpled, drowsy face. Charlie sat beside her as she fed the child, and watched them both. His horizon grew smaller and smaller. It enclosed no vast field of dream or ambition, nothing but this small room and what it contained.

'I've got everything I want in the world,' he thought.

In the kitchen Mumma and Hughie fell into a silence, listening to the radio, which, now that the noise was gone, raised its voice and was heard. They listened for a long time, and it came to Mumma that almost all the songs she heard nowadays were sad songs. There were so many sad songs – not the virile, tragic ones of long ago, but little futile, piteous squeakings against the vast and bitter world. They were like the cryings of a bird overwhelmed by the ominous and sombre sandy winds from an encroaching wilderness. Some strange rot had settled in the hearts of the men who thought, the wise and educated and accomplished people of the world. They felt that there was no permanency anywhere; that all was vanity, and nothing under the sun was worth striving for any more.

In her peasant soul Mumma thought how strange it was. Her thoughts did not have words, and her pity did not even have thought. For the first time she felt equal and even superior to these people with the riches and the wisdoms of the world, who did not know even the simplicities she had been born knowing.

She told Hughie: 'I'm tired.'

She rose laboriously and put on her slippers, and went into the dark bedroom. Her hand was out to switch on the light when it happened. Thady was there. She felt the soft neck of a little boy, and his silver head, nuzzling into her lap. He was there, as light as a feather, as insubstantial as the wind, but real. She could smell the long-remembered smell of his body, and feel the gust of his breath. It was only for a moment, but it was as though her restless, tormented, mother's heart was stilled for ever into tranquillity. She knew now that Thady had died, long ago. What the manner of his death, where he lay now, she could not think, nor did she try. It was all over, long ago, and she possessed him again, little and defenceless and entirely hers. Perhaps some other time she would find him here in this room, this dirty dark room that had now been enhaloed and enchanted as was the tomb of Joseph of Arimathea after the Resurrection. She looked up at the ceiling; neither the stained plaster nor the clotted webs did she see, only the dark and fathomless and immortal sky, and beyond it to him who chose to walk in the ways of the poor and the forgotten as he walked in his garden.

Hughie came in and put his arms around her. He was tired and clumpy and middle-aged, and he smelt of port and sausages and cheap shaving-soap, but she loved him as she had never loved him before.

'Whatjer thinking of, old hen?' he asked, rubbing his whiskery cheek on hers.

'I was thinking of how lucky we are,' whispered Mumma.

knew not that they had died long ago. What the matter if his death, there belay now, he could not think, nor did she his laws, all round could see and she possessed him again time and again and embraces and clever here. Perhaps some other time she would ... and run here in this room, which dry dark room that had now been ... studied and enlarged as was the result on thought of Artemisa after the resurrection. She looked up at the ceiling, neither the stained glass, for she could work did she see only the dark and balconies and immortal ... and beyond urged him who chose to walk in the way of the poor and the forgotten as he walked to his ...

"I right course," said put his arms around her. He was tired and clumsy and malodorous, and he smelt of port and sausage and cheap shaving soap, but she loved him as she had never loved him before.

"Won't it make no difference," he asked, rubbing his whiskery cheek on hers.

"It has done no poor Tony," we she whispered, Mumma.

Poor Man's Orange

One

And then the queer sounds would begin again, heavy, rhythmic breathing, and muffled whimpers as though someone had his head pressed hard into a pillow, afraid he would be heard.

Charlie lay awake for a long time listening. He became aware he had often heard it before in his dreams, a penetrating sound that had half-pierced the veils of sleep. He awakened Roie.

'What's the matter?'

'I don't know. Listen.'

Roie listened, 'Oh, it's only Mr Diamond. He's talking in his sleep. He always does it.'

'Wonder if he's crook? He looks funny these days.'

'Oh, go on. He's getting as fat as a porker.' Roie was cross. She scrambled out of bed to see if Motty was covered, scolding the sleeping child in a whisper when she found the bedclothes in a tangled scarf at the bottom of the cot. Mr Diamond's bed creaked, and the floor shuddered as he walked across it. They heard the pop of the gas-ring.

'He's got indigestion again, that's all. Shut up and go to sleep.'

Charlie laughed and drew her head down on his shoulder. Her fragility and slenderness charmed him, as he might be charmed by the delicate slightness of a gazelle. He stroked her cheek, and once again drowsily thought his way through the litany of his love for her, for they rarely spoke of love.

In the next room Mr Diamond waited for the kettle to boil. He waited with the fixed and avid stare of a drug addict, and all the while the pain crept downwards through his abdomen in a trembling, undulatory progression till even the bones of his legs seemed to twist and grow brittle under its impact. He knew he couldn't hold out much longer. His teeth clamped together, his face built into a square mask of determination and agony; he knew that one night he would give way and start screaming.

The kettle boiled, and he poured some water into a cup, filling it to the brim with thick, black pain-killer. Its opium smell, thinly disguised with aniseed, filled the room, and Mr Diamond snuffed it like the odours of paradise. He tossed off the filthy stuff, vomiting against the taste, and while his throat was still numb, he filled a hot water bottle and lay down again with it on his stomach.

He started to pray, 'Our Father Which art in heaven ...' mumbling the line over and over again, for he was exhausted into stupidity with pain and sleeplessness. Slowly the agony subsided. It was as though he had an animal inside his body, and it gnawed and clawed until he fed it with the pain-killer. But it wasn't an animal, it was a fish. Mr Diamond moved the hotwater bottle aside, and once again, for the thousandth time, he felt the thing that lay across his stomach. Unbelievingly, astoundedly he felt it, the shape and solidity of it, and wondered at the alien, incredible thought that this revolutionary bastard creation of his body tissue could really exist.

It was the shape of a fish, not very large, but firm and well-defined. As though in protest all the rest of his abdomen had grown soft and spongy, bulging out his trousers as though he were an alderman puffed with expensive living.

'It just can't have happened,' thought Mr Diamond, and once again he felt piteously hopeful that it was just a nightmare, and he would wake in the morning to find it gone.

Then he knew that it wasn't that he really did have a growth and sooner or later he would have to die, and go to another world even lonelier than this one, and at that appalling, certain thought, Mr Diamond began to cry harshly and loudly – he who had never wept since he was a little boy in Ireland, and his feet so chilblained he could hardly walk.

He tried very hard to stop crying, but he couldn't. The terror and the despair rushed in and seized him, and out of the past came the old cry for his mother, his father, anybody who could take the responsibility of it all off his shoulders and make him better.

'Ma, Ma,' he babbled, 'where are you, Ma?' The memory of her – the big, bony woman with the red splash on her cheekbones, her black petticoats turned up and tucked in at the waist, gutting fish so fast the knife was a flicker of silver – came at him so alive and real that it was almost as though he were a little boy again, and in trouble about something that was small, and yet seemed to fill the whole world.

'Maybe this is small, too,' thought Mr Diamond, 'but oh, God, I don't feel it that way.'

He fell into a nightmarish doze, in which he wandered again

412

through the old days that came up thick and fast as though someone were flicking them out of a card pack. An uneasiness and foreboding fear ran through them all. He chased the black bobtail pup, but never caught it. He fell into the weedy lagoon, and never came again to the surface. He fled the brindle boar, but was caught for ever suspended upon the moment when the froth-flecked snout was just behind him. The pain suddenly surged up and shook him out of his sleep, and Mr Diamond sat up and stared into the darkness, which was hot and prickling with panic. Not all his fortitude and courage could stop the terrific groan from bursting through his lips, and almost at once he heard movement next door, and the young man Charlie Rother called softly, 'What's up, Pat? You sick?'

The door handle turned, but it was too late for Mr Diamond to curse. He could see the tall shadowy figure in the dusky doorway, asking again, 'I heard you call out. Do you feel crook?'

'No,' gasped Mr Diamond, 'Just dreaming.'

He closed his eyes, sweat streaming off him with the effort of speaking normally, but when he opened them again Charlie was still there. A sickening, trembling rage seized him.

'I told you I was all right. Coming into a man's room, you bloody nigger! Go on, clear out.' He sat up and shrieked, 'Get out! Get out! Get out!'

The door closed. Mr Diamond lay back, fainting with the pain and thought of the hours ahead of him, the long minutes, the endless seconds that would have to be borne in silence.

In the morning Charlie said privily to his father-in-law, Hughie Darcy, 'I reckon you ought to go up and see if old Patrick's all right, Pop. He was making a lot of noise in the night.'

So Hughie, buttoning up his blue shirt and stuffing it into his pants as he went up the stairs, barged into Patrick's room, singing as he went, for it was pay-day, and already his tongue was hanging out like a length of red flannel with the delicious anticipation of the pub.

Mr Diamond was lying half out of bed, a grey greasiness on his face, and his eyes fallen into blue pits. A cold hot-water bottle grumbled beside him.

'Goddlemighty,' said Hughie. 'And the night last night like a furnace.'

It seemed quite plain that Mr Diamond was drunk, and Hughie

lifted him to put him back into bed. A hoarse croak came from Mr Diamond.

'Don't be touching me, Hughie.'

Now Hughie was alarmed. He hurried to close the door in case one of the girls should pass and see Patrick's nakedness.

'You know me indigestion, Hugh?'

'Like an old pal,' said Hughie, puzzled.

'Well, it ain't.'

Mr Diamond motioned Hughie to pull up the old shirt in which he slept. It was grimed with dirt, and so was Mr Diamond.

'Put yer hand on me here.'

Hughie did so, and felt the fish. For a moment appalled horror held him motionless. A cold tingling feeling ran over him from top to toe. It was almost as though death had breathed over his shoulder. He said in a small voice, 'Christ, Patrick.'

Mr Diamond hoisted himself up a little. Often the daylight brought surcease to him, and now the pain was ebbing with the onward march of the morning. He seized Hughie's arm.

'It's got me, Hugh. If I go to a hospital they'll carve me up, and it won't do any good. I'm done, Hugh. You got to stick by me.'

'Whatever you say, Pat,' promised Hughie, his eyes averted.

'I won't go into a home for the dying. I been on me own all me life, and I'm not going to be mucked about with now. I don't want anyone praying over me.'

Hughie swallowed hard. 'There might be some chance . . . you don't want to drop your bundle . . .' he said feebly. Mr Diamond lay back.

'Don't tell anyone, Hughie. You're me mate, and I trust you. I want to stick it out by meself, that's all.'

'I'll bring you up a cuppa strong tea,' muttered Hughie. Mr Diamond opened an eye in which was the ghost of an old twinkle.

'It'd suit me better if you've got a drop of muscat under the bed, mate.'

All day long Hughie pondered on Mr Diamond. He moved in a dream, his lips moving silently, his eyes focused on the inner problem and not on his work. Predominant in his mind was astonishment that Patrick should have had this thing so long, and yet no one had guessed. A growth! Hughie shied away from the real word. It was as obscene to him as some of his commoner expressions would have been to a nun.

414

And Patrick, who was so tough he never even got a snuffly nose in winter! How did it happen, this terrible secret process that uncurled in a man's vitals as softly, gently as a rosebud, until it was a dam of the life-force itself, strangulating and suffocating?

Trembling, Hughie stopped the machine. He couldn't trust himself to carry on. The sinewy strength of his own robust body, the deep chest of which he was proud, the short, strong arms, the legs like little tree-trunks were forgotten. All at once he felt that he was a cardboard man, for God alone knew whether within his own structure he was not carrying such a seed as Patrick had carried. But under his fear there was deep grief for Patrick, and indignation that this should have happened to such a good man.

'He ain't ever done anything to You!' Hughie cried to God. 'Why didn't You pick out some rotten warmonger, or stinking politician raking in the chips, instead of an old bloke like Patrick, living decent on the pension, and not doing anyone any harm?'

His eyes stung, and his throat ached. He wanted to rush up to the hospital and hammer on the door of some big specialist and cry, 'You gotta come and fix him up! I don't care if I have to work the rest of me life to pay you. You gotta save Pat's life.'

It made him feel sick. He had to go the pub for the warmth and companionship there, and it wasn't until he had had half a dozen beers that the keen edge of his pain was blunted. Even there he couldn't do anything about it. Cancer wasn't a thing you could shape up to, and knock silly. You couldn't even sneak up behind it and slam it with a bottle in a sock. Hughie felt so bad that he had to leave the happy buzz and go home. He pleaded once more with Mr Diamond to see a doctor, but Mr Diamond only became angry and told him to go to hell.

He went downstairs and sat silently at the table, waiting for his tea. Mumma peeped round the door at him several times, for she was alarmed at his un-Friday-night-like lack of rumbustiousness. Finally she said timidly, 'Feeling sick, Hugh?'

Hughie longed to tell her, but it seemed to be so much Mr Diamond's property, this terrible secret, and he had promised solemnly not to tell.

'I'm tired,' he grunted.

Mumma came a little closer; all the love in her heart springing upright like grass after the heavy weight of a building has been removed.

'I got two bob if you'd like to shout me to the pitchers,' she said.

'I can't,' said Hughie awkwardly. 'I said I'd go up and have a yarn to old Pat.'

Mumma's love retreated like a turtle into its shell. She flamed, 'That's right! Spend the night boozing instead of letting people know I've got a husband. For all they know you're only a boarder.'

And so she went on, pounding around the table and slapping down knives and forks and fuming about old booze artists like Mr Diamond who would only have to breathe on a naked flame to cause an explosion.

'Shut yer mouth!' roared Hughie. He looked at her with real hate, for it was just like a woman to berate a dying man, even though she didn't know he was dying. All at once his eyes began to sting, for at last he had put the thought into words. He rose hastily and went into the bedroom, and Mumma looked after him, amazed. She went out and spoke severely to Motty, saying, 'Your gran'pop's a bit tired. Don't you go roaring round the house like a grampus, now.'

Two

In this narrow-gutted, dirty, old house, squeezed with its elbows flat against its sides between two others, there lived seven people. There was Mr Diamond, the Orangeman, and Hughie Darcy and his wife. Also there was Dolour Darcy, who was sixteen, and her elder sister Roie, who lived in one of the attic rooms with her husband, Charlie Rothe, and their little girl, Moira, who called herself Motty. There had been two others – Thady, who had been born between Roie and Dolour, and who was stolen off the street when he was six and never seen again; and Grandma, dead a long time now, and yet curiously a part of their daily life, a shuffling little ghost, pungent as a whiff of pipe smoke, and Irish as the words that were all she had to leave them.

The Irish in these people was like an old song, remembered only by the blood that ran deep and melancholy in veins for two generations Australian. The great tree, kernelled in the rich dust of Patrick and Columbanus, Finn and Brian, and Sheena of the unforgotten hair – the tree whose boughs had torn aside the mist of Ultima Thule bore in this sun-drowned southern land leaves in which the sap welled sharp, sweet, as any on Galway quay, or the market at Moneymore. The great music that had clanged across the world, of lion voice of missionary, of sword and stylus; the music that spoke aloud in the insurrections, in the holds where the emigrants sweltered in vermin and hunger – this music was heard in Plymouth Street, Surry Hills, and was unrecognized.

For how could Hughie Darcy, stumbling up that street in the dusk, with the wind blowing dead leaves about his feet, and in his heart the helpless, defenceless despair that comes after drunkenness, know that what he sought his forefathers sought, and equally misdirectedly? The rainbow that never ended anywhere, the unbeatable conviction that somewhere, sometime, things would be better without his bothering his head to make them so.

And how could Mumma, flapping about the house in her old slippers, turning the mattresses and exclaiming at the clouds of dust in old, apt, unique phrases that came to her tongue unbidden as birds, know that those same phrases had been used for centuries,

417

rising out of the brilliant logic of the Irish? She only knew that her mother had used them, and standing there amongst the settling curds of dust she remembered that wicked, invincible little mother who had made them Australian, and said a Pater'n'Ave for her peace.

Only in the little girl, Dolour, lying on her stomach and picking her face before a yellow corner of looking-glass, was the fierce positivity of the Celt, a surging energy that made her long for the world she did not know, for thoughts she could not yet comprehend, for experience she could not yet encompass. In her was the infinite delicacy of feeling of the Irish, the very halt of the raindrop before it rolls down the stem, the spin of light on the knife-blade, the tremble of the wind harp's string as the blown air touches. She was on the threshold of articulateness, and did not know it.

All the discomforts, the vulgarities, the harsh jovialities of her little world broke against her as repeatedly and unavailingly as a wave breaks against a rock; her real life was in school, and in the church.

The church in Surry Hills was no fountain of stone, no breaking wave of granite like some of the great cathedrals. It was foursquare, red brick, with a stubby steeple as strictly functional as the finger of a traffic cop; it humped its sturdy shoulder into the schoolyard, and the children rewarded it by bouncing balls off it.

It was as much a part of Surry Hills life as the picture-show or the police station, the ham-and-beef or the sly-grog shop. Its warm brick wall was there in winter for the old men to sun themselves against, or for the feeble-footed drunk, staggering home in the dim, to lie beside. Its steps were seats for the old ladies who'd walked too far with their marketing, and them with their feet brittle as biscuits with the rheumatism. The church in Surry Hills had achieved the innermost meaning of Christianity; it was the commonplace of life, like a well-loved old coat, worn, ordinary, sometimes a little drab, but essential to living.

On Sunday Father Cooley mounted the pulpit, rather slowly, for he had lumbago. He stared full into the eye of the microphone they had installed while he'd been sick, and contemptuously clouted the thing aside. He'd always been able to blast the ears off the backbenches, and he had no intention of giving way to new-fangled inventions at his time of life.

'We're going to have a mission,' he said.

The congregation moved like grass in the wind. Mumma hurried home afterwards as excited as if someone had told her she was going to be taken to the circus. For a mission was like a tonic. It stirred the 'possum in the people, and for months afterwards they could still feel the enthusiasm, and the reawakening of faith that had become a little monotonous and habitual.

'I'll get out Grandma's old beads and have them blessed again,' she thought. For Grandma's beads, which were wooden, and big enough to have come out of a clam, had come over with Grandma from Derry in the 'seventies, and had had so many prayers counted on them that each bead was a little hollowed, like an old doorstep.

Mumma rushed straight into the house and dragged them out of the drawer where they lay entangled in the old hairnets and tram tickets.

'Gawd, it's come again!' proclaimed Hughie, for he had seen this scene so many years in succession that at the very jangle of the beads his knees ached.

'This year I ain't going!' he bellowed, and he jammed his face into the pillow with the tea-stains on it, and stuck up his rear and registered ferocious determination.

'All right,' said Mumma carelessly. 'I'll pray for you.'

Now, if there was one thing more than another that maddened Hughie, it was being prayed for. He was not good friends with God, and with the things that had happened to him, Hughie thought it was no wonder. He stood on his dignity, and the Lord stood on His, and Hughie's innate sense of justice revolted at the thought that Mumma was everlastingly trying to be a go-between.

For the woman in her innocence often said her prayers out loud as she lay in bed of a night, and Hughie would writhe in anguish as he listened to, 'He's a hard worker, Lord dear, and it wouldn't be You who'd send him to everlasting fire for missing mass, when it's the only chance he's got of a bit of a snore-off,' or, 'There's some that don't take their duty seriously, and he's one of them, St Teresa love, and nothing but a pin in his bottom would stir him to it.'

'It don't do any good,' pleaded Hughie feebly. 'All the good resolutions go west as soon as I get the breath of a bottle of plonk.'

Mumma stuck another safety-pin into the dragging hem of her old house dress.

'It's different this year, love,' she reminded. 'You got Mr Diamond to think about, poor man, and him looking so crook lately.'

So Hughie went to the mission, getting over the first great and awful hurdle of going to confession to a shadowy hump that was the visiting missioner, and explaining why he hadn't been near the church for a year. Afterwards he felt curiously airy, as though the wind might well blow through his pores, or a sneeze whisk him over the telegraph wires. And he said to himself, forgetting all the other times, 'This time I'll keep it up. What with the traffic the way it is, and the crook wine burning a man's innards into holes, you never can tell what's due next.' Then he thought of Patrick Diamond, and a deep, painful melancholy settled on him. He stared at the stable will-o'-the-wisps of the candles, and hardly saw them; he got up and sat down mechanically, and while his lips moved along the old worn path of the Hail Marys and Our Fathers, his heart was saying, 'Don't take it out on Pat, Lord, for all he is an Orangeman, and that bitter against the Church. But he's me mate, and as solid as a rock, and they don't come like Pat often. I'm the man who'll stand black for him.'

And all the many things Mr Diamond had done for and with him came to him, the shared bottle when they were both on the dole, and how Pat came across with the two and a zack when Dolour was a kid with a tooth that needed to come out, and the way when, in the depression, they'd only had one shirt between them, and it hairy as an ape around the collar with the frayed threads.

'I been a worse man than Pat many and many a time,' said Hughie, 'and I swear I'll stick by You more than I've done if only You make him get better.'

The organ mooed out a breve, and out of the dusty rafters came floating Mrs Siciliano's strong, throbbing Neapolitan voice. Mrs Siciliano was the wife of the fruiterer down Coronation Street. Every year she had a new baby, which was awkward for the choir, for it meant that for a good part of every twelve months she was not able to squeeze up the narrow stairs.

'Faith-a of our fathers!' roared Mrs Siciliano, and the congregation rose to its feet with a deafening clatter and joined in the hymn with such tempestuous emotion that you would have thought they had parked their shillelaghs in the porch but a minute before.

'In spite of dungeon, fire and sword!' cried Mumma, looking round her as though daring anyone to deny it. She saw the mouths of her family open and shut unheard, and Hughie, slouched on one leg, singing out of the corner of his mouth in case anyone noticed.

Down the front were the nuns, Sister Theophilus with her straight back, and Sister Beatrix bowed under a little black shawl, and all the little postulants in their funny hats, their clean rosy faces shining with happiness and soap. And there was Jack Siciliano, with his stomach eight inches in front of him, his head back, each candle-flame reflected separately in his glossy scalp, bellowing about it as though they were his fathers they were singing about. Mumma gave him a look.

The warm air enveloped them all. Dolour flowed backwards and forwards on the great gushing waves of sound. It was like a sea beating again and again on a beach. Her pulse was cognisant of the rhythm, but her mind was away, away. She looked at the walls, whose every crack she knew. She looked at the statue of St Patrick with the tiny church in his big capable hand, his thumb curled over the steeple; and the sad dark Byzantine Christ with the long nose and pure gold halo. When she was little Dolour used to crawl round the back of the statues to see how they did their dresses up. She found that inevitably they were like superman, with no buttons, no nuttin's. It was a blow, too, to find that the gentle angels were afflicted with great knobs on the back of the neck to hold their haloes on.

'Oh, dear Lord,' prayed Dolour, 'let me get my examination, and make Sister pleased with me.' Then she put her head down on her hands. 'And please, if I can't be a nun, let somebody like me, the way Charlie likes Roie, only nicer.'

For Dolour spent a great deal of her time praying for a vocation, though not at all sure what she would do with it if she got it.

As they went out into the hot darkness, ducking shyly past one of the missioners who stood at the steps, Dolour looked around for Suse, her friend. Anxiously, bewilderedly, Dolour yearned over Suse Kilroy, impudent child of the dirty little house down Chapper Lane, a house overflowing with unwashed whining children, begotten by a drunken father on a wife so worn down with worry and work that she was as stupid as a cow.

There was Suse, leaning back against the fence, staring at the people as they went past. She didn't care that there were holes in her black stockings, insufficiently blacked-out with ink, or that her greenish gym tunic was ripped at one side.

Dolour thought, 'Gee, ain't she pretty!' Aloud she said, 'Watcher waiting for, Suse?'

Suse was disgusted. 'I thought some of the boys might have been to this turn-out. Suppose they got more sense.'

Dolour giggled. Suse's forthrightness always filled her with shocked amusement. Even when Suse went mincing up the corridor behind Sister Theophilus, mocking her every movement, Dolour, who worshipped the nun, felt an extraordinary impulse to laugh. It was impossible for her to condemn or resent anything Suse did.

'Come on,' said Suse. Dolour hesitated, looking back at her mother, who was gossiping on the steps with Mrs Drummy, of the ham-and-beef.

'Oh, get out. She's old enough to find her own way home,' said Suse impatiently. Dumbly Dolour trotted after her down Coronation Street, which was splashed with the green and livid pink of the picture-show neons, and filled with an odour of hamburgers and terrible coffee and dust but recently laid with a sprinkle of wet tea-leaves.

'There's Ro,' said Dolour, relieved. 'I could ask her.'

'My God!' said Suse. 'What you want to ask her for? You're sixteen, ain't yer?'

'She could tell Mumma I'm with you,' stumbled Dolour weakly.

Suse snorted. Charlie and Roie were looking in a shop window, and she bowled boldly to them. 'Hiya.'

'Hullo, Suse,' Roie said shyly. 'How's your mother?'

Suse was about to say, 'Patching up the old pram for a bit more work,' but she saw that it wouldn't do. She looked quickly at Charlie. Gee, he was a looker, in that dark foreign way. She looked at his mouth and thought it a pity he had to waste his kisses on a crumby little mouse like Ro Darcy. Then she looked down and said in a low voice, 'She's not too well, poor old Mum. I got to stay home a good bit to look after her. You know how it is.'

Roie was a little afraid of Suse as a rule, but now she said eagerly, 'It'll do you good to have a little walk, Suse. Why don't you keep her company, Dolour?'

'Here, buy yourselves an ice-cream,' said Charlie, pulling his hand out of his pocket.

'He's nice, ain't he?' said Suse as they went down the street.

'Who, Charlie?' Already in her mind Dolour was buying the ice-cream, piled in softy rosy whorls in a cone. Her tongue was out to lick it; the saliva came into her mouth at the thought of it.

'Ever caught 'em making love?'

Dolour blushed in astonishment. 'Ah, hold on.'

'Aw, fooey! I'll bet he's a stinger. I wouldn't mind getting up close to him.'

Dolour said angrily, 'Aw, shut your mouth! Don't you ever think of anything else?'

' 'Course not,' said Suse, sidelong. 'Do you?'

'I just been to Benediction,' burst out Dolour. She sought for words to defend Charlie and her sister and herself. She floundered in a morass of indecision, of shyness, and a dreadfully definite feeling that Suse knew much more about everything than she did. She said helplessly, 'It's awful, talking like that about a fellow who's married.'

'Oh hell, what do you think he talks about?'

Dolour gaped. 'Charlie?'

Suse prised her hand open. 'Two bob! Jumpin' joey, we could sneak into the pitchers at half-time with that.'

Dolour badly wanted to ask what it was Charlie talked about, but she didn't get a chance. The swinging doors of the old theatre burst open, and out poured a crowd that seemed to be fleeing from a fire, but was in reality only dying for a smoke. There was a spout of music, the cry of a trampled usher, and interval was on.

'Come on!'

There were the boys, huddling in a group like a ring of mushrooms, dragging on queer cigarettes either rolled funnel-shape and showering the smoker with bits of burning tobacco, or screwed as tightly as a straw and resolutely refusing to burn. Now and then raucous shouts of laughter came from the boys, and one, pushed from behind, shot out of the group and staggered flap-armed on the edge of the gutter. They were dressed in clothes that seemed too roomy, trousers belted tightly about their slender waists, and colourful shirts with starched collars sticking up in wings round their cheeks. They were desperately self-conscious and not at all cognisant of why they were. For this reason they gave cheek to passers-by, waddled after fat ladies, and woo-wooed at girls sailing past in trams.

'Jeepers . . . no!'

But it was too late. Suse was already strolling over towards them. She had pulled in her belt tightly, so that her bosom showed, and opened the neck of her blouse. Dolour followed, shy and excited, wanting to run away, and feeling the pimple on her chin come up like a Matterhorn.

All the boys knew Suse. Out of the corner of her eye, too excited to think about it yet, Dolour saw that they dug each other in the ribs, rolled their eyes, and one hung out his tongue and panted like a dog. Suse didn't seem to mind.

'Hiya, Nipper. Howsit, Joe.'

Behind her glowing russet face, Dolour looked like a cold potato. She was so shy she didn't know which way to look, but she wanted very badly to be there, in this strange and exciting atmosphere, with the theatre blaring music at her, and brilliant light and dark furry shadow everywhere, and the air filled with the exotic odour of hair-oil, minties, and young men. She wanted to say something smart, to draw attention to herself, and she looked timidly round the group to find someone who wasn't staring at Suse. But there was no one.

They all looked furtively at each other, embarrassed and delighted. Conversation did not come easily to any of them. Their verbal range was limited to three or four hundred words, and the spaces were filled up with profanity, gestures, and inarticulate squawks of laughter, derision or protest.

'Well,' said Suse, 'ain't anyone going to ask us inside?'

'We got our own two bob,' said Dolour helpfully.

'Oh, nuts!' glared Suse. 'You know where you can put it'.

Deeply mortified, Dolour stammered, but her words were drowned in the sudden stampede for the theatre as the warning bell shrilled, and the crowd was sucked back into its vortex like dust motes. Dolour was borne along with the crowd, struggling to get beside Suse, and being left behind. She rushed forward and squeezed in amongst the boys, ducking down as they jammed past the doorkeeper in a mass. In a moment she found herself in the back row, with big feet kicking all round her, and before she could take off her hat or pull up her stockings or anything the lights went out, and a great peanut-perfumed darkness surrounded her on all sides.

'Suse! You there, Suse?'

'No, I've gone home,' answered Suse. Dolour craned to see her, wondering what she was cross about. She sat back in the seat as the picture came on the screen, and a large moist hand groped around in her lap and picked up her own grubby, surprised one. Delightful shivers of excitement ran up and down her back. To be holding hands in the pitchers, just like Charlie and Ro!

'Aw, come on, snuggle up,' said a voice in her ear.

'Go and bag yer head,' retorted Dolour haughtily. An arm crawled along the back of the seat and hooked around her shoulder.

'I been chewing musk. Like the smell?' A warm puff of breath gushed into her face. Dolour snorted. She tried to see her companion's face. There was indication of a beaky profile, and long hair marked with the inch-wide channels of a recent combing. He was not the sort of boy she would have picked out for herself, but anyway he was a boy. In a flash she transported herself into the next day, and was telling the other girls all about it, and being mysterious and maddening, like Suse. Awkwardly she tried to kink her thin, rigid shoulders into a compliant shape, and relaxed against the boy's sleeve. It was hard, for she was taller than he, but by humping her back she managed it. It was the very first time she had ever been cuddled.

'I've started,' she thought with relief and joy. 'He must like me, or he wouldn't do it.' Proudly she hoped that Suse had noticed, but all kinds of queer things were going on down Suse's end of the seat. Sometimes the whole row shook as though it were going to topple backwards, and there were the muffled reports of feet striking the back of seats in front, and the unmuffled voices of patrons rearing round and crying, 'Aw, quit it, you big-booted bludgers!'

Suse gave a whispered squeal, and a fusillade of peanuts came out of the dark like a swarm of meteorites and rattled about them. Though the screen showed Chinese refugees pinned beneath toppling walls, not one of the young people in the back row saw a thing. Their world was there, and they enjoyed it, even though they had to pay an admission fee for the privilege of darkness.

Now Suse was giggling, and the seats shook all over again. Dolour's companion was getting restive. He had turned almost completely round, and was squinting at her from a distance of two inches. His breath fluttered on her cheek like a fan, with the most curious melting feeling. Dolour's heart gave a jump. He didn't look like it, but maybe he was the one. The very first boy to fall in love with. She half-turned, and an extraordinary kiss, like a clout from a damp hairbrush, landed on her lips.

'Gee!' said Dolour feebly.

'Come on,' he said.

'Where to!' asked Dolour.

'Is this the time to give with the wisecracks?' he asked. Now his

425

voice was hoarse, suddenly breaking in the middle into a squeak that he hastily suppressed. The audience burst into a roar of laughter. Instinctively she craned to see what she had missed, and at the same moment a hand pulled up her skirt and slipped between her knees. For a moment Dolour was so astounded she did not move, or even think, and the hand, encouraged by her stillness, slid up her leg.

'Stop that!' hissed Dolour. She seized a hairy wrist, but it was too strong for her.

'Cut the capers,' said her cavalier roughly. 'Watcher think you're here for?'

Dolour had no arguments, no psychology, no tactics of any kind. Indignation and resentment flared in her, and without a thought for the hundreds of people there, the usher prowling uneasily in a circle of torchlight, or anything else, she seized a bit of loose flesh on the boy's arm and twisted it as far as it would go. The hand dropped from her leg, and an oath rent the darkness.

'You bitch!'

Dolour kicked out and connected with a shin. Her friend gave a cry of anguish. From somewhere in the theatre came a roar, 'Quit the row, or you'll get thrown out!' But Dolour hardly heard it. Blind with rage and tears she heedlessly trampled on legs in an effort to get out. She fell sprawling between their boots and the back of the next seat.

Now the audience rose almost in a body. The events on the screen went their way unheeded. Two ushers pounded down from the door, and the wandering star on the other aisle dived down from the ceiling and slid rapidly across.

'Watch it!'

There was a stampede from the back seat. Dolour was shoved down again. Somebody stood on her hand. Sobbing with fury and fright she stumbled after them, following the sound of feet running down to the side exit. The light from a torch bobbed at her heels, and a voice yelled for her to stop. Precipitated into the night, she raced down the rutted lane and out into the street.

'Suse! Suse!'

The boys had deserted Suse. Disconsolate, she was leaning up against the empty hamburger shop, where the dirty papers blew and spun in the wind.

'You're a bloody beaut.'

426

She felt in the pockets of her coat and pulled out the bent stub of a cigarette. 'And no matches, either.' Suse sent the stub whirling into the gutter.

'Oh Suse!' sobbed Dolour, suddenly aware of her barked knuckles, the knee out of her stocking, and bruises all over her. The greater pain and shock in her soul were still too unresolved to manifest themselves.

'Ah, you're mad,' said Suse, and before her contempt Dolour shrivelled. 'Go on, get back to your mother and ask her to change your nappies for you.' She turned away.

Piteously Dolour said, 'You don't know what that boy wanted to do.'

'I can guess,' said Suse.

Tears rushed out of Dolour's eyes, and she was dissolved in shame at this, her greatest humiliation, of being sixteen years old, and howling like a baby in public.

'Oh, wake up,' snarled Suse. 'What do you think boys are like?'

'They ain't all like that!' protested Dolour.

'Oh, shut up, you make me sick! Break down and be human like everyone else. You only got one life, ain't you?'

Dolour turned away and ran up the road. She was astounded to see, as she passed the post office, that she had been away barely an hour.

'They ain't all like that!' she said passionately to the clock.

She wanted badly to go home, but she was not ready for that. How could she dissemble before Mumma's eyes? How could she explain the torn stocking and the blood on her hands? She had to go somewhere, to quieten down and think up a story. There was nowhere but the church. But it was already shut up. A dark block of stone it stood there, stocky within its own shadows. Only the tall pointed sanctuary window showed dim red with the light burning behind it. The locked door seemed symbolic to Dolour. She pelted towards it, and stopped short. The confusion and shock in her soul hardened into shame. Before the penetrating gaze that pierced the door and went straight to her heart, she dropped her eyes. It wasn't possible that only an hour ago she was in there, feeling peaceful and chaste, and so sure of everything, singing her head off with the rest. She wiped her mouth hard.

'Dirty stinker,' she said savagely. 'And they aren't all like that, either.'

But she could get no reassurance from the church door, any more than she could get from her thoughts. Where were they all, the young men who wanted and tried to be clean, just as she did? Was Charlie like that? Was Roie like that, in the days before she married, willing to go any way a boy chose to lead her? Was Mumma?

Sick with disgust Dolour flew into her own doorway. Charlie was standing at the kitchen door, rubbing his arms with a towel. She glared at him, daring him to say anything about her disarray.

'Where's Mumma?'

'She went to bed.'

'Oh, well . . .' She turned away. Then she remembered something. She brought out the two shillings. 'Here. I didn't spend it after all.'

He looked at the coin lying in the dirty, blood-streaked palm.

'You can spend it another day, Dolour.'

'I don't want it!' choked Dolour, and she banged it down on the table, and pelted up the stairs to her room.

The thud of her door woke Mr Diamond from an uneasy, nightmare sleep. His mouth had hung open, and was so dry that he could feel the constriction of the tissues within his cheeks. A sickish smell of decay came from his lips, and hung about him like a miasma so that he could smell nothing else. He lay there, not even his eyeballs moving, his skin pulsing to succeeding waves of hot and cold. He was terrified lest the pain should begin again, frightened to move a muscle, willing to lie like a log for ever rather than be subjected to that unutterable torment again.

The little sounds of the night, the girl sniffling in the bedroom next to him, the whimper of Motty in her sleep, the rattle of a garbage-tin lid knocked by a prowling cat, the whine of Lick Jimmy's loose clothesline, passed over his head. They were part of his consciousness and that was all.

Into the orbit of his sight reared his stomach, huge and unsightly. It did not have the firm rotundity of Jacky Siciliano's, a healthy and hearty stomach. It was a flabby bag, obscene and meaningless.

Lying there, in the quiet and objective tranquillity that comes between bouts of terrible pain, Mr Diamond knew what he must do.

Three

Once he had made up his mind, things became easier for Mr Diamond. He was a brave man; he was not afraid of death as he was of disgracing his manhood, of becoming a shrieking, gasping wreck of a human being whose every breath was an unbearable torture. Mr Diamond wanted to finish his life with dignity.

He waited till Saturday, when they were all at mass, except Hughie, who, exhausted by Friday night's devotions, privily known to the faithful as the holy-hour-and-a-half, was snoring his head off downstairs. Mr Diamond had washed all his clothes, and folded them in a neat pile. He stripped his bed and tidied up the blankets. He did not have many belongings, and anything worth money had long ago been pawned. His pension book and his butter and tea coupons he put on the table, together with his mother's wedding lines and a postcard from Belfast bearing the news of his father's death forty years before.

Mr Diamond had always thought that a great sadness must come to a suicide when he was making preparations for the act, but he felt nothing but a little excitement as one might feel upon entering a railway station before a journey. Yet he found himself looking for little jobs to do so that he might be delayed. He cleaned his kettle and saucepan, and put all the chipped cups and plates in a row. He looked about, and there was nothing else to do.

Mr Diamond drew a deep breath. Well, no use dilly-dallying. Soon they would all be home from church, and it would be too late. He looked out of the window, at the sun gilt on the top fans of the phoenix palm, and Lick Jimmy's chimney-pot trimmed with a row of sooty bobbles that were sparrows warming their toes in the smoke. It had been a wonderful world, and there had been happiness in it, though not much of it had come to him. He thought, 'It's for the best, and I've been square, in me own way. God won't be minding it, if He's the man I've always thought Him.'

He had already stuffed up the crack under the door, and made the window air-tight with paper. The gas-ring was on the floor, stretched to the limit of its greasy reptilian pipe, and Mr Diamond lay down beside it and put a blanket over his head. As he stretched out, the thing in his stomach seemed to shift in its net of connective tissues, and fell back with a heavy dragging sensation. Almost at once the pain began, sweeping into the innermost recesses of his body and brain. The gas came hissing down the pipe, stinging his nose. Greedily Mr Diamond sucked it in, feeling the membranes at the back of his throat swell and grow taut. It seemed to take a long time for anything to happen. He rolled closer to the jets and inhaled fiercely, but with a mournful sigh the supply of gas ceased.

Mr Diamond cursed bitterly. Black specks were swimming before his eyes. He seized the gas-ring and thumped it, but only a gasp or two came out. Only too well he knew what had happened. He was always running short of gas in the middle of cooking, for he had never accustomed himself to the use of the penny-in-the-slot meter. Now, with a desperate urgency, he hurried over to the table and scrabbled amongst the coins there. No pennies! He would have to go downstairs and borrow one from Hugh. Mr Diamond almost laughed. It was a joke that Hughie would appreciate. He had a temptation to call the whole thing off and go and tell Hugh all about it.

Like the galloping of far-way horses, the pain increased in intensity, and with a sudden savage desperation Mr Diamond knew that he must not be cheated. He began to tear one of Mumma's greyish sheets into long strips.

Downstairs Hughie snuffled his way out of sleep. It was dreadfully hot in the little bedroom, and sweat lay in tiny pools around his collar-bone and in the creases across his stomach. He opened his eyes and looked dizzily into the shimmering air. There was a loud crash upstairs. Hughie was too fatigued even to swear. He lay glaring at the ceiling.

Then a muffled knocking began, a regular tapping on the wall, or perhaps the floor, so strange and unusual a sound that Hughie sat bolt upright, though he felt he had left the top of his head on the pillow. Maybe Patrick had taken a bad turn, and was banging on the floor for help. Without another thought he leaped out of bed and up the stairs.

'Everything all right, Pat?'

The door was locked; the tapping went on, and Hughie, standing on the landing in his patched underpants, felt cold with the strangeness of it.

430

'Patrick?'

Now the tapping was slower, and Hughie, drawing off to the limit of the landing, crashed against the door and tore the flimsy bolt from its socket. A wave of gas-tainted air flowed out to meet him.

It was for a long frozen moment that he stood there and watched Mr Diamond swinging from the old gaslight jet, his toes tapping against the wall. Absolute horror transfixed him. He had no idea what to do. Chittering, he rushed to Mr Diamond, lifting his body and holding the weight on his own shoulder.

'Christ . . .'

Mr Diamond was a heavy man, and Hughie buckled beneath the strain. He jerked the fallen chair towards him with one foot, 'Help! Hey! Help!' forgetting that the house was empty.

'I'm gonna be too late.'

There was no other way. He had to let Mr Diamond's swollen body dangle while he dashed for the knife on the table. For endless seconds he sawed at the sheet, cursing and praying in one breath.

He dragged his friend to the bed. Mr Diamond was not far gone at all. The dark grape colour of his face faded, and round his eyes the puffiness subsided into yellow waxy circles. Blood dribbled down his chin from his bitten tongue.

Hughie watched him, distressed beyond measure. The pity of it all ate into his soul. He wanted to bawl like Motty over a stubbed toe. Mr Diamond opened his glazed eyes and said in a croak, 'Why don't you mind your own bloody business?'

Those were the last words he spoke in that house. The doctor came, and in a little while the ambulance, and Mr Diamond was carried down the rickety stairs to the dark musky hall. Hughie was waiting at the door.

He said, 'You'll be back again before you know where you are, and me and you'll split a bottle of red ned.'

But Mr Diamond only turned his face away.

The whole house was silent with the shock. Roie wept. 'We should have got the doctor before, no matter what he said, poor old man.'

Mumma picked up Motty and stood quietly, as though protecting her. In her heart she was saying Hail Marys for Mr Diamond, and lashing herself for all the times she'd been rude to him and said hard things in return for those he'd said to her.

'For even though he did call me a pope-worshipper, I might have turned the other cheek,' she mourned, 'and him all the time with the pain on him perhaps, and it enough to get anyone's rag out.'

It was only a week or two afterwards that they heard he was dead. Though he had been expecting it, Hughie felt as though a great weight had been lowered upon him. On the top of his head and across his shoulders he felt it. It pressed his feet into the ground and made it a labour even to open his mouth.

'Hughie,' pleaded Mumma, 'come down to mass this morning and say a prayer for his poor soul.'

But Hughie only looked at her with sunken, despairing eyes, and went down to the pub and stayed there until he was thrown out at lock-up time.

So Mumma, who had been Mr Diamond's enemy, put on her old hat and went to the funeral, the only one to follow the coffin. She stood at the graveside and waited till all the perfunctory black-clad men had gone, then she said her rosary furtively, for she didn't want Mr Diamond to know, realizing that he would bitterly resent any popish prayers being said for him. And after she had finished she stood there staring at the raw clay mound and the coarse, white-striped grass which blew over the edge of it. She wanted to say something; something in her chest was struggling to be expressed, but all she could say was, 'I'll keep your mother's marriage lines, Mr Diamond. I'll put them away amongst me things, and they'll be safe.'

Four

Charlie came home early one afternoon, and there was Mumma sitting at the kitchen table with half-shelled peas all round her, and Motty sitting at her feet eating the pods with the rapidity and precision of a machine. Mumma had her glasses on. She had bought them at Woolworth's long before, and when one of the ear-handles fell off she had replaced it by a handy piece of wire that had to be wound round her ear every time she put them on.

She looked up at Charlie with the gaze of a condemned woman.

'Oh, Charlie,' she said, 'it'll drive a chill through your stomach to read what's written here in the paper.'

Mumma loved murders. She read them with shrinking horror and prawn-eyed eagerness, her lips moving in Hail Marys for the deceased as she did so, and interrupting herself with little cries of, 'Jesus, Mary, and Joseph, he cut off his own mother's head!' or, 'God help her, the poor young thing left with four children, and their father getting hung for sure.'

So Charlie said, 'Is it a murder again, Mumma?'

'It's murder all right,' said Mumma gloomily. 'They're going to knock us down, Charlie boy, and make flats of us.' And with this remarkable statement Mumma got up and stood on Motty, who yelled blue blazes.

Mumma took no notice, she was so distraught. 'It's them parlimenticians!' she cried. 'I'd like to see them tossed out of house and home and the very places where their mothers and fathers were brought up turned into factories and communist laundries and the dear knows what! Stop yer ballyhooly! You're making such a noise I can't here me ears!'

She gathered Motty up and marched off with her to the stove, where she held the child with one arm while she gathered up the washing that was draped round Puffing Billy's meagre black flue.

'Come and help me hang out the airing, Motty love, and I'm sorry I stood on yer little foot with me big clumsy hoof.' At the door she turned. 'I won't go,' she fired back at Charlie. 'They'll have to haul me out with ropes first.'

433

Charlie sat down quietly and read the paper. He was tired and dirty, his hands grained with ink, for he was a printer's machinist. There was a soft step, and Roie's hands came down over his throat and dived into the front of his shirt.

'Like me a bit, Charlie?' A kiss landed at the corner of his mouth.

'No, you're a little stinker. Shut up, look what's in the paper.'

Together they read the page. A little chill touched Roie's heart.

'It's just a lot of rubbish, isn't it? I mean, fancy pulling Surry Hills down!'

'They've been talking about it a long time.' His black nail traced the map. 'Coronation Street, Cornwall Street, Plymouth Street, Murphy . . . and all those little alleys running down to Elizabeth.'

Roie gazed at him, disbelieving. 'But people live there. Where would they go? It's our home. They can't go pulling people's homes down. What about those that own their own places, like Mr Drummy's ham-and-beef?'

'Ah, you don't want to get all boxed up about it.' He rose and stretched. 'Nothing'll happen for twenty years. You know what councils are.'

But in the laundry he bent over the tub with the soap in his hand, motionless. So they were going to pull the old place down. Charlie could almost hear the squeaks and groans in the ponderous machinery of city-building, as though it were tuning up for the job. No more web of dark alleys lined with hostile ochre walls? No more lurching lanes of corrugated iron fences, each with a little box of a peak-roofed lavatory peering over? No more tall tenements with lacy iron balconies and strings of grey washing flying like flag day?

Though home was to Charlie where his wife was, he often thought of green places, and a yard where he could go out in the cool of the day and sit and think, or play with Motty, and not have to conduct yelled conversations with a Chinese fruiterer on one side or an iceman on the other.

He scrubbed the ink out of his nails, slowly, thinking.

As the paper boy whooped his way up Plymouth Street, one house after another broke into a loud confusion of comment, and before very long heads were nodding over back fences. Soon the story was in Coronation Street, too, and Mrs Siciliano screamed and beat her breast, for she and her husband had recently put a deposit on the fruit shop, and they feared that they would lose everything.

'So they're going to put up dirty big flats,' said Mrs Campion, next door to the Darcys. 'Won't that be nice for them that live on the top floor, up and down all day. And me with me various veins that bad I can hardly lift a hoof without fear of them blowing out on me.'

'Fancy Roie pulling the pram up to the top floor!' mourned Mumma.

Mrs Campion shrieked like a cockatoo. 'Oh, no, dearie! We'll all have lifts!' She roared with laughter. 'Can't you imagine the kids hacking the ropes through, and the louts riding up and down and leaving the doors open? Oh, it's a scandal, that's what it is.'

It was all right to be funny about it, but in their hearts the people were uneasy. What did they want flats for, all herded together like rabbits with no privacy for a bit of a fight or anything? Most of the tenement people had roomers in their balcony rooms or attics, but roomers were like members of the family. It wasn't the same as sharing a dirty big building with forty other families.

'It's the washing that'll worry me,' confided Mumma. 'They say there'll be a big laundry downstairs, and we'll each have a day.'

'Maybe we'll boil all our things up together,' shrieked Mrs Campion, beating her red arms on the top of the fence in her mirth. 'I can jest see me bloomers on the line alongside Lick Jimmy's flourbag underpants.'

'Go on, yer scout!' Mumma blushed as she waddled indoors.

Roie was sweeping the crooked stairs, the broom handle almost as tall as herself. Mumma looked at the pale face of her daughter, and her slender body, and all at once she forgot about the housing problem, and remembered something she had been meaning to ask for a long time.

'I was wondering why you don't have more children,' she said, and as soon as the words were out felt upset, for they sounded angry. Roie brushed carefully at dirt that wasn't there.

'You don't need to sound like that, anyway.'

'I just thought Charlie might have made you use something,' blurted out Mumma. Roie flew into such a fury her little body shook like a bough.

'You've got a nerve, Mumma! You've always had it in for him, as though he wasn't good enough for us or something. Pity you couldn't have picked out a husband for yourself as good as he is.'

'I'm only warning you for your own good,' pleaded Mumma,

swallowing her indignation. 'Because if you're doing anything to keep the children back . . .'

'Well, I ain't!' cried Roie tearfully. 'You can talk, anyway; there was nearly four years between Thady and Dolour.'

'There was something the matter with me inside,' retorted Mumma defensively. She had forgotten all about her long wait for her children.

'Well, maybe there's something the matter with mine, too,' said Roie triumphantly. She whisked inside her door.

'Then you ought to go to the doctor about it and not go worrying people with the wrong ideas,' said Mumma angrily, after her. Roie went into her little room and sat on the bed. She giggled to herself, for she knew that Mumma suspected she was pregnant again and was using this method of getting the truth out of her.

'And I am, I am,' said Roie to herself. She could hardly believe it, it had been so long. She was twenty-four, and felt as though she had been a woman for a century. The summer of her fertility was all about her, warm and glowing. She was married to a man whom she loved in the true way so rarely comprehended by the civilized. He was breadwinner, protector, lover and beloved, and, more than that, he was the giver of children, the fertilizer of what would be without him a fallow field. Her pride in and adoration of her lover sprang out of her inarticulate recognition of him as her only bridge to fleshly immortality in her children. When he possessed her she worshipped him not only as the delighter of her body, but as the miracle-worker, the dear, familiar thaumaturgist in whose arms the new soul flashed into human clay.

Roie did not think these things; she felt them. The good simplicities of life were hers, and it would have been illogical to feel otherwise about Charlie.

The next day Dolour came bursting into the house at lunchtime. 'Oh, Mumma, come quick! There's a newspaper man down the road, and he's taking Delie Stock's picture.'

Everywhere people were galloping down to Little Ryan Street. Most didn't know what it was all about, hoping that it was a good brawl or a fire. There was already a crowd in the lane outside the sly-grog shop. Women stood there, arms folded over their aproned chests, slippered feet turned outwards at right-angles, looking shyly at the young photographer with the hat hooked on the back of his head, and the elderly, disillusioned-faced reporter who accompanied him. A couple of carters, who had hopped off their trucks to see what was happening, were there, the leather carrier's pad on their naked shoulders, great beefy hands resting on invisible hipbones five inches below the natural ones.

'Oh, glory!' cried Mumma to Mrs Siciliano, who was there, a potato still in her hand, for she had run out while serving a customer. 'And is it all over?'

'She's changing her dress,' whispered Mrs Siciliano, spitting contemptuously and then looking round to see if anyone noticed, for she was a little afraid of Delie Stock.

And there she was, the worst woman in Surry Hills, hastily dressed up in a black dress that had been a model in the shop and now looked like a sequined bag. Delie's hair had been set and lacquered about three weeks before, and now it was like a doll's wig, growing in thick clumps, some in waves and some in a fuzz, all stiff and greyish with cracked lacquer.

'I ain't changed me slippers,' she called, beaming at the photographer. 'But you won't want me feet when you can get me pan.'

A ripple of approving amusement ran over the crowd. 'Ain't she a one!'

'Been up before the beak more times than you could count.'

'She's got a good heart, that's what I say. More than you can say for some of the toffs.'

Nearby a woman began a spirited account of the flourishing brothel, one of Delie Stock's chain, which carried on business near her home, and in a fluster Mumma drew Dolour aside.

'Now, Mrs Stock,' said the reporter, 'you're a well-known citizen of Surry Hills.'

'I'll say,' chuckled Delie. 'Had me dial more times in the paper than I can remember. Got a scrapbook that'd stiffen out an elephant.'

'Well, we'd like a statement from you about the proposed resumption of Surry Hills by the – '

'Stinking mongrels!' said Delie strongly.

Somebody called out. 'What about them electric stoves they're going to give us, but?'

'Can't put yer head in an electric oven when you've had enough of life!' called somebody else.

Delie put her hands on her hips. 'That's what I mean,' she said. 'Nobody asked us if we want to be chucked out of our houses. We

437

got along all right for years here. I spent a lot of money on my place, too. Only last week I got the kitchen kalsomined a lovely blue, real pretty and only a bit streaky round the sink. Now the bloody Council comes and wants to put up flats with private fishponds or something we don't want. Where'm I going to go, that's what I want to know. Where are they going to put us while they put up these bloody beehives?'

'The Potts Point people are going to take us in,' jibed someone.

'Yes, we're all going up to the Point,' said Delie, who wouldn't have lived there amongst the gardens and the blue-bayed streets and the dignified houses if you'd paid her. For what was there in Potts Point that you couldn't find in Surry Hills, except enough quiet to give a woman the splitting headaches?

'This is where we belong,' said Delie definitely. Thus, while the rest of Sydney was reading the papers and thinking how nice it would be for the poor Surry Hills people to live in decent places at last, the poor Surry Hills people were fuming, and pitching all that was within and without the City Council to the seventeen devils.

That night as Roie sat brushing her hair before the spotted mirror that reflected the room as a dim cavern, Charlie leaned out the window. Now and then fountains of red sparks shot up out of Lick Jimmy's backyard, where he was letting off crackers in some solitary celebration, and from somewhere came the bad breath of a garbage can with no lid.

'What are you doing, Charlie?'

'Just thinking.'

She went and leaned her head on his arm, listening to the pulse of the blood in his arteries. She didn't know how to begin. All at once a gush of love in her heart made her skin tingle and tears fill her eyes.

'Oh Charlie!'

'What, darling?'

'I dunno. It's just . . . I'm going to have another baby.' She hid her face against his shirt and laughed, not being able to express in words her joy and excitement. 'You're not sorry?'

'No. I'm glad. I've been praying for it for months.'

'Me too. All the mission.'

They laughed together.

'Do you reckon prayer did it?'

'I helped a bit,' said Charlie. He held her close. 'It's funny to think of – all that, all over again.'

438

'Yes.' She sat down on the bed, longing with a vast longing for the months when she would feel the child tremble within her, and the knowledge that life was there.

'Mumma will be glad. I bet she's been putting in her spoke with the saints.'

'Embarrassing the tripe outa them.'

They rolled about the bed in their mirth, until Charlie stopped his wife's laughter with his kisses. Next door Dolour heard the laughter, and the silence, and blocked her mind quickly to the thoughts that flowed into it. She put her head under the bed-clothes, thinking, 'I hate them! I hate them!' savagely and falsely, for all she hated was her own ignorance and jealousy. Then she hopped out of bed and said a prayer for her sister to make up for her thoughts, of which she was bitterly ashamed.

Mumma was complacent about the baby, and only a piercing glare from Roie prevented her from saying that she'd known all about it. Hughie was embarrassed. He could never get used to the fact that now his daughter knew almost as much about men as he did.

'I thought we'd call it Brandan, if it's a boy,' said Roie shyly. Mumma nodded.

'It's a good Irish name, and the church and everything.'

None of them thought it was at all strange to call a child after a church, nor to thank God that their parish was not that of the Holy Sepulchre.

'You can't go putting the name of demon drink on a child,' bellowed Hughie. 'They'll call him Brandy for short.'

Roie blushed crossly, for she hadn't thought of that, and Hughie burst into song, 'Mr Booze, Mr Booze, you've got me where you want me, Mr Booze!'

They slammed the door on him, but they could still hear him proclaiming, 'Think of all the huzz-puns you have stolen, Mr Booze!'

'Never you mind, love,' comforted Mumma. 'It'll be real nice to see the pram out in the yard once more.'

'Charlie,' confessed Roie, 'he wants us to find a place somewhere else to live.' She saw the distress creeping pinkly up her mother's neck and cried, 'If they're going to pull down Surry Hills we'll all be out on our necks, and well, Charlie wants us to start looking now.'

Mumma wanted to say a lot of things, that she'd lived most of her life in Plymouth Street, and Dolour had been born there, and

Thady gone from her sight. A tumult of thoughts rushed through her mind, Mr Diamond coming down and scrapping with everyone on St Pat's day, and Grandma pigeon-toeing about and taking on the world right and left, and in the end dying in there on the old stretcher with a candle beside her. All these things came up in her mind and she wanted to say, 'This is your place, and no man's got the right to take you away from it and from me, because no matter what he is to you he's never a part of you, like me.' But instead she said dully, 'It'll be nice for Motty to have somewhere clean to play, and the children that cheeky about here.'

The joy of the new baby was all spoiled, and she went out to the kitchen and kicked Puffing Billy in the firebox and poked a block of wood down to his cherry-red tonsils. All at once sharp tears sprang into her eyes, so she leaned over Puffing Billy and coughed at his smoke, just in case Roie should come in.

Now Roie had to screw up her courage to go to the hospital and be examined. Mumma, who had never been to a doctor in her life, and had no idea what went on in hospitals, could not understand her reluctance. And she was ashamed to explain it to Charlie.

'They're only doctors,' he said. 'You're just another woman having a baby to them.'

'Yes,' stammered Roie. 'But I'm not just another woman to me.'

Like her ancestors who had preferred to die of consumption rather than have some stranger listen in to the protests of their bubbling chests, Roie shrank from having the dark, innermost secrets of her body probed, and written about on index cards. But at last she went to the great brick building, into the outpatients' department, where the merry, black-stockinged nurses flitted to and fro, and the air was full of the tingling tang of antiseptic. Almost at once the feeling of being lost and completely at sea descended upon her. There were so many strangers to meet, so many cards to sign here or there, so many details simple in themselves to attend to that she recovered the feeling she had had at school, of being dumb and stupid, slow to catch the meaning of things, desperate lest she should miss some important word.

'It's not like that, really,' she assured herself as she took off her clothes and put on the long calico wrapper like a zombie's. From the cubicle next to hers came a loud crash of glass, and a voice was raised in a lament, 'My Gawd, I've dropped me speciment!'

She sat and waited for a long time on the hard wooden forms, amongst the rows and rows of shapeless women. Some had drawn yellow faces, and others had blossomed with a ripe mellow beauty. Roie looked at their shining, ill-kempt hair, the mysterious glow in their skins. 'I'm like that, too,' she thought, and wondered. And a little shiver ran over her as she thought of all the others in that room, the mysterious hidden ones in whose hands the future was already held tight. Over and over it happened, a million, million times, and yet its wonder remained.

At last she was in the examination ward. As she clambered upon the high white table, sickness and terror nearly overcame her.

'Oh, God, I wish I didn't have to do this.'

For who could express the delicacy that filled her mind about this? The shyness and modesty that desired to keep her body for those who possessed it, her husband and children?

'He's only a doctor,' she kept saying to herself. 'I'm nothing to him. I'm only a card with me name and weight and age on it.'

Now he was here, the kind dark-eyed man with the gentle hands and crackling white coat. Roie tried to smile at him. It wasn't his fault she felt like this. It would be all over, very soon. She closed her eyes, bracing herself as she felt the cold air on her body.

Then she heard another voice, and another. To her appalled horror she saw five or six young men, hardly older than Dolour, dressed up in white coats, and crowding in behind the screen round the bed. They were medical students. She half-raised herself up, but the doctor gently put her down again.

'They – what are they doing here?' she whispered.

'They're going to be doctors some day,' said the doctor. 'They have to learn.'

'Yes,' whispered Roie. She kept her eyes closed tight, hearing what the doctor said to the students with a shame too great to bear. She felt no resentment or anger, nothing but terrible humiliation, of uncleanness and violation of her innermost womanhood. Her soul crept into a dark corner.

'I'll never feel the same again. Whenever Charlie touches me I'll think of this.'

The cubicle was empty. She got down from the table, putting on her shoes and picking up her clothes with frozen hands. Her teeth were chattering.

Then a hearty indignant voice spoke from the next cubicle. ' 'Ere!'

441

She heard the end of the doctor's reply, '. . . this is the only way they can learn.'

'Oh, it is, is it! Well, they ain't gonna learn on me! Why, I've got a son as old as that feller there, and if I thought he was going around in a fancy white coat staring at naked women and calling it learning he'd get what for!' Look at the face on 'im! Eyes sticking out like boiled onions! Yes, you oughta go red. The nerve! Give me me boots and lemme out of here!'

Roie clung fast to the table. She heard the doctor explaining that it was public hospital experience that taught these young students most.

'It's for the good of all women, you know.'

'Yeah? Then why not use all women for guinea-pigs, eh? Why only public hospitals? Do you ever go into a posh private hospital out Vaucluse or Point Piper with your tribe of pop-eyed young louts and let them have a squint at one of them pampered poodles of women? Nice stinkeroo if you did, eh? But us, we gotta come to public hospitals because we're poor, and so we can be pushed around without so much as a kiss-me-foot. We can't kick. Get outa me bloody way before I let you have it in the eye!'

Roie escaped. There was nowhere to go to hide her shock and shame except in the church, and there she hid her eyes even from God.

'They took Your clothes off and hung You up where everybody could see You, but it's worse for a girl. Let me forget, it, soon. Please let me forget it.'

She went out from that dusty shadowy place into Coronation Street, where the light beat glassily down and the heat shimmered from the asphalt. She looked furtively at the women, laden with shopping baskets, with screaming children, always carrying or pushing or dragging something. These citadels of strength, of endurance, of deep undemonstrative dignity were deemed by authority to have no dignity at all. No one would dream of subjecting a rich man's wife to clinical rape, but the poor man's wife was different.

Five

Mumma could never think what to have for tea. In Australia the meals of the ordinary people are not varied. Though occasionally a woman turns out to be a God-inspired cook, usually the housewife serves meals as though they were on a travelling belt. No sooner has the chop disappeared over the horizon than the stew looms up, and always both are accompanied by peas or beans or cabbage, and potatoes, just as the boiled custard keeps company with the packet jelly.

Every afternoon Mumma sat down with a stub of pencil and worked out what she could buy on the little money daily allotted to her. Even before she started, her forehead wrinkled into a preparatory frown, and a dim, hopeless feeling assailed her.

'What'll we have?'

Roie leaned her chin on the handle of the mop. She considered. 'I dunno. Maybe we could get some of them minces from the butcher's.'

Mumma scoffed. 'It'd be all right if you knew what he puts into them. Catsmeat most likely. And I'll bet he rolls them in ground glass.'

Roie mopped round the chairs adeptly. 'I know. Let's have sausages.'

The tension in Mumma's housewifely heart disappeared. Good old snags. They were always there to be fallen back on. She wrote down the things she wanted, and yelled up the stairs for Dolour to go out and get them.

Dolour drifted out into the butter-yellow sunshine. It was so hot that the tiny imperceptible gush of sweat to the skin was like a cool shock. Dolour held her hair like a horse's tail and lifted it to the top of her head, to let the air blow about her neck. Motty was swinging on the gate.

'Hullo, fishface,' she chirped.

'Hullo, pieface,' returned Dolour unsmilingly. She blew the child's nose, pulled up her grubby grey pants, pushed a strand of hair out of her eye, and returned her to the gate. She drifted

443

onwards till she came to the sausage shop. In the midst of a hundred shops with grease-ringed doorways, floors scrubbed down to the splinters, and high, pallid ceilings, the sausage shop stood out like a glittering box of glass. Its window bulged in a water-clear bow, boasting the rosy coils of tomato sausages, the puffy white pork, the suet-blotched Yorkshire, the giant grey horseshoes of the liverwurst, all shuddering away from the unsocial garlic. Dolour stood there for a long time, breathing in the wonderful smells and making a large misty patch on the glass. Then she passed in and bought two pounds of beef sausages, and a solitary frankfurt, which she chewed on the way home. She arrived at the gate with a pink ring from the skin surrounding her mouth. Mumma was there, her face pale.

'Where's Motty?' she called. 'Ain't she with you?'

'She was on the gate when I left,' replied Dolour, a qualm entering her soul.

'You musta left it open!' accused Mumma. 'She's got out, and there's all that traffic. Roie's gone haring off up the street looking for her. You better go that way, Dolour.'

She snatched the sausages from Dolour's grasp. Already the roar of the five o'clock traffic was funnelling deep and hollow into Plymouth Street. Dolour and Mumma stared at each other wordlessly, the same dread in each remembering heart. Then Dolour darted up the road.

'I didn't leave the gate open. I didn't!' Already into her mind rushed the words of excuse. Her swift imagination already had the child run over, enticed away by a stranger, found dead in a culvert, and before she had gone twenty steps she was in her mind confronting Roie and Charlie with fluent denials of her complicity. 'It musta come open by itself.'

The children of that district, accustomed from earliest days to play in the street, were independent and self-sufficient. But Motty was not allowed to play in the street. The wilderness peopled by the wheels and fenders of trucks was something she did not know. But she was a friendly child, whom some prowling pervert would find easier than usual to entice off the gate. Dolour began to breathe fast. She questioned the children playing in the road, women leaning over gates. She went farther and knocked on doors, thinking that the child had slipped through a broken fence to look at a lovebird in a cage, or play with a puppy. But Motty was nowhere at all.

The shadows crept longwise over the pavement, and mothers began to call their children in to tea. She wanted to run back to the house to see if Motty had been found, but she felt a mournful certainty that she had not. Almost desperately she ran across the road, dodging the cars that followed nose to tail, honking impatience.

In the meantime Charlie had come home, grimy and tired. He met Roie, running along on her swollen feet, flaring-eyed panic on her face. She stared at him a moment, almost unrecognizing, then a croak came out of her throat.

'Motty's gone, Charlie. She wandered off somewhere, a whole hour ago.' A little whimper came out of her, and her face collapsed like a child's.

'You oughtn't to be running about,' he said roughly.

'Oh, my baby, my baby!' she sobbed. Charlie took out his handkerchief and wiped her face. He felt solid and strong and he smelt familiar.

'If anything's happened to her I'll die!'

'Nothing's happened to that rapscallion,' he soothed. He walked her home, slowing her uncertain, hurrying steps, trying to be calm and unperturbed, though he was far from feeling it.

'Why, when we get inside, she'll probably be right there at the table, with Mumma feeding her bits of cake, and her spitting it out like a machine gun.'

Roie tried to laugh. They went into the kitchen, where Mumma was poking the sizzling sausages with her long fork and wiping her red eyes with the back of the other hand. She looked up eagerly as Charlie and Dolour came in, then turned away and said, 'God wouldn't let anything happen to her, darling. Not after Thady. You lie down and let Charlie take care of it.'

Meanwhile Motty had gone a long way. As soon as Dolour had disappeared she had ventured out into the street, a very small Christopher Columbus with a dirty pinny and one leg of her pants already falling down. For a moment she had ideas of following Dolour, then a lizard flashed up the fence and halted at eye-level, its heart beating perceptibly in its brown silk breast.

'Wizard,' said Motty, grabbing at it. It was gone in a wink. She indulged in the unique pastime of looking through the wrong side of her fence. She saw the rank overgrown grass, the door gaping wide, and the little yellow square of window at the end of the hall. She went right round the fence this way, looking through each crack.

So she came to Lick Jimmy's shop. She stood on tiptoe and ate

445

some of the peeling green paint that ran round the window. She wandered into the shop, eyeing the cliff-high counter, and sniffing deep breaths of the rich fruity air. Lick Jimmy was out the back, doing something domestic, so she picked up a fallen pea-pod and began to eat it. Lick Jimmy's cat sat up, bounded lightly to the floor and walked outside. Motty followed it down the alley. The cobblestones were hot to her small feet. In the niches beside tumbledown back gates grew tall thistles, which she tried to pick.

'Blast,' remarked Motty, sucking her finger.

From a low point of view, the alley was peculiarly enchanted. The high tin fences were mottled with patches of rich rust, and here and there an unbeatable larrikin creeper had sprouted up between the cobbles and plucked with all its frail fingers at the tin. Here snails lived, too. Motty picked off four systematically, and hammered them on the stones until they gave off a green indignant froth.

'Pooey,' commented Motty. She wiped her hands on the back of her bloomers and went on. After a while she met a drunk, a faltering benevolent fellow who had crept into the alley on an urgent mission. Motty stood behind him and watched gravely as the puddle crept across the stones. He gave a long sigh, and suddenly burst into song.

'You're a dirty man,' said Motty with quiet firmness. The drunk jumped and whirled round in a wavering arc, during which his feet remained on the same spot of ground. The dismayed look changed to a flush of relief. He doddered forward, carefully pulled up the knees of his indescribable trousers, and hunkered before Motty. The little girl looked unblinkingly into his rheumy eyes.

'You sweet little bastard, where did you come from?' He stretched out a hand and stroked her jetty hair. 'Ah, I wish I had a li'l girl like you. Wish I had, honest. You know what, ducks?'

'You talk funny,' said Motty.

He disregarded the interruption. 'You know what? If my wife would have kids 'stead of going to work when there ain't no need, I wouldn't waste me time getting drunk. I'd be takin' my beaut little kid to the soo to see the tigers and the hipposamus. Honest truth. Here, li'l beaut.'

He stood up and endeavoured to wangle his hand into a pocket that had grown extraordinarily tight. He propped himself against the fence and fought to get his hand over the curve of his hip. Motty watched with great interest. Now and then he nodded gravely to her as though to assure her that all was going well. Finally he brought out a banknote. He put it close to his eyes to see what it was, nodded, and beckoned Motty closer.

'You smell, too,' she said.

He looked muzzily at her dress, winked, and tied the note into the corner of his aged handkerchief. He wadded it into a ball and tucked it down the front of her dress, where it was securely held by the semi-circular curve of her stomach.

'There's one thing I got to tell you,' he cautioned, wagging an erratic finger. 'You muzzn't ever talk to strange men. Plenty of polecats about. And don't you never take money from them neither. Uncle Doug knows. Uncle Doug knows his onionses.'

He waggled his hand from the wrist. 'Goo'bye now.' Motty waved hers casually and went on. She looked back, and saw him feather-stitching away in the opposite direction.

The alley was a long one, and all sorts of queer little runnels of back lanes and pathways debouched there between the broken fences. Now, as the horizon darkened, though the sky was still bright, a figure detached itself from a fence and moved after Motty, keeping close to the long shadows, and placing its polished toes carefully on the stones. A narrow-ridged nose jutted out under the turned-down hat-brim, and a narrow, reddish chin jutted out over the butterfly bow of a pale blue tie. These were the only signs of elegance about the figure; its tight blue suit was stained and frayed about the cuffs, and its fingernails were long and blackish. It kept its eyes on Motty with an extraordinary expression of eagerness and excitement, which made its pale eyes water and its mouth move as though rehearsing enticing words. It dug in its pocket and fetched out a shilling, and then, as Motty reached the end of the alley, it darted forward and hovered a yard or two away, looking at the child's fat legs and arms.

Motty looked out into the street. A moving forest of legs hurried past, pillars in trousers, hairy bare legs with traces of yellowish leg make-up, and fleet brown ones that Motty observed with most interest. She heard the staccato clang of tram bells, and the plaintive Indian love-calls of car horns. She wondered whether she should join the throng, then she became aware that an eye was watching her through a seam in the fence.

'Pieface,' said Motty tentatively.

'Garn,' retorted the Eye hospitably. It was replaced by a stubby

447

black toe that protruded through the hole while its owner clambered to the top of the fence. A voice sounded from on high.

'Gah, what are you hanging around for, Burgess? Clear out before I tell Ma.'

Motty looked around in surprise, and saw a dark figure melt into the shadows, creeping along the fence away from them. Then she looked up and saw a coal-black face looking down at her. She noticed the blackness, but did not think it interesting enough for comment.

'That dirty old cow, always making up to kids. Only been out of boob a few weeks,' explained the face carelessly. A hand appeared, holding an ice-cream, which was systematically licked into a tall triangle.

'I'm free,' announced Motty.

'I'm a nig,' said the face. ' 'Ave a lick?'

Motty beamed like the sun. The little boy shinnied down from the fence, and popped through the gate. He was about seven, tall and thin, with his long skinny arms sticking out of a spotless but ragged white shirt.

'You can finish it,' he said magnanimously. 'I've had three today.' He turned and stared at the slinking figure, which was still hovering there, only a few yards from them.

'Just look at that dirty ole secko, will you?' he said disgustedly, and scooping up a stone he ran after it, yelling, 'Merv, Merv, the rotten old perv,' throwing stones at its feet until it skipped into invisibility at the alley end. Motty had finished the ice-cream and was now licking her hands as far as the wrists, for they felt hopefully sticky. She and the little boy sat in companionable silence, just looking at each other.

'Lexie! What you doing out there?' cried a voice from the upper regions inhabited by adults, and Motty looked up to see a dark, beautiful face above her. A crow's-wing plait dangled downwards over a grubby pink frock pinned with a large mother-of-pearl map of Australia across an olive bosom.

Motty said, 'You've got red shoes.'

The girl picked Motty up. She smelt strongly of clove carnations.

'My, you've got pretty hair. Where do you come from, you little twirp? Who's this kid, Lex?'

'I dunno. Old Burgess was hanging around.'

'I'm lost,' said Motty amiably.

448

'Ah, like fun. Never mind you come inside with me and I'll give you a cream cake.'

She hoisted Motty across her hip and went inside. A thickset, sallow woman stood at the stove, stirring a pot, in which, every so often, the scarlet of pepper floated up like specks of red silk.

'Florrie's gonna give the little girl a cream cake,' cried the black boy, dancing on the tips of his long slender toes. The woman looked dourly at Motty.

'Who's she?'

'I dunno. Where's the cakes?'

'Picking up kids! Yer mad,' said the older woman, jabbing at the bottom of the saucepan.

'You can talk,' said the other lazily. She jerked a thumb at the black boy and laughed. The boy laughed, too, and the older woman burst into a flood of passionate Italian, thumped him on the ear, and screamed furiously at her sister, who only giggled, took up a greasy paper bag from the dresser, and went out with the children to the tiny iron-framed balcony that faced the street. She spread herself comfortably on the wooden seat that had been built across the gas meter.

'Cake,' demanded Motty, stretching out her pink, licked paw.

Passers-by stared curiously at the little group on the balcony, the slovenly, beautiful girl, the tear-stained black boy, and the white child peering through the railings and painting her face with cream. This was the scene that Hughie saw as he passed by on his way home from work. He stopped, astounded at the resemblance between the small child and his grand-daughter.

Motty nodded amicably to him. 'Hullo, nice old Pop.'

The girl Florrie looked over the child with her soft, sultry eyes. Her smile was slow, revealing her glistening teeth, and the tip of her pink tongue. She was no more than seventeen.

'This your little girl?' she asked. 'I found her in the alley.'

'Christ!' gasped Hughie. 'She musta run away. Her mother'll be off her head. You little devil, I ought to skelp yer hindshoulders.'

'Ah, no!' The girl put her arm around Motty, lifting her over the railings, and the strong clove scent came to Hughie's nostrils. He became suddenly aware of his dirty working clothes, his grease-stained boots, and his unshaven chin. He stammered, and some strange nostalgic feeling came into his heart, so confusing and disturbing that he said brusquely, 'I gotta thank you, miss.'

449

'Oh, that ain't nothing,' smiled Florrie. He looked away from her, unwilling to stare, and yet unable to control himself.

'Her name's Motty – Moira, that is.'

'Mine's Florentina. But everyone calls me Florrie.'

'Yeah? That's an Italian name, ain't it?' Hughie was even more confused. 'I better be getting the little devil home.'

'Yes'. Hughie walked off, squeezing Motty hard.

'Oho.' She was tired. In a moment her head drooped on his shoulder and she was fast asleep. Unnoticing, Hughie walked past the pub on the corner, the good winey smell following him up the road, but beyond a twitch of the nose he took no notice. It was late. The pure fields of the sky were darkening, and no longer did the gable windows of the old houses twinkle and burn in the sundowning light. Mumma was leaning over the gate, saying Hail Marys for the return of her darling. When she saw Hughie she gave a squawk, and blessed herself in four rattling good thumps.

'Roie!' she yelled. The attic window sprang open with such a bang it shivered in its sash, and Roie appeared like a ghost. The next moment she flew out of the door, snatched the sleeping child from her father's arms, and burst into tears.

'God bless us, it's all over,' said Mumma, trying to take them both into her arms and glaring at Hughie. 'And you sauntering up the road as though you had all the time in the world. You oughta be ashamed!'

'Keep yer hair on,' began Hughie, but she interrupted, 'No more feelings than the boots on yer feet! Where's that Dolour?' she fumed, turning towards the house. 'A lot she'd care if Motty was run over. I dunno!'

Gladsomely she returned to the sausages, now dark fossilized oblongs in the pan. The potatoes were dry, and the eyes, which Mumma in her agitation had forgotten to remove, stared out of the pot in black dismay. But Mumma was so happy she did not care. Breaking into the militant strains of 'Hail, Queen of Heaven,' she slapped the flour in the pan and made some gravy, to the accompaniment of the peevish gruntings of Puffing Billy, who was making heavy weather of a mouthful of coke.

Dolour helped Roie to undress Motty for bed. The moment her sister's back was turned, Dolour put her arms around the child and kissed her with loving eagerness. She glanced up to see Roie looking at her.

'I did leave the gate open, Ro.'

'I guess it's the kind of thing anyone could do,' said Roie.

'If anything had happened to her,' cried Dolour, 'I would have killed myself.'

'Me, too,' agreed Roie. They looked at each other and giggled.

'Funerals all over the place,' choked Dolour.

'Imagine how busy Mumma would be,' snorted her sister. They laughed hysterically, and so Charlie found them as he came leaping up the stairs. He regarded the scene, the two girls laughing, and Motty playing peacefully with the soap, and all the anxiety and terror of the past two hours came to the top in an explosion.

'Of course no one thought to come and tell me she was found!' he shouted, wiping the sweat from his face and leaving it striped with a broad black streak. 'I musta have travelled six miles. And here are you two laughing your silly heads off.'

Motty waved her soapy paw like a sceptre at her father and said, 'Dogface!'

He pounced on her and turned her bottom upwards. 'This is the last time you're going to run away, young lady.'

'Ah, Charlie!'

He turned up her singlet. 'By gosh, what's this?'

They stared as he pulled out a large and grubby handkerchief. In the corner was a rough lump.

'She musta found it. What on earth is it?'

Charlie untied the knot, and there was a screwed-up five-pound note.

'Jeepers!' Dolour's eyes nearly popped out.

Roie, improving the moment, took the child from her husband's unresisting grasp and put on her pyjamas. 'Here, would you take her downstairs and give her a bit of a lick, Dol?'

Charlie and Roie sat staring at the miraculous five-pound note.

'Just think of the days I've got to work for that, and this zack-sized brat goes out and picks it out of the air.'

'What are we going to do with it?'

They began to remind each other of all the small necessities they and the family needed. They laughed together, and in their joy and relief at the finding of Motty loved each other all the more.

Downstairs Hughie was in the laundry, in an atmosphere of yellow soap and wet firewood and tomcats. He pottered from tap to candle-lit mirror, half-heartedly rubbing a wash-cloth round his neck. He lifted the candle and looked searchingly into the mirror. He saw there a good ruddy face, with bright and blue eyes of the clearness of glass. His hair was still thick, and hardly grey at all, standing straight up from his forehead in the Irish style. He lifted a lip like a snarling dog and studied his teeth. They weren't the best, having cost him eight pound the set back in the days when dentists measured the spaces between the teeth with ruler and T-square.

A deep restlessness had taken possession of him, a terrible distaste for his life, his work, the pettiness of his existence that added up to nothing at all. He hadn't even been to a war, having been in an essential occupation in one, and too old for the other. There was something he wanted to do, but he didn't know what it was. Get out and change his name and become someone else, perhaps.

'Guide of the wand-her-rer hee-yar below!' roared Mumma in her happiness. 'Hughie! Hughie love,' she bellowed through the closed door.

'Good-oh,' he answered surlily. He went into the kitchen. It smelt of stale food and smoke and a dirty floor, yet, even though its own peculiar smell was so strong, he could catch the whiff of burning rags and rotten fruit from Lick Jimmy's backyard. He stared at Mumma, slopping round in her slippers, each with its heel trodden down to a pancake. Her shoulders, weary with the years, were bottle-shaped, and her hips so square her dress was hitched up on the corners.

'Save us from per-her-il and from woe!' implored Mumma.

'Oh, shutup,' growled Hughie. 'Watcher got?'

'Sausages.'

Hughie groaned. 'Not snags. Not again. By God, I won't eat them, so there.'

All the trouble in his soul rose like a bubble and burst. Anger made him shake. He jerked open the oven door with such force that Puffing Billy spat a surprised little jet of soot from his flue. There, sluggishly reclining in their greasy dish, were the sad and sorry sausages, far past their prime.

'Look at 'em!' he roared. 'Dirty little frizzled-up bastards! I won't eat them, I tell yer.'

'I can't help them being dried up, dearie,' explained Mumma reasonably. 'Tea's about two hours late.'

But Hughie raged up and down the room, explaining to the walls how much he hated sausages, and how many times he'd eaten them in a month, and why he was sworn off sausages for life. Finally he jammed on his hat and surged out of the house.

'I'll go and pick up some tucker at the Greek's!' he shouted.

'And good riddance,' quavered Mumma, who was very upset, but too spirited to show it. She bent over the stove, and the tears in her eyes made the rejected sausages look twice as big.

Out in the cool evening Hughie paused. He looked forlornly this way and that, for he had nowhere to go now that Patrick Diamond was dead and the pubs were shut, and in spite of his proud boast about the Greek's he had no more than a shilling in his pockets. He was tired, and hungry, but more disturbing than these was the new feeling that had him in its grip. What was it? He wanted to fight someone, or to get drunk, or talk to an old friend – or to go into a quiet place and weep a little for his childhood, and the old days that were gone for ever. For the first time in years he thought of his mother and father, and his brothers, the way they used to be, sitting around the big table, and saying grace, and the boys kicking each other in the shins like full-backs.

He wandered along the street. Now that the dusk was coming into the air a lighted kitchen window popped into view here and there, and he heard the chatter of family talk, banging on a piano, a radio bellowing out a song. A pleasant, melancholy loneliness settled over him.

So this was what happened to a man. He found a lost child, and brought it home, and they abused him, and gave him his most hated food for tea, and after a long day's work, too.

'For it's not as though there's any nourishment in snags,' muttered Hughie. 'Any more than there is in sawdust.'

Coronation Street was long and bare, and beyond it the street lights of Redfern were a scanty nebula. Hughie crossed the road and pottered along under the verandahs, where already silent figures were bulked in doorways, shopkeepers enjoying a smoke in the cool.

When he was opposite the house where he had found Motty, he stopped and stood in the shadows. He did not know why he was waiting, but he waited, and after a while one of the upper rooms was lighted, and a window flung up. He saw the figure of the girl outlined for a moment, leaning over the sill, as though she, too, were breathing gratefully the chilling air. Then she turned away. He saw a blue wall, a hanging globe that shed a harsh light, and the uplifted arms of Florentina as she brushed her hair.

For a moment a strange incomprehensible pain seized Hughie, something so revolutionary, so without words that he was at a loss to describe it, or know how to face it.

He pulled down his hat and fled away up Coronation Street, cursing as he went.

Six

Now that Charlie and Roie had decided to leave Surry Hills, a most extraordinary civil war of the spirit went on within the Darcy household, so that the saints in far Paradise were put to the pins of their heavenly collars to decide who wanted which. There was Mumma, getting in first with the early morning mass, and asking God to keep her daughter where she was, and she with a child coming, and needing her Mumma, not some old rajah of a landlady that wouldn't lift a finger to wash a napkin, and the girl perhaps weak with the confinement.

'Your Mother will tell you how it is,' Mumma chided God reproachfully, when no still small voice spoke up in her soul. And she kept her eye sternly on the Tabernacle, until peace came to her, and she felt that faith and the housing shortage would get her her own way.

And Dolour prayed ardently, 'Oh, please let Ro get a nice little flat somewhere in a quiet street, and let me go and visit her, and I'll take the baby out and look after Motty at night so that Charlie and Ro can go to the pitchers. Dinkum I will.'

Hughie said nothing, either way, but he often looked wistfully at his daughter, her small pure face, and the thickening body, and wondered why it was that kids grew up and wanted to leave their homes, and why it was that parents didn't want them to go, and so on, round and round in circles, until he had to go and scrabble amongst the defunct shoes in the bottom of the cupboard to see if, by mischance, he had left a bottle there with an inch or two still to be drunk.

For now Charlie and Roie became aware of the great, silent, seething battle which was going on under the roofs of Sydney. The city lay in the sun, careless and indolent under its banners of smoke, its glitter of windows, its tiger stripes of black shadow and sunshine-drowned streets, and it gave no indication of the savage fight for survival that continued amongst tens of thousands of its inhabitants. They were like birds, squeezed out of a too-crowded nest and scrambling to get back into haven. They were rabbits fighting at a hole in a rabbit-proof fence, biting and suffocating and killing in their mad desire for self-safety. They were people looking for roofs in a city where every roof already sheltered too many.

Now there was another tyrant in the land, the house-owner who ground the last possible penny out of his tenants under threat of eviction. The little old ladies who put pound notes in the plate at church, and who owned rows of tenement houses, lightless, damp, and smelly; the fat profiteers who came from other countries and bought up every available property and re-let at fraudulent rents; the hard-headed business people who let houses to the tenants who could slip them a little something for the key – something sometimes amounting to the life's savings of some desperate man who had to get a sick child, a tubercular wife, or an old and dying father under cover – these were the lions in the street, preying on the needy, threatening the weak, cracking the whip with Nazi arrogance.

Day after day Charlie got up and bought the morning paper, still damp from the machines. There, in the clear light of six o'clock, with the milk-carts waggling past and some lone hawker crying, 'Close prarps! Close prarps!' through the quietness, he would read the three or four 'to let' advertisements, and the scores of 'wanteds.' And sometimes he put in advertisements himself, ringing up the office for days to see if any answers had been left for him, and finding none.

'The only way to get a place is to knock on every door and ask if they've got a spare room,' said Roie. She eased her shoes off her swollen feet, for she had run out at seven o'clock that morning to a place down by the park, advertised as having a balcony room to let.

When she got there, she found a queue of a hundred or more, most of whom had been there since the paper had slapped off the press that morning. She dawdled shyly among them, looking for some familiar face. And the faces were familiar. They all bore the same look of desperation, almost panic, and a dogged determination to outbid the other fellow.

The house was an ancient, clay-faced one, its paint covered with a velvety black bloom of dust, and wet-stains like stalactites coming down from each gable window. It was easy to pick out the balcony flat – just a verandah boarded up roughly with asbestos, which had a square cut in it for a window. There was probably a kerosene stove in the corner, and a tin dish on a bench for a sink. Nothing more

456

uncomfortable, squalid, or makeshift could be imagined, and yet the hundred people, and a hundred more whose telegrams the postman brought to the door in a huge sack at eight o'clock, were prepared to fight to the death for it.

Roie said timidly to the woman in front of her, 'Have you heard how much it is?'

The woman gave her a brief look that took in the shabby coat, the cheap shoes, and the scarf over the head. 'She'll take what she can get, like the rest of 'em. But I'm prepared to go to four pounds a week.'

'Four pounds!' gasped Roie.

The woman shrugged. 'I'm paying that now, and all I've got is a stretcher bed on a curtained-off landing. I might as well be paying it for a place of my own, even if it's only a rat-hole.'

When the woman wasn't looking, Roie went away home. She said to Mumma despairingly, 'We won't ever get a place. I know we won't. They're only for people with lots of money.'

'Never mind,' said Mumma. She wiped a rag that smelt like an old dishcloth over Motty's face, and Motty's face bloomed like a rosebud out of the vanishing dirt. 'You've always got a room here.' Roie felt comforted, knowing that not even the woman who could pay four pounds a week had a room to herself as she and Charlie and Motty had.

Mumma yearned over the girl's tired face, wanting to say something to get Roie on her side against Charlie in this scheme which to Mumma had all the absurdity of a proposed trip to a foreign country.

'It's not as if they've started to pull the roof off over our heads,' she said. 'And anyway, it's only them old, tumbledown shanties they're going to get rid of. This is a good house, if it wasn't for the roof and no bath, and the floor a bit gone here and there.'

Roie's lips trembled. She wanted to confess to her Mumma how she felt about things, but her loyalty to Charlie held her back. That afternoon they were going over to Pyrmont as soon as he got off work, and at the very thought nausea rose in her stomach and the backs of her legs ached. For already, and the child still four months away from its coming, she had been to so many places. Up and down strange streets, following clues given by workmates and strangers in trams and shops, bearing little slips of paper from reluctant estate agents, Charlie led her, and whenever they came to the right gate he would say, 'Cross your fingers and pull in your stomach,' and Roie would slump down in her coat to conceal her pregnancy. For eagle-eyed landladies never failed to give her figure the once-over. They always suspected young couples who came after a flat, in case that young couple had the best possible reason for finding a home, and were for that reason to be avoided like the plague.

They had not been to Pyrmont before. It was on the other side of the city, and might as well have been in another town as far as Roie was concerned, for to her the city was a vast wilderness, looped by familiar tracks, and a little dangerous to investigate in its remoter corners. As they crammed into the bus, rich with the smell of petrol and fat ladies, the rain started, drops, drips, beads of quicksilver slung diagonally across the windows. Down they swooped to the old Pyrmont Bridge spanning the grey stream of Darling Harbour. Once it was prodded by windjammer masts, and now was blackened by rude gusts of smoke from steamer funnels crowding into that industrialized waterway of Sydney until it was like a ships' highway, with no traffic officer. And now the bus rattled up the road that sweeps into Pyrmont village, lined with tall flat-faced houses, and queer little dumpy ones like old women resting beside the road awhile.

Roie, who had been feeling sick, woke up. The place looked familiar. The women went shopping in slippers, and the younger ones wore curling pins, and pushed prams piled with mountains of groceries. There went a hawker with a horse just cobbled together, the bottles in his tilted cart clinking musically. There were the same little shops, all crowded together, all stuffed to bursting point with foodstuffs and overspilling in piles of baskets and straw brooms. Red geraniums grew in tins on some of the balconies, and even as she watched an old Chinese came out on a verandah and fed a canary in a cage, just as Lick might have done. Roie felt almost happy. It was like home here, and close to the shops and everything. It was sort of exciting with the wharves so near, and the big ships blowing their horns just beyond the factories and silos. But before she could open her mouth Charlie said, 'It's not much of a place to live, maybe, but it'll do for a start.'

So Roie did not say anything. Silently she followed him along a crooked-elbow street where the houses, two feet behind their fences, preserved a down-at-heel, old-maidish dignity with rows of potted ferns, a yellowish passion-vine, and a dwarfish, deformed acacia, whose tender almond-shaped leaves had burst up through the asphalt itself.

'This is it.'

Roie, to hide her shyness and reluctance, looked intently at the fence, and the way the tops of its pickets had been cut into mitres, crowns and spade-shapes. She huddled forward into her coat.

'Pull your stomach in!' Charlie hissed.

'I'm pulling it in as far as it will go,' wailed Roie resentfully. The door opened and a small dark woman with a moustache and a strange poultry-yard odour appeared. She looked at them both with watery eyes, inquisitive and scrutinizing. While Charlie talked, Roie peered past the woman into the little stuffy hall, where the source of the odour was peeking along the wainscot, crooning to itself and occasionally erecting a bright greenish-yellow crest at the sight of the strangers.

'What a lovely parrot!' cried Roie falsely, for she detested parrots. They went inside, Roie pressing shyly behind her husband, for she felt uncomfortable in strange houses. Almost instantly a pink galah scuttered out of a dark doorway and pecked her ankle.

'Oh, don't be silly,' the woman reprimanded, at her startled squeak. 'It's only a dear little galah.' Roie smiled feebly, keeping an eye upon the rosy creature that circled her feet, fluffing out its quills and clashing its cherry-picker beak with malicious expectation.

'I'm Miss Moon,' said the woman. She brushed off a couple of olive budgerigars that came fluttering down from the curtains, and Charlie made a sudden embarrassed dive for his handkerchief.

'Oh, really!' said Miss Moon crossly. 'The dear little things have to follow nature. And anyway, her coat will dry-clean, won't it?'

'It's nothing at all,' said Roie hurriedly. 'Have – have you really got a flat to let?'

The woman gave her a long look, cryptic to both the young people, then she said, 'It's upstairs.'

They followed Miss Moon up the dim stairs, Roie thinking, 'Oh, I couldn't get used to all them birds . . . that smell everywhere like a chicken-house . . . and Motty would pull their feathers out, I know she would. And she's a queer sort of a lady. Mumma would never get on with her when she came to see us.'

'It's never been let yet,' said Miss Moon proudly. The top of the house had been converted roughly into a kind of a flat, furnished sketchily and yet with infinite fussiness with bamboo and rickety, useless bits of pre-Boer-War specimens of the cabinet-maker's art. From one window could be seen the parting curtains of rain, shifting like veils over the pewter glimmer of the sea. There was no kitchen.

'You'll have to share that with me, and carry the food upstairs, but of course it's no trouble,' said Miss Moon. 'The last people didn't mind at all. I had them put out for other reasons.'

'But she said – ' thought Charlie.

'Up all them stairs!' thought Roie.

From under the bed waddled another parrot, a brilliant scarlet and bottle-green creature with one blind opal eye. Miss Moon picked it up, cradling it so that the long tail-feathers spilled over her dress.

'Poor Lucky! She wants to nest somewhere, and she does like it under the bed.'

Charlie sent Roie a glance which said mutely that Lucky would be lucky to be alive if she survived their tenancy.

'It's three guineas, and cheap at the price,' said Miss Moon.

Roie gave a quickly-suppressed gasp.

'It's cheap for these days,' admitted her husband.

'You've only got to share the kitchen and the laundry, and there's a bath in the laundry,' said Miss Moon proudly.

'Yes,' faltered Roie. She dodged away from a gas bracket, where two budgies cuddled together, their little snub noses together.

'It'll be nice to have a man in the house to fix things,' said Miss Moon. 'The last man . . . it's time some of the garden was replanted, and the tap's gone wrong in the kitchen.'

She suddenly gave Charlie a beaming smile, and with fascinated distaste Roie watched her Adam's apple disappear beneath her collar and bob up again. She conceived a terrible dislike for Miss Moon. She felt that at any moment the woman was going to edge up to Charlie and stroke his sleeve.

'I don't suppose we could . . . sort of . . . discuss it?' asked Charlie shyly. Miss Moon was indignant.

'Discuss it! I don't know what you're going to discuss, I'm sure. Why, I could get eight guineas for that flat any time! And I'm only asking twenty pounds for the key.'

'Twenty!' breathed Roie.

'It's small enough,' said Charlie hastily. 'But – if we could just walk round the block – we wouldn't be five minutes, would we, Roie?'

The woman was reluctant. Her lips moved angrily. She plainly considered their hesitation a slap in the face. Roie reached out timorously and stroked the ruffled head of the ponderous parrot.

'Well,' said Miss Moon, 'only five minutes then. Other people will be coming, you know.'

They escaped from the house almost at a running pace. The air of the street, stale as it was, struck them like a blow after the fetid atmosphere of the house. They hurried up a door or two, and Roie looked hopefully at Charlie.

'Fancy asking for twenty pounds!'

'Yes, but we got to make up our minds to pay extra wherever we go,' pleaded Charlie. 'And we've got that money put by.'

'But it's for the baby,' wailed Roie. 'The hospital and everything.'

'We could save it up again. Look, Ro,' he said urgently, 'isn't this better than Plymouth Street? Look how quiet it is. And we could put the baby's cot by the window up there and we'd get the breeze straight from the harbour. And evenings we could go for walks down by the wharves,' he said eagerly.

'Three guineas is an awful lot for two little rooms, and sharing the kitchen with that woman,' faltered Roie, almost weeping. It was the first time they had ever differed about anything. 'And we ain't said anything about Motty yet!' she added.

'I don't know how she'll take that,' admitted Charlie.

'Or the baby.'

'Oh, we won't tell her about the baby.'

'I don't like her,' said Roie obstinately. Her lips trembled. All at once she felt weak and unable to think. 'I suppose you know best, Charlie.'

'I just want you to be happy, that's all.'

They stood indecisively, looking at each other unhappily. Her hand went into his. 'You want to take it, don't you?'

'I want to get away from Surry Hills, that's all,' said her husband. He had never before voiced his hatred of the place that was so great that anything at all, provided it were in some other part of the city, looked better to him. Now they were at the gate.

'Pull your stomach in!'

'Oh, shut up!' said Roie angrily. The door opened as though Miss Moon had been waiting behind it, and the galah and the cockatoo appeared, rolling over and over with claws entangled.

'Well?' demanded Miss Moon over the screeching.

'We'd be glad to take it,' said Roie.

An extraordinary change came over Miss Moon. Her dark eyes took on the appearance of melted toffee, and she looked with a strange, greedy look at Charlie.

'My, that's nice,' she said. Roie thought, 'In another moment she *will* stroke him.'

'So nice to have a young man in the house,' said Miss Moon.

They sat down gingerly in the little lounge.

'The last tenant,' said Miss Moon, mechanically stroking the galah's round, downy head, 'he wouldn't keep me company.' She stared into space with a concentrated look. 'Of course the flat has never been let before.'

'Will you want your rent in advance?' asked Charlie, nervously flashing a look of appeal and puzzlement at his wife.

Suddenly Miss Moon tipped the galah off her lap, and said briskly, 'Of course, I must insist that you take the utmost care not to have children while you're here. Children make me ill.'

She looked piercingly at Roie, with dislike and suspicion, as though Roie were obviously the kind of girl who would have children whether her husband wanted them or not.

'Loathsome, disgusting creatures,' shuddered Miss Moon. Her fingers plucked tensely at her skirt. 'Filthy little savages. I detest children.'

She looked as though she were appalled at the very thought of them. Roie felt a surge of anger and indignation at the idea of this queer little woman calling her beautiful Motty loathsome and disgusting, but she didn't know what to say, looking furtively at Charlie and leaving the job to him.

'We've got a little girl of three,' said Charlie.

Instantly Miss Moon flew into a rage, her voice growing as needle-shrill as a bird's, so that the smell of the room, the feathers lying around on the carpet, and the croonings and croakings from corners behind the furniture – all seemed to emanate from her.

'Get out! Get out of here! If you think I'm going to have a disgusting, smelly little beast of a child in my house – '

'Motty doesn't smell,' flamed Roie, half-rising from her chair, so that her coat fell open. Miss Moon stared at her, looking as though she were going to have a fit.

'You're pregnant!'

'Yes,' said Charlie, 'we were going to tell – '

Miss Moon's face was purple. She dragged at her collar, beating on her breast and going 'huh-huh-huh,' the expression on her face as terrified, as appalled as that of one who had seen a serpent.

'Bring your spawn in here . . . breeding all over the place . . . just like all your sort . . . those last people. I used to hear the talk that went on . . . oh, how I hate you filthy women!'

Roie felt sick. She wanted to get out of the place before she fainted. She said, weakly, 'Charlie, it isn't any use.'

She wanted to speak loudly in defence of the nobility of pregnancy, of the fact that she was proud and exultant to be carrying a child, and to have already borne one. She wanted to be scathing and rude to Miss Moon, as Grandma could have been rude, even on her deathbed, but she felt too sick to be bothered.

'It's a pity you haven't had a child of your own, and then you'd know what a silly old tart you are,' she said to Miss Moon.

'She's probably had one, and buried it under the rhubarb,' said Charlie, trying to be calm and self-contained and only succeeding in being pure Surry Hills. Miss Moon began to breathe in stertorous grunts, like an asthmatic dog, and her face turned darker and darker.

'She's sick,' said Roie, as she hustled out of the door.

'She's mad!' said Charlie. 'A whole lot madder than you think.'

He banged the door thunderously, and every bird in the house broke into a tin-whistle shrieking.

'I'd rather have Surry Hills than her,' began Roie in a small voice.

'Old cow! Did you see the way she looked at me?'

'No,' said Roie innocently. He was annoyed at her obtuseness.

'I don't know what she expected along with the rent,' he said, half proud, half embarrassed. Roie was silent, a giggle bubbling up from her soul, and dispersing in a moment all her weariness and nausea and relief at escaping from that horrible house. She went into the warm, slovenly, familiar atmosphere of her own place with deep pleasure. If Twelve-and-a-half Plymouth Street smelt, at least she knew where the smells came from. If it was rowdy, the row came from those she loved.

'We ought to get the place first, and tell them afterwards that we've got kids,' said Charlie.

'That wouldn't be fair,' said Mumma virtuously.

'It's as fair as they are,' growled Hughie, 'letting their rooms only

463

to people who'd murder their kids rather than let 'em be born. Pretty funny, with Australia yowling out for migrants, and not making provision for new Australians.'

'Italians, Gyppos, anything but Aussies, that's what they want,' agreed Charlie.

'I suppose the Government knows best,' said Mumma helplessly, for she had a great awe of authority. Then she burst out, 'But you'd think anyone would be glad to take a little newborn baby in.'

'They weren't glad back in Joseph and Mary's time,' said Roie with unaccustomed bitterness.

From then on all the landlords and landladies took on, in Dolour's mind, a sort of callous, Oriental look, and most of them appeared to her vision clad in striped burnouses, with plugs of coral in their noses. She hated them vigorously, until she discovered that, deep in her heart, Roie didn't mind very much.

'What do you go along for, Ro?' she asked her weary sister. 'Let Charlie do all the looking.'

'He might take something I didn't like,' said Roie evasively, and Dolour looked at her in astonishment, for she knew that in all their months of looking the only chance they had had of taking a flat was during their visit to Pyrmont. She and Roie were not used to looking into each other's eyes. They accepted each other's face as something that was inevitably on top of a body as familiar as the furniture. Now Roie turned away before the penetrating gaze of her sister.

'You don't want to get a place,' marvelled Dolour.

'Oh, smart, ain't you!' mocked Roie, angry at the discovery of her secret.

'You want people to see you're having a baby, so they'll turn you down.'

'Well, what about it?' asked Roie defiantly. She quavered suddenly, 'I don't want to go away, it's just that Charlie's keen, that's all.'

Dolour ruffled up her hair. 'I dunno. I would have thought anyone would like to get out of this dump. Anyway, what's up with you? You don't have to go just because Charlie wants to.'

'Oh, well.' Roie was angry at the look on Dolour's face. 'I'm married to him. You wouldn't understand. You're just a kid.'

She had thought the look on Dolour's face was contempt, but it was envy, and at Roie's words she turned away to hide it.

Seven

One day Mumma told Dolour to clean out the scullery shelves, and grumbling she obeyed. Outside it was a clean, windswept day, with russet leaves whirling up, up in loose-spun willy-willies to the chimney-tops, but within the kitchen was a dismal grey light, spiked with the ruby square of Puffing Billy's toothless mouth.

Dolour slowly passed a wet cloth over the soot-blackened tops of the baking-powder and jam tins. She worked as though she were at the bottom of the sea, with two hundred tons of water pressing on her, lifting her arms with the heaviness of an old woman, and moving her feet as though they wore leaden boots. Her hatred of the task drained her very blood away. By the time she came to the golden-syrup tin, with an imprisoned cockroach feebly waggling his legs in the puddle on the lid, she felt that she could fall over with sheer ennui.

'Gah!' said Dolour, lifting the cockroach with the tip of a knife and flicking him out the window. She leaned desolately on the sill, looking at the bare quadrangle of the yard, and a pair of Hughie's terrible underpants hanging forlornly under the yellow vanes of the phoenix palm. The wind, flowing over the rusty roofs like an invisible river, swooped down into the yard, brushed a wing into the alcove of the window, and swooped off again. Dolour sniffed. The wind was laden with the smells of a nearby factory, burnt sugar, and vanilla, and something foreign.

'Cinnamon!' breathed Dolour. She had never seen cinnamon. To her the word connoted a pile of transparent yellow crystals like topaz. It breathed of palaces with onion domes, and brown canals where little shoe-shaped boats floated. She lifted her wrists and shook them, and heard the jingle of bracelets. She sighed, for she had been imprisoned in the harem three years, and every day was whipped for her refusal to submit to the Sultan. Suddenly she spun round. A stranger was there, a fine handsome stranger with no shirt on, like Alan Ladd, and a striped tea-towel on his head. At his waist was strapped a gold-handled scimitar.

'How did you get here? It is death for you if you are discovered!'

465

'For you, my princess, death would be a small thing.' He came closer, she felt his warm breath on her cheek, his lips came down on hers . . .

'What the diggings is the matter with you?' cried Mumma, standing in the doorway and glaring. Dolour looked stupidly at her.

'Prancing around like a skitterbug. Sometimes I think you're a bit soft in the head,' went on Mumma unpleasantly. She came closer. 'And you've been picking your face again, too!'

It was the end. Dolour flung down her dishcloth, gave a sharp high wail like a knock-off whistle, and bolted from the kitchen. Mumma heard the retreating drum of her feet on the stairs and sighed. 'I dunno. The kid's got a bug. Too much school, that's what it is. She oughta get a job.' She looked at Puffing Billy threateningly as he belched. 'Don't you start, now, or I'll beat your black brains out with the poker.'

Upstairs Dolour beat her fists resoundingly on the iron rail of her bed. For a long time she had felt she couldn't put up with Mumma any longer, or her inspired talent for bursting in on the most luscious dreams. But underneath her impatience with her poor, down-to-earth, bunion-toed Mumma, Dolour knew that the real cause of her sorrow was that she couldn't put up with her face any longer. She propped the speckled old mirror up against the rail, and lay on her stomach staring into it, counting the spots. She found fifty-two. It was hard to believe that one face, and not a fat, expansive one, either, should have room for fifty-two spots.

Suddenly she gave a squawk of despair, dragged her hair up, and close to the hair-line, found another one.

'Fifty-three!' said Dolour in a hollow, contralto croak. Fifty-three spots! What was the use of dreaming, and wishing, and planning when she had . . . Dolour sobbed brokenheartedly. It was no good. Romance, accompanied by the skirl of flutes and the twang of harps, would never come into the life of a girl afflicted with fifty-three spots at one time. The terrible realization of it came again to her, as it had come a thousand times before, and been forgotten in the swift changes of mood that assailed her.

'No one will ever fall in love with me,' groaned Dolour. Her face hurt, too. It burned, and the skin, stretched tightly over the eruptions, felt as though she had been out in a high wind. But this was nothing to the pain she felt when people stared at her. She translated their casual gaze into contempt and pity, not knowing, in

466

the intensity of her self-consciousness, that most often they saw nothing but a lanky, half-grown girl with a sullen expression.

'They think I'm dirty,' she said, and in passion and fury cried to the ceiling, 'I will get my skin clear! I will! I won't let them laugh at me and make fun of me any longer.' And then, because none of her family ever made fun of her, she crumpled again into tears, the helpless tears that were her only defence against this humiliation.

She heard Motty's little footsteps on the stairs, climbing laboriously from one to the other, and Roie making little chirping sounds of encouragement. Dolour ran to the door and stood behind it, but Roie, who had heard the creaking of the bed, fooled her. She put Motty into her own room and closed the door, then popped her head round the edge of Dolour's. Dolour stood there, looking silly, and unable to find a word to say for herself.

'What's the matter, Dol?' asked Roie. It was no good. She began to cry again, till her face was red and swollen and plainer than ever. Roie sat quietly, stroking her sister's lank black hair.

'Why don't you go to a doctor about it then?' asked Roie.

'I can't,' choked Dolour. 'He might find out something awful was the matter with me and send me to a hospital, and I can't miss school.' She scowled at her sister to hide her embarrassment. 'I wish you didn't look like that.'

Roie did not become angry. 'I don't mind. You sort of feel different about things when they're really happening to you. It seems pretty silly to think about the way you look when there's a new life coming into the world, and no one but you can have it.' So she faltered for words while in the next room Motty hammered on the door with her stubby shoes and roared.

Roie felt in her shabby purse. 'Look, I've got ten shillings here. I've been putting it aside for one thing and another, but you can have it. You go down to the doctor, and he'll give you an ointment or something . . . you just see.'

'I don't want any money,' said Dolour sulkily and ungraciously, but Roie just smiled and put it down on the bed and went out.

Immediately Dolour decided she would go to see Sam Gooey.

Sam Gooey had a shop in Coronation Street. In its window were two jars, each containing a tapeworm of unprecedented length and adhesive power, four bottles with swollen bellies full of emerald liquid, and very many tiny pottery trays containing powdered herbs. Every time you passed Sam Gooey's doorway a gush of hot pungent air whiffed out. It bore the fumes of concoctions that Sam Gooey was cooking over the charcoal stove in his cellar, or perhaps the savoury smell of a stew, the chief ingredient of which was, according to neighbourhood gossip, the humble puppy.

There was no doubt that, even among Chinese herbalists, Sam Gooey was a bright and shining star. Had he not cured Mrs Campion of an indigestion that made her rumble day and night like a traffic bridge? And Mr Siciliano's old brother Bep, whose rheumatics were so bad he creaked when he bent – Sam Gooey and a bottle of black medicine with leaves floating in it had made a new and young man out of Mr Siciliano's old brother Bep.

She was so upset that her normal diffidence about visiting a strange Chinese and letting him look at her face had entirely gone. She hurried up through the gathering shadows in Coronation Street. It was not six o'clock yet, but the sun had long gone over the rim of the winter world. The dust-laden wind whipped back her coat and blew into her eyes. Her teeth gritted, and all her nervous system quivered with irritation and distaste.

To make it worse, she met Charlie, coming home from work. He looked taller and thinner and darker in the twilight, and his familiarity to her was as hateful as the rest of the world which surrounded her.

'Hullo, where are you off to?'

She looked at him sulkily. The uneasy dislike he aroused in her had never quite been dissipated since the day Roie married. He looked at her with his clear hazel eyes, and she felt he saw all the discontent and hopelessness that lay within her; he was ill-educated, and she had had more years at school than he, yet she felt small and young and unripe when he spoke.

'Just for a message.'

'Where?'

'Oh – ' She gestured irritably up Coronation Street, implying that it was no business of his, anyway.

'I'll wait for you.'

'Oh, for gosh sake!' she burst out. 'Nobody's going to hit me on the head with a bottle. Go on home. Tea'll be ready.'

'O.K.'

His smile as he gave her a dismissing wave of the hand maddened her all the more. He never got angry, never treated her as though she were worthy of provoking anger.

'I'm only a kid to him,' she thought forlornly, and knew that in this was her resentment of Charlie. Outside Sam Gooey's window, lit with a bilious green globe, she stood for a moment. Was it worth it? Ten bob wasted perhaps, and God alone knew what he'd put in the medicine.

'Slugs and snails and puppy-dog tails,' murmured Dolour, diving inside before anyone saw her.

But Charlie had seen her. He heard the protesting murmur within the corner pub as time was called. The bar bellowed out a roar of voices as the doors flew wide, and drinkers stepped reluctantly, and drunks doddered protestingly forth.

They stood about, arguing, pushing each other affectionately, and slowly peeling themselves away from the bee-cluster and dawdling away home. Charlie decided to wait for Dolour. He saw her go into Sam Gooey's, and wondered with amusement what Mumma could want there.

He waited a little, and Hughie appeared from the pub door, obviously the last, loneliest, loveliest of the drinkers who had refused to be hurried. He stood there a moment sticking out his stomach and wiping his mouth with the air of one who owned the place. Charlie gave him a whistle. Hughie was pleased to see him.

'Whatjer doing?'

Hughie said he'd wait, too, so they waited, walking slowly up towards Sam Gooey's shop and dawdling under the cold, wind-swept verandah, turning up their coat collars and poking their chilled fingers down into the dust-crumbs of pocket seams. Neither of them thought of looking inside the shop.

It was cold and dusty inside the shop, and an odd smell, even stranger than that ascribed to the puppy stew, curled up out of the many cracks in the floor. A hundred jars, each inscribed in red and black sabre characters, stood on the shelves, and on the counter a purple-veined wart-like thing as big as a fist swam in a bottle of spirit. This proclaimed itself as 'Cancerous growth removed from liver.' Dolour shied and was about to leave hurriedly when she saw an eye looking at her from a rent in a canvas screen pasted with pages from a Chinese calendar. Sam Gooey himself instantly appeared, smiling welcome. He was short and fat, with good health shining from his persimmon-glossy face and pouting red lips, which seemed to have been made of wax and applied after the rest of his face was made. He looked much too clean for the rest of the shop.

He wore a collar and tie, a pink shirt with a white starched collar, and neatly tailored dove-grey trousers that clung companionably to his lunar stomach.

'Yes, yes,' he chirruped in his clear, lark-like Chinese voice. 'What you want, miss?'

In his hand he had a piece of buttered bread. He put this on the shelf and turned to Dolour, ready for business. But shame had overcome her, and she could not frame the words.

'My word,' he said helpfully, 'that's a bad case of acne you've got there, miss.'

Dolour blushed with pleasure, for she knew she had acne, even though the rest of the world called her trouble plain pimples.

'That's what . . . I was wondering if . . .' she said.

'I have a look. Eh?'

He trotted round the counter and had a good look at her face. Dolour had to bend down like a hoop, he was so small. With the bright dark eyes so close to her, she was compelled to close her own, and inwardly she writhed with embarrassment at the picture she would present to anybody peeping in the door.

'Many, many things cause this acne,' said Sam Gooey. 'Sometimes one herb cure it, sometimes another herb. You come upstairs to my surgery and we have good look under proper light.'

Without thought Dolour followed him, almost treading on his heels.

'Do you think you can make up something to clear it up, Mr Gooey?' she asked eagerly.

Behind the screen they came out into what was apparently Sam Gooey's living-room. A light with a red paper shade hung in the middle of the ceiling, and through the slits in the paper showers of light fell in slivers and drop-dapples, on stiff black hair that grew straight upwards, like tea-tree, or swept back like polished leather from brows. There were, in fact, five Chinese, young and old, all busily eating, not with chopsticks, but with spoons and forks and fingers and other prosaic European implements.

On one side lay an old man with his shirt open, so that his withered mound of stomach showed. He seemed to have the toothache, for he held a poultice of some sort to his face and moaned. His little eyes, sunken in a myriad diamond-shaped wrinkles, stared resentfully at Dolour.

'Come along, come along,' chirped Sam Gooey. The Chinese

looked up, unsurprised. They were eating something dark and glutinous, with green, spinach-shaped leaves floating in it. They sang something, and Sam Gooey jovially sang something back. The old man peevishly got up, did up his shirt and shuffled into the shop, still holding the poultice.

Dolour was embarrassed, but not alarmed. The intimacy of family and neighbourly affairs in Surry Hills had conditioned her mind to many things that would alarm a girl from another suburb. Admittedly she had never seen Lick Jimmy's stomach, but she had often conducted a conversation over the fence with him while he was cutting his toenails. So she followed Sam Gooey up the rickety angular staircase into the semi-darkness above.

Before she knew where she was Sam Gooey pushed open a door, and there was a quite clean, airy room, with the window open, and the air flowing in chill and crisp from the dark street. There was a barber's chair in the middle, under a strong spotlight, and all around hundred of jars, and little saucers with seeds and leaves and chipped wood drying aromatically.

'My surgery. You sit down,' invited Sam Gooey kindly.

He went to the door and called down into the darkness. The sound of feet on the stairs immediately answered him. All at once an extraordinary feeling of expectancy and fright started in Dolour's feet and travelled clammily up her legs. She felt acutely sixteen, in a strange house, with a great many Chinese downstairs, and no one of her own to call to. It was sort of place where Fu Manchu might have lived.

Then a young Chinese girl poked her head round the door. She had a smooth moon face, the features but the merest ripple on that placid circle. Her hair was done in great puffs like a black meringue.

'This is my daughter, miss,' said Sam Gooey. The girl smiled shyly at Dolour, who gawked back. She sank into the chair. Her hat was removed with a touch as light as a feather. Sam Gooey turned the blinding white light upon her, and she closed her eyes in self-defence. He studied her skin with an eyeglass.

'I know it's awfully bad,' said Dolour, in shame and guilt, as though it were the signature of some shocking crime.

'No, no,' he tweeted soothingly. 'Don' you worry. We fix.'

He sang a long psalm at the girl, who shrilled back an antiphon. So it went on, barking nasal syllables, and words obviously based on the note of a loose guitar string, flickering above Dolour's head, while Sam Gooey's gentle pretty hands rubbed and patted and painted. The girl stood by with a smile, and when Dolour winced from the stinging antiseptic she gave a little whistling note of encouragement.

Meanwhile downstairs Charlie and Hughie waited. The street was emptying fast, and Hughie was hungry. A reproachful rumble like distant thunder sounded under Hughie's breastbone, and he smote himself petulantly.

'My God, I woulda thought the beer would keep the works quiet for a while. You sure that kid went in there?'

'Sure.'

He lounged over to the door. The tapeworms were there, and the cancer in the bottle, as well as an incredibly old, crumbling Chinaman, but there was no sign of Dolour. Charlie was astounded. The old Chinese lifted a lip, tenderly felt a solitary tooth as brown as tea, and winced.

'She went in here all right. And she didn't have a chance to come out without me seeing her.'

They stared at each other, anxiety creeping on to their faces.

'What would she want to go to Sam Gooey's for?'

Hughie lifted a shoulder. 'You know she never says anything to anybody about what she wants to do. Something comes up her back, and she just does it.'

They entered the shop with such concerted determination that they jostled in the doorway. Hughie was puzzled and distressed, and his crest of hair bristled like a poll parrot's. If Dolour had gone into Sam Gooey's and was nowhere to be seen, then she had plainly gone into the dwelling behind, and Hughie was prepared to pull the place down to get her out.

'Hey!' He thumped the counter, and the old Chinese opened his eyes and shot filmy blue sparks at him. The vibration had jarred his tooth unbearably, and he scrabbled for the cooling pudding of the poultice and clumped it against his jaw.

'You! You see a young girl come in here about ten minutes ago? Young girl with dark hair, eh?'

'She had a blue coat on,' supplied Charlie, who had one ear cocked to the laughter behind the screen.

The old man shook his head. Quite plainly he could not understand a word of English. He buried his trembling sallow chin deeper in the poultice, and plucked at the long coarse grey hairs that grew out of his cheek. He was so old his temple bones were round white bosses pressing the tight skin.

'What's the matter? Got toothache?' asked Hughie, interested in spite of himself. 'Toothee go bang-bang, allee same horse kick you on head?'

The old man emitted a quavering whinny.

'Where's Sam Gooey?' demanded Charlie. 'He's the one we want to see!'

He banged on the counter, and Sam Gooey's piece of bread fell to the floor. The old man picked it up, blew the dust off, and put it back.

'Come on out of there, Sam Gooey,' bawled Hughie, 'or by the living Hogan I'll pull the little yeller daylights outa you and wrap 'em round yer neck.'

He ramped up and down the shop, talking at the top of his voice, frightening the old Chinese into such a fit of terror that he scuttled away into the back wailing like a tomcat. There was a great commotion behind the screen. First a flat Chinese face popped round, stared open-mouthed, and disappeared; then an older, withered one protruded, much higher up, as though the owner were standing on a chair. A lot of shrill cheeping went on, and the screen shook as though in a southerly buster.

'Where's Sam Gooey?' asked Charlie. 'We want to speak to Sam Gooey.'

'Yeah, and tell him if he's done anything to my girl, I'll roll him out and cut him into fancy patterns,' bawled Hughie, now in the full swing of his beer-flavoured rage.

The screen shook violently, and the cheeping retreated. Feet thudded on stairs, and the fat flat face popped into sight again, and said timidly, 'One moment, please.'

'I'm going inside,' said Hughie violently.

'There she is.' They heard the quick rattle of heeled shoes down the steps, and in another moment she was in the shop, looking astonished and aghast and pleased.

'What's the matter? How did you get here? Gee, you've no idea, Dadda. Mr Gooey says he can make my complexion better!'

They were dumb as she showed them a pot of waxy black ointment.

'I got that much of a surprise when they said you were here. He said it's just my age. Doesn't it smell good? Come on, they'll be wanting to close the shop. Mr Gooey's that nice when you get to know him – ' She hustled them out of the door, and before they had gone two steps it closed stealthily. She was oblivious of their stares, sniffing at the ointment, and feeling her face tenderly, for it was sore from the preliminary treatment.

Suddenly Hughie said, 'You got no business going inside.'

Dolour giggled. 'I didn't know he was going to take me inside. And, Dadda, it was full of Chinamen, and one old type had his shirt undone right down to here.'

Charlie and Hughie looked with alarm at her indicating finger.

Hughie cried, 'I got a few things to say to you, young lady!'

And he said them all the way home, loudly. Dolour dragged her arm away from him, her eyes blazing.

'You shut up, you old nag. Nothing happened to me, did it?'

'It might have,' said Charlie reasonably.

She swung on him. 'You shut up, too. Following me round. Mind your own business!'

'End up in the gutter, that's what you'll do,' prophesied Hugh. 'Walking into a den of Chinks as though you owned the place. Wonder you didn't get raped, and serve you right if you were.'

Dolour resolutely squashed any fears that she had had on the same subject. 'He had his daughter there,' she flared. 'I didn't think . . . I just wanted to get my skin clear, that's all. I suppose you think it's funny, me having pimples.'

She pelted ahead of them, and Hughie scratched his head. 'Do you remember if you were peculiar like that when you were her age, Charlie?'

Charlie laughed. But Hughie was worried. He shut himself in the laundry to think about it, and was only enticed out by Mumma's kicking the door and asking irately whether he'd like his tea passed in through the keyhole.

That night Dolour applied the black ointment, as she had been itching to do all evening. Sam Gooey had said that she was to leave it on for an hour, but Dolour knew that if a little is good more is splendid, so she slathered it on to her hair-line, and left it on overnight.

In the morning Mumma called her several times, and Roie rapped on the door and reminded her of the time.

'All right, keep your hair on,' a muffled voice replied.

The men went off to work, and still Dolour had not appeared.

Then a figure, with bowed head, flashed through the kitchen into the laundry. Mumma heard a block of wood crash against it as a makeshift lock. She listened at the door, and heard a voice lifted in what was apparently anguished prayer. The tap ran interminably, and then there was dead silence. Mumma rattled the door, and a snort from a grievously wounded soul answered her. Mumma nearly went mad with the suspense.

'Oh, Dolour, whatever you've done, I'm on your side,' she cried, and the door was flung open and Dolour bounded out, whimpering.

Mumma's eyes popped like blue marbles. Her hand flew up to her mouth and stayed there. Dolour's hair was tied up on top of her head, and her face was thickly covered with a hideous black mask which had set into a kind of cement. Out of this stared in wild surmise, Dolour's desperate eyes. On the end of her nose the cement had cracked, so that the top, bright pink, peeped through.

'Glory-lory,' stuttered Mumma. 'Holy Mother, what have you done to yourself?'

'It was Sam Gooey,' moaned Dolour. 'I bought some stuff to put on my face, and now it won't come off.' She stood in front of the looking-glass on the mantel and thumped herself on the cheeks in an effort to crack it. Around her mouth it had set into circular furrows, where she had smiled or spoken before it had gone quite hard.

'I'll go mad!' she cried, seizing herself by the ears and working them violently up and down. A small chip fell off, and she picked it up tragically.

'Oh, Mumma! Mumma!'

Motty wandered in from the yard, looked casually at her aunt, got her red truck from under the table and wandered out again. She saw nothing different about Dolour, for to Motty, adults were composed of shoes, legs, shirts and trousers. Only other children had faces. Meanwhile Mumma had come out of her trance and begun to laugh.

'That's right,' cried Dolour, 'laugh. Oh, I wish I was dead!'

And she smote herself on the nose and was rewarded by another small chip. So Mumma, suffering in her heart for her poor child, and suffering even more from strangulated laughter, shut the door so that not even Roie should see, and with hot water and methylated spirits they laboured to get the mask off, Mumma clucking all the time about little heathens who ought to be thrown in the cooler for the things they did to innocent kids who knew no better.

'No,' confessed Dolour, and she told Mumma that if the mask took all her skin off it would be her own fault. Then Mumma stopped laughing, and got very angry, and they flew at each other like cats and argued interminably, until Roie banged on the door and asked what was happening, and why she couldn't come in. So she had to be told, too.

'Serves you right,' said Mumma grimly, as she put on her hat and went out to do the shopping, and tell Sister Theophilus that Dolour couldn't come to school that day. 'And I got a good mind to tell her the truth, too,' she threatened.

Dolour sat melancholy, staring at Roie. But Roie, who well remembered her own extreme and terrible sensitivity during her adolescence, did not laugh.

'The bits of skin that are showing through look clear already,' she said helpfully, perjuring herself through love of her sister.

So Dolour lurked the whole day in her room, part of the time longing to be at school and stamping with impatience at the break in her studies, the rest of the time sitting at the window lost in a golden dream wherein Sam Gooey's ointment peeled off and left her with a skin like Motty's.

'I wish . . . I wish . . .' It was the whole theme of her living, and at the very words a warm flood ran over her body and released the burning, yearning for love. Her heart opened like a window to the world and cried, 'Love me! Love me!' in so intense a voice that it seemed every passer-by must hear it.

By the next day the black cement had peeled away, taking most of her skin with it. Raw and bright pink gleamed her face, as though she had been badly sunburned.

'You can't go to school like that. You look like a peeled sausage,' groaned Mumma. But Dolour heroically packed up her books and went. She saw indications that her skin was going to be a good deal clearer when it healed, and she was making an act of self-sacrifice as a slight return to God for His kind consideration.

Dolour believed in being business-like with Them Above.

Eight

As the year wore on, Sister Theophilus called Dolour out into the corridor, and stood by the big rope of the Angelus bell. She seemed uneasy, and again and again her thumb rubbed lovingly over the worn brass figure on her crucifix. Dolour stared at her, her heart sinking, she knew not why.

'About Susan Kilroy,' began Sister, and then she was silent. Dolour waited. The clear brown eyes looked at her without embarrassment, and yet the fastidiousness and delicacy of the woman hesitated before what she had to say.

'Dolour, you're Susan's friend. You must have heard . . . certain rumours about her . . . conduct with young men. Is there any truth in these stories?'

A dreadful cold tingle crept down Dolour's backbone. She looked imploringly at the nun. She blurted out, 'People say nasty things. Just because a girl goes out with boys sometimes. People make me sick.'

Sister Theophilus sighed. She might have known better, she thought, looking at the scarlet, sulky, stupid face of Dolour Darcy, determined to die rather than tell on her friend.

'Is it I?' she asked inwardly. 'Have I made goodness too austere and chilly a thing to these children?'

It was not the first time one of her pupils had gone to the bad, but each time the blow on her heart had been almost physical. Anxiously, desperately, she had watched the developing body of Suse Kilroy, conscious that any moment now would come the temptation and the fall.

She sent Dolour back to her classroom, and on the day when Susan Kilroy was fifteen, and told her she was leaving school, she took the girl into her shabby study and talked to her a long time about the duty of the Catholic girl in a world corrupt with materialism.

Suse listened silently, shifting from one foot to the other. She wanted to say something, to tell this silly old coot that what she knew about life could be written on a tray bit. Such scorn and fury

477

rushed into her mind that it was all she could do to prevent it from rushing out in an incoherent torrent. Silly old biddy, babbling about chastity and virginity, pleading with her not to go off the deep end! Suse looked at the straight and simple habit of Sister Theophilus and unconsciously arched her chest, proud of her own unconcealed and voluptuous body.

So Sister Theophilus said good-bye to her, knowing that she had lost the battle, and no one but God could reclaim Suse Kilroy. Dolour was waiting outside the gate. She said, 'Gee, you were a long time. What did she say to you?'

'Nothin'.'

They walked on in silence, then Suse exploded, 'Old bag! What's she know about anything, anyway. Been in that convent since she was old enough to spit.'

Dolour protested, shocked, 'You don't want to talk like that about – '

'I will talk about her any way I like. Old cow. Thinks she can talk to me any way she likes just because I'm only fifteen and she's a hundred and eighty. Who're you gawking at, you bloody old hippo?'

This was to an interested woman who leaned arms like hams on a nearby fence. Dolour quaked with agony. The woman drew back as if Suse had shot her. 'Nice thing for convent schoolgirls,' she shrilled. 'Oh, yerss, I can see the ties you got on. Think I won't report it to yer teacher!'

'Ah, stuff it,' replied Suse concisely. 'Go tell the bacon factory they need yer.'

They walked on, Dolour writhing in shame and fear lest she should be involved.

'I'll never go near the damned school again, nor the church, neither,' said Suse, and she ripped off her felt school hat and sent it sailing over the post-office fence. She combed out her hair with her fingers, and the short, silky black curls sprang up. Dolour gazed open-mouthed at her beauty, the delicate hollowed cheeks, and the satin shine on the mouth. A workman passing stared, too, and Suse gave him a wink.

'You little ber-yeaut!' said the man. Suse swaggered on with renewed confidence, with Dolour pattering at her side, asking anxiously, 'You going to get a job, Suse?'

'If I gotta,' answered Suse carelessly. Dolour burned to ask more, but she dared not, in case Suse told her. Already she was sliding into an insignificant position as a girl who was still at school, while Suse blended into a glamorous and unknown world.

'Suse,' she implored, 'wouldn't your mother go crook if anyone tells her that . . . you know . . . about the fellers?'

Suse's eyes flashed. 'She'd better say something, that's all. I'll tell her a few things. She can talk. What about her?'

'I think your mother's nice,' said Dolour shyly.

The other girl snorted. 'She tried everything she knew to get rid of me before I was born. My auntie told me. But I beat her. I ain't got no time for her, and you wouldn't neither, if you was me.'

Dolour looked at her with the shocked tragic gaze of one who has been wounded. She became aware of the sinister subtle battle that had gone on from the moment of Suse's conception, and wanted to run from the knowledge.

'What's she ever done for me but land me with one stinking baby after another to wash nappies for, and give bottles to, and put to sleep. Gawd, if I ever have to put another kid to sleep it'll be for good. She can go to hell. Just wait till I leave home. I wouldn't come back if she was dying.'

'Oh, Suse!' Dolour trembled. 'You don't mean it.'

The other girl turned on her like a leopard. 'What do you know what I've had to put up with? I remember when I was ten, and Dad was in the peter and she was having another nipper. She had it too soon, and I had to run up to the hospital and ask them to send an ambulance. They wouldn't come. Thought I didn't know what I was talking about, I suppose. So Mum had the baby right there, with her biting holes in the blankets and me screaming me head off. It was dead, all shrivelled up and blue. Know what she did? She made me put it in an old tin dish, blood and everything, and carry it up to the hospital.'

Dolour wanted to be sick. 'Whaffor?' she gasped.

'How do I know? She said it was their fault it had been born dead, so they could take care of it now. All she thought was getting her own back on the hospital. She didn't care what I felt about it. How'd you like that when you was ten and didn't even know how babies were born?'

Dolour mumbled something. Her pinched pale face looked yellow in the ripe afternoon light, and with an exclamation of scorn, Suse turned and left her. Dolour went home in a trance-like state. No sooner had she reached the kitchen than she burst into hiccuping sobs, and only replied to her mother's exasperated questions by saying, 'I hate everyone! I wish I was dead!'

'Oh, is that all?' said Mumma cheeringly. 'Here you are, then,' and she presented the kitchen knife to Dolour. 'Not in here, though, alanna, because I've just scrubbed the floor.'

Dolour gave a wail and fled upstairs, and Mumma looked after her and sighed.

Dolour did not see Suse for a fortnight, then, one evening as she was coming home from Benediction, she saw a familiar figure wavering along in front of her. Her heart jumped with pleasure.

'Hullo, Dol.' Suse's voice was high and chirrupy. She tried four times to flick the glowing ash off a cigarette with her little finger, and the cigarette fell to the ground. She stood gazing at it with surprise and sorrow.

'Lookut, Dol, gone and got away on me.'

'Jeepers, you're drunk,' said Dolour, awed. Suse looked at her owlishly.

'I been drinking orange cocktail. Ain't no good, tastes like salts. Met such a lovely boy, Dol. Big blue eyes. This big.' She tried to extend her hands, but they collapsed as though they had been made of wax. She tried again and sighed. 'Gotta go home now, Dol. Right now.'

Dolour caught her by the arm. 'You can't go home, you dill, your dad'd knock spots off you.'

Suse squeaked, and was suddenly sick. Dolour held her stationary, looking up and down the road in wild anxiety lest someone should come. She was consumed with desire to shelter Suse.

'Come home with me, won't yer? You can stay up in my room till you feel O.K. Mouthwash . . . I'll borrow Charlie's toothpaste to take the smell away . . . your dad'll belt you, you know he will,' she babbled.

Suse jerked away. She began to walk with ridiculous caution down the dark alley. Dolour followed, pleading. 'Gosh, you're mad. The cops could put you in a reformatory or something. Come on, Suse. I'll go down and tell your mum you want to stay the night with me. Come on, Suse.'

'Shurrup!' yelled Suse, flapping her hand at her. There was a hot glazy look in her eyes, and at each step her ankles buckled. Half-weeping, not knowing whether to run and fetch Mumma or what,

Dolour followed, feverishly making up explanations in her mind, in case they should meet someone they knew.

'Oh, God, don't let her father be home. She's only a kid. She don't know what's she doing. Oh, God, make him not be home!'

The Kilroy house was like a cardboard box in the dusk, a dark square slotted here and there with the light that peeped from the brown-paper-covered holes in the windows. Out of the open door flowed a peculiar smell of unwashed baby, of badly-rinsed napkins strung in a steaming row before the kitchen fire, of dirt and squalidity and congestion. Dolour had a confused impression of children, big-eyed and half-naked, scurrying from under her feet, to peep like elves from behind the door and under the chairs. Blinking in the light, she came into that tiny room and its all-pervading odour. Mrs Kilroy was there, standing in her run-over slippers, with a whining baby slung across her hip. She was a little, shapeless woman with all the width in her body across the hips and buttocks. She gaped uncomprehendingly at the two girls, showing her snaggled yellow teeth. The baby whimpered, and automatically she shifted it over her other hip.

'Suse doesn't feel well,' said Dolour imploringly.

'Ah, fooey,' chirped Suse. 'I'm drunk.'

'Your father ain't going to like that, Suse,' said the woman in a voice as flat as a hammer on wood. Suse made a sweeping melodramatic gesture at Dolour.

'Watcher know! She's got the old record on again. Yer father ain't going to like that!'

She poured out a flood of filthy words about her father, and not even when she saw his huge hairy-armed shadow standing in the doorway did she cease.

'Now, Harry – ' It was the mother, a feeble squeak of protest. Dolour looked from one to the other of them, her heart thumping.

'I been waiting for you to come in,' he said. 'Tom Phelan told me he seen you going into the park with that dago from the shirt factory.'

'Now, Harry,' said the mother timidly.

'Shut yer mouth, you.'

He unbuckled his heavy leather belt. He was a gigantic man, with a bald head too small for the rest of him, so that to Dolour, looking upwards with fright-blurred yes, he seemed a malformed creature, pin-headed, with bushy brows and a face carved in deep vertical grooves. Suse's had gone white, but a piteous sort of defiance still remained on her face.

'Can't I go and sit on a park seat in the cool?'

'I was there, too,' said Dolour, piping up suddenly in a voice like the sparrow's in the wilderness. He took no notice, but reached across the table and grabbed Suse by the hair. She had it pinned up in some elaborate grown-up way, and he tore the ribbon out of it, and it fell about her face. In a moment the illusion of the woman was gone, and she became a child, in whose face terror and a blind determination were fighting. He jerked her across the table, which tilted upwards. Dolour caught a glimpse of a dirty freckled leg underneath, which was swiftly withdrawn.

'You're a whore.'

Suse said nothing. Her black eyes were fixed on his face with the dumb hatred of a conquered animal.

'You're a whore!' he shouted. With blazing eyes and face dark as a grape with passion, his immense height and hairiness, he seemed like a demon, and Dolour froze with a paralysis of terror.

'How many men 'a' had you?'

Suse's scarlet lips were pressed tightly together. He shook her violently. 'Answer me, you bitch!'

She said nothing. Once again her mother squeaked, 'Harry, you don't want to lose yer temper . . .'

Suse gave a sudden twist from his grasp, leaving his sweaty paw coated with fine dark hairs. Her escape seemed to madden him. With a bull-like roar he twisted the table out of the way, exposing two small boys, frog-eyed, huddled together like possums. They disappeared like magic into the shadows behind the dresser.

Now the man had hold of his daughter. He pushed her head down between his knees and thrashed her across the back and buttocks with the heavy strap, hitting with all his strength, a sort of demoniac lust on his face. At first she did not cry out, then she began to shriek each time the strap landed. Beside Dolour the mother whimpered as Suse screamed, as though it were her flesh that was cut. One of the smaller children began to wail loudly.

'You beast! You beast!' shrieked Dolour. She snatched up a tomato sauce bottle from the dresser and belaboured him about the shoulders, which were as far as she could reach. 'You swine! I'll kill you!'

She sobbed in great hoarse gulps, her eyes blinded with passion and only the desire to murder in her heart. If she could have reached his head she would have smashed the bottle on his skull.

Mr Kilroy reached round a huge hairy arm and swept her across to the wall. 'You pimply-faced little runt! Get out or you'll get the same!'

Whimpering, hysterical, Dolour retreated, holding the streaming bottle.

'You better go, love.' The woman pushed her towards the door. Tearlessly and expressionlessly she looked at Dolour, with a face as waxy as the baby's.

Suse lay still on the floor. Only her gasping told she was still conscious. Her father thrust his hand down the front of her torn dress and pulled out a dirty handkerchief wadded into a ball. Inside were two pound notes. He put them into his pocket, and, sitting down at the table, pulled some betting slips out of his pocket and began to study them. The mother moved timidly towards Suse.

'Leave 'er alone or you'll get a belt on the ear, too,' he growled.

The woman vanished out of Dolour's sight. For a long time she watched from the shelter of the darkness outside the door, until she saw Suse crawl to her feet, half-dazed, and limp towards the stairs. The man looked after her, then, with an expression which Dolour could not read, he shook out a newspaper and hid himself behind it.

Sick with shock, hatred and fright, Dolour ran and stumbled up the road, her face bleared with tears. She was crying loudly before she came into the kitchen of her own home. When she saw the scarlet stains on her dress, Mumma reared up with a shriek, 'Jesus, Mary, and Joseph, what's happened to you?'

'It's only tomato sauce,' hiccuped Dolour, and she hurtled into her mother's arms and blurted out the story. 'Oh, Mumma, why is everyone so dreadful? If I was Mrs Kilroy I'd put bits of light-globes into his porridge. I'd wait till he was asleep and cut his throat with the razor. I would! I would!'

'Hush, darling,' soothed Mumma.

'I'd be bad, too, if Dadda was like Mr Kilroy. I'd be bad just to show him. Oh, I wish I'd stood on a chair to hit him with the bottle, and he'd be dead now.'

Mumma rocked her to and fro. She was much too big a girl to be tucked on to her mother's knees, and bits of leg kept falling over and trailing on the ground, but Mumma tried to enfold all of her just as she had done when Dolour was little.

'Come on, you get into bed now before Hughie comes home and

starts asking awkward questions. And we'll say a decket for poor Suse and Mrs Kilroy and all the little children.'

Soothed and pampered, Dolour lay back in the narrow creaking bed and fingered her rosary beads, while Mumma knelt beside.

'The Descent of the Holy Ghost,' said Mumma. She had said half of the decade before she noticed that Dolour's responses were becoming mumbled and erratic.

'What's up with you? Where's yer respect for the Holy Rosary and Our Blessed Mother?' demanded Mumma sharply. Dolour looked at her with angry eyes.

'He said I was a pimply-faced runt, too, the big bonehead.'

'Never mind your boneheads,' said Mumma, and she squashed down her laughter and went solemnly on to finish the decade.

Suse Kilroy stayed home until her bruises were faded and the scratches where the belt buckle had torn her legs were healed, then she went out one day after a job in a powdered milk factory and never came home. Her mother whimpered a bit, but not too loudly, for she was afraid of her husband. The other children took up all Mrs Kilroy's time and she didn't have much time to think, but sometimes she dragged a port out from under the bed and took out a shrunken green woollen dress that Suse had worn when she was small, looked at it for a while, and then put it back.

Nine

It was nearing examination time, and Dolour worked early in the morning and late at night by the light of a candle to save the light bill, soaking up knowledge so eagerly, so gratefully, that Sister Theophilus was touched. She alone knew what the girl's family only suspected, that of all her pupils Dolour Darcy was the only one who wanted to get a decent job in the great world outside Surry Hills.

But one morning Dolour awoke to find her eyelids stuck together. She opened them painfully with her fingers, and the slant of light from the attic window struck them like a blow.

'Musta got a cold in them,' said Hughie, who was golloping down his breakfast. 'Looking through keyholes. Better change your bedroom.'

Dolour went a dark red for, though she had never looked through the keyhole at Roie and Charlie, she had often listened at the wall to hear what they spoke about in their private moments.

Mumma wiped her hands on her apron. 'Let's have a look at you.'

She peered into Dolour's eyes. Pink-rimmed, blinking painfully, they filled with thick syrupy tears almost instantly, but not before Mumma had seen the pearly spots on the eyeball, each surrounded by a suffusion of cloudy pink.

'You stick at them books too much. You better stay home, love.'

'I can't!' cried Dolour. 'Every day means something when you're getting near exams.' She peered in the mirror, but the stinging tears gushed out and she had to turn away.

So they got something from the chemist's. The chemist is a big man in Surry Hills. People for ever going to him and describing other folk's symptoms, and going off with bottles of medicine and boxes of pills in which they have a complete and lovely faith. Mumma got a little vial of black eye-drops for Dolour, which she put in clumsily, so that great tattoo marks ran down either side of the child's nose. And all the time her eyes became worse, so that at last she just sat with her head in her hands, a burning band behind her forehead, and prickling acid in the eyes themselves. The water that ran down her cheeks was part discharge and part tears of anguish.

'Let's have a look, Dolour.' She felt Charlie's hand on her cheek. Though he had worked hard all his life, his hands were warm, with a good smoothness. Gentle and capable, they lifted her chin.

'Maybe I'm going blind or something,' choked Dolour. 'Oh, Charlie, I'm missing such a lot of school!'

He turned her face into the half-light and cautiously she raised her lids. He saw that the pearly spots were now much larger, like minute patches of sugar on the eyeball, surrounded by a map of tiny veins like distended scarlet threads.

'You poor kid,' he said. 'I bet they hurt.'

Dolour tried to be her usual casual and aloof self with Charlie, but the ache in her heart and the scorch in her eyes was too much. She put her face into the middle of his shirt and sobbed.

'Let's go to the doctor, Dol. You can't play around with your eyes.'

'All right,' choked Dolour.

But while Charlie was getting ready, Hughie was hastily shaving, and suddenly appeared at the door and said gruffly, 'A'right boy. I'll take over,' and took Dolour's arm and marched her out of the gate. Mumma was very annoyed, but Charlie just laughed, and took Motty for a walk instead. Dolour was able to open her eyes a little behind the smoky shelter of dark sunglasses, but Hughie took her arm as they went across Coronation Street. His hand felt strong and fatherly, and Dolour sank with grateful relief into the comfort of it.

They waited for a long time in the dingy waiting-room. Hughie creaked up and down, sucking his teeth furiously, and the old women who were the other occupants of the room knitted and chatted in loud voices of their intimate complaints. Dolour sat with her head down, her tight-gripped hands shaking with nervousness.

When it was her turn, Hughie went into the surgery with her. She sat down and took off her glasses, and in the stinging white light of the window the doctor looked at her eyes. A short, fat, hard-eyed man, he looked pitilessly into them, while they swam and involuntarily jammed tight.

'Open them wider,' he commanded.

'I can't,' gasped Dolour. 'They just won't.'

He seized her face and opened her eyes forcibly, and in face of the overwhelming pain Dolour tried to co-operate. There was a pencil in his other hand, and he lightly flicked at the mark on the eyeball with it. Dolour gave a squeal of agony and the doctor spun backwards, with Hughie's infuriated hand on his shoulder.

'I got a good mind to send you through that window! What kind of doctor do you call yourself?'

'Take your hands off me,' commanded the man. 'Any nonsense from you and I'll have you up for assault, quick and lively.'

'I bet you would,' agreed Hughie. 'But you won't be a witness, boy. You'll be in hospital with a broken jaw and a shirtful of cracked ribs.'

He let the doctor go so suddenly he staggered backwards. Hughie jerked a head at Dolour, 'Come on, you.' She crept after him, fumbling to put on the protective glasses.

'You'd better go down to the hospital with those eyes,' called the doctor. 'I wouldn't treat them, anyway.'

A callous man, he had been momentarily touched by the shrinking misery on the child's face, but a moment later he had forgotten all about her.

Mumma thought that prayer might do some good, but it didn't, so a week later Dolour went to the hospital, she and Mumma together. The most terrible despair had settled into her soul. Day and night she was tormented by the pain in her head, for, like all head-pains, it was impossible to escape. But worse than that was the knowledge that all her desperate work during the year, her efforts to beat her natural dreaminess and inattention, her ambitions to succeed and get a good job – all were sliding away from her.

'You don't want to take it hard, darling,' soothed Roie. 'Why, them specialists down there might fix up your eyes in a day or two, and then you'll whizz through that exam like no one's business.'

Dolour shook her head. She knew she would never catch up now.

At the hospital Mumma went through all the form-signing, her brows wrinkled in distress above her crooked glasses, and her clumsy fingers clutching the pen with a death-like grip. Then they waited, endlessly, in corridors and rooms, in surgeries and wards, in dusk, in blazing daylight, always with the smell of cleanliness round them like a new kind of air. Mumma was terrified of doctors and the very crackle of a starched coat was enough to reduce her to stupidity. When the nurse appeared and finally beckoned to Dolour, Mumma rose too, but Dolour gave her cold hands a squeeze and said, 'You stay here. I'm big enough to look after myself.'

'It's going to be a long job,' said the doctor. Somebody held her head in a grip of iron, and her eyes were swabbed out with fluid fire. Thrust into sudden blindness, with water pouring down her cheeks and pain knifing into her eye-sockets, Dolour staggered drunkenly at the side of a nurse back to Mumma. She heard a gasped 'Glory be to God' from Mumma, the rustle of a prescription passing from one hand to another, and the nurse saying, 'Has to be done three times a week . . . ten in the morning . . . no improvement . . . operate later . . . ulceration . . . no, certainly no school . . . no reading . . . no sewing . . . no pictures.'

Something bubbled up in Dolour, and she was astounded to discover it was a laugh.

'Will I cut my throat here or outside?' she asked.

She entered into a strange world of semi-blindness, a world of passionate mutiny against her affliction, and long silences during which she found in herself the beginnings of self-discipline. Sometimes she stood by the window in Patrick Diamond's empty room, leaning on the splintered sill and looking out into Plymouth Street, which she could see but dimly through the black glasses she had to wear as a defence against the light. There was a flaw in one of the glasses, and it made everything look slightly crooked, so that the trees were lopsided, and the houses as though set on a hillside.

She saw her schoolmates go down the street, day after day, and after a while she lost interest in them. A dull fatalism entered her heart. For a long while, all her life perhaps, she had wanted to get out of Surry Hills. But that was all gone. She belonged to Surry Hills; she was from it and of it, and God had made up his mind that she was going to stay there.

Roie said, 'Maybe I could read to you, Dolour. Your schoolbooks, I mean – history, and things. Then when you go back to school – '

But Dolour shrugged. 'I won't ever go back, Ro. What's the use of bothering about it?'

Though she obediently went back and forth to the hospital her eyes grew gradually worse, and at last she spent half the night in the kitchen, bathing her eyes with cold water, which was the only thing to relieve the pain. Sometimes Mumma got up and sat with her, huddled in her old coat, her weary feet thrust into Hughie's old cobbled socks.

They talked. In the unaccustomed silence, broken only by the far-off rattle of the tram, and the trickle of the water as Dolour pressed the cloth to her eyes, Mumma, who had nothing else to talk about, spoke of her childhood.

'Would you like to know how I met your father, then?'

Dolour nodded. Out of their swollen red rims her eyes looked, seemingly sly and cunning, their clear blue turned to nothing but black dilated pupils in the blood-red ball. She knew they looked monstrous and terrible, and she hated to let anyone see them, but Mumma never seemed to notice.

'Well, it was at the icemen's picnic. You've no more idea than a hen has teeth how many people were there. It was 'way back in 1918 just after the big war was ended, and I had on a black silk skirt. Moyry, we called it. And a striped fuji blouse with the stripes going round and round as if I was a barrel.'

Dolour laughed eagerly, for she had the child's capacity of enjoying a story told a hundred times over.

'And what sort of hat did you have, Mumma?'

Mumma spead her knees wide and put a red puffy hand on each. 'Like a saucepan lid with a little crown in the middle. White straw it was, and it had three big yellow roses along here in front, and a whole bunch of green stalks, like parsley. And me hair down me back with a big black ribbon bow just here.'

There was an agitated creaking from the bedroom, and Hughie stuck his head, ruffled like a mop, round the door. He blearily surveyed the two of them, sitting silent and guilty like children caught in a nocturnal orgy of bread and jam.

'Gawd, I could do a cuppa.' His tongue came out and poked around his lips thirstily. 'And a nice fried egg.'

'Perhaps you'd like a few prawns, too,' said Mumma sarcastically, as she lumbered over to Puffing Billy, gave him a ringing kick in the fire-box, and blew his slumbering coals to wakefulness. She was delighted at the thought of a little midnight supper.

Hughie sat down beside Dolour, his strong hairy chest showing where the buttons should have been on his old flannel. He caught Dolour looking at it, and said heartily, 'Don't worry, kiddo. It's warm in winter. Ask yer ma.'

'That's enough from you, you dirty old man,' remonstrated Mumma. 'Frighten the girl off marriage for life.'

She cracked an egg smartly on the edge of the frying-pan, and the yellow globule slid out into the fat.

'Mumma's been telling me about the icemen's picnic,' said Dolour shyly.

'Did she tell yer about Herbie?'

Mumma couldn't believe that Hughie would be so treacherous. Red-faced she turned, and the egg spat and danced unheeded. Dolour's eyes would have sparkled if they hadn't been so sore.

'Who was Herbie? Mum's boy friend?'

'Herbie took her to the icemen's picnic,' said Hughie with traitorous pleasure. 'A great big yob with teeth that stuck out so far they looked like a white moustache.'

'Hugh Darcy – ' Helpless, Mumma waved the egg-turner at him. 'And me cooking eggs for you, too, you devil. He was a real nice gentleman, Dolour, and played in the band, and don't you take any notice of your father.'

'Real nice gentleman!' said Hughie, warming to it. 'Sure he wore a collar so high it cut a groove in his chin, but does that make a gentleman?'

'At least he didn't career round like a madman after the greasy pig,' flared Mumma. Unheeded behind her the egg reared up in the pan and flapped a charred wing. 'With his pants rolled up showing six inches of red underpants, like you.'

'What do you know about his underpants, eh?' bawled Hughie, twinkling a wink at Dolour. Mumma slid the egg on to a plate with such force that it skidded across to the rim. She slapped it down in front of Hughie and stood glaring at him.

'Yob or not, he was after me, Hughie, and if it hadn't been for him you might never have come up to scratch, God rest him. Died in the big 'flu he did, Dolour, and only twenty-five, poor Herbie.'

Hughie dreamily looked into the haughty face of the egg. 'Yeah, that's the place I lost me freedom, all right. What came over me, do you reckon, popping the question like a great big softy?'

'Ahhh!' snorted Mumma, grinning back at him, and buttering a slice of bread for his delectation and the egg's company. Dolour sat still, the dripping cloth in her hand, forgetting to hide her eyes from them, anxious and delighted to hear how Dadda had proposed to Mumma. For proposals were the most wonderful and romantic thing in the world, and distant music and incense went with them, she knew, for that's the way they were on the pictures.

'Aw, go on,' she besought.

'I can just see your old man sitting there,' ruminated Hughie through a mouthful, 'with his eyes popping out of his head with the heat and the beer.'

'No wonder, after he nearly broke a blood-vessel in the hammer-throw,' defended Mumma. Both of them sank into a reverie, fixing in their minds' eyes the long-gone figure of Old Man Kilker, with his double-breasted waistcoat, and his stiff collar with the turn-over points.

'Your mother didn't have any call to go slinging off at me moey, anyway,' complained Hughie suddenly, and from thirty years ago steamed up a resentment that had never really gone off the boil. 'She always did have a tongue in her head that would scare the hair off a coconut.'

'Don't go poking borax at the dead,' remonstrated Mumma, then she added softly, 'It was that nice, too, all black and silky.'

' "Pardon me, you got something stuck on yer lip," that's what she said,' simmered Hughie, and he was so annoyed he didn't even bother to chase the last of the egg round his plate with a crust. 'Stuck on me lip! And me rubbing candle-grease into it every night for six weeks to get a decent bit of scrub going.'

'Ma always spoke her mind,' said Mumma admiringly, flopping down and staring into that long-ago day, where she saw her mother, neat as a flea, wearing her waist round her hips and her boots round her calves, sitting in the shadow of the great pudding and drinking beer out of a pannikin with her little finger cocked, maintaining at the same time a brisk rat-a-tat of repartee with Hughie and Herbie, who stood near by, crumbling the edges of their straw lids and showing the whites of their eyes at each other.

'The great big ugly moosh on him!' said Hughie, whose thoughts had been pursuing the same course.

'He beat you all the same,' gloated Mumma, 'and if it hadn't been for your weak stomach, he mighta got me after all.'

Dolour, whose mind had been leaping from moustaches to stomachs in pitiful bewilderment, implored, 'But when did you ask Mumma to marry you?'

But she was unheeded. Her parents had left the room and were back on the show-ground in the little country town where they had grown up, back amidst the ripe smells of orange peel and sap from the wood-chops, and countless family parties chewing sandwiches, and old Quong, the Chinese storekeeper, wandering round with a tray of greyish chocolates and streaky pink ice-cream.

'I wouldn'ta done it if I hadn't thought I was dying,' said Hughie.

'And I wouldn'ta accepted you if the doctor hadn't frightened the dear life outa me with the stomach pump, and him with the lip so long he was nearly tripping over it,' retorted his wife. With sparkling eyes they glared at each other.

'What happened? What happened?' wailed Dolour. Her mouth opened. Surely her father hadn't taken something? She gazed at him with shock and reverence. He'd taken poison, and then the doctor had come and saved his life, and Mumma had married him, scared lest he did it again. Jeepers! She could see the scene, down by the river bank – no, under the willows – with the sunshine dappling down, and Mumma so pretty in her hat with the parsley, and Hughie pale and stiff, with the silky black moustache, and Grandma saying prayers for him. For the sake of that romantic moment she almost forgave Hughie everything, his Friday nights and all.

'I never heard such nonsense, hiding a diamond ring in the puddin'!' suddenly cried the hero of the story. 'And leading everyone on to eat it until it came outa their ears.'

'It was all in the luck,' said Mumma dreamily.

'All in the size of the belly,' scoffed Hughie, 'and the endurance of a man, seeing the puddin' was the biggest sod God ever allowed to come out of a cloth.'

'Fifteen dozen eggs,' marvelled Mumma, 'and a whole little keg of butter. And the women taking it in turns to do the stirring with a copper-stick.'

'Don't tell anyone what you're talking about, will you?' snarled Dolour. Hughie and Mumma took no notice of her whatsoever, stirring their tea crossly and looking back in wonderment at the unbelievable boneheads on that Town Council, who had thought it a good idea to have at the annual picnic a pudding big enough to stuff everyone present to the eyebrows. They could still see it, like a monstrous wet mess of black mud, with currants and dates sticking out in dreadful anonymous knobs, being scraped into the pudding-cloth, which was made of four sheets sewn together.

'Cooking it in the tank wasn't the best,' said Hughie.

'That's what gave it the taste like old forks,' agreed Mumma.

Hughie looked a little pale round the gills. 'Just thinking of it gives me a stirring in the guts, after all these years,' he confessed, and with averted eyes shoved his greasy plate away.

Mumma was reluctant to let the occasion pass without a preen. 'I was the one to get you and Herbie on the move,' she said complacently. 'I'll never forget poor Herbie trying to eat with the front of his teeth, so he wouldn't taste it, and Ma fanning him with her hat, and cheering him on for Ireland and the Revolution.'

'Was he trying to get the ring, like the charm in a Christmas pudding? cried Dolour, desperately grasping after what appeared to be the last vestige of sanity in the conversation. Hughie snarled.

'That's what we were after all right, poor mugs that we were. "I could fall in love with the man who give me a diamond ring," she said, sticking out her great paw and seeing the ring already there in her imagination. So me and Herbie went hell for leather for it, poor goats that we were. And him with a tight collar on, too.'

'He always was soft on me,' said Mumma smugly.

'Gah!'

'Eight helpings he had, anyway!' cried Mumma defiantly.

'So did I!' roared Hughie. Mumma sniffed.

'Oh, yes, but Herbie was ready for a ninth, and you down on the ground undoing the top of your trousers in front of everybody, and groaning for the priest,' she sneered. 'And when the Father came he said, "It's not God's grace that boy's wanting, it's a good lift in the tail-end for making a hog of himself." '

'Well, you couldn't expect him to know what a man would do for the love of a woman,' growled Hughie, with reluctant loyalty to the priesthood.

Mumma blushed. 'Ah, well. You looked that pale, after the stomach pump, my heart bled. And when you said, "I'm a dying man, but you got to make me happy before I go," it was the finish of me,' she said softly. And for a moment all the years between vanished, and they stared at each other, Hughie seeing the round-faced girl with some sort of yellow splodge on her hat, and the fluffy hair, and sweet pink coming and going in her cheeks with the anxiety and love in her heart. And she saw him, with hollow blue eyes and eyelashes like soot on his pale skin, lying there amongst the peanut shells with the towel tucked round his neck, and suffering so much for her.

'Wish I coulda gnawed me way to that ring,' he said sincerely.

'Shut up! Shut up! Shut up!' shouted Dolour, standing up so suddenly their tea sloshed over. Her poor swollen eyes blazing, she glared at them.

'Now what?' demanded Mumma.

'I'd think you'd be ashamed – why don't you keep all this stuff to yourself! Oh, you're awful!' cried Dolour, stammering in her disgust of the down-to-earthiness that destroyed every dram of romance in her conception of her parents. There were many things she wanted to say, but there were no civil words for them. She ran upstairs blinded with tears and passion.

The quick soft tattoo of her feet awoke Roie. The door next to hers wumped into its ill-fitting lock, and Roie sighed. 'Poor kid.'

She was sad for her sister, but the sadness did not affect her essentially. The ultimate contentment that filled her heart did not leave room for any deep sorrows, as long as its origin and propagator remained untouched. She lay in the quietness, hearing the two all-important things in her life, the breathing of her child and the breathing of her husband. Warmth radiated from the man, warmth and peace. She put her arm over him, feeling the arch of his chest, the smoothness of the flesh over his ribs. Her wordless wonderment at the miracle of his body came to her again. In her idolatry of her husband, Roie acknowledged her reverence and awe of the fleshly edifice of mankind, the dust-built, incredible temple that in its ceaseless repetition found immortality.

'Charlie, my boy,' she murmured, not alone for his ear, but for the assurance of her own heart. Out of his sleep, he murmured in answer, inarticulate, wholly-comprehensible, the primitive language of unworded sound. He pulled her closer to him, and in the complete contentment of their love they lay, their breaths mingling, sleep flowing over them resistlessly as a dream.

Dolour heard their voices and knew them for what they were. Unformed, hardly understanding, her whole being reached out for an experience that seemed to belong to everyone in the world except herself. Her body was ready for love, and her mind was not, and in the boiling confusion only one thought emerged. Desperately she needed someone who would comfort and protect, who would belong to her alone, and who would above all love her. Love? What was it? Did she know?

'Yes, yes!' thought Dolour. She clung to the window-sill, staring into the moonlight-flooded yard, where the deep shadows welled up like splashes of Indian ink. She trembled with the force of emotion within her. No one would ever want her, with her disfigured eyes, and perhaps blindness ahead of her. Ill-educated, she would be good for nothing except slavery to the factory machines, like all the others. She would never know anybody except the Surry Hills boys, the good-hearted morons of the dance-halls, the scorchers on motor-bikes, the dills who frequented the corners and developed lips like cornet-players whistling after girls.

'Oh, what's the use? What's the use?' she groaned, and dragging off her clothes she fell into bed and closed her burning, stinging eyes.

Ten

After a while it became accepted in that house that Dolour had bad eyes, just as they accepted the stairs that twisted in the middle, and the skylight that let in the wind and wet of heaven in the winter. Soon Dolour felt as if she had been at home for ever, and there would never be anything else for her but wet cloths, and darkness, and doctors, and searing swabs, and all the misery and loneliness of uselessness. The small pleasures of youth blew up like balloons before her, always unattainable. Sometimes she begged Mumma to let her go to the pictures.

'I'll just keep my eyes closed all the time, dinkum I will,' she said eagerly. 'I'll just listen. Honest I will.'

'The doctor said – ' remembered Mumma doubtfully, but Roie begged, 'Aw, come on, Mumma.'

So Dolour went to the pictures, her small thin face half-hidden behind the round black windows of the goggles. As the old smells – the peanuts and dusty plush, and rotting timber, and pressing, flurried crowds – swept up round her, she trembled with excitement. The trumpeting music, spouting out of a sound equipment worn down to a nub, seemed to her to be the essence of liveliness and sociability; the squirming, shouting children, wandering back and forth to the Ladies and Gentlemen which were placed with homely convenience on either side of the screen; the women with their hair in curlers; the battalions of babies asleep in their prams behind the seats . . .

'Oh,' said Dolour, in an outburst of childish joy, 'ain't it lovely!'

When the lights went down she was plunged into almost total darkness. Dimly she could see the greyish flickerings on the screen, so she shut her eyes and tried to concentrate on the dialogue. She kept them shut conscientiously, but when the audience laughed, and no dialogue fitted the laughter, she surreptitiously pushed her glasses up on to her forehead, and gazed through slitted eyes at the screen.

She saw there the well-loved figures of her friends, the movie stars, the legendary shadows who brought laughter and quickly-soothed tears to the millions caught in the web of their mon-otonous and over-familiar lives. But it was only for a moment. Almost instantly her eyes began to water, and Roie leaned over and gave her a poke.

'You know what the doctor said,' she reminded.

'Yes,' said Dolour forlornly. She saw that Charlie and Roie were holding hands, and in a jealous rebellion she slid away to the further side of her seat and glowered there. But Charlie reached out, took her unresponsive paw, and squeezed it. His touch was different from that of the beaky boy in the back row when she had gone with Suse. It was calm, and comforting, and not at all clammy, so after a while Dolour giggled and squeezed back.

'Don't let my wife know,' whispered Charlie. She sat there in contentment, listening to the disconnected dialogue, laughing with the laughter, and swaying to the same music that swayed Ginger Rogers. She was happy, pretending that Charlie was somebody else, who belonged to her.

When she had been away some weeks, Mumma said, 'I think you'd better go and tell Sister Theophilus you won't be back for a bit.'

Dolour was glad of the glasses that hid her lack of resignation at this final, bitter blow.

'O.K.'

Going up the narrow, shabby corridor, with the buzz of class-rooms on either side, she felt strange, as though she were a new girl. She knocked on Sister Theophilus's door, and a girl she had never seen before opened it. She saw the familiar files of desks, the blackboard with the coloured chalk scroll, the maps, the pictures of lobsters and shells and the Laughing Cavalier round the walls.

A little titter of surprise and welcome and pleasure went round the room. Sister Theophilus closed the door gently behind her. Dolour felt clumsy and awkward, all big bony legs that stuck out in every direction. She put out a hand and took it back. There was so much emotion in her chest that her voice was difficult to manage.

'I just come – came – to say I won't be coming back to school, Sister.'

Sister heard the ache in the child's voice. She had heard it so often before. Most of her girls were so glad to get away from school they couldn't go out fast enough into the world of mystery and hardship and responsibility which yet called with so alluring a voice. But now and then she had had some promising pupil like Dolour, in whose breast burgeoned a desire for things better than those with which she had grown up.

Just a little while ago Dolour had been a child, grubby-fingernailed, with cobbled holes in her stockings and scuffed shoes; now she had retreated into a girl who wore someone else's ill-fitting clothes, bobby socks, and sandals, and goggles that hid her sore, weeping eyes so well an onlooker could read nothing from her expression.

She sighed, knowing that she had lost yet another to the smoky maelstrom of Surry Hills.

'Dolour – ' She hesitated. 'Don't feel your life's ended. Things may look very black now, but – there must be a great deal of happiness for you in the future, you've been such a good girl. I'll pray for you, and perhaps when your eyes are better we can arrange some extra lessons for you, out of school hours.'

'Yes,' mumbled Dolour. She avoided the nun's eyes. She wanted to say, 'Thank you, I've always loved you, I like the way you talk, and how you never get angry or loud-voiced and rude. I want to know what you think about, and whether it's a good thing for a girl to be a nun, and . . .'

Somehow she said good-bye, and stumbled away down the stairs where the banisters were notched and chipped with the initials of the daring.

Grey and disillusionary and hopeless the world stretched before her, with no avenue of escape. She passed up Coronation Street, and the boys on the corner, chewing their sandwiches and spitting out the crusts, turned and looked at her curiously. At most girls they whistled or called out ribaldries.

And that was how it was always going to be, thought Dolour. Her developing body, taking on the aspects of womanhood, seemed to her to be an insult and a reproach, an intolerable burden, for she wanted so much to return to the safety of childhood.

But there was too much Irish in her to keep from laughing long. Often the comical and the ludicrous that lay so close to the surface in their lives, sometimes a bedfellow of tragedy itself, cropped up in her path.

One day the cat plague descended upon Plymouth Street, which had always been a dispersal ground for strays of all sorts. It was a street with a faint, pervasive odour of tomcat, harsh and masculine and arrogant, and every patch of neglected grass outside a gate harboured its basking, knife-ribbed cat. The only fat cats in the street belonged to Lick Jimmy; aloof, unsociable cats they were, not speaking English, very conscious of stomachs lined with all the fantastically hacked titbits from the Chinese butcher shop, wherein nothing even remotely resembles a joint from an Occidental butcher.

But the stray cats were different. Like loose bits of fur slung over a backbone, faces shrunken into Tartar-cheeked triangles, their narrow paws and paltry tails poverty-stricken beyond description, they haunted the alleys, an army of the lost and unwanted. They came and went in bands, for if one picked up a full stomach somewhere, the others haunted that place until they were stoned away. Those at an attractive stage of growth, or with a pretty hide, were taken in and given a home; kind-hearted folk sent others away to be painlessly destroyed; but always and always there were cats, producing kittens even in the midst of their starvation, living on and on, hanging to a thread of life so wispy a breath seemed sufficient to sever it.

Roie's gentle heart could not bear it. She was for ever picking up cats and bringing them home.

'I'll just give it a saucer of milk and then we'll put it outside the fence,' was her excuse, knowing that she could not send the thing on its way empty-bellied.

Mumma stumped to the door and flung it open. 'Look!' she commanded. On each step sat a cat, and there were eight steps. Eight rusty necks turned, and eight pink mouths opened feebly.

'That's the way they go away,' commented Mumma.

'I'll put the lot in a bag and throw 'em over the bridge,' roared Hughie. 'I'd push the lot down the lavatory, if they weren't so big they'd choke the pipe.'

Roie had a battle with herself. Finally she said, 'All right, I'll take them away to-night.'

'I'll go with you,' said Dolour quickly, anxious to get in before Charlie, for she so rarely had her sister to herself. When she went outside she found Roie feeding the cats for the last time. They ate everything, meat, fish, vegetables, bread, even a piece of half-cooked pumpkin.

'Eat up big,' commanded Dolour. 'Lizards and rats for you tomorrow.'

'Oh, shut up!' cried Roie.

Dolour held a sugar-bag, and Roie arranged the cats within, each with its head sticking out. They wriggled and squirmed feebly, all except a small dwarfish creature with a perpetual wet patch on its back, which Hughie had christened Dirty Dick. Dirty Dick didn't want to go into the sugar-bag. He had been in too many sugar-bags. He sprang to the table, fluffed up his fur, and spat from a mouth where malnutrition had formed teeth as pigmy as himself, like minute white needles.

'Oh, can it, Dick!' Dolour thrust him, with his legs sticking out rigidly to the four winds, into the midst of the mewling bouquets of cats. There was an agonized upheaval, but she held the sack in a grip about their necks.

It was ten o'clock, a dark windy night with few people in the streets. Even the stars seemed wind-blown, like flames in a draught. The two girls walked slowly down the street, Dolour adapting her long strides to Roie's lagging ones. A continual soprano wail of complaint came from Dolour's bundle. They traced an irregular and difficult course through the alleys and streets, so that the cats would not find their way back.

Roie was hesitant about plunging into many of the pitch black lanes, but Dolour was completely fearless. Brought up in Surry Hills, she felt there wasn't a drunk in the district she couldn't have handled if he bailed her up. But they met nobody, and saw nobody except lovers crammed into doorways whispering to each other.

Dolour hated the sight of their shadowy bodies, the sound of their urgent, secretive voices.

But Roie understood. 'You got to go somewhere when you're like that. Lots of boys and girls live in residentials and they ain't allowed to have their friends there.'

'Ah, fooey!' cried Dolour angrily. 'Kissing and mugging and hugging, don't they ever think of anything else?'

'Wait till you fall in love,' said Roie. 'Wait till you want to get married.'

How could Dolour reveal that dearest wish, that she wanted to get married more than anything in the world? She knew only one way to shelter it, and said in a scornful voice, 'I wouldn't get married if all the fellers in the world were after me.'

The forlornness was so apparent in her voice that Roie laughed. 'Oh, Dolour, you are funny!'

Anger seized Dolour. 'All right, so I'm funny.'

They had come out into a little street on the edge of a high embankment, along which ran a high tin wall. Down below there was a wilderness of bricks and pieces of rusty tin, where two old tenements had been demolished in the slum rehabilitation programme. At intervals along the fence, crouched like images, squatted seven tomcats, each fixing the other with a loathing eye. Dolour ran along beside the fence, pushing them off one after the other. Diminishing wails came up from the dark hollow below, evoking cooing notes from the tabbies in the sugar-bag.

'This is a good place.' Giggling like children, their disagreement completely forgotten, they hurried along the street popping cats over the fences. One house had a large garden, so Roie generously presented it with two. Finally, over a high brick factory wall, Dolour shook the clinging, malodorous Dirty Dick.

'Quick!' they scampered along for a little, then Roie tired, and loitered heavily, the weight of the child bearing down her whole body. Dolour wanted to ask her questions that she was too shy to ask anyone else, and after a struggle with herself she burst out. 'Did Mumma tell you anything – you know – before you were married?'

Roie giggled. 'Yes, she did. She told me that lysol is good for perspiry feet.'

'Ain't that just like Mumma!'

After a little while Roie blurted out, 'If there's anything you want to ask . . . about boys . . . or anything . . .'

So much embarrassment seized Dolour that she said rudely, 'What's there to know about boys, anyway?'

Roie was half angry, half relieved, but she understood her sister too well to take any notice of her. 'It's just – well, when your eyes are better you'll be going out with boys, and if you know a little bit first . . .'

'Such as what?' asked Dolour with obstinate obtuseness, for she was too embarrassed to display anything else. Roie sighed.

'Well, I knew a girl once like you . . . I mean, a nice girl with . . . well, good ideas about everything . . . and she went around with a fellow and one night he asked her . . . you know.'

'She should have hauled off and thudded him on the ear,' said Dolour briskly.

Roie was exasperated. 'Yes, that's all right, but when you love someone you don't feel like that.'

'I would,' said Dolour scornfully. She felt herself like Joan of Arc, clad in pearly armour, virginal, unconquerable. She could just see herself breaking her own heart to thud her lover on the earhole.

'Well, say you didn't,' wailed Roie. 'Say you loved your feller so much you wanted to please him, no matter what it was.'

Dolour snorted, and Roie glared. They both struggled with their inarticulateness; Dolour because she was shy, and yet desperately eager to know, Roie because her vocabulary was so small, her powers of self-expression so limited.

'I want to tell you that it isn't worth it, never. That no matter how much you love a man he won't like you any better because you give in to him. He might even think smaller of you for it. This girl I knew – well, her boy took her pretty cheap afterwards and when she was going to have a baby he cleared out and left her. That's how much he thought of her.'

'Who was she?'

'Friend of mine.'

'Rosie Glavich?'

'I'm not going to tell you. Course I'm not.'

'What did she call the baby?' asked Dolour, her unconquerable interest in babies cropping up even in this angry and uncomfortable moment. She was astonished when Roie turned away from her and said, 'It never had a name. It died ... before it was born.'

After a while Dolour said, 'I guess that was lucky for her.'

'Yes, I suppose it was,' said Roie. Dolour was staring at her, so she forced herself to stare back.

'Why did Rosie Glavich tell you all these things?' asked her sister suspiciously.

'I told you it wasn't Rosie,' flared Roie.

'Who then?' jeered Dolour. She was going to accuse Roie of making it all up when she saw to her amazement the look on Roie's face, of sudden transfixation, as though she were looking in shocked horror at some memory almost forgotten.

'Thanks, Ro,' she said, awkwardly. 'I – you don't need to worry about me.'

She thrust her hands into her pocket, and to her pleasure she found a piece of chocolate, dry and powder-streaked, wrapped up in golden paper.

'Gee, look!' You can have it, Ro, it gives me pimples,' she said gladly, and Roie took it gratefully, knowing it was Dolour's recognition of her desire to help.

502

They were near the house. On the steps crouched a small, humpy form.

'It can't be!'

'Oh, Lord!' Roie picked up the little creature by its soggy scruff, and the dwarfish figure, a perpetual frown against the hateful cruel world grooving the skin between its eyes, showed its malformed teeth and hissed. 'It must have beat us home by a short cut.'

They took it in and gave it a feed, which it ate snarling furiously, gulping down the meat in an uncatlike way, slapping meantime with a savage, sixpence-sized paw at a flapping edge of the paper. The world had united against Dirty Dick, and Dirty Dick was going to give it a run for its money.

'Gern, I'll get rid of it once and for all,' said Hughie, bending down to grab the animal, but Mumma, fat and rheumaticky and all as she was, beat him to it. She interposed her plump leg between Dirty Dick and her husband, and Dirty Dick answered in gratitude by slashing his claws across it.

Mumma gave a sharp yelp, which slightly marred the effect of her defence. 'No, you don't, Hugh Darcy. The poor little cow deserves to stay. It won't be me that can't find a skerrick of meat for him once a day.'

So Dirty Dick became part of the household, a malevolent spirit that spent half its time being pushed off the table, slapped out of the butter, and bitten savagely on the tail by the loving Motty. Not even instinct told him what affection was. When a hand was stretched out to stroke him he crouched, flat of ear and glittering of eye, a sound like a vacuum cleaner deep down in his throat. No one ever picked him up without a wound. The smell of meat drove him completely mad, and he instantly climbed up the nearest object to the source of supply. Most often this was Mumma's patient back, and many and many a time she went roaring round the kitchen begging and pleading for someone to take the devil off the back of her neck.

'I hate to think of anyone in this house who gets a bloody nose,' said Hughie, direfully. 'He'd wake up to find himself nothing but bones.'

Dirty Dick was a fine advertisement for mankind.

But Dolour was comforted by his prowling over the roof at night. He liked to sit, for ever licking at the sodden patch on his rusty back, on her attic window-sill. She never ventured to touch him, for she felt their lonely, solitary quality was the same.

Dolour never prayed that her eyes might get better. The disease was her hostage to fate; the pain and discomfort and deprivation her cupboardful of treasure, to be swapped in the future for felicity. She had the good Celtic practicality about spiritual things and saw nothing niggling in God's demand to be paid for what He might give. It was just. She gave him her fortitude and resignation under suffering and misery; in return He would give her an overflowing measure of happiness that might start any day, any hour. Sometimes in her soul she had dark, despairful suspicions that He was overdoing it a little, but she kept this from Him.

But she considered her emotions were her own, and in the privacy of the dark she often gave way, weeping with her face tightly jammed into the pillow, so that she nearly suffocated. Sometimes Charlie heard muffled clangs as her feet, drumming on the counter-pane, missed and hit the end of the bed. He grinned, for he was saving up for a surprise for her.

Finally it was bought. Mumma felt abashed that she had never grown to like him quite as she should, and she said gruffly, 'It's real thoughtful of you.'

'Listen,' said Charlie. Mumma put the black earphone of the crystal set to her ear, and Spike Jones made her hair lift. An astonished, delighted grin spread over her face. 'Ain't it clever! Lord, fancy that!'

Dolour was overcome by the sight of her present, but she did not know how to thank Charlie. She put her ear to the black plastic circle, and a minute budgerigar voice assured her of everlasting glamour if she used R-O-S-E-B-U-D soap.

'Jeepers, Charlie,' she croaked. To hide her emotion she jammed the earphones over her head, and beamed at him, looking grotesquely like a refugee from the War of the Worlds, with the horned black muffs over her ears and the large round goggles flashing heliograph signs.

Now her life was strung on the vibrating whisker of the crystal set. Every night she went to bed early, and lay in the darkness to listen-in. She listened-in to everything, and went to sleep with the earphones on, so that she woke to the gay canary chirp of an announcer whose great cross was that he had to sound like noon at six in the morning.

Without the fretting, and the tears, her eyes improved a little. There was something to look forward to now, the heterogeneous,

noisy entertainment of the radio world. She was still not of the
world, but at least she could hear its voice. When she was down the
road doing the messages, Mumma often went up and picked up the
earphones, holding them at arm's length, and bending her neck
towards them like a flamingo; they seemed to her much more
wonderful than the wireless itself, and much more likely to
explode. And probably if she had been left with them long that was
just what they would have done, for Mumma was the sort whose
very instinct was to do things wrong. She put patches on the wrong
side of the rent in Hughie's trousers, wore her hats backwards, and
could never find the dotted line she was supposed to sign on. There
was no mechanical contrivance on earth Mumma couldn't hurt
herself with, feeding her fingers into egg-beaters and shutting her
skirt into the ice-chest along with the milk. If anyone had ever
given her an electric iron she would have electrocuted herself with
it the first hour, by doing something to the defenceless thing that
no one else would ever have thought of.

Dolour could not find words to thank Charlie, so she went to
mass for him instead. And Roie, slowly and laboriously now, went
with her, getting up in the early summer morning so often that
Charlie became used to waking up and finding the short body of
Motty beside him instead of his wife's. She was a thoughtful, self-
possessed child, and liked to put her face within two inches of his,
so that he opened his unfocused eyes to find them staring into two
unwinking circlets of blue, which had obviously been committing
every line and feature to memory.

'How did you get here?' he groaned, turning his face into the
pillow.

'Mummy put me here,' said Motty calmly, which was a lie. She
poked her fingers between his teeth and pried his mouth open.

'What are you looking for, for gosh sake?' mumbled her father.

'Things,' said Motty. She clambered on to his stomach, lay back
against his knees, and looked peacefully at the ceiling.

'Flies have whiskers,' she said. Charlie, coming slowly out of the
sleep of exhaustion and discomfort that a slum night can bring,
surveyed his daughter. She was a ceaseless wonder to him, this little
being who had been nowhere, nowhere at all until he loved Roie.
He looked at the perfection of her body, the completeness of her
eyelashes and teeth, and marvelled. The number of generations
that had gone to make her, the lines of blood and bone and nerve

that converged in her – he tried to count them and failed. The great-grandmother who had been black, who had given him golden eyes and long sinewy hands – she was manifest in Motty in the wet polish of her hair that was no more like Roie's soft, sooty Irish hair than metal was like silk. And her blue eyes, with the dark thumb-prints about them, were Irish. So he stared and wondered, until he heard Roie climbing clumsily up the stairs.

At first Dolour's tender, inflamed eyeballs protested with furious tears that they could stand no light, but gradually she became used to the evening light without her goggles, and even in the noon she could bear it, inside the house, for a few moments. The pearly spots, which had been swallowed up in the bloodshot conjunctiva, became apparent as the red faded into pink, but instead of being swollen white excrescences on the eyeball, they were fading into a transparent mucus.

'They're going to get better, Ro,' she breathed. 'Oh, I don't mind if I have to wear goggles for years if only they get better a little!'

Roie was silent, not knowing what to say in case Dolour were to be disappointed. But Dolour said herself, 'I'll be able to get a job and to help Mumma out a bit.'

She said not a word of her lost ambitions, and Roie wondered pitifully if they had been put away on a shelf for ever. She was glad when they met little Mrs Drummy on the church steps. Mrs Drummy did sewing, it was plain to be seen, for her hair was covered with odds and ends of cotton, as though she were a mop that needed to be shaken out the window.

'Oh, love,' gasped Mrs Drummy breathlessly, 'ain't it a lovely morning! It's that nice to see you around again, Dolour. I been saying a prayer for you, don't you worry. Dear St Martin de Porridge, the black man, he's that good.' And she beamed as a gardener does when an unexpected seed pops up and produces a blossom. 'Oh, Lord, I gotta skip outa mass before it's finished again. We're that busy in the shop with the races on. I never see Bert at all, he's that busy with the S.P.'

She beamed and trotted into church. Dolour and Roie looked at each other, then without a word Dolour hurried after Mrs Drummy. Somewhere in her heart tears were rising, for the lost knowledge, the lost opportunities that would never be hers now. Then she squashed them down. Yes, they could be hers, some day. She was raised to be a worker, to take the amount of schooling the

Government decreed was necessary, then to scuttle out as fast as possible to get a job to help out in the family. But somehow she could put by a little every week to educate herself later on. Some day she'd leave, and do what she wanted to do, and never come within the shadow of the Hills any more.

She marched down the aisle to where Mrs Drummy, a humped, shabby little figure, was conducting a loud conversation with St Theresa. Dolour crashed in without an apology.

'Could you give me a job, Mrs Drummy?' she hissed. 'I could serve in the shop and help you out a bit.'

Mrs Drummy's eyes shone with pleasure, and Father Cooley, who had been watching willy-nilly their reflected conversation in the shining brass door of the Tabernacle, turned round, glared, and coughed thunderously. Dolour slunk back to her seat.

This was how she got her first job, down at the ham-and-beef.

Eleven

When Hughie learned that Dolour was going to work at
Drummy's, a tiny pang entered his heart, and he ate his lunch
hurriedly and went off to the pub. He boasted for a while to his old
mates – of his girl's smartness, and how she had had eye trouble and
had to leave school. Then he was silent, remembering Dolour's
passionate and tender spirit that had taken all the humiliations and
rough hardships life had imposed upon it, and yet retained enough
energy to bud forth in little ambitions of its own.

'She wanted to get a posh job,' he said.

'Nobody out of Surry ever gets a posh job,' said one of the old
mates, a melancholy fellow with a face like a goanna.

This was manifestly untrue. Surry Hills citizens had become
priests, politicians, and police-sergeants. They had soared into the
heavy income-tax division of factory-owners, black-marketeers and
garage proprietors. But in his uneasy disappointment for Dolour,
Hughie accepted the dictum of his miserable friend. The beer went
off, and Hughie retaliated against the unfeeling publican by pouring
a pint or two of harsh Australian sherry into his stomach on top of
what he had there. It made him feel even worse. He barged off
home, through a world which had dislocated itself from its horizon
and was floating some feet above the ground.

The heat was so intense, and the beer and sherry hated each
other so furiously, that Hughie felt he might die any moment.
Sweat soaked the back of his shirt in a huge irregular grey patch.
His hat was obviously made of iron, drawing down the rays of the
sun like a burning-glass focused unerringly upon his brain.

In his distress he missed his way, and blundered down the wrong
turning towards Darlinghurst. He stood staring dizzily round,
wondering how he had got there, but he was too sick to bother
retracing his steps. He saw a desolate fig-tree leaning over a fence
and casting a thick oval of shade. There was already a panting dog
lying there, but Hughie pushed it out of the way and collapsed
against the fence.

He lay there, scratching frequently, for two or three hours. No one went past on that lazy Saturday afternoon. All the windows hung open, washing drooped its spiritless legs and arms from sagging lines, and there was no sound save the muffled squawk of a radio belching out the races. Already, so early in the summer, the sun was like golden syrup, dripping languidly off a spoon. Hughie tried to remember what he had been so upset about, but he was too dizzy. His eyes felt as though he had been crying, but he hadn't.

Somewhere above him, roosting in the tree perhaps, a voice said, 'Hey!'

Hughie, unable to move his eyes for the pain in them, lolled his head and looked into the upper air.

'I'm 'ere,' said the little voice, and, upside down, Hughie saw a face protruding over the fence. A peculiar face it was, something like a Pekinese's, with a bulging, wrinkled forehead, pathetic eyes, and a nose fair in the middle like a push-button.

'Like a cuppa?' invited the face. Hughie groaned. There was a scuffling sound, and a finger poked him through a hole in the fence. He turned painfully, and there was a bluish eye staring at him through a knot-hole.

'I been watching you,' the eye informed him. 'You been looking as though you got heat-stroke, moaning away there, and sweating yourself into a puddle. 'Ere, you come inside, and I'll give you a cuppa and a powder.'

Hughie needed an A.P.C. powder. He needed anything that would turn the fermenting solfatara out of his stomach and the thumping pain out of his head. He swayed to his feet, and magically at his right hand a door in the fence creaked open, and he was ushered inside.

By the smell, he thought the large building at the end of the yard was a garage. The yard itself had plainly been used as a parking lot, for the stains of old grease blotted the soil, and a serpentine heap of inner-tubes lay in a corner like unimaginable offal.

Along the fence was a curious building of asbestos sheets, plywood, and hammered out iron. It was shaped like a fowl-house, with sloping roof patched with tacked-on pieces of boxes and petrol tins, and it was divided into many little cubicles seven foot square.

'Whazzat?' asked Hughie, politely.

'Oh, that's the flophouse,' replied his new friend, a baggy, miniature creature like a full-sized man whom someone had allowed to deflate. Hughie was no giant himself, but the little man came only to his breastbone and this in some mysterious way made him feel a lot better.

He realized, as they went towards one of the cubbyholes, that each cubicle was occupied. Here sat an old man on a chair at his doorway, cutting his toenails with the slow, cautious preoccupation of one who could not trust his own toes to stay twice in the same place; on a stretcher in another sibilantly slumbered an old woman in a hideously advanced stage of debilitation and neglect, and in yet another two aged crones quarrelled feebly.

' 'Ere.' Hughie sat down on the rickety bag bed. The air within the cubbyhole was sickeningly hot, and the sweat popped out on his brow again. He sat looking at a large glossy brown teapot on the table, surrounded by a bead-like ring of flies. He moistened his lips and felt an overwhelming urge to hang his tongue out.

'Take sugar?' The host raised his face inquiringly from a sticky brown-paper bag. Hughie nodded, dry-mouthed, as he unfolded to his feet.

' 'Scuse me. Won't be a jiff.'

'Sure,' said his little friend cheerily.

After that Hughie felt better, the uplifted, garrulous feeling of one who has been sick beyond all mortal calculation.

The interior of the cubbyhole was not very clean, and each leg of the stretcher stood in a jam tin of water. This did not amaze Hughie, though their bugs at home took no notice of such precautions, falling down from the ceiling or throwing themselves off the walls to get at their sleeping prey. A thin grey blanket, obviously at three bob a shot from the Army Surplus Stores, and a depressed, dirty pillow were on the bed, along with three racing magazines and a tobacco tin with a butt in it transfixed by a pin. This did not surprise Hughie either; he had often taken a butt about half an inch long, stabbed it through its malodorous middle and got a few more puffs out of it.

' 'Ere's yer mike,' said his host, shoving over a pannikin of stewed and boiling tea. Hughie blew on it gratefully. It did not enter his head that it was odd for this stranger to have invited him in; he had often done the same for those who seemed under the weather or the influence. It had never occurred to him that he was throwing bread on the waters of charity. The poor cow needed a helping hand just as other cows needed a boot in the jeer, and he was just as free with the one as with the other.

Soon he felt almost himself. 'Watcher mean, flophouse?'

'Ain't it a flophouse?' inquired the little man.

'My oath,' said Hughie, looking around distastefully.

'Got rats, too,' said the little man. They drank their tea in silence. Then Hughie said politely, 'How much they sting yer for it?'

'Half a frog.'

'Strewth!'

'Jest leaves yer enough to starve on,' said the old man with a sort of perverted pride.

While the tea in the pot sank lower, and the sunlight crept up the wall to disappear in a burst of twinkles under the iron roof, Hughie learned the history of the flophouse, probably only one of many in that city. Each cubbyhole was the home of an invalid or old-age pensioner, most of them once good hard workers, who had committed the mortal sin of living too long. Unable to find anywhere to live for the sum they could afford, they dragged out their lives in cold, misery, and squalidity in places such as this, erected hastily by landowners who saw a good opportunity to clean up regular small profits by charging these people ten shillings a week each for rent.

The man who owned this Surry Hills flophouse made eleven pounds a week clear profit out of his pensioners.

'What's up with you, anyhow?' asked Hughie.

The old man smote his chest. 'I got angela pectoris. It's a heart trouble. Serious.'

'Not serious enough to be worth more than a coupla quid a week though,' growled Hughie.

'Well, I got me roof,' said the old fellow peaceably. 'After you've slep' out of doors for a few nights you change your mind about the sorta roof you like best.'

'Yeah.' Hughie brooded. He wanted to go out brandishing a cudgel in defence of these poor, ragbag creatures who had no homes of their own to sleep in, or cut their toenails in. Two pound two and six a week, and they hadn't been getting that much a short while ago. That meant they had about three bob a day to feed, clothe, warm and amuse themselves. Hughie quickly translated it into beers, and in horror translated it back again even more quickly. It was plain that a pensioner could never have a beer.

'Ain't so bad for me,' said the old man placatingly. 'I got this little kerosene burner to cook on. Everyone else has to eat out, and it takes your money that fast!'

'Haven't you got any children you could stay with?'

The old man seemed suddenly to shrink, and Hughie was alarmed in case he should disappear altogether into an empty heap of clothes.

'I 'ad a boy once. But he was killed in the fust war, at Gallipoli. That's all the kids I ever 'ad. And me wife, she died on me close on twenty year ago.' He brightened up. 'You mightn't know, but I was a jockey once. Bumper Reilly they called me. Fust-rate jockey. 'Ad me name in the papers more times than I could count.'

He rummaged eagerly in the pockets of an old coat spread-eagled on a couple of nails. It was his cupboard and storehouse. He took a piece of yellow soap out of the breast pocket, two nails, and a bundle of clippings with stained, rat-nibbled edges.

'There!' The black-nailed finger pointed to the almost illegible print. Hughie held it close to his eyes, then at arm's length.

'Hum.'

'Good, ain't it?' asked Bumper Reilly, delighted. 'Look where it says Bumper Reilly rode such a race as has not been seen on the Australian Turf.'

Hughie spread a pleased grin over his face like butter. 'Fine to have things like that to look back on in yer old age,' he assented. Instantly the pathetic Pekinese look took its place on Mr Reilly's face. He wrapped the clippings round the soap, and put it back in the pocket.

'I'd like to slip yer a coupla bob for a drink, seeing you sorta came to me rescue,' said Hugh in embarrassment.

'The soap keeps the mice away, I always think,' said Mr Reilly with an indescribable look of proud rejection. Hughie sneaked the two bob on to the table. The old man saw it, but his pride had been satisfied, and he left it where it was.

There was a squall from the next cubby, and one of the old women, like a grey old mangy cat, hardly human in her poverty and raggedness, hobbled past, weeping. She was a little old animal, as unwanted and as smelly as Dirty Dick, who, having ridden the tides of life, was thrown up in this yard like flotsam of the worst possible quality.

'Never stop fighting,' observed Mr Reilly gloomily. 'Yah, yah, yah, all night long. When one dies, the other will commit suicide.'

'Look,' said Hughie impulsively, 'we gotta spare room in our place.'

The wine, oozing triumphantly up through the tea, sent forth a great warm fume of generosity and good feeling towards this poor old wreck.

'Sure,' he said, 'the missus wouldn't be objecting if we rented it to you. The roof's all in one piece, and there's a gas ring for cooking on, and there'll be plenty of tucker floating around,' he added largely, 'which we wouldn't miss, just to help you out a bit like. Seven and six would do for the rent.'

'But maybe the missus wouldn't take to me,' quavered the old man. 'I got all them parcels, you know.'

Hughie noticed what he had not noticed before, that under the table were stacked dozens and dozens of small parcels, all neatly tied with string, and clothes-line, and bits of red wool.

'Aw, what's a parcel or two between mates. A man can't help collecting a bit of luggage, and he can't always be buying ports on two quid a week. Tell you what, Bumper,' he said, beginning to feel dazed again, but in a soft-headed, happy way, 'you come round on Monday, and see the missus, and don't let her give you any cheek. Mrs Darcy's the name. Anyone who comes up all friendly the way you did and asks me in just like an old cobber is going to get what's coming to him. Me mother never raised a squib.'

'What's the address?' asked Mr Reilly feverishly, in case Hughie should change his mind. He licked a stub of purple pencil and stood waiting.

'Twelve-and-a-half Plymouth Street,' said Hughie, undecided whether he wanted to cry at his generosity or not. It was one of those moments when you leaned against your cobber and your cobber leaned against you, and you slapped each other's backs feebly and benevolently, and swore never to part. But Mr Reilly was much too small to lean against unless you were a dwarf.

He tottered home, enveloped in a golden mist of good fellowship, and it wasn't till he saw Mumma that he realized what he was in for, when Bumper Reilly and his parcels arrived.

'Ah, don't worry your head, Hughie man,' he chided himself. 'Sure, he's an old man, and that shaky a good thump on the ear would blow him over. He might be dead by Monday.'

That Monday morning Dolour had to start work. She had spent most of the Sunday learning the ways of the shop, which was one of those that open at dawn to catch the headache-powder, chewing-gum, soda-water trade, and close as late as the inspectors allow. There was a great sensation among the Drummys when it was known that Dolour Darcy, their old schoolmate, was to work for their mother. A careless, roaring crew, they thundered in and out of the shop almost without ceasing, and never a can of ice-cream in that place was emptied without their grubby fingers scooping up the last blob.

Dolour had chosen to take the early shift, opening the shop at six, when the milkmen clashed and clattered down the road with their cans. Then she was supposed to sweep and scrub it, fill the refrigerator with soft drinks, clean the counters, and freshen up the window. She was to learn that trade was so constant there was almost no time to do these things. The shop was in a good position, the focal point of a dozen poor streets. It sold milk and bread, butter and groceries, and delicatessen goods of a strictly utilitarian kind. The pickled cucumber, the olive, and the black walnut found no resting-place there; but corned beef, pressed ham, and various kinds of dreadfully pink or miserable grey sausage, which could be sold at a 'frippence-worf' and a 'zack's worf,' filled the glass window of the refrigerator.

The little shop was well aware of its prosperity. Drab of paint, its window decorated with curly strips of coloured paper hung up two Christmases before, nevertheless it appeared to bulge and burst with its contents. Straw brooms and sacks of onions and boxes of eggs and pegs gushed out of the doorway as though they were just about to leave, and inside cases of tomatoes and tins of biscuits provided handy steps and stairs to the counter for the children who were too short to see over the top.

It smelt of bacon and cheese and long-vanished tobacco, and Dolour hated it from the moment she entered it as its slave.

She unlocked the flimsy door, which was cracked with the efforts of a thousand drunks shoving each other affectionately against it. The milk carters, great husky whistling fellows, charged down the almost empty street like knights in armour, whirled into the shop, sloshed the milk into the cans, chyacked Dolour about her goggles, and charged out again, leaving behind them such an atmosphere of arrant masculinity that it was almost an odour.

She peeped timidly into the room behind the shop, in case any of the Drummys should be sleeping there, but, hollow and twilit, it was empty save for the headless form of Mrs Drummy's dressmaker shape, which stood in a corner, its pure calico bosom cruelly studded with pins. Here, too, was the sewing machine, and the little table where Mr Bert Drummy made out his S.P. books. Upstairs she could hear the stirrings of the Drummys, groans from Bert, querulous chitterings from his wife, and all the piggish snorts from the boys' bedroom. She quickly got the broom and swept out the shop, sprinkled down the pavement, and looked longingly into the sunrise that blossomed in the clear morning sky above Coronation Street. Fresh and pure, it was a fan of light reaching out of the vast chalcedony spaces and focusing like a searchlight on the city that was, after all, but an irregular red and grey speck on the vast tawny continent.

Now smoke was tufting the chimneys, for most of the houses in this street had landlords who hadn't heard of the invention of gas or electric power. She saw Lick Jimmy appear, trundling a little handcart, and trot off towards the vegetable markets. The little noises of stirring people, the little smells of breakfast, rose up in a perceptible wave.

'Ah, gee!' Dolour went inside, and put on the old pink overall that had been left over from Roie's box-factory days. Of course it did not fit her, and her long legs stuck out like a heron's. She took off her glasses and cautiously peered into her eyes. They were weak and pinkish, but no longer savagely inflamed. The lids were thickened and she had lost any looks she had ever had, but . . .

'Thank You, God,' said Dolour. She put on some lipstick. It made her pasty, unhealthy face even pastier, but it made her feel better.

Somebody pounded on the counter, and a harsh voice shouted, 'Sharp!'

Dolour scurried out, feeling nervous, for she was not at all good with change. She was out of luck, for her first customer was the Kidger.

The Kidger was an alcoholic who nightly slept with the snakes. A tall, emaciated creature, he was so bowed by his indulgences that he was bent in the middle like a fish-hook. A face as stony as a turbot's was the Kidger's. He drooled almost continuously, and his filthy coat, double-breasted and long-draped in a piteously slick spiv fashion, was streaked with the snail tracks of saliva. The Kidger was the pet and mascot of the street. He was so far gone down the path to physical and mental ruin that no one had the heart to refuse him a drink when he came begging for one; anything came well to the Kidger, plonk, plink, metho, bombo, or just ordinary whisky. He was never known to eat.

A protégé and employee of Delie Stock, the procuress, he

received a small salary and a bed for doing nothing at all. It was commonly believed that Delie sent the Kidger out to cause a commotion when the Vice Squad was getting too close, and used his arrest as a distractive measure. But she liked him, and protected him, and whom Delie protected you did not offend, if you didn't want your ribs in splinters.

This was the creature that Dolour found, lolling over the counter at half-past six in the morning. He had plainly been on the booze all night, and a cheesy pallor was added to his dreadful face.

'Why'n't yer starp in the sharp?' he demanded, his bleared eyes not even distinguishing between Mrs Drummy's dumpling face and Dolour's thin sallow one.

'Boll milk!' he demanded. She handed him a bottle, and he tore off the foil cap with his teeth, tipped it up and flooded it in a white stream over his face and coat.

'Gah!' A stream of profanity spouted out of his gaping mouth and joined the milk. He dropped the bottle on the floor and reached for another.

'Go easy,' protested Dolour, rescuing the other bottles, which teetered before his restless arm. He snatched another from her grip and stood with his hand over it, looking at her over the neck of the bottle he had in his mouth, like a dog defying all comers to take his food from him.

'That'll be elevenpence,' said Dolour, taking the mop and dabbing at the pool of milk on the floor.

Now the Kidger was feeling happier. Something like a smile made an effort to alter the concrete grooves of his face, and failed. He began systematically on Dolour, giving her detailed, filthy information about herself, what had happened to her, and what was likely to happen.

In spite of all the drunken flip-flap she had heard from her father, she had never before witnessed the stirring up of such a pool of slime as this creature's mind. For a few moments she pretended not to hear, not knowing whether to yell for Bert Drummy, or burst into tears, or what. The shock and horror of the Kidger's words had such an effect on her that it was years before she forgot them.

'That's elevenpence,' she said weakly.

Now the Kidger saw that he was talking to a bit of a girl, and he was delighted. In her pale face and awed eyes he saw the good world he hated, the respectable world he despised. He came a little closer and said a lot more, the running commentary of the brothels during the drink-sodden, nightmarish nights.

All at once Dolour lifted the mop and charged. It was so swiftly done that she had thudded him in the solar plexus before she realized she had moved. Using it like a lance, she bore him out of the door. He slid in the pool of milk and landed on his back, whereupon Dolour, unconsciously using the technique of her ancestors, reversed the mop and stabbed him with the handle under the chin.

'Gulk!' said the Kidger. He rose upon hands and knees and scuttled down the footpath for home and Delie Stock, but Dolour pounced after him, cracked him across the skull with the handle and shoved him violently into the gutter, where he lay on his back crying, his hands and legs up like the paws of a beaten dog.

Dolour was shaking with fury and distress. She went back into the shop and washed the mop conscientiously, then soaked up the milk on the floor without being at all aware of what she was doing.

The whimpering outside lasted for quite a long time, for the Kidger was hoping for someone to come along and listen to his story and be sympathetic. But everyone hastening along Plymouth Street on the way to work was in too much of a hurry even to look at him, and at last he crawled out of the banana skins and lolly-papers and filth, and wandered off, spouting such a ceaseless stream of disgusting obscenity about Dolour that it made even the citizens of that street wonder what had upset him.

Dolour served the early morning customers for two hours – the young girls who had a threepenny ice-cream for breakfast, the drunken woman who choked her way through half a siphon of soda water, the man who, she was to learn, bought three boxes of headache powders every morning. In his way he was a dope addict, but his strings were tied to the unusual horses of anacin, phenacetin and caffeine. And there were the endless cheerful, sooty-pawed children, who even at that hour were having penny glasses of the gaseous, sweet-syruped contents of the soft-drink bottles. Dolour did not wonder why it was that these children, improperly fed, never provided with nourishing school lunches, always had plenty of pennies to spend. She knew only too well the way of an overworked mother or surly father with a penny. It was one sure way of getting a kid out of the road.

She was feeling accustomed to it, even interested, when Harry

Drummy came lurching into the shop, wiping grease off his mouth and slicking down his hair in the same motion. He leaned himself against the counter on the extreme tip of one elbow, which seemed to have a nodule on the end, as a pumpkin does. Harry Drummy, whom Dolour had once fleetingly loved in their schooldays, had grown into a large youth with a pear-shaped face upon which pimples struggled to get a foothold. His hands, his feet, his wrists and knees were a matter of ceaseless confusion to him. He felt like a small boy wearing a very large suit, and this suit was his all too solid, unpredictable, unmanageable body. His manner was a mixture of shyness and rudeness, and he tried to cover it up by adopting the veneer of a larrikin, as though to demonstrate to the world that he didn't give a deener for its regard. His hair, swept straight back, was marked with savage combing.

'Howya?'

He dived into the box of stale cakes and stuffed one after the other into his face as though he were posting letters.

'Hullo, Harry.' Dolour was acutely conscious of the length of leg protruding from her overall.

'You've got lipstick on.'

'So what?'

He peered at her critically, and hung out his tongue and licked a crumb off his chin.

'Wrong colour. Brunettes shouldn't wear that colour.'

'Fat lot you know about it,' said Dolour crossly.

'Sure I do. I'm a tiger with the tomatoes. Take yer glasses off and let's have a look at yer eyes.'

'I certainly won't,' said Dolour. 'I gotta wear them all the time,' she added lamely.

'Certainly make yer look a crumb.'

He fished in the refrigerator, found a raw sausage, and ate it. Dolour marvelled how she had ever found him romantic. She watched fascinated while he stuck out his tongue and squeezed the greyish-pink sausage meat on to it in blobs from the ruptured skin. He held out the stump of the sausage.

'Have a bite?'

'Ah, you turn me up!'

'Like to go to the pitchers to-night? If you gotta coupla bob you can shout me,' he offered casually. Dolour was thrilled in spite of herself. Nobody had ever asked her to go to the pictures except Charlie, and he was so old, and married, anyway.

But she answered carelessly, 'Oh, I dunno. It hurts my eyes.'

'You needn't look at the screen,' he said helpfully. 'We can just sit and cuddle.'

'Get out!'

In such graceless conversation did they pass the time until Harry went off to work. Mrs Drummy popped in for a moment to see how things were going, commended Dolour on the orderliness of the shop, and went out to the kitchen to get the children off to school. There was an avalanche of kiddies in to spend their pennies before the bell rang, and Dolour nearly drowned under the cascades of orangeade and lime juice 'n soda.

Then, in the lull that followed, the Kidger returned, with Delie Stock. At the sight of them, Dolour's heart turned over like a fish and fluttered its fins. She had seen Delie Stock only from a distance, but she knew her reputation stone by stone. And it was quite clear that she had come down to the shop to avenge the beaten Kidger.

The Kidger had sobered up a little. He had changed his double-breasted coat for a pale yellow shirt, which had the collar turned up so that it flapped its sharply-starched wings on either side of his chin. His soulless face was completely consumed by a hyena-like triumph; he wanted to stand by and watch while his owner and mistress whaled the tar out of this upstart who had gone for him with a mop.

Delie came in as though she owned the place, looked contemptuously round as though this were the kind of dump where she'd expect to find a girl like Dolour. Dolour stood behind the counter trembling; she was frightened that if she opened her mouth Delie would give it a backhander.

'That's 'er!' said the Kidger helpfully.

'Shurrup,' commanded Delie. She leaned her elbows on the counter and stared at Dolour. Dolour stared back, paralysed, overcome by the legend that surrounded this woman.

'Slugged me with a mop, she did, and all for nuthink,' said the Kidger with the meaningless ferocity of a wounded child. Delie Stock took no notice of him.

'Didjer?'

Dolour opened her mouth and a squeak came out. Hastily she tried again, and a weak, placatory little voice explained, 'He swore at me.'

Delie Stock had been taken aback by Dolour's presence in the shop. She had expected Mrs Drummy, who could always be bullied into tears and cajoled into smiles, a process that pleased the curious mind of Delie Stock, who liked to feel her authority and be commended for her humanity. She tossed back the mangy fur collar of her coat.

'Gawdelpus! You're old enough not to mind a bitta bad language! Chrisake, if you go round bashing up everyone who swears at you you'll spend yer life in the boob.'

Delie sounded so reasonable, and the Kidger glared at her so unblinkingly that Dolour could not say a word. Her youth prevented her quick thinking; she stood there and blushed and gaped.

'Jabbed me in the belly, too,' whined the Kidger, 'and me liver's as tender as a boil on the neck.'

'I don't care,' blurted out Dolour. 'He came in here and made a mess on the floor, and he took two bottles of milk and wouldn't pay for them. Then he called me everything he could think of.' Her lips trembled. This was the limit of her defence, and she could think of nothing else.

Delie turned slowly and looked at the Kidger. 'That's true, ain't it?'

'I was gonna pay,' defended the man. 'No one's got any business taking a broom to a customer, 'specially when he's a sick man.'

'Gerrout,' said Delie.

'Stuck-up little bitches think they're the only ones on earth just because they're on the other side of a counter. Listen to the way she talks, stinking little bitch,' he mumbled, staring off at a tangent over Dolour's shoulder.

'I said gerrout!' bawled Delie suddenly, and the Kidger hurriedly got, executing a pathetic stagger on the threshold as though to impress his implacable mistress with his frailty.

Delie slapped a shilling on the counter. 'I'll pay his bill,' she said, 'and any time he comes in here giving up the breadth of his tongue you pop up to Little Ryan Street and let me know about it.'

Dolour took the shilling silently. Delie prepared to be chatty.

'Whassa matter? You look as pale as a sheet.'

'I'm fine,' said Dolour.

'What's the matter, with yer eye? Got a pig-sty?'

'They've been bad,' said Dolour. 'I've been at the hospital lots of times.'

A warm feeling came into Delie's heart. She knew that a few

520

moments earlier she would have slipped this kid a fiver to pay the hospital bill, but, after all, it was only this morning that she'd passed out three quid to someone who'd snapped off an ankle like a stick of celery down the street. A woman had to be business-like. A glowing weakness overtook her limbs at the thought of her generosity, for with the passing years, Delie Stock had become more and more sentimental.

'That's crook,' she said, nodding her head, and Dolour saw in the gesture the old woman who stood like a humped shadow behind Delie Stock, the old woman she was going to be. 'I ain't too well meself these days. Dunno why.'

'Fancy,' said Dolour awkwardly, feeling that she was to be treated to the details of some loathsome occupational disease, but Mrs Stock only said, 'I feel sorta all-over. Tired, kinda. Maybe I ought to take a holiday somewhere.' She pressed a hand to her flabby, sequined green bosom. 'Sorta heavy feeling in here.'

'Maybe you work too hard,' said Dolour mechanically, then burned scarlet. But Delie Stock did not notice anything.

She went on, heavily, 'That Kidger, you don't want to take any notice of him. He's low. Even talks that way when I'm around sometimes.'

'Gee,' said Dolour.

'Ignorant. You know,' said Delie, including Dolour in the ladylike circle to which she herself belonged. She looked querulously at the girl. 'Why'n't you use a bit of rouge? You're terrible pale.'

'I guess it's the light in here,' said Dolour feebly.

'You wouldn't be so bad if you put on a bitta colour.' Delie grew confidential. 'You know what? You got a nice little figure coming up there.'

Dolour did not know which way to look. She was terrified lest Delie Stock should offer her a job, for she had no idea how to refuse tactfully. But the woman did not. She touched her bosom again, tried to say something, and went heavily away, sinking down inside her dirty and neglected finery as though she were a bird in another's feathers.

There was silence in the shop. Dolour said shyly, 'Hullo, what can I do for you?' though there was no one there. What the Kidger had said was true. She did speak differently. The harsh chirpiness of the Surry Hills girls, the raucous laughter, and the slurred, twanging vowels of that district's argot were absent in her voice. She wondered at it, not knowing that she had grown up with Grandma's purling Irish tones her criterion, nor realizing that ever since she had been at school she had been unconsciously imitating the speech of the sisters there.

She was pleased, but disturbed, for she was enough of a Surry Hills girl to dread comment on any form of personal superiority. Almost unconsciously she began to put away her manner of speaking and to talk in the same lazy, ungrammatical way as the rest.

Meanwhile, at home Roie and Motty had gone up to the hospital for Roie's pre-natal check, and Mumma was dawdling through her housework. Mumma liked to think she was going through 'the change,' which she had actually passed through peacefully and without song five years before. Now and then she pampered herself, blaming every physical disturbance upon the mysterious upheaval that was supposed to be going on in her body, and thinking up a lot of new ones. It was an education to Roie and Dolour to hear her talking across the fence to old Mrs Campion, who, having abused and cruelly punished herself for over-fertility for a period of twenty-five years, was now suffering in real earnest.

'Twelve misses I had, love,' Mrs Campion would say, 'counting the one I had when the mister let fly with his boot when I was three months gone and him seeing snakes with God-knows-what. And now the doctors down at the hospital say I'm all in rags inside and operations wouldn't do a bit of good.'

And Mumma would look at her with her innocent eyes and say, 'It's downright cruel on a woman, that's what it is. Do you have flushes?'

'Flushes!' Mrs Campion would scream like a crow. 'Why, dearie, I have pricklings!'

And Mumma would make a concussive sound with her tongue and retreat hurriedly inside, dying to ask more, but forbidden to do so by her chaste soul. She would ruminate, silently, in her way, on pricklings and sure enough by the end of the week she had them even worse than Mrs Campion. So this Monday she doddered about the house, sweeping here, and dabbing with a duster there, for Roie had already done the washing-up, and there wasn't much to do in that small crowded house where tidiness was not considered a virtue, anyway. She went out and looked at the step and sighed, for it had been done only yesterday, and now it was freckled all over with purple where Motty had been squashing a beetle.

522

Mumma hated to bend, for bending brought on not only flushes and pricklings, but what Mrs Campion cryptically referred to as whirligigs.

'You see black specks floating round in front of you,' she explained. 'And when you straighten up again, yellow flashes and whirligigs in front of your eyes, something awful. But it's only to be expected, and I suppose a woman's lucky that it only lasts five years.'

Mumma got the sandsoap and the floor-cloth, and cursorily wiped the step. She straightened up cautiously. The black specks were there all right, and she waited patiently for the yellow flashes, but they were apparently off plaguing someone else.

'Oh, well, they'll come in their own good time,' murmured Mumma, 'please God,' for she was a little disappointed. Then she gave a squawk of horror, for something worse than whirligigs was standing there – a strange, peculiar little man with a face like a Pekinese dog and so intense an expression that she almost expected him to burst into tears.

'You the missus?' he quavered, over the armful of brown paper parcels he held.

Mumma relaxed. 'We really don't want nothing to-day,' she said.

'Mr Darcy sent me,' said the little man. 'I'm Mr Reilly.'

'Oh, yes,' said Mumma civilly but uncertainly, for Hughie had mentioned sending no one.

'He said you'd show me the room,' said Mr Reilly, his Adam's apple tremulously bobbing. Mumma gaped. Which room? Was he here to mend Roie's gas-ring? Or the roof in the kitchen? Or the leaking copper in the laundry? While she turned over the questions in her slow mind, wondering which one to ask first, Mr Reilly piped up, 'The spare room he said I was to look at.'

Mumma was completely bewildered. It was clear that Hughie had said something to her about Mr Diamond's room that she had forgotten, but nothing came to her recollection.

'Well,' she said doubtfully. 'I suppose . . .'

She stood aside, and Mr Reilly flitted past on the sandshoes that had been so carefully whitened with window cleaner. The dark hall, haunted by cabbage and fish and onions, seemed to him beyond compare, and he looked eagerly at Mumma.

'Mr Darcy said it was upstairs.'

'That's right.'

Mumma eased her hips past him and stumped laboriously up the stairs. Half-way up she held on to the banister and tried to see whirligigs, but they were not for her. She turned, further questions about his business with the room already on her lips, but Mr Reilly was pressing behind her like a small excited dog, and in embarrassment Mumma hurried up and flung open the door of Pat Diamond's room. It had the forlorn air common to all empty rooms; its windows tufted with dirt, and the tenuous, delicate fabric of dust-strung cobwebs draping the corners of the roof. The old bed was there, dipping in the middle, its legs splayed out, and there was the picture of a racehorse tacked over the mantel by Patrick's own hand.

The smell of the place, its emptiness, and its dank airless coldness brought a lump to Mumma's throat, remembering the nightmare that had been here. She looked down at Mr Reilly.

'Well, this is it,' she began dubiously. 'Now, what – '

Mr Reilly darted past her into the room. He saw the gas-ring standing rusty and unused on its grease-stained table, the window that could be pushed open to air and sun, and the bed that was perhaps not so much more comfortable than his own little trestle with its legs in the jam tins for fear of bugs. But it was a bed with space about it, so that he would not be afraid to fling out his arms and legs without crashing into the wall.

Tears came into his weak old eyes. He fumbled for his glasses and hid behind them, then he looked at the woman peering and frowning at the door.

'It's lovely, missus,' he said. 'Lovely.'

'I've done me best with it,' agreed Mumma, mollified. She waited for a little while, but Mr Reilly did not seem to be going to say anything, so she prompted, 'Now, what did you say Mr Darcy sent you along to see me for?'

Mr Reilly unloaded his parcels cautiously on the bed, as though they all contained rare and brittle china, then he straightened up, and a look of humility, joy, and disbelief that could not be duplicated by anyone except a homeless, familyless man who had just found a comfortable room at a rent he can afford flamed all over his face.

'I'll take it right away, and I'll pay you the rent as soon as pension day comes round.'

A dreadful procession of emotions moved over Mumma's face as she realized that in spite of her delight in her home with no strangers in it, Hughie had gone and let Pat Diamond's room under her very nose, and to this peculiar man who looked like a dog. He wasn't even clean, and for all she knew he would bring things into the furniture, to join the starveling bugs.

'Oh, no you don't,' she blurted out. 'This room isn't for rent. I dunno what that Hughie's thinking about. He made a mistake, that's what he's done.'

Mr Reilly's Adam's apple disappeared beneath his collar. Tears trembled on the pink rims of his eyes.

'But Mr Darcy said – ' he croaked.

'I don't care what he said,' exploded Mumma, suddenly feeling pains in the back of her legs, and flushes and pricklings and whirligigs, all at once. 'He might wear the pants in this house, but he isn't going to let my rooms over me head. The nerve of him! Go on, get out of here this blessed minute.'

'But I ain't had a home for years,' wailed Mr Reilly. 'Oh, missus, you don't know what it's like! And Mr Darcy said – '

Mumma hardened her heart. 'Teach him a lesson, the straddy. Come on now, out of that!'

Sorrowfully, his head bent, Mr Reilly began gathering up the parcels. Mumma hovered for a moment, then stumped down the stairs. When she was half-way down there was a bang, and the staircase was blotted into darkness. Mumma felt herself go hot as fire all over, the very worst flush she had ever had.

She rushed up the stairs and hammered at the door. But Mr Reilly had shot the bolt. She could hear him breathing heavily.

'Oh, you fladdy-faced little tripehound!' roared Mumma, rattling the knob so loudly she could not even hear herself. 'You did that very knacky, but I'm not the one you can put it over! Open this door! Oh, I'll knock the priest's share out of you when I see your face again. I'm going to get the police this minute!'

A little voice squawked, 'I'm going to wait for Mr Darcy, that's all, and if he says I've got to get out, I will.'

Mumma would have liked to take a running kick at the door, but the landing was too small. She stood and rattled and pleaded and roared for a long time, but not another sound did she hear. Then she stooped and put her eye to the keyhole. Judging from the darkness within, Mr Reilly was doing the same thing.

'Snoop!' said Mumma haughtily, and she lumbered downstairs, talking to herself and making all kinds of fantastic plans for luring

Mr Reilly out of his fortress. First she thought she would let Mrs Campion in on the secret, and ask her advice, but at the fence she paused. Mrs Campion was such a gab-bag, and only the Dear knew what she would make of a strange man in Mumma's spare room. It almost seemed like evidence for a divorce.

So she went to the other fence and hooted for Lick Jimmy, but Lick was not back from the markets, where he had got into a dice game and lost all his oranges and bananas at one throw.

Mumma couldn't even enjoy a cup of tea.

'I'm bothered,' she admitted, and sat down on a chair at the foot of the stairs like a fat old watchdog, waiting for Roie to come home.

After a little while she heard the creak of the gate, and Motty shrilling some incomprehensible song.

'Good heavens, Mumma,' cried Roie, 'whatever are you doing there?'

She looked waxen, and breathless, and her little feet bulged out of her shoes as though she had dropsy.

Mumma gasped out the story. 'I'm that upset, Roie, and I haven't a stirring in me head what to do. Do you think we ought to get the police?'

'I dunno.' Roie considered. 'You know what people are like, seeing coppers come in here. Dad'll be home early, and anyway, this Mr Reilly can't steal anything or hurt the room even if he does stay there.'

'But the look of him, Ro!' moaned Mumma. 'He might be queer in the head, and come down and let us all have it with the axe.'

So they cooked up a great plan. Roie went quietly up the steps and placed a chair in a strategic position just where the architect had made a slip with the pencil and caused a sort of kink in the straight flow of the steps. It was a mantrap for anyone sneaking down to give his landlady the axe.

'There'll be such a clatter we'll have plenty of time to run,' she assured Mumma. Roie did not take it very seriously. She gave Motty her lunch without a qualm, while Mumma roamed up and down like a caged tiger, addressing Hughie as though he were present, and informing him that the dogs wouldn't pick his bones after her.

Suddenly Roie hushed the chatter of her daughter. 'I heard something, Mumma.'

There was a stealthy sound. Mumma's face went pale as a candle. Roie grabbed Motty. The next moment there was the sound of a crashing chair, the thud of a falling body, and an eldritch scream.

'We got him!' cried Roie jubilantly.

'Run, quick!' cried Mumma, but Roie bravely went into the passage, peering into the semi-darkness for the stricken form of Mr Reilly. She gave a shriek.

'I should think you oughta scream,' remarked her sister severely, painfully unwinding herself from the newel post. 'Of all the barmy tricks!' You and Mumma ought to have your heads read.' She came limping out into the light, rubbing her elbows.

Roie started to giggle. Dolour glared at her and Mumma, whose face was inscribed all over with guilt and consternation.

'You ought to be more careful,' she snapped, heaving some of the blame on to Dolour's shoulders.

'How would I know that some bullet-headed calonkus would leave a chair on the stairs?' shouted Dolour. 'Wonder me glasses weren't smashed.'

All the nervous strain of the morning, of Delie Stock, and the Kidger, and a too-early breakfast, and the disappointment of not being able to sneak upstairs and privily try the rouge she had just bought, made her temper flare. But they took no notice of her at all, but poured out the story of Mr Reilly and the bailing-up in Mr Diamond's room. Dolour was delighted. She was all for going up straight away, climbing along from her window to his and over-powering Mr Reilly by force.

'After all, he's only little,' she said reasonably.

'No,' said Mumma ominously. 'We'll wait for your Dadda, and if there's anything left of him after I've finished with him, he can get rid of his friend Mr Reilly.'

By the time Hughie arrived home he had forgotten entirely about Bumper Reilly, and when Mumma confronted him with the locked door and a torrent of accusing words, he felt quite sick. For once his wife had caught him at a loss. He stammered out an explanation of Mr Reilly's kindness, and the terrible situation at the flophouse.

'After all,' expostulated Hughie pleadingly, 'he's a clean old bludger, and you often said yourself that – '

'Clean is one thing he isn't,' stated Mumma. 'Sure you could grow enough potatoes to tide us over a strike in his ears.'

'Well, what's ears?' exploded Hughie, losing his patience. 'What are you doing gawking into his ears, anyhow? Hasn't a man got any privacy?'

He banged on the door. There was silence, and Hughie looked around to see the four pale faces of his womenfolk grouped at the bottom of the stairs.

'Hey, Bumper, you old cow,' he bellowed. 'It's me. What are you doing bailing us out like this?'

There was a muffled gasp from someone very near the door on the other side, and the lock clicked. Hughie pushed inside, and Mumma and Dolour began to inch cautiously up the stairs.

'Oh, Mr Darcy!' cried Bumper. He stood in the middle of the floor in the piteous condition of one who had been through terrible hours of nervous strain. 'You did mean it, didn't you?'

'Well, I – ' stammered Hughie, wishing to hell he'd never seen the man, let alone been bound by chains of gratitude.

'You didn't say she was yer wife, you just said the missus,' babbled Mr Reilly. 'How was I to know? She was going to throw me out into the street, and I already guv up me place at the flophouse and I got nowhere to go now.'

'You took it pretty much for granted,' growled Hughie.

Mr Reilly's throat moved convulsively. 'I won't never make a noise. I swear I won't. You won't even know I'm in the place. I don't drink and I don't smoke. Everyone will tell you I allus pay my rent and don't never rampage around. And it's such a beaut room.'

A little placated, Mumma snorted out of the dusky stairs. She and Roie and Dolour began a heated controversy.

'I don't see why he can't stay, poor old coot,' began Dolour.

'But maybe he's one of the those nasty old men who look through keyholes,' protested Roie, who hated the idea of having a listening ear on both sides of her room.

'If he looks through mine I'll jab a knitting needle in his eye,' promised Dolour heartily, taking no notice of Mr Reilly's audible gasp at this information.

'I'm not giving way to Hughie, I don't care what he says or promises,' said Mumma sulkily.

Meanwhile Hughie was wondering what all the fuss was about. Mumma had been glad enough to receive a little extra money from Patrick Diamond, and what was the difference in this poor little dingbat except that Pat had been big enough to roll out into two of him?

He began to think pleasurably of a place of refuge where he could go when he had a few in and Mumma was being a bit obstropolous, somewhere where it was possible to shoot a bolt and have her safe and sound and steaming on the other side. He looked critically at Mr Reilly. There was nothing the matter with him that a scrubbing brush and soda couldn't fix.

'I knew that if I could only hang out until you came I'd be right,' babbled Mr Reilly. 'I knew you was the boss.'

Tired as he was, and confused as he was, Hughie knew that his new lodger had hit the nail on the nob. Give way now, and there was no knowing what liberties Mumma would be taking. He had to make a stand, even if he didn't particularly like the ground. He winked at Mr Reilly.

'You can take yer coat off, boy.'

He went downstairs and told them Mr Reilly was staying.

'If you was going to let it you could have picked someone nicer,' said Roie. 'There's Tonetta Siciliano looking for a place so she can get married, poor kid.'

'She could have had it, and welcome. Better than that old ratbag,' backed up Mumma.

Hughie looked defiantly at the pair of them, then bent his fierce blue gaze on Dolour. 'Well, what you got to say for yourself?'

Dolour was sulky. The first excitement of Mr Reilly's advent over, she had remembered that he had stolen all her thunder. Her first day at the new job, and all the things that had happened, and nobody had even asked her how she had got on. A fat lot they cared if she had to beat off old drunks with brooms. No one would even think they were her family. She hated them all.

'Oh, go to hell!' she blurted. She glared at the astonished faces and bounced out of the room.

'Now what's up with her?' wondered Roie wearily.

'She's growing up all within herself, and I can't say I like it,' agreed Mumma. 'Raving like a cat in the measles one minute, and on with the day-dreaming the next.'

'Ah, yer makes me sick, every goddam one of yer, picking and poking, scroogin' and scrabblin',' growled Hughie. He stamped out to the lavatory, and after five minutes of futile wrenching at the door, remembered that his home was no longer his own. He had to go inside again and go through all the strain of preserving a stony silence while Mumma, tight-lipped and offended, got a cuppa tea ready.

Twelve

So Mr Reilly became an inmate of that house. He was an irritating shadow whose ways took a lot of getting used to. Because he was terrified of meeting anyone and annoying them by his very presence, he was always peeping round the edge of his door, waiting for the strategic moment to streak down the stairs and into the yard or the street. This unnerved Mumma, and she began doing the same thing, sneaking round her kitchen door to make sure she would not catch Mr Bumper Reilly in the act of flying past.

Daily she placed the broom and dustpan at the foot of the stairs, and daily they disappeared as though pixies had swooped upon them, to be followed half an hour later by the slight clang of the garbage lid as the dirt was interred. It was like having a ghost in the house. Twice Charlie had reported seeing his face suspended on the darkness under the stairs, where he had retreated when he heard the younger man enter the house. And Dolour, who went off to work so early, had never seen him at all.

She began to develop a dreadful curiosity about Mr Reilly, and desperately thought up excuses for going across the landing and hammering on his door. But either he wasn't in, or he wouldn't answer it, for it never opened, though once, seven shillings and sixpence slid on a sheet of paper underneath it, as though to infer that her knockings could only be for the rent.

'But what does he do all day?' wondered Mumma.

'Rattles paper,' answered Roie. 'He makes noises like a rat in a paper bag all day and all night.'

'Ah, it's the poor old cow's parcels,' said Hughie comfortably. He had finished his tea and was sitting in his Jackie Howe, which is a singlet with the sleeves out of it, and called after a famous shearer of the blade days.

'Parcels? What of?'

'How would I know?' asked Hughie. 'He had a lot the day he came here.'

'And he's always got one under his arm when he comes into the house,' added Roie.

530

Hughie frowned at her. 'And what business is it of yours, always sticking your nose into other people's parcels?'

He shook out the paper, making a white wall between him and the family, which immediately went into an animated discussion on what the parcels might contain. Dolour thought he might be a dope-peddler, and briskly prophesied a police raid, and Mr Reilly getting hauled off to the pokey by the scruff of his little neck, a vision that gave Mumma such a fright that she sat quite silent and yellow for some time. In spite of her big talk about policemen, Mumma was dead scared of them.

Very slowly and solidly, like a blancmange setting, a conviction formed in her mind that she must find out the contents of Mr Reilly's parcels. Once the decision was made, she felt quite differently towards the old man. From a spirit-like creature who haunted unoccupied portions of the house, he became a man. He was a human creature who ironed his collars with a flat-iron disastrously heated over the gas-ring; a man who stayed an unconsciously long time in the lavatory; who was too timid to come and ask Charlie for a hammer when a nail came out of the wall and his coats fell down, but knocked it in with the heel of his shoe instead.

Like Dirty Dick, Mumma felt that God had made him to be put up with, so she adapted herself round his presence like an oyster round a pearl, though Mr Reilly was no pearl. In time she even thought how tough a go he must be having on his little allotment of weekly money, because he was obviously putting out a shilling a week in insurance for his funeral, in the decent dignified way of the poor. So she went out and slapped down an enamel plate at the foot of the stairs, with such a loud emphatic bang that Mr Reilly couldn't help hearing. On the plate lay sheepishly some warm potatoes, a cold chop, a hard-boiled egg, and a tomato that Mumma had thought twice about. She bellowed for Mr Reilly, and as she waddled back into the kitchen she heard the upstairs door open stealthily.

Within ten minutes there was a musical clang from the garbage tin, and Mumma hardly waited for Mr Reilly to skip back into shelter before she went out and investigated. She was confronted by the polished bone of the chop. Mumma felt that was satisfactory, and ever after that all the odd bits went to Mr Reilly, silently, without even an overture of friendship. In this way Mumma salved Hughie's conscience about his rash promises.

The last weeks of Roie's pregnancy passed in a dream. The days were like a calm golden river flowing down to a heavenly sea. Such contentment filled her as she could not explain, nor did she want to. Sometimes she sat for an hour not thinking, not doing anything but breathe, a rich, wonderful delight welling inside her. Sometimes she would hold Motty and just stare at her, soaking her senses in the child's silken brown skin, the plum bloom of her lips, the warmth of her hair. At night she lay quietly in the curve of Charlie's arm, lost in a haze between sleeping and waking, so rich, so ripe a tranquillity emanating from her he could feel it like a perfume or a flavour.

'Asleep, Roie?'

'No.'

'What are you thinking of?'

'I dunno. Us. Motty and you and me.'

She was like a tree at the prime of its harvest, a creature that had withstood storms and the bare lonesome winters, that had flowered delicately, felicitously, and now stood drooping, laden, lost in a delicious dream that nothing could break.

He leaned over her, seeing the white triangle of her face on the pillow, the shadow of her eyes, and the glossy gleam of her eyeball. He traced the outline of her mouth with his own, feeling her lips relax and smile under his.

'What's the matter, darling?'

He wanted to tell her that he loved her, that he worshipped her, that she was his life-spring and his end and beginning, but he was dumb. The two races that met in him – all their powers of fiery and passionate articulation that had poured themselves out in place-names and chants and laments of unequalled beauty – were silent before this need to speak.

'You know, don't you, Ro?'

'I know you, that's why.'

And so the days and nights went on, fluidly bearing her closer to the birth.

One night about a fortnight before her confinement was due, she was alone in the house except for Motty and Hughie, who had come home dead drunk and was snoring on the bed, still fully clothed, with a trickle of spittle down his chin, and his dirty shoes turned upright at right-angles.

Mumma did not like going off to Benediction, for Charlie was working a late shift, and Dolour was helping Mrs Drummy to clean out the shop window, but Roie laughed away her fears.

'Don't you worry, Mumma. I won't put a fast one over you.'

She liked the unaccustomed stillness of the house, the way the street noises seemed to vanish down a long corridor, till she felt that the old house had drifted out to sea and was rocking quietly there on the fathomless quiet. She sat for a while trying to brush her hair, for now she found it difficult to lift her arms above her head. Twice she toiled up the stairs and caught the bugs that had scuttled out in the darkness to feast on Motty's soft skin. And once she went in and looked at Hughie, wistfully hoping that he would wake and speak to her. His mouth was wide open, showing his teeth, and with every snore his cracked tobacco-stained lip fluttered like a leaf in the wind. Roie put a blanket over him so that he would not be chilled.

She went back to the kitchen, and suddenly she was paralysed by a piercing scream from Motty upstairs. It gave her so much of a shock that even the child in her womb leaped and shuddered.

'Motty! Motty, I'm coming! It's all right!'

She scrambled clumsily up the stairs where once she had bounded two at a time. The screams were ringing one after the other now, interspersed by a gabble of cries and sobs.

Roie burst open the door and flicked on the light. She saw Motty sitting up in her cot, blood on her cheek streaming down in a blackish map. Her eyes were screwed up tight, but she was beating with both fists at the thing that crouched on the blankets in front of her.

Roie dragged Motty out of the cot and retreated a step, but the rat merely scuttled to the end of the bedding and sat there, its teeth bared. It was as big as a kitten, an old, scarred warrior with one ear and a dozen shining cicatrices on its hide. Its eyes gleamed like garnets, and its teeth seemed all bunched together in the front of its mouth. It snarled with a kind of self-possessed ferocity that petrified Roie, as she stood with the howling Motty over her shoulder.

Suddenly it leaped out of the cot and flashed across to the door, but it had swung shut after Roie. It bounded against the panels, as though it knew the way to liberty, and the rattle of its filthy claws on the wood made the girl shudder. It slowly turned and looked at her with an almost human intelligence and defiance, then it darted into the old fireplace and squatted in the ash-pan.

Motty had stopped yelling, so Roie put her down on the bed and

533

wiped away the blood. There was a ring of toothmarks on her cheekbone, but only one had penetrated the flesh. At the sight of the wound a deep, devouring fury seized Roie. She panted with rage. That this carrion prowler should bite her baby! She glared at the rat, and out of the duskiness its garnet eyes glared back.

If Motty had been younger, she might have died as other babies had died in that locality, awaking in the night with a feeble cry, and dying with the same cry, their throats torn into holes, their faces gnawed, and even the tiny bones of their fingers exposed through the nibbled flesh.

For all those babies Roie was enraged to a savagery unknown to her gentle nature. She slammed shut the window through which the rat had come. Then she went to the door, and, keeping her eyes all the time on the fireplace, screamed down the staircase to her father.

'Dadda! Dadda! You got to come!'

But Hughie was unconscious in his methylated sleep, and not even a whisper penetrated.

Roie shut the door. She cautioned the wide-eyed Motty to remain on the bed, and Motty, already recovered from her fright, sat there motionless, her bright eyes following her mother. Roie scrabbled in the corner, where there was an old walking-stick of Patrick Diamond's, kept as a sentimental souvenir by Mumma.

It was a heavy stick, with a broad, splayed rubber point.

She approached the fireplace, holding it like a hockey stick. She gave a sharp poke at the half-seen body of the rat, and the thing scampered out across the floor. It was a small room, and the rat ran along the wainscot, leaping up and falling back every few inches as though looking for an opening. But Roie knew it had come over the rooftops and through the window. She had it imprisoned. Quietly she followed it. It flew into the shadow of the bed and crouched against the wall. But there was a little opening between the bed and the wall, and Roie leaned across and looked down. The eyes shone up at her, like cigarette ends. She stabbed downwards with the stick, and the tip hit something soft. There was a squeal, and Roie made an inarticulate sound of triumph.

The rat pounced out now, between her feet, and Roie stumbled backwards and nearly fell. It whisked under the narrow base of the dresser, and she got down on her knees and slashed about with the stick, muttering to herself an unheard chant of 'I'll get you, you swine, you beast. You won't get away.'

Once again there was a squeal, and the rat rushed out and began to dart round and round the room on an endless orbit, eluding Roie's frantic swipes with the stick, and tiring her to a standstill. She sat down on the bed, wiping the sweat from her face. Motty's face was bleeding again, and she wiped away the blood saying to the child, 'Lie down. Keep still. It'll be all right soon.'

She waited till her breathing grew easier, then with a quiet, vicious determination she went after the rat again. She had hurt it. Tiny bubbles lay spattered on the floor, and the sight of that blood made her crazy to catch it and beat it into pulp.

The chase went on for twenty minutes more. Once she caught the rat glancingly with the point of the stick and threw it off-balance into a corner. She gave it a savage whack across the back, and it squealed piercingly, opening its mouth wide and vomiting dark blood. But it was alive as ever, and flickered into the fireplace and jumped agilely up against the flue, knocking down a cloud of soot.

She was sobbing with frustration and weariness now, scared that the beast would elude her and get away somewhere. She poked and slashed in the fireplace, and the rat crowded in a corner, snarling with a high whining sound. The stick thudded again and again on its body, but at such an awkward angle she could get no force to her blows.

Then suddenly, desperate, it flung itself out in one almost invisible flash of movement, jumped at her and ran up her skirt on the underside. Roie felt its sharp claws clinging to her bare leg. She screamed and screamed, beating with the stick at the bulge under the cloth, nearly mad with terror and horror that swamped her like a wave.

'Dadda! Dadda!' she shrieked, and Motty joined in and shrieked too.

She thrashed with the stick. Sometimes the blows fell on the rat and sometimes on her leg, and all the time she felt the cold scaly body slithering and scrabbling for a foothold on her flesh. Then with a thump it fell to the floor and crawled a little way and faced her, squealing on a high-pitched note.

'Beast! Beast!' sobbed Roie.

The rat knew it was helpless and cornered. Its hindquarters dragged and it did not try to crawl away. It stood there, almost with its paws up begging for mercy. A dark ruby of blood quivered on the end of its nose.

Roie hit once and it collapsed. She hit it again and again, until its pelt peeled away and a sharp white splinter of bone stuck out of its shoulder. Still she went on hitting it mechanically, till it was a red squashed mass in the middle of a thick pool. Then she stopped, trembling, realizing almost with shock that there was no need to hit any more.

She saw the fleas jumping off the body, like tiny black seeds struggling in the sticky blood.

Then she stumbled to the bed and lay down beside Motty, shaking so much that her teeth chattered. Motty crooned to her, patting her cheek with her soft, suede-like hand, marking with her fingers the streams of sweat that ran down her mother's face. So they were when Charlie came home.

'I got angry,' was all Roie could say. 'I shouldn't of. It bit Motty, and I got angry.'

Charlie put them both into the bed. He sponged the wound on Motty's cheek with iodine, and cleaned up the floor. He brought up a hot drink for Roie, but she was already asleep, her face fallen into the bluish hollows of exhaustion.

He stood for a while looking round the poor room, the worn oilcloth, the walls rippled with the tide-marks of old rains, the furniture whose every crack was infested with the black crawling cities of the ineradicable bugs. He looked at his child, only one of the hundreds of children maimed or marked with rats, those scavengers whose very presence in a modern city was an affront and a disgrace. He knew now that they must get out of it, no matter the obstacles, no matter the circumstances, they would have to get out of this to some place where the air was clean and the houses fit for human living.

He threw open the window, and there was the scrabble of claws on the iron roof, and the flashing of shadows over the high brick wall. They were waiting out there, as the other had waited, for darkness and silence. Charlie shut the window and fastened the catch so that no one could open it till he could nail some fine wire-netting over the entire window space.

'As soon as the baby's born we'll go,' he promised Roie, who lay sunken in sleep as in a stupor.

Then suddenly he remembered the man who had slept through it all, for the father who had not heard his daughter's screams when she needed him most. He ran down the stairs and into the bedroom, seizing Hughie by the shoulder and dragging him upright.

'Open your eyes! Open your eyes!' shouted Charlie, shaking him till his head wobbled back on his shoulders.

'Wasadoing?' mumbled Hughie. His eyes rolled open, laggardly, so that the whites showed. There was blank incomprehension on his face, and a breath as though from the mouth of hell came from his lips. 'Wasadoing, boy?'

Charlie dropped him back on the bed. He left his eyes half open, but he took up the rhythm of his snoring almost where he had left it off.

The younger man unclenched his fists almost by force. He stood for a little while staring down at Hughie's face, feeling sick and ashamed for what he had been going to do. He went outside and walked up and down in the cramped dark square of yard, trying to recover his self-respect.

Roie went to the hospital the next morning. She woke feeling heavy and unwell, and it was not long before she felt the old familiar pain, a little ripple, the gentle opening of a door. It made her happy, and she began to smile as she dressed, showing Charlie and Mumma the bruises on her leg where she had hit at the rat.

'I won't go to work,' said Charlie. But Roie laughed.

'I'll be all right. Don't forget, I've had practice.'

And Mumma, too, shooed him off, fussy and important in her anxiety, and assuring him that if three women couldn't attend to getting the girl into hospital, then the world wasn't worth a mallamadee.

She bustled off downstairs, her lips already forming the syllables of prayers to the Blessed Mother, for this was plainly women's work. Roie put her arms round her husband, feeling that it was for her to comfort him now.

'It's not like having the first one, Charlie. I know what happens now.'

Charlie had never thought of the black abysmal terror of the young girl in parturition, to whom every normal phase of birth is a shock and a catastrophe. She put her soft cheek against his chin.

'I love you, Charlie.'

'Not more than I love you.'

'Wait,' she said. 'There's another pain coming, a big one.'

He held her in silence, seeing the blood flee from her cheeks and the blue appear under her eyes as though by magic. He felt the ripple in her body, and the answering shudder in the child. It was the closest he had ever felt to her; the nearest approach he could make to the mystery proceeding within her.

'Good-bye, Charlie.'

He worked all the morning through, against the shuttling clatter of the flatbed, where the shiny sheets flopped out with hypnotic regularity.

'Any 'phone calls for me?'

'Nope.'

The hours went on, flat-footed hours that came in wearily and trudged out bowed and laden with his anxiety.

'Any rings for me?'

'Nope.'

It was nearly twelve when he looked up suddenly and saw Dolour, bewildered and flustered by the machines, threading her way towards him. He searched her face for news. She mouthed something, but he couldn't hear. He thrust his face at her.

'What's the matter? What's up?'

She looked at him dumbly, and he took her by the sleeve and led her to the door.

'She isn't too good, Charlie. The baby isn't going to be born for a long while.'

'I'd better come?'

'Yes.'

Outside her lips began to tremble, and she gasped, 'I mustn't cry here, I mustn't cry here,' pushing up her glasses and pressing her fingers against her eyes. He put his arm over her shoulders.

'Don't you worry, Dolour. Nothing's going to happen.'

'It's all right for you,' she croaked. 'She isn't your sister.'

He looked at her with such pain that she was silent, and so they went to the hospital.

Mumma was there in the waiting-room, sunken into a queer shapeless heap like a clay statue that has been out in the rain. The beads slipped through her cold fingers, but the prayers she murmured were unheard by her own ears. So they waited.

The sounds of the big hospital went on around them, the soft trundle of trolley wheels in the corridor, a muffled laugh, the rubbered tread of nurses, the clinking of cups and bottles.

Sometimes they talked, reassuring each other of the excellence of the hospital, and how even the big specialists sent their private patients here if they foresaw any trouble.

But mostly they were silent, lost in a deathly quiet that seemed to retard the dragging feet of the passing moments.

At five Hughie came in, wild-eyed, dirty and tousled. He said in a hoarse whisper, 'What's wrong? I read the note you left. What's wrong?'

'They're operating on her,' said Mumma. 'She's got a good chance.'

At the words Dolour gave a loud snort of agony. She threw herself down beside Mumma and hid her face on her mother's knees. Mumma stroked her hair mechanically, and unheedingly.

A sister came into the room, and they stared at her with dilated eyes, as rabbits at the approaching rabbiter.

'The child's alive,' she said. 'It's a fine healthy little boy.'

'Michael,' whispered Mumma.

Charlie was on his feet. 'What about my wife?'

The sister had a gentle face. She had seen so much trouble and pain, and it had given her a tranquil strength that could be communicated to others. She put her hand on his arm.

'I think you should all go home. Your wife is still under the anaesthetic, and it may be some hours before we can give you any good news. Go home and have something to eat.'

Dumbly they went.

What happened that night and the next morning? Speaking about it in after years they could never remember what they had done. Gone to the church, yes . . . and Mumma had cooked something, and they had tried to eat it . . . and they had sat round for a while, talking about other things. Somehow the interminable hours had slipped away, somehow. Now and then Charlie had gone out and rung up on the street 'phone, with all the gossips leaning over their gates and clucking sympathetically.

'No change?'

'No.'

Mumma got Motty from Mrs Campion, who had had the child all day, and washed some of the dirt off her. The child suddenly took on a great significance, and they all stared at her as though they had never seen her before.

'Mummy coming home soon?'

'Yes, and she's got a present for you, a little brother.'

So they talked, and hid their frightened faces, and tried to be ordinary, so as not to upset each other.

'She was so happy this morning.'

'When she comes home she ought to have a holiday.'

Mumma seized on this eagerly. 'Yes, you can put the baby on a bottle, and I'll look after it, and you and Ro can go to the beach like you did for your honeymoon. It did her so much good last time.'

Then, all at once, they were back at the hospital, and Father Cooley was there in his surplice, with the purple stole over his shoulders. As he came out of the room they looked piteously at him. Hughie's face was pulled into long vertical lines like a bloodhound's, and his hair stuck up stiff as a brush, it was so long since he had taken a comb to it.

'Did she speak to you, Father?'

'She's still unconscious.'

'Couldn't she make her confession?' stammered Mumma.

'She ain't never done anything wrong,' growled Hughie, turning his face away.

During this time Charlie and Dolour said nothing, standing and staring at the priest as though he were a stranger.

A nurse came out of the room. 'We're ready now, Father.'

'We shoulda brought Motty,' said Mumma.

'It doesn't matter,' said Charlie. They went into the little room with its shrouded lights, the spindle-legged high bed, the strange sharp smell of anaesthetic, and the wax candles seeded with flame. It was a nightmare in which not one, but all of them participated. Who else was there? A doctor perhaps, two nurses, but they saw no one but Roie lost in the whiteness of the bed.

They had washed away the sweat of her long agony, and brushed the hair she had torn and tangled. They had taken away the bloodstained clothes and her depleted empty body was wrapped in a clean white nightdress. Her hands lay upon the counterpane, quiet and at rest. It was hard to tell that they had writhed and beaten and scratched the skin from each other only the day before.

She was a stranger to them all, already withdrawing into the mystery they could not comprehend.

Clumsily they knelt around, while the priest, old, fat, often rash and reckless in his judgements – the clumsy old exile from a land he had almost forgotten save as a legend – cast off his earthly traits and significances and became the bearer of God and God's mercy.

540

'She coulda been saved,' burst out Hughie in his anguish. 'Rotten dirty doctors – '

'Sssh!'

Roie did not know anyone was in the room, yet she was acutely sensible of the feelings in her hands and feet. She felt the cool smoothness of the oil on the feet that had walked in foolish and evil places, and on the hands that had been careless and impatient so often. Now it was on her eyelids, and she struggled to raise them and see. But there was no battle left in her. Her spirit, finding those doorways closed, turned away and went to the portals of the ears. But the oil was there, too, the gentle seal of the oil against the sounds of the world.

She lay within herself, in a silence so dark and deep she wondered at it.

Yet sharp and clear she saw once again the things her memory had kept in its subtle archives – a wagon-load of cherries, a dog run over, the smiling face of Lick Jimmy, the chattering machines at the box factory where she had once worked. And she saw, too, the pale young face, and dark eyes of Tommy Mendel, whom she had loved, long ago, and felt again the bitter sorrow and guilt of the loss of his child.

The old days came crowding up around her, insubstantial, and yet part of the fabric that was fraying and tattering as the seconds ticked past. Not one person stood out above another, not Charlie, or her mother, or her children. They were all part of her life, which was unravelling like a ragged banner, and blowing out on some incomprehensible wind.

Suddenly, like a trumpet's sharp blow on the ear-drum, realization came to her. She was dying. It was no dream, no imagining. She was leaving the pattern of her life, the common pattern already experienced by a million, million women, and Charlie would have no part in what she was, any more.

She screamed, 'Charlie! Charlie!' but her husband, his face upon her hand, heard it only as a whisper.

A great agony of grief and yearning seized her, a terrible longing for him, his hands, his eyes, the touch of his mouth and warmth of his body. She was part of him, and he of her, and the pain of this last and most terrible amputation seized her in its grip and burst with her through the dissolving dark.

Thirteen

It was hard to remember afterwards. They had stared dumbly at the doctor as he explained what had happened. But what were technicalities to them, caught unstruggling in the simplicity of death like a fly in syrup? With throats aching and eyes burning they looked at all these strangers who were trying to be helpful and kind, and when they said anything at all it was disjointed driftwood from the confused stream of their private thoughts.

'It was only yesterday she said good-bye to me.'

'Twenty-four ain't old enough.'

'It isn't fair! It isn't fair!'

Hughie sat with his face as red as a beet, his eyes jammed shut and his lips pursed out to stop them trembling, saying nothing; but in his heart he was yelling, 'Oh, God, it's me that ought to be dead instead of my little girl. Maybe it was that fright she got, and me lying down there stewed as a pig and not lifting a finger to help her. Oh, God, I wish I was drunk. I wish I was drunk.'

It was dusk when they left the hospital, and on all their lips was the taste of Roie's, smooth and cool and waxy. They peered bewilderedly into the blue dimness where the scanty constellation of lamps already glimmered. Dolour pressed close to her mother like a dog, or a little child. She had made no sound, but she was breathing quickly and loudly.

'Maybe we ought to get a taxi, Hughie.'

He looked round despairingly. 'I dunno.'

They waited for a long while, but no taxis stopped, so they set off walking down the windy hollow street. After a little time Dolour stopped, and shaking, clung to a fence.

'I can't go no farther.' She broke into violent sobbing.

'We can't go giving in to it, lovie,' said Mumma in a voice so strained it did not seem like her own. But in their bewilderment, their astonishment and defencelessness, there seemed nothing else to be done.

Suddenly Charlie said, 'I'll be home later. I want – I'll be home later.'

Without waiting for a reply he strode off along Murphy Street.

He did not feel himself moving. Rather, the street flowed past him, the lemon-yellow windows, the shadow-striped balconies, the cats that whisked over the broken-toothed fences. He felt the pavement under his feet, the cold air on his cheek, and that was all.

Soon he was in Oxford Street, blinking at the flood of light. For a long time he stood aimlessly watching the trams crawling like beetles up the hill and rattling away around the corner. The crowds milled about him, and somewhere a newsboy droned like a bee.

He could not stand there for ever, so when a tram came along he swung aboard, hunching like an old man in a corner of the great, clumsy, open-sided thing. Time meant nothing to him. Staring out the doorway, with the light and the dark rushing past alternately – here a pedestrian's pale face, there a half-lit balcony, a palm-tree, a running dog, a man pushing a barrow – he was aware of nothing.

Soon the city was left behind, and the harsh smell of the sea washed into the tram like a tide. Awaking like a man from sleep he saw patches of sandhills, creamy in the dark, and low scrub that clothed the land like sparse fuzzy hair. He stared at this for a long time, and then, all at once on the right there reared up cubical and monstrous, like blocks of darkness, the smokestacks of Bunnerong. They were the chimneys that empowered Sydney with light and energy, built away out here on the coast because of their dowry of ash and smoke. They seemed to him ominous and sinister, and he turned to the sole remaining occupant of the compartment and asked, 'Where's this?'

'La Perouse, boy.'

He recognized with astonishment that the man was coloured and remembered then that La Perouse was the aboriginal settlement that clung, ignored and forgotten, to the proud hems of Sydney. In the shabby little houses there was light, and sometimes the sound of a radio, or the bell-like laughter of a half-caste girl. He stood and listened to the intermittent hum of living behind those walls, then he went up on the hill and down to the low sandstone shores of Botany Bay. It was almost dark there, and the sea below but a breathlessness in the darkness. It tossed out its edges, scroll after scroll that unfolded across the terraces of rock and tinkled away down the crevices in irregular music.

And there were stars, too, a vast white webbing just without the eye's range, as though the Milky Way had overflowed its boundaries and flooded to the horizon.

Charlie stood there and looked at nothing at all. He was acutely conscious of the structure of his body, of the bones mounted and subtly balanced one upon the other, of the latchings of the foundations of his skull. As though he had never heard it before he heard the tremendous shaking of his heart. Thus he waited, like a man who has received a stupefying blow, and is waiting for the reawakening nerves to shout the pain to his mind.

'Roie,' he said, questioningly, stiff-tongued, and as though that were the signal, the pain that hung about him converged, dripped, and drowned him in a terrible grief that flung him to the ground, with the whole weight of the world pressing upon his back and shoulders.

In that moment his life was completely ended. The centre of his world had gone, and life itself became illogical. His very existence was a contradiction and betrayal of the death in his heart.

So he lay, motionless, while the dew settled imperceptibly on his clothing and dripped down his hair.

The impossibility of what had happened made him feel that perhaps he had gone crazy, that he was imagining it all, that any moment he would wake and find Roie beside him, laughing at him.

And then, remembering her like that, the pain grew worse until he thought that he would go mad, with the knowledge of his empty room, his empty bed, the realization that all was for ever wasted; her body that had comforted him, her breasts that had fed his child, her womb that had been the doorway of his physical immortality; her voice and smile, and little yearnings and contentments, everything that she had been, all gone, lost for ever, dwindling away to its component atoms . . .

'Roie! Roie!'

Surely she must speak to him, whom she had loved most of all. He looked into the sky, into the windy wastes of stars that would be so alien and frightening to a girl who had spent her life in little crowded streets and rooms where there was no space to turn round. Where would she go, where could she go, in those vast meadows of darkness where a million, million years stretched between one beacon and the next?

'Why didn't You take me, too, so I could look after her?'

She had never been anywhere by herself since he had married her, and now she was alone.

Then he thought with joy of death, and in a false and unreasonable eagerness jumped up and ran to the low cliff-edge, stumbling over the grass clumps, whispering that he had not thought of this before. He began to scramble down the rocks towards the soft sibilance of the water, then, as though a hand had arrested him, he stopped. Somewhere across the wasteland from one of the little houses there sounded the wail of a child, and almost with shock Charlie remembered Motty, and the boy, the new-born.

It would not matter. They were so young, and Mumma would look after them as long as she was alive.

But the moment of piteous exhilaration was gone. He knew he could not kill himself, not only because he had children to hold him back, but because his own life, though his spirit had suffered so mortally, was mysteriously left to him.

He would have to live, no matter what it cost him.

He climbed back to the top of the cliff and sat there, bowed, drenched with dew, throughout the night, lost and dazed, unable to think, to plan, to do anything but suffer.

The stars were swallowed up, and like the great hoop the Milky Way swung over beneath the water. The light, the world's first, crept up the sky, leaped the ragged islands of New Zealand, and saw that the Australian coastline reared like a wall. It lapped it, besieged it, cliff and bay, and drew it upon the dusky sea like a monstrous golden boomerang.

Charlie saw an old man coming over the grass towards him, leading a goat. The man was an old aboriginal, bent at the knees and the elbows into a comfortable workaday shape, and the goat was a fleecy nanny with striped, insolent eyes.

'You up early this morning, boy,' he greeted. 'Bin fishing?'

Charlie shook his head, unable to trust himself to speak, wishing that the old fellow with his pleasant squatty nose and his deepset bloodshot eyes would go away. He looked down and saw that his clothes were soaked and dank, covered in grass-seeds. Even his shoes had been scribbled across by the gossamer trails of snails that had crawled over him, mistaking his stillness.

'You look bad, son. Bin on the booze?'

'Yeah.'

It seemed the easiest way out of it.

'You like to come over to my camp for a cup of tea and a wash-up? Boy, you look a mess all right.'

Charlie went with the old man to a little humpy built beside the road. On a bench outside were rows of carved boomerangs and peculiar little shoes and trinket boxes made of shells, for sale to tourists. The old man and the goat went inside, and the goat made itself comfortable beside the fire, staring all the time at the stranger with its inimical eyes.

'Sit down there. You shibbering.'

Charlie sat down docilely. The hot tea, sticky with goat's milk and brown sugar, made him feel a little better. He washed his face in the tin dish, outside the door on a box, and turned to the curved sliver of mirror propped up on the ledge.

'I got a comb somewhere, too. Boy, you bin on a bender all right.'

The old man's face was full of kind brotherliness. He was delighted to have someone to talk to so early in the morning. He walked round Charlie, brushing at him with the flat of his hand, and clucking anxiously. He did not treat the young man as a stranger at all.

Looking in the glass, Charlie knew why. In the night age had crept upon him, sharpening his bones, stretching the flesh into haggard pits and furrows. Bloodshot and sunken, his eyes looked out of sallow hollows. His great-grandmother had been black, but looking at him now one would have said he was a half-caste, come to the right place at La Perouse.

In the brilliant, blinding light of that new day, he knew with pitiless reason that he would have to go on. There was no dodging anything, not the loneliness, or the pain, or the frequent agony of the long solitary nights, or the responsibility of his children.

Nothing could be avoided except by death. Though Roie was gone he would have to live.

He thanked the old man for his tin dish, and his hot tea, and the comb with the gapped teeth.

'You come back again some time. Me and you go fishing,' promised his host in his soft, sibilant voice. 'You just ask for Angus McIntosh.'

'Yes, I will,' said Charlie.

Fourteen

A week after Roie's burial Dolour lifted her head from the pillow and knew she would cry no more tears. She was emptied of emotion. A vast coldness spread outwards from her heart until even her flesh seemed chill. She said, 'I'm going back to work, Mumma.'

'I wish you didn't hafta, darling,' said Mumma painfully. 'But I'm that short with Hughie off work and everything.'

The scalding tears gushed out again, and she quickly turned away to the sink, her swollen red hands trembling amidst the grimy suds.

'Oh, Lord,' she prayed, 'don't let me give in to it. It'll get better some day, just like it did when Thady disappeared, and Ma died. I got to keep me end up so I can look after the baby when it comes home.'

So she struggled through the days, waiting for the healing that was so long in coming. There was little help from the others. Hughie, after his first fierce grief, had been continually drunk, and yet in his drunkenness there was no surcease from pain. He sat at the table with the tall bottle before him and his head in his hands, and now and then his blurred babbling ceased and he ran into the bedroom, rooting frantically amongst the old clothes that were jammed into boxes and suitcases under the bed until he found something of Roie's – almost anything. Once a stubbed shoe, another time a grubby powder puff or a bit of blue ribbon with a tarnished medal on the end of it. The sight of these things seemed to drive him into madness. He would weep and whimper over them, his head on the table, and his gnarled hands knuckling into the wood in his agony.

'Roie! Roie! Tell me it's all a dream!' he would cry, grasping at Charlie's shirt as he passed. 'Tell me I made it all up myself !' And he would in his stupor pretend that Roie was coming through the door, stumbling to meet her and clasping the empty air, until Charlie's throat ached as though it were constricted with iron bands.

And at other times Hughie would follow Motty round, as she

went her way, heedless as a bird of the suffering that surrounded her, for in a few days she had accepted the story that her mother had gone to heaven and would come and get Motty some day soon.

'It ain't no good, Hugh,' said Mumma pitifully, her heart aching for him even more than for herself. 'Nothing's going to bring the darling back again. We got to go on living without her, that's all.'

And she looked pleadingly at him, longing for the comfort and sympathy that he had never given her, and which she was now denied again.

Hughie's face crumpled like a child's, and he cursed Mumma for putting into words the inescapable truth. He made a sweep at the table and knocked over the bottle, jumping on the fragments and smashing them into topaz gravel. Then he crawled into his bed and slept the sleep of the emotionally exhausted, his face sunken into the grooves and pits of an old, old man's.

The hospital had kept the baby for a month, the other women giving their plentiful milk with sympathy and generosity to the motherless child. Mumma went up often and looked through the glass at the smudgy red face, fast asleep with lids folded like poppy petals, or wide awake and yelling.

'Come with me, son,' she pleaded with Charlie. 'You can't blame the baby for it.'

'I don't blame it,' was all Charlie answered, but he would not go with her.

Mumma knew everything about babies, but nothing according to the clinic. Dutifully she listened to the sister's advice, and painstakingly laboured through the booklet of directions given to her. But to Mumma directions were only for bottles of medicine and tins of condensed milk. You couldn't bring up a little live baby that way. Mumma knew that what babies need most of all is love, and this she was prepared to give for twenty-four hours of the day. In addition she brought out of her memories of her own childhood the story of the bit of a black goat that had supervised the weaning of herself and her ten brothers and sisters.

'A nice old nanny she was,' said Mumma, 'and we kept her at the bottom of the yard. I remember her coat, just like a dog's, short and shiny. And a raggy scrap of a tail, and little sharp feet. And talk about milk! She didn't cost anything to keep either, she just ate all the rubbidge.'

'Wouldn't be possible to keep her in our little yard?' said Hugh. Mumma fired up at once.

'I don't see why anyone has to know about it,' she cried. 'Only Lick Jimmy, and Mrs Campion on the other side, and they wouldn't let a yip outa them when they knew the milk was for the baby.'

So they asked Lick, and Mrs Campion. Lick, who had been brought up with a water-buffalo putting its shaggy head over the mud threshold of his long-ago provincial home, thought nothing of a goat in a Surry Hills backyard. 'I give you all sclapee,' he promised, and Mumma, with delighted thoughts of the richness of milk from a goat fed exclusively on specked fruit, nearly cried.

As for Mrs Campion, she said heartily that no bloody health inspector would hear from her, and beside, the smell of goat would sorta clean up the smell of tomcat.

So it was that Anny came to live with the Darcys. She had belonged to a mate of Hughie's who lived up the north line where there was more room. She was young, glossy-pelted, in milk to her first kid, and her neat sharp hoofs clattered contemptuously on the cobbles of the yard. She looked round in amazement, chewing rapidly all the while, so that Hughie said, 'Gawd, don't she remind yer of Grandma!'

Anny looked the yard over thoroughly, bent a cold yellow eye on Motty, who had wandered delightedly to interview her, then stood on her hindlegs and began stripping the dead fans off the phoenix palm.

'There!' sighed Mumma in relief. 'She's taken to us.'

Anny took to them with her whole heart. She ate their washing, chewed up the picture books Motty left about, and walked into the kitchen whenever she felt like it. Because the little yard was no place for a healthy animal, she soon began to smell, and she filled the whole rear of the place with an elusive odour, which clung to Mumma until even Mrs Siciliano, who could not live without garlic, twitched a nostril when she came near.

'He'll have good bones,' thought Mumma to herself, 'and lovely little teeth, like Thady had.'

Real excitement possessed her when she thought of the child. It was like having one of her own again. She looked at Charlie, and the old jealousy raised itself. Fiercely she resolved that the baby should grow up loving her better than its father.

'Because he won't pull himself together,' she argued self-defensively. 'A whole month gone, and still you can hardly get a word out of him. And he's that stubborn about Motty.'

For Mumma had wanted to rearrange the house, putting herself and the two children in the upstairs room, and Charlie downstairs with Hughie. A curious streak of unreasonable cruelty in her gentle nature argued that she had put up long enough with broken sleep from Hughie's drunken rip-roarings, and since she was taking the responsibility of the children from Charlie's shoulders, he ought to pay for it some way. But Mumma did not know she felt like this.

She said, 'You can't work all day at your job and then come home and be up with a little one when he's got wind, or teething, Charlie.'

'I can look after him,' said Charlie. The anguish of his confused and jangled feelings made him long to lash out and shut up this old, interfering, and yet eagerly kind woman. But he forced himself to speak quietly.

'He'll need a bottle at two in the morning,' cried Mumma, desperately and untruly.

'I'll wake up all right,' said Charlie.

Suddenly Mumma exploded. 'Oh, it's all right for you, thinking it's so easy!' And she voiced what had been troubling her for so long. 'You'd sleep all night and let the little thing howl himself sick, you're that cold and unfeeling.'

Charlie said nothing.

'Your wife dead for a month, and I ain't yet heard you say her name,' blazed Mumma. 'What's it matter to you, with your heart like a lump of concrete and your face all shut up so that a body's got no idea of what you're thinking?'

Dolour came in from the laundry where she had been painting the old tin bath for the baby's use. 'Mumma, what's the matter with you?'

She put her arm round Charlie's shoulders, looking accusingly at her mother.

'How do you know what Charlie feels? I suppose you think a person has to go round behaving like Dadda before he feels anything. You ought to be ashamed of yourself, Mumma.'

Mumma looked at her daughter aghast. In every family quarrel, Dolour had been on her side.

'It's all right, Dolour,' said Charlie. She saw his face was thinner now, his skin so sallow it made his eyes look yellow. Any good looks he had had were gone. He looked sick.

Dolour had never thought of Charlie as a young man, or even as a man. She had been jealous because Roie loved him more than she loved her sister; she had disliked him because he was impossible to aggravate or provoke; now, for the first time she became aware that the flesh under his shirt was warm, that she could feel it burning against her bare arm.

He was young, not ten years older than herself. He had been kind and good to her many, many times, and she had been ungracious and ungenerous in her reception of his kindness. She had taken it for granted, as they all did, that Charlie would cope with any domestic crises, that he would hump Hughie into bed when he was drunk, fix the laundry tap, sole and heel their worn shoes. She could hardly remember what it had been like before he had come to live with them.

Before the startled look on the girl's unprevaricant face, Mumma was puzzled and angry. But the moment for accusation had gone, and she said humbly, 'I'm sorry I didn't put a tooth on it, Charlie. You were a good husband to Roie, and I'd be the first to have a piece of anyone who said you wasn't. It's just that I'm all on edge.'

'Yeah,' said Charlie. He went upstairs and sat on the narrow bed with his head on his hands. It was as bad as ever. He was like a man with an incurable illness. Now, after all these weeks, the pain was so severe that he could not bear to be alone. Like Mumma he knew that one day he would feel differently, that he would live and enjoy life once more, but he thrust that thought away, feeling it disloyal to his wife.

Motty came up to him. She thrust her head between his hands and looked at him unwinkingly.

'You got a headache, you poor man?'

With a groan he buried his face in her soft neck. 'I got an awful headache, Motty.'

It was impossible to sit still. He put on his coat and went downstairs. Mumma was astounded.

'You're not going out, Charlie? Not when the baby's coming home this afternoon?'

'I'll be back in time.'

It was a compulsion with him to live in his memory, a fierce unavailing attempt to make Roie alive once more, if it were only in mirage. He stood on the Quay, looking at the oily water. Here they had stood together waiting for the Manly ferry.

The ferry swished in, and he went aboard, into the sun-dappled saloon, looking for the seat where he and Roie had sat that day they went on their honeymoon. He sat there alone, closing his eyes, trying to feel the warmth of the little blue-clad figure with the bead waterlily on her bodice.

'Roie, can't you speak to me, darling? Just a word, just a word to say you're all right. My sweetheart, my darling! Where are you?'

The ferry musicians came sawing and squawking past, and he fled from the thoughts their blithe disharmonies brought him, lapsing into dullness and mental silence. What was the use of it all?

He had not been to Narrabeen since Roie and he honeymooned there. Four years ago, and he had not taken her anywhere much. Narrabeen had not changed. A solitary figure, he wandered along the empty miles of sand, unmarked by any footprints except the tiny triangular ones of the seagulls who, scarlet-legged, frosty-winged, yelped in anger at this intruder. Now the tide was coming in. The long clear sheets of water, curling at the edges, slid swiftly and silently over the smooth sand, and from afar out beyond the breakers came the sonorous bass of the swelling tide, a prolonged note on a vast organ.

Here they had pelted into the water. Here Roie had screamed and pranced like the child she was. He suddenly wanted to see that little pink house where they had lived for that enchanted fortnight and he clambered up the dunes, over the rippled sand where every ripple cast a black wave of shadow.

The house looked shabby now. The stucco was faded and stained with mildew, and the garden wild and rank. Even the shell borders of the little path had disappeared. The whole charm and delight of the place had vanished.

He turned away, confused and despondent, and saw in the hollow of the dunes below two lovers lying, still as statues, the dark head pressed against the fair, half-asleep in the pool of shadow. As he looked, the girl opened her eyes, and saw Charlie standing there. Over her fair, flushed face a look of resentment and anger came, and she held the boy's head against her so that he, too, would not see their secret paradise had been overlooked.

Their absorption in each other, their innocent happiness, was almost too great for Charlie to bear. He plunged away down the dune and caught the bus back to town, defeated, despairing.

Meanwhile Mumma had gone up to the hospital and brought the baby home, a little mummy swathed in the good Australian way in woollens and shawls, though the weather was stifling. Its small, surly red face glared out of the woollen cap that had slipped ludicrously down over its invisible eyebrows. Mumma looked often at that face, feeling slightly timorous, for it was many years since she had had sole control of a baby.

'You're not going to be a naughty boy for your nana?' she asked placatingly. The baby blew a bubble of milk, and made a glunking, sinister sound. His eyes stared unseeingly, in the fixed glare of indigestion.

'Oh, baby,' sighed Mumma. She folded him closer to her breast, and, half-suffocated, brought almost to boiling point by his wrappings, Michael Rothe stoically endured until he reached home.

Motty and Dolour waited at the door. Motty, streaky-faced, ominous of demeanour, chewed a grass stalk with steady champings. Already she hated the baby. The mystery of her mother's disappearance, the equal mystery of the strange baby's arrival in the household had left her with only one clear thought – she was going to bite it.

This she did. Michael had hardly been laid in Dolour's soft and delighted arms before Motty climbed on the step and bit his cheek so hard that a purple ring of toothmarks was left on the tender skin.

'You little skrimshanker!' shouted Dolour, hauling Motty away before she amputated her brother's nose. The baby roared so loudly Mumma was nearly deafened. Motty screamed with fury, and Dolour scolded. In the midst of it all Charlie came in the front door, and Anny came in the back, marching up the hall, a piece of potato peel poking out of her mouth like a tongue. Motty stopped yelling and looked at Anny's potato peel with delight.

'Ain't she a bloody old hardcase?' she chuckled. Now it was Mumma's turn to roar.

'Oh, what do you expect?' asked Dolour angrily. 'Dadda talking the way he does, and Motty hanging over the gate all the time. What do you think she learns out there, prayers?'

'I'll slap her,' said Mumma reluctantly, looking furtively at Charlie to see if he were taking any notice of the baby. She sighed, and went off to make ready a bottle.

Charlie had hardly looked at his son. The noise, the smallness of the passage, so low of roof, so close of wall that it seemed to be crowded with women and children, made him wish with a sick urgency that he had not come home. He stood there indecisive, alien, hating himself and everyone else, while Dolour took the hot bonnet from the child's fragile face, exclaiming at its downy hair and the softness of its cheek. Her heart swelled with pity for this little one, and for Roie that she should never have seen the child for which she gave so much. She said harshly to Charlie, 'There's nothing you can do, Charlie. Go and have a rest. It's that hot.'

He said, not looking at her, 'I want the kid to sleep in my room.'

Dolour nodded. 'I'm going to take Motty in with me. I'll watch out Mumma doesn't . . '

She had no need to finish the sentence. Almost unnoticed she had ranged herself on Charlie's side against Mumma's fierce maternalism.

Charlie went out on the verandah, sitting on the gas-box in the corner under the ragged shadow of the vine, hiding himself from the curious stares of passers-by. The whole world seemed poised on a pivot, palpitating in the heat. From the sky like grimy glass came the smell of dust, speaking mutely of the drought-bitten hinterlands, of the cattle-skulls gaping out of the soft-sifted soil, the deserted towns half drowned in sand, the earth grinning and cracked, and the very flesh and blood of the continent whirling out in a cloud to the sea, and nobody caring a tinker's whether it did or not.

But there was something else, too, an expectancy, an awareness, which even he in his numb apathy could not help but feel.

After the unbearably hot day, the old men on the balconies were snuffing the air and saying, 'Here she comes!' The southerly buster, the genie of Sydney, flapped its coarse blusterous wing over the city, a hearty male wind with a cool and spirited breath. The women undid the fronts of their frocks, and the little children lifted up their shirts and let it blow on their sweaty bottoms. Even the dogs crawled from the oven-hot shade of the parched trees and hung out their tongues like banners in the cool. Now there was movement everywhere, the trees tossing their arms upwards, the torn shop awnings undulating, and the scattered papers on the road taking flight, leaping upwards in gleeful tackings, up, across, over the roof and round the garret chimney, until like a ragged flock of cubist birds they disappeared into the rents and ravines that the southerly had torn in the high far roof of cumuli. Doors slammed, windows rattled, and Lick Jimmy's clothesline spun round like a top.

And the birds, too, exploded into the sky. There was no telling where they had come from. They pelted out of the dusky sunset, no more than black dots, as feckless, as disorderly, as swift as insects bursting from a hedge. There were starlings in a loose-flung flight, like a cast net, a rocket of sparrows, and then, far up, the strong-winged, disciplined webfoots, the ducks with necks outstretched, the heavy geese, and the wild black swans; they passed up there where the colour and the light were fading from the after-sunset, leaving behind them the eerie sound of their voices, discordant, forlorn, like distant bugles.

Up the path came Hughie, his feet turned well out so that he would not fall over. He sat down beside Charlie without a word. He reached into his back pocket, and a silent, venomous struggle went on with the cloth. At last, breathing triumphantly, he managed to get the bottle out.

'Have a drink.'

The stuff stung like turpentine. Its odour came up into the back of the throat and hung there like a thick and choking curtain. But it crept into the blood and made the rest of the world draw off and hesitate, a little unreal.

'Have another one.'

So they sat, while the saffron faded from the sky, and inside the close and musty house Mikey wailed feebly for his dinner.

Fifteen

Dolour knew no other way to hide her sore heart, so she plunged into work, and in a little while she was so adept at managing the shop that Mrs Drummy was content to leave her to it while she worked at her dressmaking. In spite of Mr Drummy's S.P. activities, the Drummys were so plentiful, and so reckless, that there was invariably one of them in hospital with his leg strung up to the rafters, or trotting about wearing a chin-warmer of plaster. So Mrs Drummy always needed money. If it wasn't one thing, it was another; there was Bernadette learning typing and shorthand at a business college in town, and young Michael frightening the wits out of his parents by saying he felt the vocation stirring in his heart, and them knowing it cost a thousand pound or more to make a priest out of a boy.

So Mrs Drummy sewed, roughly and hastily, slashing out patterns and fitting cheap and unsuitable cloth over the lumpy contours of her clients. An endless parade of bottle-shouldered down-at-heel women trailed through the shop to the sewing-room, and between the clangs of the bacon-cutter Dolour heard scraps of sentences, and words that had come loose from their moorings: 'She's that high-stomached . . . got one hip bigger than the other . . . me bust has gone down something awful . . . petersham ribbon and a few stiffeners . . . green's me colour . . . they pulled down her house and stuck her in a tin shed out at the housing settlement, and her only two weeks from her time.'

It was much cheaper for most of those women to get Mrs Drummy to run up a frock on her machine than to buy one, for hardly any of them were stock size, bearing the imprint of too many children, too frequent scones and tea, and bad, damp houses. Also, it was that nice to choose your own colours.

Dolour learned a lot about colour from those customers of Mrs Drummy's. Her mind, coming out of the numbness that follows pain, wondered why they chose hard, insolent blues, jam-label greens, and sometimes even red, which had no relation to their faces or hair, or to anything they wore. It was a long time before she realized that they had a peasant gift for looking at a garment as a garment, and not as a part of a person's entire appearance. When they looked in the glass they saw the dress, perhaps, or the hat, but never the two as part of a whole.

'It suits,' they often said, not 'It suits me,' which would have meant something altogether different. No, it suited. It satisfied. It was a little bit of contentment in a discontented life. It meant that, even though you had a husband who belted the daylights out of you every week-end, you still had a dress that pleased you. There was something deep and primitive there, and Dolour remembered Grandma telling her of the red woollen petticoats that the village women wore, tucked up above legs that, when peat-gathering in the cold wetness, were as pink as a turkey's.

'It was a consolation,' said Grandma, 'to have such a petticoat, a warm thing to think of, even though the baby had the whooping cough, and Himself digging up the seed potatoes to eat.'

Dolour had expected to find those days in the little shop lean and sorry ones, but somehow in the bitter loss of her sister her ambitions and their frustrations were almost forgotten. She was kept so busy she did not have time to think, for Mrs Drummy appeared to help only at lunch-time, when the hungry crowd banked up four deep at the counter, squawking for milk and sandwiches.

Speckled all over with odds and ends of cotton, as though she had been caught in some unique pastel snowstorm, she would rush out and take charge in her own muddled but competent way. When things became really hectic, Mrs Drummy ordered down reinforcements from Heaven, and often Dolour heard such things as: 'Saint Teresa, three egg and one ham, be at my side. St Anthony do thou me guide. What was that about the pickles, Joe? No cauliflower. Right-e-oh, Joe. Oh, Holy Mary, me feet are that cruel to-day I can hardly put up with them. No, dear, the foundry boy wants them in a box, and six warm pies. That's the style. And you got his milk? Ten half-pints. Dear Lord, and the kids'll be in soon and the lunch not even in the oven having a warm. St Francis Xavier, pray for us.'

There was something good about that little shop, bursting with its commonplace opulence, its eager air of rubbing shoulders with everyone, like a scrubby friendly cat. And it gave Dolour a sense of power to be able to put an extra lick on top of the ice-cream cones she put into the dirty little paws that stuck pennies over the top of the counter.

Shyly she watched the young men who came in, their slender

557

necks protruding like stalks from the collars of their Frankie Sinatra jackets, their knobbly wrists invariably ending in hands that were dirty and stained from the factories and machine-shops where they worked. Dolour felt sorry for their hands until one day, handing the bags of cakes across the counter, she saw that her own were greasy and grey. No matter how many times she washed herself, she couldn't keep clean. The cases of soft drinks, sparkling from the factory, were dumped in the alley an hour or two, and when she went to bring them inside to the refrigerator they were frosted all over with glassy black dust. At the back of the Drummy shop a chimney pointed an enormous blackened finger at the sky. It was so tall that rain-clouds trailed their ragged plumes over it in winter, and on the days that the dank, dirty city frost lay on the soggy ground the starlings vanished into its smoke like midges, looking for warm copings upon which they could huddle awhile. It was no wonder that Mrs Drummy's clothes-rope, slung between her shop and the next, twenty feet up, was harsh and hairy with soot.

Mrs Drummy loved cleanliness, a thing that Dolour had never known much about. She wiped up water as soon as it was spilt, and not in all her life would she have polished up a grease-spot with a wad of paper and left it at that. Every Saturday she cleaned the windows, and as she left one side slippery and shining, tiny clots of soot came from nowhere and settled upon it in an impalpable velvet bloom.

Furtively, Dolour began to imitate her, washing her overall every night, and ironing it in the morning before she left. And now, instead of dipping her head in the tin basin of sudsy water, and rubbing it dry, she washed her hair long and lovingly, sneering at the black water with a triumphant sneer, as though she had temporarily defeated the dirt of Surry Hills.

Mumma scoffed at her, but in private she boasted to Mrs Campion over the fence. 'She's got the nice ways of the nuns,' she bragged.

Often, now, as she came home from work, Dolour found Motty playing in the street, the seat of her pants black and wet and filthy from the gutter, her hair in tangled witch-locks and on her face the look of a mutinous angel. Motty fought silently, viciously scratching and biting, using her toenails as well as fingernails, occasionally spitting out a word straight out of the back alleys. In some extraordinary way she had retreated within herself, and nobody could communicate with her real self. Her father took little notice of her, Dolour was away all day, and Mumma's attention devoted to the baby, so Motty, like a little wandering cat, walked by herself.

'You shouldn't let her out on the road,' expostulated Dolour, holding the wriggling child between her knees and looking carefully through her hair for 'things.' 'You know Roie wouldn't like that.'

'I know,' sighed Mumma, 'but Mr Reilly leaves the gate open, and Charlie don't seem to care, and she does look after herself, Dolour, you can't deny it.'

'She's only four,' said Dolour. 'There!' she pounced. 'She has got things in her hair! You've been wearing other kid's hats!' she accused the sulky Motty, who stuck out her tongue and jerked her hips in the immemorial gesture of contempt. 'Kerosene on your head to-night, young lady!'

'They'll go away,' said Mumma comfortably.

Dolour snorted. In some strange way it seemed as though the place were falling to pieces without Roie, as though she had been the gentle binder on the toppling walls of their family. With the hopeless, angry desperation of the young, Dolour watched Motty run wild, and, even worse, Charlie's complete apathy to life. On the surface he seemed the same, but to her acute and sensitive vision he seemed to be rotting away within. All that had been strong and admirable in him had become hollow, melancholy, and completely negative. She watched him, and was angry, and did not know that the ancient fatalism and defeatism of his aboriginal blood was being thus mysteriously manifested in him.

But in his grief Hughie felt drawn to Charlie as never before. He was like an old dog, tolerated, kindly treated, and then suddenly admitted into the inner friendship of the master. It was good, when Mumma was nagging, and the domestic turmoil of the place overpowering, to go up to the attic and know he would be welcomed. His heart, opened up, with the warm air of human contact blowing through it, healed a little.

'A man don't want women round him all the time,' he said. He held up the bottle to the light. A curdy black sediment clung round the shoulders like a moraine. Hughie shook his head. 'Gawd knows what they put in it down at Delie Stock's. A coupla shovelfuls off Bondi Beach, be the look.'

So they drank, and the dead marines mounted up in the corner, where Roie's clothes had once hung. After a little while the lagoons and islands in the kalsomined walls merged into a marbled pattern, and the curtains became a weaving film of light, in and out, in and out, so hypnotic, so dizzying that Charlie could not take his eyes from it.

Hughie's voice washed back and forth with the sound of surf, sometimes hollow, sometimes like the little voice on the other end of a long-distance telephone.

'Put a hump on himself like a ferret . . . shaping up to me . . . I let loose with the old one-two and he fell on his ombongpong . . . me father came from Kerry . . . often he told me about the little cows . . . big as them St Bernard dogs . . . wish I had a cow . . . it was that long ago . . .'

The bottle on the table gathered into itself the rich heavy light of autumn, the sunset that gilded the curly edges of the wooden shingles on Lick Jimmy's roof and turned to yellow flags the shirts that flapped on his line. Charlie stared at it, stupid, unable to think or dream, unable even to distinguish between the sounds below, Motty screaming with rage, the baby thumping a spoon on the table, Dolour clattering about the yard in the too-big shoes she wore in the wet.

It was like the time between sleeping and waking, suspension in a world of no thought, no feeling, no anything. Charlie fell into it as he would have fallen into a deep pool, with complete emotional exhaustion. Hughie's voice was no more than the humming of a blowfly in a corner. There was nothing in the world. Although his pain had dulled and blunted, the pulse of life had not come back. The night would never be a time of contentment any more; the day would never bring the good hard normal joys of work and fulfilment, and hope that things would be easier sometime.

All at once a hideous localized emergency filled his brain with stupid alarm. He got to his feet and, pushing Hughie aside, lurched down the stairs. The fresh air struck him like a blow, and the yard spun round giddily. The distance from the door to the drain lengthened to a hundred yards. He let go the door and staggered towards it.

The sound brought Mumma from the stove, where she was leaning with her forehead pressed against the mantelpiece, stirring at a pot. She looked interestedly out of the window.

'He'll bring up his liver and all its trimmin's in a moment.'

Dolour was setting the table. She slapped down the forks with angry vigour.

'Trust him to do it right on teatime. I dunno how you've put up with him all these years.'

Mumma went on stirring. She said, with a tiny shade of triumph, 'It ain't your dadda. It's Charlie.'

Dolour stood frozen. She went to the window. Within reach of her hand was Charlie's face, deathly yellow, his eyes closed, and streaks of sweat running down his cheeks. Dolour could have reached out and wiped those streaks away, or pushed up the dark curly hair from his wet forehead. As she stared, her mouth open, dumbfounded, his head drooped, and she saw the back of his neck, young, clean, and in some extraordinary way submissive, to what she did not know.

'He's drunk,' said Mumma complacently.

A terrible fury against her mother rose in Dolour's chest, suffocating her.

'Charlie doesn't get drunk. He never gets drunk. What are you talking about?'

'He can't hold it like your father,' said Mumma.

'Charlie?'

'Yes, Charlie,' said Mumma angrily, turning and facing her, the spoon dripping on the floor. 'Why not Charlie? He's a man, ain't he?'

'What's that got to do with it?' blazed Dolour, trembling with shock and disgust and anger. She heard Charlie begin to be sick again.

Mumma went on stirring. 'It's natural for men to get drunk when they're upset. You might as well get it into your head right now.'

This time there was no mistaking the complacency in her tones. In Mumma's simple heart a great problem had been solved. Charlie had not shown what were to her the orthodox signs of grief at the death of his wife, and she had resented it. Now that he had, he was established in her approval and sympathy.

'That's not true,' cried Dolour. 'You've always been jealous of Charlie because he isn't like Dad, and now – now he's going the same way you're glad!'

She rushed outside, and there was Charlie, white-faced and shivering, walking slowly towards the door. She waited till he was

561

within reach, then she hit him as hard as she could across the face. He looked at her, dazed.

'How can you do it?' she cried. 'Don't you see what Dadda is? Do you want to be the same as him when you're old?'

He rubbed his cheek slowly.

'Oh, Charlie,' cried Dolour, not knowing what to say, and choking over the words that did come out, 'Surry Hills is full of fellows who – it ain't fair to Motty or Michael – you got to pull yourself together somehow.'

He said thickly, 'What do you say "ain't" for, when you've had a better education than any of us?'

She heard his slow footsteps lurching heavily from one step to another, until they reached the landing and vanished into the sound of a slammed door. Dolour stood in the yard for a long time. Mumma stuck her head out of the scullery window.

'If you've got nothing better to do than stand around on your big flat feet, you can come in and feed Mikey.'

'Oh, shut up!' said Dolour.

It was beginning to rain again. The saffron faded from the sky, and strong and pungent rose the smell of wet and rotting vegetables from Lick's shed. The house seemed to draw into itself huddling under its misshapen roof as though it were afraid of getting damp. Dolour ran the tap hard over the drain and went inside, depressed and melancholy. Her hand still stung and shame and dejection filled her soul. She looked at the room, the crumbs trodden into the floor, the chairs with their seats pushed down into terrible hernias, the plaster blotched with old grease marks where her father had thrown his dinner at the wall. Motty sat at the table, her hair like Medusa's locks, her little beautiful hands thick with grime. Mikey crawled around her chair, napkins bunched behind him in a wet grey bustle, his wrinkled little legs red and raw from their chafe. With a sob Dolour picked him up. He had a sickish smell of the unwashed baby, the smell that hangs like an aura over a hundred thousand slum houses.

'Mumma,' she began. Desperately she struggled for words but there were none. Her mother's broad, patient back was there, the rhythmically stirring arm, the feet planted at right-angles to bear the weight that had become wearisome with the years. How could she expect her mother to understand? Dirt was dirt, and life was life, to be plodded through patiently, uncomplainingly, doing what

562

you could and not bothering your head about the rest. And her mother was right. Her method was logical. Mrs Drummy wore herself to a shadow trying to defeat dirt; her mother accommodated herself to it. But what about Motty? What about the baby? As she thought these things, Motty suddenly jabbed herself with the fork, and from her red rose lips burst the words, 'Bloody basket!'

'Oh, Motty,' chided Mumma, 'you mustn't say them things.'

'Once,' thought Dolour, 'she would have clipped my ears, if I'd said that.'

Yes, once Mumma would have minded, but now it was different. She was tired of battling against things without making an inch of headway. It was the same with Hughie; it would have been the same with Roie. The slums would have sapped her, too.

'But Charlie ought to be different,' thought Dolour in anguish. 'He wasn't born here. And I'm different. I am! I am!'

But deep down within her she knew that she was doomed from the start to become just like them, worn down like a stone with the flow of her environment. For how did you get away from it? What were the first steps? Did you have to break every bond of emotion and warm family love before you could become like other people and lead a life wherein cleanliness and quietness and privacy were intrinsic, and not luxuries? A lump in the back of her throat hurt. 'I could get a job somewhere else, and board out. But I wouldn't want to leave Mumma, and the babies, and Charlie.' At the thought of Charlie a flush of shame stained her face. 'He'd never look after the kids properly. And he might get married again and some rotten woman would knock them around, just because they weren't hers. Oh, God, why do You make it so hard for everyone?'

Desolately she knew that the elder people of that house were finished already, that all volatility of spirit was gone, and there was no one left to pull them together except herself. Motty was a little larrikin; in all her brilliant beauty there was no grace or gentleness or kindness; nothing but the piteous brazen fearlessness of the slum children, like little lion cubs snarling at a world that had already shown itself inimical. With a shaking of the heart Dolour could see Motty as she would be thirteen years hence, another Suse Kilroy, a fragile, brittle creature with no more morals than a butterfly, resentful with a deep and bitter resentment against the life that had been begrudged her since conception.

'You didn't ought to have hit Charlie like that,' said Mumma.

'No,' said Dolour, 'I didn't.'

They heard the merry footsteps of Hughie on the stairs and down the hall, and with a sigh Mumma shovelled his dinner on a plate and stuck it in the oven with another plate on top of it. Puffing Billy's oven was peculiar to himself, a bulging stomach ornamented with a tongue-shaped latch and hinges as big as handfuls of knuckles. While one side of the oven tray was red hot, a fly was dawdling about the other side, which explained why Mumma's scones were always either burned black, or semi-liquid.

Hughie was feeling good. The warm generosity that drink and companionship always lit in him burned high. He wished he could corner Mr Reilly in the hall so that he could whack the little fellow on the back, and pour a drink into his herring guts. For Charlie, stretched like a log on the bed, was no longer of any use to Hughie.

'Funny how a fellow that age can't take it,' he ruminated as he floated down Plymouth Street, remembering how when he was Charlie's age, not yet married, free as a bird and with twice as much kick, there wasn't a pub in the north-west whose threshold hadn't some mortal wound from his boots as he was thrown out. Hughie felt sorry for Charlie and his drab life.

But he was too late to get in for a drink at the Foundry. As he arrived he saw the beefy great lump of a publican clank the doors together, and the clots of customers dispersing in the twilight. As though he had been a balloon, and it pricked all of a sudden, Hughie's high spirits leaked out of him. The air was chilly, and he had no coat. The blister on his heel, where one of Mumma's catastrophic darns had rubbed off the skin, spoke up shrilly.

'Gawd!' groaned Hughie.

There was nowhere to go except home, and his soul cringed at the thought. He wandered down Coronation Street hoping to meet one of his mates, but there was no one to meet except an occasional stranger hooked around a post, waiting for the feeling to come back to his feet. A flood of kids gushed out of Jacky Siciliano's fruit shop and fled up the street, leaving the footpath miraculously littered, all in an instant, with peanut shells and banana skins. Jacky Siciliano's broom appeared, with Jacky close behind it.

'Some day I catch-a those little devils and beat off their bum-as,' he threatened with a broad grin. Then he leaned on his broom and said sadly, 'You know, Hughie, what? Tomorrow my little girl, my Tonetta, get married.'

'You don't say,' said Hughie, in spite of himself interested. 'Why, she's only a kid!'

'Sixteen,' said Jacky Siciliano proudly. 'She marry ice-cream.'

'Yeah?' said Hughie, puzzled.

'She marry Jupiter Giaquinto, the ice-cream,' explained Mr Siciliano.

'Yer don't say!' Hughie remembered Jupiter's father, a tiny wrinkled Italian like a sausage left too long in a shop window, trotting about with a wheeled box containing pink, green, and chocolate ice-cream, and followed by three or four small sons, each with a tray of cones slung from his shoulders.

'Jupiter, Mars, Mercutio, and Venutio,' remembered Hughie, and all at once there was Roie swinging on the gate, a big girl of twelve with short white socks and a hole in her bloomers, chanting the names of the four little happy Italian boys. Abruptly he barged away from Mr Siciliano, his head down, knowing that if he thought about it the pain would be too great to bear. She was on every street corner; she leaned out of windows shaking tablecloths; she hid in the bottle; she was written all over Coronation Street, and he could not get away from her.

'Hullo,' said someone, and Hughie glanced up, opening his eyes wide so that the tears would not fall out. There, sitting on the verandah of the little yellow house, was the girl Florentina.

At the sight of her Hughie felt so strange a shock that he wanted to be sick. It was as though the years had fallen from him, and left him naked and shivering, or as though the familiar old world had changed and become something quite new and alien, and a little terrifying because it was so. The wine in his stomach curdled and water rushed into his mouth; he was dreadfully afraid he would be sick before he could get away. But all this passed in a moment so short the girl did not notice it.

'How's that little girl of yours?'

'Eh?' For a second Hughie gaped at her, then he remembered Motty. 'She's the same little devil.'

He went on staring. She had been in his mind for so long, deep down, almost lost under all the worry and sorrow, but still there with her deep Assyrian hair, and the eyes that were sombre even when she smiled.

'Florentina.' Once he said it he felt silly, and a dark red stained his skin.

'That's right. You going anywhere? Then come in and have a drink.'

Dumbly he followed her into the little room that opened off the verandah, a room strange and mysterious to Hughie with its half-seen pictures, its dusty darknesses, and its smell of scent and wine. Almost under his feet unrolled what appeared to be a black rat. It flashed white eyeballs at him, and white teeth shone in a mouth as dark as grapes.

'It's my sister's little boy,' explained Florentina. 'Go on, Lex.'

She stirred him with her foot, and the boy vanished silently from the room. Hughie looked at her, not understanding anything, only wanting to be sick, and wanting to cry because of his loneliness, and growing old, and the way the wine was acting up.

This was the way he fell in love, when the last years of his middle age were disappearing like sticks on a stream, bobbing ever onwards like sticks on a stream in spate, with him grasping after them with one hand, and with the other drawing the coat tighter round shoulders that felt the autumn chill. He had forgotten youth, and long forgotten the enchantment of love. Once or twice it had happened to him, but the years that stretched between were so many that his infatuation hit him with a strength that knocked him dizzy. The loss of his daughter and all its shifting and opposing tides became so identified with his finding of this other young creature, with the same slender arms, the same heartbreaking, mysterious sense of youth, that he could not distinguish one from the other.

But now it was only a beginning. He went home in a daze, and there was Mumma, crossly washing up, slamming dishes about and slinging her hips from side to side with a fury that had been impressive in her youth and was now only ludicrous. He stared at her, appalled that he should be married to this old woman.

'If you had my bunions,' she said reproachfully, 'you wouldn't have me standing around for hours waiting to put yer dinner on the table.'

Hughie told her what she could do with her bunions with such viciousness that she turned round and gaped. He stamped into the bedroom, and Mumma timidly went to the door.

'Don't you want yer dinner?'

He put his face into the pillow to get away from her, her red hands rolled up in her wet apron, her face puffy from the stove, her teeth showing snaggled and yellow behind her half-opened, aston-

566

ished lips. He wanted to yell, 'Shut yer mouth! Get out of here! Go and cut yer throat!' but he knew it would be no use. Mumma would be with him until he died. So he said nothing. Mumma went back to the dishes. Slowly she watched the grey greasy suds ride about her swollen wrists. And it had been a nice dinner, too. She looked at it forlornly sitting there on the plate.

'I dunno.'

Suddenly she attacked Puffing Billy, dragging his lid off and stirring savagely amongst his half-digested clinkers.

Puffing Billy decided he had had enough. 'Tachah!' he remarked. He spat through every crevice, enveloped Mumma in a choking fog, and gave up the ghost. Mumma gave him one look, threw down the poker, and marched out of the kitchen.

For a long time Charlie lay in a stupor. The air was so chilly that the sweat, drying on his body, made him colder than stone. He was aware of the chuckling croonings of his son being put to bed, of Mumma's hands pulling a blanket over him, but he could not even mumble acknowledgement. The hours went by in half-unconsciousness, with no memory, no pain, no grief. He fought off returning sobriety, knowing it would bring so much to hurt. But it came, anyway, and he raised himself on the moonlit pillow, looking at the empty one beside him.

He shaped in the air the slender contour of her cheek, her little chin, the shell shape of her sleeping eyelids. He stroked her long soft hair, dark as darkness itself, remembering all the times it had lain like silk on his soft chest.

'Roie, my girl.'

Then a terrible despair seized him. He sat upright and looked at the room, blocked with black and striped with moonlight, the angle of Lick Jimmy's roof standing like a gallows in shadow on the wall. He smelt all the smell of that slum attic, the wet in the wood, the dirty nappies on the chair. A kind of horror seized him. What did it all mean? What was he doing there? He sprang out of bed, walking aimlessly about the room, his mind a chaos of despair. The little confines of the wall stayed his step in either direction. God was nowhere. Roie was nowhere. He was lost and destroyed and there was no way of recovering himself. He flicked on the light, going automatically to the cot where the baby slept. He looked at the puffy pink face with a bubble of milk on the cheek as though he had never seen it before. He listened to the tiny sound of the child's breathing with wonder. For this Roie had died, for this Motty was motherless, and he was alone.

Yet with clumsy hands he pulled the blanket up about the baby's neck, and turned the cot a little to shield its eyes from the light.

'What am I going to do?'

There was a little tap at the door. It hardly penetrated the thickness of his thoughts. The handle turned, and his gaze went to it, incurious.

'Charlie, can I come in?'

Dolour was bundled up in her old rain-spotted winter coat, the hem of her nightdress drooping about her bare feet. Her pale mouse face looked at him anxiously.

'I'm sorry I woke you up, Dolour.'

But before he could say anything else her face crumpled up piteously like a child's, and out of her closed eyes two big tears squeezed.

'Oh, Charlie,' she sobbed, 'ain't it awful!' She turned away, hiding her face with her hands. 'I'm sorry, Charlie,' she said when she could speak. 'I know no matter how bad I feel you feel worse. I'm sorry, Charlie. It's just that sometimes I feel I can't bear it if I don't see her soon.'

'I know.'

They stood looking at each other in the bald light, the great pain between them, the pain that was different from Mumma's and Hughie's because it was young and uncomprehending and impatient. The tears came into Dolour's eyes again. She gulped them down in her throat. He put his hand under her chin and she tried to look at him with her red eyes.

'You look a bit like her sometimes.'

She tried to smile. 'I won't ever be as pretty as Roie.'

From somewhere a little comfort had entered her heart. She went over to the child, picking a bug from behind his soft crumpled ear and squashing it without a qualm under her bare foot.

'Filthy brute, feeding on my Mikey.' She slipped her hand under the blankets. 'You've let him get wet again, Charlie.'

'I can't keep up with him,' said Charlie. For a little while all the pain and terror had left the room. He watched with greedy relief the calm commonplace movements of the girl changing the baby and tucking the blanket down. She stroked the downy cheek.

'Gee, he's nice. Wish you'd let me have him in my room.'

'Haven't you got enough with Motty?'

'I love kids,' said Dolour. She blushed. 'Anyway, Motty and Michael aren't just ordinary kids. They belong to me, too.'

She gathered up the soiled napkins from the chair. 'You want to go to sleep, Charlie. You're looking that peaked lately.'

As she passed Mr Reilly's door she could hear the stealthy rustle of paper. He was doing up his parcels again, at two in the morning. The light went off in Charlie's room, and Dolour went quietly into her own. For a little while she hung out of the window, breathing in the knife-sharp air. The sky was freckled with stars, blacked out here and there by the squares and angles of buildings. Dirty Dick sat humped on the fence.

She turned away. Her fingers traced the line that Charlie's had. 'Do I really look like you, Roie?'

A little peace stole into her heart. It seemed that Roie could not be lost as long as someone looked like her.

Sixteen

One day Mrs Campion barked alluringly at Mumma as she was hanging out the clothes.

'Jer hear about Lick going! Poor little stinker! It's not going to be the same street without him.'

Mumma gaped. She was not one to gossip, but she always kept her ears open. Mrs Campion, reading her face, was delighted. She reached over the fence and gave Mumma a puck in the chest.

'You mean they're going to pull his place down?' gasped Mumma.

'Naow! He's going back to China!'

Fancy! Mumma waddled inside and sat down to have a think about it, wiping her face meantime with her apron. It was bad enough to think of Lick Jimmy going away, but worse to think of strangers next door, for in Plymouth Street, where the houses were built so closely that your neighbours could spit in your pockets without even trying, it meant a great deal to live next door to amiable people.

'Nasty kids maybe,' said Mumma gloomily, visioning dead cats thrown on her roof, and mud on her washing, and maybe a bait slipped to poor Dirty Dick. Or perhaps there'd be a father who'd take a fancy to Hughie, so that he'd always be nipping in with half a bottle, and there'd be rows, and she'd be dragged into it, and life in the backyard would be unbearable. Mumma felt very vexed with Lick, for what was the use of going back to China at his time of life, and with a war on, too?

'He'll hardly put his foot to the ground before they'll be lopping his head off,' thought Mumma angrily, for her Chinese history had stopped back in the days of the Old Buddha.

She put the baby in the pram where he lay, blinking in the sunshine, the light glistening on each separate hair on his downy head.

'Nana's little dotie,' said Mumma admiringly, tickling him under his lowest chin, and he broke into a loud tuneless song, showing his new teeth like tiny shells. He had eyebrows now, like dark feathers, and his grubby face was of a glossy waxen texture, like Victorian

570

mantel fruit. Mumma thought nothing of this. She was dead scared of fresh air blowing on babies. They swallowed the wind, she said, and belched themselves blue in the face for days afterwards. They had to be well-wrapped all the time, and taken outside only when necessary. In Mumma's babyhood, in the emigrant days of fifty years before, babies had always been kept in a room with a fire, where they could get a good warm, and when croup and whooping cough carried them off like feathers on a gale, it was the will of God and nothing else.

So with her anxious love she swaddled and coddled Mikey, and only Mikey's solid Irish constitution defeated her.

She pushed the pram down the street to do the shopping, and the parcels mounted up and up until Mikey's eager inquisitive face appeared like that of a bodiless sprite over a heap of groceries. Almost nobody knew that Lick was leaving, and she found a quiet pride in being the bearer of such interesting news. So the story went from fence to fence, and everyone remembered how Lick Jimmy had always given the kids attention instead of serving the grown-ups first, as other shopkeepers did, and how he was never a scrooge with the specked fruit. And Mumma remembered how he'd given Roie all that awful pink silk when she got married, poor little fellow, not knowing much about the colours a girl could wear, and how he'd made Dolour kites when she was smaller, and he'd always remembered to give her and Hughie a pot of ginger for Christmas, though he was a heathen, and felt different about the holy day from everyone else.

Plymouth Street was full of a warm feeling about Lick Jimmy, and for a little while all the Sicilianos' customers forsook them and dealt with him, much to his grave amazement. They asked him a great many questions about his trip to China, but Lick, who had never troubled to learn much English beyond weights and measures, and how to make sure he was getting the right money, let it all flow over his head and smiled gently and chirped, 'What else, please, eh? You wantee palsnip? You wantee cabbagee, only lempence, velly cheap?'

'When are you going, Lick?' pleaded Dolour, who had loved him best of all, and could not imagine the street without his soft shuffle, and his bowed blue back plodding along behind a heaped wheelbarrow as he came back from the markets.

'Ahhh, soon,' promised Lick.

'You might have told us before,' said Dolour, almost tearfully, for

Lick was bound up with so much of her childhood that she felt he would be taking the spellbound years back to China with him.

But Mumma often thought of how cold China was, for she had read about it in the Far East, and slowly there came the idea that it would be nice to give Lick a little something to remember them by. Timidly she broached this to Hughie, and as she expected Hughie's chair crashed back on all fours from its tilted position and he guffawed, 'Who ever heard of giving a Chow a presentation? If you want to give anyone a present, you can give me one.'

'He was kind to Ro,' was all Mumma said, 'and now he's going away.'

Hughie was silent. Another one to go away – Thady, Grandma, Patrick Diamond, Roie, and now Lick. Almost violently he said, 'You can have the chicken feed this week.'

The chicken feed was the shillings and pennies in Hughie's pay envelope, the sixteen shillings he kept for himself, except on those occasions when he really got drunk, when he helped himself to the housekeeping money as well.

So with that, and the money Dolour scraped up, and the little bit Mumma scrooged out of the house money, they bought a cardigan. Mumma, doubtful, had chosen a dark-blue guaranteed to make Lick's complexion look like aged soap.

'Bit herring-gutted, ain't it?' asked Hughie critically.

'He's only little,' said Dolour.

'True enough,' agreed Hughie. 'He's got a behind on him like a two-year-old child.'

'Never mind the behind,' snapped Mumma. 'It's the shoulders I'm thinking of.'

She marched into Lick Jimmy's shop. Though he was going away Lick did not seem to be making any effort to clean up. The same old calendars showing Eastern pin-up girls with high-necked gowns and thread-thin, crimson lips, spotted the dusty walls. The strings of papery garlic swung in a curtain behind the window, and on the counter his cat suckled five blind bullet-headed kittens in a crate half-full of lemons. There sat Lick Jimmy, peacefully smoking his pipe, his shapely hands, with long thumbnails like transparent horn, placidly shelling peas.

Mumma did not know what to say, so she put the parcel on the counter and blurted, 'This is for you, Lick.'

Lick looked at the parcel. He smiled, shook his head, and gave it back to Mumma.

'Velly nice,' commented Lick, 'but no money.'

'What say?' asked poor Mumma.

'Lick got no money,' said Lick.

'I'm not asking you to buy it,' cried Mumma, light breaking. 'It's a present.' She jabbed Lick in his skinny blue chest, then poked herself in her abundant black one. 'From us, see?' She took a deep breath, then spoke his own language. 'It's a plesent, Lick.'

Lick did not understand. He tried to read the meaning of the mystery in Mumma's face. She seemed to be cross, and he did not know what he had done, so nodding and smiling and mumbling he took the parcel and put it on the shelf amongst the wilted celery and leprous cucumbers he had put aside for the pig-man. Then he said doubtfully, 'You wantee somesing? Spud? Pummikin?'

Mumma was deeply disappointed. She had pictured Lick putting on the cardigan and beaming all over, for once acting like an understandable human being.

'It's because you're going to China, see,' she tried again.

Lick beamed. 'Lick come from China all li,' he agreed happily. He looked round for something to please Mumma, and fished a passion-fruit from a box.

'For bubby,' he said, and Mumma, a little mollified, returned to her own place, where Dolour was impatiently awaiting her.

'Well, how did he take it? Was he thrilled?'

'He was so grateful he could hardly say a word,' said Mumma thoughtfully.

Nobody knew just exactly when Lick Jimmy was leaving, but Mumma kept a close watch from her upper windows, and there came a day when he hung out on the line a collection of patched quilts, sacks stitched together, and archaic blankets, and beat the blazes out of them with a broomstick.

'There now, he's going to pack,' she said, satisfied. A few moments later she was rewarded by the sight of Lick toddling out with a brand new high chair, painted a bright glossy blue. She couldn't call down the stairs fast enough for Dolour to have a look.

'I suppose he's taking it back for his grandchildren,' said Dolour.

Mumma was determined that Lick wouldn't get away without her saying good-bye, and she and Dolour watched the shipping news for those vessels coming from China.

'Here's one,' said Dolour one night, and her gloom deepened as she heard excessive activity in Lick Jimmy's house that night. A jumping jack bounded in a shower of sparks across the yard, and

573

through the veiled windows they could see all sorts of twinkles and sunbursts.

'He's telling all the devils they ain't got tickets,' chuckled Hughie.

Next morning Lick went out early, and all the Darcys hung out of their windows and waved to him. He seemed dumbfounded, trotting down the street and turning round at intervals to see if they were still watching.

'I wonder where his luggage is?'

'Work yer head. He's sent it by carrier.' They watched the little figure dwindle to a matchstick in the glossy sunshine.

'Well, that's that,' declared Hughie, melancholy. 'Now I suppose we'll get a load of Greeks, pelting us with fish-heads.'

They all went off to work, and Mumma was left alone to cope with the two children. Motty had a bad cold, and went whooping about the house, whingeing between whoops and clinging to Mumma's leg like a limpet.

'Mother of heaven, won't you let me to meself for a minute, lovie!' exploded Mumma. Then she picked Motty up and cuddled her, saying, 'Ah I've forgotten what it is to be little, Motty, so you mustn't be hard on me if I'm cranky sometimes.'

Heavily she climbed upstairs, Motty on one arm and Mikey on the other. Sometimes Mumma felt very tired, but since Roie had died she had had no time for 'the change.' Life went on over her head, but she was too busy attending to other people to notice its passing.

As she went past she gave Mr Reilly's door a kick. There was a steady rustling going on inside as though Mr Reilly were having a lovely time unwrapping parcels, but at the thud of her toe against the door the rustling ceased with the abruptness of a mouse that hears a footfall.

'I beg yours, Mr Reilly,' she called, 'but I'm going to put the children to sleep, so please don't make any noise if you don't mind.'

Behind the closed door there was the silence of death.

Mumma put the baby down with the bottle of milk, and tucked him up.

Wearily she undressed Motty and put her into Charlie's bed, where she squirmed and whined rebelliously. But Mumma's big rough hand had motherly magic in it. She patted Motty's back with a monotonous, hypnotic rhythm, humming meantime a song her ma had sung to her long ago, a song that had come over on the convict ships, and was old long before that:

'Now, all you young dukeses and duchesses!
Take 'eed of what I do say.
Make sure it's your own that you toucheses,
Or you'll meet me in Botany Bay.'

Now and then she stopped tentatively, and Motty opened a threatening blue eye.
'Ah, yer little tripehound. All right, then:

'With a tooral-i-looral-i-addity,
And a tooral-i-ooral-i-ay!
With a tooral-i-ooral-i-addity,
Oh, I'll meet *chew* in Botany Bay.'

Now, out of the sultry heat of the early morning came rain, and with the soft rattle on the roof Motty went to sleep. The baby was already fast asleep, a trickle of milk on his chin. The attic was dusky with the dimness the clouds had brought, and gratefully Mumma stood at the sill and breathed in the coolness. She watched the beads of quicksilver that streaked across the cranky-paned window, the raindrops bowling along the telephone wires, and the damp, sooty birds that huddled together under cornices and clung upside-down to the guttering. The houses across the road looked shut-up and unwelcoming, with their closed eyes, and even the doormats taken inside. Mumma forgot all about the big wash awaiting her downstairs, the unswept kitchen, and the dishes still lying on the table. She gazed unseeingly at late workmen going past on bikes, with tool-kits on their shoulders under rain-capes, so that they looked like a great many hump-backed little Frankensteins.

'Oh, Roie, darling, is it going to be all right? I get that worried about Motty, and her the little firebrand she is. Do I look after them the way you'd want, and will I live long enough to see them able to watch out for themselves? Look after them going over roads, darling, and other places where I can't be. And if Motty gets the whooping cough and the baby gets it, too, make that Charlie let me have him by my bed so I can see he's covered at night.'

575

So she prayed, shutting her eyes and trying to find Roie in that dim quiet room, longing to have her arms round her daughter, to feel her reassuring flesh.

'Oh, if only I could have my life over again, with you a little child, and Thady my baby.'

She felt the panic of sorrow rising in her heart, and she gabbled Hail Marys to still the flood, for there was too much housework to be done for her to give way. Then all at once a most extraordinary occurrence drove every other thought out of her mind. Two taxis drew up outside Lick Jimmy's, and every possible kind of Chinese personage tumbled out, holding newspapers and umbrellas over their heads, and talking at the tops of their voices.

'Glory-lory-ory!' said Mumma.

First came Lick Jimmy himself, squeezed up as narrow as a bookmark by the buffeting he'd had in the cab. He galloped in and unlocked the shop door. Mumma was by now paralysed with astonishment. She tried to fit the facts together, and every second piece was left over.

Lick Jimmy was very delighted about something. He pranced out again and held one of the lopsided umbrellas over two young men who, laden down with suitcases, rolls of blankets, an empty birdcage, and a large basket, followed him to the shop. After them came a stout middle-aged man, very prosperous, and with a certain critical air as he peered through his horn-rimmed glasses at his surroundings. Then came two pretty girls, with hair so sleek that not even the rain dulled its paint-like gloss. They wore Chinese gowns, and one carried a very fat small boy with basin-cut hair and a smart English style tweed suit.

In the Irish way, watching a good spectacle by herself was not enough for Mumma, so she ran out and thumped on Mr Reilly's door.

'Come and look through the window, Mr Reilly! You've never seen such goings-on!'

The sepulchral silence of Mr Reilly's room was unaltered.

'Quick, or you'll miss it! It's the fun of Cork.'

She gave a last despairing kick at the door, but Mr Reilly said not a word. She rushed back in time to see a third taxi arrive. It contained nothing but luggage, a large frying-pan, a bunch of artificial flowers, and a box with the head of a live white fowl sticking through the battens. The middle-aged man paid off the first two taxis with a baronial air, and clucked round the third, making sure that no chickens or new-born puppies were left in it. Then the second taxi heaved once more, and out of it climbed the oldest Chinese woman in the world, a mere morsel of a black-eyed creature with a face as big as Mumma's hand, so scribbled over with years that it no longer looked like a face at all, but a piece of vellum, creased many times. Painfully she hobbled on her stumpy feet to the door, and was received with assisting arms and loud cheeps of welcome.

'I suppose they forgot her,' ruminated Mumma.

The door of the shop slammed, and almost instantly there was a deafening burst of crackers. Windows flew open upstairs, and the fowl gave a death-cry.

Mumma could no longer see anything, so she went downstairs, pausing on her way to kick Mr Reilly's door and call out reproachfully, 'You're a fine one. You've missed the sight of a lifetime.'

She muddled through the dishes, thinking excitedly, 'Maybe they're going to take the shop over. Maybe he leaves for China tomorrow.'

But she had to know for sure, and as soon as possible she had a peep to see if the shop was open. And it was. Mumma took her string bag and went in. The rain had stopped, and the road was steaming in the sunshine. Already one of the girls was scrubbing the shop step, but at the sight of Mumma she and the bucket wafted out of sight. Lick Jimmy and the young men were engaged in incredible activity behind the counter, knocking in nails and jerking them out again, and talking all the time at the tops of their voices. All Lick Jimmy's gravity, his solemn and remote air had vanished. His little lemon face had broken into smiles, and he showed his snaggled teeth right to the cheekbone.

Mumma had to ask for onions four times before he gave them to her, giggling to himself. The young men, subdued into silence by Mumma's presence, stood shyly at one side. Their clothes sat curiously upon them, their slender necks unsuited to the stiff collars of the Western breed. Like Dolour, Mumma liked Chinese, and shyly she peeped at their beautiful wrists, their eyes set gently in the flat of the face, the russet blush in the creamy cheeks.

'When are you leaving, Lick?' asked Mumma. 'To-morrow?'

Lick nodded vigorously. 'All flamlee now!' he giggled, his eyes, which were beginning to turn a little blue with old age, crinkling up with utmost pleasure.

Mumma couldn't make head or tail of it. Just then the smallest stranger, now visible as an incredibly fat young godling of eighteen months, with eyes like black glass, and a body completely naked except for Lick's new blue cardigan, which trailed on the floor like a State robe, appeared from behind the screen. Mumma was dumb-founded. In two seconds she had added up all the little sacrifices contributed by Dolour and Hughie and herself towards the 'plesent' for Lick, and the sum was ingratitude.

'I've a good mind to ask for it back!' she exploded, and marched back into her own house, leaving the onions and the three Chinese all looking at each other bewildered.

Mumma was very upset indeed. More than that, she felt a fool, and all day long she fulminated against herself, and the Chinese, and Dirty Dick, who invariably occupied the place where she next wanted to put her foot. But it was not until Dolour came home that she could express herself fully.

Dolour was delighted. She rushed into the shop to fetch the onions Mumma had forgotten. After a long time she returned like a whirlwind, crying. 'You are a dope, Mumma! Lick never said he was going home to China at all. Mrs Campion must have got it wrong. All he meant was that his family was coming from China.'

'All of 'em?' gasped Mumma.

'No, just some of them.' Dolour began to count on her fingers. 'The old lady is Lick's missus, and the big fat joker is their son, and the two young men are his grandsons, and the girl with the smallpox marks on her face is the granddaughter, and the other one is his granddaughter-in-law. She's married to the grandson with the scar on his chin. And the little boy is their son, and his name is Loger Bubba.'

'What?' gaped Mumma.

'Roger Bubba,' giggled Dolour. She pranced round the room. 'Isn't it fun? And none of them can speak English so as you can notice it.'

'How did you find out, then?' said Mumma suspiciously.

'Oh, we made signs,' replied Dolour carelessly.

Mumma whacked Puffing Billy turbulently across his waistcoat with the poker. 'He took that cardigan for false pretences,' she said, and for three days she believed it.

The Lick family settled down peacefully in the little shop in Plymouth Street. Though Lick had kept it as clean as his old sinews had permitted, still they found more dirt, and for days the house seemed to smoke clouds of dust. They crawled out on the roof and slapped mats furiously, talking all the time, and laughing their heads off. They washed their hair in the backyard and sat round endlessly combing it with quince-seed lotion, while they yelled witticisms to those in the house, and those in the house shrieked them back.

Mumma had grown up with noise. The Campions were so close that Mr Campion's drunken roarings sounded in their very ears, and the night his batch of home-brew burst its bonds and bottles, the Darcys had felt the fusillade keenly. So Mumma did not notice the rowdiness of the Licks. They were clean, and minded their own business. They never squizzed through the fence, or lit fires when the wind was blowing Mumma's way.

'It's real homelike with them around,' admitted Mumma grudgingly, and indeed it was impossible to feel lonely. Mr Bumper Reilly lived within the house, but might not have been there at all. The Lick family lived outside of it, but they gave off like a glow the atmosphere of congeniality and family warmth.

Very soon Motty was wandering in and out of their household, and Loger Bubba was coming as far as the Darcy doorstep. Loger Bubba, that worshipped Eastern godling, shocked Mumma.

'He doesn't wear nappies,' she confided to Dolour. 'And he needs to.'

But Mumma really didn't mind. She just followed Loger Bubba round with a floor-cloth, waiting for the worst.

Seventeen

Because of her dark glasses, and because she was not pretty, only the queer boys with long noses and pimply chins came Dolour's way. She swung violently between hatred of their raucous voices, their empty heads and right-angled elbows, and understanding of their awkwardness. Half-educated, with minds that revolved round amusement parlours, girls, and timid bets at the S.P. shop, some of them would grow up into that repulsive product of the slums, the middle-aged larrikin, standing over weaker men for money and drinks, dodging work wherever possible, praying for a depression so that they wouldn't have to work. But the majority would just become ordinary working men, unambitious, garrulous, who would spend all their days spilling out of foundries and factories and garages, and spilling into pubs and mean little houses; who would always do even the most fundamental things, such as eating and fighting and making love, in the most unskilled manner; who would never learn anything from those who had gone before, and never want to. They would grow old without knowledge or complaint that they had never really had any conscious life at all.

Dolour learned a few things about them, that it was their nature to give any girl a try, that romance with them was just a word you heard on the pictures, that it was pansy to have good manners. She understood why all these things should be, but before their inner minds she floundered. What did they think about? How did they get the way they were? Didn't any of them want to be sailors, and see the world, or save some of their money and go elsewhere to live, or talk about something that was real and lasting instead of superficial and ephemeral? Did they wake up in the night and yearn for love, as she did, of abiding and tender love, and not something that was composed of dirty blankets and a bug-ridden bed over a squalid street?

Again and again she looked at Charlie, sunk in his quietness, growing older and shabbier, drunk often, hardly ever taking part in a conversation with anyone, and wondered piteously what would become of him. For she felt that he hadn't been like those other boys when he was younger, and it seemed a contradiction of all her fierce faiths that he should have so surrendered to life now. Maybe all men were the same at heart, living for the flesh, and the moment.

But she denied that passionately, in church, on the street, to herself at night-time, feeling that she could not be alone in her longing for the pure and dignified things of life.

So she went on, a child one hour and a woman the next, seeing the world often as a bright and lovely place with every possibility of great happiness for those who searched for it, and sometimes as a bog that crawled and seethed with hidden dreadfulnesses. Then the walls of the houses would seem transparent to her eyes, and she would see other Kilroys beating their wives and their daughters; mean, dirty women blowing their noses on their aprons, and letting their children play round garbage tins heaving with maggots; women who suckled their children to three years old in an effort to prevent another conception, oblivous to the ill-nourished and imbecilic look of the child; fathers who violated one daughter after another as they grew to the age of twelve or thirteen years, and mothers who stood by and allowed it; grimy-fingered old hags up dark alleys who would abort you with a crochet hook for ten shillings – all the commonality of sin was laid before her in the streets. She saw the reverse of the tapestry, hidden, unfinished, grotesque, thinking it was peculiar to Surry Hills, and not knowing that the whole world was the same, if you wanted to look for those things. In these bad times she did not see any of the good and heroic things that were going on about her, the tubercular mother fighting to feed her children, the kindness and generosity of the poor to the poorer, the old man tending his blind and crippled friend on the park bench, the returned soldier with no legs, sitting in the window whittling wooden toys, as un-bitter as a bird. She did not see that for every sin in Surry Hills there were a thousand heart-warming words and deeds.

There was nobody to ask. Mumma wouldn't know, and Hughie would be embarrassed, and Charlie wasn't the right one. Sister Theophilus would do her best to help, only Dolour didn't know what to ask. She couldn't even find the words to ask Father Cooley, in the darkness of the confessional. What was it she wanted to know? A million things, and yet they all added up to a reassurance from some grown-up and trustworthy person that life was beautiful and noble, as she had once believed it. Perhaps Roie could have told her, in her halting way.

One day she heard from the younger Drummys that Sister

Theophilus was leaving St Brandan's. She could hardly believe it, for Sister Theophilus was the bell-tower, the foundation stone, the polished floor, the hum of prayers and the sweet spiralling smoke of the Gregorian chant. She had been there twelve years, and that was nearly all of Dolour's life.

'It won't be the same without her,' said Mumma mournfully, pausing with a half-peeled potato in mid-air. 'I remember the first day I took you to school, and you bawling so loud I could see your tonsils.'

'Yes,' said Dolour softly, remembering the awful moment when Mumma's head, going away down the sloping street, disappeared bit by bit behind the wall, until it was only a tuft of brindly hair. Then Sister Theophilus, so tall that it was years before the child knew her as anything but a long brown skirt and a pair of shabby polished shoes, took her by the hand and led her along the polished corridor.

'You've got warm hands, and a silver ring,' said that small Dolour.

'Yes, darling.'

'And I've got pants that button up,' boasted Dolour.

Long after Dolour could remember things about Sister Theophilus. Often she had fallen over and barked her knees, and was taken into the convent kitchen to have them bathed. She remembered the dark-green linoleum, and the red from the fire reflected in ruddy pools, a round clock like a plate, and a diminutive lay sister standing up on a box to stir the saucepans at the back of the range. And all the time the reiterated, halting notes of 'The Jolly Farmer' coming from the music-room at the back of the convent.

And once, too, she had a terrible cold that took chips out of her ribs every time she coughed, and Sister made her sit on the verandah and drink hot cocoa, which she took sacramentally out of a cup with no cracks in it. Of all the things and people connected with her happy schooldays she best remembered Sister Theophilus, her grace, her dignity, her warmth and maturity, and now she was going.

'You oughta go round and say good-bye,' said Mumma. 'I would meself if it wasn't for the toes sticking outa me shoes.'

For days Dolour thought about this, but somehow she felt herself a stranger now. The two years that had risen between her and her schooldays had thrust her willy-nilly into a too-soon maturity, and she felt long grown up. Besides, she used lipstick now.

She shrank from going into the school, into the old scenes, and hearing whispers from the children who had once known her, and answering kindly questions from the nuns. Besides, what would she say? She was too old to blurt out her feelings, too young and brash to put her thoughts into the right words. And soon it was too late.

Mrs Drummy, rushing in from one of her numberless visits to the church, gasped out, 'What do you think, Dol? I just saw Sister Theophilus and that poor dear old Sister Beatrix going off to the station with some luggage.'

Dolour stood with the wet cloth clutched in her hand, and said nothing, but kind Mrs Drummy, always ready to put the sentimental touch to things, said 'Why don't you hare off to the station and tell 'em good-bye, love?'

Once Central Station, and Plymouth Street, and all the network of veins that ran between them had been one great cemetery, and even now, so tradition said, the trains thundered over the rotting bones of those old nameless ones who had died in their fetters and been buried without tear or trumpet in an alien land. But there were no unquiet ghosts in Central, only tremendous cavernous spaces, and echoing bells and whistles and voices, and the ceaseless clank of pennies in the public lavatories, and the great indicators presiding over all, like the dials of some incalculable machine. Dolour stood beneath them bewildered, pushed and shoved by the battling crowds, wondering how she could hope to find the sisters in this wilderness.

But she forced down her confusion, and made her brain work sensibly, for they were going to a southern town, and there was only one platform they could be leaving from. Yet when she reached the platform there were so many porters driving beetle-backed little trucks with long snakes of luggage-laden trolleys behind; so much noise and battling, and suitcases left in the way; so many screaming children besmearing their grandpas with kisses and toffee-apples; so many old ladies already dying for a cup of tea, and them not in their seats five minutes, that Dolour wondered why she had come. Then she saw them, tidy and quiet in their black mantles, with mittens covering their hands, and their small polished suitcases sitting sedately by their polished black toes. Dolour had often theorized about the contents of those suitcases. Hughie reckoned a pair of sandshoes and a spare set of pyjamas, but Dolour thought privately of a nightie with long sleeves and a high neck, and perhaps a toothbrush and a starched white handkerchief.

They were so quiet, so self-contained, speaking to each other so rarely, that she hesitated shyly and uncertainly, wondering if it would be good manners to go up to speak to them, or whether they'd be allowed to answer, and what she would say if they did. Her heart yearned over Sister Theophilus, sitting by the elderly Sister Beatrix, a little pale and grave. As never before the ordinariness, and yet the difference of these women came to her. All her life she had loved the nuns, for the ordered regularity of their lives, so foreign to her own, and now in her near-maturity she realized what she had loved most of all.

It was their womanliness. They had not been shut away from the world. Their locks were all on the inside of the wall. They had shut away the world from them; all its rowdiness and dirt and self-striving and self-adulation was no more to them than the hum of traffic in the distance. Yet there in the cleanly uncluttered convent they had developed as women and human beings. The rub of character against character was there, the instinctive antipathies and impatiences. The difference was that they subdued all these things to live in amity with each other. This was the secret strength she had sensed in them. They had sacrificed all things that the world loved most, but the greatest sacrifice of all, the most wearing, the most subtle, the most fretting was continual self-discipline, hour by hour, minute by minute; the unremitting watch on themselves lest they give way to irritation, weakness, or any shadow on the perfection they set themselves.

The nuns did not see Dolour lurking in the chaff-dusty shadows behind the weighing-machine, with her eyes glazed and her mouth open, but other people did, and smiled, thinking her some Protestant girl with a terror of the 'robes.'

The whistle blew, and before Dolour could awaken from her dream, the nuns said good-bye to each other. A swift pressure of the hand, and a kiss on Sister Beatrix's old red cheek, and Sister Theophilus, together with three of the strangers from other convents, had gone into the carriage. She jumped out quickly from behind the weighing-machine, thinking, 'I'll wave as the train goes out. She'll see me. She'll just think I came too late,' but as the nuns on the platform turned, she shrank back again, a shy smile trembling on her face in case Sister Beatrix saw her.

But Sister Beatrix, her face scarlet as a beetroot, and her mouth set even more grimly than it had when she was trying to teach fractions to Dolour and thirty other boneheads, was stumbling along, a young nun on each side of her, and not noticing anybody. Even as Dolour's mouth opened to say, 'Good afternoon,' Sister Beatrix's face crumpled up for a moment and tears rushed down from behind her glasses. Then she was borne away. Dolour was so astounded by this revelation of grief and pain of parting that she did not notice the train slide away, switching its long black tail round the corner, its wail floating back like a banner of smoke. She had not known that nuns ever cried, particularly Sister Beatrix. She had not known that twelve years of living and working together could make Sister Beatrix feel about Sister Theophilus as she felt about Roie.

Mournfully she walked up into Surry Hills again. Here and there were empty spaces where houses had been demolished. Where the dank cellars had sweltered, and the rock faces sweated in the darkness, the sun now shone, and the blue convolvulus, the periwinkle, and the tasselled ragwort blew. And here came again the dispossessed, the honey bee, coming from nowhere to the earth where no flowers had grown for so long. Here and there stood an idle steam shovel, drooping its sardonic jaws like a prehistoric monster frozen in the act of chewing the cud. But Dolour hardly noticed.

She knew that at least she had one thing in common with Sister Beatrix. In Sister Theophilus she had lost a friend and protector, almost invisible, who could never be replaced, and who had left her alone in a world she would have to face for herself.

All day she was sad until Harry Drummy asked her to go to Luna Park with him, and every other thought fled her mind.

She rushed frenziedly home to see whether Mumma had ironed her blue floral, and she had.

'I'm going to have a bath,' decided Dolour. It was an important decision, for bathing in the Darcy household was fraught with both danger and adventure. Since they had been using the old tin tub to bathe the baby in, they had been climbing into the wooden wash-tubs, a difficult business, for the tubs, with their chewed, pitted bottoms and slanting sides were never made for comfortable accommodation of the human body. Hughie, who had developed an astonishing liking for baths lately, always ended his ablutions with a curious bruise on the base of his skull, where he had thrown his head backwards and almost fractured the bone on the grim beak of a tap. Charlie never spoke of his experiences, but he usually looked clean, so apparently he managed all right. And Mumma accepted the inevitable and point blank refused to endanger her life by jamming herself into so small a receptacle; she much preferred to 'have a rench' with a nice basin of hot water.

But Dolour made it a ceremony. She had hardly entered the laundry and kicked the block of firewood against the door before the whole dank, soap-smelling, candle-lit place was transformed in her mind to a beautiful bathroom like those you saw on the pictures. She dreamily heaved bucket after bucket of steaming water into the deep wooden box of the tub, occasionally plucking out a splinter that floated to the surface. The stone floor was already covered in lagoons from the leak in the pipe, and everywhere the candlelight winked at itself.

'I've got mirrors all over the wall,' she murmured.

She took off her clothes, sniffing curiously. Suddenly she leaped at the wood box, hauled out the spitting Dirty Dick by his repellent scruff, and dropped him haphazardly out of the window. It took all Dolour's imagination to transform the smell of wet tomcat into that of expensive bath salts.

'When I get out I've got my lovely pink – no, lilac dressing-gown to put on. It's satin,' she thought, her knees jammed up against her chin, and her neck crooked forward so that the tap wouldn't peck her. It was hard to admire herself in such a position, but at least she could see that her legs were smooth and hairless. By an acrobatic feat she tilted up her toes and warmly appraised her toenails.

'When I'm rich I'll polish them. And I'll wear slippers with very high heels and lots of feathers on them.'

Languidly she soaped her neck and chest. It was very difficult, craned forward like a striking hawk, and the knobs of her backbone kept bumping on the hard tub. All at once she had a wonderful idea. She leaned forward and tried the water in the copper. It was still hot. She hopped in. The water came up round her chest, for it was a huge, antiquated copper built to take the washing for a family of twelve. By kneeling she had very much more leeway than she had had in the tub.

'I'm in a sunken bath,' she decided, 'And there are lovely green plastic curtains hanging all round me.'

The next moment the door crashed open, and Hughie blundered in, blinking at the dimness and roaring at the top of his voice. Dolour's green curtains disappeared even faster than they had come.

'Some silly galoot's gone and left a candle burning in here,' yelled Hughie amiably. 'Want to burn the house down, I suppose, and me in it. I suppose that would satisfy the dirt on yer liver.' This last to Mumma in the kitchen, where she had ventured to remonstrate with him on his midweek merriment.

Dolour shouted, 'I'm in here, Dadda! Go on, get out!'

Hughie lifted the candle like a wavering star and stared at the empty tubs. Dolour, shocked and furious, cowered down in the copper. A pleading note quavered in her voice.

'Go on, Dadda! Clear out, will you? I'm having a bath.'

Suddenly Hughie spotted her. His eyes sparkled with mischief. He leaned an unsteady elbow against the doorway and said conversationally, 'Well, now!'

Dolour squirmed. 'Aw, go on, Dad!'

'That's a fine idea you've got there,' said Hughie agreeably. 'But tell me, what are you doing to keep your crankcase off the hot bottom?'

'I'm sitting on the soap,' said Dolour, surlily.

'Ah, it's you that's got the brains,' approved her father. He came a little closer, and Dolour bent herself into the shape of a depressed S and sank into the water to her chin.

'What's that you've got on yer head, may I ask?' asked Hughie politely. Dolour gave a squeal of despair.

'Mumma, come and take him out! Mumma! Gosh, you're awful!' she cried to Hughie. 'I bet other girls' fathers don't come into the laundry when they're having a bath. Mumma!'

'Tell me what you've got on your head, then,' wheedled Hughie. There was a moment of explosive silence, then his daughter capitulated.

'Me bloomers.'

To keep her hair from getting wet she had thrust her head through one leg of her bloomers and twisted the rest of the garment into a knot at the side. Under this macabre headgear, which came down to her eyebrows, Dolour's eyes shone ferociously. Hughie nearly had a fit. He rolled from side to side, kicking the door wide open so that the laundry was fully exposed to the kitchen. Dolour was afraid that at any moment Charlie would come in to see what all the noise was about.

But Hughie, who wouldn't have hurt her feelings in a million years, couldn't resist pulling her leg a little further. He began to gather bits of firewood.

Dolour whispered, 'What are you going to do?'

'That water looks a bit cold, me darling. I'm going to heat it up.'

He thrust the wood into the firebox and began ostentatiously blowing. Dolour squawked.

'Here, have a heart! You'll boil me! You brute! You devil, you know I can't get out! Mumma!'

'We could slip in a few onions and carrots with you and there'll be a first-rate stew,' said Hughie helpfully, sitting back on his heels and grinning happily into the anguished face of his daughter.

'Mumma!' bawled Dolour, and Mumma, upstairs with Mikey, heard the call and pounded down the stairs with the sound of thunder. She seized Hughie by the arm and jerked him from the room, slamming the laundry door so that the whole house trembled.

'You're so shook for something to do that you've got to tease the poor kid like that, Hugh Darcy, and her so modest!'

'Take some of the starch out of her,' protested Hughie, still with a twinkle.

'You've got to remember she isn't a child now. She's nearly eighteen, and a young woman,' scolded Mumma.

The laundry door slammed back, and Dolour, bundled hastily into her clothes and still wearing the bloomers on her head, exploded into the kitchen. Mumma hid a grin at the hauteur with which she tried to sweep past Hughie.

'Don't take it so hard, love,' chuckled that sinner. 'I used to change your nappies when you were little.'

'Oh!' Dolour fled up the stairs, with a horrid chant of, 'I used to change your nappies!' following her all the way.

Down at Circular Quay Harry Drummy waited for her, draped mournfully over the rails in the peculiarly filleted manner of his kind, and eyeing off all the good sorts who were pushing and screaming their way on to the Luna Park ferry. He was game to bet a peanut to a deener that Dolour wouldn't turn up in a pair of them grouse shorts that showed all the fellers what she had and they couldn't get. He couldn't make out why it was he was always stuck with drack types like Dolour Darcy, then, rubbing his hand over his grievously nubbly chin, supposed it was because he had pimples. But she had had pimples, too, when she was younger, and he made up his mind he'd ask her what she'd done to get rid of them. Just as well she didn't have them now, or the pair of them surely would look tricks moting around together.

Yeah, there she was, in a warby kind of a blue dress, and low-heeled shoes. Not an ankle-strap in a cartload, for her. He looked critically at her legs. She coulda worn them, too. And them dark sun-glasses she wore! Gawd! Bitterly Harry recriminated against the heavens that gave him hickies, and girls that no one else would envy him.

A sick feeling entered Dolour's heart when she saw Harry standing there, his hands thrust into his pockets like packages, and a little, saliva-stained fag stuck on his lower lip. Of all the nice boys going to Luna Park, tall, brown, bright-eyed, jolly-looking fellows, she had to draw this droob.

Then she thought that it wasn't his fault he was a drongo. You had to be fair. He didn't want to have pimples, or a thin neck, or that hair all snowflaked with dandruff. Perhaps he would grow out of it some day, and then she'd be glad that she'd been tolerant with him when he was young. Anyway, he had asked her to go out with him, and they could have a nice time if she wasn't too critical.

'Why don't you take off them black windows?' he snarled in answer to her hopeful beam.

For a moment she hesitated, for her eyes were still shy of light, and she had worn the glasses so long that they were a protection for her soul.

'O.K.' She took them off, and showed the long, colt-like eye-lashes that had mysteriously grown while her eyes had been bad. She blinked in the wind, and saw Harry looking at her and blushed.

'You know,' he said in surprise, 'you ain't half as funny-looking as you were a while back.'

'Thanks. Pity I can't say the same for you.'

She flounced on to the little water-beetle of a ferry that rocked and reeled with the weight of screaming teen-agers who besieged it. Girls with the faces of flowers and the voices of peewits clung close to the slick hips of sailors who had hooked their caps on the corners of their heads; compact family groups stood bracing their legs, long and short, against the onslaughts of the younger passengers; an occasional oversea serviceman stood, the whole weight of Empire pressing on his uniformed shoulders while his eyes roved shyly amongst the unattached girls, who, in twos and threes, giggled and shrieked and rubbed their blue, goose-pimpled legs, for the evening was chill.

Soon they had chuffled alongside the ramp that led to the fantastic, shoddy fairyland of Luna Park, and Dolour and Harry were borne along in the rush for the gates, excited and half suffocated by the smell of scent and sweat and plain old humanity. The hot-dog man, his face glazed red as a clown's with high blood pressure, warbled monotonously, 'Carm an' getcher dargies! Carm an' getcher dargies! Mustid dor termarter! Carm an' getcher li'l' red dargies!'

With sparkling eyes Dolour and Harry gazed on the arena, and their feet jiggled in time to the merry-go-round, which swung in pallid green circles to a syrupy, steam-punctuated waltz.

'I go for the Big Dipper meself,' cried Harry with boyish gladness. 'Oh, boy, that Big Dipper! You have a milkshake before you go on, and when you come off you spit up half a pound of butter.'

'Oh, you!'

Face pink with anticipation and excitement she looked at Harry. She had forgotten about her eyes, and they rewarded her by forgetting about their sensitivity. Her long hair blew out on the sea-wind like a black flag, and the blue dress, blown close to her body, showed curves Harry hadn't known she possessed. He thought, 'Gee, she ain't so bad!' A tiny tingle of excitement ran over him, and he haw-hawed coarsely, not knowing what else to do, or how to express the half-comprehended instincts that filled him. He was delighted and flattered when a passing soldier reached out and pinched her on the thigh. She shrieked, and Harry growled perfunctorily.

'Wantjer big ears flattened?'

'Who's gonna 'elp yer?'

'Ah, pull yer 'ead in!'

Honour was satisfied. Almost with pride he pushed her into one of the Big Dipper cars. Round and round they rode the tilting horizon, deafened by their own shrieks and the shuttling clacket of the machinery, suspended above the jewelled round of the amusement park both sideways and upside down until they were finally decanted in the throes of terrible seasickness. They clung to each

590

other, breathless, shrieking with senseless laughter, and praying.

He thought, 'Gawd, I could puke quicker than wink.'

She thought, 'I'd be all right if I could sit down for a moment.'
They smiled at each other brightly. Harry took her arm, more to
support himself than anything else, and they strolled away uncertainly. But after a few moments, so great was the youthful resilience
of his digestive tract, Harry felt better, and he slid his fingers up her
arm until they rested against the slight curve of her bosom. A wary
prickling ran over Dolour. She wanted to jerk free, but she felt a
little shy about doing that. Harry was a good Catholic boy, and not
like those other louts at the pictures, and he had his hand there
most likely by accident, and she might hurt his feelings if she pulled
away. So she left the fingers there, feeling uncomfortable and
cautious and indecisive, all of which Harry interpreted as
acquiescence.

He thought, amazed at his own dumbness, 'I shoulda given this
sheila a go before.' But he said, casually, 'How'd a hamburger go?'

'There,' said Dolour triumphantly to herself, 'it was just an
accident,' and for some reason felt just a little disconcerted.

The blue fumes from the grill wafting over them like grease-
laden incense, they waited in the queue of hungry hands that
reached out for the hamburgers, each cosily nested within its half-
burned bun in a posy of greasy onions and rusty shredded lettuce.
Harry champed with bits of onion falling out of his mouth, and he
finished by opening wide and throwing the last corner of bun into it
with bear-like dexterity. Dolour tried hard not to watch, but it was
too fascinating. A deep melancholy, which had been in her heart
from the very beginning, welled up and nearly overcame her.

Forlornly she followed him into the little boat that bobbed at a
doorway, ready to take passengers through the River Caves. It was
cool and quiet and damp in there, and the noise of Luna Park
sounded like the muffled squawking of magpies. The light slid
silver and unearthly down the concrete stalactites and the silky,
chuckling water. Her yearning for romance rose up again, and she
thought, 'Poor old Harry.' He snuggled up against her, his long
angles trying to accommodate themselves to her shorter ones. His
hair brushed her cheek like a greasy mop, and he smelt of
brilliantine and onions, but then, she did, too. She had a wild
impulse to start talking about something to distract him, but he
looked so pathetic and homely, and she knew no other girl would

ever let him kiss her. Anyway, at least it would be an experience, and there were lots worse than Harry. She opened her eyes and saw a green, corpse-like face leaning over her, swallowing.

'I wish he was someone else so I could slug him,' she thought. His soft wet lips descended on hers, and she peeped through her lashes a moment to see him looking cross-eyed and concentratedly at the top of her nose. She shut her eyes quickly, trying to imagine the kiss different – exciting, wicked, enthralling, or even merely pleasant. But it wasn't. It was like kissing a wet hamburger.

'God,' gasped Harry, 'I could go for you!'

He was amazed at the effect the kiss had had on him. He wanted to get her by herself in some dark place and forget all about everything and just be himself. For a long time he had envied those mates of his who just had to look at a girl and she'd fall into their arms, so they said. Although he had had lots of furtive back-alley experiences, hot and frightened and uncomfortable, they'd all been with little tarts who'd get behind a back fence with any boy. Yet here was Dolour Darcy, with the reputation of being cold as an eel and a bit of a nark as well, plainly falling for him like a stone. He was about to go further, eagerly, when the boat shot out into the light, and with a wrench of anger and frustration he realized that he'd have to wait.

Dolour was feeling noble that she'd let Harry kiss her, particularly since it had been so ghastly. And even though it was only Harry, she was flattered that he could go for her. He might have looked a moron, but he had good taste, was what she felt, though she did not think it. She smiled encouragingly at him, longing with a great longing to hear him say something romantic or tell her she looked pretty, or that he liked her dress.

Harry was having trouble. He swallowed once or twice, wanting to change the subject and regain control of himself, so he blurted out, 'How did you get rid of your pimples?'

'I went to Sam Gooey,' said Dolour wanly.

The evening never recovered its lustre. It was the same as all the others when she had gone out with neighbourhood boys and known that she was not a success, and, even worse, could not persuade herself that she wanted to be a success with them.

No matter how much she tried to blame it on the boys and their gaucherie, she could not help feeling that the fault lay within herself. Some deep humility made her search her own personality for the trouble, for it was plain that most girls got on all right with boys, and not because they were all Suse Kilroys, either. In books and films there were plenty of girls who went out with boys and had a good time, with no awkward silences or feelings of discomfort.

'I wish I was prettier,' yearned Dolour. 'It would be different then.'

Her heart went out to Harry, apologizing because she couldn't feel romantic about him, and thanking him because he could go for her. He put his arm round her and squeezed, raking his sleeve buttons painfully across her hipbone. Their feet jockeyed urgently for the same place, then Harry squashed her to his chest and kissed her again, there in the darkness behind the fairy-floss stall, where there were lots of other clotted figures doing the same thing. For the first time Dolour felt a pleasant kinship with these figures. People who saw her and Harry wouldn't know that she was putting up with it just to be nice. They'd think she was just a girl getting kissed by her boy friend.

'Poor old Harry,' she thought remorsefully, and kissed him back, getting the flavour of hamburger with renewed poignancy.

'Christ,' thought Harry, 'she ain't so bad. And I ain't so bad, neither.' He snuggled up closer to her, his cold damp nose poking in her ear. Dolour resisted a desire to struggle. 'What about clearing out?' he asked hoarsely.

'Where to?' she asked cautiously.

'I know where there's a party on. Like to go to a party?' He thought, 'I ain't ever walked in to Shirley's place yet with a sheila of me own. Give 'em a shock.'

Dolour was delighted. It was like the stories you read, where the girl went out to dinner and then on to a night-club. Going to Luna Park for a hamburger and then on to a party wasn't so different.

'Is it someone I know?' she asked eagerly. But she hadn't ever met Shirley, who lived in the second house on the right, by the biscuit factory in Pump Lane. She felt a little shy, wondering if her dress were nice enough, or whether her nose were pink from the cold wind. But Harry's kisses, catastrophic as they had been, had bolstered her self-confidence, and all the way over on the ferry she submitted to his cuddles and assured him, in answer to his reiterated inquiries, that they would have real dinkum fun at the party.

Harry was choking with excitement and confusion and delicious anticipatory guilt. His mentality was such that it was totally unable to cope with any but the simplest problems of life, and that was the way he liked it. He suited himself. Consequently he was shocked that Dolour had been under his nose for so long, and he hadn't done anything about her. Of course she wasn't what any fellow could call a whacko-the diddle-O piece, but she was a girl. And kid she didn't know what it was all about! It was true what the blokes said, the quiet ones were the hottest, and he'd find out how high she could send the mercury to-night.

On the other hand, if she'd just been stringing him along, he could leave Shirley's early, before the fun started, and she'd be none the wiser!

But Harry had miscalculated the time. Shirley's mother, who worked as a late-shift waitress in a fish café near the railway, started at six o'clock, and Shirley had had two clear hours to get wound up.

The tall old house was all in darkness, cocking its gable roof rakishly at passers-by, and wearing its chimney like a top-hat.

'Round the back,' said Harry confidently. Dolour's feet slipped on glassy tiles as they felt their way through the pitch darkness, which was filled with the sharp smell of woodsmoke from neighbouring chimneys. She was a litte shy and nervous, thinking of all the strangers she would meet. The house had a basement, a yellow-lighted well beside the steps. Two cats erupted like rockets out of the well, and rushed screeching past Dolour's legs. By the time she had collected herself the basement door had opened, and she and Harry, blinking and dazzled, were inside the big cavernous cellar, which seemed to be full of young people, great splodges of black shadow, a naked globe strung over a nail on a serpentine flex, and a gramophone belting out a raucous dance tune. The first person she saw was a girl she'd been to school with, Connie Croucher, and even though she'd never liked Connie, the pleasure of seeing a familiar face amongst all the strange ones was great. She waved gladly, and was astounded when Connie looked dismayed, and melted into the crowd as though she'd never been there at all.

'What's up with her?' she asked Harry indignantly, but Harry was tugging at her sleeve, trying to introduce her to Shirley, a small, round, fat-faced girl with cat-like eyes, which she considered were like Ava Gardner's. She narrowed them now at Dolour, protruded a wet lip and crooned, 'Make yourself at my place, love'. Dolour disliked her on the instant. She felt four sizes bigger than Shirley, with great, long hanging arms. Besides, Shirley wore the tightest red sweater in the world, and smelt slightly of plonk. Dolour looked closely at her. Shirley was tottering on the brink of being properly stewed, and she was no older than seventeen.

'Here you are.' A glass was thrust into Dolour's hand, and almost instantly a tall pimply youth in a king-sized Frank Sinatra jacket, whirling past with a girl in his arm, snatched it from her grip and poured the liquid down his throat. 'Catch it, Minnie.' He tossed the glass back to her, and Dolour, flustered, missed, and it splintered on the stone floor. Shirley broke into a shrill flood of complaint. Most of her expressions would have been welcomed by the Kidger into his select vocabulary. Coming from her round, childish, scarlet bud of a mouth, they sounded fantastic. Suddenly she spat at Dolour, 'What are you grinning at, you big gollion?'

'I wasn't grinning,' gaped Dolour feebly, then rage flashed out of her, and she cried, 'You dirty-mouthed little ape, you can keep your rotten party.'

Shirley's face crumpled like paper; she emitted a little wail and whimpered, 'She hasn't got no reason to come here slinging off at me. I didn't ask her. And I ain't a nape, neither.'

Dolour was overcome by her own rudeness. It was true, she hadn't been asked, and there was no reason why she shouldn't have left quietly without insulting her hostess. But there was no time to say she was sorry, for Shirley was borne off, weeping winy tears, in the arms of the boy in the Sinatra jacket, and Dolour herself was pushed down into a chair, and a red-hot saveloy was placed in her unresisting hand. Somebody lifted up her hair and nuzzled the back of her neck, and shuddering with nervous titillation she glared round into a bold, long-nosed currant-eyed face which smacked its lips and whispered, 'Hullo, silk pants. What you got that I ain't got?'

'This,' snapped Dolour, and she jammed the burning saveloy into her admirer's vest pocket, beside his dazzling yellow silk handkerchief. She jumped up and looked round for Harry, but Harry had disappeared. In that hollow, dirty grotto of a place, smelling of damp and old timber and cats, she couldn't even see the door. The candles were guttering down in their bottles, the electric globe was a blinding hoop of brilliance, somebody was being sick in a corner, and extraordinary things were going on in the shadows. Dolour felt her heart stick in her throat. For a moment she felt she was asleep and dreaming the sort of dream she would try to forget in the

595

morning. Paralysed, she stared, unwilling to look, and yet unable to take her eyes away. Shrieks of laughter came from the alcove near her, and Shirley appeared momentarily, her sweater pulled over her head, so that she staggered blindly this way and that.

'Gimme another boll soda water,' she was yelling, 'or I'm a goner.'

'My God,' giggled someone near her. 'Don't she know it isn't grandma's day any longer? And her just out of hospital after the last!'

Clutching her soda water, trying to drag off the cap with her teeth, Shirley was pulled off into the dark by another boy. Her sweater flew out into the middle of the floor like a scarlet bird.

An arm slid around Dolour's waist. It belonged to Harry, who was pressing up against her with a curious mixture of defiance, trepidation and persuasion on his face.

'Come on, kid,' he whispered. 'Be in it.'

'Harry,' she said, hardly hearing him. 'They're – what are they doing?'

'What we ought to be doing,' said Harry, and everything left his face except a hot glazy-eyed eagerness, and he slid his wet lips over hers like a slug. Dolour was a strong girl. He was bigger than she, but she shoved him away, spitting her loathing and terror, and stumbling over a couple on the floor, she groped along the wall for the door, which had melted into the cobwebs and dusk. Harry seized her.

'Don't be mad, what's the harm in it? Everybody does it. I'll look after you. Gawd, why don't you break down and be human!' He was ashamed and a little frightened, but he had to disguise it by roughness. Dolour fought him off, sobbing with rage and shock, and some of the others, with shrieks of joy, saw their unequal battle. In a moment she was surrounded by a ring of half-lit faces, so young, so fresh, so unmarked by corruption that for a moment she thought it must have been a hallucination.

'Come on, be in it, chick!'

'Where did you find it, Harry?'

'He got it outa a Sunday-school book.'

'Christ almighty! It's a virgin, that's what it is!'

It would not have been so shocking if they had looked bad, but they didn't. They were just ordinary boys and girls from sixteen to twenty, that you might meet on the street any day of the week. They were healthy young animals, cynical beyond belief, amoral, shameless, and for all she knew all young people were like that.

Harry was like that – Harry, from a good family like the Drummys, and a Catholic boy as well. Maybe it was a common thing to sneak into each other's houses in the absence of parents, and indulge in the wild, incredible promiscuity that can only be approached with a mature body and an immature mind. She stared at them wildly, wanting to be sick, and with a deadly fear creeping over her. But they meant her no harm. She was the canary in the cage full of sparrows, and they couldn't help teasing her. She was funny to them, and they began to have fun with her, pulling up her skirt to see her legs and holding her hands so that she couldn't protect herself. She was that comic object, the one virtuous person in a degenerate gathering.

Harry stood by, terribly ashamed of Dolour, more ashamed of his friends, not knowing whether to laugh or to protest in case he was lumped in with her. Suddenly she got her foot free, and the long-nosed boy received such a kick under the chin that his jaws clopped together with a loud loose sound.

'I oughta fix you for that, you bitch!' He seized her by the front of the dress, which ripped out in his hand. 'And I'll do it in front of everyone, too!'

'Leave her alone, you bastard!'

Harry, plum-faced, boiling over with his uncatalogued emotions, spun him round and lashed at him so amateurishly that everyone laughed. They fell on the floor, struggling like two beetles, and while they were doing this some of the others pulled down Dolour's dress and wrote a filthy word in lipstick across her bosom. Then they opened the door and pushed her out into the dark, amongst the squalling cats and the icy wind, and the strange obstructed darkness of the yard. Her glasses had been smashed, she had lost her purse, and she was physically and mentally on the verge of collapse. A moment later Harry, dishevelled, his nose dripping red, hurtled after her, with a chorus of good-natured mocking obscenities following him. She ran away from him, hysterical with relief and disgust, wanting to be sick. She barged into the side of the house and struck her face stingingly upon the corner. Harry took her arm to lead her up the dark path, but she ripped it away and ran, stumbling on the dew-wet tiles, and finally crashing through the gate into the dim street. She heard a passing woman say, 'That little sweep Shirley Hubis! I wonder her mother don't tumble to what goes on behind her back!'

'I didn't know,' appealed Harry, rushing through his pockets for a handkerchief. He blew his nose with his fingers, sending a shower of ruby drops through the air. 'Honest, Dolour, I didn't.'

Dolour tried to get away from him. But she was too distressed to run. She leaned over a fence and was deathly sick, not caring at all that he was watching.

'You won't tell Mum?' he pressed anxiously. 'Dinkum, I hadn't the faintest that they'd go on like that.'

'Oh, go away,' gasped Dolour, and grumbling and disturbed he went, to stand on the corner and watch until she moved into Plymouth Street. He thought, 'By God, if she opens her big mouth I'll tell the world she was right in there with the rest of them. I'll put her pot on, the bitch, thinking she's so holy. I'll tell every feller I know she's easy, and she won't be able to go down the street without having the acid on her.' But underneath he wasn't really frightened that she would tell. The habit of minding their own business was too deeply ingrained in the young and the old of Surry Hills. Pulled up as witnesses by the police, they preferred a fine or jail rather than have their heads kicked in as top-offs when they came home. He watched a little longer, then decided he'd go along to Siddy Doust's place to clean up a bit, in case the old woman got the wind up when she saw his bloody nose.

Dolour's feet were weighed down with lead, and she shivered spasmodically, holding up her torn dress, and keeping to the shadows so that no one would one see her dishevelment. Now that the terror was over, she was numb with the reaction from shock, her common sense and sense of direction so destroyed that she would just as soon have crawled into a dark doorway and huddled there all night as gone home. Nothing was real any more. In a sense, she felt the same as she had after Roie's death, as though the world had stopped.

All at once she saw Charlie, walking unsteadily in front of her, and at the sight of his shabby familiarity her numbness thawed. 'Oh, Charlie!' she cried, and in a moment was in his arms, crying loudly like a child, not caring that people might hear, or that he might not want her there.

'What's the matter, Dolour?' He let her put her face on his shoulder and sob, soothing her as she might have soothed Motty, feeling an aching compassion for all her pride and independence that had vanished in the stress of some crisis he did not know. 'What's happened, darling?' The word slipped out of him un-noticed, for he had never held any crying girl in his arms except his wife. He saw the bruise on her cheek, and as she moved, the torn dress, and the beginning of the obscene word upon her white skin.

'Dolour! Who did that? Did something happen to you?'

Now he was alarmed. She shook her head. 'No, nothing happened. Only – Charlie – oh, Charlie, people aren't all bad, are they?'

Out of her great need, out of her shattered ignorance and assaulted innocence she begged him whom normally she would have been too shy to ask. He was a little drunk, but because he understood her he didn't ask any more questions, but answered hers, 'Most people are good, Dolour. No matter what they tell you, or what you see, most people are good.'

'And people can love each other, and it isn't terrible and filthy like – ' She could not continue, but began to sob again.

He knew what she wanted to know, but although he sought desperately he couldn't find words that satisfied him. 'No, Dolour, no!' He felt her stop sobbing, though her face was still hidden. He did not know what provoked this tumult, but he knew that her need was desperate, that he had to tell her plainly without any obscuring delicacy. 'What's between a man and a woman was meant for marriage. Otherwise it's like a picture jagged out of a frame, all wrong, and hard to see the right way.'

'I want to see it the right way,' whispered Dolour.

'Lots of people have wrong ideas, but you mustn't get them. There's nothing more wonderful than to love a girl and have her own you and you own her, because it's not only your body that matters then, but your soul and mind and everything you've got.' He had never said anything like that before; the words were torn out of his own experience, and for a moment an echo of his terrible grief trembled on the brink of his consciousness, but he ignored it. 'Dolour, don't you ever let anybody tell you any different. That's the way God meant us to look at it, and because people smear it all over with their filthy paws doesn't make it change.' He was floundering again. 'You believe what you know is true, and some day you'll find that you've been right all along.'

She was quiet now, almost drowsy, the physical strain of her experience expressing itself. His arms were warm and sheltering. He was not Roie's husband, he was not even a man; he was just a human being older and wiser than herself, who had given her the rope when she was drowning. She thought, 'All along he's been there, and I didn't know.'

She did not know that her innocence, like Mumma's, was

intrinsic, that she could not help her violent reactions to those things that affronted her chastity. She only knew that after she'd thought about this, after the shock and horror were all gone, and she was able to look Harry Drummy in the face again, she'd be able to think about Shirley's and not feel soiled. Shirley would slip into her right place, as she, Dolour, had slipped into hers. What Charlie said was right. It was what she had always felt. Life was good, and love was beautiful, and she would not mind any longer keeping aloof from everyone rather than waste herself on love that fell short of perfection.

But just now she wanted to sleep.

'You can't let Mumma see you like that,' said Charlie. 'I'll go in first and talk to her in the kitchen, and you can sneak upstairs and fix yourself up.'

Mumma was unsuspecting. Anyway, she was worried, for Anny was sick. Mumma had her in the kitchen, lying on a sack in front of Puffing Billy. The devilishness had died out of her golden striped eyes, and her feet were cracked and hard. She hung her head, with long silvery streams of spittle looping to the floor.

'What's the matter, Anny, eh?' Charlie smoothed the dry, rough coat. Anny made a feeble attempt to bite him, then struggled up and limped into a corner of the kitchen. Dirty Dick appeared momentarily, like a smelly ghost, and slunk across the floor. A brief twinkle came into Anny's despairing eyes, and she lifted a back hoof and got him fair and square in the ribs. 'I'm afraid she's going to die, Charlie,' said Mumma mournfully.

'I could take her down and let her loose in the park,' suggested Charlie. 'The poundkeeper would find her and she'd get a good home.'

Dolour came soundlessly in. She had changed her dress, and scrubbed the word off her chest. There was nothing to tell of her experience except the blue welt on her cheek.

'You're that late,' scolded Mumma, 'and what on earth's the matter with yer face?'

'Cracked it on a swing over at Luna,' lied Dolour.

'Gallivanting around when I'm worried outa me wits with the kids yelling, and your dadda as drunk as an earl, and Anny gone sick on me,' complained Mumma.

'Poor Anny.' The goat had been dry a long time, and there had been no need to keep her cooped up in the backyard, except that

Mikey loved to play with her. It seemed to Dolour that their treatment of Anny was typical of the spirit of Surry Hills. They could have sold her, or given her away. She could have been bred again and provided milk for some other child. But they just didn't bother. They just left things as they were, as Mumma left the curtains torn, and Hughie left the floor unmended, and Charlie allowed Motty to go her own sweet way. It was always too much trouble to do things immediately; far easier to take a risk on the future. So Mumma let her teeth rot in her head, and Mrs Campion just didn't bother to get her children inoculated for diphtheria, for they mightn't ever get it, anyway. Laziness was the core of the slum. Dolour grasped after this thought, but her brain was too fatigued, and it skipped out of her reach. One day she would think about it. And she was just as bad, for she hadn't bothered about Anny, either, accepted her unquestioningly as a part of that little, imprisoning yard, as though she were a clothesline.

'She needs fresh feed. She'll be all right,' said Charlie, stroking the animal's delicate hairy nostrils.

'Poor Anny.' The tears rolled down Dolour's cheeks. They were the reaction to her experiences that evening, but there was no bitterness in them any more.

'I never seen such a fuss over an old goat,' scolded Mumma, but her glance was sympathetic, and together with Dolour she watched as Charlie took the limping, stumbling animal down the dark street to the shelter of the park.

Eighteen

In all that great village of Surry Hills, which clung to the proud skirts of Sydney like a ragged, dirty-nosed child, there were little eddies and pools of streets and blocks, peculiar to themselves, like towns within a town. Mumma knew all the women in her street; she knew whose children had things in their hair, and who stayed longest in confession, and quite often why. She knew all the little shops in Coronation Street, and which ones were good for tick, and which weren't, the measly-minded vultures. But out of her locality, in the next street but one perhaps, she felt strange, with the people looking at her, and the women criticizing her.

So Hughie, when he went to Florentina's house, felt that no one round there would recognize him. He had been in the pub on the corner, but that was all, for there were no friendly faces of old mates there, and the barmaid had aloofly ignored his uplifted finger. Two blocks away from his own street he was a stranger. Not that the possibility of discovery had ever occurred to him for a moment. His life outside the doors of his home had always been his own; he had gone his own way and come back when he felt like it, and always found Mumma still there. He would have been amazed at the idea that it was any of her business what he'd been doing.

Now, in the lopsided dream that had arisen out of the incomprehensible alchemy of his own mind and body, he rarely thought of Mumma at all. She was part of Number Twelve-and-a-half Plymouth Street, dirty, monotonous, hardly animate, Dolour was a prating voice, cheeping away in the distance, barely heard and never understood. And Charlie, sullen, silent, growing thinner and older and sallower by the day, was just a stranger who appeared sometimes to keep him company with a bottle. He came into the house and went out, blankly, his mind so filled with the girl that he could not think while he was working, or laugh with his mates, or do anything in the world without entangling his thoughts about her.

Sometimes he would stand in wonder and look at his thick, unsupple hands that were weathered and beaten, scarred and battered. How could they be worthy of the shoulders soft as suede, the dove-like softness of the throat of Florentina?

He was bemused with her, walking gape-mouthed through life, unable to think or plan. It was like waking up, and finding he had only dreamed he was middle-aged and fettered to a life of no more value than ashes. She was the glass of water in the sand, the rain at the end of the burning day. She had given him back his youth, and like a drug he had to possess her to preserve the illusion.

It did not matter that she was a prostitute. In Surry Hills and other places like it the curious inversion of the moral law that made the policeman an object of contempt and the basher someone to be looked up to and respected, accepted the harlot as a commonplace. The reputable people of Surry Hills were too proud to be snobbish with the disreputable. They felt themselves on a level with everyone else. The grocer on the corner was a good, church-going fellow, but mean and dirty with his children; the chromo next door got her money easy in dark doorways, but she was always ready to shout you a feed when you were down and out. It all balanced when you came to the end, and God alone knew whom He was going to ask inside when he had the lot of you clamouring outside the walls of Heaven. So when a prostitute got old or tired, there was almost always someone ready to marry her, and later on, when she had a houseful of nice kids, and the same troubles as everyone else, hardly anybody remembered her youth except with good-natured tolerance. So Hughie accepted Florentina, because he had to, for his passion ignored everything but its food. If she had been diseased he would have accepted her just the same. His was the frantic monomania of a man who will rape the woman he wants rather than be frustrated of her; but being Hughie he begged and prayed instead, when he had no money, that she be accessible to him. It was only in these moments that a tiny corner of his soul, almost hidden in the darkness, hated itself because of the humiliation of grovelling to a girl young enough to be his daughter.

But Florentina was always accessible. Lazy, good-hearted as an animal, she would never have turned down any man because he didn't have enough money. Besides, in some subtle way, Hughie fed her ego. She would have been content to loll and watch him, and often she felt an indolent resentment at Seppa for continually holding out her hand.

'You're mad,' said her sister, the thickset Italian woman, standing before the glass and plucking fiercely at her black moustache. 'If you want an old man hanging around, why don't you pick one with money?'

Florentina hardly heard. Lying on the unmade bed, dreamily watching the rain, she murmured, 'Aw, he's that mad about me, Seppa. He's like a dog. Honest, he is.'

The other woman snorted. 'And you'll get about as much from him.'

Florentina rolled over. 'Aw, shut up, Seppa. I bring in the dough, don't I? You ain't losing anything.'

The black boy sidled into the room, his chocolate eyes rolled askance at his mother for fear of reproof or a blow. Out of the mirror her face glared at him, 'Out the back, you black bastard!'

Florentina reached out an arm as the boy skittered past.

'Ah, don't be such a bite, Seppa! Ain't his fault he's black. He was got on a dark night, eh, Lex?' She muzzled her face into the child's slender neck, soaking in his adoration. 'Here,' she put a chocolate into his mouth. 'Go on, Lexie. You better go before your mumma chips an ear off you.'

The elder woman looked at her with disgust in which jealousy struggled to show its head. 'You make me sick, Florrie. You're like a bloody cat, purring and stretching whenever anyone strokes you.'

Florentina laughed. Her sister slammed out of the door, and she relaxed in the dimness, her ears lulled by the gurgle and splash of the rain, the swish and roar of passing cars, the sucking patter of feet on the road. Her mind was a stream that flowed silently, placidly, deeply and narrowly. Like a flower, benevolent, beautiful, unrelated to morality or inhibition, she bent this way and that before the wind, and thought nothing about anything.

She had grown up in the shadow of the great markets, her road strewn with blue-mouldy oranges, yellowing cabbage leaves, and apples brown-sugared with decay. There she had knelt, black-curled and angel-faced, coaxing out the lost kitten cowering beneath the wagon, or feeding broken sugarcane to the children who were not so fortunate as to have for a father a man in the wholesale fruit business. She could not remember when she was a virgin, if she knew the word. She dreamed her way through life, floating along on the stream of her own drowsy intelligence, her own human-kindness, passing from one man to another and not being polluted by any of them. As long as they were kind to her, she did not mind who they were. When she was sixteen her father died, and she went to live with her sister Seppa, who had been on the streets a long time, and there she stayed, happy, incurious, waiting for life to happen to her.

Minutes or hours passed, half in sleep, half in waking dream, when there was the sound of wet boots on the balcony and a bang at the door.

'Push it. It ain't locked,' called Florentina sleepily. Milkman, iceman, or customer, it did not matter to her. 'Watcher want?'

Hughie stood there blinking in the dimness which, even after the dull grey of the streets, was that of a cave. He was at once abashed and excited at the sight of the girl on the bed, and dragged something out of his pocket. He wanted to say something significant and memorable, but he only growled, 'You can have this.'

'Gee, love!' She took the bangle, a streak of yellow light. He had bought her a present, and almost nobody ever bought her a present. Affection for him flooded her easy heart. 'Ain't you a duck!' She tried it on, twisting her dark wrist this way and that to catch the light. 'Don't it shine, Hughie! Just like a Christmas tree with all that stuff on the branches.' She put her arms round his neck.

'Where's the kid?'

'Oh, I dunno. Around. You don't want to worry about Lex. He never sees nothing.'

Over his shoulder she could see a plate of apples on the table. 'Gee,' she thought, 'I'd like a pear. I could go for a pear, one of them brown winter ones. Hope Seppa remembers to bring home the garlic. Last time we had stew there wasn't none, and it ain't the same somehow. When he's gone I'll get up and wash me hair. I'll do it right up with a lot of curls and a green ribbon round it like that tart I saw down town last Satdee arvo. I need a new dress, too. That blue one's nice but the colour's all gone funny where I spilt the wine on it. I better get out to-night and get meself some money, Seppa picking on me all the time like an old hen, think I never brought anything into the house. That's a nice cop on the beat along Oxford Street. Never said a word to me. I sure do go for them blue eyes, like sparks. I could wear me new bangle with a new dress. I think I'll get green after all. Green makes Seppa look like an egg-yolk. Gee, she's getting fat, poor Seppa, must be all them spuds she eats. Hope she remembers the garlic.'

Hughie lay with his face in the pillow, spreadeagled, trembling.

She looked at him pityingly, and got him a drink. He gulped the red-hot spirit gratefully. He said, not looking at her, 'You shouldn'ta let me.'

This remark, which rose mechanically like a bubble from the submerged reef of Hughie's moralities, always left Florentina silent, not knowing what to say, for nobody else ever said it to her. She lifted the glittering bracelet and held it to her cheek.

'I sure do like you a lot, Hughie.'

Hughie groaned. He sat with his head in his hands. He knew he would have to have money, if he were to continue in this frail precarious heaven.

'I'm sick of this place,' he said hoarsely. 'Working me guts out for nothing. We'll go to Melbourne. You'd come to Melbourne with me, Florrie?'

'I sure would like to go to Melbourne,' said Florentina meditatively, staring into the kitchen, where she could see the white eyeballs of Lex blinking in the shadows. Melbourne's the place where you can make money, all the girls said, just like Brisbane during the war. All them swank hotels, and me going in with a high-class feller, and one of them strapless evening gowns like the movie stars wear, and me hair long with a silver ornament in it, just here. But Seppa wouldn't ever leave Surro, and I sure would miss little Lexie. When Hughie's gone I'll light the fire in here and me and Lexie'll finish up the chocolates and have a good warm.

'What's that, love?' she asked Hughie.

She wondered what he'd been talking about, but it didn't matter, anyhow, for there was Seppa, stumping in, streaming with rain, a kit of food in each hand. She glared at Hughie, and Hughie, grabbing his hat, muttered, 'Well, I better go through.'

'Hope you don't get too wet, duck.'

He plunged away into the silver sheet of the rain, and Florentina turned to her sister eagerly, 'Bet yer forgot the garlic!'

Hughie battled up Coronation Street, cursing the people who hissed past in big cars, water swinging up in grey circles from the wheels. The rain squelched up in his shoes and bubbled out through the rotten stitching on the uppers. He felt nothing, thought nothing except of what obsessed him. He did not even think that he had been physically unfaithful again. Unfaith meant nothing to him, for his marriage, with his past, had disappeared in his mind. He could only think of himself, a man with no name, no trappings, no responsibilities, nothing except manhood. Yet his physical unfaithfulness did not bring any content, nothing but a deeper and wider hatred of life, of himself, and all the things that he knew. It bred confusion, and Hughie's mind was not made to cope with confusion.

As he skipped across the muddy road before the onslaught of the trucks the money in his pocket jingled. He had just enough there for a few drinks. The bangle, shoddy and all as it was, had taken all his pay. He wondered indifferently what Mumma would say when he told her there wouldn't be anything for the rent and the housekeeping this week, and bitter gall came up in his throat as he thought of her, and that intolerable house, and the yelping clamour of the children.

Well, she didn't have much to complain of. She had Dolour's money, and Mr Reilly's rent, and whatever Charlie would bring in.

'Let bloody Charlie keep the place for a while,' growled Hughie to himself. 'Wake him up a bit.'

All at once he saw in a fruiterer's window a pale yellow pyramid of marmalade oranges, the ironically christened poor man's orange that starred the winter orchards. Their skin was so smooth and shiny, their pith so plushy, their juice so tangy that they might well have been little wild grapefruit. But they were so bitter that they made Hughie's face screw up wryly at the very sight of them. Dolour loved to eat them, going round chewing at them, oblivious to the looks of loathing on the faces of her family.

'I'll get the kid a dozen.'

But he only had enough money for a few drinks, and what use was it trying to carry a paper bag in this weather? Ten steps and the oranges would be bouncing all over the road.

'I'll get them again.'

But he knew it was a toss-up between the drink and Dolour, and the knowledge that she didn't have a chance was so cold, so bitter, so self-contemptuous that he swallowed hard as though someone had hit him, and plunged into the steamy maelstrom of the pub.

So it went on, for week after week, until one day Harry Drummy said to Dolour, 'Aw, come on, let's go to the pitchers to-night.'

'Go and get your head read,' retorted the girl furiously. 'I wouldn't go out with you again unless I had a diving suit on.'

Harry was piqued. He'd been a bit sick of her frigid silence over the last months, and anyway, she'd brought it on herself, the way she'd led him on.

'Pretty choosy, ain't yer?'

Dolour sulkily slammed the milk bottles into the refrigerator, trying meantime to think up something smart.

'So bloody stuck-up no one's good enough for you. Pity yer old man ain't a bit the same way.'

Dolour wiped the wet cloth energetically down the counter, flicking crumbs his way. 'What are you babbling about?'

Infuriated, the boy picked the crumbs off his shirt. 'About that wop chromo your old man knocks about with, that's all.'

Dolour stood with her mouth open. 'Go on, you're mad.' She dipped the cloth into the bucket of water.

'Oh, am I? I seen him down at her place meself. That yellow place on the corner of Elsey Street.'

Suddenly Dolour could stand the sight of his hateful, jeering, pimply face no longer. She blazed, 'Don't you say things like that, you dirty-minded jerk!'

Mrs Drummy popped out of the inner room. Her face was anxious. 'What ever's the matter, love?'

Dolour was silent. Her lips trembled.

'I just happened to mention her dad and Florentina, that's all, Mum,' said Harry, injured. 'Thought she knew all about it. Isn't as though it's a secret.'

Mrs Drummy looked from Dolour to Harry. 'You shouldn't of told her,' she said weakly. 'It's uncharitable talk.'

All at once Harry got mad. 'Swanking around the way no feller was good enough for her. Why doesn't she look at her own family?'

Dolour hardly heard him. She appealed to Mrs Drummy. 'It isn't true, is it?'

Poor Mrs Drummy didn't know what to do. She said cautiously, 'Well, dearie, I'm not the one to say it is or isn't. You know my friend, Mrs Croucher, she lives next to Florentina's, and I seen your father myself going into Florrie's place but you know how it is, maybe he had to go on business or something.'

'Business!' guffawed her son. Mrs Drummy turned on him like an infuriated rabbit. 'You get to the back of the shop, you big yob! And keep your nose out of Dolour's business. If I hear you slinging off at her again, I'll knock you bandy, honest to goodness I will!'

'There, you don't want to get upset, dear. You know how men are. You can't trust any of them, not even the old boys. Don't I know what my Bert would get up to if I took my eye off him for a moment. Anyway, it mightn't mean anything. Just like I said, there's lots of things your father could go there for.'

'What, for instance?' asked Dolour bleakly. Mrs Drummy floundered.

'There isn't anything,' said Dolour. She took off her overall and folded it mechanically, staring at nothing. 'Dadda! And he must be about fifty.'

'Well,' said Mrs Drummy helpfully, 'he's a strong, healthy man.'

Dolour's face crumpled. 'Oh, stop it! Stop it!' she cried, and with a look of unutterable disgust, she grabbed up her things and ran out into the street.

Nineteen

Dolour was trembling with fierce hatred of her father and fierce love of her mother. She felt sick with passion. For a long time she stood at the open window of the attic, unable to think or plan to do anything constructive. The disgust in her heart was a huge indigestible lump that completely demoralized her. How could he! She said it over and over again, grasping the sill so that the splinters went into her palm.

'How could You let him?' she cried passionately, putting her head on her hands and crying bitterly. She had often felt shame before, for her father drunken on the street, for her mother's shabbiness, for her own poverty in school, lack of clothes, of shoes, of threepences to give to the basketball fund or the bazaar. But this – to have everyone laughing at them because silly old Hughie Darcy was making a fool of himself over a prostitute.

She tramped up and down the room, face crimson, her eyes getting painful with the tears, imagining herself going down and facing Florentina and telling her to get out of the district or she'd kill her.

'And I would, too! I would! I would!'

And then her mind went off at another tangent, and she saw herself taking Hughie aside and talking to him sensibly and calmly, telling him of all her mother had been to him, and putting before him the wickedness of what he was doing. But she knew that she couldn't possibly do any of these things, that she was helpless, her hands tied before this inexplicable manifestation of adult character.

She felt that it wouldn't have been so bad if her father had fallen in love with a decent girl, whose very decency might have lent some romantic aspect to the affair. But a prostitute! And falling in love! Dolour castigated herself bitterly for using the expression, for what did love have to do with it? She felt as though she were sucked down in a current of evil, the old feeling that it was there, invisible, all-pervading, a dreadful miasma that she could never escape.

She forgot that she had loved her father, that he had been kind to her, and generous often, that he had been her protector when she was young, and her unnoticed guardian since she had grown up. All at once he became a man and nothing else.

'I'll run away,' she babbled. 'I won't stay in the same house with him.'

And she imagined how all these weeks people had been coming into Drummy's and going out and jerking a thumb and saying, 'That's 'er. That's his daughter,' forgetting that the same thing had happened so many times that it was hardly more than a subject for idle gossip. But to Dolour she was the centre of all the scorn, the laughter, and the jeers. She made up her mind that her mother would never learn the truth from her, wiping her eyes and blowing her nose with such savagery that Mr Bumper Reilly, snoozing in the next room, awoke with the trembling conviction that it had been the trump of doom.

That day Mumma was feeling very happy. She sat on the step, Mikey on her spread lap, rocking gently back and forth, and enjoying the savour of the stew on the stove and the warm mellowness of the sunshine with equal pleasure. Now and then she turned Mikey over and listened approvingly to the wind bubbling out of him. 'Was it at you, Mikey?'

There were very many things for her to do. The tubs were half full of nappies that she had started to wash and forgotten at some interruption. Motty had not been washed all day, and her legs wore socks of dirt. And there were pants to be patched, and a shirt with the elbow out, which Mumma had looked at helplessly a dozen times and then put away in the pathetic hope that Hughie would forget about it. But in spite of all these things, Mumma just sat and enjoyed the sunshine, and played with the little boy. She knew that Motty was happy, dirt or no dirt, and as for the nappies, well, another hour in the tub would do them a world of good. She buried her face in Mikey's fat neck. 'Wouldn't your mummy have loved you?'

At the thought of Roie tears came into her eyes, but they were not sad tears, for in the way of things the sorrow had been blunted, and now she could speak freely of her daughter and remember things about her that made her happy instead of grieved.

'He kisses your pitcher every night, darling,' she said.

She put the baby down in the yard, and went inside and yelled up the stairs for Dolour.

'What are you doing loafing up there when I'm run off me feet with the work?'

In an instant Dolour had forgotten all her love and passionate defence of her mother. She protested, 'You are not. You've been sitting down there ever since I came home.'

She flounced into the kitchen and surveyed the desolation with despair.

'What a pigsty!'

Mumma was angry, because she was guilty. She made a back-handed swipe at Dolour. 'Talking about your own home like that!'

'Well, what else would you call it?' flamed Dolour. The two women looked at each other with real, though evanescent dislike.

'Well, why don't you get down on your knees and give it a scrub, seeing you're so fussy!' demanded Mumma scornfully. She gave Puffing Billy a kick in the teeth. 'Let me tell you a few things, young lady. You're too big for your boots, that's all. You always did have ideas bigger than your stomach could hold. Just because you've got a better education than any of us, forgetting that your poor father slaved to give it to you.'

Dolour was scarlet with emotion. 'Don't you poor father me. I'd like to see him fall off a tram.'

Slam! Mumma's heavy hand hit her across the ear and almost knocked her flat. Bells ringing, drums beating, Dolour collapsed into a chair.

'Don't you talk about your father like that! It's a pity the nuns can't hear you, and them thinking so highly of you.'

Dolour began to cry, talking in a loud high voice through her sobs so that hardly any of her words were intelligible.

'I hate him! I hate him! Oh, I wish he was dead!' She rubbed her ear, which felt as though it were swelling to the size of a plate. 'I'm not the one you ought to hit. Why don't you have a go at his girl friend? You're so smart with your fists you ought to have a go at Jack Hassen.'

And so she sobbed and hiccuped her way through childish threats and inanities until Mumma seized her by the shoulders and cried, 'What are you babbling about?'

Dolour had gone too far, so she said defiantly, 'He's got a girl friend, that's all. Everyone knows about it.'

Mumma's mouth hung open, her face as pale as soap.

'Don't you dare say such – '

'I'm not daring anything,' said the girl sullenly. 'He's been knocking around with her for months.' Then she began to cry again, her head on the table amongst the pots of jam and the torn tea-towels and bits of tape and old receipts that Mumma had left there when she was cleaning out the dresser. 'Oh, Mumma, I didn't mean to tell you.'

'You ain't sure?' asked Mumma. She searched her daughter's bleared face. Dolour nodded.

'Mrs Drummy said so. I guess that's what he bought the new shirts for.'

There was a long silence. Fearfully Dolour looked at her mother. She stood there stirring the stew, round and round and round, looking at nothing. She said, 'Do you reckon Charlie knows?'

'I dunno. I dunno who knows. Oh, Mumma, isn't it awful? Everyone laughing about it. He's an old man!'

'Mrs Drummy don't gossip,' said Mumma finally.

They were silent a little while, then Mumma said, 'The baby's out there in the yard, and Motty, she's out in front, with a dirty face.'

'I'll go,' said Dolour, anxious to escape, and she went out and found Motty, and took her into the yard, where she kept both children quiet, listening all the time for any sound from the kitchen, fearful and a little in awe of what might happen.

Mumma, left alone, showed every sign of a person suffering from shock. She stood so still it seemed she could hear the very ticking of her body, staring straight ahead of her and not seeing a thing. For a while she wandered aimlessly about the kitchen, putting on saucepan lids and picking up scraps of food, wiping her vegetable knife with detailed care. She could not think. Her mind was like an empty room, with many things in it, but none moving.

After a while she did the thing she always did when great trouble came to her. She put on her old brown coat and went down the road to the church. She must have gone along the street, perhaps even spoken to people, but she did not know it. She came to herself as she dipped a hand in the conch shell full of holy water at the door.

There was nobody in the church, for it was a busy hour. Mumma squeezed in between the seats and knelt down. The coolness of the place, the homely dust on the great arching beams, the comforting red glow of the sanctuary lamps was there. Always they had brought her peace before, but now they did not even register.

For Mumma had never considered Hughie with another woman. He was hers, and she was his, for better or worse, and although she had always had the worse end of the stick, that was marriage, and nothing could be done about it. Mumma had the true, traditional Irish regard for matrimony; in itself it was an important and significant and holy thing, and this very holiness made possible all the things that had been done in its name in Ireland and other places where people almost strangers, with no passion or magic between them, had become husband and wife and been true, and raised children, and died at last lamenting each other.

Mumma knew that marriage, the sacrament, was more important than the people committed to it, and thus she had never imagined, not even for a moment, the possibility that she should look at another man, or that Hughie should look at another woman.

The horror and shock of it lasted for a long time. Then, like a stirring in that empty room of her mind, came the grief, the terrible humiliation that she had loved and worked and suffered for this man, and now, at the end, had been thrown aside. She had put up with his drunkenness, his fecklessness, his complete disregard for her happiness and comfort, and the poverty he had brought with him. Yes, she had been the injured one, the one who had borne, and not complained, and yet she was to be discarded, and the worst of it was that Dolour knew it. This was Mumma's bitterest knowledge. She did not know why; she only knew that her most intrinsic dignity had been laid waste.

Mumma tried to awaken her wild Irish anger, but it was crushed, silent, and unwilling to give even a wag of its tail. The grief and the shock, appalling in their pain, surrounded her, drowned her, and her spirit sank beneath them in a despair that not even she had known before.

She knelt there a long time, a shapeless clod in the gathering shadows; thick red hands over its eyes, skirt trailing in the dust of the kneeler, and the patched soles and run-over heels turned up to the gaze of any passer-by. Out of that hour of pain came many, many thoughts. She had given up her name for that man. Along with all the other things she had carelessly and indeed even joyously given up had been her own patronymic, and yet Kilker had been a name that had fought its way through the famine, and the black plague, and the Troubles, and survived to travel steerage to Australia nearly ninety years before. An unbeatable name it had been, yet she had thrown it away at Hugh's bidding, put it on a shelf and never so much as took it out and gave it a shake and a kind word.

And her own name, her baptismal name, what had happened to

614

it? She was a stranger to it. No one ever used it any more. She was a nonentity, a creature who had entered marriage a person, and within a year was nothing but Mumma, an institution.

'Where's it all gone?' cried Mumma's soul. 'Where's me hair that was so curly, and so pretty, and the way me complexion never got a spot on it, and the bust that made even a five-bob blouse look like the front of a ship? Where's the times I went out with Roie on one hand and Thady on the other, and Roie with the great ribbon in her hair, and Thady's legs so fat and round that everyone smiled? Oh, God, what have You done with all the years?'

And Mumma's memory stumbled from tumbledown shanty to bug-ridden residential, to evil dirty cottage; up lanes she'd nearly forgotten, to countless gates where she'd waited for Hughie, dreading to see the stammer in his step as he came up the road. And she saw the red geranium she'd once grown in a pickle bottle, and the little canary that had choked on a bit of banana, and the lovely hat with the flowers she'd worn for her wedding.

And Thady came into her thoughts, playing marbles on the footpath the way he'd been before he'd disappeared; and Roie, kicked and bleeding the night she'd told her Mumma she'd been going to have Tommy Mendel's baby.

Oh, there were many things. Mumma stared straight into the face of God and they rushed through her mind, pell-mell, like birds flying – the great sadnesses, the disappointments, the endless anonymous monotony of her life that was no more than a passage and a buffer for the other lives about it.

'It makes you wonder what a body's born for,' she said.

She got up. Her bones seemed to have set into a clumsy, bowed shape, and it was hard to genuflect. She stood for a moment on the steps, blinking in the last of the sunlight. The street flowed past, almost unseen, and it was with difficulty that she brought her thoughts and her eyes to Mrs Drummy, coming up the steps.

'Why, Mrs Darcy!' said Mrs Drummy. 'You ain't got your hat on.'

Mumma put up her hand, and there was her bare, tousled head.

'Neither I have,' she said in a tone of incredulous wonder. She looked bewildered at the other woman for a moment, then her lips began to tremble and she put down her head and hurried away.

Twenty

Never again at any time did Mumma mention Hughie and Florentina. Like Patrick Diamond, who had ignored his cancer, so did Mumma ignore this incredible eruption in her married life, hoping that because it was ignored it would go away and stop bothering her.

Before her dignity, her silent, self-contained dignity, Dolour felt childish. Her anger flickered out into doubt and uncertainty, her disgust into bewilderment. For what was it all about? Dolour did not know. Hughie was just the same to them as he always was, coming home tired and dirty-faced, ready to snap their heads off till he'd got his boots off and had a snore-off on the couch. He still yelled at Motty one moment, snatching her up and cuddling her extravagantly the next. When he was drunk he still hung tearfully over Mikey, trying to ease the pain that came when he thought of Roie, and he always thought of Roie when he was drunk.

She and Mumma stared at him as though he were a new man, and the mystery was that he was still the same old Hughie. Had he been like this all the time, faithful to them in his way, and yet running off in his mind after other women? Dolour was so confused that she felt sick. For the greatest puzzle of all was how a man could have a wife and family and go on living with them, and yet love another girl.

For to Dolour's mind the issue was clear-cut. If you loved someone you went away and joined your life with theirs. You could not travel two roads at once.

Sometimes she hated her father so much that when he brushed against her she shrank away, and the moment afterwards yearned for him when he looked puzzled and hurt. For Hughie, in his confidence that nobody knew about his association with Florentina, acted as though he were innocent. In effect he was innocent, and would be until found out.

So he looked at Dolour and said wistfully, 'You're getting that cranky. Why don't you turn in that job and get a better one?'

'We need the money,' she answered coldly and obstinately.

'You ought to go to night school,' he said with unwonted timidity. 'I know how you feel, and you having to leave school and everything when you was getting on so well.'

'Maybe I don't want to go to night school,' she said, and turned away.

'Next year I'm on to a better job down at the factory and I could shout you to a course in typewriting and shorthand or something down in the town, like Gracie Drummy,' he pressed eagerly.

Both Hughie and Dolour knew very well that any extra money he might earn would go the way it had always gone, but once the thought would have pleased her as much as the act, and she would have thrown her arms round her Dadda and given him a hug.

But now she did not say a word, leaving Hughie bewildered and affronted.

Just as he had ceased to be Dolour's father, to become a man, so did he become a man to Mumma, who had for twenty-five years looked on him as that anonymous humdrum creature, a husband. At night as he lay snoring on the far side of the bed, she crept over and put her hand on him, feeling his flesh that was still warm and smooth, and his shoulder still strong and shapely. She felt almost sinful as she did it, quick to alarm at his snort or snuffle, ready to roll away to her side of the bed to pretend sleep.

'What did you have to do it for?' Her thoughts went round and round, wondering what was the matter with her that he went looking elsewhere. She was old, of course she was, but so was Hughie, and Mumma could see nothing but unnaturalness in a middle-aged man's chasing after a young girl.

'It's just as if I got sweet on a young feller like Charlie.'

At the very thought an embarrassed giggle came out of Mumma into the darkness, and Hughie grunted inquiringly. Mumma lay as still as a mouse, hoping he would not awake, and yet longing for him to do so, so that she could have it out with him, furious denunciation and denial, abusive admission, and perhaps forgiveness. For Mumma knew that even if there were no repentance there would be forgiveness.

She thought sometimes of Dolour's outburst about the kitchen being dirty, and how the girl spent all her Saturdays scrubbing and washing, and she thought, 'All very well, but after twenty-five years of married life it's as much as you can do to keep yourself clean.'

Suddenly doubt entered her mind. Giving your face a lick with a wash-cloth, and a bit of a rinse round the neck and arm-pits wasn't the way the advertisements in the papers spoke of being clean. He could talk, anyway. Him with all his new shirts. They didn't hide the grey in his whiskers. And as for that Florentina, all of them Italian girls ran to fat, and got hairy around the face. But Mumma made up her mind that she would smarten up a little, just to show Hughie what he didn't have the sense to appreciate.

Hanging out the nappies – for Mumma was too bothered to train Mikey otherwise, and so he was still using them – she pondered how she should do it. She hauled on the dry sooty rope, and away up between the walls flew the clothesline, the nappies flying like signal flags from some unimaginably drab battleship.

'That's the way it is,' said Mumma, watching the soot, like bits of black lace, sifting down out of the paint-blue sky. There was a flicker of movement in the open doorway, and Mr Bumper Reilly's little face appeared for a moment, upside down like a mirage. Mumma squinted until she realized that he was peering round the side of the door. Delicately she went inside, and not till a scamper of creaks on the stairs told of a mission accomplished did she go outside.

'He's no company,' sighed Mumma.

She got the mirror, a thing she hadn't done for years, and for a long time looked at her face. It seemed to her that she was fading away. It wasn't sickness, or thinness of body. Rather were her bones sinking into each other, joint upon joint, so that her frame was forced outwards into a squatness it surely hadn't possessed when she was young.

'I'm not going to be a neat old woman like Ma was,' mourned Mumma. 'And I ain't got the skin she had, that white you would have thought she was a lady.'

For a while she thought of her Ma, saying a little prayer for her rest, and then remembering that rest was the last thing Grandma would ever have wanted, and changing the prayer in a hurry, 'Make heaven to her liking, dear Lord.'

She was still there when Dolour came in from lunch, dragging a shrieking Motty by the hand.

'I found her down the road with her pants off. She was carrying gravel in them, and throwing it at motor cars,' she said giving the turbulent one a shake.

'Watcher doing, Nana?' asked Motty, opening wide her tearless eyes.

618

'Looking at me teeth,' said Mumma sadly. She rolled up her lip for Motty's inspection. Dolour shuddered.

'Jeepers, what an awful-looking lot of clothes-pegs. Why don't you get them out?'

'I was thinking of it,' said Mumma. 'A person can't look their best with a mouthful of old snags.'

Dolour understood instantly. 'I can just see you with a lovely set of white teeth,' she said. Enthusiasm filled her. 'I'll pay them off for you, Mumma. Gee, you'd look nice. Fatter in the face.'

They looked at each other like conspirators. Dolour burst out, 'Show him a few things! You don't have to depend on him to buy new teeth for you.'

It had been so long since Mumma had good teeth that she couldn't remember what she looked like with them. They had started to go when Roie was on the way, and by the time Dolour was born they were crumbling like old monuments. It was a long time since she had had a toothache, for the nerves were all dead, and the teeth just lay like yellow stumps in the gums. But she hadn't forgotten her childish horror of dentists, ever since a drunken dentist in her childhood had planked her down in a chair and, holding her jaw in a steely grip with one hand, crushed a molar to pieces in complete disregard of her hysterical shrieks.

'I think maybe I'll wait till the weather's colder, so I can wear me coat,' she said uncertainly, looking at Dolour hopefully.

'No you don't,' said her daughter. 'You're going as soon as I can get an appointment for you.'

'Me shoes are that awful,' protested Mumma, and they argued back and forth across the lunch-table, Dolour holding Michael on her lap and poking spoonfuls of vegetables into his mouth. He was a remarkable eater. He would obligingly eat all his dinner, and then, after his junket or jelly had been amiably taken, eject an unsullied mouthful of pure carrot. Now the food oozed out as fast as she put it in, and she scraped it up and determinedly put it back again.

'Want to grow up a squib? Want to be as thin as a stick of celery?'

Mumma sighed. Roie wouldn't have bothered to make the child eat. But Michael went to Dolour when he tumbled from his chair, cried for her, 'Do-Do-Do!' when he was sad, and laughed at her approach.

'You'd think she was his mother,' said Mumma privately to herself. 'She's that queer, interested in babies at her age.'

But she had been the same way, doting on all her small brothers and sisters until they'd been carried off by colic or whooping cough, and lamenting over them until a new one had come along, for Grandma had been indefatigable.

Motty decided she had had enough, spat out a bone, and dived for the door.

'Hey, where are you going?' asked Dolour.

'Out,' replied Motty briefly. She remembered a child down the road who had a string of red wooden balls, and Motty considered that it would be easy enough to take them off him. At the thought she bunched her filthy, scratched little fists.

'You come back here,' commanded Dolour. Motty spat juicily at her, and ran.

With lips grim Mumma rose and went after her. Most of the time Motty was entirely out of her control, but she did not admit it in front of Dolour. Dolour sighed. She went on feeding Mikey, kissing the back of his soft neck and murmuring words that meant nothing except that she loved him. So they were when Charlie came in, pushing open the door half apologetically as though he no longer had any place in that house. When he saw the sleek dark head bent over the fuzzy one, his heart stopped for a moment.

'Why, Charlie, what are you doing home?'

'Breakdown. Thought I might as well come home.' He sat down, wearily.

'You finish giving Mikey his milk and I'll get some lunch for you. I gotta go back soon.'

From the stove she watched him covertly as she lapped an egg with the sizzling fat. He stared at the child sucking at the mug as though he had never seen it before.

'I hope he notices that Mikey has a dimple,' thought Dolour. 'I hope he sees that his hair goes up in the front like Roie's and his chin's like hers. Gosh, I don't know why he isn't interested in Mikey.' Aloud she said, 'I'll take him now. You eat something.'

Once she would have been uncomfortable along with Charlie, looking for things to say, or excuses to leave the room. But now she sat companionably silent, buttering him a piece of bread, pushing the salt along before he needed it. Furtively he looked at her, wondering how she was content to stay in this place that once she had rebelled against, wondering what she thought of when she was alone.

Dolour said, 'You ought to go away for your holidays this year Charlie. You look rotten.'

He did not answer, and she burst out, 'And no wonder, leading the sort of life you do, lying around all the week-end half stewed and never taking any interest in anything. And I'll bet the last time you were in church was at Roie's funeral!'

His eyes blazed at her. 'Oh, shut your trap!' He pushed the plate away and he and Dolour glared at each other over the baby's soft hair like two dogs. Dolour felt a pang of pleasure that she had awakened him from his apathy. In her mind she quickly revolved whether it would be better to backtrack like Mumma, or attack tooth and claw, like Grandma, but before she could decide he said, 'I'm going away for good. Perhaps that'll satisfy you.'

The words were ordinary ones, but as though they had been in a new and magic language, a door slammed shut in Dolour's mind and she knew what she felt about this man. He had been the barrier to all the world about her, the last fence to protect her against its coarseness and cruelty, the last link she had with delicacy and sensitivity and self-respect. She recognized that she had bitterly opposed his downward path not only on his behalf, but on her own, because he had represented all that was stable in her unstable life.

'How can I do without you, Charlie!' cried her heart, and the tears gushed into it, and she bent over to hide them. She said in a strangled voice, 'I don't know that I blame you. You ain't – haven't ever fitted into this place.'

'I've lost myself somewhere,' he said with difficulty. 'You know.'

'Yes, I know.'

'I thought if I cleared out of it, it might be easier. The kids won't miss me. Mumma'll look after them. I'll send her their keep.'

Dolour was silent. Then she said, 'Money isn't all a father gives to his children. And Motty needs someone all to herself, even if Mikey doesn't yet.'

'Motty?'

'Haven't you noticed?' asked Dolour painfully. 'Motty isn't the kid she was when Roie was here. She's the cheekiest kid in the street. Mumma can't do a thing with her. And neither can I.'

'But Mumma – ' Charlie was astounded.

'Mumma can't look after kids the way she looked after Roie and me. She's old now. She says God will give Motty grace in His own good time, but what she needs isn't grace but a good hard switching three times a day.' She looked appealingly at the man. 'I dunno how to put it, Charlie. Mumma loves Motty and Mikey, but as long as they're happy she doesn't care about keeping them clean, or putting warm clothes on them, or watching out they don't play with kids that have the measles – or anything.' Suddenly the tears came to the top. 'She's on the street all the time and I just can't forget the way Suse Kilroy grew up, or the way Thady disappeared. There's such awful men wandering around and – ' she gulped. 'I suppose you'll say I've just got an imagination.'

Now he was confused, appalled that he hadn't thought of this before, ashamed that he had had to be told, guilty that he had been going to leave these children without a thought for their future except physical provision.

He said, 'I'll go out for a while.'

Dolour rose, too. 'Don't go to the pub, Charlie,' Then she blushed and grinned. 'I sound like Mumma talking to Dad. I guess it runs in the family. Go on, get drunk, and see if I care.'

He said wonderingly, 'You do care.'

He saw her for the first time as a young woman, and not as a child who looked a little like his dead wife. She was grown-up. She was old enough to have borne the child she carried, she was old enough to get married and go away and never be there for him to talk to any more. He had forgotten that there was nothing to keep her there, while there were two children to keep him. He said, not knowing what else to say, 'You're a good kid.'

Dolour's eyes fell. 'I'd better get back to Drummy's.' Inside herself she was saying. 'I'm not a kid. I never will be any more.'

Right up to the last moment on the Thursday when Mumma had her dentist's appointment she maintained the illusion that she was going, alluring Dolour along by frequent references to herself as a sight for sore eyes with her glittering double row of new teeth.

'Do you think I could have a tiny speck of gold, about ten bob's worth, in the front ones, darling? It looks so tasteful.' And, 'After all, a body hasn't been able to smile properly in the last ten years, what with the awful spectacle it's been, and the cold air playing jip with the aching ones.'

Dolour eyed her with suspicion. She had her doubts of Mumma's glibness and careless courage. 'I'm going with you, you know. Mrs Drummy's given me the afternoon off.'

Mumma looked at her like a trapped animal. She hadn't quite decided which excuse she thought best, but she hadn't banked on Dolour's presence complicating everything.

Dolour said grimly, 'I'm going to press out your dress now.'

'It's got egg down the front,' protested Mumma feebly.

'How on earth did you get egg on it?' demanded Dolour angrily.

'I dunno,' faltered her mother. She flared up momentarily at the expression on Dolour's face. 'Don't you look at me in that tone of voice, young lady, or I won't go at all!'

'Oh, won't you?' said Dolour, tipping up the shiny black bottom of the flat-iron and touching it with a sizzling wet finger. Mumma stamped after her. 'No, I won't, if I don't want to.'

'All right,' said Dolour. 'Stay home and look awful and have Dadda run off altogether with his girl friend.' Mumma went pale, for that had not entered her mind. Dolour stretched out the dress and rubbed at the egg stain. 'And then you'll have to go to work in a café washing greasy dishes all day.'

'You stop that talk,' quavered Mumma. She pressed her hand to her face. 'Oh, me nerves are all jumping and bumping fit to kill. I'll go next week.'

'And what a fool you'll feel when you remember that you could have had the whole thing over by then,' said Dolour, clouds of steam from the wet cloth rising around her. 'You go and get your stockings on.'

Miserably, talking to herself, condemning Dolour one moment and proudly thinking how much the girl thought of her mother the next, Mumma dragged up the stockings and jammed her feet into the boat-shaped shoes.

'Oooer!' she began, and then, hopefully, 'Oh, Holy Mother, me bunions are that bad I could cry.'

'Probably your bad teeth poisoning your whole body,' returned the hard-hearted girl from the kitchen.

Mumma scowled. 'It's a grand lot of sympathy I'd be getting from you, my girl, and me in me death agony.'

'Here you are, put it on,' said her callous daughter briskly, 'while I do my hair.'

Mumma snatched the dress, hating it, and then remembering she had worn it for Roie's wedding, and holding it to her breast tenderly.

'It's one thing I'll never send to the ragman.'

Upstairs she could hear Dolour bumping about, and a sudden glint flashed into her eyes. With great agility she climbed on the bed and groped about in the clots of dust on top of the wardrobe. There was her navy hat, approximately the shape of a jelly-mould, and

623

trimmed with a flute of pink ribbon. Ordinarily she loved her hat, but now she detested it. Cunningly she tipped it over the wardrobe, where it fell down into the mouldy darkness on top of all the other things that had accumulated there throughout the years, for the wardrobe weighed two tons, and could not be moved by anyone except a giant.

Giggling, Mumma continued to get dressed. When Dolour came down she was rubbing her nose with a powder puff and saying docilely, 'I suppose I'd better take a lot of clean hankies.'

Dolour was delighted. 'I'll fix that. You do look nice, too. Now, where's your hat.' She sprang upon the bed and rooted round in the well of the wardrobe. 'That's funny.' She pulled open the door, and half a dozen garments fell out and engulfed her. 'You're going to have gas, and it'll be over and done with before you know it,' she cheered, fighting her way out of the clothes and diving into the musty depths of the wardrobe.

'Gas!' sneered Mumma silently, looking with real enjoyment at Dolour's heaving form as she struggled with the fifty old shoes, cardboard boxes, and fallen, dust-stiffened garments on the wardrobe floor.

'It's not here,' said her daughter, red-faced and puzzled.

'Well, I dunno,' said Mumma. 'I musta wore it last Sunday.'

There were not many places in that room for a hat to hide. Dolour peered under the bed, snorting at all the dust and papers which had been swept under there. She came forth snorting with Motty's shoes.

'There, I told you she didn't lose them.'

'I wonder where it could be, dearie?' cried the false Mumma. 'We're going to be late if we can't find it soon.'

Slowly Dolour went over the room to the shelves in the corner, then whizzed round to face her mother.

'Hah!' she cried. Mumma wiped the expression off her face with lightning speed, but it was too late. Dolour stalked towards her. 'You hid it!' she accused.

Mumma decided to brazen it out. 'Be that as it may or isn't,' she proclaimed, 'I ain't going without me hat for no one, so if you can't find it you can wait till next week to get me teeth out.'

'Oh, you're a heart-breaker!' raged Dolour. 'After I went to all the trouble to get you an appointment, and got the afternoon off and everything! I could murder you!'

Mumma sniffed triumphantly, but she had reckoned without the spirit of her daughter.

'All right,' cried the girl. 'You can't go without a hat, but I can!'

She yanked the dark felt sailor off her head and planked it down on Mumma's amazed and tousled head. It curled up at all sides, and made Mumma look like some exotic type of long-haired padre. But she was too angry to laugh.

'You're coming if I have to drag you every foot of the way.'

Mumma peered into the glass. 'I won't go. I wouldn't be seen dead in it.'

'You'll be found dead in it if you don't pull yourself together. Think you're smart, don't you! You're just like a kid!'

Mumma had two pink patches in her cheeks. A fine and glorious temper was working up in her, but before she could frame it in suitable words, Dolour jeered, 'You're just scared, that's all. You're frightened. And you're supposed to be Irish! Oh, I'm ashamed!'

Before this insult to the nation Mumma folded up her lips so tightly they disappeared altogether, so that she looked like a missionary about to thunder hell and damnation. She took up her withered little purse and marched out, Dolour following her and silently giggling. At the front door Mumma's brief rage flickered out.

'I want to go to the back again,' she appealed.

'No you don't,' said Dolour inexorably, and she marched her Mumma down to the tram stop. It was a lovely afternoon, and Mumma should have been glad to have the children off her hands for the afternoon, for Mrs Campion was looking after them, and had promised not to feed them any rubbidge, but she wasn't, she was too mad. By the time she reached the dentist's the loathsome white-tiled place with its smell of antiseptics, and the clink of instruments sinisterly penetrating the bright bareness of the waiting-room, she was in a lather of fear, her eyes sticking out, and her fingers boring holes in her handbag. Dolour watched her sympathetically, but she knew that at the first sign of weakening Mumma would be up and off like a hare.

'You don't want to be frightened,' she said kindly. 'Remember how brave you used to be when you brought Roie and me here to have teeth out.'

Mumma gave her a look that seared her to the bone. Just then a patient tottered through from the surgery, a blood-red handkerchief pressed to his mouth. Mumma reared up on her chair.

Dolour forgot all her psychology. 'Gee, it'll all be over in a minute or two, Mumma, and it won't hurt. And you will look lovely with your new teeth, honest.'

Mumma nodded voicelessly, and when the nurse appeared she followed her without a word. Dolour relaxed. She fished in her pocket for her rosary beads, and began mechanically to say Hail Marys for her poor mother with the funny hat on, hoping the dentist wasn't the hairy old shocker he had been in her day. Though the door was closed, she could hear the clink of glass on porcelain, and the slight sound of the gas apparatus.

'Don't let him hurt her,' prayed Dolour. 'She's that upset with Dadda and everything.'

The next moment there was loud masculine exclamation, the crash of a breaking glass, and a shudder of the door as though someone had tried to come through it without bothering to open it first. Dolour jumped up, just in time to catch Mumma as she hurtled through, bug-eyed and yellow-pale, but still with all her teeth.

Behind her appeared the red angry face of the dentist, and a flustered-looking nurse.

Mumma's face twisted up like a child's and tears popped out of her eyes.

'I ain't going back in there,' she sobbed. Dolour looked apologetically at the dentist.

'I had hardly begun to examine her teeth when up she bounced out of the chair,' he expostulated. Dolour patted her mother's back. Suddenly she seemed so small, so old, that the girl gave up all hope of new teeth for her.

'She's had a lot of trouble,' she whispered.

All the way down the stairs Mumma kept sobbing, but deep down in her soul she was crowing. Dolour wiped the tears off her face and pulled the awful hat down further over her forehead.

'Me teeth are jumping like grasshoppers,' moaned Mumma. 'Oh, I can't face the tram.'

'We'll walk then,' soothed Dolour.

They passed down the crooked lanes where the slattern houses leaned close as though gossiping about dark secrets. Some had sandstone steps, cunningly placed out in the footpath to trip the drunken or shortsighted. They were worn down almost to the road level. On the balconies sat old people, sunken-mouthed, hair tightly drawn back, taking the sunshine into their brittle old bones. There was a smell of age everywhere, and of stones that had soaked up the dankness and mouldiness of winter and were now opening their pores and giving it back.

'You're ashamed of me,' lamented Mumma.

' 'Course I'm not.'

'My feet hurt that much,' said Mumma in excuse. Dolour sighed, for Mumma seemed to hurt in so many places.

'When I get my next pay we'll buy you a nice new pair of shoes,' she said.

'What about the coat you was saving up for?' asked Mumma hopefully.

'That can wait.'

Suddenly they came upon an extraordinary thing. It was a patch of blue sky where it had no business to be at all. In this place the skyline had not been seen for eighty or ninety years, and yet there it was, bright and bare between two goblin houses that looked forlorn and surprised because they had nothing to lean against.

'That's what they do to yer,' proclaimed Mumma sorrowfully.

A heap of rubble lay where the old houses had once been, and its squat shape was imprinted upon the aboriginal clay that had not been seen by the eye of man for so long. And now they saw that the houses on either side were empty-eyed, staring at the sun for perhaps the last time.

'Yairs,' said a woman leaning over a nearby fence. 'The whole terrace is coming down. Next month we go out on our heads, and my father and mother lived here before I was born.'

'Fancy,' said Mumma sympathetically.

'Old Mrs Farrell lived in that place,' said the woman, pointing with her thumb to the empty space. 'Blind, she was. Knew it like the back of her hand. Now they've pushed her into one room out at Lilyfield. Fell down the stairs the first day. Doesn't know a soul to give her a hand with the cooking or shopping. Here we all took an interest in helping old Mrs Farrell.'

'Well.' She booted a rooster back into the hall as it came striding through the house to freedom. 'That's progress for yer, love. That's progress.'

Mumma and Dolour went silently on, Mumma with a vast dread pressing on her even more painfully than her bunions.

Dolour said, 'But it might be years before they get around to Plymouth Street.'

'I dunno why they can't leave us alone,' said Mumma dully. 'I ain't ever heard anyone out Surry Hills complain about the way they lived.'

Now it was sunset, and a breeze awoke in Redfern and came leaping up the gutters, bowling the bits of paper before it. They turned into Coronation Street, a bedlam of noise, with the trams crashing and clanking round the corner, their flanges reverberating against the points as though they hated them, and the wires overhead singing on an infinitely high note. Mumma stopped before the window of a ham-and-beef-shop, where Mr Kontominos, in the midst of clearing his window for the day, was resting amongst the pickled cucumbers and the sausages, cleaning his nails with his long fork. He ducked and smiled at them.

'Oh, look at the nice brawns,' admired Mumma, looking at the glazed pink circlets of heterogeneous meat. 'Your Dadda would just love one of them for tea.'

'Let him go and run after his own brawns,' snapped Dolour.

Mumma was abashed. She wanted very much to go in and buy the delicacy, but she felt that after her carryings-on this afternoon, she had better pull her horns in a bit with Dolour. Dolour spied some tomato sausages sitting in the window-corner.

'Oh, isn't that the stuff Ro brought home one day? Charlie liked it, didn't he?'

Before Mumma could object, for it gave her the repeaters, Dolour had darted in to get some. Little Kontominos was just about to close up. He was a small, sweet-faced Greek whose hair had slid backwards over the crown of his head in an orderly retreat from life. He seemed to be worried, going to the door to peer up the street.

'What's the matter, Mr Kontominos?'

'Big trouble,' he muttered, and was wrapping up the sausages when all at once there was a roar and the trampling of many feet. Dolour found herself being pushed towards the door. The sausages were thrust into her hand, and the shilling plucked out of it, and Mr Kontominos's door banged behind her, and the bolt crashed into its socket. Bewildered, she shrank into the doorway, looking at the mass of fighting men who surged about in the street.

'Mumma!'

But where was Mumma? Panic-stricken, Dolour tried to get out of the doorway, but a bottle crashed at her feet and a splinter stuck into her ankle. The next moment two threshing figures reeled against her, and the tomato sausages were squashed into a pink blob against her chest. She shoved, and the two figures toppled out into the stream of the main battle and were swept away.

What the fight was about nobody, not even the contestants, could have said. It had started with somebody spilling somebody else's beer down a third party's coat in the Thatchers' Arms down the street, and before the police arrived four hundred men and women were involved. Now the police were here, and the majority of the crowd had turned on them, determined to prevent their arrest of anybody at all. Blue forms, crushed by superior numbers, shot up off the ground here and there, and whistles cried piercingly for help that never came.

An old woman, who had been tottering down the street with a little billy of milk, was knocked down and trodden into the pavement, and Dolour heard the shrieks of children dragged away from their mothers and lost amidst the forest of hostile legs. Ever and anon, above the roar, could be heard the blithe pipings of old men who, safe up on their balconies, leaned over rails and exhorted everyone to 'ave a lash.

'Mumma!' roared Dolour, reverting to the strong-lunged terror of her youth, and as though in answer she saw the red face of Mumma, far out on the stream with one arm jammed above her head, and a little withered handbag still clutched in it. Dolour flung herself into the crowd. Blows flew past her face, and now and then she came hard against a pair of men locked like wrestlers, crudely trying to kill each other, and not making the slightest impression. Now a punch on the shoulder thrust her hard back against a fat lady who shrieked and jabbed her in the stomach with her elbow. Mad with rage, Dolour stamped on a foot, but it didn't belong to the fat lady, and the anguished face of a friend and neighbour swept past her on the tide.

At last she reached Mumma. Mumma was spent and gasping, squashed so hard on every side that she had almost popped out of the top of her corsets.

'Oh, Dolour,' she gasped, 'I'm going to faint.'

Frantically Dolour held up her head above the crush, for she knew that if Mumma slipped and sank beneath the trampling feet she would be killed. Sobbing, sweating, she pushed off the wild faces, beating men in the chest and slapping women off Mumma until all at once she was jammed in a corner against something hard and metallic. The sound of a key in a padlock was lost in the chaos of screams, oaths, and crashing glass, for already the brighter spirits in the crowd were smashing the ends of bottles and using them as wicked weapons. The metallic bars behind her parted, and a hand rudely dragged her and Mumma inside the shelter. The same hand ruthlessly thrust back a little ragged man, who scrambled to follow them, and the grids clanged together.

'Quickly.'

Half-dead, Mumma and Dolour staggered into a dark shop. In the show-cases dimly winked brassy gold and shoddy silver. The old-clo' smell of the pawnbroker's establishment was there.

'Oh, Mr Mendel,' sobbed Mumma, 'I'm on me last legs.'

The old pawnbroker took them into the room behind the shop. It seemed to be furnished in untold luxury, with a carpet smooth under their shoes, and a polished table which showed not the usual film of bloom, but gentle reflections from a red-shaped reading lamp.

'Jeepers, lookut all the books!' gasped Dolour, her eyes wandering in awe over the shelves. There was in this room the smell of old leather, of floor polish, and a strange, sweetish tobacco.

Mumma fell into a chair. Even in this moment of stress Mr Mendel's noble white hair was neatly brushed, his black silk coat falling in classic folds about his gaunt frame. Though outside bodies crashed against his thoughtfully grated window, and hoarse yells and imprecations filled the air, he took no notice whatsoever, pressing brandy on Mumma with a courteous air as though she were his guest and nothing else mattered. Anyway, brawls had occurred outside Mr Mendel's shop so often they were merely a part of the occupational perils of his profession.

Dolour became aware that her leg was bleeding profusely. Her torn stocking was blackened with blood, and a great slow gout was bulging over the side of her shoe. In a moment it would fall on the carpet. All Dolour's fright, her anger, her physical stress, her terror for Mumma's safety, became concentrated on one small point – she could not let her blood soil the beautiful blue carpet. She held her ankle, not knowing what to do with it, pressing her grubby handkerchief against the wound.

'It's nothing,' she said, embarrassed. 'A bottle hit me. It's just a bit of a mess.'

She giggled, abashed, as she saw, hovering in the farther shadows of the room, another man. He was pale, fattish fellow, with dark and sullen eyes, a soft white neck, and a look, deep down under unfamiliar contours, of familiarity. Dolour's gaze fastened on him piercingly. In a moment she was twelve, with short socks, and shoes with henpecked toes, and there was all around her the gaudy rowdiness of the Paddy's Markets – and Roie – and she was looking at a scarlet shawl on an old-clo' stall.

'Tommy!' she cried, and then was unsure, and turned her face away and blushed. She was aware that a most extraordinary change had come over her Mumma. Lying back in the chair, smelling strongly of brandy, and still looking pale she was, but the next moment her face flushed darkly and she turned her head as though by compulsion and stared at the young man.

'My nephew Tommy,' said Mr Mendel, motioning the young man closer. He limped forward diffidently, not wanting to show himself, and yet putting a bold front on it.

'Hullo, Mrs Darcy,' he said.

'How are yer?' said Mumma, not wanting to know at all.

'Gee, Tommy Mendel!' marvelled Dolour. 'I'd forgotten all about you. You went clean outa me mind.'

'Thanks,' he grunted.

Dolour stared at him, trying to find the slender, delicate boy he once had been in this sickly-looking fat young man. He could not have been older than twenty-six or seven, but he looked well into his thirties. His belt was stuck out a little over a balcony of stomach, and she had grown so much in stature that she thought he had grown shorter. Tommy stared covertly back, trying to place the tall dark girl as the stumpy-legged, loud-voiced child he remembered. Disconcerted, he looked at Mumma.

'How's old Ro these days?'

Mumma's face was sickly. 'She's been dead over eighteen months,' she said. Dolour stared angrily at Tommy, whose life had gone on without his knowing that Roie was dead, or hardly caring that he knew. He was astounded.

'My God, what knocked her off? She couldna been more than twenty-four!'

Cripes, Roie! The first girl he'd ever had. He remembered her soft hair and the way her eyes glimmered in the dark, and her soft lips, not knowing how to kiss, but wanting to. That kid! Dead as a doornail. Dead as she ever could be. Tree shadows, and the cool, nedley grass, and trams casting yellow flares across the grass, and Roie crying and not knowing how to say no. And now she was dead for all that time, the way he well might be next year with his chest, and the way coughs hung on, tearing the guts outa him all winter. And the bad taste he had in his mouth when he got up, and his bell burning like acid after he'd had a drink, the way he might have been an old bastard instead of only in his twenties.

He stared at Mumma, waxy with shock and fear, and Dolour thought, 'I was wrong. He does care. I remember him going out with Roie. He musta liked her, even though nothing came of it.'

'Get some water and some cloths to bathe the girl's ankle,' said old Mr Mendel curtly, but Mumma heaved to her feet, crying, 'Don't you touch her, you – you – ' To see her mother there, her face puffy and scarlet with rage, her eyes glittering, defeated by her inarticulateness, struggling for words to express an emotion Dolour couldn't understand, appalled the girl.

'Mumma, whatever's the matter?'

Mumma seized her by the arm and began pulling her towards the door.

'Not that way,' said old Mr Mendel quietly, guiding Mumma towards the back entrance. Mumma struck his arm down, pushing rudely past him, and dragging Dolour willy-nilly, so that she had time for no more than an appealing, bewildered glance at the old pawnbroker before she was stumbling down the steps into the cool quiet of the clean cobbled yard, where a frangipani-tree bloomed whitely in a mist of fragrance.

'Mumma, he was kind to us!' she cried, but it was no good. Her mother pushed her through the gateway, and the gate slammed like a final word.

'You must be mad!' cried Dolour furiously. 'Acting like a lunatic! I'm going back in to thank him.'

Then she saw to her dismay that Mumma was crying like a child, her face screwed up, and the tears pouring down without any effort to stop or hide them.

'My little girl!' she sobbed. 'My poor little girl!'

And she went on sobbing and lamenting in words that had no meaning, and sentences that had no relation to each other, till even in that locality where people fought and screamed and made love

632

publicly, women came to scullery windows and men looked over back fences to see what was happening.

At last Dolour managed to get her up the lane which abutted on Plymouth Street, and there, Mumma, exhausted by her grief, subsided a little, hiding her face on Dolour's shoulder and saying, 'You'll be ashamed of me, but it's been bottled up that long.'

'What has, Mumma? Tell me what's the matter,' whispered Dolour, unutterably distressed.

'That feller,' said Mumma, and in the bitterness of her soul she burst out with that which had been a secret in her heart for seven years or more. 'That Tommy Mendel. I hoped and prayed that I'd never have to lay eyes on him again, and now I have I feel just as bad as I usta.'

'But what's he done?' whispered Dolour.

'If it hadn't been for him maybe Roie wouldn't have died,' said Mumma, and she gave a great gulp and forced down the sorrow that was rising like a flood in her chest once more. 'I've tried to forgive him, and I've prayed for him, but somehow when I saw him there tonight, large as life and not even caring what he'd done – I coulda spit in his eye,' ended Mumma forlornly.

A chilliness seized Dolour, a feeling that forbade her even to speak.

'He got around her, and she had a baby by him,' blurted Mumma, unable to go any longer without sharing her trouble. 'And before it came them sailors caught her in the street and kicked her, and it died.'

'Roie!' breathed Dolour, trembling. 'Roie!'

'I thought you mighta guessed, when she was so sick,' said Mumma, 'but anyway you're big enough now to know what she went through, and it wasn't her fault, neither, poor little innocent, thinking she was in love with him,' and she wandered off into comforting denunciations of Tommy, not noticing Dolour's silence as they went slowly between the tall bare fences and the swinging, dilapidated gates.

'The doctor didn't say that was the reason things went wrong at the birth, but I always felt it mighta been. Oh, Roie! Roie!' and Mumma broke down and wept miserably, her feet hurting, and her dress all torn with the brawl, and the hat feeling like a barrel-hoop on her forehead, and her teeth still in, and no hope of nice white glistening ones any more.

'I suppose Motty is giving Mrs Campion what-for,' she said,

brightening a little. In some strange way she felt relieved, as though Dolour had lifted a load from her shoulders.

Dolour went up to her room, sitting on the bed with Mikey, and not seeing anything. Her last dream had fallen. So even Roie, gentle, delicate little Roie, had known the darkness and despair, the unutterable grief and sorrow of disillusionment when it comes in early girlhood.

'Nothing could have made Roie a bad girl,' said Dolour to the darkening room.

She had expected to feel disgust, anger, disappointment, anything but what she did feel, an understanding at last of love and its pitfalls for the innocent and trusting, of the agonies Roie had suffered, and that perhaps had made her what she was in her wifehood and womanhood. It had come at last, that understanding, and she did not know that it marked the end of her childhood and the opening door of her maturity. She pressed the child into her shoulder's hollow, breathing in the smell of its flesh, and it was as though she embraced Roie, her sins, and tears, and the anguish of her last good-bye, her defenceless shrinking before the hard and callous world.

'Charlie had the best in the world when he had you,' she said to her sister.

In the next room Charlie stood listening, thinking she was speaking to the baby. He wanted to go in and watch her attending to the child, and know that if he spoke she would understand him, and if he was silent she would know why. He had been so long without human companionship, marooned on the isle of his own grief and self-absorption, and now he needed the comfort of her presence, the balm that her quietness would apply to wounds that were healing a little.

For the first time in a long while he stood up straight, as though the load had grown lighter – or he had grown stronger under the load.

Twenty-one

So it was Christmas again, and those that were left were still together, which was the main thing. Down in Pump Lane, and all the way up the crooked elbow of Grave Street were fallen bricks, and fences standing up round nothing at all, a sad confusion to the drunks who went looking for steps to sit on and found only emptiness. But in Plymouth Street the old plane-trees put on their yellow leaves for Christmas, and the houses nodded together as they had done for nearly a century.

'They might get tired of it before they come to us,' said Mumma darkly, as she creaked cautiously about the house at six o'clock, with the clear untarnished sunshine splashing on the floor and showing up the dirt something terrible. And although it was the third Christmas since Roie died, and the day brought back memories sharp and sorrowful, Mumma burst into *Adeste Fideles* and swung open the scullery window, letting in a frightful smell that nearly lifted the hair off.

For there was Lick Jimmy standing in his yard burning fishbones and singing like a tomcat.

'Merry Christmas, Lick,' coughed Mumma.

'Melly Clismus, Misser Darcy,' chirruped Lick. 'Loger Bubba just gone in to see you.'

'The dear little fellow,' said Mumma warmly, picking up her floor-cloth. But she had hardly reached the kitchen door before a small tornado struck her amidships, and a large tornado took her by the shoulders and turned her round.

'Don't you look!' cried Dolour.

'If you do we'll kick you in the bottom,' cooed Motty. So Mumma waited, with Motty's black shiny head burrowing into her, and her grubby hands clutching her thighs.

'You can look now. Merry Christmas!' cried Dolour, and there on the table, arranged in a nest of tissue, was a pink woolly cardigan. With sparkling eyes Mumma looked on its softness and prettiness, but she was overwhelmed with flailing arms and enthusiastic kisses. Tears came into her eyes.

635

'Ah, you're good girls,' she said. It was almost like having Roie again to have the two of them giving her a surprise together. 'But you shouldn'ta bought anything for me. I don't need anything.'

Every Christmas she solemnly cautioned her family not to buy her anything, and every Christmas she hoped they wouldn't take any notice. Then she had a terrible feeling, for as she straightened out the cardigan she saw it was much too small. It hadn't been built for her bottle-shoulders and fifty-inch bust, and once her arms jammed into the sleeves they would bend like boomerangs. Her disappointment was so great she nearly cried, but stronger than that was the knowledge that she couldn't let Dolour and Motty know. She stammered, 'Me hands are all black from the coal. I'll try it on after I got the dinner going.'

'Aw, come on, Gran'ma!'

Mumma didn't know what to do, but just then Hughie came out of the bedroom, his hair sticking up, his braces hanging down his back like a tangled tail, and a yawn unrolling down his face like a blind.

'Compliments of the season,' said Mumma shyly, looking at him yearningly, as though expecting that her prayers had come true and he would stump over to her and give her the kiss that would tell her he was her own husband again. But Motty jumped at him and yelled, 'What did you get for me? You promised me a doll's pram with a red handle and real wheels.'

Hughie looked helplessly at Mumma. He was ashamed to tell Motty that he had never had any intention of buying her a doll's pram, in spite of his lavish drunken promises, so he pulled away from her clutching hands and said, 'We'll see about that some other time,' and went into the laundry and shut the door.

Motty stood as though he had slapped her face. Her eyes filled with tears and her lip stuck out so far that it nearly cast a shadow. She threw herself at the door, kicking it and wrenching at the knob, yelling, 'You're a bloody liar! You didn't get it! And you promised! You promised, you dirty, stinking old liar!'

Dolour and Mumma were filled with dismay.

'Don't you go speaking to your grandpop like that, Moira, or you'll get a belting. The like of it!'

'Look, Motty, look!' Dolour pulled a package out of her pocket. 'I got you a present.'

Motty glared through her tears. She tore the paper off rudely. It was a string of green beads, each painted in red and gold like a tiny Chinese lantern. Motty clutched them to her breast and howled, 'Oh, I told Roger Lick and Betty Brody and Fatso Kennedy and everyone I was getting a doll's pram!'

'He could have got her something,' said Dolour bitterly.

Mumma tightened her mouth. 'It's her father's job to get a doll's pram, not Hughie's anyway,' and she lifted a foot to land a good one on Dirty Dick's rusty tassel of tail, recollecting his needle claws just in time to draw her foot back smartly.

Hughie sluiced his face over the tub. The water was dank and already warm from the sun-drenched pipes. He spat it out and wished he had a drink. There was a sickish feeling in his stomach, and his head was stuffed with wet paper. He sat for a while on the laundry step, blinking at the blazing sky and swallowing at the poignant smell of Lick's fishbones.

'I coulda saved up for it,' he groaned. 'Sixpence a week ain't much. Poor kid. I ain't much good to her or anyone else. I coulda pawned something,' and his thoughts went dolefully to Mr Mendel's shop where most of his clothing already hung.

'It's going to be God's own misery in the winter,' he thought, for he knew that he could never redeem them. Then he forgot all about Motty and the rest and not having a present for any of them, with the worry that was in his mind about Florentina.

He was physically exhausted, and the wild flare of passion for her had almost gone, but he couldn't see that it was his fault. She just didn't take much notice of him any more, that was the reason. Once, above all the others, she had liked him best. But now it was different. He was just another customer, and not a particularly welcome one, either. Always the woman Seppa hung round, scowling, reluctant to let him in. And the black boy Lex dogged Florentina like a faithful hound.

'If she's got someone else, someone special,' he thought with piteous ferocity. But the fear of losing her was not as great as the fear of realizing that he was too old and too poor to hold her interest.

'She's only a bitch, anyway,' he said, and rose to his feet feeling strong and contemptuous, for the moment, above all women and all male weakness. Lick Jimmy's shrunken face popped up above the fence.

'Too much pooey for you?' he inquired, waving with his eyebrows towards the smoke.

637

'Ah, shurrup,' growled Hughie. He stumped inside and there was Mumma teetering precariously on the rickety table, with Motty and her brother sitting expectantly underneath it, waiting for the crash. She was trying to unhook the Christmas pudding from the rafter where it had swung, a shrivelled black cannonball, shunned by flies and looked at askance by cockroaches, for the last six months.

'For gawsake,' protested Hugh, seizing his wife by the legs, 'do yer want to smash at me feet like a cup?'

She wanted to be dignified, but she was too delighted, and she said, 'Oh, get out!' and passed the pudding down and lumbered to the floor.

For the first time in a long time a pang of pity entered his heart and he thought, 'Poor old cow. She don't get much outa life.'

She said appealingly, 'You'll come to one of the Masses, Hugh?'

'Say the eleven o'clock,' said Hughie, avoiding her eyes by busily examining the pudding-cloth for toothmarks. Mumma sighed, for it was a sung Mass, and what with all the getting up and sitting down and forming fours that went on, it was a trial even to a devoted Catholic like herself, let alone Hughie. She had known all along that he wouldn't go, Christmas and all as it was, but she had hoped wistfully that her instincts were on the wrong track.

'Well, we'll get going then,' she said, resigned. 'Your breakfast's in the oven, don't let the egg get leathery, and the pudding's to go in the pot at half-past nine. And you gotta be careful with Mikey if he's in the yard that he don't eat any broken glass.'

'Ah, I've had kids, too, haven't I?' suddenly thundered Hughie, and Mumma backed out, vowing to herself that for all she cared he could sizzle like a sausage for the want of a prayer.

She and Motty and Dolour went sedately into the church, into its brown silence, and with pleasure Mumma sniffed the archaic smell of the incense, which had been floating in invisible clouds among the rafters ever since Holy Thursday. All along the row of brass candlesticks twinkled the stars of the candle-flames, and the altar cloth was starched so stiffly and ironed so smoothly that the stars were dimly reflected there, too. Even Motty, such a restless, difficult little pagan, was awed. She twisted around and stared up at the choir-loft, and there was Mr Siciliano leaning over, looking with beaming interest at the latecomers. He had once been slender and romantic with hair like black Florentine silk, but now he had an equator, and a bald spot from which radiated locks grey and straight, except at the ends where they kinked desperately in memory of the old days. Mr Siciliano had little claims staked out all over church. There was Michelangelo at the altar, and in the front row were Rosina and Violetta in their Children of Mary blue cloaks and over with the Holy Name Society was Gio making big black sparkling eyes at the girls, and towards the back was Mama, with Tonetta, expecting a child herself, helping her to keep an eye on Julio, Albertino, and Redempta, and Van, who was named after Mama's favourite film star.

'This next bambino,' thought Mr Siciliano, 'we call him Finito, and perhaps God tak-a the hint.'

'Yoo-hoo, Mr Siciliano!' cried Motty benevolently.

'Sssh!' hissed Mumma, and Motty's protests were drowned in a wild moo from the organ as it chased the choir into full flight.

'Look, there's Daddy!' cried Motty, dragging at Dolour's arm. She looked, amazed, at Charlie's dark head, away over in the transept beside a pillar, as though he had slunk in a side door so that no one would see him. A warm, glad astonished feeling filled her heart, she did not know why.

'Well!' said Mumma, reluctantly letting some ironic remark pass by just because of the season and her circumstances, 'I won't say it ain't time.'

'*Et-a in terra, pax-a hominibus!*' cried Mr Siciliano's harsh soaring tenor, which all the years of shouting 'Fin-a broccoli, lempence da punch! Two-a pob da grapis!' had done nothing to impair. In between the triumphant phrases he scowled at the basso, Mr Dugan from the fish-and-chips, who was booming away like a bee, fighting with the organ for the lowest place, and the contralto, who sounded as though she were singing down a bottle. But the good hearts were there, and Father Cooley, moving round the altar and trying not to bellow when he genuflected, so bad was his back, felt proud of his people, especially when they joined in the singing. It was strange, those labourers and shop people and ordinary down-at-heel housewives singing the archaic and hallowed music of the Church, which had once run in square notes along monkish paper.

'Oh, Lord,' prayed Father Cooley, 'the times have changed, but their hearts haven't, and there's so much good in them I feel small.'

He raised his eyes to the dazzling brass doors of the Tabernacle, and was rewarded by the reflection of his youngest altar boy, Michelangelo Siciliano, dangling his rosary beads from his ear.

After Communion Dolour sank into herself, shutting the doors one after another until she was deep in her own heart, wondering, asking, answering. The great problems that had once seemed such insuperable obstacles to her rose again, but her peace of mind was not disturbed. The mysteries remained, but she saw them as mountains to be climbed later, not now, when she was too young and too small. From somewhere patience had come. Once she had wept because the great miracles of religion were all repulsive when she looked at them closely. Calvary was a butcher's block, and Joan of Arc a charred skeleton, and who'd be able to look on Stephen, the beautiful young man with his blue Israelite eyes pits of bloody dust, and his brains trickling over the broken stones? But now it was different, and she couldn't understand why.

'I've grown up,' said Dolour wonderingly.

Somewhere in her heart she found her sister, for in possessing God she possessed all the dead. She felt as though Roie were only standing in a dark room. Or perhaps she was the one in the darkness, unable to see the bright figure lost in the light.

'Roie,' she whispered. And, all at once, with a shock not of shame or guilt, but only of astonishment that she had not consciously realized it before, she said, 'I love Charlie.'

A blush burned up from her inmost depths and she buried her face in her hands. 'Roie, I love Charlie!'

Now it was all explained, her loathing and terror of the wicked and vulgar and ludicrous things in her life, her amazement that love did not seem to be the joyous and cleanly thing she had dreamed. She had matched all those boys with him and they had fallen short; she had stacked all her own experiences against the sweetness Roie had known with Charlie, not knowing she had done it. All men were not like Charlie, but she hadn't known why until now.

She had never heard of anyone loving a dead sister's husband, she did not know whether it was wrong or impossible or foolish. She only knew that he did not love her and probably never would. At the thought of the battles unfought, the sorrows unexperienced, the years to be travelled, alone, uncompanioned, tears sprang unasked into her eyes, and she stared at the altar and hardly saw Father Cooley lifting his hands laboriously and blessing them in a voice which suddenly sounded old and tired.

'Never mind,' whispered Mumma, and her warm hand gave Dolour's arm a squeeze. 'He'll realize he's doing wrong and come back to us after a while.'

Dolour blinked away her tears and nodded and smiled, knowing that Mumma was talking about Hughie, for whom she had prayed and yearned all through Mass.

Outside Little Ryan Street a small crowd had collected in the hot sunshine that beat down and ran like honey into every crack and cranny. Mumma and Dolour and Motty stood there gawking with the rest.

'What's 'appening?'

'Oh, it's crool! Who'da thought it, eh, and her with the stren'th of ten when it comes to bashing johns over the ned.'

Mumma's new hat, a grey straw with a lovely bunch of poppies and sweet-pea and those little blue cornflowers that nobody ever saw nowadays, was as tight as a nut on a bolt, but she stood as though it were a crown, conscious of her Christmas newness, and the white shine of her soul. For once Motty had stayed clean, and for the moment her little face looked up out of her white sun hat like an Italian angel's, as richly coloured as wine. Mumma held her hand so tightly that Motty was compelled to direct her energies in subtle directions. She sneaked a piece of red chalk out of her pocket and began furtively to draw cats on the skirt of a woman standing in front of her.

In the shadowy depths of Mrs Stock's house there was a crash and a frightful torrent of blasphemy as someone fell down the stairs.

'I remember the time old Mrs Purcell had the stroke up there,' breathed someone, 'and the coffin got wedged on them stairs. Had to take her out, all stiff and cold, before they could get it down.'

'Glory-ory!' gasped Mumma. 'You're not telling me that Delie Stock's dead?'

But the next moment a flustered ambulance man, red in the face, with a great streak of dirt across his white coat, appeared, and behind him in the stretcher was Delie herself, half sitting up and haranguing the stretcher-bearers with the full of her tongue.

The little crowd backed into a compact heap, it was so strange to be seeing her, the immortal, the indestructible, getting shovelled into an ambulance as though she were an ordinary old woman.

'Go on, get out of here!' croaked Delie, vermilion patching her floury-white cheeks, and her dark eyes, sunken with pain and sickness, coming to life for a moment and shooting sparks. 'It ain't a monkey-show. Who're yer gawking at? By God Almighty, I'll move yer meself!'

641

And she heaved on the stretcher and the blanket fell off, showing the rest of her clad in a fancy pink silk nightdress splotched all over with spilt food and medicine and God-knows-what, and the hem of it pitch black from long trailing in the dirt.

'Lie still, madam,' said the second ambulance man, pushing her gently down again. Delie erupted like a volcano, screaming curses, then all at once she shrank into herself, clutching her chest and coughing hard as though there were something sharp stuck into her chest-wall. Tears came into her eyes, whether with coughing or emotion none could say, and suddenly her face crumpled up and she sobbed, 'I ain't coming back, you know. I ain't coming back here any more.'

'Now, now,' soothed the man, motioning his companion to lift the stretcher into the ambulance.

'Now, now me big black foot, you starched bastard,' sobbed Delie. Out of the doorway of the ambulance, looking like a raddled, sick old bird in all that white-enamelled austerity, she looked at the crowd with a yearning, longing expression. They were nothing to her; she had battened on their menfolk, starved their children, lured and bullied their daughters. She had fed them filthy liquor and taken them down every way she knew, but they were Surry Hills to her, the little scuttling beetles who had looked up to her as their spokesman, who came to her when they were in trouble. They were her people, and she would never see them again.

'Well, here's mud in yer eye,' she croaked. An old woman in the crowd darted forward and squeezed her foot, which was all she could reach.

'They can't kill you, Delie, never you fear,' she cried. Delie brightened up amazingly. The warmth of the crowd's feeling touched her in that chilly place where she had gone since she learned that her heart would never get better.

'Carm on, give us a kiss, you old ratbag.'

The old woman's puckered lips touched her cheek as she bent forward.

'That's more like it.' Her gaze took in the crowd. 'There's ten cases of bombo in me backyard, and youse can split it up between youse.'

The ambulance door clicked, and amid a ragged cheer Delie Stock left Surry Hills.

'God bless 'er,' said Mumma. 'She's a bad woman, but she's done

642

more good than a lot who'd like to think God's got a pair of wings on the hook for them.'

She spotted the red hieroglyphics on the skirt of the woman near by and, full of horror, dragged Motty away and up the street before she was discovered.

'And you just after going to Christmas Mass and seeing the little Baby in the crib and everything,' she scolded. 'Just wait till the Sisters get you in their dear kind hands when school opens,' she added pleasurably. A look of inward absorption came over Motty's face. She had inspected the Sisters minutely as they filed into church, and it seemed to her that they had stomachs to be kicked just like anyone else.

It was still early, and so Mumma hissed over the fence to Mrs Campion for her rabbit, which Mrs Campion had been keeping on the ice for her. Mrs Campion was busy cooking, her blouse undone nearly to her middle, her red face downy and dewy with sweat.

'Gawd,' said Mrs Campion, lifting up an arm and scratching under it lingeringly. 'You oughta see what the family give me for Christmas, love. A lovely fur. Real rabbit. It's that warm I nearly 'ad a fit when I tried it on for size.' She sighed with pleasure. 'Watcher get?'

'A pink cardigan,' said Mumma complacently. 'The high-class sort. Only it don't fit. Too small. I dunno what musta come over Dolour.'

Mrs Campion sympathized. 'Never mind, love. It just goes to show you don't look as big as you are.'

'No,' agreed Mumma, the thought dawning pleasurably, and she pulled in her middle as though to prove to Mrs Campion that she was right.

'And 'ere's yer bunny,' said her neighbour, swiftly handing the frozen red corpse over the fence. Mumma whisked it into a tea-towel and waddled inside. Nobody in the house would eat rabbit, but Mumma reckoned that well covered in gravy they wouldn't know the difference. She hurriedly dissected it and hid it under-neath the roasting fowl from which delicous odours rose in such profusion that Mumma's breakfastless stomach burst into a soprano song of praise. Chook came only once a year, and Mumma loved it.

She was happy. She went again and again to look at the pink cardigan, and the box of face powder, ostensibly from Motty, and the green hankies from Michael, which she loved as much as if

Mikey himself had toddled out, a spare napkin under his arm, and bought them himself. Mumma didn't expect anything from Hughie, for he never gave anyone anything, but she did think Charlie might have come across with something. She went about her cooking and table-laying steaming gently about this, for Charlie, even though he was off work such a lot, must have had a little bit put aside, and he could have spared a thought for his mother-in-law who wore her feet to the bone looking after his children.

'I can't stand the mean ones,' she confided to Mikey, who was trotting about with a mouth full of pumpkin seeds, which he spat out one at a time with an effect like shot. He was a beautiful child, his hair still silvery white and his eyes sparkling like blue beads. He grinned and Mumma melted.

'I didn't get anything for him, either, come to that,' she admitted, 'but that's different.'

It was no good. Though she tried to be sober for Roie's dear sake, the happiness of Christmas overcame her, and she sang loudly as she went about her work. As she was dishing up, Hughie popped his head in the door.

' 'Course you know Mr Reilly's coming to dinner,' he said.

Mumma couldn't believe her ears. She looked in dismay at her husband. 'Hughie, you didn't oughter! Not without telling me!'

'It sorta popped out last night when I was having a drink with him,' confessed Hughie, a little shamefaced. 'Poor little cow, up there with not a soul in the world to call his own.'

'You got no right,' burst out Mumma. 'You know I like to keep Christmas dinner in the family. I suppose you'll be asking Lick Jimmy in next.'

Hughie didn't know what else to do, so he got angry. 'That's a nice thing to hear from you, just back from Communion and everything. You can sling off at me being tired out and missing church, but I got more feeling for the poor lonely little bastard upstairs than you or any other holy moses in this house.'

He slammed out of the door, and Mumma stood upset and undecided, feeling that perhaps he was right and she was mean. A hotness came over her at the very thought, and she put the plate of food she had just dished up into Dolour's hands and said, 'That'll be for Mr Reilly, then.'

'What about you?' protested Dolour.

'Oh, there's plenty here yet,' said Mumma falsely and mournfully, and she scraped the last few dried peas out of the pot and added potatoes and a few shreds from the rabbit's bones, and splashed some gravy from the pan over all. She could have cried as she saw the little, forlorn heap of food in the middle of the plate's white desert, and she resolved to leave it just like that, just to show Mr Bumper Reilly that he couldn't come bursting into the middle of other people's Christmas dinner without depriving them. Then, as she heard his timid squeak outside the door, her natural generosity overcame her, and she hastily spread out the food over the plate, arranging the potatoes so that it would look as though she had as much as everyone else.

Mr Reilly was shaved to the very bone. He had been up since six o'clock preparing for this great event, and his collar, though unironed, was as white as paper. His little pug face had shrunken until a saucer could have covered it, and out of it his weak eyes looked apologetically.

'I bought along a little something, Mr Darcy, for your kindness,' he said, tendering a long parcel. It was two bottles of the cheapest, most potent port, which he had bought out of the remains of the six pounds he had earned the previous week when the Council, out of the charity of its heart, had put old-age pensioners to a week's sweeping of paths and weeding of parks. The rest of the money Mr Reilly had put towards an interesting purchase which he intended to use at the very end of his life.

'I don't want any of your porpoises' coffins,' he often said to himself, his little chin trembling with pride.

'God keep the man!' roared Hughie now, and he kissed the bottles resoundingly on their cool smooth side.

Mumma sniffed. She slapped down the last plate and said gallantly, 'Well, Merry Christmas, Mr Reilly, I'm sure.'

At the sight of the steaming food Mr Reilly's eyes watered, and a piercing arpeggio sounded from under his waistcoat.

'And plenty to fill that little tin-can, too,' said Hughie cordially. They all sat down in the dizzy heat, with Motty sitting between Dolour and Mumma, and fixing baleful eyes on Mr Reilly, who dropped his gaze to his plate. He was terrified of Motty. She reached out with her short legs as far as she could, but Mr Reilly had tucked his underneath the chair. Dolour gave her a sideways glare, which Motty understood perfectly.

'You take them away from me and I'll cut holes in your stockings,' said Motty, her brown paw flying protectively to her beads.

Dolour did not dare to look at Charlie for fear she would blush, but he kept stealing looks at her, wondering if she were cross with him for something. He had a present for her, and he didn't know how to give it to her. For the first time he felt self-conscious with her.

Mumma, standing her knife and fork up on their feet, beamed round the table. She was so hot she felt she would pop, but it was Christmas, and the pudding was hubble-bubbling in the pot in the most satisfactory manner. With a sigh of relief she turned to her meagre helping.

'Criminy!' Hughie dived into his plate and held up a leg dripping with gravy. 'I can just see this bolting across the paddock with a pack of dogs yelping after it.'

Mumma blushed guiltily, and Mr Reilly cheeped helpfully, 'Some fowls have tremenjus shinbones.'

Mumma flared up. 'And some people never know when to be grateful.'

The suppressed resentment in her soul surged up through the happiness, and she yearned to crack Charlie over the head with a plate for not giving her anything, and tell Mr Bumper Reilly off good and proper.

'Ah, shut up!' snarled Hughie. 'Here.' He poured out a cupful of the port and shoved it at Mr Reilly, who snorted it down to drown his embarrassment. He had already been shouted a couple of beers that morning, and the port hit them and gave off an umbrella-shaped canopy of smoke. The fumes rose to his head, and he saw Mumma's face as a full red moon, sinister and unpleasant.

'And don't you go listening to my door, neither,' he said challengingly, choking down a mouthful of seasoning and almost hearing it sizzle as it struck the burning lake in his stomach.

Mumma was shocked, as if a mouse had snarled at her. She rose from the table, taking her plate with her, and Charlie suddenly broke his silence and said, 'Oh, sit down, nothing's the matter.'

'I beg yours,' said Mumma haughtily. 'You're a nice one to be complaining about anybody, and you so tight-fisted you couldn't even buy anyone a present.'

Mr Reilly gulped down another cupful of port, and Hughie kept him company.

'Oh, Mumma,' protested Dolour, 'how do you know Charlie hasn't got you anything?'

For she had helped him to choose a gift for Mumma, and was terrified in case Mumma alienated him before it was given.

'Insulting a guest,' shrilled Mr Reilly suddenly. 'Owww!' Motty had managed it at last, and her hard-toed little shoe made a chip in Mr Reilly's brittle shin. 'You little hell-cat, you want your bottom heated.'

Mikey, who had been gazing from one to the other with trembling lip and wide-open eyes, could not bear the angry voices any longer. He began to howl like a wolf, and Dolour picked him up and hugged him tightly.

'You ought to be ashamed of yourself, Mumma,' she hissed, and Mumma waddled out to the scullery with the air of an affronted queen. There was a great washday smell, the clang of a dropped lid, and a chump from Puffing Billy, then the pudding appeared, a steaming black boulder of a thing, strangely depressed and gibbous, and exuding a limp smell of wet dates.

'Strike!' gasped Hughie. 'It's a sod!'

And so it was. The water had got to it, and it lay upon the plates in crumbling slabs. But to Mr Reilly's starved eyes it looked rich and rare, and he wolfed it greedily.

'You'll vomit if you eat like that,' prophesied Motty darkly.

Her lips compressed with her hunger, and the great disappointment of the pudding that had been made with such high hopes, Mumma sat down.

'There's six threepences and four sixpences in it,' she said, morosely, and brightened a little when there was a murmur of approval at her generosity. Motty began to gobble furiously. But the first find was made by Mr Reilly.

'Now you'll have good luck all the year round,' said Mumma begrudgingly.

Mr Reilly brought the little silver thing close to his eyes and beheld the image of some old Roman saint who had hung up his head on a gate-spike some nineteen hundred years before. It was a holy medal, which Mumma had put in by mistake, and sick with rage and disappointment and port Mr Reilly rose to his full five foot three and proclaimed, 'I'm an Episcopalian.'

'Be careful of your language,' flared Mumma.

'Don't you speak to my missus like that,' cried Hugh, the pudding suddenly acting within him in a dreadful fashion, and he leaned across the table and snatched at Mr Reilly, who jammed his chair back and squawked with courage that amazed himself, 'Keep your rotten Christmas dinner!' and made for the door. It was so exhilarating not to be frightened that he turned at the door and yelled, 'And don't think I don't know you snoop through the keyhole when you think I'm not noticing!'

Hughie choked down another cup of port and began to rampage round the room, sick with remorse at poor Bumper's hurt feelings, and furious at his unpardonable breach of the laws of hospitality. Mumma sat answering up bravely for a while, and trying to eat her pudding. Finally she gave it up and cowered in her chair, tears running down her face, for the dinner had been awful, and the place just not the same as it had been when Roie and Grandma were there.

For a while Charlie took no notice, for he had found out that fights in that house boiled up quickly and ebbed just as fast, except when some outsider put his spoke in. But after a while he grew sick of it. He jumped up and thrust Hughie out of the room. Hughie had been a valiant fighter in his day, but he was like clay in the stronger grip and longer reach of the young man, and all he could do was to pick up the depleted pudding as he was borne struggling past, and whang it at the fence, where it dribbled in a wet black star instantly covered with a swarm of rapturous ants.

Hughie was livid. The humiliation of being marched out like a misbehaving child, and by someone who wasn't even a member of the family, went to his head, where it formed an explosive mixture with the beer, the port, and the orange cocktail he had been surreptitiously slugging all the morning.

'You shoulda left him alone, Charlie,' wailed Mumma as a boot thudded against the locked door. 'Oh, he'll perform now! And I went to Communion this morning and now I'm angry, and me tongue with wicked words tottering on the tip of it.'

Hughie's distorted face appeared momentarily at the scullery window, as he jumped up and down trying to catch a glimpse of Charlie. Motty shrieked with delight, and the baby hid his face on Dolour's shoulder.

'Come on out here and I'll smash yer black face in!' roared Hughie, and then, to some invisible onlooker, 'And you, too, you ice-slinging bonehead, come on in here and I'll pull out your tripe and feed it to the cat!'

648

'That's Mr Campion,' shuddered Mumma, 'and him sixteen stone if he's a day.'

'I'll go out and shut him up,' said Charlie, but Dolour put her hand on his arm.

'You know it's no use. He'll get over it if he doesn't think anyone is listening.' She struggled for words. 'Mumma, Charlie's bought you an electric iron for Christmas.'

'I wouldn't use one of them dangerous things,' said Mumma sulkily, and, remembering her manners, added reluctantly, 'Not that I don't appreciate the thought.'

'That's a nice way to put it,' cried Dolour, suddenly losing her temper. 'I don't suppose you realize how much electric irons cost! I suppose you think Charlie didn't save up for weeks to get it for you. Don't say thank you, will you?'

'Oh, what's it matter?' asked Charlie. He pushed his chair back. 'I'm going out for a while.'

They heard the front door slam, Dolour's lips trembled. 'You make it so pleasant for him, don't you?'

'Getting awful careful of his feelings, ain't you?' sneered Mumma hotly, and was too angry to see how Dolour turned away to hide her face. Meanwhile Hughie, having insulted one neighbour, had turned on Lick Jimmy, and they could hear him trying to climb the fence and falling back on the garbage can, his voice rising to a scream of fury, 'Rice-eating magpies, ain't yer never heard of the White Australia policy? Yi, yi, muckakili!' he chanted in hideous travesty of Lick's language. Mumma flushed scarlet.

'That's the end!' she declared. 'I'm not having him insulting poor little Lick after all he's done for us. That finishes it. I'm going to get a policeman.'

Dolour sighed. It was Mumma's grand gesture, and never carried out. Mumma would no sooner have put Hughie or anyone else in the cold cells on Christmas Day than she would have jumped off the Bridge. She bolted down the passage out into the street, and Dolour resignedly began to stack the dishes. It was just another fiasco to her, and she burned passionately to be out of it and away from it for all time.

Now, in all her life, Mumma had gone for the policeman only four or five times, and had always taken great care not to find one. But this time there was one just outside in Plymouth Street standing dutifully in a shady doorway, wiping his neck with his handkerchief and longing for the evening. It was too late for Mumma to draw back. He had heard the shouting voice, and saw her distressed red face. In less than no time she was waddling up the road beside him, trying to keep her anger up to fever heat, and feeling nothing but a Judas.

Meanwhile Dolour had gone into the yard. 'You'd better shut up. Mumma's gone for the cops, and she means it!' she threatened.

Hughie couldn't believe such treachery, but all the same he climbed down off the fence, mumbling, 'I can't stand a bar of a Chow.' He bolted inside, and, not waiting to take off his boots, shot into bed and pulled up the quilt, closing his eyes and pretending to be asleep, for in spite of all his bravado, Hughie didn't like the cops.

'I been sick in bed all day, d'yer hear?' he bellowed at Dolour. 'I been sick in bed all day, or I'll beat yer brains in.'

'Poor Gran'pop,' crooned Mikey, sticking his elfin face round the door, 'Poor Gran'pop want basin?'

While Hughie was a mere recumbent statue, Mumma was coming up the path with the policeman and failing heart. She didn't want to put Hugh in, God knew she didn't, but with the day all spoiled, and the rest of it already booked up for his arging and barging, she felt she couldn't bear it.

'I'm getting old now,' she sobbed. 'I ain't just up to it.'

'Don't worry, missus,' said the policeman kindly. 'A night in the cooler will do his blood pressure a world of good this hot weather.'

He marched down the hall, and just as he did the door over his head opened, and Mr Reilly, who had been chewing over his wrongs, and repenting his retirement from battle just when things were going so well, bounded down the stairs, leaned over the rail, and screamed, 'Come on out here, Hugh Darcy, and I'll turn yer long snout inside out! Let me finish what I begun, and the cats can clean up the rest!'

The policeman's calm hand settled comfortably into the back of his collar.

'Come along, me boy,' he invited, and Mr Reilly, mentally paralysed by the miraculous eye of the police force, went down the passage as quiet as a dove under the appalled eyes of Mumma and disappeared down the street before she could get a twitch out of her tongue. Mumma tottered towards the kitchen door and met her daughter.

'Dadda's in bed, quiet as a mouse,' whispered Dolour.

650

'I got a policeman,' confessed Mumma, awestricken. 'And he's gone and taken Mr Reilly.'

Their hilarious shrieks rang out, causing Hughie to pop his head over the bedclothes in bewilderment.

Mumma's eyes glistened. 'I'll bet he's left his door open!'

'Mumma!' warned Dolour.

'Oh, ain't I?' retorted her mother. 'After I've wore me head to the bone wondering what's in them parcels of his.'

She lumbered up the stairs, and Dolour darted after her.

'It isn't fair, Mumma. It's his own business. Gee, you're mean.'

'It's not going to hurt him, me knowing what's in his parcels,' cried Mumma, slapping Dolour's hand off her skirt.

Full of triumph she pushed through the door she had not seen open for two years or more. 'Ha!'

The small attic room was half full of parcels, big and little, tied with rope and string and tape. They reached almost to the ceiling in the corner. Mumma and Dolour gaped at each other in a wild surmise.

'You mustn't, Mumma,' cried Dolour. 'It's not honest.'

'Go on out then if you're so finicky,' jeered Mumma. 'You don't have to look.'

She picked out a large, oddly-shaped parcel and began to untie the string. Several others crashed down about her feet. The odour of old food and dirty clothes wafted round them. Behind a hanging tea-towel Dolour could see a solitary sausage on a plate, black with flies. In a saucepan on the gas-ring was something clotted and brown. It crawled with ants. Distressed at Mr Reilly's undisguised poverty, Dolour looked back at her mother, who was avidly taking the paper off the parcel. Inside was a squashed shoe-box. Mumma looked at it a little timidly.

'Maybe there's a bit of body in it,' breathed Dolour. Mumma took off the lid, and Dolour craned forward to look. Inside was an old brassière, a cotton slip with torn blue lace, and a blood-stained handkerchief. The two women stared with popping eyes.

'Maybe he *has* killed someone!' twittered Dolour.

Mumma pointed a shaking finger at a tiny parcel on top of the others. 'What's in that one?'

'Looks like a big toe,' said the callous Dolour. She dragged off the paper, and there was revealed a baby's shrunken sock.

'That's Mikey's!' said Mumma indignantly. 'I missed it in the wash when he was round about eight months, and gave Anny a kick in the ribs for eating it.'

'I'd like to know what else he's got,' cried Dolour angrily. 'What about that blouse of mine that someone snowdropped off the line, and my new red belt that I blamed Motty for taking out in the street and losing?'

'You want to look for them?' said Mumma righteously.

'No,' admitted Dolour sullenly. 'And he can have this, too, if it makes him happy. Mikey's too big for it, anyway.'

She wrapped up the sock and put it back, and Mumma arranged the shoe-box unobtrusively underneath. Not speaking to each other they went downstairs, and washed the dishes in silence. Now and then vast questions rose to the tops of their souls like bubbles, but for some reason they did not speak about the parcels again. If anything, a certain respect for Mr Reilly, unique in his eccentricity, had stolen into the house, and the very air was tinged with it.

Late in the afternoon Hughie, who had succumbed to his rage and his mixed cargo, awoke, and Mumma told him what had happened. Feeling righteous, he went down and bailed Mr Reilly out, and Mr Reilly, piteously confused about the whole business, and pathetically grateful for such a good friend, begged his pardon for creating such a commotion, and sneaked upstairs to have a good lie-down.

Christmas had been a bad one for Hughie, and there was an indigestible lump inside him not caused entirely by Mumma's cooking.

He came now to the blistered yellow house in Elsey Street, his body sticky with sweat. The hairs on his legs tingled with discomfort, and at the back of his neck the cuts from his holiday haircut stung with the salt. As he raised the knocker he felt again, with amazement, the lack of interest in this house, in Florentina, even in himself. On the surface there was a mechanical repetition of his old eagerness, but underneath, and not far underneath, there was the deep fundamental exhaustion he too had never felt before. It was not only physical, it was moral and spiritual. After all this time of walking in an unreal world, of impatiently thrusting behind him all his real life, he was beginning to drag back to that world – or perhaps it was sucking him back into its tide.

'Well, what do you want?' The woman Seppa did not come fully into the light of the door; in the habitual way of those who always expect unwelcome visitors, she stood in the shadows to one side.

'She in?'

'No, she ain't.'

They stared unwinkingly at each other like two cats on a fence. Hughie hated her – her moustache, the thickness and greasiness of her skin, the knowledge that she was what Florentina would grow into. In her, her younger sister's tidal drift had become a fixity of purpose, a gimlet-eyed commercialism. Seppa did not bother to wear bright clothes. Her sense of economy told her that men would come her way whether she decked herself or not. She detested Hughie mainly because Hughie detested her, and made no attempt to invite him in to wait. In the dimness behind her he saw the white roll of the black boy's eyeballs.

'Hi, there, Lexie.'

'Hullo, Mr Hughie.'

'You get out back there,' ordered the woman. She tried to close the door. 'Florrie's out and she won't be back for hours. Want to make something of it?'

'She's gone out with Topper. Topper's living here now,' chirped up Lexie eagerly. Seppa's eyes glinted expectantly. She hoped Hughie would say something, and juicy phrases of abuse rolled round her tongue in anticipation. But to her disappointment he merely looked stupid and blank and remained silent. A dull apathy soaked him. All he wanted was to take off his shirt and undo his shoelaces and have a cool-off somewhere.

'Ah, you got no guts.'

The door slammed. Hughie dawdled off up the road. It was surrendered to the sunshine and the somnolence of after-Christmas dinner. Here and there a group of old men clotted a shady balcony, cheeping over old times and hooting on their withered noses with saxophone sounds. A ragged urchin stood outside the closed doors of Drummy's squeaking on the glass panes with a sixpence and hopping from foot to foot as the pavement grew too hot for him. Hughie tried to feel angry, or disappointed, but he couldn't. Deep within him there was some depressive area of emotion, like the buffer depression that runs before a cyclone, but he could not find the energy to examine it. He came to Delie Stock's lane, and along into its furry black shadows he went, feeling sick with the heat and the food and the bad liquor. He peered through the palings, seeing a sliver of the Kidger's bent roach back, then another of his lolling pale face, and yet another of a dirty hand clutching a bottle with the neck knocked off. Hughie raised himself cautiously above the fence.

'Hey,' he called 'any chance of getting a boll?'

The Kidger came out of his trance and made a feeble gesture. The yard was a wreck. Little Ryan Street had taken Delie's parting largesse. They had stormed into the yard, broken open the cases, and snatched every bottle. They had even lifted off the lid of the copper where she did a bit of private adulteration, and dipped out the nauseous mixture with cups and peach-cans. A dim, broken sound of revelry from the end of the street showed that it hadn't all gone yet.

'Come on in and help yourself,' said the Kidger. His hair was matted as if he had poured syrup on it, and his face was the face of a corpse. Out of his bright pink shirt, streaked all over with spilt wine and vomit, his neck rose long and pallid, like a duck's.

'Gawd, you look in a bad way, boy,' said Hughie, eagerly going in. The Kidger suddenly dropped the bottle as though it were hot, and began to cry like a child, without raising his hands to his face or doing anything to mop up the tears that welled stickily out and dribbled on to his unspeakable shirt.

'Poor Delie, she ain't never coming back,' he babbled. 'She's got it that bad in the chest.'

'Ah, yer don't want to take it so serious,' soothed Hughie, looking covertly round the yard. He saw a bottle sticking out from under the woodheap and cracked off its top. A blast of methylated air nearly blew his hat off. He inhaled thankfully.

'Tell me about it,' he invited, sitting down beside the Kidger and expertly blowing off the glass splinters.

'I been with her for fifteen years,' mumbled the Kidger, wiping his eyes on the back of his sleeve. 'I been her useful for that long I don't know what else I can do.'

'Wish someone would give me a chance to get me claws on to the business,' said Hughie dreamily. 'Christ, what's she put in this?' he added, spitting out a mouthful of froth.

'Lemme whiff it,' blubbered the Kidger. He took a forlorn sniff. 'You got some of the lemon essence lot there.'

But the distraction was too slight, and he staggered across the yard and lay down on the woodpile like a yogi, sobbing to himself and picking incessantly at the shedding bark of the logs.

Hughie kept on drinking. He wanted to feel big, and by the time dusk fell he was beyond all measurement.

When Charlie came home the house was quiet, so quiet he could hear the ping-pong-ping of the iron roof complaining under the sun. He peeped into the stifling bedroom and there was Mumma, a shapeless hump in her slip, snoring beside the starfish figure of his daughter. Mumma loved to camp after dinner, but she didn't often get the chance.

He went upstairs and there was silence there, too. He stood on the landing for a while, then he went into his own room and got the little parcel, turning it over in his fingers and wondering if it were the right thing to get for a girl like Dolour. Maybe she would have liked some scent, or a bright scarf. Roie would have.

Feeling diffident, and in some strange way pleased and a little excited, he looked in at her half-open door. She was asleep, and it was typical of her that on that burning day she had taken Mikey to bed with her, his pink puffy face squashed on her arm, and his naked body gently shining with sweat.

Charlie thought, 'I'll put it over there, and she'll see it.'

But instead he stood there looking at her, defenceless in her sleep. He felt guilt because she was defenceless, and yet he was unable to look away. It was almost the first time he had looked at her because she was Dolour, and not because she looked like her sister. All at once she awoke, alarm and surprise on her face.

'What's the matter, Charlie?'

Stammering, he held out a little figure. 'I got this for you. I was going to put it on the table.'

'Gee!'

Dolour slid her arm out from under the baby, and cautiously got off the bed. Barefooted, flushed with heat and sleep, she pushed back her hair and eagerly took the parcel.

'Oh, Charlie . . . I didn't expect . . . you shouldn't have bothered . . . it must have cost an awful lot!'

It was a little bone carving of a Chinese water-seller with a yoke bearing two swinging buckets. His feet were bare, his trousers rolled up, and under the conical hat his goat-tufted turnip of a face was so cheerful, so completely indifferent to the troubles of this world that Dolour laughed with glee. Charlie smiled with relief.

'Oh, Charlie, I love it! I'm going to call him Ah Grin. How did you know I liked little Chinese things?'

'I've seen you with Loger Bubba,' he chuckled. Dolour had almost forgotten what he looked like when he was happy. Holding Ah Grin in her hand she looked at him, forgetting that she didn't wear her glasses now, and that what she felt was plainly written in her eyes. She thought, 'Oh, Charlie, I'd like to put my arms around you and tell you – ' She dropped her gaze and said, 'Nobody else would ever think to give me anything like this. It doesn't seem to fit in with – ' She made a small despairing gesture around the small, ugly room, whose bone-bare cleanliness only emphasized its ugliness.

'Dolour, why don't you leave home?' he asked impulsively.

'Oh, I dunno.' She flushed. 'I suppose I will some day, when the kids are bigger.'

'How old are you now?'

'Twenty in March. Why?'

'It's funny a girl of your age so interested in someone else's kids,' he said, half-tenderly, half-jokingly, watching the blushes chase each other over her face and wondering why.

'Mumma needs a hand. Anyway, it doesn't matter much. I'm too old to get any more schooling. I'm only good for shopwork and the factories and I might as well be here as anywhere else.'

'You'll be getting married one of these days,' he said, and was amazed to feel all at once an extraordinary anxiety grip his heart. Like a child she dropped her head, but not before he had seen the tears in her eyes. 'Why, Dolour, what's the matter?'

'Nothing,' Dolour said, trying to pull away from the hand under her chin. 'Nothing, Charlie. Honest.'

'You don't like the little Chinaman,' he accused. 'You'd rather have had something to wear.'

'Oh no, I wouldn't. I love it. I'll always keep it,' she whispered, terrified lest he should pull her closer and she would not be able to bear it.

'Then what's the matter? Are you in love?'

Almost at once he saw he had hit her in a vulnerable spot. She jerked her chin away from his fingers and said, 'Of course I'm not. You've got a nerve!'

But it was written plain in her flushed face, her angry, resentful eyes and trembling lips. She was not old enough, or experienced enough, to dissemble, and, more than that, the honesty of her nature would always make her face transparent to those who wished to read it.

But this was not what shocked Charlie. He was appalled to find that this was what he had been unconsciously looking for in her ever since they had spoken of Motty's future in the kitchen. He didn't know what to say, standing there like a fool, his arms hanging at his sides, not knowing whether to put them around her, or to say something, or just to go away and leave her to her tears.

'I'm sorry,' he said. 'It's none of my business.'

'No, it isn't,' she cried, and he went out, knowing that she would cry and then pick up Mikey and comfort herself with him.

He sat on his bed a long time, staring at the wall, his mind a confusion, and a deep shame waiting to engulf him. For he didn't know whether Dolour was to him just a young girl, whose sympathy and youth and virginity had called to the starvation within him. For four years his adoration for his wife had expressed itself in unbroken companionship and tenderness and frequent passion, and never been rebuffed or discounted, and when Roie died his body had sickened and hungered. It was not through desire alone, but for a much subtler reason. The tongue had been taken from the nightingale, and white paper from the poet, the eyes from the seeing man. His had been the rich and contenting routine of husbandhood, broken like a snap of a thread, so that his soul had been thrown willy-nilly into solitariness.

And Dolour, the passionate, mutinous child, the soft-hearted and mercurial girl, and now the young woman secret within herself? What could she see in him, who had perhaps once been lovable, but now was only driftwood, a man whose courage and spirit had no fixed abode? It was only her romantic imagination, her sympathy for him, her love for his children that she had extended to include him, too. So he argued with himself, and did not notice that in all this time he had not once thought of Roie as a part of his life, only as a part of that which had gone.

The cool wind sighed up the street blowing the heat away like a monstrous balloon until it floated out to the Tasman and was absorbed in the ragged clouds.

Hughie rose and reeled down to Elsey Street again. He waited a long time, shivering in the wind, with his lumbago prickling like a fiery belt and his eyes watering with the intensity of his glare. Hughie did know why he waited. He just wanted to be sure. Of something. His lips were dry and cracked, he was sobering up with unpleasant quickness, and his stomach rumbled that it needed hot food to keep away a chill.

'Ah, shuddup,' said Hugh to his midriff.

During the time he waited he had a hundred arguments with unseen and inaudible persons, plunging down into the muddied well of his emotions and coming up with false and furious reasonings. The bitterest taste in his mouth was the wry, ironic one of the knowledge that he had to spend the last and most exultant flame of his mature life on a prostitute. Rich men could have girls clean and decent in themselves. They could have girls privily, and know no other hand would touch them until they came again. But he had to fall in love with a woman who had been on the town since she was fourteen. He had never been anywhere in the running; all his life he had been sixth-rate, failing in crises, sickening in emergencies, flying to the bottle when he was needed. There was in him the unconquerable ability to be missing at the right moment. So it was typical that he should spend his passion and infatuation on a little bit of street flotsam.

And now she had a pimp, somebody to pick and choose her men for her, to batten on her earnings, and finally, when she grew old or diseased, to pitch her out. And in the incredible, fantastic way of women, she would take it. At the thought of this man, this Topper, whose shadow had been over his life for some time now, the most terrible murderous jealousy rose in Hughie's throat and nearly choked him.

About eleven o'clock he saw the girl come along Elsey Street with a man. She walked slowly, her head down, and her manner weary. For a moment Hughie's heart melted, then he remembered that she had never been his; she had never been anyone's, not even Topper's. She was largesse to all the world, and like fairy gold she melted from sight as soon as she was given. The man with her was big and young, but like a fox terrier giving challenge to an Alsatian, Hughie took no notice of the other's size. He wrenched at the fence in his maniacal rage, and a rotten paling came away in his hand.

'By God,' said Hughie, as though God Himself had given the weapon. As Florentina and the man came closer, he stepped out of the darkness to meet them, standing there motionless, the paling down in the shadow beside his leg.

'Well, how'd yer make out to-night?' His voice was thick, and the smell of wine hung round him like a cloud. He might have been any abusive drunk. The couple walked on, ignoring him, and after a moment of shock and resentment Hughie ran after them, a squatty figure against their tall slenderness. On the wall his shadow showed like a gorilla's, with one long deformed arm hanging to the ground.

Florentina said something to the young man, who leaned against the wall, his face still unseen, but his shoes twinkling in the lamplight. Hughie found his eyes fascinated by them. He loved fine clothes, suits that fitted like a glove, ties that hooped out in a blaze of colour, stickpins with lumps of red and blue rock in them, but he never wore anything but old hand-me-downs from Joseph Mendel's. The sight of the shoes maddened him even more.

'Go away, Hughie,' said Florentina. 'You don't want to be bothering my friend.'

Hughie spat out a filthy word pregnant with his scornful disbelief. Neither Florentina nor the young man took any notice of it; they had heard it fifty times a day all their lives. A flood of blasphemy poured out of his mouth, aimed at the girl, but rooted in his own misery, his realization of his failure, his complete and utter futility.

Florentina half put out a hand to Hughie, but the stranger struck it down with a casual, un-self-conscious viciousness. Hughie looked at her with such hatred on his face that, bewildered, she backed away. She walked off quickly, and Hughie galloped behind, continuing to abuse them both in a voice that grew louder and thicker until it awoke the echoes in the empty allotments and caused a window to clang upwards and a voice to yell, 'Put a sock in it, can't yer?'

Suddenly the young man left Florentina and came back. In the lamplight his face showed lean and ratlike, with pale protruding jaw and keen, zinc-grey eyes. It was the face of the petty racketeer, the black-market tout, and the successful man of unobtrusive criminal affairs. He had a pleasant, persuasive voice.

'Look, mate, sling yer hook before something falls on yer head.'

It was all Hughie needed. His common sense had long fled, and he had rushed on towards this moment like a river rushing towards a ravine. He raised the paling and jabbed the young man in the belly, intending to crash him over the skull with the other end as his head came down. But the rotten thing snapped like a carrot, and he stood defenceless.

'She's a whore!'

'Sure, pally.'

The street tipped up and hit Hughie on the back of the head. Quick as a cat he bucked out of the way of the boot that flashed towards him, but the wine slowed his legs, and the young man leaped on his back, twelve stone of larrikinism that had cut its teeth on such brawls. He seized Hughie by the back of the neck; his long sharp fingers stabbed in on either side of the windpipe and he ground the older man's face into the pavement, up and down across the footpath. People came out on the balconies, blinking in the light, and leaned over the rails to watch.

'It's a bloody shame! He's only a little feller!'

'Ain't he got go in him, but! He oughta be on at the Stadium.'

Hughie got one boot in the young man's side and gave a desperate downward rip towards the groin. As the other fell back with a whistled groan, Hughie leaped on him, half-blinded by blood, savage as a tiger. But he was too old. In a second he was underneath again. Their skulls met with a sharp crack, and Hughie's teeth closed on the other's ear. It was good, warm and rubbery, and with delight he heard the grunt of the man as his teeth went through. Like a dog he dragged at it, then his dentures flew from his mouth, shattering on the street. An anguished curse against God went up out of Hughie's heart. He struggled for the gouge, but the strength ran out of his limbs like milk, and his heart swelled up and hit him under the chin. The light was blotted out, and a fierce agony exploded against the side of his head. He lay hardly conscious, aware of the boot crashing into his side as he might be of a drum beating a long way away, his mind pulling up the darkness like a blanket until he lay lapped in its shelter.

The young man flipped his hand, sending a rain of blood-drops across the street as he dabbed at his ear. He went to Florentina, who stood against the fence, half awed, half fascinated, lifting her eyes to his with the unquestioning docility of a child's.

'You and your old bastards!'

His fingers closed over her arm, thrusting downwards between the two bones. She squealed in torture. He looked at her closely while he thrust deeper, relinquishing her with a laugh and striding ahead to fit the key in her door. Florentina followed after, looking backwards covertly at the sprawled figure under the light, her eyes dim with the tears that would never be shed. A moment or so later she would have forgotten why she wanted to cry.

Most of the people on the balconies went inside, after Hughie had lain still for more than five minutes. They knew that sooner or later he would get up and stagger away. Anyway, the excitement was over.

When he opened his eyes the street was empty, save for a dreadful old ratbag of a woman with bare blackened feet sticking out from under her long skirt. She was squatting beside him chewing at nothing at all, and staring at him with eyes filmed with white.

'You got that much of a belting from that Topper,' she said. 'You better come into my place and I'll give you a drink.'

Hughie rolled over. His ribs felt like an iron cage that had been heated. They pressed against the flesh with a hooping, outward movement that he could hardly bear. He tried to get up several times before he succeeded. An old arm, hard and strong as a stick, hoisted him to his feet, where he stood swaying, the light in the wire-protected globe fuzzing like yellow fur.

Suddenly he was sick, an awful blood-streaked convulsion that made his stomach feel even worse.

'Gawd, he's torn yer guts loose from their moorings,' remarked his witch-like companion with eager interest. She put out her arm to support him, but with a groan Hughie avoided it and staggered up the street. He heard her calling after him, 'Hey, you forgot yer tats! Don't you want yer teeth?'

It was endless miles to Plymouth Street, which seemed to lie on the other side of the city. By the time he reached his own dark gate he was whimpering with the pain of exhaustion, and the fearful irrevocable humiliation.

'Well,' he gasped to the bright sky, 'You got Your own back.'

Mumma was in the kitchen, pottering about soaking porridge, and wondering what it was she had forgotten. He reeled past her, hideous in his mask of dirt and blood, and she stood there yellow-faced, not saying a word, holding the saucepan in her hand. He managed to get into the laundry, and Mumma, listening, heard the scrape of a match, and then his sobs. The tears ran down her own face as she listened.

661

After a while he felt better and, lifting up the candle, he stared at his toothless face in the mirror. The blood came straight from his savaged heart, and what hurt most of all was the realization that the steps could not be retraced, that he could never recapture his youth any more, that time was final, and not all the human pride or anguish in the world could gainsay it.

He lay beside Mumma in the darkness. He would not touch her, and she would not touch him, yet each felt the bodily warmth of the other. They breathed the same air, and that was all. Mumma tried to be triumphant, to be hard and revengeful, pleased that he was beaten and bruised, proud of herself that she had been silent and not reproached him ever. But all that her heart could cry was, 'Oh, Lord, let it be next week, or next month soon, so that we can forget it all, and be like we usta!'

Twenty-two

Almost with a shock Dolour watched Lick Jimmy's papery fingers putting the jar of purple immortelles into his window. So it was winter again. Once the seasons had been to her as the slow turning of a book's pages, each with its unique delights and troubles. But this last half-year had gone like a dream, and she realized with an ache that it was because she had grown up. There were so many things to think of that she hadn't noticed the bed-bugs sluggishly sidling into cracks and crannies for their cold-weather hibernation, or the wet-stains on the walls growing green-velvety with renaissant fungus, or Mikey in the house all the time because he couldn't play in the flooded yard. It was winter again, and at the thought the piercing, dusty wind whipping up Plymouth Street seemed to gain an added shrill bitterness.

And Lick was older, too. He had always been old, but since his family came to keep him company he had settled contentedly into his years, allowing the plum bloom to creep over his kind, diamond-shaped eyes, and the frost into his stiff black hair, which he kept covered now with a little flat tweed cap, like a lid. He had shrunken against his own brittle bones, so that his blue coat flapped, and sometimes even his shoes fell off, which made him giggle gleefully.

'Oh, Lick,' thought Dolour sadly, 'why has everything got to change?'

Yet she did not want to go back to the old days, for she had not loved Charlie then. It had happened to her, and secretly, tenderly she hugged it to herself, feeling her womanhood flower and her heart open day by day. It was a mystery she could not comprehend, for Charlie had been there with them so long, and in all that time there had been no love for him latent in her. It had come unbidden, like a child into the womb, and as though it had been a child she cherished it, for it was all she had. Charlie would never love her, for she could find nothing in herself to love.

As her eye trouble had disciplined her to the limits of her fortitude, as the loss of her ambition had taught her to look further than the moment and at the same time to make the best of what she had, so did this unacknowledged and unreturned love make her conscious of the divine principle that it is better for the soul to love than to be loved. Yet the bitter consciousness of the loneliness that would be hers if he left them, the jealous terror in case he should marry again, and her continual battle against sin in relation to him were always with her, so that she dreaded her solitary hours and the thoughts they bred. Sometimes they came upon her like darkness itself, shrouding all her brightness and hope, crushing her beneath a despair she could hardly combat. Was it to be like this all her life, empty of all she most wanted? No husband was to be hers, no children; she could never pour out her whole being in adoration of another. Her sweet saps were to be curdled, her bloom withered, and all for nothing. She thought, desperate, 'Oh, Roie, you were luckier than I am! It was worth it to die, to have what you had!'

And at other times the temptation came to her to belong to Charlie in dreams, for she could belong to him no other way. She lay in her bed and listened to him moving in the next room, her body crying out with incredible, insupportable longing for his hands in her hair and his lips on her throat, so that she got out of bed like an old woman, walking up and down the room with her hands against her ears, tormented beyond control, and yet piteously determined that she would not sully him by sinning with him in her thoughts.

She did not know that he sat in the darkness and listened to her footsteps, wanting to go in and speak to her, longing to wake Michael so that she would hear the child's sleepy whimper and come in to see what the matter was. He hated himself for his thoughts, calling her a child, and knowing that she was not, telling himself that she was only infatuated, and knowing that might have been true of anyone but Dolour. For a long time he had not known what he himself felt about her, but now he knew, and the knowledge was bitterer than the confusion.

He had thought that in his emotional instability he had identified her with Roie because she looked like her sister, that his body wanted her because of their propinquity, and his mind because she was the only solid and understandable creature at which he could grasp. But that was not true. If he had never met Roie he would have loved Dolour as she was now. He knew that God had picked her up gently as a child, saying, 'This one I will teach the inner meaning of life,' and put her down softly on her own feet to go her own way, knowing that her idealism was not that of the escapist, who shuns realism, but was strong and untainted enough to come hard against the utmost brutality of evil and retain its integrity. Charlie knew that whatever happened to Dolour she would not be conquered, but his heart bled at the griefs that still lay before her, dreading that she might fall into the hands of some man who would savage her instincts and blaspheme her innermost sensitivities. Charlie had faith in God's care of Dolour, but he wanted to be there to make sure.

He fished under the bed for the bottle there. It fell and bumped across the floor, and Charlie stood ashamed, grinning wryly, knowing that Dolour would have heard. He let it lie where it was, thinking, 'It's all in the frame of mind, anyway. It doesn't make me think clearer, or feel better, or get things straighter.' But a moment later he had persuaded himself that as she'd believe he was drinking, he might as well be doing it, and he fumbled round after the wine in the darkness, and found it with the gratitude of a man finding a lifebuoy in a desolate sea.

It was six months since Motty had started school and in all that time not one day had passed without her causing a commotion. She was small, a pocket-sized girl, yet what could one do with a pocket-sized girl who could transform herself into a spitting, shrieking, biting, swearing tiger at will? From the moment she got up they bolted the door lest she should run out and disappear, and so, frustrated, she hid. Mumma's back ached with dragging Motty out by the leg from under beds and behind chairs, while she screamed blue murder. Taking her to school was a trial of strength, for outside the gate she sat down hard, pulling back with her strong little arms and digging in her heels, so that she had to be dragged every inch of the way by brute force.

The sisters had never seen anything as bad as Motty before. They had struck wildcats, but Moira Rothe was a werewolf. In the schoolroom she rampaged at will, tearing up books, slapping her companions, and throwing herself on the floor purple with rage and suffocation. Even when she was subdued by force she put up the sort of fight Dirty Dick would have put up if matched with a lion. A grown-up could crush her only by sheer weight and strength, reducing her to a panting, tearless, glittering-eyed little animal at bay, with no words, no defence or excuse, nothing but hate.

'I never in all me days seen a child like her,' wailed Mumma to Mrs Campion.

She was an outlaw, and she tore Dolour's heart to pieces. She felt that it was her fault, for alone of them all she had realized the way Motty was heading. She should have made Mumma send her to school the year before, instead of letting her get away with, 'Oh, she's only a baby. You don't want her in there bothering her head with reading and counting at her age.' She should have managed, some way, to get her into a kindergarten, instead of allowing Mumma to let her run the streets.

Motty's treatment of her brother was that of a sultana with the lowest rank of black slave. Still, he trotted after her adoring her visibly and audibly. He and Loger Bubba liked to play together, sitting placidly in the sun conversing in Australian-Chinese and pressing gifts on each other. Motty like nothing better than to storm in, kick their games to pieces, and crash their heads together. She was kind to nobody except Dirty Dick, and he and she treated each other with a sort of silent, mutual respect, understanding each other very well.

Mumma tried everything with her, affection, indulgence, force, bribery and corruption. Mrs Drummy said that St Joseph did wonders with difficult children, and Mumma tried him, but Motty left him standing. Some days she vanished directly after breakfast, and not all the searching up and down streets and in neighbours' backyards brought to light a shred of her. For all they knew she was kidnapped and raped and murdered and her body stuffed down a sewer. But when sundown came Motty would turn up, filthy, exhausted, and ravenous as a wolf.

'Beat it out of her!' growled Hughie, but belting never did a thing with Motty. Sometimes after she had been given what-for with a strap she would crawl under the table, and Dolour would cautiously lift the cloth to see her squatting against the wall, Dirty Dick in her arms, the pair of them staring fixedly into space, pondering perhaps on the incomprehensible cruelty and dictatorship of adults in a world that seemingly was not made for children.

Then Mumma would weep a little, filling up a kettle or stirring a pot meanwhile, for she never had time for weeping as a separate process. 'Oh, I done my best, honest to goodness I have, and I'm at my wits' end what to do about her.'

'Perhaps we could take her to a doctor,' suggested Dolour helplessly, for how would you get Motty to a doctor when she didn't want to go, except by tying her hand and foot with ropes and heaving her into a taxi?

'Maybe she's a bit wrong in the head,' said Mumma, blessing herself for fear she was right. But Motty's eyes were brilliant with intelligence. It wasn't her head that had gone wrong, and Dolour knew it. But it was no good trying to explain to Mumma.

'It's that black blood in her,' said Mumma, 'making the child into a savage.'

Acid words rose to Dolour's lips, but she did not say any of them, for Mumma had an opinion inside her head, which was tantamount to saying that she had a billet of hardwood resting snugly against her frontal bone. She thought, 'It isn't the drop of black blood that makes her that way, for where could you find anyone gentler than Charlie? She was all right when Roie was here, and she'd be all right still if Roie had lived.'

She put her arms round Motty, expecting a forearm jolt in the face, but instead Motty gave her a quick hug, and wriggled away, as though embarrassed. Yet often in the middle of the night, when Motty woke frantic with nightmare, Dolour would take her into her own bed and cuddle her till light came, with Motty clinging like a bear, choking with sobs that shook her to her calloused, dirty little toes.

'What's the matter, Dolour's girl? Aren't you happy? Tell me and I'll fix it up. Would you like to go away with Dolour and live somewhere else, in the country, with lots of room to play in, the trees to climb and dogs to play with? Would you?'

But Motty wouldn't answer, and Dolour knew that the dark hid a face that was tightly shut-up, like a book hiding God alone knew what jealousy and loneliness and piteous rebellion against a world too big to be managed. So she would talk on, half to herself, 'Soon they'll be pulling this place down, and then we'll have to go. And if Nana and Grandpop won't come, you and I will go away somewhere, and Mikey, too.'

So she spoke to comfort the child, forgetting that she herself had never walked across a paddock, or touched any horse except the baker's weary old mare, or heard the sea boom at night, or watched the wind shake silver out of the gum-leaves.

The worry of Motty was so great that to some extent the pain of her love for Charlie was ameliorated, for she didn't have time to think about it.

It was a bad six months. Something seemed to have happened to Twelve-and-a-half, Plymouth Street. The old simple, warm contentment was gone, and there was nothing left but uneasy anticipation of worse things to come. Mumma's bunions were playing up something cruel with the cold and the wet, and Mr Reilly caught a kidney complaint and there was no getting into the lavatory for anyone else in the house. And Hughie, though he made a brave attempt to be as he had always been, had all at once become an old man.

'And no wonder, with his teeth gone west, and him not doing a thing about it,' scolded Mumma.

For his face had fallen in round his toothless mouth, and the ruddiness had drained out of his skin, leaving it sallow and baggy. But he couldn't be bothered to get new teeth, all that money, and going to the dentist and having his moosh stuffed full of concrete to get an impression, and all the rest. He just couldn't be bothered, but chumbled uncomplainingly on Mumma's tough steaks and gangster chops, and learned to smoke a cigarette without sucking off the end.

The doom was on the house, and at night the old planks creaked and croaked to each other, 'Ninety years, and you and I remembering when the Surry Hills were green, and the wild swans nested along the swamp in Coronation Street.' And, 'This house stood by itself then, and where the Licks live, and the Grogans and the Brodies, the orchard stretched, full of loquat-trees where the pink parrots held parliament.'

It was almost a relief when the Casements, in the boarded-up shop on the corner, got their removal notice. Perhaps it wasn't so bad for them, for they were elderly folk, with their children long since flown, so that they wouldn't have to put up with getting the kids to a new school, and disagreements with new neighbours over who bashed whom. But Mrs Casement was distraught. 'I'm too old. I'm too old,' she kept saying. 'I've bin here forty years, and me curtains won't fit any other windows.' To get Mrs Casement out of her house was like digging up an old tree. She was so used to ducking her head under the dwarfish doorway to the bedroom that for the rest of her life she would do it whenever she saw a bed. She liked the little yellow window over the stairs, and the white fleur-de-lys in the dangerous, slippery tiles in the backyard. The clothes line was just her height, and she'd never be able to find another window-sill with a dip in it that just fitted her pot of mint and parsley.

'And where am I going to hang me canary in me new kitchen, wherever it's going to be?'

She sat in the doorway complaining and weeping a little at the sympathy of her neighbours, enjoying her temporary fame in a miserable way, for it wasn't often that she had the chance to be the focus of Plymouth Street conversation. Nobody took much notice of old Mr Casement, who was pottering around the yard, his chin shaking, and a terrible churned-up confusion in his mind. He wanted to cry, but what with all the women coming in and out, bringing batches of scones and cups of tea, and biting his wife for something to remember her by, he couldn't find a place to be private in. Already he felt his roots becoming dry and shrivelled, as though he'd be dragged out of his own soil and thrown on a heap of weeds in the sun. He was much older than his wife, and he didn't know what he'd do if they sent him to Hargrave Park. For this was the terror of most of the evicted people, that they would be sent to the squalid housing settlements where worse slums had been created than any the Council had pulled down.

'Them little army huts,' thought Mr Casement in panic, 'and people fighting and screaming and banging on walls, and pinching the washing, and Jessie expecting me to go in and tell 'em off. I just ain't up to it these days.'

He went again and again and looked at the spot on the ground where Keithie, their youngest, had crashed off the wall and broken his skull, and him only four and a bit. For thirty-five years Mr Casement had grown candytuft on that spot, and not allowed anyone to walk there, and now they were going to come and trample it all over, and tear it up with steam shovels. At the very thought Mr Casement's eyes filled with sticky, difficult tears, as though Keithie were going to be killed all over again.

'I wish I was dead,' he moaned, and didn't know that a fortnight after he left Surry Hills he would be already buried, his soul shocked out of its fragile shell by the violent disruption of routine.

The Casements had hardly gone before the men arrived to pull the shop down, and they pulled it down with such ease that it was a wonder to those watching that it had stood up so long. Mumma and Mikey stood in the crowd, curious and morbid, to see Mrs Casement's living-room exposed to view, like a doll's house. Down came the wallpaper, striped with scarlet roses and lettuce leaves. Up came the floor that was most surprisingly black in squares where Mrs Casement hadn't bothered to clean under the furniture. A window fell out and crashed in a million diamonds across the candytuft, which was now a green slimy smear over the tiles. The plaster shot up in spurts of white smoke, sprinkling the heads of the crowd like a dying benediction. The workmen, stripped to their brown middles in spite of the winter wind, sat astride the beams sucking tea out of enamel pannikins, while the sun filtered down through the naked roof on rooms it had never seen before.

'They had bugs awful bad,' said Mrs Campion mournfully. 'I guess it's one way of getting rid of them.'

Mumma picked up a piece of red-rose wallpaper and sneaked it into her pocket. She was going to keep it in memory of Mrs Casement. Unhappily she went home, wondering, sick with trepidation, not knowing whether to curse or pray.

'I suppose they mean it for the best,' she said drearily.

She couldn't be bothered cleaning up the kitchen or getting dinner ready, so she made a cup of tea, and was still drinking it when Hughie came home. They didn't look at each other, but Mumma poured him a cup and sugared it heavily, listening without criticism to the drainpipe noises he made as he drank it.

'Won't be long before we get the boot, too,' said Hughie gruffly.

'What do you reckon they'll do with us?' quavered Mumma.

She snorted into her tea with her worry and distress and anger at all the interfering boneheads who couldn't leave decent people where they were.

'We'll make out,' said Hughie. 'We've always made out.'

She looked at him blindly and hopefully, and for the first time he saw her not as the girl she had been, or as a dumpy, rather dirty middle-aged woman, but just as a person whose exterior didn't matter much. Roie had gone, and Thady had gone, and some day soon Dolour would get married and leave them, and he'd be alone except for Mumma, sticking around as she had always stuck around, wanting to make things comfortable for him, and not much else.

'It ain't been much of a life for you,' he said, uncomfortably looking down at the syrupy pool in his saucer.

'No, it ain't,' thought Mumma, remembering herself in childbirth, and Hughie crashing in drunk and lying across her feet until the midwife pulled him off; remembering hungry days, and ashamed ones, and days muddied with sorrow and annoyance and humiliation. The words were there, ironic, acid, waiting to spill out and encompass him, to burn him down to the ground like an old building.

It might have been the greatest feat in the world, to force back those words and say nothing, but it wasn't. She looked at him, and she knew there was no bitterness in her heart, no resentment, nothing at all but a trembling hope.

'Ah, well, we're still together, Hughie,' she said.

Like summer, withdrawing into the upper air, leaving her warmth and mellowness half as a reality, half as a memory, Hughie felt his youth leave him for all time, unregretted. He was strong yet, a healthy, hearty man, with plenty of kick in him, and, Hargrave Park or not, he'd give them all a run for their money. They hadn't been kicked out of Surry Hills yet; it might never happen, even if it did, they could always come back. It was a free country.

'We ain't licked,' he said, and crammed half a scone into his mouth. 'No, we ain't licked yet, old chook.'

'You will be,' said Mumma, 'if you don't get yer tats in and stop golloping.'

'Ah, shuddup.'

He came over clumsily, and put a buttery kiss on her cheek, and Mumma thought, 'Ah, I don't mind where we go, if only he's with me. But You've taken Your time with him and me, Lord, and no mistake.'

Twenty-three

As though the dust rising from the Casements' fallen dwelling were the dust of an implacable, pursuing rider, Charlie knew that he must shake himself out of his apathy and do something. Motty could not go on as she was; he could not go on as he was. Before the next Christmas perhaps the pattern of their lives would be broken, and he had a desperate desire to aid his destiny a little, not wait for it to happen to him as though he were a log of wood or block of stone. But he had forgotten how. Faced with decision, the old confusion of thought and spirit overcame him. He knew only one thing, that he could not live in the same house with Dolour any longer.

He listened at walls for her voice, and her light footstep on the floor. He watched her covertly as she washed the dishes or swept the yard, seeing how in this little while she had become beautiful, with a wistfulness he had never noticed before. Once perhaps, before his marriage, he could have borne her continual presence, but not now, when he was fully a man, accustomed to the physical expression of love as an accompaniment to the spiritual.

Could he go to her and say, 'I love you, and want to marry you, but it is forbidden?'

For Charlie had thought of something of which Dolour was ignorant, that according to the Church they were within prohibited degrees of relationship.

He had to go away before it was too late, and he had spoken to her.

Now, as never before, Roie seemed to be closer to him, as though she had put her sister in his way. He walked the streets, and she was with him, not loving him less, but more, so close that he could have put out a hand to touch her.

'Roie, what'll I do about Motty if I go?' he asked.

The two ends of the rope were there – Motty to keep him, and Dolour to send him away, and the bitter thing was that he knew Dolour was the only one to coax Motty back to a normal childhood. He laughed with the irony of it, and then suddenly, on an impulse, went up the worn, lopsided steps of the church and into its stillness. He had not been there since Christmas, and he had not

672

even bothered to work out the riddle why, since he believed that God was there, he had not come near Him. Now he felt dirty and unshaven, a spiritual tramp, as embarrassed as though he'd gone to see the nuns with ragged clothes and hair down the back of his neck. He was uncomfortable, looking at the Tabernacle half apologetically before the sensation was swamped in his misery. He sought for Roie in that presence, knowing she was there somewhere, but feeling himself too coarse and corrupt to touch her.

'What'll I do, darling?'

She was still his darling. His simplicity was too close to earth for him to confuse the two loves. What he felt for Dolour was not what he had felt for Roie. His adoration for the dead girl still lived, its colours a little dimmed, its perfume a little nostalgic. It had made him what he was, and was part of him for all time.

Again he had the impression that Roie had given him Dolour, and again and again he came against the stone wall of why, why, why, when it was impossible, when he could never marry her according to the laws of the Church, which for Dolour was the only way. He could feel himself getting exhausted, falling into the ready panic that called for drink and stupor to alleviate it. There was no way round the problem, and no one to ask about it.

He became aware then that for a long time a curious sound had been the background to his thought and, startled, he focused his attention upon it. It was the creaking of boots, up and down, up and down. He raised his head, and there was Father Cooley marching up and down the aisle with his head bowed over his breviary, but for all that looking like a policeman on the beat. Now and then a Latin mutter, strongly tinged with Galway, escaped his lips, and as though apologetically his eyes looked up under their grey bristly shelves and fastened on Charlie's. Father Cooley looked weary and old; the broad heartiness had left his frame, and Charlie suspected that under the concealing flow of his soutane he was thin and a little bowed. Actually Father Cooley's back was so bad he wanted nothing so much as to give in, bend over like a safety-pin, and limp away and lie down with a hot-water bottle, for which weakling thought he condemned himself to another twenty-five turns up the church, not skipping the corners. He reckoned another three looks at young Rothe would do the trick, and they did.

'Can I speak to you, Father?' asked the young man, and Father Cooley shut his breviary with a business-like air.

'You can that.'

The visitors' room at the presbytery looked like a parlour, and so it was, bare-floored, drab, smelling slightly of cabbage, and with a picture of the Pope looking cadaverous and eager-eyed over the mantel. Father Cooley sank gingerly on to a chair, suppressing a cry of pain as his lumbago stabbed him like a tack. He though, 'Holy Mother, I've left me flannel off. No wonder it's at me.'

Charlie said, all thumbs with nervousness, and the need to blurt out everything, and yet with the feeling that Father Cooley was a priest, and not a man, 'I wanted to ask you about Motty – Moira, my little girl. She's . . . hard to manage. I thought perhaps you'd give me some advice.'

'A beautiful child,' said Father Cooley immediately. 'I remember her well. Bit right through my trouser leg the first time I met her in the playground.'

Charlie was uncertain whether Father Cooley was chiding him, or pulling his leg. He looked diffidently at the priest, and the priest's blue eyes twinkled back, so that Charlie laughed. Father Cooley felt relieved. He hated the ice-breaking business, and couldn't understand why these people felt there was any ice left on him after all these years of attending to their intimate spiritual troubles. So he took the Irish way, and gave Charlie a prod.

'Your face isn't one I see at Mass every Sunday.'

Charlie shook his head dumbly.

'On the other hand I've frequently seen it down the street with the wrong sort of look on it. It wasn't like that while your wife was alive.'

'I don't feel the way I did when she was alive,' said Charlie, and was amazed when Father Cooley became very angry, stamping up and down the worn bit of mat in front of the fireplace, saying, 'And why should you? You're older, you've got more responsibility, and you should have more sense, too, and yet, God help you, you've fallen down on the job.' Charlie was dumbfounded. 'Oh, you've not come to me before, and your mother-in-law, poor woman, hasn't asked my advice either, so you can take that look off your face. But I've got eyes in my head, and the Sisters have been having their troubles with Moira, and I can tell you I've been wondering when you'd wake up to yourself.' He suddenly levelled a stumpy finger at the young man. 'I'll tell you what'll happen to Moira. She'll go the same way as plenty of other children in this locality, into a reformatory. She's an uncontrollable child already, and the blame for it is at your door.'

674

'I've always been kind to her. I've always provided for her,' defended Charlie.

'Kind to her! Is that all a child's wanting? Do you think she's a kitten, perhaps? Oh, it'll do for some children, and little harm will come to them, but not for that tempestuous little creature.' He was silent, rubbing his leg fiercely, as though Motty's bite still pained him.

Charlie burst out, 'Well, if it's my fault, I want to fix it up. God knows I don't want Motty to grow up the wrong way, but what can I do about her?'

'Do something about yourself first,' said the priest. He slapped his breviary down on the table. 'Ah, it's bad enough to see these poor lads about here cracking like rotten sticks when misfortune hits them, but it's worse to see a man who's had a better start in life sliding into the backwash as though he hasn't an ounce of courage or fortitude in his whole body.'

Charlie thought, 'How do you know what sort of a start in life I had? Would you call knocking around the bush with a half-crazy bagman a good start? And how would you understand how I felt when Ro died?'

But Father Cooley didn't give him a chance. He saw he had Charlie pinned, and he went after him like a bulldog. 'You're falling to pieces like an old book, and the worst of it is that you're feeling sorry for yourself as the pages fall. Who are you to be sorry for yourself? You're young, and healthy, and your life's hardly begun. Buck up and get hold of the pieces and pull them together, and maybe your children will feel you're not just a column of air for them to grasp.'

'I thought of going away,' muttered Charlie.

Father Cooley snorted. 'So, you're going to pass the buck entirely! Mrs Darcy's to have the care of the little ones, I suppose, or Dolour, hardly more than a child herself.'

'I've got to go,' said Charlie desperately.

'And why, may I ask?'

Charlie blurted, 'I've fallen in love with Dolour.'

Father Cooley was silent. He went up and down the mat a few times thinking. 'So this is at the bottom of it, not the child's welfare.' Then he said, 'And what about Dolour? Does she think the same about you?'

'Yes, she does,' said Charlie. 'I haven't said anything about it, but I know she does.'

'I suppose you would,' admitted the priest, with a twinkle which he quickly suppressed. 'Well, she's a fine girl, a good girl, and old enough to know her own mind. You've been thinking of marriage, then?'

'She's my sister-in-law,' said Charlie, astounded, thinking the priest had forgotten.

'That's true, she is,' said Father Cooley thoughtfully. He ruminated, 'Now, here's a fine excuse. Shuffle off the children, be the martyr, off into the wide world with the head bowed and damn Mother Church for her stony heart.'

'So, if I can't marry her I can't stop in the same house with her,' said Charlie, his eyes asking, 'You're enough of a man to understand that, aren't you, even though you're forty years older than me, and long forgetting the cry of the flesh to be comforted?' He went on, 'I just wanted to know what to do for the best, Father. I've got myself so muddled up I don't know what to do.'

'The Sisters tell me she's grand with the children,' commented Father Cooley meditatively. 'Perhaps that's what the little one wants, a mother of her own, and not the feeling that there's no one in the world to belong to.'

'You'd think they were her own the way she's always working for them,' said Charlie. A wild rage against the frigid and implacable laws of the Church filled him. What right had they to keep him from Dolour, and Dolour from him, and Motty and Michael in their separate places? Anybody else, and he could go away with her and marry her in a registry office, and no one would know the difference. But he knew that wasn't what Dolour would ever do, not even if she had to spend the rest of her life alone. And it wouldn't do him, either, there was no real use in fooling himself. He had not been a good Catholic for a long time, but the ticklish conscience of the Catholic was there, never sleeping, never to be destroyed, always ready to raise its obstreperous fist and jolt the drugged or dreaming spirit back to life.

'It would be best for you both, not regarding the affection between you. She's a grand girl, and too good for many who'll be after her. The kind of girl who would make something of her life, given half a chance,' said the priest. His pain caught him with an iron grip across the loins. He thought, 'If I don't sit down I'll fall down, and if I sit down, I'll never be able to straighten out again.'

'Yes,' said Charlie dully. 'She's made for better things than she's got here.'

'I suppose,' said Father Cooley, keeping the wince off his face by a great effort, 'you could forget all these bad days and leave the grog alone if you had such a woman to think of.'

Charlie said nothing. Rub it in, he thought, but I don't need you or anyone else to tell me I've turned the game in these last years.

'And the children, you'd take them away, and they'd have a chance to grow up in the atmosphere children need,' went on the priest pleasurably, as though he were planning, and not merely babbling on about an impossibility. 'It's no life here for children. Even when the old place is pulled down, and the new Surry Hills built, there'll still be streets for them to play in, and the city smoke, and the criminal element always waiting to show its nose like a rat out of a hole. For there's people here who will make slums wherever they go. They won't be different, even though the shape of the house is changed.' He could see the wonderment on Charlie's face, the resentment at the salt in the wound, so he said hastily, 'It would be a fine thing for all four of you, but there's the impediment. We've got that impediment whichever way we look at it.'

'That's right,' said Charlie.

Father Cooley contemplated him. 'I'll give him a little more rope,' he decided, with a flicker of mischief. 'I suppose you're thinking the Church is hard in matters of this sort?' he asked.

'It's all just a question of law, isn't it?' said Charlie angrily. 'I'm no relation to Dolour. Marrying her sister didn't make me her brother. I can't see what'd be wrong in it no matter what way I look at it.'

'Ah, there could be things that make it wrong,' replied the priest. 'You must remember the Church has lived for longer than any of us, and has had plenty of time to think about things. She doesn't bother to make her commandments just for a whim, or just to let her children know she's holding the whip.'

Charlie sought for words, but he could only show his despair on his face.

'On the other hand,' added Father Cooley suddenly, 'You'll go a long way before you find an old lady who hasn't collected a great deal of commonsense throughout the years, and the Church is no exception.'

He became aware of the silence in the room, of the young man's yellow eyes looking at him, waiting like those of a watchful dog. This is where he'll show himself, thought the priest, and went on, gently, 'If you'd come to me earlier I might have been able to save you a lot of anxiety by explaining that very often a dispensation can

677

be obtained in such a case as this. But no, that was too simple. You had to leave it unsaid, and worry yourself to a rag, all because you didn't have the gumption to come and ask the man whose job it is to know most about such things.'

And he went on grumbling and scolding, watching Charlie furtively from under his eyebrows, and feeling his heart melt as though it were under the burning eye of God Himself to see the flush under the dark skin, and the whole expression change from bewilderment and anger to one of hope and exultance, chasing each other swiftly and excitedly until a torrent of questions burst from the young man's mouth. Father Cooley thought almost with pain, 'Ah, Lord, do me a favour and make it come out all right for him, and the young girl, and the little devil with a bite like a dingo.' He held up a hand.

'I'm not saying we'll manage it. I'm saying it's possible. But I feel, myself, that with things as they are, and especially with the children needing a proper family life ...'

'We'll go to the country,' said Charlie. 'I was brought up there. There's plenty of jobs I can take a hand at. Or I could find a place with a small-town printery – '

'Whist-a-whist! It's not me that has the say. The case has to go to the proper authorities. I'm only the man who'll present it to them. I'm the go-between.'

'Father,' said Charlie. He stood up, wanting to say many things, unable to express any of them, feeling an almost exhausting relief and eagerness, and an urgent desire to get away by himself and think about it.

Father Cooley cautioned him, 'Don't say a word to the girl yet. It'll be a week or so before I can get an answer for you. Don't talk to anyone about it except God.' He sat down painfully at the desk. 'Now, let's get the facts down.'

Charlie stood staring at the bristly white back of Father Cooley's head, trying to read the thoughts therein, and feeling, no matter how much he tried to control it, that all would be well. His mind leaped out to Dolour, probably putting Mikey to bed now, leaning over his cot with her soft hair falling in a curtain down the side of her cheek. In his mind he took hold of her by the shoulders and turned her round saying, 'Oh, Dolour, I'll love you the more because I loved Roie. There's no conflict between you and her, and couldn't be, because you know how I felt about her, and I know how you feel still. I'll take you away and we'll start again, with the children. There's so many wonderful places to see in this country, beautiful places to live where the trees grow, and the lakes and rivers run, and the sea is always to be heard even on the quietest night. You don't know what life is yet, Dolour, the way you've been shut in here by the greyness and the dirty buildings, and the people living the lives of parrots, squabbling and screaming because they're unhappy and discontented and don't know it.'

He was suddenly aware that the priest was speaking to him, and with a wrench he brought his thoughts back to the old man, who declared crossly, 'There's plenty of time for that later.'

Charlie flushed and grinned.

'And now,' said Father Cooley, 'doubtless you'll be wanting my company in the church.'

Charlie opened his mouth to say, 'I'm not ready. I haven't examined my conscience. Next week – to-morrow – ' but Father Cooley went to the cupboard and got out his purple stole, and with the air of one laden down with broom, bucket and scrubbing brush, briskly led Charlie back to the church and the confessional.

Charlie spent the days in an agony of anticipation and terror lest something should happen and Dolour should change towards him. He could not show his feelings in case the permission for the marriage was not given, and yet he could not altogether hide them. Sometimes he grabbed Motty and held her to him saying, 'Things'll be different for you, sweetheart,' and kissed the insolent, darkly suspicious look off her face, receiving either a hug or a blow in exchange. Or he followed Michael round, laughing at his quaint and stolid amiability, so that Mumma nudged Hughie and whispered, 'What's up with him now? Taking notice of the kid! And he's not drunk, neither.'

Dolour noticed the difference with a pang, thinking that perhaps something important had happened to him which would change the course of his life and therefore hers. But he was no different towards her, except perhaps to avoid her glance. She stood looking after him and wondering, hardly noticing Hughie standing there with a brown paper bag in his hand.

'Lookut I got, Dol.'

He grinned, and with his toothlessness looked like a shabby old leprechaun, so that she marvelled how it was she had ever hated him. For the signature of his lifetime of hard work was on him, on his calloused hands and his strong bent legs and his tousled head, and she wept inwardly to think she could have begrudged him the little pleasure he had found in being drunk and rumbustious.

'Oh, Dadda! Fancy you remembering I like poor man's oranges!'

'Saw them in Lick's window,' boasted Hughie. Something sad and fugitive came into his eyes, shadowing their blue and devilish glint for a moment. It was almost as though the sharp aromatic smell of the oranges had made him remember something better forgotten.

'What's up, Dad?'

'Nothing. It's just that me liver goes all goose pimples when I think of eating them things.'

She laughed. He looked at her admiringly. He liked Roie's sort better, just big enough to get into your arms, and the shy timid look to her. But Dolour was someone to be proud of with her straight back, and the way she looked you in the eye no matter if you was the Pope himself. He thought, 'The right bloke had better get her, or I'll stiffen him out, as God's my judge.'

To cover his embarrassment he said, 'Watcher know? Just seen young Charlie coming out of the presbytery. Suppose he was having a couple of pints with the Father.'

He rolled off, roaring with laughter, gathering up Mikey and Motty on the way, and, one under each arm, bore them shrieking with joy into the sun-striped backyard.

'Whatever could he be doing in the presbytery?'

The mystery of it bothered her all through teatime, and she couldn't help stealing glances at Charlie as he sat silently eating. He didn't seem to be cast down. It was only now and then that she felt she detected an air of intense excitement about him. But what had he to be excited about? What had he been doing?

It was with relief that she finished the dishes and went to her room, sitting on the bed and brushing her hair, still thinking and puzzling. She was there when Charlie came in. He pottered about, looking out of the window and picking up Ah Grin and putting him down again. Dolour watched him with an aching heart.

'What's wrong, Charlie?'

'Dolour, remember we had a talk once and I was thinking about going away?'

With cold hands she put down the brush. 'Yes, I remember.'

680

'Well, I've made up my mind. I'm going to go. Outback.'

She was not old enough to hide her feelings, but she tried, looking at him and saying in a voice which quavered a little, 'I guess you'll be happier somewhere else.'

She tried to say more, but the words wouldn't come. To her helpless shame tears welled into her eyes. 'I'm an awful cry-baby, aren't I? I don't know what's the matter with me lately. I guess – I guess it's because I'll miss you.'

'You'll stick by Motty and Michael as long as you're around, Dolour?'

A little irony came to her face. She'd be around. He wasn't tied by his love or anxiety for the children, but she was, and would be until she was earning enough money to take them away with her somewhere. But what would she do without Charlie? It was no use trying to be brave. The pain was as great as if her heart were pulled in half. The emptiness, the fruitlessness of her coming years, magnified beyond calculation by this shock, fell upon her and crushed her, and so she looked at him, not knowing it was all written on her face in letters an inch high.

He wanted to encompass her in the tenderness he felt for her, but this was not the place. Not this squalid room where Mumma or Hughie might burst in upon them at any moment. He said, 'You and I haven't ever been out anywhere together, Dolour.'

She was astounded, blinking back her tears in puzzlement.

'Let's go out for a walk to-night. A tram ride. Something.'

The strangest feeling stole into her heart, more delicate than she could describe, more poignant than she could comprehend. It was like the quiet time when the great instruments rested, and the players waited, patiently, for the conductor to raise his hand, and the music to flow.

But she did not say anything but 'I'd like to, Charlie.'

Twenty-four

Here on this long low shadowy shore, first of the coast to be seen by white men's eyes, the coarse grass blew, bleached and melancholy.

Botany Bay.

Name of glamour, name of grief! A great round harbour, it rose up out of the dusk into the light of the moon, a sheet of pewter. The wind blew from the city behind and, meeting the cold breath of the sea, it funnelled upwards with a sound like a vast sigh. Perhaps it was the same sigh that had come from those rotten leaking ships that had limped into that bay a hundred and sixty years before . . . the sigh of the exiled felons who would never see home any more.

'It looks like the end of the world,' whispered Dolour. She whispered because there was a heaviness in the air, an uneasiness that weighed on the heart. It was as though a very thin and palpitating tissue divided this night from the past. The cry of the convicts was all round them, the heartsickness of the innocent penned with the guilty, the weeping of women who had stolen food for their children and would never see those children again.

Dolour wanted to cry 'It's all right! It's all right! Sydney wouldn't be the same if it hadn't been for you!'

She wanted to show them the city behind her; the stony forest, the fantastic lichen that crept from the moonlit shores out over the foothills, here and there poking up a shoot in the form of a radio tower, a brazen-scaled steeple; there dwindling away into the earth-hugging film of the little slum houses of the 'Loo, or Surry Hills, or Erskineville. It was like a sea, this city. It had bays and peninsulas; it broke in a foam of tumbledown cottages about some massive sandstone outcrop. It receded like a defeated wave from the northern hills.

It was a strange memorial to the forgotten and defiled, yet everywhere they had left their mark upon it. Sydney's cobblestones were worn with the tramp of chain-gangs; her road cuttings still bore the scars of their chisels, and the walls of those cuttings were still streaked with the rainbow slime that the thirsty convicts had licked long before.

There was no convict blood in Dolour, yet she felt a fierce pride in these, the wicked, the hating, and the hopeless who yet had been the components of a miracle. It was right that this wild and brilliant land, this last, lost fabulous continent should have such a beginning in all that was best and worst, and most passionate and vital in mankind. For the felons, in spite of starvation and flogging and despair, had survived. They had survived.

The wind was colder now. It blew her long dark hair across her face and Charlie's, and at that subtle touch he put his arms round her, kissing her as though he were a starved man. He had not had a woman in his arms for three years; with joy and gratitude he felt once more the delicate lyre-shape of hips and thighs, the slender waist and broad arch of the breast fashioned so precisely for life and life-giving.

'Dolour,' he said, 'come with me when I go.'

She was silent. She bowed her head on his shoulder, trembling.

'What's the matter?' he asked. 'Don't you want me to love you?'

She had no words, but the beat of her heart drummed over and over again, 'Thank You, God.'

He looked at her face in the moonlight, her features that had changed in his memory from the smudged contours of girlhood to strength and beauty, with broad planes and winged eyebrows, and eyes that lay deep and calm in darkened sockets. He had been familiar with that child, but the woman was a stranger. He knew nothing of her deepnesses, only that he loved her.

'Charlie.'

She opened the top button of his shirt, rubbing her cheek against his chest. He laughed.

'Roie used to do that, too.'

Dolour felt that she should pull away from him, that she should be hurt or dismayed. But she could not feel any of those things.

'Is it only because you miss Roie?'

Down below the water chuckled on the sandstone ledges and tinkled off with the sound of a thousand waterfalls. 'No.'

A little pang of jealous pain caught Dolour's heart. In spite of what he said, she knew that she was second-best. She had wanted most of all to be first-loved, and best-loved, but that was not to be

683

hers. Then it was all swallowed up in a burst of love for Charlie, for her sister, and their children, and the children she herself would bear.

'Roie is part of me, and part of you,' she said. 'This won't make any difference to what we both feel for her.'

She knew the poor man's orange was hers, with its bitter rind, its paler flesh, and its stinging, exultant, unforgettable tang. So she would have it that way, and wish it no other way. She knew that she was strong enough to bear whatever might come in her life as long as she had love. That was the thing, the backbone of endurance itself, and she who possessed it needed no other weapon.

She kissed him, timidly at first, and then answering antiphonally his love, feeling him tremble, and confiding her trust in him by her very defencelessness. So this was passion, not the shoddy imitation of it that she had feared and witnessed, that blasphemed the fundamental nobilities of life, but passion that walked hand-in-hand with innocence, a magnificent delight that encompassed all tenderness, all self-sacrifice, all richness of giving.

'Roie knew,' she thought.

They walked up from the city, through the dark alleyways where cats sprang hissing from the garbage tins and the walls glittered with their crowns of broken glass. Here and there a drunk lay in a doorway, or a woman showed a pale face from a balcony or dim-lit window. Music spilled across the street like the yellow light that spilled from the tall corner-lamp slung in its archaic wrought-iron bough. But mainly there was silence, as though already Surry Hills felt its doom, and down in the earth the old grass-roots were stirring, ready to clothe this soil with the verdure that had been there a century before.

They came to the top of Plymouth Street and saw, where the old ochre shop had stood on the corner but a week or two before, a square of stars. There was a sharp clatter of falling bricks as a stray dog slunk across the allotment, and then silence once more.